MOON and the MARS

MOON *and the* MARS

KIA CORTHRON

Seven Stories Press
NEW YORK • OAKLAND

Seven Stories Press
140 Watts Street
New York, NY 10013
www.sevenstories.com

College professors and high school and middle school teachers may order free
examination copies of Seven Stories Press titles. To order, visit www.sevenstories.com or send a
fax on school letterhead to (212) 226-1411.

Library of Congress Cataloging-in-Publication Data

Names: Corthron, Kia, author.
Title: Moon and the Mars / by Kia Corthron.
Description: New York, NY : Seven Stories Press, [2021]
Identifiers: LCCN 2021011365 | ISBN 9781644211038 (hardcover) | ISBN
    9781644211045 (ebook)
Classification: LCC PS3553.O724 M66 2021 | DDC 813/.54--dc23
LC record available at https://lccn.loc.gov/2021011365

Printed in the USA

9 8 7 6 5 4 3 2 1

for my foster ancestors
Mary Edwards
Halvin Edwards
Virginia Brown

CHRONICLE ᴼᶠ THE LIVING ᴬᴺᴰ SOME ᴼᶠ THE DECEASED
1857

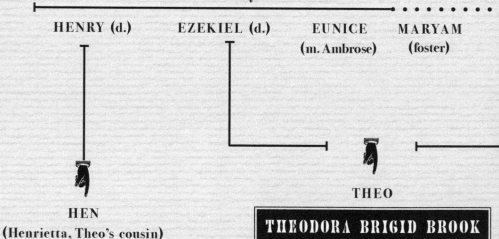

BROOK FAMILY

LIODA (GRAN-GRAN)

JEDEDIAH (GRAMMY)

HENRY (d.)   EZEKIEL (d.)   EUNICE (m. Ambrose)   MARYAM (foster)

THEO

THEODORA BRIGID BROOK

HEN
(Henrietta, Theo's cousin)

CAHILL FAMILY

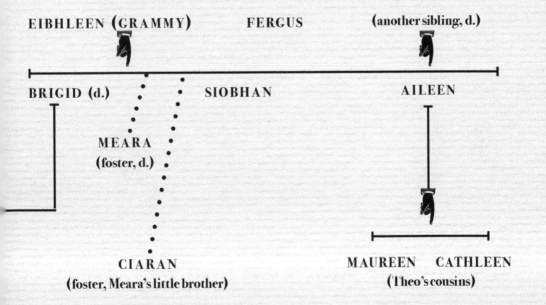

EIBHLEEN (GRAMMY)   FERGUS   (another sibling, d.)

BRIGID (d.)   SIOBHAN   AILEEN

MEARA
(foster, d.)

CIARAN
(foster, Meara's little brother)

MAUREEN   CATHLEEN
(Theo's cousins)

1857

Lucky

Mutt I am.

Irish and the black, black and the Irish, colored, Celtic, County Kerry, Afri-*can*!

What you sayin in there? call Grammy Brook from the front-room.

Nothin!

Talkin to yourself again, mutter Grammy Brook to herself.

Throw the cover off, jump outa bed, *brrrrr*! Woke up alone in the bed I share, alone in the bed in the bed-closet in the apartment in the tenement a Grammy Brook. Come out to the front-room grinnin.

Whatchu grinnin for? she ask, smilin. Then hold out somethin warm, somethin sweet: johnnycake! Happy birthday, birthday girl.

Thank you, Grammy!

Careful—hot.

Ah!

Toldja—*hot*!

How old's Miss Theo today? ask Mr. Freeman.

Seven!

Seven. That's a good one. Mr. Freeman nod, Mr. Freeman our boarder sit in the chair havin his bread n coffee breakfast, his bed-roll rolled up, rolled to the corner. Our apartment have two rooms: front-room and bed-closet. Our apartment have two rooms, two windas—both windas in the livin room facin the street, none in the bed-closet. Gran-Gran sit in her chair nex to the front winda near the door, Gran-Gran always at her winda lookin down on Park street. Gran-Gran is Grammy's mammy.

So whatchu gonna do today, Miss Seven? Grammy ask, ironin her whites for the whites. The wet ones hung all over our apartment.

Door fling open, in come Hen. My cousin Hen, carryin in the pail.

Three, Hen say, then dump the water into Grammy's pot on the stove. Hen strong! Hen only nine years of age, carryin the full water bucket:

heavy! Soon as Hen empty it, she turn back around, head out our apartment, down the stairs for more.

I'd better be getting on to work, say Mr. Freeman.

All right, say Grammy.

I just want to say again how much I appreciate it, Mrs. Brook—you not raising the rent.

Didn't get mine raised, no call to raise yours.

The barbering business not what it used to be, Mr. Freeman say, more to hisself. Then put his tin cup on the shelf and our barber boarder out the door.

I'll sing a song for you, Grammy, *that* what I wanna do for my birthday!

Good girl. Grammy switch irons. Grammy tole me why ironin need two irons: one to use hot till it cool while the other *gettin* hot on the coals.

Hark! the herald angels sing!

Oh, that's that new pretty one.

That song *old*, Grammy! Two years old, that song come to be when I was five!

New to old me.

Glory to the newborn King!

Your papa woulda been proud a you.

I knew she say that! Every time I have a birthday Grammy Brook smile teary and say my dead father her dead son Ezekiel woulda been proud a me.

In come Hen. Four, she say, emptyin the water into the pot. After five, I gotta get to work myself, Hen say and gone. When the water come to boilin, Grammy'll dump it in the washtub and put in more a the white sheets and white towels for the white folks.

I gotta go to the necessary!

Bring me back a paper. Then Grammy careful count out her coin, sigh. I remember when it was the *penny* press. Now hard to find it under two.

But you gimme two cent and a *half*, Grammy.

The half-cent for *you*, birthday girl.

Thank you, Grammy!

Mijn gelukwenschen met uw verjaardag, say Gran-Gran, still lookin out the winda. Gran-Gran and Grammy useta be slaves with Dutch masters. I look at Grammy.

She wishin you good wishes.

Thank you, Gran-Gran! I'm seven!

Gran Gran blink, not turnin her head from whatever's happenin out on the street.

We live on the fourth floor: top! I skip down the steps, out to the back courtyard water-closets to wait in line, one two three four five six seven eight *nine* in front a me! Nine colored, our tenement all colored, nine in front a me, *I gotta go!* There's Hen at the pump, *Hen!* I wave but she act like she don't see me. Eight in front a me, *I gotta go!* Hen finish fillin the bucket and start luggin it back up to our apartment, seven in front a me, *I gotta go! gotta go!*

The little Brook girl hoppin, she gotta go bad, say Miss Lottie who live crost the hall from us. Then everybody let me go! Then I run out to see whatever's happenin out on the street. The mornin boys hollerin.

New intelligence on the Bond street murder!

Bill passed for wagon road to the Pacific!

Latest on President-elect Buchanan's picks for his cabinet! Read all about it!

I buy a two-penny press for Grammy Brook, run it up to her, run back to the street back to Park street, right on Baxter street. Five-story tenement and on the third floor: Grammy Cahill.

Maidin mhaith, Grammy!

Maidin mhaith, Theodora Brigid, say Grammy, smilin because she pleased I'm practicin my *Good mornin* in Irish.

It's my birthday!

I know, little sprout. Seven is it?

I'm grinnin, noddin.

Lá breithe shona duit.

What's that, Grammy!

Happy birthday.

Lá breithe shona duit, Theo! say Maureen and Cathleen.

May the saints be with ye, say Cousin Aileen, who's my cousin Maureen and my cousin Cathleen's ma.

Go raibh maith agat!

That's how ye be thankin *one* person, Grammy correct me. More than one, ye say *Go raibh maith agaibh.*

Go raibh maith agaibh!

No, thank *you* for bein the livin spirit of herself, your dear mammy.

(I knew she'd say that! Every time I have a birthday Grammy Cahill smile teary and say I'm the livin spirit a my dead mother her dead daughter Brigid.)

Ye're after catchin me in the nick, *mo leanbh*, headin out to work. But I'm ready for ye. And she hand me a bite a cake.

Barmbrack! I chew it—still warm. Now Cathleen hold out her hand.

A little something for the birthday girl, say Cathleen.

Ah! say everybody. Cathleen made me a doll! Little doll, jus tall as my wrist to my fingertip. My cousin Cathleen and her sister Maureen and their mammy Cousin Aileen is seamstresses, Cathleen musta made my doll outa scraps from her work. Cathleen make pretty sewn things! Her mammy and sister work at the workshop but Cathleen gotta work the piecemeal at home: Cathleen's fifteen years of age, and when she was six, she climbed a tree and fell and her legs stopped workin.

Go raibh maith agat, Cathleen!

You're welcome.

Grammy Cahill headin out to work carryin her wares table, me skippin nex to her. Out to Baxter, then block and a half back to Park, set up her table, then send me to the grocer on Mott to pick her up a little flour. Crunch crunch through the Febooary sleet. Cross the road, I can do it! Look right and left for the carriages and carts. Look down for the horse manure and tenement manure. Look everywhere for the people rushin, pushin—hog runnin loose, everybody jump out the way! Buy the flour, back to Park, give it to Grammy. Then head six doors down the street: O'SHEA'S BOARD & PUBLICK.

Mornin, Auntie Siobhan!

Well, good mornin to *you*, Miss Theo. Wonderin when you wander by, it bein the ninth of Feb.

I come near every day! Look what Cathleen gimme!

Aw, what a pretty doll baby. Care for a little birthday nog?

Yes! I can pay for it! Grammy Brook gimme a half-cent for my birthday!

You save that for candy.

Thank you!

Better spend it today. Government claimin they'll be endin the half-penny later this month.

No!

Spend it today.

I sit in my auntie's tavern sippin my nog. Nutmeg! And a birthday apple! I'll save it till later.

Tell me a story, Auntie Siobhan!

Em . . . Let me think.

(My colored family says *um*, my Irish family says *em*!)

A *birthday* story.

Right. Your mother's birthday was—

May the twenty-fourth!

May the twenty-fourth. Woke up to a glory of a Wednesday and I said to my sister, Whyn't you take off from that tyrant, we make a day of it in the park? The tyrant was—

Mrs. Bradley!

Told ye this one before, have I?

No!

Brigid was a day-maid, another girl lived there but your mother-to-be came home nights. Like all the fancy folks, Mrs. Bradley lived uptown—

Forty-first and Fifth!

And if your mother'd been older she'd never a done it, played hooky from her place of employ. If *I'd* been older I'd never a suggested it, but her newly sixteen and me two years behind so there we were, plannin the mischief. Walkin down to City Hall—

To the park!

And who we run into goin the other direction but Lily the cook! Brigid begged her to tell Mistress Scowlface she fell ill, promisin to return the favor one day. Your mother'd been workin for the beast a year, screamed at near daily, her face slapped for a vocal tone not pleasin to the lady or for disturbin the library's alphabetical, placin a Charlotte Brontë before an Anne. Lily'd had her own troubles with the witch, don't the Irish and the black always suffer it all? So Lily wished your ma a happy birthday and went on her way, and there we be: your mother and I and soft grass and crackers and whiskey. Laughin at some rough n tumble we'd seen at Mott street and Pell that mornin or at the people walkin by or at Brigid scrunchin up her face and makin her boss lady's voice and *that* she just happened to be at when we look up to see none other than you know who!

Mrs. Bradley yell at my mother?

Herself was takin an afternoon stroll with her aul chum Mrs. Hyde, *another* one. Everything stops still, them starin at Brigid, the one supposedly home runnin a bout of fever. Then the old mistress heads straight toward my sister, chargin, her hand ready aimed to slap your poor mother's cheek! Gets within three feet of her—and falls! Flat on her face, Lady Bradley is sherry-drunk middle of the afternoon—*she* of the Temperance Society! Then her companion comes to her aid, but appears aul Mrs. Hyde's not exactly treadin steady ground neither! Finally Brigid helps her employer to her feet, and Mrs. Bradley yanks herself away, stumblin again with that, and the ladies depart. When they're beyond hearin, we're rollin, our stomachs torn up with the laughter! But next day, your mother trembles to show up for work, fearin she'll be given her walkin papers.

My mother get *sacked*?

Auntie Siobhan shake her head, smilin.

The she-devil musta worried Brigid might someday have a mind to reveal that peculiar episode in the wrong company, so not only was your mother's position secure but thereafter her tenure on Forty-first and Fifth proceeded appreciably more agreeable.

Not fair!

We turn to the man just entered the tavern from upstairs, tenant a the boarding-house.

Ye can't just raise the rent every February the first, Siobhan!

The law says otherwise, my auntie answer him. Don't go into effect till May, ye make your decision. 'Tis a wee increase, be no effort ye'd just re-budget your monthly liquor allowance.

Here I slip off the stool, out the door, leavin em to their shoutin.

How do ye, Theo!

Round the corner in the alley I see Nancy, smaller n me, standin with her brother, Elijah, smaller n her. They sleep in the alley crates since their mammy caught the influenza from the white folks she worked for and died. Nancy and Elijah skinny like sticks, eyes on my birthday apple. Now *my* eyes on my birthday apple. I take a nibble: sweet! Then give the rest to Nancy and Elijah who attack it, hungry-greedy. In my head I see Saint Peter in heaven markin this good deed on my list.

Your rich auntie give it to ya? ask Nancy, *crunch*.

One of em, I say. Now off to see the other.

Uptown I head: twenty blocks north, forty blocks and more, up to the country. At Fifty-ninth, Broadway change its name to Bloomingdale, still I keep goin. Eighty-sixth and Seventh, *knock knock!* Nothin. *Knock knock!* Then I remember: today's Monday—my auntie at school!

Good mornink, Theo!

I turn around.

Good morning, Mr. Schmidt! It's afternoon now!

Ah, you're right! he smile. Tell your aunt sank you again. She's a nice landlady.

I will!

Seneca Village where my Auntie Eunice lives where her tenant Mr. Schmidt lives is Seventh avenue to Eighth, Eighty-second street to Eighty-ninth and some say higher. Mr. Schmidt lives in the house my auntie and uncle used to live in before they built the new one. Crost the field, I see Mr. O'Kelleher drivin a hog home. I wave. He wave back.

I run over to Colored School No. 3. My auntie at the front a the class nod her head to the back for me to sit, then she ask everybody, What's one over two times five over six?

Everybody *click click* scratch their slates.

When dismission time come, my teacher-auntie and me walk back to her house hand-holdin. I tell her what Mr. Schmidt said to tell her he said.

It's because I didn't raise the rent. February first is Rent Day, to warn the tenants if the rent's to be raised in May. If it's too much, May first is Moving Day, but Mr. Schmidt won't have to worry about that. Now why in the world would you be paying me a call on February ninth?

I grin. Look what Cathleen gimme!

What a pretty doll. You should leave it at home to play with so you don't lose it.

I won't! I can carry it around, not lose it!

All right, stubborn, don't cry when it's gone.

Won't be gone!

Auntie Eunice cookin. We got her house all to ourself because Uncle Ambrose a seaman, more months away than home. Teachers ain't sposed to be married but Auntie Eunice say she The Exception Proves The Rule and somethin else about bein a good convincer and childless. I look out the winda.

We in Seneca Village, Dolly, I tell my dolly. *How* the colored people come again? I ask my auntie.

Seneca Village as we know it began when land here was sold to a colored, then another colored, then another. In Seneca Village, the negroes are the landowners. But we get along fine with our tenants, those Johnny-come-latelys from across the Atlantic: the Irish and the German searching for America. Why don't you read me some Thoreau.

I read *Resistance to Civil Government* while she stir the stew, then she wipe a tear and say, Your papa loved that book. Then she tell me read a little *Winter's Tale*. I do, then: When you plan on going to school, Theo?

Which is a very often disagreement between me and my auntie. I say nothin. Auntie Eunice been teachin me to read since I was three. I tried school once for a week and didn't care for it so didn't go back. I know she know but I say nothin because impolite to insult somebody's livelihood.

After supper, Auntie Eunice step outside with a bowl and no coat, come back in with a mound a freshly fell snow. Open a cupboard. Vanilla, sugar: vanilly snow!

For the birthday girl, she say and hand me a spoon.

I snuggle up with Auntie Eunice for the night. In the morn, she go to school, and I turn south, walkin ninety-six blocks back downtown to below First street. In the Thirties, a nativist man gawk at me: that look I sometime get from them ones claimin they the First Americans, descended from the original white people. Then he bark: Mongrel!

No! Mutt! I giggle and run.

Don't let the ignorants worry you! my grammies and aunties always say. And between Seneca Village and my downtown home's a whole lot a blocks a ignorance. Plenty a mutts where *I* live, home is black and Irish every day every minute crossin all kinds a paths, don't the rest a the world only wish they got our harmony?

Near dinnertime, Park street bustlin in the pre-noon winter sun. Newsboys callin the afternoon editions—and there my grammies talkin together! Grammy Brook makin laundry deliveries, Grammy Cahill with her table set up peddlin anything she find to sell. Right now appears they dickerin on a shirt.

Grammies!

They see me, drop their haggle-faces to smile.

I take a hand a each one. Green eyes and flowy light-brown hair the Irish gimme, but my nose and lips took a bit a thickness from the colored. High yella, my skin betwixt: not rich dark like my father's people nor rosy fair like my mother's

Long lashes just like your mammy, Grammy Cahill say.

Dimple-smile just like your papa, Grammy Brook say.

These I collect to make a picture, otherwise I don't know what they looked like. My mother dies three days after I'm born, father two years after her. Last summer, couple nights I stayed with Nancy and Elijah the back alley. Their mother passed not long before and no rent money, now they sleep the street. I try cheerin em up: Look at the Milky Way! But I don't speak a weather, rain and the comin snow. I don't remind em beddin under the stars is fun n rare for me because any night a the week I got a choice of roofs: my colored grammy's tenement or my Irish auntie's boarding-house or my colored auntie's uptown house or my Irish grammy's tenement. Mutt I am: orphan lucky.

The grammies start up the bargainin again so I move on. Adventures await! And them bounteous in Five Points, Manhattan, New York City, when a birthday girl got a whole half-cent to squander on em.

Arrivals

Late to work!

Grammy Cahill runnin around, puttin her wares in her bag.

My dearest friend and fiercest competitor Maeve better not've taken my spot!

I'm *never* late to work! Cathleen smile. She say that because her legs don't work so *her* work is *here*, home. Her needle nimble attachin collar to shirt: skill. Cathleen on the couch like usual, me under the couch playin with Dolly doll: four days past my birthday, I ain't lost her yet!

Rap rap!

Now who could that be? say Grammy, headin to answer. She ask that because nobody livin here would knock, and the landlord a just barged in, and the sub-landlord a just barged in specially with the doors in the tenement apartments broken off their hinges not lockin anyway, so who rappin the other side?

Maidin mhaith—Good morning? Cahill?

He pronounce it perfect! *Cah*-hill, rolled over the tongue fast! Head taller n me, his hair black and wavy, skin fair and rosy, eyes shinin bright blue but tired. And accent straight off the Isle. Grammy frownin, starin the suspicion. Then her face sudden soften altogether.

Ciaran?

The boy nod.

Ciaran *Moore*?

The boy nod.

Ciaran? Cathleen's mouth a O.

Ah! And Grammy grab him, hug him.

The spittin of your sister, ye are! Oh, so cold! Let's warm ye!

Grammy hold him tight, rubbin his arms. His arms hang straight down his sides, boards. Now Grammy lean back, her hands still graspin above his elbows.

Look at this lad! How old ye be?

Eight.

Eight years of age!

Nine July.

Eight and a half years of age! Girls! Come meet your cousin Ciaran!
Ciaran, this is Cathleen and Theo—Theodora Brigid.

Fáilte, Ciaran! welcome Cathleen, smilin bright.

My cousin how?

Not by blood, Grammy answer me. By love. Meara's brother.

And Grammy tell me the story I already know, not takin her eyes off Ciaran.

His poor parents near dead with the hunger, their three little ones they're after buryin, all those little girls. And me settin sail for America, the landlord offerin us escape from the Famine, but his mother and father too far gone, his mammy askin mightn't I bring Meara her eldest with us, sole survivor of her babies? Thirteen years of age his sister Meara was, year younger than Brigid year older than Siobhan, those girls all close just like his mother and me, We'll take her, sure we'll take her! All us wailin the fare-wells, and I'm thinkin next time I see Meara's mother's in heaven. Meara writin monthly hopeful and hearin nothin back, oh her poor parents sure be buried. Then one day comes the letter: Caoimhe and Riordan still in the land of the livin—and expectin another! And here he stands! Miracle baby, we called him! Baby Ciaran, born durin the Hunger. Shoutin the gratitude from their knees they were, his dear mother and father!

Dead, say Ciaran, and his eyes look dead when he say it.

Your poor aul fella, Grammy say, shakin her head. Didn't quite make it. Ah, in our families, the Famine was a widow-maker! Your mammy after losin your da, I'm after losin my Seamus, my niece Aileen her Malachi. That was Cathleen's poor father, Malachi. But somehow amongst us the mothers survived—

Dead.

Grammy stares. Your mammy?

Bump in her belly. Lump in her belly, hard. And bleedin.

Year ago! I remember, then she came bouncin back strong! Fearin she's not long for the world, she's after writin to Meara, askin her to take you. Meara scrape together the money for your passage, send to your mother, Meara cryin for her mammy but long to meet her baby brother who never arrived. Then your mammy's after writin she's feelin better!

Better. Then worse. Then dead.

When?

Two days before Christmas. Two days after New Year's uncle put me on a boat. Five weeks, six days.

Cathleen say, Crossing the Atlantic?

Five weeks, six days, Ciaran repeat.

Docked on Staten Island, were ye? Grammy ask. Early this mornin?

Ciaran nod.

And found your way to us, say Cathleen. What a clever boy!

So clever! Grammy's eyes shine.

Ciaran pull out a piece a paper, show to Grammy. Grammy read it, show to Cathleen.

Letter's a year old, Grammy say soft.

From my sister, say Ciaran. Her whereabouts, your whereabouts.

Grammy nods.

I'm after goin to her house. Fire, people on the street is after sayin. Her house burnt to the ground, they're after sayin.

Grammy nods. Seven months ago. Ah, these wood tenements is nothin but kindlin! Just after the Fourth of July, 'twas. I wrote. Ye didn't get the letter?

Ciaran stare.

I wrote! Ye didn't get the letter?

Ciaran shake his head.

Well, ye're not to fret, Grammy swallow. You'll be stayin with us.

Now my mouth the same O Cathleen's was! Our apartment is one front-room and one bed-closet *that's it* now here's what we got:

1. Grammy Cahill
2. her niece Cousin Aileen
3. Maureen, Cousin Aileen's daughter who's eighteen
4. Cathleen, Cousin Aileen's daughter who's fifteen
5. Great-Uncle Fergus who's Grammy's brother
6. me (when I'm not at Grammy Brook's)
7. now Ciaran

You must be starving! say Cathleen.

Grammy catch her breath. *Starve* is a word she don't throw around devil-may-care. She look in the stove.

Lump of coal left! I'll make the porridge, ye must be achin for a bite.

Do you need a nap? ask Cathleen. Bed closet's right through the doorway.

Is it a bath ye first be needin? ask Grammy. Theo, would ye fill the pail?

Seein my sister I first be needin.

Everybody stop. Seem like Ciaran missed Grammy's meanin: 'tweren't only Meara's *buildin* come to ashes.

Ciaran, say Grammy, a tear startin to fall. Oh, Ciaran . . .

Out the door! Down the stairs, through the other door to the street. Walk down Baxter, cross at Park street, busy Park! Crunch, crunch, light snow lass night. Mary Bree on the corner a Park and Mission place, barefoot with her broom. I wave.

How do ye, Mary Bree!

She don't see me. Talkin to a gentleman, hopeful customer, but the customer walk on. I get closer.

How do ye, Mary Bree!

How do ye, Theo! *Dia duit!*

Dia duit! I say. I taught Mary Bree that greetin, she oughta know some Irish since her name's Mary Briana O'Doolin. I like your gray shawl, Mary Bree!

Thanks! I found it!

Mary Bree only six and that shawl still a little small for her, fulla holes, lookin like a part a somethin bigger got ript up. Still, before she didn't have *no* cover over her dress, and Mary Bree work in the outdoors, street-sweeper, tidyin away the weather and the debris for the gentry steppin at the corners. Mary Bree rub her right foot gainst her left leg, then left foot gainst right leg, warmin em, hopin they change blue to red.

Where your Grammaw Cahill be? She not in her spot.

Late, gatherin her wares. Then company come.

What company?

From Ireland.

From Ireland?

Little brother of Meara—the one died in the fire lass year with her husband and girl.

I remember that story!

Grammy wrote to Ciaran and his mammy bout the fire and bout everybody dyin but they didn't get the letter.

What his name?

Ciaran. *Kee*-er-un, that got three beats but fast it almost sound like two: *Keer*-un.

Sweep your walk for ya, ma'am?

Yes, thank you.

And Mary Bree get to work, grinnin, sweepin the corner so the lady can cross, not get dirty snow on her fine boots. Coal! A big lump right there in the street, no one else see it. I grab it quick! Give it to Grammy! Sometime hard to pick which grammy, but not now: don't wanna go back to Cahill's, the Meara tears! Like lass summer, everybody sad! I never much knew Meara. When I was toddlin, she met a sailor passin through town, marry and back to Boston with him. Then she miss New York so here they are again, her and him and a girl two years of age, and year later fire took em all. Most I remember about Meara is she come back to die and leave my family sad. I liked her little girl though, Regan. I taught Regan Pat-a-Cake!

Grammy! Grammy! I can't wait, hollerin, runnin up Grammy Brook's tenement steps, *Grammy*! Fly through the door, Looky what I got! I hold up the coal, knowin she be pleased because coal's gold.

Everybody standin quiet. Grammy Brook and Auntie Eunice and Hen and Mr. Freeman and a new one.

Come in, chatty girl, say Grammy, and close the door behind ya. I smell Grammy's hog fat n string beans on the boil. My belly growl.

The new one got skin night-dark, smooth. Tree-tall—I see the washtub out, she musta pulled her legs in tight to fit in that bath. Eyes shine like black pearls, and though the torn dress and bloody scratches speak a hardship, her thick lips open soft to smile.

Maryam, this is my granddaughter Theodora. Theo, this is Miss Maryam.

We are sisters, say Auntie Eunice.

Auntie Maryam, Grammy correct herself.

My father's sister? I ask, suspectin not.

Yes, say Auntie Eunice, you can say that. We shall say that.

You my father's sister, Miss Maryam?

Ain't that what you just heard, say Hen.

She'll say that, say Grammy, if anybody ask, but nobody likely to, and don't you go voicin it out in the street.

I won't.

And not to your Irish kin neither, Hen just gotta add.

I won't!

I know she won't, say Grammy. She's a good girl.

We don't need a good girl, say Hen, we need a quiet girl.

Shut it!

I, start Miss Maryam. Everyone look to her but she stop. Hen scratch her head and soot fall off. Soot most a her body, Hen musta just come from work, *she* oughta get in the tub. Chimney sweep, the customers take her for a boy.

Auntie Maryam will be staying with us, say Grammy, and I look at our front-room and bed-closet, which is the whole a our estate.

1. Grammy Brook
2. her mother, Gran-Gran, at the winda
3. my cousin Hen who's ten
4. Mr. Freeman our barber boarder
5. me (when I'm not at Grammy Cahill's)
6. now Miss Maryam

Grammy take her string beans and seasonin off the stove.

Everybody suppin. Grammy say, What were ya? Before?

Miss Maryam take a pause, then: Lizzie Hathaway. Hathaway Plantation, South Carolina. I work the fields. I's twenty-five. Or -six. Or -seven.

In the street a driver hollerin at his horses. Every time he crack the whip Miss Maryam jump.

Lizzie they names me but my mammy secret names me Maryam, Maryam I is.

Grammy take a think.

Let's make you New York born. Been workin a upstate farm, just come back home to be with your family. Us. Let's make you a washerwoman. Let's make you twenty-six.

Year younger than I, my baby sister! say Auntie Eunice. Do you know when your birthday is?

Spring. My mammy say I comes with spring.

March twentieth then! say Auntie Eunice. The first day of spring.

Your family name, say Grammy, will be Brook, *our* family name. My mother, husband, and me given the master's name, Broek—Broek with an *e* that the master shortened from *ten Broek*. When emancipation come to New York State thirty years back, we made it plain old Brook.

Mancipation thirty year *back*? say Miss Maryam, makin the third O-mouth a the day.

What's that? I point. Somethin hangin from her neck.

Miss Maryam finger the little leather pouch, square and somethin surely inside it.

From my mother, she say. From Africa.

Africa? say Grammy, smilin like wondrous. And passed down all these generations!

One generation. My mother born Africa.

But? Grammy start, eyes to the ceilin, figurin somethin.

They made the trans-Atlantic trade illegal in aught-eight, Auntie Eunice say, voicin whatever Grammy was tryin to solve. Which only means the trafficking continued covertly. Illegally.

Where's your mother now? Hen ask.

Miss Maryam look to Hen, eyes full a water, and when a tear from each eye start to fall, she quick wipe em away.

Auntie Eunice change the subject, start talkin bout makin a new dress for Miss Maryam so she don't gotta wear the dress she come in, start talkin bout city livin, love your neighbor but don't let em swindle ya. Auntie Eunice stay with us tonight, which I'm happy about! Even if the apartment now got *too many*. When Hen take Miss Maryam down to the w.c., I ask, Where Miss Maryam come from?

You heard, say Auntie Eunice. South Carolina.

I mean how she come to *us*?

It's organized, say Grammy. There's volunteers. Hosts. We volunteered to host. Didn't know when our guest would come, or if. All that's a secret.

Where's Miss Maryam's mother?

Must be sold or dead, say Auntie Eunice, don't bring it up.

I think about Miss Maryam's teary eye to talk about her ma, about Ciaran's eyes dry like the desert to talk about his ma and pa. Orphan lucky: I not known mother nor father so my eyes never too wet, never too dry, just right! Hearin stories bout my mother from Auntie Siobhan is fun! And I like when Auntie Eunice have me read the book my papa loved, but none a that ever make me long for the dearly departed. It jus give my eyes the twinkle, the only thing waterin bein my mouth, ponderin what kinda special treat a grammy or auntie might have in store for somebody happen to be the spittin image of the beloved dead that begat em.

Tour

Here's a room with my family. The Brook and the Cahill, both grammies, both aunties, Cathleen and Hen, Maureen and Cousin Aileen and Gran-Gran and Uncle Ambrose and Great-Uncle Fergus, everybody warm eyes on me.

There they are, Auntie Siobhan smile.

Right through there, Auntie Eunice wink.

Door. And on the other side's my mother and father, I get to see what they look like! Walk to it, my hand reachin for the knob, *Ow*!

Wake on the floor!

Sorry! Sorry!

Even in the dark, I see Miss Maryam's eyes shinin wide, scared.

Don't be squintin no nastiness, girl, Grammy warn me, never openin her own lids.

Our bed ain't big but before we sleep good: Grammy and me, Hen crossways below our feet. In the front-room, Mr. Freeman got his bedroll and Gran-Gran on the couch. As Gran-Gran got older Grammy wanted her to share the bed but Gran-Gran didn't wanna, too crowded, so jus Grammy and Hen and me: perfect. Now Miss Maryam squeeze in between Grammy and myself, and turns out Miss Maryam's fitful in the night.

Nex time I wake's bright day, alone in the bed-closet, hearin the chatter. Hen and Mr. Freeman already gone to work, but the front-room still busy with Gran-Gran starin out the winda, Grammy peelin potatas, and Auntie Eunice who musta come over early sittin next to Miss Maryam on the couch, Bible crost their laps.

Good morning, sleepyhead.

Mornin, I say to my auntie, yawnin.

Sorry, Theo. I's fitful in the night.

Didn't bother me, say Grammy. There's a biscuit for ya.

Biscuits in hog fat! Soft and hot, the butter melt in my mouth and all round it too!

Sunday, I say to Auntie Eunice. Thought you be in church.

Caught an early service, Auntie Eunice reply, eyes on the page.

Yooooh. Yooooh-kuh.

Yoke, very good! say Auntie Eunice to Miss Maryam, who's tryin to read. *For my yoke is . . .*

Miss Maryam starin, her lips movin, tryin to figure it out, so Auntie Eunice say: When two vowels go walking, the first one does the talking.

Miss Maryam take in the lesson.

Easy?

Yes!

Now Miss Maryam's eyes take in the bookshelf. Yall *all* read?

Auntie Eunice nods. I look at our library. Five books: *Narrative of the Life of Frederick Douglass, an American Slave*; *Uncle Tom's Cabin, or, Life Among the Lowly*; *History of the Expedition Under the Command of Captains Lewis and Clark to the Sources of the Missouri, thence Across the Rocky Mountains and Down the River Columbia to the Pacific Ocean*; *The Tempest*; and the Bible they're readin. For all but the Bible, Auntie Eunice was the buyer.

I learned to read from that Bible on your laps, say Grammy. Been in our family generations.

Auntie Eunice flip back to the first page to show Miss Maryam.

Births

Lioda ~~Broek~~ Brook
b. 1779

m. Moses ~~Broek~~ Brook
b. 1780 d. 1808

Children

Jedediah Brook
b. June 5, 1806

m. Abner Brook
b. 1802 d. 1841

Children

Henry Floy b. Dec. 23, 1824 d. July 2, 1849   m. Jennie Tiller d. Mar. 3, 1851
   Children: Henrietta b. May 17, 1847
Ezekiel b. Oct. 2, 1828 d. Sept. 5, 1852   m. Brigid Cahill d. Feb. 11, 1850
   Children: Theodora Brigid b. Feb. 9, 1850
Eunice b. July 26, 1830   m. Ambrose Bennett
   Children:

Our family genealogy, my auntie smile.

Master never catch you?

Reading? Grammy ask. Miss Maryam nod. Grammy say, Never illegal for slaves in the North to read.

Read till my eyes went bad, say Gran-Gran, eyes on the street.

My mother attended the Society for the Propagation of the Gospel, Grammy say, smilin eyes on Gran-Gran.

Masters embraced their slaves' reading, say Auntie Eunice. Helped them with their business.

Literate slaves gave a master high status, say Grammy.

Where your slave dress go? I ask. I notice Miss Maryam wearin somethin new, not fancy but better n what she come in. I only got my one dress, light brown. It never get too raggedy since my Cahill family's seamstresses and my Brook family can sew.

I had material, I made that new dress yesterday, say Auntie Eunice, smilin at Miss Maryam. Pretty on you.

Gimme the slave garb, I'll pass it to my Grammy Cahill, she sell old clothes.

Stop tellin grown-ups what to do, say Grammy Brook.

Stop dropping the esses from your verbs, say Auntie Eunice.

Sometime I say the esses. And sometime Grammy drop hers.

Stop with the back-talk! say em both.

Theo read? Miss Maryam wonder, and I grab a book, findin a page.

Oh yes, Auntie Eunice say. I began teaching her when she was just—

> Abhorrèd SLAVE,
> Which any print of goodness wilt not take,
> Being capable of all ill! I pitied thee,
> Took pains to make thee speak, taught thee each hour
> One thing or other. When thou didst not, SAVAGE Oww!

I stare at em, the sting a Grammy's hand still ringin on my bottom.

What you doin? Grammy snap. Put that Shakespeare back!

What's wrong with you? bark Auntie Eunice. Say you're sorry!

Reckon they mad I'm showin off. That particular piece Auntie Eunice have me read enough I got it near by-heart, so no stumblin.

Or maybe in trouble for hollerin *slave* and *savage* in Miss Maryam's direction.

Sorry! order Grammy.

Sorry, I mutter.

For my yoke is easy, and my burden is light.

Excellent! Auntie Eunice beamin at Miss Maryam readin that baby-simple Bible scripture. I suck my teeth, then notice Grammy closer behind me than I thought so run out the door before her palm find my backside again.

Auntie Siobhan got a nice big bed in her boarding house and happy to have me for company a few nights, but Thursday afternoon I run into Hen who say Grammy made gingerbread.

How do ye, Grammy!

How do ye, sweetie-pie, say Grammy, ironin.

Then I see the gingerbread pan. Empty, nothin but crumbs!

Hen said there was gingerbread!

Was. You ain't been by since Sunday, Theo, I didn't know whether to save any.

I look at Miss Maryam, who freeze in the middle a chewin.

Lemme whip up some porridge for ya, say Grammy, and I know better n to say I don't want any blamed porridge!

Whatchu thinkin bout Eunice's invitation? Grammy ask Miss Maryam while I pick at the mush in my bowl.

Miss Maryam say nothin.

Eunice got a couch.

I look up. Think but don't say: Miss Maryam gonna live with Auntie Eunice in Seneca Village? Give Grammy and me and Hen our bed back?

But Miss Maryam eyes fill, fit to cry.

Dontchu worry, say Grammy. You feel more comfortable here, you stay.

I feels . . . I feels harder the slave catcher find somebody your parts. All these folks, I thinks I be lost in em.

There been escaped slaves hid in Seneca Village, I offer.

You keep that business to yourself, little lady. If Auntie Maryam feels better here, here she'll stay.

A little quiet, then Miss Maryam say to Grammy real soft, like she fear she askin too much: How you spells Maryam?

People spells it different.

How the Bible spells it.

M-A-R-Y-A-M.

Miss Maryam smile. Then, I washes! and she start collectin the dishes.

Oh, thank you, Maryam, say Grammy. *Daughter*, she add, returnin the smile. Miss Maryam take my bowl and not even notice I only ate half, tired a porridge! Still hungry!

Nex mornin, first thing I hear Miss Maryam: Good mornin, Theo! She walkin through our apartment door carryin the pail, smilin bright at me. Water to drink and water to cook and water to bathe means runnin down to the courtyard pump, fill it, lug it heavy back up to the fourth floor, pour it into our washtub, that's one bucketful. Down, pump it, lug it, pour it, that's two bucketfuls. Down, pump it, lug it, but Miss Maryam was a slave so guess that kind a labor all in her everyday.

Don't you speak? Auntie Maryam just said good morning to you.

Good mornin, I say. Good mornin, Grammy. Good mornin, Gran-Gran.

There's a biscuit.

And butter! I sit and eat while Miss Maryam lug up a fourth pailful, a fifth.

Thank you, Maryam, that'll do me. Now where *you* off to?

I dunno, I answer, gunny-sack over my shoulder. Look for coal (which I know Grammy won't argue with).

Sometime I thinks, wonder what Theo do all day? You likes I come with you?

Grammy and me stare. Far as I seen, except to the back courtyard to fetch the water or use the water-closet, Miss Maryam ain't set foot outside our apartment since she come exactly one week ago.

I arrives New York the dark. I sees nothin cep what I sees from this here winda.

Sorry, I got work to do, I gotta collect the coal—

It's all right you show your auntie around a bit first. Take a shawl, Maryam.

Down the steps I fly, fourth floor to the ground, swing the door open. Wait for her, feelin my hot bull-breath, mad! Finally she appear: *Ah!*

Her face a marvel. Then I get it. This be Miss Maryam's first real live view of it: Five Points. Horses clompin and wagon wheels clickin and a stray hog and feral dogs and sometimes a dead rat or horse and customers flowin in n out the grocery-groggeries and cats on the prowl and the smell a baked bread and the smell a rotten vegetables and the smell a cigars and the smell a horse dung and people shoutin people laughin people people.

Careful, I warn, though wide-eyed Miss Maryam already got her hand on her dress, ready to tug it up if the manure piles reach above her ankles. Mostly horse waste for sure but also seepage from the tenements, which Miss Maryam prolly figured out. Not our fault. The cesspools sposed to be cleaned by the city regular, but they're cleaned by the city rare.

Why it call Five Points?

See there, that intersection: five points comin together. Park street—*our* street—crossin Baxter street, then there comin in on the side is Worth street. The neighborhood grown out from that junction. My other grammy lives right round the corner there: Baxter.

The Irish?

I nod. Five Points is mostly Irish. But there's the colored tenements in Park street where we are, and the colored shanties in Baxter street near the African Society for Mutual Relief and just across there's the dead-end Cow Bay: all colored.

The China war—highly interesting particulars of the American operations at Canton!

Serious affray in Kansas!

Relocation of the quarantine! Updates on Staten Island's Sailors' Hospital and Retreat!

So many! Miss Maryam say, all wonder at the newsboys.

Whole lot more round the ferry landins and the train depots, I reply, startin to enjoy my tour-guide knowledge. *Sun* or *Dispatch* or *Herald* or *Daily Times*, the *Daily News* or the *Commercial Advertiser* or the *Day Book* or the *Christian Advocate and Journal*, or the *Tribune* or the *Leader* or the *Examiner* or the *Ledger* or the *World*.

Latest on the Irish riots in Jersey! calls a *Herald* boy.

Or the *Irish-American* or the *Evening Post* or the *Evangelist* or the *New-Yorker Staats-Zeitung*—that's just a *few* a the dailies. For weeklies, you have your *Dispatch* or your *Caucasian*—ah! You might be partial to *Frank Leslie's Illustrated Newspaper*: all drawings!

Fresh sha-a-ad!

My clams I want to sell today, the best clams from Rock-a-way!

Miss Maryam smile at the Irish peddlers.

What *that* be? Her pointin to a big buildin.

The Mission. And that one there the House of Industry.

What *that* be!

Streetcar. The New York and Harlem. Follow these tracks, I'll show you where it all starts, jus below City Hall. City Hall's in the Second ward which is right nex below to the Sixth ward, and Sixth ward is where we stand, where Five Points is. You know what people call where we live? The Bloody Ole Sixth!

Then I take Miss Maryam down to City Hall.

Grass!

Miss Maryam look delighted and occurs to me this the first greenery she seen since comin to New York, though the green mostly yella and brown, whatever bits peekin through the Febooary dirt-snow.

The park, I say. City Hall Park but everybody jus say *the park* since it's the main one in Manhattan. When people got the leisure for a fancy picnic day, they take the ferry to Brooklyn, Green-Wood Cemetery.

Maybe we goes there!

Grass in Seneca Village where Auntie Eunice live, I remark. Miss Maryam act like she don't hear me but then she sure hear the trumpet blarin, make her jump. Band on the balcony, beckonin in the visitors. Buildin take up a whole block, Broadway and Ann. Miss Maryam stare at the big letters.

Bar—Barn—

Barnum's American Museum. I hear they got jugglers and glassblowers, elephants and dancin fleas. I hear they got people eats other people and bentriloquits, Siamese twins and snake charmers and Tom Thumb, I wanna go! I never been, under ten get in fifteen cent!

Ain't that somethin! say Miss Maryam, awed by it all. I say nothin else, figurin if Miss Maryam stayin with us and if I mention the museum time to time maybe one day she take me. I lead her back up to the Bloody Ol Sixth, where a horse n carriage speed by, Miss Maryam barely leap out the way jus to step into a pile a horse droppins.

Ha! A woman laughin, lookin at Miss Maryam scrapin her shoes, the ones she said was give to her by the Underground Railroad people minute she arrived in the city before bein sent to Grammy's. I give the chortler my hard eyes but her mind already elsewhere. Enjoy an apple, madam?

Two ladies in fancy wear huddlin close to a gentleman for protection from the neighborhood. They hold cloths over their noses and mouths.

Who them?

Takin a tour, I tell Miss Maryam. The rich people say *doin the slums*.

A policeman lecture em: And *this*, ladies and sir, is the Irish apple woman you've famously heard tell of.

Now the fruiterer frown suspicion, chew her pipe stem, twirl it in her lips. Newsboys rush to the tourists.

Madam, New York premiere of a Verdy opera at the Academy of Music! About a *fallen woman*, read all about it!

Sir, news on the markets! Beeswax sales up, coffee up, ashes, candles—

Shoo! say the constable to the newsboys, and they do. You too, filthy urchin.

I ain't a urchin, I snap back. Orphan with family! Jus had a bath last week! I think but don't add, Which from what I hear's prolly more recent than them gentry starin at me. Now a hullabaloo nearby. A gentleman runnin. Stop them! Thieves!

Christmas! the officer tour-guide yells at the boys runnin and laughin. He wants to chase after em, but senses his sightseers don't wanna be left alone.

Street arabs, he mutters, then back to his lecture.

Clean your shoes, Miss? A chorus of hopefuls at Miss Maryam, a white bootblack and a black, one boy a little bigger n me, the other a little smaller. Miss Maryam smile shy, shake her head. Then take me aside.

Why he saze Arab? Why he saze Christmas?

Street arabs what they call the robbin n stealin urchins.

Why they call that?

I shrug. Christmas is the name a the boy leads that gang.

Einen schönen Tag noch.

Mr. Freeman! I call, seein our barber boarder polite farewellin a white man leavin his shop. *Dia duit*, Mr. Freeman!

He smile. *Dia duit*, Theo.

Remember Miss Maryam from our front-room?

Yes, I saw her this morning. He tips his hat to her. Good day again to you, ma'am.

Miss Maryam smile wide.

Mr. Freeman was speakin German! Then Irish! Mr. Freeman know languages!

Helps with the clientele.

Everybody come to his barbershop!

Everybody but colored. Our fair patrons stipulate that the scissors and combs that touch *their* hair never touch black. Thus negroes are the barbers, not the customers.

Miss Maryam wanna know why street arabs called street arabs.

Not certain really. Since they're street urchins, I suppose it's a reference to nomadic Arabs. Though I imagine their survival penchant for theft would be an insult to their namesake.

A ruckus from inside the barbershop.

The majority of our Irish regulars are *old*-family, been here generations. A couple budding figures of our city's fine Tammany Hall crew are being serviced by my fellow barbers even as we speak, and it appears they've once again set fire to each other's beards. If you'll excuse me.

Mr. Freeman go back in. Music comin from nex door, music that'll get louder tonight.

Grock— Grock—

Grocery, I say, lookin at all the signs she tryin to read, practically every other Five Points establishment say it.

What it mean?

Food, they sell.

A woman stagger outa one of em, cursin to herself.

But mostly spirits.

Thank you for the tour, Theo! Now we best gets the coal for your grammy.

Sweep-oh!

That's Mr. Samuel! He the chimney-sweep master!

Miss Maryam flinch. *Master?*

See?

Miss Maryam look every which way but where I'm pointin.

There.

That his slave?

No! He's the *master*!

Miss Maryam's mouth: O. *Colored* master?

I nod. And the white man he talkin to's a customer he tryin to rein in. *All* the sweep-masters is colored, chimney sweeps is colored work. The apprentices too, see? There's Hen. Hey Hen! Apprentices is boys small enough to fit in the chimneys. Except Hen's a girl.

Yella! we hear and turn round. Another chimney-sweep master and his two apprentices lookin tired. That master I don't like, he beat his apprentices. I don't know why he callin Mr. Samuel yella, *I* get called yella sometime but Mr. Samuel and his apprentices is all dark-complected. Mr. Samuel's maybe-customer gone on his way, so I run up to him.

How do ye, Mr. Samuel!

How do *you* do, Theo. Who's this?

Miss Maryam—I mean, Auntie Maryam, she's my auntie, Hen's and my auntie, stayin with us. Miss Maryam, this is Mr. Samuel, Hen work for him. And that's Jeremiah.

Good mornin, Miss Maryam, say Mr. Samuel, smilin friendly up at Miss Maryam. He's decked out: feather hat and cloak, soot fallin off him. Most a the masters dress dirt-dandy. Miss Maryam's tall, Mr. Samuel small, so his head bout high as her chin.

We're not yella! Jeremiah yells back. He's the other apprentice, year older n me. Hen jus busyin herself blowin soot outa one a the brushes.

He thinks the new patent sweep machine is cowardly, Mr. Samuel say, eyes on the other master disappearin round the corner. Fears it might give me an edge: competition.

It's in that bag, Miss Maryam! I point to the big leather sack Mr. Samuel carries.

The new patent sweep machine has mechanical arms that reach up into the chimney so I don't have to send my apprentices up on roofs to fall off and break their necks, like what happened to a kid or two *my* apprentice days. All right, let's go, Mr. Samuel say to Jeremiah and Hen. To Miss Maryam he tip his sooty hat. Pleasure to meet you, ma'am. Miss Maryam smile. Then they move down the street.

Miss Maryam say, Okay, we best gets that coal now.

I'm thirsty, and Miss Maryam follow me into O'SHEA'S BOARD & PUBLICK.

Mornin, Auntie Siobhan!

Mornin, *mo stoirín*.

That's Irish for my little darling. And my Grammy Cahill call me *mo leanbh*: my child.

Miss Maryam's eyes froze wide, starin at my auntie and the Irish customer she sellin a bottle to.

Who's this?

Miss Maryam, livin at Grammy Brook's now. This is Auntie Siobhan, Miss Maryam—I mean *Auntie* Maryam!

But all that do is make Auntie Siobhan frown, I forgot she already *know* all my aunties! Two: her and Auntie Eunice. I mean cousin! She's my cousin!

You and your cousin like some cider?

Auntie Siobhan pour our glasses. Miss Maryam look like nerves. The customer gone, so only the three of us left in the saloon, and Auntie Siobhan touch Miss Maryam's hand gentle. Miss Maryam near leap to the ceilin. Auntie Siobhan say soft: Your secret's safe with me. And Auntie Siobhan don't move away till Miss Maryam fall to ease. Then Auntie Siobhan wipin glasses.

I likes your establishment.

Thank you! You read the sign out front? *O'Shea's*?

Miss Maryam can't read.

Well, that's what it says. O'Shea was my husband. He liked his bottle. I was seventeen, him thirty-seven when we wed. Three years later, he's dead: one drink too many. Twenty-three I am, three years the sole proprietor, saloon *and* boarding-house. And my medicine cabinet, I carry a few cures: tablets, tinctures, tonics, and if the remedy that rectifies ye's whiskey, I got a few bottles a that too. You lookin for a place?

Miss Maryam stare confused, then her eyes to the floor. Don't know.

You'd like it here, Miss Maryam! My friends Miss Sally and Miss Fiona live upstairs, wanna meet em?

Miss Maryam follow me up the steps, *creeeeeeak, creeeeeak, knock knock!*

Who's at my door, crack a dawn!

Theo, I say soft. It's near noon.

The door swing open.

Theo! Miss Fiona smilin, not crabby like she sounded fore she knew it was me.

This is Miss Maryam, stayin at my Grammy Brook's. She might live at the boarding-house!

Well, you'd be welcome. Care to see my room?

Miss Fiona swing her door wide. Bright, bed, bureau. A little table.

Pretty! say Miss Maryam.

What's all the commotion? we hear from crost the hall.

Miss Sally standin at her door, open wide. Bed and bureau with big circle lookin-glass.

Potential new boarder, say Miss Fiona, tippin her forehead toward Miss Maryam.

Fiona got the table, Miss Sally say. And the nice daylight.

And *you*, say Miss Fiona, got the vanity with mirror.

Which I share with Fiona, say Miss Sally.

She does indeed, say Miss Fiona.

Hel*lo*!

We turn. A white man just come up the steps, wobblin. Lookin nativist, uptown. He stare between Miss Fiona and Miss Sally.

The brogue and the black. Had Ireland last night. I like Africa now.

He point a thick, shaky finger at Miss Sally who slap it away.

Not in that state. No regurgitating in the middle of business.

Get yourself a bit soberer, say Miss Fiona. Then we'll be seein ye.

With cash, say Miss Sally. Then Miss Fiona turn the drunk around, give him a little shove to send him staggerin back down the stairs.

It's a nice situation here, say Miss Sally to Miss Maryam. Good neighbors. Gertie down the hall's a maid to some fancy Gramercy Park people.

Lucille and her daughters upstairs take in the sewin, say Miss Fiona.

Most the boarders go out on the street, day work, say Miss Sally.

But Sally and I prefer the convenience a workin at home, say Miss Fiona, glancin back at her own bed.

Speakin a which, say Miss Sally, *I* need to be gettin ready for a little day work. She look at me. Anybody care for a peppermint stick first?

Miss Maryam and I suck on sticks, sittin on Miss Sally's pretty bedspread while she at her vanity, candy hangin out her mouth, starin into the mirror and applyin her cosmetics. Miss Fiona stand nearby, drinkin somethin the color a tea that's not. Miss Sally put cream on her face, on her arms, and everything start gettin lighter.

What that be? ask Miss Maryam.

Skin lightener, say Miss Sally. An asset, with some customers.

Miss Maryam finger the jar. Miss Sally take a gander at Miss Maryam's dark dark complexion, then say: I make it, sell it. You like an order?

Miss Maryam look at Miss Sally, look at the jar. Maybe. Maybe.

Give ya a sample, and Miss Sally rub a little on Miss Maryam's hand, turnin it high yella. Miss Maryam smile, but we leave without a purchase, out into the crisp air.

I feels we needs to get that coal now, Theo.

How do ye, Theo!

Nancy! This Miss Maryam, my auntie. That's Nancy and Elijah.

How do ye, Miss Maryam! You the rich auntie?

No, them's the other ones, I say.

Look!

Elijah stick his hand in the pocket of his pants. Then he take to cryin.

He had walnuts in there, say Nancy, but they musta fell through.

And there Elijah's fingers wigglin through the hole in his pocket.

On the way to the coal gatherin, Miss Maryam say, Peoples just gives us the coal?

I shake my head. On the streets close to the coal-yard, pieces falls off on accident while they're deliverin it.

Oh. Theo. You know what Miss Sally, Miss Fiona does for their work?

The men buys kisses from em. Miss Sally tole me.

Miss Maryam make a little chuckle, I don't know why.

If the coal-yard coal's been picked over, we can go to the docks. Sometime pieces falls off after bein taken from the barges—

We go *home!*

I turn round. Miss Maryam frozen behind me, like seen a ghost.

We gots to get home now!

This time she say it quieter, but harsh. I don't know what she talkin about!

Then I see what she sees.

$500 REWARD

Ran away, or decoyed from the subscriber, living near Beltsville, Prince George's County, Md.

MULATTO WOMAN, MARIA!
From 30 to 35 years of age, and very stout.

NEGRO BOY, DALL!
Dark Mulatto, 13 years of age, stout and well grown.

Negro Boy, Lem
11 years of age, Black, has a scar on the side of his breast, caused by a burn.

NEGRO BOY, BILL
Generally called "Shag," 8 years of age.

NEGRO BOY, BEN
2 years of age. Also,

NEGRO MAN, ADAM
About 30 years of age, 5 feet 4 or 5 inches high, stoutly built, full suit of hair.
He ran away on Saturday, the 22d of August, and I think has returned and induced his
Wife and Children off. I will give $600 reward for them, no matter where taken, if lodged
in Jail, or secured so that I may get them again, or, I will give

$300 REWARD for ADAM
If taken separate, and a proportional reward for either of the others, if taken separate, in any case
they must be secured, so I may get them again.

Baltimore, February 9, 1857.

ISAAC SCAGGS.

You can read it? I ask.

She whisper hard: I know what that kinda poster mean.

Miss Maryam, that ain't you. That slave catcher handbill lookin for Maria the Maryland mulatto.

She stare at it, like tryin to piece out the words.

That letterin. Look like more n Maria.

The rest is men. Boys and men. From Maryland, not South Carolina.

Miss Maryam catch her breath, thinkin.

Ever you sees South Carolina, you tells me?

I nod.

Soon. Soon I reads it myself.

When we get home, nobody there but Gran-Gran starin out her winda. I get my doll which I hid behind the flour bin, take her to the bed-closet floor playin with her. Then Miss Maryam come in, sit on the bed.

I likes your doll.

I nod, say nothin. I liked playin with jus *myself*.

Your Irish auntie gots a nice place.

Didn't look like you wanted to be there at first.

Not knows if they likes colored.

I was there.

Maybe caint tells you's colored.

Miss Sally's colored.

I never meet Miss Sally till we goes upstairs.

I shrug. Don't matter in Five Points, long's you got the money to pay.

Then I make Dolly do somersaults.

Nancy and Elijah is orphan?

I nod. I make Dolly dance.

No place they lives?

Live on the street.

Rags.

They ain't orphan lucky like me.

Nobody is.

My eyes snap to Miss Maryam, not knowin if she mean to be mean. But she jus lookin sad, lookin down.

Nex day is Saturday. I spend it with my Irish family but nobody hardly notice me, all tendin to that new boy. Ciaran's eyes now more red than dead, constant wet since it been clarified his sister got burned and buried. Still no tear he let fall, a hard stone not cracked by any Cahill kindness. After supper, I leave for the street. There Nancy and Elijah.

How do ye, Theo!

How do ye, Theo!

How do ye, I say, takin in that Nancy and Elijah got somethin new. Somethin the color a the slave dress Miss Maryam come in.

Where them gunny-sacks come from?

Auntie Maryam! say Nancy.

Auntie Maryam! say Elijah. Now I won't lose stuff from my pocket!

Auntie Maryam, say Nancy, tell us we can call her auntie, like you!

I tear off to Grammy Brook's. Who told Miss Maryam she could start bein friends with *my* friends without me? Who said Nancy and Elijah can call her Auntie Maryam, *I'm* the one sposed to call her Auntie Maryam and I'm *not*! I'll introduce her as such but to her face I'll say it never: she ain't my blood!

I storm in jus when everyone make a big laugh so they don't see the fury sparkin out my ears. Mr. Freeman tellin a story, somethin funny happened at the barbershop got everybody's attention. Hen look clean, Grammy musta made her bathe after her week's work. Mr. Freeman's hands movin, Grammy, Auntie Eunice, and Hen listenin close, smilin and waitin eager, then suddenly our barber boarder hit the funny line and everyone roarin. Grammy and Auntie Eunice and Hen and Mr. Freeman got the jollies but not Miss Maryam. Miss Maryam smile but it don't feel easy. Somethin keepin her out of it, keepin her away, outside the circle a joy and warm, some kinda deep-down hurt I spy, and all at once I know she made them gunny-sacks for Nancy and Elijah so they be just a little bit happy, feel just a little bit taken care of because them and Miss Maryam is orphans very very very unlucky.

You wanna biscuit and gravy, sweetie-pie? Grammy ask me.

One left, say Hen. You don't take it, it's mine.

Oh look, say Auntie Eunice. She's going to read the Bible for us.

That's a good girl, say Grammy.

Thank you, sugarplum, it's helpful for Auntie Maryam to hear reading aloud, say Auntie Eunice.

That Bible been in my family *generations*, Grammy tell Miss Maryam again.

Wait. Theo! Why do you have my fountain pen? ask Auntie Eunice.

Theo, careful with that ink near the family Bible! say Grammy.

Theo, what are you *doing?* ask Auntie Eunice.

Theo, stop, girl, stop! Grammy movin to me fast.

Auntie Maryam! I cry, wantin her attention. She turn to me, everybody froze, everybody starin at the Bible page I'm holdin up.

Births

Lioda ~~Brook~~ Brook
b. 1779

m. Moses ~~Brook~~ Brook
b. 1780 d. 1808

Children

Jedediah Brook
b. June 5, 1806

m. Abner Brook
b. 1802 d. 1841

Children

Henry Floy b. Dec. 23, 1824 d. July 2, 1849   m. Jennie Tiller d. Mar. 3, 1851
     Children: Henrietta b. May 17, 1847
Ezekiel b. Oct. 2, 1828 d. Sept. 5, 1852   m. Brigid Cahill d. Feb. 11, 1850
     Children: Theodora Brigid b. Feb. 9, 1850
Eunice b. July 26, 1830   m. Ambrose Bennett
     Children:
Maryam b. Mar. 20, 1831

Stories

Sunday mornin, Ciaran sittin on the cold grave-yard ground sobbin a sea's worth.

You after writin I could stay with ye! Sayin we make a family here, *how? So many Irish in America* writes you, *Beautiful America* writes you, it's *not!* Dlrty, no green, I miss—

All a sudden Ciaran's shoulders pop up like a cat. His head swerve round, catchin me ten yards behind, observin.

Maidin mhaith, Ciaran.

His eyes a fury.

I'm Theo, remember? From Grammy Cahill's. Lately I been mostly stayin at my other grammy's so maybe you forgot. It's *Thee*-oh, like *Hail Mary, full of grace, the Lord is with thee*-oh, not *Tee*-oh, some Irish mess that up. Your sister and my Auntie Siobhan and my mother was boon companions, raised like sisters since they come to America, so you and me's near cousins. Well, I reckon that make you my near-uncle but you ain't old enough for that, *hehe!*

He say nothin. I point.

That's my mother—Brigid, see? With the little Mary lookin over her, I jus come by to say Mornin to my mother like I do some Sundays. Her and me never met, but Grammy Cahill say it good I try keepin up my end a the relationship. And your sister and her husband and your baby niece right nex door, even though they ain't our blood, your sister *almost* family, close enough we invite em share our grave-yard space.

Now some kinda surprise happen in Ciaran's face, like what I jus said don't register friendly as I intended.

Well, I'll leave you alone to jabber with your sister.

I turn and walk away, feelin Ciaran's eyes singein my back. Not every Sunday do I come. But when I wrote Auntie Maryam's name in the family Bible lass night, seein my mother's name reminded me been a while since I visited, not since winter set in. I turn the corner outa Ciaran's sight, but

I reckon he don't know I'm still in earshot because all at once I hear him givin full voice to the wail again.

Back to Park street where Grammy Cahill set up her table, I wait for her to finish negotiatin a customer.

Mornin, Grammy!

Mornin to *you, mo leanbh.*

Ciaran cryin at the grave-yard!

Well. Still all new to him, only found out about his sister thirteen days ago.

He sittin on the cold cold ground and it only Febooary the twenty-second, he gonna catch his death!

He'll be all right. *You* leave him be. Born this side the Atlantic, but sure you inherited the gift of the gab.

I don't gab!

Leave him be. Here, this pot'll be grand for my stew. Take it home.

I take it home where Cathleen seamstressin, attachin sleeve to shirt.

Why're you looking like you just lost your boon companion?

Grammy say I'm a gabber and I'm not! I was goin to visit my mother's graveside—

Aw . . .

And there Ciaran at Meara's graveside—

Cousin Meara. She was a generation older.

Well, I was jus not interruptin Ciaran at Cousin Meara's graveside, now he's mad like I were sneakin up on him, I weren't! If he say different, he a liar, I was bein respectful!

Leave him be.

I sigh loud and storm to the door. At the door, I turn around. Cathleen back to her needle-pullin, not even care I'm upset!

All he talked to was his sister! And his brother-in-law and baby niece grave right there, ignorin em!

He didn't know them.

He didn't know *her.*

He knew his sister by her letters, knew her by their parents' love.

But Regan—

You remember the baby? Cathleen finally look up, flash of a smile, then it fade, her shakin her head. Poor little newborn. Regan never got to be a person. The idea of a baby succumbing to a fire might bring a sad picture, but how can you *love* an infant you've never held? How can that precious angel ever feel *yours*? Poor Ciaran.

Cathleen sigh and suck her bloody finger, she always hold pain into herself so till now I didn't know the needle even stabbed her.

Two days later, I'm up early outside Centre street and Pearl where the last-nighters at Matt Brennan's saloon and John Doscher's saloon left a holy mess. And it was Monday—shoulda been quiet! Lotta glass pieces for my gunny-sack, few metal frags, I take em to the scrapman. Two bits! he gimme. Grinnin at my quarter, Lady Liberty sittin holdin a flag and lookin off behind her, *Aaargh!*

My head snap: who grumblin? Ciaran, givin me the evil eye again! From where he standin and how he glarin, I suss it: in line behind me but didn't get as much from the scrapman.

Quality or quantity?

What?

Did he say he low-pay ya because your product was poor or because weren't enough of it?

Ciaran shrug.

I can show ya where there's plenty a good goods. I can tell ya best time for huntin and gatherin.

Proceedings of yesterday's Tammany Hall powwow!

Market news—latest cotton statements from Augusta and New Orleans!

I wanna do that.

Newsboy?

Ciaran stare at em, no answer.

I know some newsboys, I could—

No you can't, you're a girl, there's no newsgirls. Then Ciaran turn and walk away: rude!

❧

Nex day Mary Bree bawlin on her corner.

It don't sweep, the competition takin all the customers!

I see why she cry. Half the straws of her broom gone, and what's left worn down to near nothin!

Farms! I say, and me and her hand-in-hand up to the junction a Broadway and Eighth. Slip into a barn: straw! Gather a bunch, under our clothes gainst our skin, *ouch! ouch!* head back downtown. Mary Bree's face all happy-grin. In a alley, we try tyin up the straw round her stick but jus make a mess, Mary Bree cryin again! Then I say: Cathleen! Up to Grammy Cahill's, Cathleen pause her parts-sewin and wrap up Mary Bree's broom in a jiff.

Go raibh maith agat! Mary Bree grin.

Cathleen smile. You're welcome.

Theo's teachin me Gaelic!

Irish! Cathleen and me both say. Mary Bree frown.

Once I say *Maidin mhaith* to a customer, and she say *That's very nice Gaelic* and I say *It's Irish* and she laugh and say *No, you're Irish, the language is Gaelic.*

Ignorance, Cathleen mutter. *Irish Gaelic* you might call it, or just *Irish*, but not just *Gaelic*, which is ancient and an umbrella: Irish, Scottish, Isle of Man Manx. Americans trying to say Irish are so stupid we don't even know our own language, now I ask you: *Who's* the dunce?

Mary Bree back on her corner, grinnin, wavin to me. I wave back, my pride shinin, the good deed I done, and jus beyond I notice a bootblack I ain't seen before. Walk up to him.

I hope you talked to the bootblack captain.

Ciaran gimme a look like I'm some buzzin gnat he ready to swat.

There's rules. Captain set the prices. The bootblacks don't like intruders comin along lowerin the rates.

Thank ye for your all-important wisdom, he say and look off, like lookin for customers. And I can tell by his sneer-face he don't appreciate my wisdom at all!

I'm *tellin* you—

Then he pick up his boot brush and leave! I follow. I'm tryin to help him, he need my knowledge!

Turn a corner: where he go? Runnin toward Bayard, then I spy him to the right, Pell street, talkin to a man drivin his hog. The farmer shove Ciaran away. *Look like I can afford to hire a hand?* The farmer walk on. Ciaran stare after him. Ciaran don't see me, his breath slow, steady, left arm hangin, right arm crooked holdin his hip. But not mad. Jus starin at his feet, head hung, eyes to the ground so long I finally quiet move away.

$$\backsim$$

Snow! Six inches! Thursday mornin, run crost the street, *bam!*

Hen gigglin her head off. She snowballed me! And she sposed to be at work! Then we snowballin each other. Then I run inside O'SHEA'S BOARD & PUBLICK.

Auntie Siobhan! Auntie Siobhan!

Yes, *mo stoirín?*

My cousin Hen snowballin me!

Oh! Some hot cider then?

While Auntie Siobhan pourin, a customer say, Seem you got the luck, Siobhan. Survived the license law.

Luck? I work night n day and *still* barely make the increase they chargin for a liquor license now! Damned temperance Republicans! Any trick to impoverish the Irish!

Tell me a story! I say, sippin my apple nectar.

That pull my auntie outa her tirade. She smile.

Well. Snow weren't just invented your generation, ye know, your mother and I were pretty fond of it ourselves. I recall she were about fifteen years of age and me thirteen, I'm walkin down Chatham street, mindin my own affairs when all the sudden a poundin! And the bombardment not lettin up—your mother, that rascal, been out half an hour stockin up her cache!

Haha! *Then* what?

But before she answer, Ciaran pop up from behind the counter! Facin Auntie Siobhan, his back to me. Tell *me* a story, he say. My sister.

Ha! My auntie look delighted. Just as I'm returnin the barrage to my assailant, who should come up from behind and whack me back a the head? Two on one—and me the youngest! But neither *your* sister nor *your* mother could pack a snowball tight as yours truly. Soon they're *both* beggin on their knees for mercy!

But though that story become for Ciaran *and* me, once *he* appear my auntie seem only to have eyes for *him*, warm eyes on *him*.

What you doin here!

Ciaran know I'm talkin to him but he don't turn round, keep his back-side to me.

Arrangin my glasses and my bottles, say my auntie. Very kind of him.

But don't he have to bootblack?

Both! Ciaran say too quick, still not lookin my way.

I stare. Then fast yank my belly up on the counter. Ciaran try turnin his face quick but I'm quicker, I see it: black eye.

Ha! Pears the bootblack captain taught ya a lesson, toldja!

Theo! Say you're sorry!

I stare at Auntie Siobhan. *I* didn't give him that black eye! The bootblack captain—

Then that's between him and the captain. Then she turn to Ciaran but her eye half on me. What's got into her, I can't say. My niece is usually such a good girl.

I look at Auntie Siobhan. I look at Ciaran. And just a flash of a second seem like his mouth corner turn up, like he think it funny! I snap back to Auntie Siobhan.

My story! *My* story! Then I run out, runnin.

Theo! I hear on the street.

Grammy Cahill callin, standin in the door of a tenement where must be a recently departed, she goin to do business with the survivors about the estate a the deceased which usually be a rag or two.

Mornin, Grammy.

Haven't seen ye a few days. Wanna come sleep at Grammy's tonight?

I ain't sure with Ciaran there, but I miss my Grammy Cahill! I nod!

Grammy gimme a kiss. Then she kiss me kiss me till I laugh. This a kissin I known my entire life and Ciaran jus new, she can't be offerin Ciaran *this* kissin!

Bean soup supper in a circle: Grammy and Great-Uncle Fergus and Cousin Aileen got their chairs, Cathleen and Maureen on the couch, and on the floor's me and Ciaran, him and me inchin away from each other far as we can go. Cold! Coal runnin low, my feet ice! Crost my legs is the new blanky Grammy bought from Mrs. Flynn, her dead twins shared it. Little hole here, little hole there, too raggedy to sell on her table so Grammy brung it home, but the air blow through to my bones! In the night, I sleep nex to Grammy, her warm arms fold round me! And

Cousin Aileen my other side, Maureen crossways at our feet, Cathleen stay on the couch. Ciaran gotta share Great-Uncle Fergus's bedroll, the front-room.

Nex mornin coffee, and me and Ciaran get porridge, Cathleen already at her needlework. Everyone else gone but Grammy. My sort of cousin don't even look at me so I don't even look at him: don't look, don't speak.

Don'tcha speak? Grammy ask.

Our answer is no answer.

Well, ye're *goin* to. Who plans to start?

Me and Ciaran's eyeballs glance at the other, glance off. I sigh.

Maidin mnaith, Ciaran.

That's a good girl, say Grammy.

And a good mornin to you too, *Theo*.

My mouth fly open. He never said my name before and now say it like poison! I hit him!

He hit me back!

Stop!

Grammy's fists holdin our fists.

Out with ye both! And be back in an hour with coal!

Sun come out, and most the snow melted soft or dirty or gone. Ciaran and me near the coal-yard. Take me a long time to get here because I'll not walk the short course with him. But he musta also found a long way around avoidin me because I still beat him by a minute. I got my gunny-sack. I see he's wearin dead Liam Flynn's ripped coat, fillin the pockets. We work a long while, not a utter. But then I see somethin. Ciaran made a mistake. I should jus let him make that mistake, get him in trouble with Grammy. But then he does it again!

That's a rock.

He keep goin like I never spoke.

I *said* that's not coal, it's a rock.

Still pretend he got no hearin.

I *said*—

I *know*!

He start slammin his rocks *and* coal on the ground, throwin away everything he gathered!

I know what coal looks like, I don't care!

Then he slam his bottom on the ground, cross his arms.

Grammy gonna be mad—

Aaargh! He slam his back on the ground, lyin down, glarin at the clouds.

Prolly I should say nothin. Except I wasn't finished my sentence. But Ciaran musta figured out I'm about to finish my sentence because just as I open my mouth again, he sit up, open his faster.

I'm handy. You think farmin takes no cleverness? Knowin when to plant, when to rest the soil, when to harvest, how much. What's clever mean here? Knowin how to survive in the dirt! Filth!

You slept with pigs.

That's how we're after keepin em back home! So they don't get stole, don't wander off. *And* they're a mite cleaner than anything *human* in Five Points!

I'm tellin Grammy you said that.

Heathen.

What you call me?

Blasphemer. Next to your mammy's grave and not even bother to go to her, speak to her.

I go to her! That day, *you* was there with your sister, I was jus waitin later so's I be alone with my mother, come back—

Protestant, are ye?

Half Catholic, half A.M.E. Zion.

Ciaran suck his teeth.

Don't suck your teeth at me!

Ciaran suck his teeth again. I walk over and hit him. He don't hit back. I'm after askin you a question. No love have ye for your own mother?

I wanna hit him again, but then I see he's really wonderin. Didn't know her.

Ciaran jus keep starin.

Didn't know her! Not my father neither. Make me a sinner? Because I love no one I never knew?

Ciaran think on that. You don't care?

I shrug. No feelins one way or the other. I got my Grammy Cahill and my Auntie Siobhan, my Grammy Brook and my Auntie Eunice, I don't need no mammy nor da.

He look at me. Then look down. Hurts. When you *do* care. Then he look up: Not carin. You have the luck.

I know! I giggle and, because my gunny-sack's full up, head back to Grammy Cahill's.

Overnight: nother four inches! I help Grammy Brook deliver some whites to the whites, then see Mary Bree on her corner. Make a stack a snowballs, gonna surprise her! Wait for her to walk sweep for her cus tomer. But coughin so much while she offerin, the fancy couple move away fast. Mary Bree wear boots she made outa rags, soaked through.

How do ye, Mary Bree.

How do ye, Theo, then her fallin to a coughin fit again. I don't unload my ammunition on her. Later me and Hen'll have a time.

Nex day's Sunday first a March: spring comin! But no sign of it outside, flurries and the ground still mostly white except for the black a the dirt, yella a the urine. I head to the graves. My father in the A.M.E. Zion cem etery, my mother in the Catholic. In the latter there Ciaran be, whisperin to his sister, not seein myself. I ain't no heathen but Ciaran's a little right about me not visitin my mammy regular. These two Sundays in a row's highly unusual.

I walk right by him, not botherin to tiptoe since lass week I tried to be respectful and all I got in return was nastiness.

Now Ciaran look at me. He don't seem mad today, jus curious what I'm up to. I march right up to my mother's grave.

Mornin, Ma, I say. Then start hittin the marker with my snowballs! I throw a thousand snowballs! *Bang bang bang!* I'm laughin and laughin. I look at Ciaran, I say, She like it! Auntie Siobhan said so! And I keep up the poundin.

Ciaran's eyes on me. Then his lips turn up, near a smile. The first kind liness I ever got from him! I can't stop laughin. I can't stop bombardin my mammy!

Remember, I ask the grave, when you and Ciaran's sister Meara was ambushin Auntie Siobhan? Well, *your* turn now, Ma! Haha! Snow for *you!* You like snow, *I* like snow! I'm your daughter, Theodora, remember? I'm that baby you had then died, but all grown now, see? I'm seven! See?

I turn to Ciaran. Look! I got her right on the nose!

But Ciaran not smilin no more. What he is is not mad, jus starin at me. I washed my face only two days ago so can't be very dirty, I touch it. Some thin warm. My cold flesh but somethin I didn't know was there, somethin warm, and wet, and salty. And the water in my eyes and in the streams on my cheeks already turnin crystal, turnin ice.

Bad Week for Black

Outa there, squirrels! Kep me up half the night!

Grammy Brook bangin on the ceilin with her broomstick. The scurryin overhead stop. Then start.

Garret? ask Auntie Maryam.

Grammy nod. They're up there.

How you gets up there?

Grammy pick up one of our wood chairs. We got three chairs, two at the little wood table plus Gran-Gran's at the winda. Grammy take a chair outside our door, the corridor. Set it down, we look up to the ceilin: trap-door. Auntie Maryam stand on the chair, unlatch trap-door, stick her head up so it disappear through the ceilin. I never notice that trap-door before!

I gets rid of em, we hear from inside the garret.

How?

I sees the holes they gets in. I patches em up.

How?

Auntie Maryam bring her head down visible to answer Grammy.

I needs some a your ironin cornstarch.

Grammy think on that. Then nod.

I needs vinegar.

I can get some.

You find some pebbles? Auntie Maryam ask me.

What's pebbles?

Little rocks, then Auntie Maryam show with her finger and thumb how tiny.

Okay!

I gets rid of em.

Catch one before you patch up all the holes, say Grammy. Squirrel stew: Sunday dinner!

I run out to the street to find pebbles. Squirrel stew! I never ate a squirrel before. It taste furry? Soft? I eat squirrel's bushy tail? Where I find them pebbles!

President James Buchanan sworn into office!

Blood in Kansas: Sheriff shot during meeting with Governor Geary—read all about it!

Whatchu suckin on?

Hen standin outside Mr. Freeman's barbershop, suckin on a sweet.

Taffy, she say, her head tilt toward the shop. I gotta go to work. Then Hen take off to find Mr. Samuel her master sweep. I go in.

Another one? say some customer gettin a shave. Come get your candy, girl!

Five colored barbers tendin to five white customers who look richer n Five Points.

That little darky not so dark, say the candy man to Mr. Freeman who say nothin, keep trimmin the man's hair. I say nothin, taffy's a long chew.

There's a whole lot lookin like her roamin round here, say another customer.

Buchanan inaugurated yesterday, say another customer. He your man, Longworth?

Well, there weren't much choice, say the candy man. I certainly don't favor these radical Republicans.

Fillmore?

Candy man Longworth say, You know he took twenty-one percent of the popular? The Know-Nothings nominate our former president without his knowledge nor his enthusiasm, and he takes twenty-one percent of the popular vote!

Trim my sides, Ben, say another customer to his barber.

Who'd *your* man be? Longworth ask Mr. Freeman. If Ethiopians had the franchise.

A few do, Mr. Longworth, the propertied ones, but since that doesn't encompass me, it would not seem to matter.

I'm still chewin, headin for the door, then hear, Stop, Theo.

I turn. Mr. Freeman still ain't looked up from Longworth.

Wait till I'm finished here.

Blast it! say Josiah, one a the young barbers, lookin at a shavin strop snapt in two.

When Mr. Freeman's through with Longworth, he take me in a little room in the back.

I'm here and I'm a grown-up who lives with you, but in future what happens if a grown-up offers you candy and there's no grown-up around who's a relative or who lives with you?

Umm. I look for a grown-up lives with me or relative?

You say *no*.

Oh.

Repeat what I just said.

Anybody offer me candy

Or a ride, or to show you something.

Anybody offer me anything not relative or lives with me, I say no. Unless grown-ups I know around.

Good. I need to get back to the next customer.

Mr. Freeman! The president innogerated yesterday?

He was.

How come the election was November the fourth but the innogeratin not till March the fourth?

I suppose they have to give the new president time to get to Washington City in case he's from far away. Though this one was only coming from Pennsylvania.

Oh. Mr. Freeman! What that man mean, lots a people look like me? Nobody look like me!

He means your coloring. He means in Five Points it's not infrequent for negro and Irish to come together, like your mother and your father.

Oh. Mr. Freeman! Why that man call you Eatey-ope?

Ethiopian. It's another term for colored. Like negro, like black, like African, like a man of color. I don't know why Ethiopian, maybe because those are the Africans people remember from the Bible.

Auntie Eunice's church is African Methodist Episcopalian: African!

Now you let me get back to my customers?

Can I have Josiah's shavin strop ript in two?

Why? You wanna go up and knock out those squirrels in the attic?

What's *attic*?

Garret.

No! Auntie Maryam doin that. I want the strop for Grammy Cahill, sell at her table.

You let me get back to my customers, I'll save it for you. Come in the afternoon when it's quiet.

I think I know a place where I might could find some pebbles for Auntie Maryam: the park! Run down to City Hall. I see a little stone! Between the dirt, I gotta dig. Another one! I think about what Mr. Freeman said. I will follow that rule not take from grown-ups I don't know—except for the scrapman. If I bring him scrap, I'm sure takin his money for it!

Here some pebbles, Auntie Maryam! Jus her and Gran-Gran home.

Goooood, she say, lookin in her pot on the stove.

What's cookin?

Cornstarch n vinegar n water, I makes my glue.

Auntie Maryam, I come up to the garret with ya? I never seen it before.

These be good pebbles, Theo! Now go get s'more.

More?

More! She grin, stirrin her brew.

I eat molasses n bread then go back down to the park to collect more pebbles then it's middle a the afternoon, I come back up to the Sixth ward the barbershop. Afternoon no business, the five barbers havin a rest, sittin in their five barber chairs readin the paper. Their faces covered by their paper, droppin em from their face when I walk in, then pick up their readin again: the *Sun*, the *New-York Dispatch*, the *Herald*, the *New-York Daily Tribune*. Mr. Freeman lookin at me over his doubled-over *Frederick Douglass' Paper*.

Back for the strop?

I nod.

There's two worn out. That do ya?

I nod happy. And the one snapt in half!

What can you do with that?

Grammy Cahill always think a somethin.

Ha! says Josiah, then reads: *I must humbly invoke the God of our fathers for wisdom and firmness to restore harmony and ancient friendship among the people of the several States and to preserve our free institutions*, I know *one* damned institution ain't free!

Who's invokin God? I ask Mr. Freeman quiet.

Buchanan, inaugural speech.

How about this? say Ben, the other young barber besides Josiah. *A difference of opinion has arisen in regard to the point of time when the people of a Territory shall decide this question for themselves. This is, happily, a matter of but little practical importance*—since the question in question is slavery, obviously he ain't asked nobody black.

Obviously he ain't asked nobody *white*, say another barber. The territories he speakin of is bleedin.

What territory's bleedin? I whisper to Mr. Freeman.

Kansas, little girl, that same barber answer. Slave-mongers comin in to attack the Free-Soilers.

Missouri worried their slaves gonna escape over the western border to free land, Kansas Territory, say Ben.

Free soil, snort the fifth barber. White Kansans just wantin to stave off some big damned slave plantation takin root. Bleedin Kansas just about the common white man gainst the rich white man, far as they're concerned *free soil* got nothin to do with the black man.

What's that? Hen ask nex mornin at Grammy's, lookin at a ball big as a grown-up hand, pebbles glued together. Hen didn't get back till late lass night after gone a couple days. Sometime she take a mind to sleep in the street with the urchins.

It's Auntie Maryam's thing against the squirrels, say I.

And workin already! say Grammy at her ironin. I hear less squirrel pitter-patter. Don't forget to save a critter or two for stew!

How come you glue all those little rocks together? Whyn't you just get one big rock? ask Hen, which is somethin I been wonderin myself.

Fill the holes, gots to be the right size, say Auntie Maryam. I glues some down here, then finishes up there nex to the hole: exack.

Grammy, you like President Buchanan? I ask.

Doughface, say Grammy.

Doughface! Hen and me giggle.

Doughface is a Northerner allied with the South. Well, what else you call a Pennsylvania Democrat?

Democrats is bad? I ask.

Democrats against abolition, yes! say Grammy. Democrats is bad.

Know-Nothins is bad?

Know-Nothings called themselves right.

Republicans is bad?

Republicans is new. Run the gamut. Some got courage: no slavery! Some cowards: no *expansion* of slavery.

Scurry scurry. We all look up.

Theo. I found some pretty beet seeds cheap. You bring em up to Auntie Eunice? Ask her can I borrow some salt for our Sunday squirrel stew?

Okay!

I need it before Sunday and today's Friday. So if you stay the night with her, you be back tomorrow. Or early Sunday.

Okay! Auntie Maryam, can me and Hen come up to the garret with you? We never seen the garret before.

I seen it, say Hen.

When!

Sometime.

Where's that tomboy not been? say Grammy, lickin her thumb and testin the hot a the iron, *sssssss.*

Scurry scurry.

Grammy look up and grin: Meat!

⌁

I know Auntie Eunice'll still be at school so I wander way up to Jupiterville, One Hundredth street and Seventh avenue. I never know if this still Seneca Village or Seneca Village suburbs, but Mr. Hesser sure a part a the settlement. His house big—two floors! And barn, gardens, chicken coop, goat stables. He won't mind I walk round his property collectin pebbles for Auntie Maryam, listenin to the music scales inside. When the piano stop, I knock.

Theo! Come in, come in!

Even though I'm not one a Mr. Hesser's pupils, he gimme a exercise when I come to visit him, run my fingers on the keys and talk about sharps and flats. Him and Auntie Eunice and Uncle Ambrose is friendly neighbors. After my lesson, Mr. Hesser always make me a snack. Today is potata slices to which he add onions and bacon: German fries!

Hour later, I'm in my auntie's parlor, which is her fancy name for *front-room.* She lookin at a paper in her hand.

Auntie Eunice! I went to Jupiterville today!

Did you. How's Mr. Hesser?

Grand! He gay me a piano lesson!

Wish we could afford to give them to you regularly.

And German fries!

Hm.

He been in New York longer n Mr. Schmidt? Mr. Hesser don't sound German like Mr. Schmidt.

Yes, Mr. Hesser's been here a long time, he and Uncle Ambrose's father were friends.

Uncle Ambrose's father who's buried in the Seneca Village cemetery?

Yes.

Grammy gay me beet seeds to give you. They're purple! Can we go plant em?

Spring. I'll set them out in the cold until then.

Grammy said can she borrow salt for squirrel stew Sunday after Auntie Maryam catches a squirrel in the garret? You know there's squirrels in our garret? You know a garret's a attic?

Yes.

You know a cellar's a basement? You know Mr. Hesser got a whole cellar under his big house? He got a chimney. He got a sewer! How Mr. Hesser get a whole town to hisself?

It's not a whole town. He bought those seven lots and called his Seneca Village property Jupiterville because his name is Jupiter Zeuss K. Hesser. Mr. Hesser is very wise, he cultivated that land, he built that home *to last*.

I wait while Auntie Eunice dab her eyes. And now I see Auntie Eunice ain't looked too happy the whole time since I come.

Why you cry?

She swallow.

This paper? It's a warning of eviction. It came today, and it cautions that there may not *be* a Seneca Village much longer. We've been struggling with the city, *the fight is not over!* But it's very hard. They want to take our land.

Why!

They have other plans.

But where everybody go? You and Uncle Ambrose? And Mr. Schmidt your tenant? And Mr. O'Kelleher's pig farm? And Jupiterville?

Gone! The city doesn't care where!

Auntie Eunice wrap the seeds up in a pouch and take em outside, under her front doorstep. I stoop down with her.

I was twelve in 'forty-two, say my auntie, when Charles Dickens came to town. Marching around Five Points with a police escort, I don't know if I ever saw him, I wouldn't have known who he was if I did. It was his notorious visit that set off the blasted slumming craze of the idle rich, Dickens finding Five Points to be a more wretched place than the East End of London he was so famous for portraying—this was my home! And then I met your uncle Ambrose. And he introduced me to *his* home: greenery and space and friendly neighbors, many landed *colored* neighbors! Generations they'd been here! And more recently the Irish, the German, everyone harmonious.

Like Five Points!

Well. Cultures here not quite overlapping in the way of your father and mother, but the cooperation, the goodwill: yes! And clean! Space! At first, I couldn't believe it. And when I finally did, I made the mistake of believing it would be forever.

Why they wanna remove the Seneca Villagers off their land? Who they wanna come live here?

Trees!

But there already trees!

They want *all* trees, they want no people of color and no immigrants and no poor. They want to tear down our homes and build a park! An enormous park in the middle of Manhattan, *not* touching the bordering Fifth avenue mansions of course, heavens no! The park will serve as the aristocracy's front yard, their scenic pleasure.

I look around at the Seneca Village houses. I think about City Hall Park, I love the park! But after I visit, I like goin home.

Nex mornin I wake, no Auntie Eunice beside me in the bed. I hear a poundin. Come out to the kitchen: Auntie Eunice poundin out biscuit dough! Now she don't seem sad. Her face look mad. On the table nex to where she work's a mornin edition.

Theo, she say without lookin up, her voice low. Do you know who Dred Scott is?

Shake my head.

Dred Scott was a slave. *Is* a slave. Dred Scott's master was a U.S. Army surgeon who took him along to various military assignments—fort in Illinois: free state; fort in Wisconsin: free territory. Mr. Scott was in free Wisconsin four years, wedding a wife and having a daughter, hiring himself out during long periods when the master was away. The master returned and took Mr.

Scott and his family to slave states, then the master died. Mr. Scott and his wife had scrimped and saved to purchase their family's freedom, and requested this of the physician's widow, who refused. Mr. Scott took them to court, basing his claim on the family's previous residences on free soil, and won. *He won!* But the fiend mistress appealed to the Missouri Supreme Court which, *two years after Mr. Scott and family had gained their freedom*, overturned the ruling, placing them back in slavery. Another trial, this time regarding the physical abuse Mr. Scott had endured. Another unjust outcome. So, the U.S. Supreme Court. The decision came yesterday.

Here Auntie Eunice pick up the newspaper, slam it down.

Damned Taney!

Auntie Eunice cussin make me jump more n her slammin the paper! Flour flyin, then fall soft.

Who's Taney?

Roger Taney, the Supreme Court chief *in*justice. Not only does he deny Mr. Scott his freedom but Taney takes his breach of righteousness much further. Dissolving the Missouri Compromise, meaning western land guaranteed free is no longer, *and*—it was just professed that negroes never were and never will be U.S. citizens.

Auntie Eunice point to some words in the paper. I read em out loud: *so far inferior, that they had no rights which the white man was bound to respect*—

If we are not citizens, then how did we have the right to claim freedom suits? Freedom suits work?

Of *course* they work! Hundreds and hundreds have been filed, and there have been *many, many* victories! Freedom awarded! Do you want an egg with your biscuit?

I clean my plate. After breakfast, Auntie Eunice quiet a while. Then she say, The freedom suits *won't stop*. Do you know why?

I shake my head.

Because we won't let them.

Then she snatch my dirty plate so fast I have to grab my last crumb a biscuit n yolk!

I go out to the outhouse, then collect a few more pebbles. When I come back in, my auntie at her table scrawlin.

Whatcha writin?

Finishing a letter to Uncle Ambrose.

Uncle Ambrose get your letter middle a the sea?

No. I write letters to him, and he reads them when he returns. It makes me feel like he was here, and it makes *him* feel like he was here.

She stop writin, like she thinkin. Then turn to me.

Auntie Maryam is free only because she escaped to a free state. She wasn't *born* in a free state, she didn't sue in court, she *escaped* to here and thus her freedom is undocumented. This is *only* since the blasted Fugitive Slave Act of 1850! Before then, escape to free land, you're free. But now. Some evil mercenary slave-catcher could recognize Auntie Maryam, kidnap her, deport her back down South, property of a master monster. *Free* colored people have been sent down, it's happened! The bounty hunter making a false claim— well, his word against a negro's, and weren't we just declared non-citizens?

Auntie Eunice swipe a tear. I think about the white customers in the barbershop, the white men I pass on my way uptown to Seneca Village. Might one of em be itchin for a bounty windfall?

Be kind to Auntie Maryam. The news about Mr. Dred Scott will go very hard for her.

I nod.

And *you* be careful! Never talk to strangers! Avoid back alleys! Stay in crowds!

I nod.

Would you like to read my letter?

I stare at the curvy words.

Go on. I've taught you cursive.

Saturday the 7ᵗʰ of March, 1857

My dearest Ambrose,

It has been a very trying week. I received an eviction warning yesterday regarding the City's determination to destroy our village in order to make way for the proposed central park. You may wish to comfort me, to remind me that they have said such things before, but you surely have not forgotten the incidents regarding the firewood, the "park's stones."

I look up.

My auntie say, A couple was taken into custody for chopping trees for firewood when until very recently the activity was perfectly legal. Mr. O'Kelleher was arrested for peddling the so-called "park's stones," when he has for years broken rocks and sold the gravel to the city for paving.

I say nothin about my pebbles. I'm glad the coppers didn't find me! Continue.

And last week our dance hall was raided by police. Though we didn't partake ourselves, I'd always enjoyed hearing the distant festive music wafting through the Saturday night air. This foreboding against our community and land, against <u>your family's land</u>, the soil that holds the graves and spirits of your beloved mother and father—these threats are beginning to feel more real. And I have barely begun to put my head around the imminent closing of my cherished Colored School No. 3.

Last Sunday, our dear pastor informed the congregation that the peril for our community is far greater than homelessness. It's these horrid voting requirements for colored men, only <u>colored</u> men. If a negro must prove his residency for three years at a freehold estate worth at least $250, how many black voters would we have left after the destruction of Seneca Village? One might say it matters little; as it stands the numbers are deplorable, merely 91 of 13,000 negro New Yorkers having the franchise. But we must start somewhere, and an appropriation of our village by the authorities would subtract 10 from that already pitiable colored voter roll. Ambrose, you voted for Senator Frémont of California, the first Republican on the presidential ticket! It may be your last chance to ever cast your ballot against slavery.

Speaking of which—that defender of the curséd Fugitive Slave Act Buchanan was sworn in Wednesday! And now the Supreme Court has at long last handed down a decision for poor Mr. Dred Scott, the ramifications much worse than we had imagined. All in all, I would have to say this has been a very bad week for black folks. I can find hope only in the prospect that such severe reactionary measures may very well be evidence of the Court's own sense of threat—that times are changing.

I miss you exceedingly today. The scent of your pillow

That's the gist, say Auntie Eunice, snatchin the letter back quick.

Nex mornin's Sunday. I get up before dawn with pebbles in my gunny-sack and a pouch a salt and head downtown before Auntie Eunice wake up and make me go to the Seneca Village A.M.E. Zion with her. When I get home to Grammy Brook's, she gone to the big local Mother Zion, and Hen not around. Gran-Gran at her winda, and Auntie Maryam ironin the whites for the whites. I give her my long face.

Mornin, Auntie Maryam.

Mornin, Theo! How's *you* today?

Sad.

How comes?

Mr. Dred Scott lost his case.

Yes, I hears that. Auntie Maryam dribble starch on a sheet.

I got some more pebbles for ya.

Done! Squirrels is gone! You likes to see the garret?

Yes!

I didn't expect *that*! Auntie Maryam don't seem sad at all. She take the candle in the stove, *whoosh*! pick up one a the table chairs with her other hand. I follow her out our door. She set the chair down, stand on it, unlatch the trap. Look down at me.

Everything in the garret a secret. You keeps a secret, Theo?

I nod!

You keeps a secret, Theo?

I stare.

What happens the garret *gots* to stay secret. You keeps the secret?

I nod. I say nothin but now the garret feel scary! What up in the garret, *ghost?* Auntie Maryam lift herself into it. I get on the chair, she lift me into it.

Dark! But we got the candlelight. Ceilin low, my head near touch it! I crawl behind Auntie Maryam. In the middle, we sit.

Don't hear no scurry scurry, does you.

I shake my head.

I gots rid a the squirrels! Plug up all holes cep one, one the critters leaves by. When I comes up this mornin, no squirrel! So's I plugs the lass hole there, see all the cornstarch pebble plug-holes?

But what about the squirrel stew!

Squirrels gone. Your grammy say, You catched one for my stew? I saze no, I gots rid of em too fast! I's sorry disappoint your grammy, she gon pick up shad, dinner be shad fish and cabbage.

What Auntie Maryam say make me feel sad. And feel bad that I feel sadder about I don't get to taste squirrel stew than I feel sad about Mr. Dred Scott.

You wants a secret? Auntie Maryam cup her hand over her mouth, whisper: I likes our squirrels. Look!

Auntie Maryam shine her candlelight on a pile a thisnthat. Acorns and a string, pine cone, heel of a sock. Twig and tree bark, jagged piece a liquor bottle and pine needles and a bitta fur and a dried leaf and a bitta lettuce and a raggedy handbill.

I thought you don't like them posters, Auntie Maryam! They're bad!

No! Good! Good squirrels, they takes it down! There's white peoples likes it, likes them posters. There's other white peoples don't likes it but if they tears it down, they goes to jail. The colored peoples don't likes it but if they tears it down, white peoples thinks *they* must be escaped, *they* goes to jail, then deport to the South: slave! So all the peoples leaves poster be, but squirrels sees the poster, squirrels tears it down! Nobody puts squirrels in jail!

Auntie Maryam pick up the poster and the bottle shard, I crawl-follow her. She bring us to one a the cornstarch plugs, then she remove it. The daylight flood in.

Ready? she say. Then she lift up the candle, touch poster to flame, the poster burn up! Crumble to ashes into the bottle glass.

Auntie Maryam grin. Blow, Theo. Blow!

I blow hard. Ashes fly out the hole, into the sky. Bits n bits of ashes, pieces a nothin floatin all over Five Points.

Then a scratchin behind us in the garret, our faces snap to it.

Auntie Maryam, ya missed a squirrel!

Dorothea! I thinks you's gone with the rest.

But Auntie Maryam smilin at Dorothea.

Auntie Maryam, you give the squirrels names?

When I sees they brung the poster, I knows they's my friends.

Oh. Then I whisper, I bet Dorothea taste good.

But like Auntie Maryam don't hear me, her eyes only on Dorothea. Then her fingertips start tap tappin gentle near the exit hole.

Dorothea come flyin to us fass, I got to cover my mouth, shut me from screamin! Out the hole, she fly to the nex-door roof. Dorothea already found herself some other bushytails to chatter with! Happy she home with her own peoples, free. Then, while Auntie Maryam fass cover the hole again with the cornstarch plug, I remember how much I love shad and cabbage.

Holidays

Lookin like an angel in white altogether, say teary Grammy Cahill.

I look down. I do! Standin on the chair while Cousin Aileen puttin pins in Maureen's First Communion dress, passed down to be Cathleen's First Communion dress, now *my* First Communion dress!

When I'm through, say Cousin Aileen, it'll fit her grand.

Found a bunch! Ciaran walk through the door grinnin, holdin a armful a papers. Don't know who'd've just dropped them in the street, he say. Then he jus drop em on the floor, all different kinda papers.

I'll take the *Tribune*! smile Cathleen from the couch.

The *Herald*, say Great-Uncle Fergus from his chair in the corner.

Irish-American for me, mumble Cousin Aileen around the pins in her mouth.

Ciaran stare at everybody, glance down at the pile, look up at everybody. Then, seemin unsure, start handin out the papers.

You gave me the *Herald*, say Cathleen.

This the blamed *Times*! snap Great-Uncle Fergus.

I didn't ask for the *Sun*, frown Cousin Aileen.

Ciaran! say Grammy, and snatch up a *World*. Read.

Ciaran look at Grammy, look at us, look at the paper, stare at the paper like some kinda magic might come along save him.

Mmmmm. Mmmmmaaaaaaaaay—

Grammy cross her arms. *School.*

No! Ciaran speak it not like refusal but like horror, like sent to the firin squad.

Till you're readin, Grammy say, while Great-Uncle Fergus hand out to everybody their requested daily. When ye pass my readin test, Grammy go on, ye can quit.

Theo don't go!

I know how to read! My Auntie Eunice taught me, she's a teacher.

Ye come here holdin the letter from poor Meara in your hands. How'd ye make out what it was sayin to find where we lived?

Memorized it, he mutter to Grammy. Back in Kerry, a neighbor's after readin it to us. Wrote our reply for us.

I can teach you to read, Ciaran, I offer.

He gimme the glare. Plenty enough I read!

Today's date that be, say Grammy, pointin to the paper in her hand. You're seein M-A and readin *May*, it's *March*! March the tenth!

One week till Saint Patrick's Day!

You're jumping and clapping while all officialdom's brawling, Cathleen say to me. Irish factions wrangling over the parade.

Always the in-fightin. Great-Uncle Fergus shakin his head, eyes in his *Herald*.

And worse, say Grammy, the religionists hopin to take it *all* away, turn Saint Pat's into a quiet church day. 'S if it makes them more Catholic than the rest of us!

No parade?

Oh, there'll be a parade, Grammy say to me and wink.

A thousand saints, mumble Ciaran. Saint Finbar, Saint Ailbe, Saint Brigid of Kildare—

That's my ma's name!

Every day be *some* saint's day, why you've not toasted the others?

But it's Saint *Patrick!*

And?

Grammy chuckle at my gasp. America's after makin Saint Patrick's. Back home, we would give him the day, but that were all the acknowledgin. But here. Born in Britain, snake charmer of Ireland, Saint Patrick's spirit come to Irish America to be crowned Saint of all Saints! Then she turn to Ciaran: I'll take ye down to the school tomorrow, get ye registered.

Most everyone in America reads, say Cousin Aileen to groanin Ciaran. The educators and the God-fearin made it their mission.

You'll be grateful, lad, say Great-Uncle Fergus. I learnt it too late. I don't complain! Street cleaner, scrapin up the muck: the horse apples and the garbage, thanks be to God, not a bad livin! But if I could read when I was a young one—maybe a different path, Irish drives all the public transport because they's the ones deciphered the street signs. Irish lately been hired for police, goin into *politics* even, what kinda possibility for a young literate one!

Listen to Fergus, Grammy say.

If we were *all* literate, mutter Great-Uncle Fergus into his *Herald*, we could *all* move up, give the dung-dredgin back to the coloreds.

I like you're the street cleaner, say Ciaran. Sure, I'm very interested in enterin that line of work.

School! say Grammy.

Look at me! I say to my other grammy that evening. I'm doin the jig! This my Saint Patrick's Day dance!

Take down those dry whites.

I start pullin em from the clothes-line. When did colored do the dung-dredgin?

Grammy, Auntie Maryam, and Mr. Freeman look at me.

My Great-Uncle Fergus the street-cleaner is after sayin if all the Irish could read, they do the politics, give the dung-dredgin back to the coloreds.

Stop with the *after*s! say Grammy. It's not: he's *after saying*. It's: he *said*, stop Irishing up your grammar!

They took them, say Mr. Freeman. Service jobs. What negroes *used* to do, when the Irish came, the bosses started giving the work to *them*.

Why?

You figure that out yourself one day, mutter Grammy.

Two days later, Grammy Cahill at her table smilin big at me.

I'm only after sellin the last half-strop, *mo leanbh*. The two halves ye give to me last week each brought in two cents, the two whole ones nickel apiece! Good girl! And Grammy gimme a warm hug for gettin the shavin strops from Mr. Freeman, then send me coal huntin. Roundin the corner, I hear the newsboys callin.

Murder in Worth near Hudson: Irish woman of alleged bad character has throat cut by alleged West Indian negro sailor!

Felonious assault against Sixth ward police captain Dowling!

New gold deposits discovered in Mexico, read all about it!

Crost the street, I hear, No! Don't need no more!

One a the newsboys. I know what he's sayin is his paper need no more newsboys, and the boy he's sayin it to is Ciaran. I walk up to him.

You're spose to be in school.

Supposed. Ye can read but ye can't speak?

School!

School dismission for dinner.

I stare at him. Thinkin: I forgot about dinner. Wait . . . It's ten in the mornin, no dinner dismission yet!

You go to school, *I* find work. And he walk away.

I'M TELLIN GRAMMY!

Would that be the hundredth time this week you were sayin those words or the thousandth?

Lease *I* can *count* to a hundred!

SO CAN I!

I CAN READ!

AM I *SPOSE* TO BE IMPRESSED?

COME HERE!

The lass yellin come from neither Ciaran nor me. Auntie Siobhan standin behind us.

Now.

She storm us to her saloon, mutterin, Can't even go on an errand without the fuss.

Sittin on bar stools, don't speak. I side-eye Ciaran, see he side-eyein me. *Speak!*

I hate it! he tell her, shiny eyes. I hate the nuns and I hate the prayers and I hate the ABCs!

And this verdict you've come to after all of a day's education?

Ciaran cross his arms, eyes hard.

I know it's not all frolic and delight, but you should know what we've gone through. The Protestants offered what they called school, which was just proselytizin to their taste, and if Irish didn't like it, we could just stay gropin illiterate in the dark. Catholics made our own education! Ain't it grand?

I wanna work! I wanna be a newsboy!

You need to read to be a newsboy.

I don't! I can count, I know how to count the coins!

Auntie Siobhan pick up a paper from the counter.

You ever hear a newsboy call out *Getcher paper, two cents!* No. Ye hear robbery and murder and the price a cotton and the entertainments. Newsboys buy the papers, skim the headers, then pick out a tantalizin one, call it out. Newsboys are salesmen, and the product they're sellin's the latest intrigue in printed word.

I'm tellin Grammy you were missin school.

No you are not, Auntie Siobhan say.

He only went one day! Grammy said—

If he promises to go tomorrow, there's no need in tellin Grammy. Do you promise to go tomorrow?

Friday tomorrow. Maybe I wait till Monday, start a new week.

Then I cannot be held responsible for any gabbers gettin the news to Grammy in the meantime.

I'm not a gabber!

Tomorrow then! But Ciaran's face all surly, like he surely don't appreciate everything the Catholics did for his education.

Grand. Now I have a story to tell ye both.

In the old days when Auntie Siobhan would tell me a story bout my mother, I'd be happy! But the old days was the days before Ciaran come, which are gone.

Our first Christmas in New York was prayerful. While she say it, Auntie Siobhan tear off two neat squares a the newspaper, foldin em sharp then foldin em again. Gratitude we'd escaped the Hunger, gratitude we'd survived the coffin ships crossin, set foot in America whole if skin n bones. We needn't material gifts, the gift of life was unexpected surprise enough. But your sister Meara was born with her own gifts. She handed us each a little box folded from newsprint. Inside was a word she tore from the paper. The word inside your mother my sister Brigid's box was *laugh* because she was a jokester, always had us hootin! The word inside my box: *clever.*

Now Auntie Siobhan hand us each a box she jus made right before our eyes! Bottom and four sides, but no top.

Go raibh maith agat, Auntie Siobhan!

Ciaran say nothin but his lips part, starin at his paper crate like some jewel.

You each have a lidless box. If you brought them together, if you wanted to *share,* you could slip the two one inside the other to make one covered box.

Ciaran and me look at each other.

Didn't think so. Then if ye want a cover, ye each have to make another box yourself. Ye seen how I did it. Practice!

❧

I collect the coal, and by the time I'm bringin it home, it's the afternoon. I'm walkin Park and notice Grammy Cahill's table not there. Go in our tenement, up the steps.

Cluck cluck cluck!

Shut it before she take her leave! snap Grammy.

I come in and shut our door fass behind me. It wanna bounce back open but I lock it with the brick stop. There Grammy standin and Cathleen on the couch and somebody new.

Grammy! Where you get that chicken?

A Saint Patrick's miracle, *mo leanbh!*

But Saint Patrick's not for five days!

And we'll have a feast! I named her Nuala: means *longed-for*.

Nuala start runnin in circles, *cluck cluck!*

I like that name! I giggle. Nuala, we longed for ya!

Don't get too attached, say Cathleen.

Then Ciaran saunter in, the after-school hour. He see me, freeze, eyes saucers. His face a question: *Did you tell?* I give no clue.

How was school? Grammy's eyes fixed on Nuala as she ask it. Ciaran glance at me: *Her question a trap?* I give no clue.

Grand, Ciaran say careful.

Glad to hear it, say Grammy. Come meet Nuala, our Saint Patrick's guest of honor.

Where Nuala come from, Grammy? I ask.

Man at my table offered her, cheap. An aul one, barely layin anymore, and her few eggs not good. Were lamb plentiful, Nuala's poor feathered life be spared, at least for a wait-and-see regardin her yolks. Saint Patrick's ought to be lamb stew but, pity for Nuala, no stray woolen creature is after chancin across my path.

I know farm work, say Ciaran. When the time come, I'll do it.

You two keep that door closed! Don't want herself findin the way to the corridor, neighbors wavin her in through *their* doors.

When the time come, I'll do it, say Ciaran, then put his right fist over his left and twist to prove it.

⸻

Saint Patrick's Day! Tuesday, March 17, people everywhere! Us squeezin into Twenty-third and Fifth, me and Grammy and Auntie Siobhan and Cousin Aileen and Maureen and Great-Uncle Fergus and Ciaran and zillions!

Who's on that horse, Grammy?

The grand marshal, James Keelan.

Who's he?

Some bigwig from the AOH. They run the parade.

What's the AOH?

Ancient Order of the Hibernians.

What's Hibernian?

Latin for *Irish*. Look at all the horses! All the Irish soldiers!

I love the Irish soldiers! Grammy, they're playin the drums! Who's that?

The Saint James Temperance Society.

Who's that!

The Father Matthew Temperance Society.

Who's that!

Some politician hopin to trade a handshake for a vote.

Who's that!

Another Father Matthew Temperance Society.

Is there anythin you *know*?

Shut up, Ciaran, I have to report back to Cathleen! I wanna hit him but he's the other side a Auntie Siobhan and my arm won't reach.

She does indeed, say Grammy. Cathleen'll be wantin to know all the details.

Who's *that*? I ask Grammy, my glare on Ciaran.

A division of the AOH.

People cheer the division of the AOH. The men in front carry their green-and-orange sign, the other man hold a banner: WE VISIT THE SICK AND BURY THE DEAD.

Lookit *that!*

Eight white horses two-by-two pullin a float. Ladies in long dresses sittin on the sides, man playin a harp, a big head risin above the middle. But before I get a chance to ask, Who's the big head statue man? some people behind say, The counties are comin!

Cork. Then Sligo. Then Kerry Kerry Kerry, I yell! Us! Even Ciaran near smile, sure a rare shape for his face.

❧

What other floats were there? What music were the bands playing? How many people were marching for Kerry?

I'm answerin Cathleen's questions while Grammy peel a potata. About time to bid aul Nuala farewell, she say, pickin up the sharpknife and lookin to Ciaran. You or me?

Ciaran stare at her, for a second turnin shamrock green.

In the courtyard, he hold Nuala by the neck. She ain't cluckin now, she squawkin.

Thought you was gonna twist her neck.

Grammy's after sayin this is quicker. Sorry, Nuala. Then he lay her down and he slash quick, but the end don't come quick. Nuala screamin. Ciaran hold her neck, cut her head off, her feet still runnin in the air.

Let her go! I never seen a chicken runnin with its head cut off before!

I hurt her, no need to shame her too.

Then Nuala's legs slow, slower, stop.

You're good at farm work.

Never I kilt a chicken before, but once I seen it done. Not us. One time we had a chicken but we're after keepin her. Eggs.

I know where farms is. Right on Manhattan Island.

Small farms uptown, they need no help. Or have it already. I asked.

You didn't go high enough.

Sixties! Eighties!

Higher! Hundred ten, hundred twenty: Harlem. *All* farmland.

He look at me.

Twelve and a half cent the New York and Harlem Railroad, two bits both of us.

Both of us?

I'll come with ya! I been to a Hundredth, to Jupiterville, but no higher. I never been on a train before! I wanna see the big farms, the drawbridge! They say there's a drawbridge way north, over the Harlem River. I never seen a drawbridge before! I never been to Harlem before!

Whyn't ye?

Nobody gone with me.

Sure you always travel alone.

I shrug. They only jus started lettin colored on some a the streetcars, I don't know bout the New York and Harlem Railroad. And Harlem's white, don't know what they think about colored. Or Irish. But we find out together, run away fass together if we have to!

Ciaran tilt his head like a puppy with a question. Then some other thought grab his head.

Yesterday a man call me a white nigger.

Sometime the nativists call Irish that. Sometime the nativists call colored smoked Irish. I'm both!

Now a question mark floatin over Ciaran's skull.

My papa was colored. I'm half-colored, half-Irish.

Look like this be new information to Ciaran. He take a think on it.

And where come the quarter for the streetcar?

Scraps! We'll collect em to sell, we might have to save up—

And were I to get work, you'd be needin to come home alone.

I'll walk down to my Auntie Eunice's, she's Eighty-sixth.

Ciaran's eyes on me, but his mind makin calculations someplace else, Nuala's blood drippin through his fist.

We walk back up to the third floor. Grammy has me help her pluck Nuala's feathers. Ciaran don't have to because his chore was kill Nuala which he done, so he sit practicin makin boxes outa newspaper.

What's the news? ask Great-Uncle Fergus.

Important from the Dominican Republic, say Cathleen, glancin at the paper on her lap. *Persecution of American citizens, the U.S. flag trampled underfoot—*

Next, say Great-Uncle Fergus.

Domestic troubles among the wealthy. Supreme Court, before Honorable Judge Roosevelt. Quarrel for the custody of a child—

Next.

A Glance at Life in a Southern City: Private letter from a Northern traveler—

Next.

At the Broadway Theater—

There's several, say Maureen. Which?

The Broadway theater that's just called the Broadway Theater, Cathleen tell her sister, Broadway between Pearl and Anthony. *A dramatic spectacle entitled 'The Usurper of Siam' was played for the first time in this city last night. The audience was composed in no small part of juvenile New York, who were attracted, not by the play, but by the elephants Victoria and Albert, who were announced to appear in the leading rôles.*

Can we go?!

Is it Broadway Theater money ye have? Grammy answer me, then she turn to Ciaran. Them papers you wouldn't know how to read, but it's box-makin I see ye've discovered.

Auntie Siobhan taught him, I say.

Sure that's clever, Ciaran! say Cousin Aileen.

She taught me too!

What was your favorite float today? Cathleen ask me.

The one with the eight white horses and the ladies in dresses and the man with the harp and the big head statue man. Who was that big head statue man?

The bust? say Grammy. 'Twas Daniel O'Connell. The Liberator.

You're not knowin Dónall Ó Conaill? say Ciaran.

He's after fightin hard for us, say Grammy. Catholic emancipation.

Catholics was slaves?

Meant somethin different in Ireland, Grammy answer me. The right to sit in Parliament, and one day he did. Workin for tenants' rights, toward repealin the Act of Union with Great Britain.

Never before ye're hearin of Dónall Ó Conaill the Liberator?

I said I didn't!

Sure then the half of you that's Irish be your legs, not your head.

Ciaran! Enough a that carry-on. Nobody's *half.*

Ciaran sprised as me Grammy snapped at him. Finally!

But she *herself* was sayin—

That's her affair, say Grammy. What herself calls herself. Her blood's Irish as anyone in this home.

Cahill Irish blood, I say, and blood's thicker n water.

And for that, Grammy gimme a whomp on my backside!

Sit down, both a ye!

Since the front-room's fulla Grammy and Cathleen and Cousin Aileen and Maureen and Great-Uncle Fergus (but not Auntie Siobhan who say Saint Paddy's Day bring her business a pot o' gold so she jus have to toast Saint Paddy at the saloon), that mean only place for me and Ciaran to sit down's the floor. Grammy sit in her chair.

You know what else is thicker n water? say Grammy. Mud.

Then she pause but we know we better keep that pause quiet.

When we're after departin Éire, nothin left but the hunger and the mud. Like a sister your dear mother was to me, and when the landlord's after buyin our passage, and she ask will we take your sister Meara, sure we didn't think twice. From out of the mud our family grows: your big sister becomin my mud daughter, Siobhan and Brigid's mud sister, and *that* mud just as precious as blood.

Then Grammy turn back to plucked Nuala, reachin into her neck to yank it out. Make a wish.

Ciaran grab his end fast, so either Ireland knows the wishbone or someone told him here—so fast I don't got time to make any wish cep wishin I get more n half. *Snap!* I'm mad and waitin for Ciaran to gloat, but he jus stare at his bigger part like this luck for him is wondrous and rare.

❧

Week after Saint Patrick's, I wake up at Auntie Eunice's, then walk south from Seneca Village. Nearin downtown, somethin catch my ear:

Crowds rush to try world's first passenger elevator!

Otis's elevator featured at 'fifty-four world's fair now accepting passengers at new store!

Five-story emporium sending customers to the top in steam-powered car— read all about it!

I wanna ride the elevator! But I'm scared! I wish someone ride it with me but my grammies and my aunties and my cousins all workin—wait. There's Ciaran. It's Tuesday, what's Ciaran doin not in school? What's Ciaran doin talkin to the street arabs smokin their cigars but not sharin with him?

Ciaran!

Ciaran see me: fly! The street arabs roarin merry. Not that boy Christmas's gang, but another one.

Ciaran! CIARAN! I WON'T TELL, IF YA DO SOMETHIN FOR ME!

Ciaran stop.

Thousands! The screamin, the pushin, take a lotta muscle and boldness and nearly losin each other twice, but me and Ciaran make it inside, in line for the mechanical lift. Black iron like a cage, look like a cooker could boil us! A man standin in the contraption to drive it. Sofa for the ladies. Ciaran and I stare, watchin passengers get in. They take a breath when the driver close the door, then a jolt and somebody scream, us on the ground shiver and laugh. Steam push the carriage up through the ceilin! Plenty don't trust it, jus here to watch, but others got the heart of adventure. At first Ciaran not so certain, jus certain he not wamme tell Grammy bout him hidin from school. Here he seem shaky in the crowd, but gettin closer to the black box, airship to the roof, his eyes start to dance.

Hour after gettin in line, we at the front: squished into the compartment. The elevator man slam the door shut, my heart poundin as he pull the lever and *whoosh!* The thing lurch, my belly lurch, hold my belly tight, we rise! Pullin up and away from the first-floor people, the people gettin smaller, then disappear. Every floor we stop and magic: the door open, a whole new picture from the lass time door opened! Some man on every floor to talk about the new picture: here's the porcelain, here's the glassware. A few people get off at the floors to inspect, a few get back on, door slam shut. I worry elevator might forget it spose to stop at five and fly us through the roof! To the sun! But after five, the elevator man close the gate, and it start rattlin back down. Not pausin at the floors this time, fallin free, I hope we don't crash through the ground! My stomach feelin sick, and I look at Ciaran. He smile lookin out, the bottom risin up to us, then turn to smile at me. He don't know I'm sick, not a mean smile. His smile is *I thank you.*

When we hit the bottom, we bounce back up a bit, gasp! Then laugh. Then the door crash open, and Ciaran take my hand tight so we don't get lost from each other navigatin the crowd to the street.

Walk a couple blocks, Ciaran smilin, thinkin a our adventure.

Whatchu doin talkin with the street arabs when you spose to be in school?

Ciaran let go a my hand and the smile.

You gonna get in trouble with the street arabs. They're robbers!

I'm them.

You're not!

Orphan.

But we're orphans with family!

You with family, not me. Blood thicker n water.

When he say it, Ciaran not look at me. His eyes full a lonely, like forgot all about Grammy Cahill sayin so's mud. And Grammy's meanin was *he's* mud. And Grammy's meanin was Mud's love.

Extra! Fire in West street, a five-story store: Corse's Flour and Feed, Sailmakers Jones and Wilson, Trowbridge's Freight Crockery Dealer!

Ciaran's eyes on the newsboys which he can't be since he can't read.

I could teach you.

This I offered before, but maybe he like my voice better this time because now Ciaran turn to me.

❧

The followin Sunday is March the twenty-ninth, the organ playin at Transfiguration R.C., right here in Five Points, Park and Mott. We at the front a the church, my belly growlin. Here come the bread!

It taste good!

Then the priest do the Latin.

Wine! Wine! What it taste like?

Walkin home after my First Communion, Auntie Siobhan hold my hand and say to Grammy, Did ye see herself scrunchin her face up like she's tastin vinegar? Then throw her head back laughin.

I don't like wine!

May the saints watch over ye, Cousin Aileen bless me, smilin.

Two weeks later's Easter, the one day both my families say I *have* to go to church: back to Transfiguration R.C. for the sunrise service with Cahills, Mother Zion (the big A.M.E. on Leonard and Church) with Grammy and Hen, Auntie Eunice goin to her Seneca Village A.M.E. In the afternoon, Auntie Eunice arrive for dinner, and brung someone with her.

Uncle Ambrose!

He pick me up, hold me high above his head.

Lookit this big girl! Gettin heavy!

When you get back!

Last night.

Just in time for Easter! say Auntie Eunice, all smiles. What a surprise!

Ashore for a few days. How does my niece do?

I been teachin Ciaran from Ireland from my other grammy's to read! That's a good deed I'm doin, Auntie Eunice? Like you teachin Auntie Maryam?

That's a very good deed. And Auntie Maryam is progressing *very* speedily in her reading.

Auntie Maryam grin at Auntie Eunice, wide and shy, and now Auntie Eunice innerduce her to her husband.

Like the good works they say in church, me teachin Ciaran is all unselfish, get nothin out of it myself.

Oh you get somethin out of it. Chance to boss somebody around.

Shut up, Hen! (Though she makin me think how Ciaran sometime cross his arms durin the lesson, and I need to remind him *I'm* the teacher, *you're* the student!)

❧

Couple weeks later, I wake up to a baby cryin. Run down the steps. Third floor, man and woman movin in, infant bawlin in her arms.

Mornin! I call. The baby stop cryin, look at me.

Mornin! say the lady. You live upstairs?

I nod. I'm Theo!

We're Mr. and Mrs. Jewel, your new neighbors. And this is Charlotte. Mrs. Jewel put down Charlotte, who barely big enough to stand.

Mornin, Charlotte! I say, and she move her fingers like to wave. I run outside. Five Points streets even wilder n usual! Ciaran appear, his face don't know what to think!

Moving Day! I tell him. People removes today! February first is Rent Day, three-month warnin of an increase, and if ya can't afford it, May first Moving Day!

People pushin carts fulla things every direction, some carts pulled by horses, some carts pulled by goats, some carts pulled by people, carts crashin, things fallin, horses whinnyin, the outside side steps leadin to the second-floor apartments got people scurryin down carryin stuff, scurryin up carryin stuff, people on ladders takin down business signs, other people paintin new signs, callin and screamin, and Ciaran and me jus watchin it all like a play!

Reckon time for me too, say Ciaran. Remove.

Where?

Harlem. Farm work.

A screech. Brawl eruptin yonder among the street arabs: two rollin on the ground, the others cheerin and laughin.

Grammy might not let ya. Grammy might say you're only eight and a half years of age.

Nine come July.

But first we need to finish the readin lessons, you never know when Grammy gonna test ya.

Yesterday I'm after askin her to test me. I passed.

I stare at Ciaran. He never tole me he was takin the test! I start to open my mouth but before I get a word out I see Mr. O'Kelleher, Auntie Eunice's neighbor from Seneca Village, pullin a overflowin cart: crates and pots, a table, a chair near fallin off, what's he doin?

Mr. O'Kelleher! Mr. O'Kelleher!

I run after him. Why's Mr. O'Kelleher rollin a cart a his belongins into Five Points?

Mr. O'Kelleher!

All a sudden he turn around look right at me, shinin eyes full a so much sad I'm startled a step back. Then he go on with his task. I walk slow back to Ciaran but Ciaran's gone.

Slept at Grammy Cahill's last couple nights so tonight I stay at Grammy Brook's. Nex day, I head to Grammy Cahill's table in the afternoon. Still Moving Week so a lotta unruly, plus busy Saturday so I wait for Grammy to get through some hagglins before I speak.

Grammy, yesterday Ciaran tole me he be nine years of age in July so he thinkin bout headin to Harlem workin on a farm!

Ciaran's gone. He's after leavin early this mornin.

Jus beyond Grammy two horses pullin two carts near collide, rear back and neigh, then move on.

All by himself? I ask, but my voice surprise me, dropped to a whisper so I gotta repeat it.

Somethin him and your Auntie Siobhan's after cookin up, you have to ask her. I'm wantin to stop him goin but. Grammy's eyes wet. Sure I'll miss him.

I tear off to Auntie Siobhan's. All I been wishin is Ciaran gone so this is grand, but leavin and not say bye? We had times together—the elevator, I taught him to read! Fly through the door a O'SHEA'S BOARD & PUBLICK. Before I say a word, Auntie Siobhan take a look at my face, and her face go sad.

Oh, *mo stoirín*, he already left. You missed him.

Rude! Not even say bye to me. And he wasn't even goin to school after Grammy told him to! *I* taught him to read! *I* taught him to read!

I know. You're a good girl.

She pour tea in a glass and put it in front a me.

Few days ago, Ciaran was here while I was talkin to a mister and missus not a year out of Ireland. They longed for the farmland, like home. And been savin, they were ready. Hated the crampedness of Five Points, they were ready. Don't know how they'll fare, Harlem full a nativists might shun the Irish, but maybe they'll find some acreage away from any nasty neighbors. All they needed, said they, was a farmhand or two. Ciaran: right place, right time.

Why Ciaran always wanna be workin!

But before she answer, a couple customers come in, and she go to em. One aul one tell her a joke and she laugh hard, her curly red hair bouncin on her shoulders, but I can tell she's a little sad. There's somethin funny in my stomach. Ciaran in my stomach, but maybe I drink enough tea, I wash him out. This I know: I'm orphan lucky with my family, and now lucky got my Irish family back to myself.

Auntie Siobhan, tell me a story!

It feel good to say it: like the old days, jus me and my auntie! She take a think.

We were at the dance hall. Your mother was sixteen, me fourteen. I was still a shy dancer then, but Brigid tore up the floor, and I'm sittin drinkin a cider and notice my sister out there spendin a lotta time tonight with one particular gentleman. Somethin dark, somethin handsome. Your father, this would be their meetin. Then Meara runs in, Meara's fifteen and has a letter, news from home. Letter from Kerry! she's yellin, wavin it proud. I've a new baby brother!

Then Auntie Siobhan reach under the bar.

He left somethin for ye.

A tiny little newspaper box. The newsprint on top got part of a word circled, rest a the sentence crossed out, foldin over the side.

Theo~~logians denounce Cathol~~

I shake it.

Somethin in there! What is it!

I don't open other people's parcels, she say, then: What can I do for ye? to the man just entered.

I open. What had been jigglin was the bigger half of Nuala's wishbone. And there with it's the tiniest piece of newsprint, just one word: **Mud**.

Pinkster

Saturday mornin, Grammy Brook pull it out the ole trunk, hold it up: red coat n trousers.

Pinkster, I grin.

She wink at me. Pinkster *Eve*. Then turn to Gran-Gran. Think it still fit, Mama?

Gran-Gran just stare out the winda.

Gran-Gran don't know tomorra's Pinkster, I whisper.

She will, say Grammy. I like to make a blackberry pie. Think Auntie Maryam wanna go pickin with ya? Get her out n about?

I run down to the courtyard. I love berry pickin! But I don't see Auntie Maryam at the pump or in the w.c. line, and she never go nowheres else, even after I give her the Five Points tour. I gotta go in the w.c. line! When I'm done, I run back up to Grammy's.

I don't know where Auntie Maryam is. She weren't at the pump or the w.c. line.

Oh, say Grammy at the stove, maybe she was *in* the w.c. Come have some porridge.

She couldn'ta been *in* the w.c. because I never seen her come *out* a the w.c. while I was waitin.

Mornin! say Auntie Maryam, walkin in behind me.

Where *were* ya, Auntie Maryam?

The w.c.

But I didn't see ya.

I heats up the irons.

Get you some porridge first, Grammy say to Auntie Maryam while standin front a Gran-Gran, showin the coat n trousers. Looky, Mama.

Now Gran-Gran turn to her.

Pinkster, say Gran-Gran, grinnin.

Pinkster tomorra, Auntie Maryam!

She look at me confused.

You not know a Pinkster?

Pinkster's North, Auntie Maryam wouldn't know it, Grammy answer me, foldin the red suit up neat. Pinkster was New Netherland: New Jersey, Long Island, Staten Island, New York State, Manhattan. Pinkster come from the Dutch.

Pinksteren, say Gran-Gran.

Pinksteren, Grammy nod. Seventh Sunday after Easter, somethin religious for them, but what come to be Pinkster was American, African and American. Mama was born Manhattan 1779, saw Pinkster through its heyday to its outlaw.

Outlaw?

You didn't know of our illegal doins, Grammy smile at me. Eighteen eleven Pinkster was abolished, then 1827 slavery in New York abolished and Gran-Gran brung back Pinkster.

What Pinkster is? say Auntie Maryam.

Time for celebration, say Grammy. Time for reunion! Slaves sold to the country could come back to the city a few days every year, be with their relatives.

Reunion with *family*? Auntie Maryam's mouth open.

Festiviteiten, say Gran-Gran.

Holiday: no work! say Grammy. We'd meet at the Common.

What the Common is?

The park.

City Hall Park, I chime in.

'Twas a carnival, say Grammy. Tossin coppers. Leapin, racin.

Saturnalia, say Gran-Gran. Grammy hold out the red suit for Auntie Maryam to see. Auntie Maryam touch it gentle.

Pinkster in Albany, Gran-Gran smile. I was sixteen years of age. A girl!

Auntie Maryam's mouth wide, hearin Gran-Gran talk sentences.

Grammy smile. Pinkster bring back Mama's memories. When she was sixteen, her Manhattan master hired her out: two years upstate. Albany— the heart of Pinkster! A week of preparation before Pinkster week. One a the slaves was crowned King Charles. The Dutch paid a painter to create a portrait a the black king, hung it durin his Pinkster week reign when he was ruler of *all*: black *and* white.

Auntie Maryam gapin again. Grammy chuckle.

Don't know nobody colored wanna go back to slave days. But under the Dutch, we married, had families. Under the Dutch, plenty a slaves set free after years a service: reward for good behavior. In Albany, our King Charles'd march through the street, everybody cheerin. Then collect his revenue.

Shilling from every black man, two from every white, say Gran-Gran.

Eventually only colored participated in the merrymaking, say Grammy, colored made Pinkster our own. Sojourner Truth was upstate New York, had a *mean* Dutch master: whipped her, promised her freedom then took it back, sold her *son*—but after she escaped, ever grateful to the whites rescued her, she claimed her only regret was missin Pinkster—fellowship of her black people. First half the week for the celebration, second half for recoverin from the celebration!

Why it stops!

Grammy sigh. The British gradually gainin power, she answer Auntie Maryam, British changin the idea a slavery. I reckon too much colored congregatin become a threat. Then Grammy turn to Gran-Gran, warm eyes. Olden days was *King* Charles. But my mother, eldest to keep Pinkster here, now every year crowned *queen*.

Queen Lioda! Gran-Gran beamin.

Pinkster in Albany, Grammy say. Mama's first taste of freedom. Now let's get these whites for the whites behind us so we can usher in the revelry. And Grammy start takin down pilla-cases from the clothes-line.

My letters! cry Gran-Gran.

Okay, Mama, okay. Then Grammy take some ole letters outa the trunk and bring em to Gran-Gran, start readin em quiet to her, Dutch.

You wanna go blackberry pickin with me, Auntie Maryam? There's blackberries Seneca Village. Auntie Eunice'll help!

Reunion with family, Auntie Maryam say soft to herself, like jus the idea of it, God musta come down and cast a miracle.

Knock knock. Auntie Eunice open her door, eyes red.

Grammy say pick the blackberries for the blackberry pie!

Auntie Eunice stare at me. Then step back in her house.

Let us repair to the grove, she say quiet, takin her gunny-sack.

Grammy say maybe Auntie Maryam like to blackberry-pick with us, I tell Auntie Eunice under a tree thick with fruit, but cep for the day I give her her Five Points tour, Auntie Maryam never travel nowheres but Grammy's apartment and the courtyard.

You're eating more berries than you're collecting, Auntie Eunice say, eyes on the berries she pickin.

I can't wait till Pinkster tomorra. I love the thirty-first a May!

Pinkster is not always the thirty-first of May, because Easter is not always the twelfth of April, Easter is a moveable feast. And Pinkster came from—

Pinksteren!

Pinksteren is the Dutch word for Pentecost. *Pentecost* is derived from the Greek *Pentekoste*, which means fiftieth, Pentecost being the fiftieth day past Easter.

Aaaah! That bee almost stung me!

When Christ ascended into heaven, he promised his disciples the Holy Spirit would enter into them. In fifty days, the disciples were surrounded by tongues of fire, speaking in foreign languages: *glossolalia.*

Glossolalia, I giggle.

Somebody else laughin, we look up. Two police patrollin, stroll up the hill. Auntie Eunice glare where the coppers gone.

And then come Pinkster!

The Dutch religious observance of *Pinksteren* became the secular celebration of Pinkster for us, African descendants. Pinkster is a *negro* celebration. Tomorrow morning, I will go to A.M.E. Zion before the festivities, my *African* Methodist Episcopalian church. We must always keep the faith.

What that mean?

Say it right.

What's that mean?

It means we must keep practicing our religion, our faith in God. And when things look most bleak, that's when we must especially strive—*look at this grove!*

Auntie Eunice is lookin north, lookin south, eyes shinin. I peer up in the direction of Jupiterville, over to Auntie Eunice's house, down to where Mr. O'Kelleher used to live.

Why Mr. O'Kelleher have to leave Seneca Village, Auntie Eunice?

Ants!

Auntie Eunice pointin at my sack on the ground, a whole line a ants marchin into it! She snatch my bag and run it to the stream, plunge it. Ants roll off down into the water. Some try to swim, but not for long.

Why you cry, Auntie Eunice?

Eviction is *hard*, she mutter to the drownded bugs, her tears lookin warm but voice ice cold.

೨

Back to Grammy's, my gunny-sack got a weight to it.

Look, Grammy! I got *lotsa* pie berries!

Grammy on the couch, eyes on the red trousers she's stitchin. Good girl, she say to me. Then to herself, Suit's got a little threadbare after all these years.

Auntie Eunice say she be by tomorra after church.

Every year I have to take these in. You're gettin *too thin*, Mama.

Nathan, Gran-Gran say, sittin in her corner, lookin over her ole letters.

Her beau! I cover my warm face, fall over gigglin. Auntie Maryam look up from the white she's ironin.

Nathan Reems, Grammy say. Neighborin farm, my mother was sixteen, him nineteen. They married, and she carried his child, but little girl born still. When two years later her master come to take her back to Manhattan, she wailed. And every Pentecost she return to Albany for Pinkster, but time apart made it hard. Emancipation come 1827. By then Mama was forty-eight, Nathan fifty-one.

And you *twenty*-one! I say.

Gran-Gran'd married my papa long before, Nathan'd married another.

I whisper to Grammy: Gran-Gran lookin at her letters but can't see no more. Can't read no more.

She know what they say, Grammy say aloud.

This pile finish, Auntie Maryam say. I gots to go to the necessary. And she walk out the door.

How old Gran-Gran?

Seventy-eight.

Old!

Older. Slave years is more n free years. But thank the Lord she still with us. Nathan, Gran-Gran say, shakin her head, smilin.

You think Gran-Gran liked Nathan Reems better n my great-granpapa, your father?

Take the blackberries down to the courtyard, run em under the pump.

I go to the courtyard to clean the berries and I don't see no Auntie Maryam. Where she been hidin?

Drag my gunny-sack back up to the fourth floor, but before I go through Grammy's door, I look up. Ceilin trap-door's cracked open.

More squirrels?

I turn. Miss Lottie who live crost the hall from us lookin at me. I stare at her. I stare at the ceilin door.

I think, I start to answer. I think—

You need a chair, get at em?

I nod.

She go in her apartment, bring a chair out. Might as well keep it for tomorra, she say and go back in her apartment. That because everybody in the tenement invited to Pinkster, and if they wanna sit, they need to bring their own seats.

I set my sack in the corner, stand on the chair. Quiet I push the trap-door wider open, lift myself into the garret.

Some tiny gap in the ceilin slat. My eyes get use to the dark, and now I see Auntie Maryam mutterin on her knees. And fall forward on the floor!

Auntie Maryam! Auntie Maryam!

She snap up, see me crawlin fast under the low ceilin to her.

Auntie Maryam, you fainted!

No! Pray.

I saw you prayin but then you fainted! Fell over flat on your face!

That way I prays, she say. That way I keeps my faith.

How come you pray in the garret?

Likes to pray by myself.

You come up here every day?

Auntie Maryam show her right hand, fingers stretched out.

Five times every day?

Secret?

Okay! I'm good at secrets, remember? I never tole no one bout your squirrel friends who never come to be squirrel stew, remember? What's at?

A little slip a some kind a animal skin, got scribbles on it. Auntie Maryam quiet a second.

Before I comes North, I reads. Not English. But I reads. Then she slip the parchment in the pouch always hang round her neck.

⁓

Nex morn: Pinkster! No whites for the whites today, Grammy not work today, rest! All she do is dust and sweep and straighten and scrub and mop and cook and bake.

Grammy and Auntie Maryam and Hen and me bring up pails and pails a water, and everybody have a bath, Gran-Gran first! (Mr. Freeman washed already—his barbershop.) All us same water, chimney-sweep Hen the dirtiest go last. Then Grammy tell me: Tell em.

I run out to the street, past the newsboys, past a coupla early staggerin drunkards, past the hot corn girls. I run to the barbershop: don't forget Pinkster! To the chimney sweeps: don't forget Pinkster! To the colored scrap people: don't forget Pinkster!

What's Pinkster?

I turn. There Mary Bree, street sweeper the winter, hot corn girl the summer.

Holiday. For colored people.

Oh. Then she yell her wares: *Here's your nice hot corn, smokin hot, smokin hot just from the pot!* Her hot corn smell good!

Is it good? Don't know why I ask since I got no money.

Don't know, she say, I got no money. Then she yell some more. I wish she gimme a cob free, but know she say no. She don't take none free herself for fear her matron beat her. Her arms lookin skinnier n last time I seen her.

You wanna come to a colored holiday, Mary Bree?

Yes!

First Mary Bree need to finish sellin her corn batch so she don't get in trouble. I go lookin for more Pinkster people and find little Nancy and Elijah. Then us four head to Grammy's.

Everybody goin into Grammy's tenement! Every colored body. On the third floor, Mrs. Jewel our new downstairs neighbor stand in her doorway with Charlotte the toddler. Mrs. Jewel's belly stickin out a little. She look like wonderin what all the commotion is, and I remember she weren't here for Pinkster before.

Mrs. Jewel! Pinkster! Bring Charlotte!

Neighbors in our tenement come, everyone bringin meat and berries and cakes and beer and cheese and liquor to our hearth, center a festivities, and Miss Lottie's hearth crost the floor take up the spillover people. Mary Bree and Nancy and Elijah eatin, happy. The doorway to the bed-closet covered with a sheet, and I know Gran-Gran in there restin, every once in a while Grammy check on her. But mostly Grammy enjoyin herself, laughin with the guests, shufflin up ole times.

Pinkster *sona*, Theo!

Pinkster *sona*, Mr. Freeman!

That Irish? Mary Bree ask.

Yes! Mr. Freeman wishin me happy Pinkster. This is Mary Bree, Mr. Freeman.

I know Irish.

Ah! say Mr. Freeman. *Dia duit*, Mary Bree.

Dia duit, mister!

You seen my boss? I turn around, there stand Hen. I ain't seen him. I need to see him.

I shake my head. Too crowded, I catch no sign a Mr. Samuel the sweepmaster. Corn! I take half a cob. Sweet! Then somethin tappin my bottom. It's Charlotte my neighbor toddler, grinnin up at me! I give her some corn kernels. She's so cute!

Have you seen Auntie Maryam? ask Auntie Eunice.

Now when Auntie Maryam disappear, I got a good inklin where she be, but I can keep a secret. Shake my head which is no lie: I ain't seen her.

I move through the crowd out to the hall, look up. The ceilin trap-door cracked—and now I see Auntie Maryam's eyes lookin right down on me!

No peoples in the hall? she whisper.

I look around. Shake my head.

Quick she slip down. Now a squabble commencin the steps below.

Be a mistake!

My mistake.

I run down the steps. There Mr. Samuel lookin at Hen, her two steps above. With Mr. Samuel short, they now eye-to-eye.

Evenin, Mr. Samuel!

Good evenin to you, Theo. Will you please tell your cousin she'd regret it, departin my employ for Cornelius Hornbell's stable?

Not a stable, Hen say low. Her back to me, but I hear in her voice that her eyes got the glower.

Treats his apprentices like animals. Beats em. Feeds em when he feels like it.

I got family, he ain't got to feed me.

Hen—

He say I'm fast. He say you not usin me no more, you use the contraption—

The new contraption mean I don't send you down the chimney, closed quarters you can't breathe, or fall break a bone. Like *I* did, your age.

I *like* slippin down the chimney.

But Mr. Samuel miss this lass bit a sass, lookin up behind me and breakin into a smile.

Miss Maryam! I haven't seen you since the day Theo introduced us on the street.

Miss Maryam's several steps higher and tall, so Mr. Samuel have to look very high up to her.

I likes to stay close, she say, eyes on her feet.

Mighty pretty pouch you have.

And now she see she didn't close the pouch tight after she jump down from the garret, the little scribblin peekin out! She quick stuff it back in.

As-salāmu 'alaykum.

Auntie Maryam startle. Stare at Mr. Samuel.

My first sweep-master was from Africa. He kept his faith. The Koran.

She keep starin at him. Then: *Wa alaykumu as-salam.*

Mohammedan!

We look up to see who's yellin, standin a couple of steps above Auntie Maryam.

Sister Maryam! Auntie Eunice go on. Do you not love Jesus?

Peace be upon him, say Auntie Maryam. A great messenger.

Great *messenger*? Do you not mean our *savior*?

Happy Pinkster, Theo! Mary Bree grin, appearin on the steps above Auntie Eunice, blackberry juice all round her mouth.

Who is this?

Auntie Eunice starin at me. I say nothin.

Didn't I tell you Pinkster is a holiday for the descendants of *Africans*?

From up in Grammy's, we hear fiddlin.

It's startin! say Hen, tryin to get through everybody up the steps.

Yesterday afternoon I paid *rent* on *my house*!

Auntie Eunice sit down hard on her step, tears streamin. All us froze.

I was at City Hall paying *rent*, I went with the remittance on our home, our home we *own*! The ground sold to Ambrose and me, now the city claims it's theirs, city property, claims we are *leasing*, so long as they *permit* us to stay, we and *our tenant* now owes *them* rent!

How can they—? start Mr. Samuel.

Began a year ago, other owners have been leasing since then but. But somehow Ambrose staved them off, our friend Mr. Hesser of Jupiterville who has an acquaintance in City Hall staved them off for him, for us, but *now*. *Now*. Oh, sometimes I miss Ambrose so badly!

Searching for you all!

We look up at Mr. Freeman, top a the stairs.

It's starting!

All our eyes on Auntie Eunice. She swallow.

I would like to be alone, she say quiet. Please. Go.

Hen's fastest up the steps, then me takin Mary Bree's hand. I turn round at the top to look down, see the grown-ups talkin soft to Auntie Eunice.

Grammy's front-room packed tight, people spillin out in the hall. Hear the fiddlers, hear the African drummers circle in the middle, I can't see em! Then Auntie Maryam come, pick me up on her shoulders, and Mr. Samuel pick Mary Bree up on his, Hen already done managed to slip through legs to the front. Since Auntie Maryam's tall and Mr. Samuel's small, I'm highest! Everybody made a big circle round the musicians, I wave to Nancy and Elijah crost the circle, grinnin wide.

By the time the chimney sweeps come out for their African dance, we all managed to nudge to the front, so me and Mary Bree standin on the floor when Mr. Samuel go to the center. The stompin and the slidin, Mr. Samuel in perfect rhythm with the other sweeps!

In Manhattan, whisper Mr. Freeman who now I see is nex to me, Pinkster was once known as the Sweep Chimneys' Holiday.

When the sweeps done, they clear the floor, and the drummers start a fast hard beat, then all at once stop. Look at Grammy, who stand near the curtain in the doorway separatin bed-closet from front-room.

Introducing, she say, Her Majesty Queen Lioda!

Then Grammy tear away the curtain, and Gran-Gran appear in the red coat and trousers, wearin a big hat with a big feather stickin out of it, grinnin ear-to-ear. Everybody cheer!

Welkom! say Gran-Gran.

Is breá liom Pinkster! Mary Bree's gettin good at Irish.

Is breá liom Pinkster *freisin*, I return because I love Pinkster too!

'iinah yawm rayie 'alays kadhalk? Mr. Samuel say to Auntie Maryam, who look surprised and delighted Mr. Samuel know his Arabic beyond the friendly greetin.

Na'am fa'allan, she reply. I don't know what they're sayin, but they're smilin at Pinkster so I think it also mean we havin a happy day.

Mijn volk! say Gran-Gran. *Mijn volk!*

My people, my people, I hear in my ear. It's Auntie Eunice behind me! Glossolalia! I say.

She laugh, give me a hug.

Know what I just realized, sugarplum? We haven't lost yet. Not until Ambrose and I leave our home, and we won't. We'll fight them, and we'll *win*. This fall you'll come for Halloween treats just like last year.

Okay!

I turn back to the start-of-summer Pinkster show while already thinkin bout the jack-o'-lantern cookies. My auntie holdin me tight, kissin top a my head. And now I feel the drops, warm and wet, fallin on my scalp. I'm hopin them's what grown-ups calls tears of joy, but I don't ask for fear a the answer.

Riot

Stop him! Stop him!

Butcher yellin. Man on the run, musta stole from the butcher! I see no meat so musta stole money! Here come a Municipal chasin after the robber. Here come a Metropolitan chasin after the Municipal chasin after the robber! More Metropolitans, more Municipals. A Metropolitan shove a Municipal, a Municipal jump the Metropolitan.

He's gettin away! the butcher scream.

Now all the uniforms wrestlin: two different New York polices tumblin in the summer heat over who get to arrest the robber.

He got away! the butcher pout. The Munis and the Mets still brawlin, people laughin. One a the laughs I reckonize, standin in the doorway a O'SHEA'S BOARD & PUBLICK.

How come there's two different polices, Auntie Siobhan?

Sure the Municipal Police *are* the city police! Always been! Now the state tryin to replace em with these Metropolitans, never!

Why?

Oh, claims of Democratic partisanship, what they *mean* is too many Irish! And what's the Metropolitans but *Republican* partisanship? DID YOU SEE IT, UNCLE?

Auntie Siobhan callin out to Great-Uncle Fergus, who happen to be crost the street doin his street-cleanin duties. He keep his head down on his broom and shake his head, like he find it all foolhardiness.

Ye heard about the skirmish a few weeks back? we hear from inside, some man customer. The Municipals and the Metropolitans in a knock-down, drag-out right there on the steps of City Hall!

Auntie Siobhan throw her head back hollerin the laughter, then go inside.

Hey Paddy! call out some white man standin with another white man and scraggly beagle. My dog just shit here, clean it up, Mick. Here, boy! And he whistle at Great-Uncle Fergus like *he* the dog. Great-Uncle Fergus quick fire him a look, but keep workin. He always pay sharp attention to the street cleanin, don't wanna give no boss no excuse to excuse him from employment.

Shut up! I snap to the white men since I got no job to worry bout bein excused from. They look at me, frown.

You a paddy or a nigger?

Come over here and find out, I say, tightenin my fists. They laugh and move on.

Great-Uncle Fergus's eyes still on the sweepin, but I glimpse a smile where wasn't one before.

❧

That evenin my great-uncle teachin me to box.

When the damned Know-Nothin bastards come, know how to hang a left, he say.

Hook or uppercut?

Start with the jab. Strategy's all-important.

You Know-Nothin swine! and I hang my left jab in the spar. Stupid nativist nothin-knower!

Not every nativist is a party to the Know-Nothing party, but many of them are, say Cathleen, glancin over her newspaper.

American thugs, say Great-Uncle Fergus. Come on, aim for my chin!

Extra! High court rules Municipal Police Force unconstitutional!

All three of us turn to the winda, then me and my great-uncle run to it. The evenin boys hollerin.

Municipal Police Force to be disbanded tomorrow, Metropolitans taking over the city—read all about it!

In the night, fracas from the nex-door apartment: screamin and shoutin and a dog barkin and a baby cryin and pots clang-bangin gainst the wall, keep me awake. Cousin Aileen to my left sighin, Maureen crossways at our feet scrunchin her pilla over her head.

Wonder what the MacSweeneys fightin about? I loud-whisper to Grammy on my right.

He was a Municipal, gainfully employed, now not. I reckon that be a cause of marital worriment.

Nex mornin the street quiet. I go see Auntie Siobhan in her tavern, tea with Miss Fiona.

You ever seen it like this? my auntie say, eyes on the street. The Points. Like a funeral.

No Irish they hired to this new Metropolitan force, say Miss Fiona. Except the odd Irish *Republican*. Did ye know how many Irish were on the aul Municipals? Near two of every three! Twelve-dollar-a-week jobs!

Auntie Siobhan! How come Great-Uncle Fergus never got a twelve-dollar-a-week job with the Municipals?

The Democrats offered those jobs in return for *favors*.

Couldn't he a done some favors?

They never asked him.

Maybe they disband the Central Park police too! I say, hopin.

Believe the Central Park police is a whole different matter unto themself.

No Irish need apply there neither! say Miss Fiona. Not for police, not for construction. Didn't they fill the park last May? Twenty thousand in City Hall Park protestin, the damned Republican domination of the board, do ye know who they plan on givin all the new Central Park jobs to?

Not Irish?

Correct! And here we are, blazin third a July. Quiet this hour, but I heard some rumors. What do ye suppose the fireworks be startin early?

Auntie Eunice! Auntie Eunice! Knockin on her door in Seneca Village where she ain't yet been evicted from. Auntie Eunice!

I turn the knob.

Theo?

She come out from the bed-closet, adjustin her dress like she just slipped it on this late in the day!

Auntie Eunice, I have news!

Surprise: out from her bed-closet come Uncle Ambrose home from the sea! (Who also appear to be jus slippin into his day clothes.)

I heard there's gonna be new Central Park jobs not given to Irish so maybe they be given to colored!

Auntie Eunice and Uncle Ambrose stare at me, then take to laughin stomach hard. *I* take to laughin. I didn't know I made a joke!

You always sayin you miss Uncle Ambrose on the sea all the time, Auntie Eunice. So if he get a job at the Central Park—

If we *were* offered—Auntie Eunice sudden hard, not laughin no more—which we won't be, but if we were, we'd refuse. Do you think after they evict us—?

Your auntie was just talking about whipping up some sugar cookies, say my uncle. That be a good idea?

But while she whippin em up, I get sleepy in a chair, the MacSweeneys' squabble kep me up all lass night. When I wake up late afternoon, I'm on the bed in the bed-closet. I come out to the parlor and see Auntie Eunice and Uncle Ambrose lookin over the letters she wrote to him when he was on the sea, talkin quiet, sighin. After a minute, they look up to me.

Staying for supper, sleepyhead?

No, I answer her. Both my grammies have deviled eggs for the Fourth, and if I help make em, I get a extra egg early! But I have time for a sugar cookie fore I go!

❧

Fearin the MacSweeneys might be at it again, tonight I stay with Grammy Brook. But I'm woke by a commotion from outside. Seein I'm all alone in the bed-closet, I go out to the front-room. The windas wide open in the heat, and Grammy and Gran-Gran starin out Gran-Gran's winda, Auntie Maryam and Mr. Freeman starin out the other. I squeeze between my new auntie and our boarder.

All kinds a ruckus in the street. People yellin, arms wavin wild. Our little wood clock say 12:15—jus turned into Saturday, Fourth a July.

The blasted police factions, sigh Mr. Freeman.

But they disbanded the Municipals, I say.

Municipal *sympathizers* against the Metropolitans. *And* the Dead Rabbits versus the Bowery Boys.

Who's the Dead Rabbits? I ask Mr. Freeman.

Your mama's kin, Grammy answer me.

Who the Bowery Boys? ask Auntie Maryam.

Five Points Irish-American gang, say Mr. Freeman. Democrats who apparently are in hot water with the other Irish for supporting the Republican Metropolitans.

I sure like to know where Hen is, Grammy worry.

And right then Hen fly through the door.

Riot on Chatham! Mob goin after the Metropolitans. Fists and stones and kickin, I saw one copper bleedin and the horde chasin another!

And you didn't have sense enough to come home? ask Grammy.

I did! I'm here!

Yes, after you followed the crowd *there*. Both you girls: when the mob movin one direction, *you* move the *other*!

Eventually things quiet in the street. Rest a the night, everybody inside sleep wake sleep wake.

Come daylight on the Fourth, the mean people's gone—Sleepin off their drink, Grammy Brook say—and people gettin ready for the holiday. Grammy has corn! I help her shuck it, then help her make the deviled eggs and she gimme one! Auntie Maryam cuttin up a tomata. Then Auntie Eunice and Uncle Ambrose walk through the door.

Heard some shenanigans happened downtown last night, say my auntie. Your mother's family join in?

I don't know.

As I recall, Siobhan sure had a way with a brick-bat.

Eunice, warn Grammy.

Brick-bat? ask Auntie Maryam.

Something used for a missile, say Mr. Freeman. Fragment of something dense, hard.

Such as a brick, say Auntie Eunice.

Usually about the size of your hand, Mr. Freeman go on.

So not dangersome like a brick? ask Auntie Maryam.

Hurled down from a height, from a tenement window? say Mr. Freeman. Oh, it's dangersome.

Walkin to Grammy Cahill's in the early afternoon, dodgin the firecrackers in the street. Cloudy sky, hope it don't rain, the city cancel the *big* fireworks!

My other grammy just started makin *her* deviled eggs so I get my second one already! The street gradually gettin more crowded, people lookin to celebrate. I have more eggs and pickles and crackers, and around five I think about goin back to Grammy Brook's for a second supper when somebody from the street holler, There goes one! Then the screamin and all us at the open winda, we only got the one at Grammy Cahill's, everybody starin out cep Cathleen on the couch and Great-Uncle Fergus who went out for somethin.

Below us a Metropolitan runnin for his life. A rough bunch followin, throwin everything they get their hands on.

I know that copper, Auntie Siobhan say. Native-born. Father was an American-Republican.

Republican?

No, *American*-Republican, somethin different, from back in the 'forties. Know what they were?

What?

Anti-Catholic. He better be runnin a lot faster.

And now I notice Auntie Siobhan's clutchin a brick-bat.

Hullabaloo: bunch a Metropolitans arrive, and everybody start flingin things out their windas. And here come some Bowery Boys joinin the Metropolitans.

That nativist, I say. That's the one whistle at Uncle Fergus, tell him pick up his dog's poop.

I barely have the words out when Auntie Siobhan send her brick-bat from our third-floor winda down hard on that nativist's skull. He wobble, put his hand on his head, look at his fingers: blood. Then look right up at Auntie Siobhan, raise his pistol.

Aaaaaaaaaah!

All us jump back, *BANG! BANG!* First bullet whiz past us through the open winda, second aimed higher hits the glass. The winda shattered, shards all over our front-room. When I pointed out that nativist, I didn't mean for Auntie Siobhan to knock him! but shoulda guessed she would. And when she knocked him, I wouldn'ta figured he shoot at us, but what else?

Then Great-Uncle Fergus stagger in, holdin his bloody head. Grammy run to him, her hand tight on his wound while Cathleen tear up material from the seamstressin while Cousin Aileen murmur calm to him *May the Saints watch over you* then Maureen wrap up his skull while Auntie

Siobhan searchin the cupboard searchin under the couch gatherin more ammunition.

We still got em! say Great-Uncle Fergus shakin his fist. We still got em! Hold still, Uncle! say Maureen.

I look out the winda, wonder: Where all these people from? Wall to wall, these ain't just Five Pointers. There's spectators. Our riot must be famous all over the city!

The hollerin the poundin the breakin glass the gunfire go on till eight in the evenin when some kinda ceasefire happen. I want to go to the fireworks, but Grammy say, No! Not fireworks enough for ye today?

Oh, Great-Uncle Fergus murmur, his eyes rollin around, blood soaked through the bandage. Everybody careful walk him down the steps and out the tenement, him staggerin and I smell his whiskey breath but this is a different kinda stagger. There's people on the street but not fightin, lookin dead tired. And somewhere I hear wailin, which sound like somebody dead *dead*. The drug-stores full a bleeders so Great-Uncle Fergus and us gotta wait. If people's really bad off, they get took to New-York Hospital, but if they can walk, they walk themself to the pharmacy because pharmacy you're treated then released but New-York Hospital you're treated then jailed.

Nex mornin, Five Points is quiet. Grammy and Cousin Aileen and Maureen sweepin, pickin up the shards.

Pray cheap window glass comes to my table, Grammy mutter.

Runnin around, I collect plenty a Saturday trashed papers to sell to the scrapman. Mary Bree and Nancy and Elijah and the other urchins and the street arabs got good riot stories from up close, so I spend the day on the street takin in the particulars.

Sunday night, I stay at Grammy Brook's, and nex mornin early I see Great-Uncle Fergus in the street with his dirty head bandage walkin a bit wobbly as he sweep up the horse apples.

Midday there's potata soup at Grammy Cahill's, Great-Uncle Fergus havin his dinner. He eat sittin on the floor, Cathleen on the couch wrappin his head in a fresh dressing, Grammy pourin out soup for her and me.

Did we win the riot?

Great-Uncle Fergus and Cathleen look up at me, Grammy starin down at me.

The Dead Rabbits. Us fightin the Bowery Boys.

No such thing as Dead Rabbits, Great-Uncle Fergus say. The Roche Guard, we follow Walter Roche.

Wh——?

Saloonkeeper, he answer before I finish askin. Just a friendly club. Till we were pushed.

Somebody actin the cod, thinks up *Dead Rabbits*, say Grammy. No one agrees from where it come, but the newspapermen decide it's more colorful, no matter it's a lie.

The Roche Guard whipped the Bowery Boys?

Not that simple, say Cathleen. Walter Roche was once appointed to local office with the influence of Police Justice Matthew Brennan. So when Roche's rivals, councilmen James Kerrigan and Pat Mathews, caught wind that Matthew Brennan was backing the struggle against the Metropolitans, James Kerrigan and Pat Mathews threw in with the Bowery Boys against Matthew Brennan and Walter Roche's folks.

Huh?

Politics.

But ain't all those folks you jus said Irish?

All Irish, say Great-Uncle Fergus. All Democrat.

Deaths, Grammy say. Six, accordin to the papers.

Then double that, say Great-Uncle Fergus.

No dead Bowery Boys, or whoever they be, say Grammy. Only the Roche Guard and sympathizers diggin graves. And the law only pressin charges against the Roche Guard sympathizers.

While the other done the worst damage! say Great-Uncle Fergus. *They* had the guns!

How come *all* the Irish weren't fightin to bring back the Municipals?

The Municipals? Great-Uncle Fergus say to me. The Municipals ain't *never* comin back!

I thought . . . I thought we were fightin to bring the Municipals back.

You're startin to give me a headache, *mo leanbh*, sigh Grammy.

Then what we fightin for?

Justice! say Great-Uncle Fergus and Grammy like obvious. Cathleen jus look tired.

After Great-Uncle Fergus go back out to his street cleanin and Grammy go back out to her table, I sit quiet while Cathleen do her seamstressin. I play with what's left a Dolly Doll, fallin to pieces.

I'll have to make you another sometime, Cathleen murmur. Here's two pennies. Bring me a paper.

I do, and soon as she look at the *Daily Times*, she laugh out loud. Entire front page, six columns a newsprint, all dedicated to our riot.

RIOTING AND BLOODSHED

THE STREETS BARRICADED.

THE CITY UNDER ARMS.

Six Men Killed and Over One Hundred Wounded.

THREE REGIMENTS CALLED OUT.

Riots in the 6th, 7th and 13th Wards.

"Dead Rabbits" Against the "Bowery Boys."

Metropolitans Driven from the 6th Ward.

THE FIGHT AT COW BAY.

Chimneys Hurled Down Upon the Populace.

That's not funny!

Now turn to page two, she say, and I see six full columns again.

THE PEACEFUL CELEBRATION.

The Fourth of July as Honored in the City and Its Suburbs.

MILITARY AND CIVIC PROCEEDINGS.

Quiet Comfort at Seguine's Point.

GOV. KING AND MAYOR WOOD HOB-NOBBING.

Entertainments, Exhibitions, Innocent Ebullitions.

A MORMON CLAM-BAKE.

No Rain, No Row Before Midnight, and No Fireworks.

The fourth of July was celebrated on Saturday very much in the usual fashion. Despite the rain the glorification commenced early on Friday evening, and from that time till after midnight on Sunday the air was resonant with the bang, pop, whiz, crack and crash of all sorts of explosive material in the hands of the patriotic. The day itself could scarcely have been pleasanter.

Uptown's a whole different city, she say, pullin her needle through.

Look! They postponed the fireworks fearin rain, now they're sposed to happen tonight! I can see em, City Hall Park!

Pretty side of the park for ticketed patrons, she say, uglier side for us. Then Cathleen yank the thread so hard the knot rip right through the cloth.

Panic

In the store, I ask for the yarn and give em the two nickels Cathleen gimme.

Thank you, dear, my cousin say when I bring it back to her.

Grammy and Cousin Aileen and Great-Uncle Fergus gonna like the winter hats you make em for Christmas!

Well, business hasn't been bad lately, I was able to save for the yarn. Now I just need to find the time to knit them.

But it's only the twenty-fifth of August! You got four whole months!

I have work quotas, that doesn't leave a whole lot of spare minutes in the day. Remember: the gifts are a surprise! Then Cathleen put her finger to her lips like *Sh!* And I put my finger to my lips like *I can keep a secret!*

Tell me what's interesting in the *Herald*.

I pick it up. *The steamships* City of Washington *and* North Star, *which arrived here last evening, left Liverpool and Southampton on the twelfth inst.*—What's *inst*?

Stands for *instant*. Means recently, the twelfth of this month. What else looks interesting?

I turn to page two. *The Burdell Estate: Mrs. Cunningham Declared Not to Be the Widow of Doctor Burdell*—

What else looks interesting?

I skip to page five.

There was a pretty good sized panic in the stock market this morning. Large lots of stock were offered—more than were sold; and it will be seen that the sales were unusually large. The movements at the Board of Brokers were hastened by rumors which were current in the street at an early hour in relation to the suspension of a large moneyed institution. At a later hour it was announced that the Ohio Life and Trust Company had suspended and closed its doors.

That ain't New York news! That's Ohio.

That bank is in New York. I suppose its first branch was in Ohio. What else looks interesting?

A late September late morning, I'm on the street when suddenly come a pourin, come a chill. Runnin home to Grammy Brook's when I see Mary Bree lookin forlorn on her sweeper corner.

How come you stand in the rain, Mary Bree?

I gotta wait for the customers.

Ain't nobody comin in the storm!

I gotta wait.

Theo!

I look over to Mr. Freeman standin in the doorway of his barbershop.

Get in here before you catch your death!

I look at Mary Bree, her eyes startin to look as watery as the rest a her.

Both of you!

And Mary Bree take to a grin jus for bein included. Both us race into the barbershop.

Ship a Gold? say Josiah, applyin shavin cream to a white customer's cheek.

Ship a Gold, say the man, holdin a *New-York Daily Times* which jus redubbed itself *New-York Times*. Officially *S.S. Central America*, lemme tell ya how it earned its moniker. Ship docks in San Francisco and they fill it with gold. Then ship sails the Pacific south: off the coast a California, off the coast a Mexico, past all a Central America till it docks Isthmus a Panama: skinniest strip between the great brines, barely forty miles ocean to ocean! Portage the cargo across, and there lies the mighty Atlantic and the *S.S. Central America* waiting.

Gold headed where? ask Josiah.

Here. New York. So the vessel embarks north. Little stop in Havana before sailin up the coast. And off the Carolinas, it hit.

Hurricane, say Ben, eyes on the haircut he givin another white man.

Hurricane, say the storyteller. The crew fought the tempest for days, but on the twelfth, the good ship sinks. And with it twenty thousand pounds a gold.

Everybody: *Twenty thousand pounds a gold?*

Twenty thousand pounds a gold bars and twenty-dollar gold coins bottom a the sea. The man spit in a cup, then add, And four hundred twenty-five people.

Twenty thousand pounds of gold? say my Cahill family that evenin. Cousin Aileen and Maureen brung a little seamstress work home with em, so them and Cathleen all sewin.

If I's a pirate, I'd dive to the bottom a the ocean and get it!

Needn't be a pirate, Grammy tell me. Pirate's a robber of the seas, but nobody left to rob from. Just be lost and found.

I used to wanna be a pirate, say Maureen. I used to wanna be Anne Bonny. Who's Anne Bonny?

Irishwoman, my cousin answer me. Bastard daughter of a man and his servant, he took her to England, dressed her like a boy, called her Andy. They ended up in Carolina Province before it was South Carolina state. She married a not very good pirate, then left him for a pretty good pirate and must've liked bein a boy because she dressed like a man and joined him and his band sailin the West Indies, Anne Bonny bold enough we know *her* name but not theirs, ravishin the ships of the Caribbean, *aaaaarrrrgh!*

Everybody laugh.

You take me with ya, Maureen? Piratin?

But what I ask wipe the smile right off her face.

I'll only be on the ship if the pirates in need of someone skilled in the fine arts of hemmin and bastin, she grumble, bitin her thread hard.

Week later, I wake from a nap in a new bed-closet.

Auntie Eunice, I like it here! I like your apartment! I like Greenwich Village!

Thank you, sugarplum, she say quiet.

Can I read your letter to Uncle Ambrose?

Thursday, Oct 1

My dearest Ambrose,
It is not even eight o'clock but I can hardly keep
my eyes open after this longest of days. It was, as you

know, Eviction Day, the cruel deadline that the city set for the final death knell to our lovely Seneca Village. Even as the metaphoric walls have been closing in, I have prayed for divine intervention, some bureaucratic error that would bring back our community, bring about justice. I believe it was with the official closing of my beloved Colored School No. 3 last week that I finally surrendered to bleak reality, packing my school supplies and crying the entire night.

At first light this morning, I walked to the door, and found a letter that had been slipped under it from dear Mr. Hesser, expressing his appreciation for our long friendship and his uncertainty regarding his immediate future now that Jupiterville, that wonderful refuge of beasts and Bach, is no more. I then stepped out to take a last look around. And there they stood, the mounted Central Park police surrounding our hamlet, should any of our good neighbors dare dispute the "wisdom" of the Powers That Be. Soon my sweet little Theo arrived, and with the added assistance of our kind, now former, tenant Mr. Schmidt, we loaded the cart to head south.

Theo and I have just put everything away here at our new home in Little Africa (or, as the rabble have dubbed this corner of Greenwich Village, "Coontown"). It is some consolation that our neighbors have all been very warm and welcoming.

As we departed our cherished neighborhood late this morning, I turned around and glimpsed a wealthy gentleman on Fifth avenue, someone evidently hopeful of increased land value now that the Central Park is to be the new front yard of his mansion. He should have been dancing at the sight of our final expulsion but, on the contrary, he appeared openly distressed. Perhaps he was feeling a bit of guilt, though that would seem unlikely as those investors prone to sympathy have long ago mollified their consciences in countless justifications of the park as a common good.

And then I remembered our current state of affairs. Nowadays one would be hard pressed to pick up any paper without seeing "panic" splattered all over the front page. And it occurred to me that these recent remarkable events were quite likely the cause of the aforementioned aristocrat's perceived affliction. As I looked upon our beautiful village for the last time, the refuge where we negroes have felt freedom for generations, I reminded myself that God works in mysterious ways, and found comfort in the possibility that perhaps one of those ways might very well result in this dear patrician's financial ruin.

Always,
Your loving Eunice

                                              ❧

Extra! Extra! Run on the banks! Read all about it!

Circus! The gentlemen in their shiny top hats, ladies in their fur coats like winter and today only October the ninth! Shovin, shoutin, everybody wanna get in the bank!

Ex*cuse* me, sir, *I* was here first!

Do you *mind?*

Does anyone know if the banks will be open tomorrow? If we don't get in today, may we enter in the morning? Saturday?

For all we know, the banks may never open again!

I've heard they've nearly run out of specie!

No!

Don't be a fool, they can*not* be out of specie!

Madam! Was that *your* cane in my back?

Mr. Samuel! Mr. Samuel! I was jus walkin by the Bowery Savings Bank. Rich people! Rude people!

Yes, he tell me, the rich aren't used to bein *inconvenienced.*

Standin behind him's Hen and Jeremiah. After all the fuss on Pinkster,

Hen never did leave Mr. Samuel for Cornelius Hornbell's stable. But her and Jeremiah both lookin pretty bored now.

Nobody need their chimney sweeped?

Unfortunately, Mr. Samuel tell me, the *haves* are now distracted by other matters—the fear of being a *have less.*

They want their specie! What's specie?

Gold. Or silver, they want their money in coin, metal—not paper.

But aren't bank notes more?

Paper money's the *idea* of value. When reality strikes, paper's nothin but paper.

In the afternoon, I ask Cathleen: Did you know specie's specie but paper money's nothin but the idea a value?

Cathleen on the couch got the yarn in her lap, eyes on her knittin. That Ship of Gold you mentioned? I've read up on it. The California gold discovery fueled speculation, and speculation precipitated inflation: a bubble. Eastern banks were depending on that gold. Twenty thousand pounds of gold valued at twenty dollars an ounce at the bottom of the Atlantic. Do you know that arithmetic?

Emm . . .

Six million four hundred thousand dollars. You can close your mouth now. We should all learn to be good swimmers, she wink.

Cathleen, you're almost finished Great-Uncle Fergus's hat! You're fast!

Well, with the seamstress work drying up—she sigh—seems suddenly I have plenty of knitting time.

❧

The Crimean War, say Miss Fiona, throwin a whiskey shot back in Auntie Siobhan's tavern Saturday afternoon.

That was over a year ago! say some man, bloodshot eyes.

What's the Cry Me In War? I ask.

Russia and France and Britain and Ottoman in some holy war over the Holy Land.

And what's that to do with the New York aristocracy in conniptions? Auntie Siobhan ask Miss Fiona.

War! Inductin into the military European farmers away from their crops, European soldiers *destroyin* enemy European crops. Who d'ye think then made a bundle sellin grains to every side of the conflict, never takin sides? America! And that war ended a year ago, that bleedin bloody income stops flowin to the States and you ask what's *that* got to do with *this*?

※

At the barbershop no customers, the barbers sittin in the barber chairs, readin their papers.

Farmers out west hit hard, say some new young barber I never met before. Land prices declined, less people settlin out there if nobody buyin what the land produce.

That because a the Cry Me War? I ask.

Mr. Freeman nod. Never happened before: this global connectiveness for prosperity or failure, we are now for the first time part of a *world economy*. Railroad securities plunged, all those speculators betting on a continuous flow of settlers, on steady economic growth in the frontier— well, suddenly Westward ho!'s turned to Westward: no! You heard how many train lines in default? Illinois Central, Erie & Pittsburgh, Fort Wayne & Chicago, the Reading. That's not even mentioning the ones gone altogether bankrupt: Delaware, Lackawanna & Western; Fond du Lac.

※

Dred Scott, say Auntie Eunice Sunday, lookin up from the paper she's readin at Grammy Brook's. Grammy have less whites for the whites lately with all the whites clutchin their purses tighter, so she sit with Gran-Gran at her winda, lookin out at the newsboys workin overtime, more *Extra!* editions, headlines changin by the minute. Meanwhile Auntie Maryam moppin again even though she mopped yesterday, like she always feel she need to work for her keep. No chimneys to sweep so Hen sit around whittlin, don't know who taught her. Bet she stole that penknife.

The population of the North is more than twice that of the South, Auntie Eunice go on, and slaves make up nearly *half* of those already meager Southern census figures. Given that Southern plantation owners obviously have no intention of relocation, much of the westward expansion has been made up of former inhabitants of the populous North longing for space. Until last spring Kansas was experiencing an onrush of a thousand new migrants a day! But with March came *Dred Scott*, opening up the possibility of the territories becoming slave states, and this decision caused a major hiccup in the previous steady flow of newcomers. There are many Northerners morally opposed to slavery. There are other Northerners indifferent or pro-slavery but loath to remove to a West where they must compete with wealthy slave-holders, might become embroiled in hostilities against wealthy slave-holders. Thus, like dominoes: a disgraceful Supreme Court ruling causing a plunge in western settlement causing a plunge in railroad usage, plunging land values and causing a failure of banks which had financed railroad and land speculation, causing *that*.

Auntie Eunice point to the winda, noise on the street, the raised voices of white gentlemen pretendin sober come to replace the raised voices a Five Pointers admitted drunk. Auntie Maryam stop her moppin to come look down on em, little smile formin on her lips.

One thing I know, Grammy say. Whenever the rich make a crisis, you know what gonna fall to the poor is catastrophe.

⁓

Tuesday seem *all* the rich runnin to their banks! Wednesday I wake up hearin *Bank Suspension Day! City banks announce suspension of specie payment until further notice!*

Meeting of Boston Bank Presidents!
Conditions of Finances in Virginia and Tennessee!
Runs on the Savings and Discount Banks!

Wait—I know *that* newsboy's voice. It's a girl's. I run out the door, down the steps.

Hen! When you get to be newsboy?

Hen grin, hair tucked under a hat and holdin papers, then wave at someone behind me: Auntie Maryam standin in the doorway of our tenement, half hid behind the wall. Not too many colored newsboys, ain't *no* girl newsboys. But seem the only business boomin now's the newspapers, sellin out quick and not long to wait for the next *Extra!* special edition. Lotsa people on the street movin around but not workin. Not the fruiterer not the scrapman, not Grammy Cahill with her wares. Not the worry-face gentlemen walkin through, everybody solemn, only the newsboys and Auntie Maryam appear delighted. I walk back to her.

Auntie Maryam, I say soft, you never step outside our tenement cep to the back courtyard. I never see you near the street.

I has to see it, she say. Witness. Wednesday, October the fourteenth, eighteen and fifty-seven: the white peoples' terror.

They did it! come a gentleman staggerin from a saloon, tears streamin. Suspended specie! I'm ruined! Ruined!

What Auntie Eunice saze, *Dred Scott* part a the cause a all this? Auntie Maryam go on. Where I's from, never happen. Never no argument amungst the white folks, slavery always were, always be: agreed. Look like times is changin, *inshallah*.

And now here come Ciaran walkin down Park street, lookin around, confused by all the confusion.

Ciaran! I wave and yell. *Ciaran!* He see me, break into a big smile. I walk over.

I thought you was on a farm in Harlem.

'Twas. But they're after losin their money, had to let me go.

Still he look a little happy, like maybe he come to see Five Points as home. So here we be: Auntie Maryam smilin and peekin from the doorway and Ciaran on his homecomin and Hen grinnin shoutin the *Extra!*s and me in the middle of em all on the street, four orphans observin the woes and desperation a the Panic of 1857 but feelin nothin but a sighin ease.

1858

Depression

Mothers hold their children's hands for just a little while, and their hearts forever, Grammy sigh, standin in Deirdre Boyle's doorway.

Not one day you could've waited, Eibhleen Cahill? My little girl Colleen still warm in the grave and here ye are to bid on her dress!

It's just a few words of comfort my granddaughter and I've come to offer the bereaved.

That's good, for the dress were my baby's one and only and sure she were buried in it! Then Deirdre Boyle take to bawlin. I'm only after givin her the blanket I knitted for her Christmas, and my precious daughter barely sees it into the new year!

The poor angel, say Grammy.

And I forgot her rattle! Meant to lay it next to her, now she's nothin to play with!

Except all the other little angels in heaven God's taken with the scarcity.

Deirdre Boyle wipe her eye with the heel a her hand. Well, it's not me alone with the keenin. The priest is after comin last night to give aul Padraic Murphy his last rites.

Grammy say, Wouldn't poor little Colleen get a little joy, lookin down from heaven to see that rattle in the hand of another wee one?

Grammy leave the Boyles carryin the rattle and a chipped porcelain Virgin she bought to sell. In the street, she move us to a corner, countin her coins in private, January wind whippin the snow.

Mornin, Eibhleen.

Grammy look up. Walkin by's Maeve, Grammy's dearest friend and fiercest competitor. Grammy's eyebrow raise.

Mornin, Maeve. Where're ye off to s' early?

Ah, here and there, and Maeve disappear into a tenement.

Grammy? You think maybe we oughta wait a extra day before we come for the dead's belongins?

And let my dearest friend and fiercest competitor Maeve get there first?

Grammy stuff her change inside her dress. Now then. As I recall, dearly departed Padraic Murphy's survivors reside in Mott street.

⌒

Jus before dark, I'm walkin by a alley, see a whole bunch a urchins huddled up together. Mary Bree sleep near the edge of em, and in the middle's Nancy and Elijah under some newspapers.

Theo! Nancy call. We got a dog!

Skinny, dirty white mutt between em stick its nose out from under the papers.

She's Lucille, say Nancy. She keep us warm!

Ark! say Lucille.

Can I pet her?

Achoo! say Elijah. She *like* to be petted!

Ark ark! Lucille say when I pet her.

Where you get her?

She jus follow us! say Nancy. When the baker give us a roll, we give Lucille some crumbs, she follow us, she love us! *Achoo!*

⌒

This is my niece Theodora, Auntie Eunice say nex day in their new apartment in Greenwich Village Little Africa. Theo, these are the Peterses. They may be staying with Uncle Ambrose and me for a time.

Good day to you, Theodora. The woman Peters smile.

Greetings to you, Miss, say her husband.

You were speaking of your employment with the St. Nicholas Hotel, Mr. Peters?

Yes. Well. The man look down. Hard times, not so many travelers comin through New York.

And not so many porters the hotel is in need of?

Everybody quiet.

Mr. Peters. Mrs. Peters. I sincerely empathize with your troubles, it's hard times for all, we negroes *especially*, which is why Mr. Bennett and I have elected to take in boarders. However, that would be a most moot effort were our lodgers unemployed, penniless—

The woman Peters take out a little pouch, *clink clink*.

Savins, she say, and hand it to Auntie Eunice, who count it. Then my auntie smile. Take out a key from her dress pocket, hand it to Mrs. Peters.

The evenin, Uncle Ambrose come home tired. In the livin room where the Peterses'll sleep, Auntie Eunice serve us and them a biscuit each, little bit a gravy. In the bed-closet after, Uncle Ambrose say, I'm a skilled seaman! And now can't get a job as butler.

They got a depression on the ocean too, Uncle Ambrose?

He shake his head. Not the ocean. Now I'm a seaman of the inland. Canal to the Lakes, loadin foodstuffs from Ohio, Michigan, Wisconsin, Indiana, Illinois, western New York, and haulin it back to the city.

How come the foodstuffs don't just come in a wagon?

Rugged terrain. Faster, easier on the water: why they built the Erie Canal. He sigh. Sure do miss the whalers. One whale could yield forty-five barrels of oil, fuel to light ten thousand lamps! *Twenty* thousand! Sperm whales the most valuable. And we could boil the blubber into oil right on the ship! The whalebone sold for springs, needles. America dominated the world market! I missed my wife, but steady work. Eh, Eunice?

We have the boarders now. We'll manage until something comes up.

What happen to the whalin, Uncle Ambrose?

Began costing more than businessmen were willing to invest in. Oil alternatives developed: Alcohol. Lard. Linseed. Coal. The work dried up. *So* I trade the wide open sea for the winding Erie and eventually find it again: peace on the water. Till some smug speculators have the whole country crashing. Drowning.

When Uncle Ambrose go out to the necessary, I help Auntie Eunice wash the dishes in cold water, can't spare coal for hot.

I'm sorry Uncle Ambrose lost his sea peace, he gotta stay home.

Hm? Oh, thank you, Theo, say Auntie Eunice, but she don't look sad about it at all, hummin lively like she near ready to dance.

Auntie Siobhan, how come your saloon near empty? I say nex day, sippin tea at the bar. There's more drunk people than ever, good business!

Don't know where they're gettin that penny-a-glass rotgut, but expect to see them all droppin like flies any day now. Auntie Siobhan shrug. Who can blame them? Drink what ye can afford when the other choice is wake up every day hungry and sober—then my auntie take her little glass and throw her head back swallowin.

Herself does tell the truth, sigh the customer nursin his drink at the table.

Funny you say that, given *you* appear quite well fed as of late.

The man don't look at her, don't answer. Pick up his glass, throw the drink down his throat.

You and your Methodist friends.

Now he turn to her. Man's gotta eat, Siobhan.

Ho ho! He didn't think I'd spy him, Theo. (Sayin my name, but never take her eyes off him.) Comin out *the Mission* lookin nourished and content. And all he had to do to fill his belly at *the Mission* was denounce the holy Catholic church!

Didn't. All the matron wanted was me to affirm the true way to heaven's through the Scriptures—

The Scriptures! Protestant flim-flam!

I could go to the Mission, I chuckle. I'm half-Protestant.

Auntie Siobhan's eyes turn to me sharp. Do, and you'll no longer be a niece of mine.

❧

Outside, snow blows! Mary Bree sweepin the walks. And there Lucille with her!

Mary Bree, how come *you* got Lucille? Where Nancy and Elijah? I lean over to pet Lucille but Lucille *grrrrrrr*.

They dieded.

I look at Mary Bree. I look at Lucille. I look at Mary Bree.

Caught a fever. Then somebody say they dieded, then I see Lucille come barkin up to me.

Grrrrrr, say Lucille, eyes on me.

But she growl to everybody else now, say Mary Bree. Hungry.

Aw, don't cry, *a chuisle mo chroí*, Grammy Cahill say that evenin, me bawlin on her lap. Two little angels gone straight to heaven, where it's always warm and plenty to eat.

I can't stop my sobs altogether but they do take a rest, seein Nancy and Elijah floatin around in their little white gowns and little white wings and little white haloes playin little white harps. I don't know what dead Colleen Boyle looked like, but I send in a gurglin baby floatin by. Then Nancy pull out a little white fiddle, and Elijah pull out a little white banjo, and all the other kid angels bouncin to the music till a street arab angel try to steal Elijah's white banjo, then Nancy wallop the robber with her white fiddle, and I laugh right through my tears!

❧

Nex day's Sunday, the wind whippin through the walls, through the cracks in the winda from when it got shot through in the riot though we covered most of it with a board. Everybody at Grammy Cahill's bundled up huddled up, no coats but we gettin warm together. Full house: me and Grammy and Cathleen and Auntie Siobhan and Ciaran and Great-Uncle Fergus and Maureen and Cousin Aileen, the sewin shop got no more work for em so Cousin Aileen and Maureen mostly home these days. Me on the couch next to Cathleen, her combin my hair. No seamstressin and no more yarn for knittin (but Grammy and Cousin Aileen and Great-Uncle Fergus loved the hats she made em for Christmas, and she surprised me and Ciaran and Maureen with hats too!), and she already read the scrap newspaper I found her, and Cathleen always like her hands busy so now givin me the plaits.

We'll be out tryin to drum up the work again in the mornin, say Cousin Aileen, like she say every day. Saint Joe be with us, she add, her eyes on our Saint Joseph the Worker statue.

Tried the dry-goods stores, have ye? They're always in need of girls for the mendin.

Every day, Cousin Aileen say to Grammy.

There's Lord and Taylor. Or Stewart's. A. T. Stewart's an Irishman, ye know. Irish millionaire!

Ye said that yesterday, Auntie Eibhleen, say Cousin Aileen. And the day before. And he's an Irish *Protestant* millionaire.

Still—

I go to Lord and Taylor, say Maureen, and Ma to Stewart's, hopin for one or the other.

I'm only suggestin Stewart's as he might be inclined to favor an Irish girl—

Which one a the thousands clamorin at his door, do ye think?

I could do without the cheekiness, Aileen!

Sorry, Auntie Eibhleen. We'll be out lookin in the mornin, bright and early—and Cousin Aileen cross herself for good measure.

Ye know things is bad when Siobhan's here, mindin the Sunday liquor-ban law, which no one else minds, mutter Great-Uncle Fergus.

All my business gone to the bloody moonshiners, she say. I'll open up later this evenin, send up a prayer.

As I recall, Niall O'Shea could *always* bring in the customers.

Maureen! say Cathleen and Cousin Aileen and Grammy.

It's true!

Auntie Siobhan's eyes narrow at Maureen. *Niall O'Shea* never had to compete against a depression.

Who's Niall O'Shea? ask Ciaran.

My uncle, I say.

Not your uncle! say Auntie Siobhan and Cathleen and Cousin Aileen.

'Twas, say Grammy, but thank God he was dead before ye seen much of him. Niall O'Shea was Siobhan's husband.

An *aul* one, he was, say Maureen.

I was seventeen, him thirty-seven when we wed, say Auntie Siobhan. He was handsome, he owned a publick. And I was young. Too love-blind to see he was a drunkard himself, didn't anticipate that regular bruisin and breakin my body would be a part a the marriage contract.

But! say Grammy, he died suddenly three years ago, rest his soul. Forty, leavin my then twenty-year-old girl with a name and a business, so I'd say he well served his purpose on this earth.

How he die? Ciaran ask.

A harsh fever come on him one evenin, took him quick, say Grammy.

The fever, *interestingly*, come on just after Siobhan served him a bowl a vegetable stew, say Maureen.

Maureen! say Cousin Aileen, then turn to Auntie Siobhan and Grammy. It's her hunger talkin, bringin in all the ugly.

Grammy say, Let's just all stop speakin a Niall O'Shea.

Niall O'Shea, say Auntie Siobhan, had rules, and one of them was food gatherin is women's work. A wiser man, she add with a funny smile, might've made an exception for mushrooms.

Knock knock!

Well, thank ye kindly! Grammy say to the knocker at the door, then come back with a wood box: flour! marmalade! cheese! oats!

Little door-to-door gift from our Tammany friends! smile Grammy, moist eyes.

Always I hear Tammany Hall. Where Is It?

Not a *where*, Great-Uncle Fergus answer me. A cooperative. Provide assistance to the poor. Helped me get my street cleanin job.

We'll dole this heaven-sent fare out gingerly, say Grammy. Make it last.

Which, since we already had broth, mean we ain't get a crumb outa that box tonight.

The mornin: porridge! Somethin I'm tired of in normal times and crave in the scarcity. Smellin it, every time Ciaran's belly growl, mine growl louder, then Cathleen's louder still, we laugh waitin for breakfast! Then Great-Uncle Fergus gettin ready to go out clean the streets, and Cousin Aileen and Maureen gettin ready to go out searchin for work, so they all served first and not much, which is a lot more than the few spoons me and Cathleen and Ciaran each get after. I know Grammy goin out too, see what scraps she might collect, and here she scrapin bottom a the pot for us with no servin left for herself. Me and Ciaran and Cathleen eat our spot a meal slow, bit by bit.

Grammy?

Hmm?

How come Cousin Aileen and Maureen never go sewin at the House a Industry?

Grammy and Cathleen gasp!

D' ye know what they *do* in that House of Industry?

I stare at Grammy.

Adopt Irish children away! And not just orphan urchins. Little ones abducted from their own livin parents! Sent to Protestants in the West. To be slaves!

Ciaran and me gasp!

Just steer clear of it and nothin you two have to worry over.

I eat my lass grain a porridge.

I don't even know how much seamstressing goes on there anymore, say Cathleen. They used to offer work to women, but now they seem to concentrate their efforts on saving the children of Five Points. Cathleen give her own words a little eyeroll.

Even if they *did* still offer the jobs, grumble Grammy, ye think we'd be travelin with the likes of them? *Kidnappers?* Matter of principle!

Grammy wavin her arms in the excitement, which startin to look thinner n Mary Bree's broomstick.

Now breakfast over, Ciaran and Cathleen and me's stomachs seem to be growlin louder than before, this time nobody laughin. Before Grammy put the bowls in the cold dishwater, she lick em clean, even though they was already licked clean enough by me and Cathleen and Ciaran.

〜

Your Irish auntie do got a point bout the Mission, say Mr. Samuel, shiverin on the street, tryin to drum up the chimney-sweep work, no more apprentices. Food and clothes they offer only upon professin the *right* faith, Methodist as they see it. Wanna know how *I* see it? He lower his voice: Your Auntie Maryam on the plantation had to keep her Islam between her and God, she *survived*. Whatever she *say*, God know where her *heart* is. *Survive* might not be a word in the Commandments but that's because God assume you got sense enough to do that *first* so you be around to follow the other Ten.

What about House a Industry?

When that Reverend Pease first come to preach, just a little time in Five Points taught him sin derives not from lack of God but from lack of work. He begun that House of Industry, built it himself after the religionists abandoned him for refusin to make it a House of Proselytizing. Pease never required any oath of Methodist loyalty. You think this neighborhood's bad now? Shoulda seen it before. The drunks lyin everywhere, whether passed out or dead only the rigor mortis or lack thereof divulge *that* secret. Not quite the hunger we got now, but the hopelessness led to death just as easy. Then in come this new thing: job trainin for indigent women, be ya Methodist, be ya Catholic, be ya Jew. Long, far as I could see, as ya be *white*.

But don't House a Industry adopt Irish children away into slavery?

Foolishness! say Mr. Samuel. Then shrug. True, the focus seems to've changed from the ladies to the orphans. Suppose the Mission *and* the House of Industry got into the adoption business, but *slavery?* Little Miss Brook, if you know nothin else in this life, know this: there's only one people in the United States of America that's snatched into slavery, and Irish ain't it.

Now Mr. Samuel move off callin *Sweep-oh!* and hopin. Then I get a start rememberin what he just said about Auntie Maryam. I guess they come to be friends on Pinkster because nobody else outside our family she let know she come from any plantation.

I wander over to Broadway, wonderin if Cousin Aileen and Maureen might get in to A. T. Stewart's Dry Goods. The street packed: ladies everywhere! Ladies and girls, worse n when Haughwout's opened with the passenger elevator! Each one beggin, pleadin, cryin for a job—if Cousin Aileen and Maureen somewhere in there, I hope they don't get crushed!

⁓

Two days later, here I sit in the Jewels. Downstairs neighbors moved in lass Moving Day, first time I ever been in their apartment. The coffin two feet square. I thought a coffin's spose to be long-shaped, I whisper to Grammy Brook.

Two babies side-by-side, she whisper back. Sharin one box save a little wood, what the family could afford.

Mrs. Jewel sobbin, Mr. Jewel's arm round her. People keep walkin up to em, talkin soft. After a while she wipe her tears. This how I know they always be together in heaven, she say, then break off wailin again. Charlotte and the other baby, one she had in November: Clementine.

One was two, one was new, Grammy sigh soft.

Supper that night is some beans, half a hard biscuit, dab a grease. Huddle together in the cold, except Gran-Gran refuse to leave her winda. I'm thinkin a Nancy and Elijah and Charlotte and Clementine and Colleen laughin, runnin around the warm heaven playground, when Mr. Freeman clear his throat.

Caleb.

We look at him.

My apprentice. Nineteen years of age, married, expecting their first child. We had to let him go. I'm not the shop owner but I'm the manager, it's my job to . . . I told him he'll be welcomed back when times get better. Business was waning *before*. White men. Hating the Indians, wanting to show they can grow a beard when the Indians can't. Or the lately women's rights talk, the white men wanting to keep their beards, show off their manly man-ness—this is how the barbering business plummeted *before* the Depression, and *now*. My apprentice, Caleb, wants to take care of his family, he and his wife went to the Association for Improving the Condition of the Poor—

Not for us, say Grammy.

The room go quiet.

In any case, they only take the worst destitute.

And who are *we*?

Mr. Freeman, Grammy start.

Mrs. Brook, I have heard the Association for Improving the Condition of the Poor is serving *three times* as many this winter than usually—

Servin those who pass their inspection. Servin the people *they* deem worthy—

Okay, say Mr. Freeman to Grammy. He think, then after a while sigh, say: You're right.

Inspection? Auntie Maryam ask Grammy.

Before they offer their services, *food*, they require a home visit. They'd want to confirm we are *penniless*. They'd ask our neighbors about our work ethic, our drinking habits.

We ain't drunks! I say.

No, but that's *our* business, not theirs.

You're right, Mr. Freeman sigh.

Judgment, say Gran-Gran, eyes out the winda.

Might not be *our* choice, Grammy say, but if ever was a good reason for our neighbors to stay drunk, hunger's it.

But the Association got *food*—

So let em into our privacy? Grammy snap at me. Never! Matter of principle!

I think a moment. What about Tammany Hall?

Grammy and Mr. Freeman stare at me.

Maybe they bring us a box a food. Like at Grammy Cahill's.

Tammany Hall, say Grammy, eyes all narrow, is a system. The New York Democrat Party machine, beehive of corruption. Not interested in us.

It started anti-Irish, say Mr. Freeman, but when Irish became the plurality of the voters, Tammany knew where its bread was buttered. In exchange for the groceries, on Election Day they'll expect your menfolk to vote Democrat early. And often.

In bed, my stomach growlin again. I see Auntie Maryam awake.

Was slavery worst?

In the moonlight, I see her thinkin. Then nod.

Whippins, she whisper. Labor dawn to dusk, hot sun, no rest. But Hathaway Plantation, food we always have. Not enough. But *some*thin on the plate.

Then quiet so I figure she gone to sleep.

Once, she start again, I sees a mother wail like Mrs. Jewel, her baby sold. Nex baby die, she bury it, wipe a tear, go on. Lease she know *that* baby ain't a slave. Lease she know where *that* baby be.

In the night, I hear Auntie Maryam sniff sniff, think she cryin. Then see she jus smellin the smell a that greased biscuit still on her fingers.

❧

Soup kitchen! Long line, shiverin, holes in my soles: wet snow touch my feet! This mornin, Grammy Cahill open her cupboard, sigh: Nothin in the press. It's time. Now us in the line for stew! And it's the city, neither House a Industry nor the Mission, jus regular charity!

Emmet Burke, say Great-Uncle Fergus. Conan Magrath. Maggie O'Sullivan.

Not Maggie! Grammy say. I'm only after seein her last week!

Boarded the ship two days ago.

Not so many, say Cousin Aileen.

Finn Moriarity. Aoife O'Brien. Then Great-Uncle Fergus stop.

Not so—

Not sayin there's many! he snap to Cousin Aileen. Sayin there's some Irish after survivin the famine, after survivin the coffin ships, now find life in America such a treachery, they board again to turn around: back to the Isle.

Never hungry like this there.

You don't remember the Hunger! Grammy say sharp to Ciaran. The *Great* Hunger.

Never this bitter cold in Ireland, say Great-Uncle Fergus. And there were sod for the fire. And once the blight passed, soil for crops!

Nothin would turn me back around, say Cousin Aileen. Except the babies. Another chance to be with the four babies I'm after buryin there, these hard times remind me of it! Your dear starved brothers and sisters, she say to Maureen, swipin a tear.

The family in front a us take a step forward, thus so do we.

This will pass, say Auntie Siobhan. Just like 'fifty-five.

'Fifty-five! say Great-Uncle Fergus. D'ye recollect *that* winter? And here we are, sufferin from another panic only three years later!

D'ye think there'll be whole pieces? worry Cousin Aileen. Not just broth? A whole bit a meat or vegetable I might bring back to Cathleen?

I brung a cup, Maureen whisper. We might have to turn on the tears to make them believe us, but how can they refuse a hungry invalid girl?

If not, we could go to the House a Industry and fill our pockets, bring it home to Cathleen.

All the grown-ups turn to me lightnin fast, lightnin eyes.

I won't go! Me and Ciaran won't go so we can't be adopted into Irish slavery but *grown-ups* can. Mr. Samuel say *God* know where our Catholic heart is, our job is survive first.

And when the want ads say *Work for Protestants only, no Papists*, shall we denounce our faith then as well? ask Cousin Aileen.

Or *Housin available, no Irish need apply*—will ye be turnin your back on your faith and family at that time? ask Auntie Siobhan.

He's my brother!

We turn around to see who's yellin. A push, a push back.

And ye think that gives him the right to cut into the line?

Mary Bree ain't been on her corner, I say. She *always* on her corner but I ain't seen her two days.

For the first time today, my gift a the gab Irish kin fall silent. The family in front a us take a step forward, thus so do we.

That evenin, I stroll by the House a Industry, the tall buildins side-by-side in Worth street, six stories! The wind whippin, I start walkin back to Grammy Brook's, but pass an alley and somethin catch my eye.

Mary Bree!

There she lay, eyes open, lookin blue lookin froze. Lucille dog stiff beside her. I touch Mary Bree. Nothin.

I can't carry Mary Bree *and* Lucille, I gotta pick one. Mary Bree on my back to the House a Industry, knock. A lady answer, and seein Mary Bree, her voice take to flutterin the fear, and some other lady come, and they rush me and Mary Bree in, take Mary Bree and wrap her in warm and put her by the fire, they let me by the fire too! Then gimme soup! A doctor come in and pick up Mary Bree, and nex thing I'm wakin on the rug, mornin light and nothin a the fire left but embers. I hear a lady's voice, soft. Talkin soft to Mary Bree. Mary Bree awake!

Mary Bree!

Mornin, Theo, Mary Bree say soft. Where's Lucille?

I forgot about Lucille! I say: I'll get her!

The lady help me find my way to the door.

Would you like to stay here and go to school with us, Theo?

I say, No thank you. I'm orphan with family. Then I run out before she can adopt me into Irish slavery! Or colored slavery! Either way, I'm on the market!

I hear the woman call after me: No dogs!

I didn't know where else to take Mary Bree, scared she might die. Now she lived, maybe they sell her! I got a idea. I'll bring Lucille back to the House a Industry, they say No dogs! and they throw Mary Bree out with Lucille: they be free! *Or* I'll say Mary Bree's my sister, we got folks!

Lucille still in the alley froze, but maybe she can get Lazarus'd like Mary Bree. I take her to Grammy Brook.

Grammy! Nancy and Elijah and Mary Bree's dog Lucille froze. You make her live?

Grammy Brook inspect Lucille all over.

Sorry, punkin, she's gone.

My eyes water. We bury her?

Ground winter hard now. You say a prayer though, wish her luck on her journey. And give her *gratitude* for comin to see us on her way.

I do, though I don't understand the gratitude. Grammy send me down to fetch water from the pump and soon's I'm back send me out to search for coal and soon's I'm back send me up to Little Africa Greenwich Village to borrow salt from Auntie Eunice and soon's I'm back it's suppertime. Sure wish Lucille coulda been around for our soup supper: first meat in two weeks! Grammy and Auntie Maryam and Hen and Mr. Freeman and Gran-Gran all smilin.

What's this meat, Grammy?

The meat of *gratitude*, say Grammy. Which don't answer my question, but I can tell that's all the answer I'm gonna get. I look at everybody else, who is none of em lookin at me.

After supper, I wanna go see Mary Bree, but Grammy say gettin dark, cold: stay home.

In the mornin, I knock on the House a Industry. It's a different lady, and I keep askin about Mary Bree but she all confused, then finally the lady I remember from before appear in the doorway.

Theo! Come in! Warm yourself by the fire. Would you like some oatmeal and bacon?

Mary Bree is a very lucky girl, she say as I chew my pork strip. First, you saved her life, bringing her here two evenings ago. And then yesterday afternoon, we were visited by a childless couple who happened to be in town, a couple desperate for a little daughter. Mary Bree embarked with them to Wisconsin this morning.

I stare at her.

The woman smile. Mary Bree seemed very happy. I know you're sad as you'll miss your friend, but her new parents are very good people, the mother a teacher. Mary Bree will no longer have to sweep the corner. She will go to school. She will have shoes!

This woman seem nice, I don't think she lyin. I try to think Mary Bree not sold into Irish slavery. After I finish my oatmeal, the lady walk me to the door.

Mary Bree's Irish, I say. Catholic. Her new parents Catholic?

The lady still smilin tender. Now she stand on the warm inside hallway and me the cold sidewalk. I'm waitin for her to answer my question but gentle, gentle, she close the door.

Knot

Come March, the Depression let up a bit: spring mean a little outside construction day work, mean not have to heat up apartments. Grammy Cahill back with her table. And there Auntie Eunice *at* Grammy Cahill's table! Not often I see both sides a my family together!

Mornin, Grammy! Mornin, Auntie Eunice! Whatcha doin?

Bargaining, say Auntie Eunice.

Grammy show her some scrap cloth. Looky here, she say, then take out what Cathleen made her for Christmas. Cathleen got a little fancy with the grown-ups' hats.

See the tiny flowers? Lace? Delicate, it is.

I stare at Grammy. She tryin to sell Cathleen's gift? That hurt Cathleen's feelins!

Very pretty hat, say Auntie Eunice, if I were in the market for one. I asked about material for a *dress*.

The hat's not for sale, but the seamstress's skills are. What a pretty frock she'd make! Grammy wink: The family discount for ye.

A *wedding* dress? say Cathleen that afternoon.

Don't fret, Grammy say, stashin money in our floor-board hole. You're a seamstress who made our home warm with your lacy doilies. All a weddin dress is is sewin and lace.

Cathleen still lookin worried but think on that.

When is she coming?

She never leave Grammy Brook's apartment.

Cathleen stare at me. Well, *I* can't leave *our* apartment! How shall I make it?

That evenin, Auntie Siobhan come by for supper with a rope.

Met her when Theo was showin her around the neighborhood last year. Tall. Colorin dark. Like Eunice and Zeke.

Cathleen never met Auntie Eunice or my father!

I did. Your mother married your father right here in our apartment so I could be at the wedding.

Give this rope to Eunice, or your other grammy, Auntie Siobhan say. Tell them to wrap it around Maryam for measure, and mark it. They'll know.

Mornin of the weddin, I'm carryin the dress in a bag to Grammy Brook's.

Now isn't that *beautiful*, Grammy Brook say.

I grin like *I* made it. There weren't anywhere near enough a any one material, so it's a patchwork dress with Cathleen's fancy roses and lace, lookin prettier n any rich people's weddin dress I ever heard tell of!

Worth every penny, say Auntie Eunice, who ain't easily won over. Cathleen is as clever as any tailor! But, alas, *that* well-paid work is reserved for men.

Auntie Maryam beamin, turnin her shinin eyes to Auntie Eunice: *Your* penny.

Auntie Eunice smile. Two dollars given the family discount, which I could afford with my new job. My wedding gift to you.

Ain't we like the gentry, Grammy smile. Every bride *we* know just wear her Sunday best for the wedding, and here we got a special gown.

My foster sister spent the first quarter-century of her life in slavery, Auntie Eunice say. An indulgence she deserves. Let us try it on!

While Auntie Eunice help Auntie Maryam slip it over her head, Auntie Eunice say, The dress is something new, and I'll loan you my good heeled shoes, something borrowed. Here's a blue patch in the dress, so we only need something old to have your wedding good luck complete.

Now Auntie Maryam wearin the dress. It hang too long.

Auntie Siobhan told Cathleen Auntie Maryam's tall! I say, tearin.

Too long we can trim and hem, too short: outa luck, say Grammy. Your Irish cousin was wise. I'll fix it.

People will start coming in a couple hours, say Auntie Eunice. Maryam and I shall go downstairs, and I'll do the hemming. Mother, you wait here for the guests.

So beautiful! Mrs. Jewel say when she see Auntie Maryam standin on her chair in the dress. Mrs. Jewel below us invited to the weddin, and said if we need to use her apartment before, we welcome. She smile wide, but always carry the moist eyes since her baby girls died January. Auntie Eunice standin on the floor, sewin bottom a the dress.

Whatcha hummin, Auntie Eunice?

Wedding March in C Major. They were performing it at the Academy the other night. Mendelssohn composed it a decade and a half ago, a lively tune set as incidental music to Shakespeare's *Midsummer Night's Dream*, but it wasn't until January just past when it was played at the wedding of Princess Victoria that suddenly white Americans are selecting it for their own weddings. And *I* thought they fought a war for independence *from* the British. Auntie Eunice chuckle and bite down on the thread.

You like your new job? ask Mrs. Jewel.

I am blessed to be employed in these hard times. Ambrose, my husband—He finally was offered a position as a seaman again, and while I miss him, I know he is most gratified by work on the water. I was once gratified by my teaching, the company of my students, but Colored School No. 3 was closed during the annihilation of Seneca Village, and I fear my chances of being hired by another school, especially as I am a married woman, are slim indeed. I would have been quite lonely with Ambrose's absence if it weren't for our lovely boarders the Peterses, but the husband has managed to find intermittent work, and they have let us know they'll be looking for their own apartment and removing come Moving Day, first of May.

Somethin old, say Hen, walkin in. Grammy tole me to bring it to ya. Then she hand Auntie Maryam a string.

What's that? I ask Hen.

Papa! Auntie Eunice smile. A violin string she saved from my father. He was a fiddler.

But, start Auntie Maryam, who try handin the string back to Auntie Eunice.

Auntie Eunice smile. I already was given a string on *my* wedding day. *This* one is for Mother's *other* daughter. Auntie Maryam smile, eyes a shine.

Two little girls, say Mrs. Jewel, her own watery eyes on Hen and me. Gettin so big.

I'm eight years of age! My birthday was Febooary the ninth! And Hen's turnin eleven in May! Auntie Eunice, you never finish talkin bout your new job!

So one day, I was strolling up and east from Greenwich Village, and I paused by the Academy of Music. I was very excited by its grand opening three years ago, such a magnificent building, and I stood there on the corner of Irving and Fourteenth street and listened, as I often have. If the wind is right, I can hear long excerpts. That day it was a brand-new operatic imagining of *Macbeth* by Giuseppe Verdi, a wonderful composer living in one of the Italian states. On a wild whim, I was inspired to walk right up to the stage door and ask if there might be any openings. And the incredible coincidence: just that morning, they had fired a colored girl they'd accused of stealing. *If* she was guilty, she may well have had her reasons. I'm conflicted as to the circumstances leading to my sudden employment, but for now I have regular pay, I am distracted from what otherwise would have been a daily nothingness, and I am inside the Academy of Music, I hear every note clearly! God does work in mysterious ways!

Very mysterious you're a teacher and God make you a maid, say Hen, sittin on the floor whittlin.

Don't be impertinent, say Auntie Eunice.

Wish God gim*me* a job. *People's too poor to buy papers, we ain't sellin like we useta*, say my boss. But don't see him lettin the news*boys* go.

Mrs. Jewel excuse herself to go down to the w.c. Auntie Eunice keep hummin and hemmin.

We gonna sing *Wedding March?*

It's music, no words, Auntie Eunice answer me. White folks play it at the *end* of the wedding, organ preferably. For the beginning, they have as late adopted *Bridal Chorus* from the opera *Lohengrin* by Richard Wagner, a composer living somewhere in the German Confederation.

We gonna sing *Bridal Chorus?*

Again, no words, no *English* words. It goes like this: Hm hm hm-hm. Hm *hm* hm-hm.

I know that! say Hen. I heard it the back alley.

> *Let's tie the knot,*
> *Shit on the pot.*

You will *not* sing that! snap Auntie Eunice. (But I think I see my auntie hidin the teeniest smile.)

Can we hum it? I ask.

Yes, but don't think about Hen's words when you do.

How come you cryin, Auntie Maryam?

Everybody turn to her. She look at me since I's the one asked the question. Wishes my mother's here. Wishes my sister's here.

We all stare. She never mentioned no sister before.

My mother tells me I has a older sister, sole when she a chile, when me a baby. Then my mother dies, my mother don't see Hty.

Auntie Eunice hold her, and Auntie Maryam cry more. When Auntie Maryam first come, we didn't know if her mother died or was sold, but eventually she told us. *Hard slave life* was all she said for the cause.

Okay! say Auntie Maryam, and like that, she dry up her tears and back to standin on the chair just before Mrs. Jewel return through the door.

Half-hour later, me and Auntie Eunice and Hen and Mrs. Jewel standin among the crowd in Grammy Brook's apartment, people near thick as Pinkster. Grammy and Gran-Gran and Mr. Freeman, the neighbors and the barbers and the chimney sweeps, everyone eyes on Auntie Maryam as she walk through Grammy Brook's open doorway in her patchwork weddin dress. Everybody smilin bright lookin at the smilin bride, and the one smilin brightest, waitin on the far side a Grammy's front-room for his about-to-be missus, stand Mr. Samuel Wright, no chimney soot, cleanest I ever seen him. And I think a the smile musta been on the faces a my mother and my father makin vows in Grammy Cahill's front-room, and I start hummin that *Bridal Chorus*, and Auntie Eunice then everybody start hummin with me, and Hen shoot me a secret grin mouthin silent *Shit on the pot*. When Auntie Maryam get to the front, Mr. Samuel offer his crook'd arm and Auntie Maryam crook her elbow into his, her wearin Auntie Eunice's borrowed shoes that make her taller than she already is, then they face the pastor useta preach in Auntie Eunice's closed-down Seneca Village A.M.E. Zion. After they pronounced married, Mr. Samuel look up at his wife, his slave-turned-free bride, then stretch up on his toes to reach her lips, and everybody laugh and cheer.

Sunday, March the seventh, a year and a day since the Supreme Court called *Dred Scott*, since Auntie Eunice wrote to Uncle Ambrose 'twas a Bad Week for Black. But today, lookin at the weddin guests with bodies skinnier since Pinkster, faces bonier, but smiles warm as June make me think if there any such a thing as a *Fine* Week for Black, this surely be it.

Luck of the Irish

Ciaran standin on the corner a Bayard and Baxter, grinnin ear to ear.

Gift from my sister!

Then he show it: four-leaf clover.

Kneelin before her this mornin, then I see it. Little green shoot thrust up from the soil overnight, through the frost, right in front of the grave-marker! Herself *knows* I visit every Sunday morn—Meara's spring gift to *me!*

He gaze at it. Shamrock's the triumvirate, Holy Trinity, he go on. But a *quad*-petal: there's the luck!

I hold out my penny hot yam. Wanna share? The cent I got from some man, askin me for directions. I only need half.

Ciaran's eyes twinkle.

See? he say. Prosperity already!

Sittin and eatin, then hear: *Go!* We follow the voice to the alley.

Bunch a kids racin, most I know: the street urchins includin Jeremiah who useta apprentice chimney-sweep with Mr. Samuel, the street arabs includin Christmas who say givin him that name was the lass thing his mother did before drank herself to death—all the kids enjoyin a little spring sun. March the twenty-first, first official day a spring was yesterday (when we have a little cake for Auntie Maryam's given birthday at Grammy Brook's), though still an undertow a winter chill. Ciaran and me jump in. Eleven races, Ciaran win every time! Even when some kids leaves and new kids comes! I woulda been madder bout losin to him weren't there a whole lotta others losin to him too.

Your sister Meara's clover brung you luck for sure, Ciaran!

He shrug. No luck. Always I was winnin the races back in Kerry.

Boy, say a man.

We didn't notice no grown-ups amongst us till now.

Want a job?

❧

The alley behind Baxter behind MacDermott's Saloon is Ten Pin Alley where the bowlin happens. Late March sun get the grown-ups playin outdoors too! Crowded, mostly men

Little distraction from the depression a the Depression, remark a onlooker.

The wood pins fat, shape like a duck. The wood ball size of a man's fist, fit in a man's hand. Even the best men, tough to knock all ten pins down at once, everybody get three tries each round. The man who brung Ciaran here (with me followin) takes the bets, his brain like a machine figurin out the numbers, no mistakes. When a player want his cigar lit, Ciaran quick with the match. When a player need to quench his thirst, Ciaran in n outa MacDermott's lightnin fast, not spill a drop a liquor. Ten days later Ciaran raised up to pin boy: settin up the pins, retrievin the ball. Ciaran contribute to Grammy Cahill's household plus save some hisself.

Good Friday morn, I find Ciaran on Franklin street, sack a popcorn in his hand, starin into space.

Can I have a piece?

He hand me the whole thing, like he Moneybags! I eat fass before he change his mind!

Feelin lucky, he say, little smile on his face.

It's not a lucky day, I say, my jaws full. Today our Lord Jesus Christ is crucified. But Sunday surprise: he gonna rise!

You don't go to church.

On Easter I do!

Somethin else lucky. John Kelly kissed his ball last night and last bowl made him the big winner. Seven pins, then one pin, then two pins. Seven, one, two.

I shrug, stickin the remainin kernel in my mouth. Ciaran jus keep smilin. And I see between his fingers that four-leaf, him twirlin the clover gentle.

Sweep-oh! Sweep-oh! I hear nex mornin. *Freeze tonight, winter not over, chimneys need cleanin, sweep-oh!*

Mornin, Mr. Samuel! I mean, Uncle Samuel!

Good mornin, Theo. *Niece* Theo.

You look happy! That because Easter's comin, Jesus gonna rise Sunday? Or that because you're still happy bein married to Auntie Maryam?

Both! Also—he lean over, whisper: The policy come through—seven, one, two. I hit the number! Fifty cent!

I say nothin but think: Ain't the numbers runner goin gainst the law? Ain't the policy racket a sin?

Then Easter at Grammy Cahill's: Pork! Potatas! Pie! And I realize I got *no* dispute with the street lottery!

After dinner everyone layin around fat n happy, I see Ciaran standin at the winda, lookin out. I stand nex to him.

You always give the policy man the score a the lass round a the winner a the bowlin alley game a the night before?

Not always, just when I'm feelin the charm.

How you know it gonna win?

Don't know. Just sense it. Luck needs two things: luck, plus Mind of the Lucky. That four-leaf might've brought fortune, but more important: I've a mind assured fortune's headed my way.

Forever? Luck resta your *life?*

Ciaran chuckle, eyes still out on the street. Luck and milk both *eventually* go bad.

In the evenin, Ciaran go out to the bowlin alley. Cathleen done fell asleep one end a the couch, me leanin against Grammy on the other.

You know Ciaran got a four-leaf clover givin him luck?

He showed it to us that Sunday mornin it happened, Grammy say, my sweet Meara's gift to her brother. Right in the middle of the Depression it blossoms.

Luck of the Irish!

Where'd ye hear that?

I shrug. Street.

Hmph. Somethin the nativists cooked up to disparage us. A few of us got rich, strikin out with the forty-niners, so the Americans start spattin *Luck of the Irish!* Couldn't *possibly* have anythin to do with brains, with plannin and patience and prudence, *no,* if the Irish is thrivin, must be chance fortune. Sure strikin gold you need knowhow *and* a bit of luck, so bless the ones who know what to do with it when it come! For luck and mutton both eventually go bad.

A week later, she's askin after Ciaran: Why is it he keep skippin supper? He's providin plenty for our meat and potatoes, but not around to taste it himself.

That evenin, I head to the bowlin alley. Longer days now, bowlin till past seven. I stand in the crowd. Ciaran lookin a little tired, stoopin, ready to set up the pins, return the ball. After a while, the players start arguin about somethin, and I go to him: Grammy wanna know why is it you been missin supper.

Workin.

But after the bowlin alley close—

Birds.

What?

But before Ciaran can answer, the men done with their squabble, everybody back in the game. They wrap up their last match jus after sunset, and I turn to glimpse Ciaran disappearin round the corner. I run! Follow him three blocks, then see him take the outdoor steps down to the basement a Casey's Publick House. Inside is packed with mostly Irish men and some colored men and a couple German men, men and cigar smoke, steins a beer and tumblers a whiskey, *sportin men* Great-Uncle Fergus'd call this crowd, everyone out-yellin the other. Now the horde crush back against the wall, allowin a big circle a cleared floor in the middle, and finally I catch sight a Ciaran crost the ring. He don't see me, hands in his pockets, he don't move nor talk. Suddenly everybody roarin and cheerin. Ciaran's eyes with the dark circles focus on the big circle, on the somethin about to happen in the middle. And now two men stoopin crost the ring from each other, each holdin a rooster.

Nex day Ciaran sleepin late at Grammy's, no one botherin him, big bread-winner. When he wake at eleven, he look straight at me.

Like ice cream?

On Broadway up near the fancy stores, he order strawberry for me, vanilla for himself. I'm happy lickin off my spoon! Ciaran tastin his sweet white, but eyes on the street, the goin-ons, like plannin, like some rich man plottin his nex move to make hisself richer.

That rooster died.

Take a second fore he notice I spoke, then turn to me.

Not the one *I* bet on, he say, one with the white tail. I been watchin, known he was a champion.

The other one! Pile a feathers and blood!

That's the way it works.

Not the way it works! *People* don't die from *boxin!*

Sometimes they do. Then he take out that clover, gazin at it. Didn't seem to bother you last year when I cut off Nuala's head for your Saint Paddy's chicken dinner.

That was different! That was nourishin!

He jus twirl that four-leaf in his fingers, eyes back to the street.

⤳

Week later, I'm walkin in Baxter, all a sudden everybody runnin. I run with em, see where it's all goin! Right to the alley behind MacDermott's: brawl! Near as I figure, one a the duck-lookin pins was rotten wood, and one a the balls smashed it to pieces, then everybody jump into the fracas! I see Ciaran lookin at it all, not happy, guess there be no bowler winner tonight, no score, no number for Ciaran's policy playin. Nightfall, I leave to sleep at Grammy Brook's.

Walk to Grammy Cahill's nex morn, there Ciaran out on the outside step, legs pulled in to his body, arms huggin his shins, face down in his knees, his whole self small as he can make him. Bandage round his right hand.

Your rooster lose?

Yes, he say, not lookin up. I start to go inside to Grammy's, and he lift his face.

Raid. The police.

I say nothin, but since Ciaran's doins suddenly more interestin, I sit nex to him.

They waited for the big bout, midnight. Match'd barely started, caught us in the act. I was lucky, the Metropolitans only arrestin the grown-up gamblers which, by the by, there *is* a special children's section of the Tombs, but I reckon they weren't in the mood last night to run after kids. My rooster. He weren't so lucky.

If the match weren't finished, the birds still livin, ain't they?

It finished, just not the way 'twas planned. White-tailed cock. Distracted by all the confusion let down his guard a second, and the challenger moved in. Pulverizin. I knew my rooster was lost but . . . all the winnin he's after bringin to me, I owed him. Went in, hopin to end the torture, let the champion die in dignity, peace. The opponent pecked a chunk out of my hand before turnin to turn white-tail crown-to-toe soppin red.

Ciaran closes back into himself.

You mighta been lucky not arrested, but all n all, seem your luck's runnin pretty thin now. Maybe you better stop bettin a while.

At first, I can't place that sound comin from Ciaran, face all hid. Then I make it out: laughin! What's so funny! And he lift his face up to look at me, cheeks rosy from the mirth.

That I'll do, he reply to my suggestion. Then get up and walk away.

I walk over to Park street, Grammy's table.

Grammy, you better talk to Ciaran, for his luck's runnin out, and I think he need to stop bettin. I told him this, and he jus take it like I'm jokin!

Ciaran has nothin left to bet with. Put all his money on a cock last night.

ALL OF IT?

All of it.

I stare at Grammy. I didn't know she even knew bout the rooster wrestlin!

Well, you know what else? He didn't go to his bowlin job today! He's home when he oughta be workin, he gonna lose that job!

He lost it. He's after goin to his employer this mornin, who took one look at his bandaged hand and knew it'd slow down his gatherin of the fallin pins. Sacked. *Yes,* Grammy suddenly focused on a customer walked up, *these are some lovely suspenders, will hold your trousers up well!* She don't seem bothered at all about Ciaran lettin hisself go from riches to rags! I wait for her to make her sale, which take forever with the hagglin.

You ain't mad Ciaran got sacked, Grammy? You oughta be mad! We gonna go hungry again!

What's today?

Thursday.

What else?

April the twenty-second.

April the twenty-second. So yesterday was one month to the day Meara give Ciaran that clover. I've an inklin he thought the luck was due to run out. And once he lost his Mind of the Lucky, well.

Can't he get it back?

Grammy smile. We survived winter of 'fifty-eight. I pray the Depression over before the next cold season, but till then at least I know we'll make it. Enough supplemental income that lad provided to stock potatoes and onions and salt, I'll never fault him after all he brought. Suppose he figured with his luck runnin low, time to chance it all, God love his gumption! And the memory we've stored: what a marvel of a month!

✺

Friday night I stay with Grammy Brook, then Saturday mornin walk into Grammy Cahill's tenement, but stop before I go up the steps, hear a snifflin. Dark in the tenement corridors, I can't see, but then somethin in a sob sound reckonizable.

Ciaran?

The sound halt a second, then the sobs comin harder. I go under the steps, where he stand. Still hard to see him, but my eyes now a little use to the dim.

How come you're cryin?

Lost my clover!

He bawlin more. Take a minute, then it hit me.

Oh! That why your luck run out!

He shake his head.

I just lost it this mornin. 'Twas still in my hand whole time my luck was dyin.

Oh. Then how come your luck run out?

I don't know! I don't care! He sob, then stop up the sobbin, quiet down.

Somethin I see now I didn't before. Only luck that really mattered was my sister giftin me, now it's gone! Don't know what I'm to tell her when I visit tomorra, then Ciaran off wailin again.

I think maybe he wanna be alone, so I leave him and walk up to Grammy's. Cathleen doin her seamstressin, Great-Uncle Fergus home for midday dinner, eatin soup. I open the door to the press, fuller than I ever seen: potatas and onions and salt and flour and oil and garlic and pepper, the bounty Ciaran brung. No breakfast this mornin, and now my stomach growls.

Cabbage stew your grammy made on the stove, say Great-Uncle Fergus. I'll pour ye a bowl, if ye're hungry.

I already known there was cabbage stew, the sweet smell of it all over the front-room. The bounty from Ciaran, workin so hard he hardly around to partake a the fruits. And every Sunday seein his sister, snow or shine. I can't remember the lass time I visited my mother.

No thank you, I utter.

~⁀⁀

Sunday mornin April the twenty-fifth is sunny and warm. I figure Ciaran'll still be upset, havin to tell Meara he lost her clover, so I walk up respectful and quiet and ready to wave to him so he'll know I ain't sneak-spyin, just on my way to my mother's grave even if she got a right to receive me arms crossed: *Long time no see*. I catch a glimpse a Ciaran's back, him facin Meara's grave, and I tiptoe solemn, but on accident my toe catch a big stone and I fall flat on my face! Ciaran startle, look at me.

Sorry, Ciaran! I was tryin to come up quiet and respectful, wanted to say Mornin to my mother. I wipe the moss from my cheek.

And now I see Ciaran don't look sad at all. Bright smile.

Look!

And there Meara's grave covered in dandelions. Some of em's yella fresh, some of em's fairy dust. And I see what he's seein: dandelions all over the grave-yard but nothin nowheres thick as the ones over Meara.

She forgive me! Sent a sign to prove it!

I look at my mother's grave. Hardly any dandelions. My eyes burnin hot.

You think—you think Meara mind sharin some a her flowers with my ma?

Sure! say Ciaran, and pick a bunch a the pretty yella ones which don't at all seem to dwindle the forest atop Meara. He give em to me, and I lay em neat all over my mother's earth.

Ma. These are from Meara and me. And Ciaran.

Then Ciaran hold out one more—a white fairy-dust one.

In Kerry, we'd make a wish and blow.

Five Points too! I say. Then we close our eyes, lips puckered and ready.

Room of Hope

You like the Twentieth ward, Auntie Maryam?

Yes!

Me and her out in the country garden she planted, yard a her and Mr. Samuel's house uptown: West Thirty-second. *Off* West Thirty-second, built in a courtyard behind a tenement, away from the street. Summer crops a-ripenin: the cabbage and the peas. Corn!

I gives you cabbage and peas and corn for your grammy, we gots plenty! and Auntie Maryam spread out her arms to prove it. Her voice sound like a smile even though I don't see it. The net hangin from her garden hat so thick can't make out her face, her garden gloves cover her hands though now and again she slip em off brief, let the earth pour through her fingers. Weedin and pickin up stray straw. The stray straw from a West Seventies farm, Mr. Samuel gathered it. Chimney-sweep the winter, but sellin straw for mattresses is summer colored work.

You're good at gardenin, Auntie Maryam!

I's the ace ricer, South Carolina.

And cotton-picker?

Auntie Maryam shake her head. Rice and cotton two different skill. Take trainin.

If Mr. Samuel get tired a the straw sellin, he can sell buttermilk! I offer. Then we get buttermilk free!

Mr. Samuel lucky he gots the partnership with the farmer for the straw, the buttermilk colored men gots to enter into a contract for the cow *stop*! I's much obliged for your help, Theo, but what you jus pulled was *not* a weed, why don't you stays with collectin the straw?

Inside Auntie Maryam put some cabbage and peas and corn in my gunny-sack, then pour us coffee, slice the bread. She make good bread! Sweet! Auntie Maryam and Mr. Samuel's house *big*: front-room plus bed-closet plus bed-closet—three rooms! The little bed-closet Auntie Maryam call the Room of Hope.

Auntie Maryam, like never was no Depression *your* house!

When the hard times come and the banks run, Mr. Samuel have some specie hid away. The land values drop, he gots a regular gentleman chimney customer lookin to unload property, Republican gentleman friendly to negroes.

Lotsa negroes your street, Auntie Maryam! And you and Mr. Samuel got a yard!

She nod, sit back, stare out her little winda on her little garden. 'Twas a devotion. Mr. Samuel grew up Five Points, never he think to remove. But I longs for the air, this he do for me, space the only thing I miss bout Dixie. And my hands knowin the magic, knowin how to make soil deliver.

Then I'm shuckin Auntie Maryam's corn for her while she churn the butter. Now her eyes turn to me.

I gots to go out little while. You help me?

I nod! I love helpin Auntie Maryam! She open a big jar a the concoction, I can smell her recipe: almond oil, shea butter, beeswax. I know how to spread it thin, cover her right arm, not a peep a her real skin show through.

Fine work, she say, smilin.

While I spread the linament over her left arm and hand and back a her neck, she stare into her little round lookin-glass set on the table, plyin it to her cheeks and chin and forehead and eyelids. Auntie Maryam look funny, light-skin her face and neck and hands and dark everywhere else! But face and neck and hands the only parts shows when she out n about so them's the only places she need to potion. After Auntie Maryam and Mr. Samuel make their newlywed nest, she decide time to start leavin the house on occasion, and here's what I reckon: Auntie Maryam remember Miss Sally, colored boarder to Auntie Siobhan who make herself light and pretty for the gentlemen, and Auntie Maryam wanna be with the fashion. Auntie Maryam Africa at home, mulatto in the street.

I amble with her to Miss Philippa's, down in Little Africa Greenwich Village near Auntie Eunice. Miss Philippa I see right away don't waste nice on nobody, but do acknowledge us with a civil greetin, gap between her front teeth. Auntie Maryam hand Miss Philippa some coin, and Miss Philippa pass to Auntie Maryam a little pouch. Miss Philippa give a few instructions, and that's pretty much all the words they use up.

I think a droppin in to Auntie Eunice's, then remember she be workin at the Academy of Music now, so I stroll with Auntie Maryam back up to the Thirties. She sigh.

Guess you's big enough. There's days I worries, slave-catcher right round the bend, but other days figure it never be, why Master bother? Years I'm ripe and bein cultivated, yet not once he planted in me, nothin fertilized to increase his crop a darkies. You understand?

I nod, but I don't know what Auntie Maryam's talkin about. In the distance, the thunder rumble.

And I knows Mr. Samuel and me only married a short spell—

Your anniversary lass week—July the seventh: four months!

Four months. Still. She swallow. Miss Philippa know her herb, gonna help me fill the Room of Hope. And Auntie Maryam's right fingers gentle caress Miss Philippa's pouch, left hand caress her belly. Then the sky open, sheets hammerin, we race to her house.

Even in the rain, Auntie Maryam's light-skin cream barely smudged. Wamme help clean you up, Auntie Maryam?

No, I gets to it.

I look at her. Usually she like to wash the high yella off second she walk through the door. Then I remember Mr. Samuel gone before crack a dawn, didn't get to catch a glimpse a his light wife today.

Cloudburst big, not lettin up. Gettin toward dark and no Mr. Samuel.

He got sense enough wait out the storm, she say. You too, may as well stay the night. Then she pull out a deck: Pick.

First I don't know what. I never done no cards before! Never been close to no heart no diamond. Fraid I'm doin it wrong, still I go deep in the pile, glance it fast so she can't see! Leave it back atop as instructed, Auntie Maryam shuffle, shuffle, pull it out: deuce a clubs. How she *do* that!

Broth and bread, then: Time to hit the hay.

But she ain't hittin no hay. Auntie Maryam take to her rockin chair, light her smoke, waitin for Mr. Samuel. Hen carved it for her, Hen gettin good at the whittlin: stem, bowl. I never seen Auntie Maryam smoke before but now she enjoy her pipe like she was born to it. I stand at the doorway a the Room of Hope which is where I'm sposed to hit the hay, but I'm not ready to.

I help wash the dishes, Auntie Maryam?

I gets to em directly. She puff, eyes on the dark out the winda. I never seen Auntie Maryam lazy at Grammy's, I like it! But wonder why she prolongin a chore?

Then I know: she don't wanna stick her hands in no water yet

Now you *really* look like my auntie, Auntie Maryam!

She turn to me, eyebrows a question.

Or my mother! I giggle. Cep my mother was Irish, you couldn't look like *her*!

Auntie Maryam's eyes stuck on me. I chuckle but my laugh startin to lose air. I wanna stop, but her eyes don't let it.

Both us pretty—light light!

Her puffin stop. Eyes narrow. You know why I do this, Theo.

I stare. Auntie Maryam never stern to me like that before! I nod.

Then why you natter on?

I don't know what answer I'm spose to give to that. She sigh, back to her rockin, eyes back to the winda. Me and the crickets wait.

I'm a homebody, likes my walls round me. But sometime gots to show my face in the world, the odd errand. I knows you likes cleanin the light-skin off but sometime I likes to wait for Mr. Samuel.

(Which is jus what I reckoned, waitin for him to see her pretty and light, but figure best keep that reckonin to myself.)

Now Auntie Maryam look to the lookin-glass, starin at her fair cheeks. No smile. She speak soft, like more talkin to the mirror than to me. No kidnappin *me* back whip n chain, South Carolina ain't *never* find their dark-skinned Lizzie. Not on the street nohow.

Then we both quiet till my yawn sneak up and bellow.

In my dream, I'm walkin down Broadway with Auntie Maryam, and here come the slave-catchers. Then I see Auntie Maryam forgot to put on her light-skin disguise! Scared for her! You seen Lizzie? one of em say, I shake my head no no no but surely they see my heart pound through my chest. Then Auntie Maryam beside me take to laughin, hold her belly, rollin on the ground, the funniest joke! I start to smile, then feel my water.

Wake up, slip outside to the Irish shantee, which is somethin I recently heard Great-Uncle Fergus mutter, but when *I* said it, Cathleen and Cousin Aileen snap, Call it *w.c.*! *outhouse*! *privy*! Outside no more rain, jus the mud.

Walk back when I'm done, on the stoop's a pail a water for cleanin dirty feet. Rub em till they glisten, then step inside. A murmur from the other bed-closet, Mr. Samuel musta come home while I was emptyin myself. Creep back to the Room of Hope, notice the other door ajar. Mr. Samuel washin the light-skin off Auntie Maryam. In the chimney-sweepin winter, Mr. Samuel always carry the soot filth, but now washed, him darker n me but lighter n his wife and on the bed they sit together, her face already clean brown, now he work her arms. He do it soft, his skin movin slow gainst hers. Faces close to each other, eyes warm at each other, and where he washed off the light lotion and her brown flesh peekin through, he kisses, his lips gainst her clean soft elbow, brown soft lower arm, muscle and fat, slow and mellow, her shinin deep dark brown skin delicate and strong. And the gentle and the tender and the smilin get to feelin so much like somethin private, like somethin ought to be only between man and wife that I get the blush and scurry-quiet back to my own room g'night.

Portent

Jump outa bed, run to the front-room: bright sun shinin through the winda, through the hangin whites for the whites, clear blue October sky.

Peak tonight, Grammy!

So say the papers, reply Grammy Brook, sittin, squeezin out a soppin pilla case.

Seventeen eighty-six, say Gran-Gran. Seven years of age, but I remember.

Her eyes out the winda like usual, cep stead of em lookin down on the street, they turned up to the sky.

That was my first one. Another 1805, 1807, '11. 'Forty three, *that* was a big one. Recall it, Jedediah?

Eighteen forty-three, mm hm, answer Grammy.

Portent, say Gran-Gran.

What's portent?

Sign, Grammy answer me.

Like O'SHEA'S BOARD & PUBLICK?

No. Sign as in harbinger. As in foretellin.

Good sign, bad sign, mutter Gran-Gran to the sky.

Good sign! say Grammy. What else could it be? Lookit all these whites for the whites! The stars lettin us know: hard times is over!

10:15 A.M.

Racin in the alley, I hear em! Round the corner just in time to watch Ciaran win gainst some boy I never seen before. Lotta days I catch Ciaran in the run, only time he don't seem worried bout a job. After he lose the bowlin work lass April, he go back to the race, tell me maybe the bowlin boss see he's faster n ever, hire him back. But I think Ciaran forgot he was hopin for pin boy, he jus dashin for the thrill a the win, which he do every time.

Every time, mutter the new boy, shakin his head.

What's your name?

Friedrich.

Where you live?

Elizabeth street. We just moved in.

Between Bayard and Canal?

Yes! How'd you know?

I know because he's blond blond, and Elizabeth between Bayard and Canal is German, but before I get a chance to say it we turn for the nex match, Ciaran winnin gainst a little urchin girl Molly, then beatin Yacob who live with his family in the Jewish block Baxter between Chatham and Park. Ciaran thumb-rub a apple he jus took as prize, give it a shine and preparin to bite when we hear: You ain't raced *me* yet.

Everybody turn round to where the alley meet the street. There stand Hen.

Ciaran! This my cousin Hen. Hen! This my near-cousin Ciaran.

He never loses! pout Friedrich, even though himself got high hopes as he already beggin for a rematch.

Whatchu got to wager? say Hen.

Ciaran's the undefeated so all us shocked when Hen take the first race! Hen's eleven and Ciaran only ten, but age never stopped him winnin before. *Beginner's luck!* he snap. But after *Two outa three!* and *Three outa five!* Ciaran finally exit the alley stompin mad, and Hen take a big victory bite a his apple. While she chew, she say, Grammy said Auntie Maryam offered beets from her garden, go fetch em.

She tole *you* go fetch em.

I gotta see about a job, then Hen toss her naked core and gone.

11:30 A.M.

On the way to Auntie Maryam's, I pass Grammy Cahill's table.

Peak tonight, Grammy!

Sure a good omen, *mo leanbh*. I been countin the signs since Wednesday. The new moon that night, and I blessed myself. Thursday I seen a funeral and walked three steps with it, both these in the prevention of misfortune. And Friday—

Yesterday!

Friday yesterday I found a horseshoe, spit on it, and tossed it over my head—good luck! And now the peak comin. No more Depression: I say, the tide's a-turnin!

12:45 P.M.

I walk up to Auntie Maryam's, her tendin her autumn garden: beets and broccoli and brussels sprouts. She pick some a her yield for Grammy, then we go inside: tea and bread

You think it's a good sign, Auntie Maryam? I point to the sky.

Yes! See what it do! and she show me her cut-out from a paper. Auntie Maryam read good now!

Fugitive Slave in New-London—The Slave Free.

We understand there was a sudden and stirring breeze of excitement in New-London yesterday. A coasting vessel arrived in port with a fugitive slave on board—said slave having smuggled himself with a jug of water and a ham on board the schooner, as she lay at the wharf of one of the North Carolina ports. He continued to "lie low and keep *dark*" until the vessel was far on her voyage home. The Captain arrested the runaway, not by due process of law, but upon his own responsibility, conducted him to the Custom-house and delivered him into the charge and safe-keeping of Collector MATHER. News of what had been done soon got into the street. State-Attorney WILLEY was forthwith impressed into drawing up a writ of *habeas corpus* to be used if occasion required, while Judge BRANDEGEE and Dr. MINER started for the Custom-house. They found the Customs Collector and his sable companion sitting very quietly and peaceably together in improving social converse. The Judge asked the Collector if he held the colored gentleman by any legal authority? The Collector said, No. The Doctor asked the darkey if he desired to go back to old North Carolina? The darkey said, No. Then cut and run, said the Doctor. And cut he did, drawing a bee-line for Canada.

3:15 P.M.

Grammy Cahill home from her table just a minute to stash money in our floor-board hole. I tell her and Cathleen bout the colored man escaped, bout the good portent Auntie Maryam seen in the *New-York Times* when in come Cousin Aileen.

News!

No day work ye picked up? Grammy ask, already soundin disappointed before she hear the answer. Cousin Aileen and Maureen finally hired back to the seamstress shop, but Cousin Aileen only irregular.

Better! Just got on at a new store. The pay higher!

Grammy and Cathleen and me clap and cheer. I'm sittin with Cathleen on the couch pushed gainst the outside wall so Cathleen have a easy view a the sky.

How'd ye manage it, Aileen?

Mona from the sewin shop kindly let me in on it. There's liftin now, crates and the like, and arrangin the merchandise for display in preparation for the openin on the twenty-eighth of the month, not three weeks away! Which'll be when the seamstressin'll come in. Sixth avenue between Thirteenth and Fourteenth. Oh thank ye, St. Joe!

That's far north for a dry-goods store, say Cathleen to her mother.

'Tis! R. H. Macy and Co., it's to be called.

Good omen, Grammy say to me and wink.

4:30 P.M.

Customers lined up outside a O'SHEA'S BOARD & PUBLICK. I go round the back door and slip in. Auntie Siobhan servin em fast, and somebody else servin too.

Who's her, Auntie Siobhan?

That's Roisin, helpin out today for it's s'busy.

She pour a coupla drinks, then when my auntie stoop down for more bottles, she talk fass to me.

Let me tell ye, *mo stoirín*, bad times is good business, people needin to drink. But a sign a good times to come is *better* business, everybody hankerin to toast! And this Depression, long spell since people feelin the celebration, not since Star a Bethlehem has the sky offered such a blessin!

Then she turn to the patrons all hollerin at her, drunk and aimin to be drunker, but throw to me over her shoulder: Be back here seven. I'll take ye to the top!

6:30 P.M.

Extra! Peak viewing tonight!

Best seen seven and a quarter to eight o'clock, read all about it!

There Ciaran and Hen on the street, not racin. Talkin. Lookin up.

Evenin, Hen! Evenin, Ciaran!

Evenin, they both say, Ciaran lookin content, Hen her regular ole showin no cards.

I brung Auntie Maryam's harvest to Grammy Brook since you didn't.

Good, say Hen. I got that job. Hotel, guest attendant.

I got a job! say Ciaran. The Spanish Company.

What's that?

Dunno, he answer me, but I'm hired: errand runner! They like I run fast!

Sound like *that* job shoulda been *mine*, Hen say, dry. I expect Ciaran be mad, Hen referencin her beatin him at the races this mornin, but he jus smile, and I notice his vision appear dropped from Hen's face to her little protrudin chest.

Auntie Siobhan tell me come by seven, she take me to the top!

Now both of em turn to me.

7:00 P.M.

The streets is packed and Auntie Siobhan's saloon near empty cep one customer, teary-eyed and in his cups.

Fools! Lookin to the sky while the fire uptown already forgotten!

Sure your skills as floor-sweeper will transfer elsewhere, Timothy Kildare, say Auntie Siobhan. And these days there's work to be had!

Not so fine a position I'll ever get again. They paid me decent! Treated me fair!

Then Timothy Kildare turn to us kids.

Did ye know the Crystal Palace hosted the 1854 Exhibition of the Industry of All Nations? America's first World Expo? Elisha Otis introduced his passenger elevator there!

Ciaran and me glance at each other. I didn't know the mechanical lift began at the Crystal Palace! I passed it many a time, Forty-second street between Fifth and Sixth. I turn back to Timothy Kildare. Till he mentioned it, I forgot the buildin burnt to the ground Tuesday. Four days ago.

I'm closin up, Auntie Siobhan tell Timothy Kildare. Ye can come back and continue your lamentation when the show's over. Eight and a half o'clock, I'll re-open then.

As Auntie Siobhan's helpin Timothy Kildare to the door, I see it: frame of iron, walls of glass, I heard you could behold Queens County, Staten Island, and New Jersey from the Crystal Palace high dome observatory!

Two thousand people in the cross-shaped buildin when the blaze started, and the flames moved fass but nobody killed—Miracle! say everyone. And now everyone talkin bout hard times over—the signs! But livelihoods and fortunes lost in the ashes, I can't see how ruin by fire's ever a good omen.

To the top! Auntie Siobhan say, after lockin the door behind Timothy Kildare. We follow her.

Auntie Siobhan's boarding-house is four floors includin the garret apartments, and in the back a the fourth floor's a tiny little room, and in the tiny little room's a ladder, and the ladder lead to a ceilin trap-door: the roof. From there, me and Auntie Siobhan and Hen and Ciaran can see down on Five Points, see everybody on the ground lookin up. Then we look up.

I remember hearin a fancy lady doin our slums tell her policeman guide she wanted to be outa the vicinity before dark. Once night falls on New York City hardly ya see your hand front a your face. Five Points, there's the occasional streetlamp, a little light spill from the night shops and taverns, but not much, and all that dark jus make our comet shine brighter. Comet Donati been on this visit since she come knockin soft and shy end a August. Now bold, her head big and bright, swish tail take up half the sky!

Tonight's peak mean she startin her farewell. From here she'll fade till she disappear from the northern half a the world, and not long after gone from any view on the globe. The scientists debate her orbit, but she might not return for two thousand years. Between now and then, she'll be swingin around other stars and other galaxies, makin her trip of a few billions a miles. But for tonight, she ours. For a moment I glance down on the street to see everyone lookin up, smilin! Cep over there near the corner, Timothy Kildare sittin on the edge a the sidewalk, the wood planks, face down in his hand. I look back up.

Clutch my auntie's hand. It's a good sign! and Timothy Kildare all despair missin it. That Crystal Palace fire mighta hinted a gloomy foreshadow, but 'twas days ago, and things change fast in New York. Now we got this *flyin* fire in the sky! What else could it bode but blessins? At least for now. At least this moment everybody on the planet, one family altogether all sharin our great comet, what a potent portent to be right place right time! 1858. Earth.

1859

Business

Mice!

Jump up outa Auntie Siobhan's bed: I don't like mice! Hear em in the wall, bang my fist: Get outa there, mice!

Stop! The wall hissin at me!

Then a piece a the wall move, and there Auntie Siobhan. *In the wall!*

I woke up, you was *gone*, Auntie Siobhan! I thought you have mi—

Sh! She wave me in, then quiet pull the movin wall closed. I'm in the wall! Tight space, candle for light. My auntie clutchin a note-book to her chest. On the floor: money! Five- and ten- and twenty-dollar pieces!

You're nine years of age now. Grown enough to keep a secret.

I nod.

And it's the switch for ye if ye don't!

I laugh. Then see she ain't kiddin!

You're rich, Auntie Siobhan! All this money!

Expenses I got as well. How's your arithmetic?

Piles a coins with a wood chip on top. I pick up the pile with the chip say LQ. What's LQ?

Liquor, my liquor bill. How much?

I count and tell her. She check it against what she got in her book.

Grand. Next?

What's LO? What's TR?

Lamp oil, tenants' repairs. Stop askin questions and count.

After I finish countin the GS for glasses and steins, Auntie Siobhan frown at her book, say, Count again. I do: same numbers as before. Now *she* count. Smile.

Your figures differed from mine, but yours were the accurate. Seems I got myself a real live calculator, second set of eyes. Come this time every mornin, I'll give ye a nickel for the recount.

And she hand me my first five-cent piece!

The expenses I tally only Thursdays—

Today!

But the gross earnins I need to assess daily. Nickel either way.

Okay!

Secret! Everything behind the wall's nobody's business but ours. Got it?

I nod! and think a how Grammy Brook's garret was my secret place with Auntie Maryam, my aunties always trustin me with their secrets!

Down in the tavern, Auntie Siobhan fix us each a tea. A rappin from the back. My auntie go to answer, and I wonder what customer she got already eight in the mornin and how come they at the back door?

This is my niece Theo. Theo, this is Mr. John O'Mahony.

John O'Mahony got a tall forehead before his hair starts. Hair black, curly hang to the bottom of his neck. Mustache thick, beard black hang to his chest. Stern face!

Mornin.

Good morning to you, miss.

Auntie Siobhan stoop behind the bar counter. Mr. O'Mahony comes every mornin for his tea, she say, then stand, little wood box in her hand. Now I see another one he got. They swap boxes, then he tip his long forehead at me, then at Auntie Siobhan, put his tea box in his coat pocket and leave through the back.

How come you and Mr. John O'Mahony swap boxes?

I have his tea ready for him in today's box, and he returns yesterday's emptied box with the payment inside.

Won't Mr. O'Mahony's tea in his pocket spill out on his coat?

Box filled with tea *leaves*. Brews it himself.

Mr. John don't want no spirits?

Auntie Siobhan shake her head, wipin glasses. He just like his tea in the mornin.

Was he mad?

Auntie Siobhan frown.

He look mad.

Not mad. Serious. Mr. O'Mahony's a scholar.

He go to school? *Grown man?*

I mean he's bookish. Reads and writes. Always on the path to knowledge, ye needn't a schoolhouse for that. Reckon aul Eunice still tryin to put you through the academy.

Auntie Siobhan add a spoon a honey to her tea and mine too.

He tried it. Trinity College Dublin, but never finished, smarter than the headmasters, I'd wager. He studied the ancient tongues: Sanskrit, Hebrew, and of course Gaelic, Mr. O'Mahony's specialty. Teaches Latin and Greek now and again. Look.

Auntie Siobhan pull out a book from under her counter.

THE
HISTORY OF IRELAND,
FROM
𝔗𝔥𝔢 𝔈𝔞𝔯𝔩𝔦𝔢𝔰𝔱 𝔓𝔢𝔯𝔦𝔬𝔡 𝔱𝔬 𝔱𝔥𝔢 𝔈𝔫𝔤𝔩𝔦𝔰𝔥 𝔍𝔫𝔳𝔞𝔰𝔦𝔬𝔫.

BY THE REVEREND GEOFFREY KEATING, D.D.

TRANSLATED FROM THE ORIGINAL GAELIC,
AND COPIOUSLY ANNOTATED,

BY JOHN O'MAHONY

Mr. O'Mahony!

The Brits been tellin their made-up story of Éire for centuries, *mo stoirín*, but *this* is truth, Ireland by the Irish! Auntie Siobhan seem very delighted, gazin at the book fond and wipin her drinkin glasses squeaky clean.

Out into the Febooary wind whippin the snow. On Mary Bree's old corner's the new girl Hannah since Mary Bree got adopted away to Protestants in the West by the House a Industry, which I warned Hannah about who nodded scared and solemn. Hannah say she's ten years of age though she don't know, don't remember her family. Mary Bree had dark hair but Hannah's hair's blond, Hannah's hair's a nest of a mess!

Mornin, Hannah!

Mornin, Theo! I'm goin back home! Ireland!

When? (Hannah never lived nowhere but Five Points but she wouldn't be the first New York–born Irish to call the Isle *back home*.)

Soon's the Fenians come! But *sh!* Secret.

What's Fenians?

The people gonna conquer England. Irish warriors gonna take back Ireland, then we all return. Ireland for the Irish!

Ciaran come racin by grinnin, wavin at me as he keep dashin on down the street and round the corner. Ciaran all happy with his job, runnin errands for the Spanish Company.

How you find out about Fenians?

Hannah shrug. I hear.

If you heard people speakin on it, don't sound like a secret, sound like news. How come the newsboys ain't chantin it?

Hannah shrug. The wind *whoosh*. Hannah's toes through the holes in her shoes turnin blue.

My auntie gimme a nickel. Wanna hot potata?

We jus turnin to head to the yam man when Ciaran holdin a parcel come grinnin and wavin and runnin the other direction back to the Spanish Company.

The nex day Cathleen doin her needlewoman work, Grammy Cahill countin her coins and smilin.

Good times, Grammy?

Good times, *mo leanbh!* The bad days over. I was after frettin when that Macy's let your Cousin Aileen go, but then the new workshop picked her up, we're all in business! Grammy put her money under the floor-board, the secret place.

Are we goin back home to Ireland when the Fenians conquer England and save Ireland for the Irish?

Grammy Cahill and Cathleen stare at me.

I don't wanna leave Grammy Brook but I don't want you to leave me neither!

Don't know what ye're pickin up from the street, granddaughter, but I promise you no one from this slum apartment has the money to be movin any time soon.

Hurrah! and I do a little Irish jig.

They gimme the job! say Great-Uncle Fergus, bustin through the door. The Central Park!

They hirin Irish? Grammy ask, all wonder.

Great-Uncle Fergus nod, grinnin. Reckon that demonstration of discontent in the park about the Park couple years back come to some good in the end.

But what about your street-cleanin job, Great-Uncle Fergus? I ask.

The Central Park offered me more. Done with shovelin the blamed coach-horse manure off the cobblestones of Five Points. You'll now find me shovelin the blessèd workhorse manure of the construction crew in the Central Park, and the earnins to show for it!

Middle a the night, I slip outa Grammy Cahill's bed to the front-room chamber-pot, which we only use at night: daytime, we go down to the public privy. Ciaran awake, sittin near the winda with the moonlight floodin in, readin. I don't like people awake when I'm usin the chamber-pot, so I take it just outside the door. When I come back, Ciaran ain't budged, like he ain't even seen me walk through. Ciaran got good at readin!

What's that?

Take a few seconds before he glance up, like he jus notice I'm here. He look at the paper cover, old n yella: *Graham's Lady's and Gentleman's Magazine.*

A story.

That magazine 1841: before we were born!

Hm.

What's the story called?

The Murders in the Rue Morgue.

That sound like a bad story!

It's a good story about a bad thing. Go back to bed before Cathleen and Mr. Fergus wake up.

This I know won't happen because Great-Uncle Fergus in his bedroll snorin too loud to hear us, too loud for Cathleen on the couch to wake and hear us.

Who's that? I say, pointin to somethin about Auguste Dupin

He sigh. August Doopin, who can look at the facts and deduct the possibilities one by one till his reasonin sum up the solution.

Huh?

A species of story the writer made up. Now Ciaran gaze at the cover, all thoughtful. Some sailor gave it to me. *Used* to be a sailor workin for my company's contracted shipments, now works in the office. Read when he got bored on the sea.

My uncle Ambrose was on the sea too! Maybe he met your boss!

Maybe. Then Ciaran go back to the story.

That the name a the person got murdered?

No answer.

That the name a the person got murdered?

What!

I point.

No! That's the name of the author!

I thought it was the person got murdered, don't they call murder bodies John Doe and John Roe?

That says Edgar A. *Poe*!

Oh. Who died in the story?

Ciaran gimme a look like *Go away*, but I'm not goin away.

Did the murderer murder the murdered man with a gun?

Ciaran stare at me. Then his voice go softer, but not friendly soft. 'Tweren't a man got murdered. Were two ladies.

Oh.

A grown woman who lived with her gray-haired mother. The police found the aul one on the ground, thrown out the window.

Her daughter did it!

The daughter was strangled and stuffed up the chimney.

Bet Mr. Samuel'd get paid extra for cleanin *that* chimney! I chuckle.

The mother's body was a pile of broken bones, her throat slashed so deep when the copper picked up her body, her head fell off. Bone's hard to cut through, perhaps the killer had to saw it, the blood gurglin from the old lady's neck, in her mouth. Then the daughter. Must've been stuck tight up that chimney, her twisted body stiff with the rigor mortis—

Not scary! Not scary! I holler, hands over my ears runnin into the bed-closet, seein Grammy wake and starin as I dive under her.

I'm up in the early mornin after wakin all night from bad dreams. Run to Auntie Siobhan's, hopin I ain't too late for my nickel in the wall!

But when I get there, she already in the tavern havin a chat with Miss Fiona and Miss Sally, who usually ain't up s'early and look tired. On the bar *The History of Ireland* sets open.

After the worknight, we always take our sleep, ye know, say Miss Fiona, but Sally and I been up discussin this.

We waited till we heard you stirrin around down here, say Miss Sally.

Today's Saturday the nineteenth, say Auntie Siobhan, and I gave ye full warnin on the first.

Ye did indeed, say Miss Sally. Fiona and I been discussin it ever since—

I don't raise the rent every year, some do! I didn't burden ye with an increase last year durin the Depression—

Neither assuage the adversity with a *de*crease, say Miss Fiona.

*De*crease?

Ye knew we were strugglin—

Weren't we all? I spent a day or two in the soup line m'self—

We spent a lot *more* days, Auntie Siobhan's tenants say together.

Your saloon's packed now every night, say Miss Sally.

'Tis, Depression's over. Which you both well know since after droppin coin in my coffers, a goodly number of my customers then head upstairs, to *your* financial benefit.

Ye money-grubber! say Miss Fiona. Aren't ye rich enough, Siobhan?

If ye don't fancy the new rate, Moving Day's May first.

Then Miss Fiona and Miss Sally *hmph!* on their way back upstairs to sleep off the worknight.

Auntie Siobhan—?

But before I get it out, I hear the rappin on the back door.

A few minutes late ye are, John. Come to expect ye just as the church is ringin eight bells.

I heard talk. Sounded like you were having a meeting—*achoo!* I didn't want to interrupt.

Nothin important, Auntie Siobhan say as she reach under her counter for the wood tea box. Comin down with a cold, are ye?

Maybe. Mr. O'Mahony sniffle. Him and my auntie make their trade, then he move to leave.

John.

He turn.

I'm enjoyin it. She hold up *The History of Ireland*.

He smile crooked, like embarrassed, then go out through the back. Auntie Siobhan gazin where Mr. John left. After all the earlier arguin with Miss Fiona and Miss Sally, now Auntie Siobhan's frown replaced with a little smile.

How come Mr. John come through the back door, Auntie Siobhan?

He and I have a special arrangement. Don't want some rumor spread all over Ireland we're open for commerce eight a.m. (By *all over Ireland*, I know she mean all of Five Points Irish, like when my Brook family tell me not to spread their business *all over Africa*.)

Is Fenians in *The History of Ireland*, Auntie Siobhan?

Her still smilin where Mr. John left, then frown, turn to me. What?

Is Fenians in *The History of Ireland*?

They are, as a factual part of literary heritage, though they're lore.

What's lore?

Rip Van Winkle.

I like that story!

Well, long, long before Rip Van Winkle 'twas the Fenian story cycle. Oisín was out huntin with his father Fionn mac Cumhaill and the Fianna warriors—

Fenian warriors.

Fenian we say now, Fianna is old Irish. So Oisín was out huntin when a beautiful woman entered ridin a white stallion. She introduced herself as Niamh of the Sidhe and said she'd always loved Oisín, and she brought him with her to Tír Na nÓg, the Land of Eternal Youth. He was very happy with Niamh, but missed his Irish loved ones terribly, and after three years she told him: You may take my horse and return for a visit, but mind that ye never let your feet hit Irish ground. He was very glad to return to Ireland, but now all's changed. No family, no friends, his grand castle home a shambles. Here's the rub: time moved slowly in Tír Na nÓg. What was three years there was three *hundred* years in Éire, all his loved ones long dead! But even in his awful sadness, Oisín had a kind heart, and when he saw some aul one tryin to move a large stone, he leaned over to help—and fell! When he touched Irish soil, he aged three *hundred* years, and died!

I don't like that story!

Well, Oisín got to live three centuries with the love of his life. That's longer than you or I or anybody we know'll get, and Auntie Siobhan tap my nose with her finger.

But it only feel like three years to him! And the love of his life was bad luck!

Auntie Siobhan chuckle. Wouldn't be the first nor last time for that, she say, then back to readin *The History of Ireland*.

Can I do our secret doins for my nickel?

Auntie Siobhan's eyes never lift from her book: Too late, already done. Told ye: need to be here early, and she turn the page.

I walk outside, mosey over to the Spanish Company. There Ciaran be, feedin their horses tied up in front. He catch me in a glance, not pausing his work.

How come the Spanish Company got no sign over its door?

Because it's office work, he mutter without lookin up. A corporation, not some dry-goods store anyone off the street can just step into.

Ciaran open up another big sack a hay, pour it out.

You finish that story?

Ciaran nod.

It wasn't that scary. I know a scarier story. It's about Oisín in Ireland, who fall in love with Niamh who take him to the Land of Eternal Youth but he go back home to visit and three hundred years past, he touch Irish soil and die. They're the Fenians and they come back to conquer England and save Ireland for the Irish!

Ciaran rise a eyebrow at me like I'm loony.

It's in *The History of Ireland*! Auntie Siobhan readin it. Auntie Siobhan enjoyin *The History of Ireland*, that's what she told Mr. John O'Mahony, who translated it, when he come this mornin for his daily mornin tea, he come every mornin through the back door, they got a special arrangement she don't want all a Ireland knowin about.

Hah!

Huh?

Hah! Preparin his tea for him every mornin, caressin his blessèd words, secret special arrangement. And now sharin a love story—she's in love with him!

I frown. How *you* know?

August Doopin's not the only soul to cleverly assess the situation and make the conclusion. Siobhan, John—they even rhyme!

I consider it. Then say, I'll ask her.

Don't ask her! These things are secret, none of your business!

None a *your* business neither!

True. Then Ciaran go back to feedin the steeds.

They don't even hardly talk. Mr. John O'Mahony don't hardly talk.

Didn't say it was requited.

What?

I didn't say he was in love with her back.

She's not in love all by herself!

Come here, boy! call a man from the door a the Spanish Company, and Ciaran run inside.

I stay the night with Auntie Siobhan to make sure I get my nickel nex morn. Then we move down to the tavern. Mr. John don't come.

Because it's Sunday and you're closed? I say, even though I know usually Auntie Siobhan ignores the close-Sunday laws like all the other saloons.

No, I have his tea every mornin. Reckon he's laid up with that cold, sigh Auntie Siobhan. Which is exactly when he needs his tea! She look a little sad.

I stay a couple nights at Grammy Brook's, who's sneezin like Mr. John, and by Tuesday night she hardly sleep with bein stopped up. So nex morn, she send me to the drug-store for medicine.

Either Philip White's or Doctor McCune's.

Auntie Siobhan sell remedies too. Her inventory's mostly spirits, but she have a few—

I would *like* to patronize Philip White's pharmacy, or Doctor McCune's if you please. And Grammy gimme the coin.

All my colored family like to support Mr. White or Dr. McCune, the colored pharmacists. My Irish family also fond a Mr. White for whatever antidotes Auntie Siobhan don't have (which is most of em), for Mr. White always kindly extend credit.

Walk to the corner a Gold and Frankfort where Philip White's drug-store is. Full with people gettin potions, plenty of em sneezin. As I get in the line, somebody walk by me leavin, jus finished his purchase. I look up just in time to see 'twas Mr. John! I never seen him before outside of

Auntie Siobhan's tavern! I run out to wave to him, but he already gone. I head back inside where I lost my place in line to another.

Wait a minute. What's John O'Mahony doin here when he coulda bought his medicine from Auntie Siobhan! He's perpetratin the competition! I mean not exactly the competition, but if he require her love, wouldn't he make do with whatever remedy she got?

I don't have to bring up nothin bout love to Auntie Siobhan jus to let her know Mr. John is takin money should be hers down the street. I run into O'SHEA'S.

Auntie Siobhan!

She ain't here, say Roisin Feeney, who helped Auntie Siobhan durin the peak comet busy-ness and since Auntie Siobhan hired regular. Said back in an hour before the evenin crowd.

She upstairs or outdoors?

Roisin shrug. She's the boss, I don't ask her business.

I run up to the third floor to her room. *Auntie Siobhan!* Listen quiet but no sound from the secret wall place. *Auntie Siobhan!* Down to the second floor.

What's all that hollerin about? Miss Fiona holler weak from her room.

Evenin, Miss Fiona!

Evenin, Theo. Miss Fiona sittin up in her bed.

Your voice sound sick, Miss Fiona.

That I am.

Whatchu readin?

It's a grown-up book.

What's *Confessions of a Lady's Waiting Maid* about?

Never you mind, then she set the book on her table facedown. Now why you hollerin all over creation for your aul auntie?

Lookin for her.

That don't answer my question.

Mr. John O'Mahony's buyin medicines from Mr. White when he shoulda bought from her!

Miss Fiona chuckle. I know your auntie likes a full till, but her business is robust enough I don't think she begrudges others. How else could Five Points ever satisfy the copious clientele? And the herbs—just a side trade.

I *know*, but . . . But Mr. O'Mahony, he and Auntie Siobhan got a *special* relationship—he . . . they . . .

Miss Fiona frown. Then a little smile cross her face. Under the suspicion Siobhan might be sweet on the fella, are ye?

My hands clasp over my mouth: spilled a secret! How she figure it out? What's your evidence?

Smilin and sellin him daily tea and smilin and sayin him and her got a special arrangement and smilin and readin his book—You know Mr. John O'Mahony? Translator a *The History of Ireland, From the Earliest Period to the English Invasion*?

I do.

And when I asked about Fenians comin to conquer England and save Ireland for the Irish, she smile and tell me a love story!

What *you* know about Fenians?

Oisín followed Niamh to the Land of Eternal Youth but come back to Ireland and turned three hundred years of age and died but now the Fianna Fenians comin back to conquer England and save Ireland for the Irish!

Miss Fiona do some froggy coughin, then blow her nose, then froggy cough again. Come sit with me.

I jump in under the warm covers!

Not too close! Nowadays they claim touchin a sick person ye might get sick yourself.

There's a inch between us.

All right then. So: In the beginnin were the Celts. From them come our Irish language, our Irish story cycles, culture. Christianity made landfall the A.D. 400s, *Catholic* Christianity, and with it come writin, our recorded history commences. Kingdoms emerge, powerful monks livin on rich church estates. Then the Vikings, usherin in international trade. Then the Normans, descendants of the Vikings bein French and Italian and British. By this point we're up to the eleventh and twelfth centuries. Till now, settlers stayed and adapted—no matter how belligerent their arrival, if they stayed they just become Irish. And then, 1171, Henry the Second of England lands in Éire, and Henry the Second of England brings about somethin new.

Conquest?

Conquest. First military, then economic. We were formidable, mind ye, but in the end—*Divida et Impera* said Julius Caesar, and with Ireland not bein a political whole but an array of separate sovereignties, *Divide and Rule* was very efficient. After the carnage, the next subjugation was to bring in English settlers and grant them estates while turnin the Irish into peasant tenants and grant holdings on their own land. The Irish Rebellion of 1641 laid the ground for Oliver Cromwell—

Here Miss Fiona and me turn two different directions, spittin off the side a her bed.

Sound like your grandmother taught ye right, but ye needn't've spewed *that* big a wad. Clean it up.

Cromwell, Miss Fiona go on as I clean, and his evil design to Protestantize the entire populace and resettle Catholics in the West, far from England's borders and on the most barren land, *so:* the uprisins. In the 1790s we come close with help from the French, but a terrible storm turn our continental allies around. Next: Rebellion of 1798—my grandfather!

He led a *rebellion*?

Rank-n-file, but nothin lowly in that. Peasant he might've been, but *he* knew the history! And instilled it in me. What d' ye think happened?

Ireland lost?

Squashed! Then the brutal *moppin* up process—punishment of the *dissidents*, which were defined vaguely and broadly. Next: Rebellion of 1803, Robert Emmet and his famous speech from the dock just precedin his execution, proclaimin we need to wrest our independence from England with our own hands. His housekeeper and co-conspirator Anne Devlin was arrested and tortured.

Tortured how?

No need in incitin your nightmares with the specifics there, all you need know is our brave girl never breathed a word to her enemy tormenters. Then the tithe resistance of the 'thirties, *that* one I recall! I was a young one but observed my grown kin refusin to pay a tribute to the damned Anglican Church of Ireland. And *then*, sigh Miss Fiona, the 'forties.

The Hunger.

The Hunger. Forced off productive soil and onto bad, payin rent for the privilege of livin on our own land, land that could barely support any crop but potatoes, and when the blight came . . . While the Irish revolutionary spirit's had its fits and starts over time, 'twas the Famine anchored the hardenin of our hearts, sparked the fire in our blood that can*not* be extinguished.

Miss Fiona's eyes fill, thinkin on a faraway memory.

After a while, I say quiet, But what about Fenians?

I was just comin to that. A few years before the harvest went sour come to be the Young Irelanders, followers of Daniel O'Connell.

The Liberator!

Miss Fiona nod. But durin the Famine, they broke away from the Irish Confederation. And when the Young Ireland rebellion of 'forty-eight fell short, those not apprehended had to flee, exile themselves. Mr. John O'Mahony was one of the exiled.

Mr. John was a Young Irelander?

Ran first to Paris, then he came to settle in New York, concentratin on his scholarly pursuits. But now—*now*—Miss Fiona turn to me. Secret?

I nod! All my grown-up ladies trust me with their secrets!

Now Mr. O'Mahony's one of the underground organizers of a new disorder, quietly, quietly. Fenians. Takin the name of the ancient lore warriors as a blessin to the modern livin ones. When my parents named me Fiona, 'twas the same root. Same spirit.

Mr. John don't seem like no warrior! Mr. John O'Mahony seem sad-serious, all in his books.

Sure he broods. His mind on a higher plane. Spent time in the asylum, I heard.

Mr. John's a lunatic?

Miss Fiona honk-blow her nose. I think translatin the history book took a toll. And naturally the Brits banned it, keepin it from the Irish—all seem to weigh heavy on him. A sadness hard to pull himself out of.

I don't want Auntie Siobhan in love with a crazy man!

Way the world is, I think everyone not blind or evil must be a little crazy. But I don't think ye have to worry. Siobhan and John'd make an unlikely pair. Him intent on bringin us back our history, our culture, our land—enrichin the Irish. On the other hand, your auntie the capitalist just seem intent on enrichin her own self. *Achoo!* Oh, don't you go ballin up your fists at *me*, little miss, ye know it's true!

Then Miss Fiona *achoo! achoo!* nine of em, and by the time she done, my fists loose.

You think Fenians be the rebellion that'll stick, Miss Fiona? Save Ireland?

We shall see. Plenty of Irish in America sendin their coin home to the cause, I can tell ye.

Fenians in Irish lore, and now *real* Fenians in Ireland!

She smile. 'Twas the Irish in *America* took the name Fenian, the Fenian Brotherhood. Everything set in motion in Ireland last St. Paddy's Day, but the namesake's a bit more formal there. Christened as a *revolutionary* alliance, but the people confused the *R* so it came to be the Irish *Republican* Brotherhood.

Then Miss Fiona get quiet.

My grandfather saw terrible things in 'ninety-eight, unspeakable acts done to civilians. Most from the imperialists, but the rebels made their own share of barbarity too. *Revolution* must happen, *change*. And unfortunately there'll always be *some* goin to the vile side, ends justify the means—*no*. We revolutionary republicans just need to remember there was virtue in the inspiration, and to keep that virtue in the implementation.

Downstairs the tavern startin to be busy, Auntie Siobhan back from her errand-runnin, now tendin the saloon with Roisin Feeney, Roisin lookin like she startin to get the sweats like Miss Fiona. I wanna talk to my auntie, but know she shoo me away with all the customers callin to her. Even in her rush labor, she got a smile for everybody, and smile often even when she ain't in service—Auntie Siobhan happy with the good times, money rollin in. Nobody want depression but I wonder if might be somethin to what Miss Fiona said. Capitalist: not sure what it mean exactly, but sure didn't sound nice in Miss Fiona's voice.

Nex day I come earlier to Auntie Siobhan's and *still* miss my nickel, she already down in the saloon checkin her liquor stock. I'm startin to wonder if maybe she get up before I arrive on purpose, her fingers wary to let loose of even that paltry five-cent piece.

Mornin, Theo.

Mornin.

Sorry bout your nickel. I had to get up early and get ahead of the day. Roisin took sick in the middle of last night, leavin me short-handed and behind.

Oh.

And Fiona sick. And Sally I heard coughin last night, who's next?

I seen Miss Fiona last night.

Hm. And what might the two of you had to say to one another?

It's a secret.

Auntie Siobhan's eyes on her task before, like barely polite interest to me, but now she look up.

You oughtn't be keepin secrets from your auntie!

You tole me don't tell secrets!

She sigh. Ye're right. Then she go back to her bottle-countin. Then: Talkin about *me?*

I stare at her.

The rent increase is a smidgen!

Talkin bout Fenians! (Hands over my mouth!)

Oh. I already told you about that.

Not the same story.

Then might this be the one about the Fenians alive and well today, the new warriors for Ireland?

I don't like Auntie Siobhan's smirk. She go back to her stock check. Then she laugh outright.

Oh, *mo stoirín*! That's a lot more fairy tale than the one I offered. At least in my story, Oisín had it pretty grand for three hundred years. There's nothin'll come of this you speak of.

It's real!

Oh, I never said it weren't real. The Fenians, the *Irish Republican Brotherhood*, how's that for a lofty moniker? We Irish been dreamin freedom seven hundred years, never short of the fantasy or the attempts to realize it. And where are we? Independence came only for us who finally abandoned the aul Isle, makin the best of it an ocean away. There's but one way to win in this world, my love: beat em at their own game! Then Auntie Siobhan take out a pouch from under the counter and shake for effect, *clink clink*: Money!

Mr. O'Mahony buys his cures from Mr. White's drug-store!

Auntie Siobhan stop still, stare at me. All a sudden I feel bad, breakin her heart. I wipe the tear come to my eye.

Sorry! Sorry, but I don't think Mr. O'Mahony love you like you love him, elsewise he'd buy his remedy from you an a the competition.

Auntie Siobhan still starin. Then throw back her head, roarin the laughter.

Theo! She try to say more but too caught up in her funny fit. Oh, *girlín, you* are the grandest medicine to start the day!

Rap on the back door.

Come in, John! she call, twinklin eyes on me and my warm, red cheeks.

Mornin, Siobhan.

I'll get your tea.

Auntie Siobhan reach for his box under her counter. Appears your cold cleared up.

He nods. Somethin from Philip White's drug-store.

Oh? Auntie Siobhan very skilled in signalin her merriment to me but not to him. They trade boxes. Mr. John O'Mahony go to leave.

Your book.

He turn back around, and I see Auntie Siobhan's smile changed from mirth to warmth.

I finished it. And I liked it. Very much.

Mr. John O'Mahony stare at Auntie Siobhan, then look down.

The original Gaelic. There were holes, the narrative. He sigh. I wrote it in haste! I wanted people to see it, our history, our *real* history not rewritten by colonialists, *I tried to do right by Ireland!* I should've—

And he look to the floor again, starin at it a long time, ponderin on whatever he should've.

You *did* do right by Ireland, John.

He look to her, unsure. Then grateful. Then he leave.

I wanna spend the night with Auntie Siobhan so *for certain* I'll be here for my nickel tomorra, but I have supper with Grammy Brook and afterward she say too cold, too late to be runnin around. But nex mornin I make sure I'm at Auntie Siobhan's room seven and a half o'clock!

Come in, *mo stoirín.*

Achoo! Achoo! Achoo! Laid out on her bed's her secret note-book a figures and her box a tea for Mr. O'Mahony.

Aw, Theo, the sickness finally come to me, Roisin and me *both* on our backs. I'll have to run to the druggist for some kind of concoction later before the busy hour. Or close our doors till this all passes and suffer the financial consequences. She blow her nose. Reckon ye're here for your nickel.

I nod.

All right. This chamber-pot needs emptyin, let me do that. Auntie Siobhan labor to move her feet from her bed to the floor.

Wamme to empty it?

No, I want you to do your job for my business.

She tear out a clean sheet of her note-book, hand me the page and her feather-pen, then point to the wall. Go in there. It's Thursday, expense calculation day: add the piles and write em down. Don't look at my figures! I need *your* sums free of the influence of *mine*. Mr. O'Mahony'll be here momentarily, you bring his tea to him for me? Don't want anybody to see me like this.

She drop a nickel on the bed. There, ye're paid in advance. Then Auntie Siobhan pick up the chamber-pot, sick-waddlin out the door.

I go in the secret wall room, doin the sums. I don't think Auntie Siobhan's avoidin Mr. John because she's sick and don't look pretty any more than she'd avoid anybody else. I don't believe Ciaran deducted his reasonin right—she ain't *in* love with him. But tellin him bout his book, *'twas* heart in her eyes. Different kind a love.

I write down the figures and come out. And there Auntie Siobhan's note-book on the bed. I hear no sign a footsteps outside the door so I peek.

All the numbers I just checked in the secret room. LQ for liquor, LO for lamp oil, TR for tenants' repairs. RF I figure is the pay for Roisin Feeney, all the money amounts matched what I just counted. But there's one symbol that didn't have a pile a money in the wall, symbol she never showed me before: IRB. It take me a few seconds to figure out them letters. The amount she contribute to *that* seem pretty generous.

I pick up the box for Mr. John—way too heavy for what it's meant for. Look inside. Sure there's the tea leaves, but I feel under: coins. *Lotta* coins. Exactly the plentiful amount Auntie Siobhan marked down for the Irish Republican Brotherhood. I remember my auntie lass night shakin that *clink-clink* pouch at me: *Money!* Knowin how to keep her secrets, her business bein *her* business. Quietly, quietly goes the Rebellion, say Miss Fiona.

The church bells start to toll eight. Mr. John mus be rappin at the back door. I slam Auntie Siobhan's note book closed, then slip the nickel she left for me in with the cash under the tea leaves. Run downstairs with Mr. John O'Mahony's Fenian tea box which holds the secret of him and Auntie Siobhan and me, all us together tryin to do right by Ireland.

The Weeping Time

Whatcha singin, Auntie Maryam?
  We useta sang it in the fields.

> *Oh, Mary, dontchu weep, dontchu mourn*
> *Oh, Mary, dontchu weep, dontchu mourn*
> *Pharaoh's army got drownded*
> *Oh, Mary, don't weep!*

Auntie Maryam singin her ole slave work song while workin in New York: now *she* do whites for the whites! Her washtub in the corner, scrubbin sheets and hangin em around the front-room. She still not like leavin her house n garden, put on her light-skin on days she gotta pick up the laundry, carry it back. I'm glad to be up and helpin her after bein in bed three days. Hour after I gave Mr. John O'Mahony his tea box Thursday morn, I took to sneezin and sniffin, I never got closer n an inch to anybody and *still* got the sick!

In come Auntie Eunice bringin the end-a-Febooary chill with her, dressed like church. Have you seen this?

Me and Auntie Maryam look at the newspaper she holdin open.

No, you couldn't have, it's an Albany paper, though no doubt the ad appeared in *some* city rags. A woman in the congregation, her sister visiting from upstate, brought several to church this morning.

FOR SALE.
LONG COTTON AND RICE
NEGROES.

A GANG OF **460** NEGROES, accustomed to
the culture of Rice and Provisions; among whom
are a number of good mechanics, and house servants. Will be sold on the 2d and 3d of March
next, at Savannah, by

JOSEPH BRYAN.

The Negroes will be sold in families, and can
be seen on the premises of JOSEPH BRYAN,
in Savannah, three days prior to the day of sale,
when catalogues will be furnished.

I've never heard of such a large auction! Do you know of this Joseph
Bryan?

Auntie Maryam shake her head.

Well, he's just the broker. Do you know Pierce Butler? The Butler Island
Plantation?

Auntie Maryam make a startle. Georgia? she whisper.

An island off Georgia, in the sea.

Auntie Maryam swallow. Jakey. Jakey took with Master on business.
Days and nights, days and nights. After they comes back, the slave quarters: Jakey tell us bout Butler. Jakey sees families. *Generations.* Jakey saze
they stays together. Jakey saze Butler never sell!

He's selling now! Or *one* Butler—brothers John and Pierce Mease
Butler each inherited half their grandfather's estate, *he* was the patriarch
you speak of. *Senator* Pierce Butler, one of the signers of the U.S. Constitution, the man who never sold his slaves, also was the legislator who
wrote *into* the Constitution the Fugitive Slave Clause, precursor to today's
Fugitive Slave Act. It turns out one of the grandsons, Pierce's namesake,
is money-reckless, gambling debts and the crash of 'fifty-seven and an
expensive divorce from his English actress wife. And the primary asset
Pierce the younger is willing to part with are four hundred sixty negroes—

Negroes sold in families! Don't that paper saze that? cry Auntie Maryam.
That's somethin. That's *some*thin!

Auntie Eunice say nothin.

Rest a the afternoon Auntie Maryam workin her laundry, nobody talkin. After a while, Auntie Maryam kneel, forehead on the floor, third time outa five today. I figure Christian Auntie Eunice be bothered by Auntie Maryam doin her *Allah*s, but my blood-auntie jus clasp her hands close her eyes, doin her own prayer, lips movin.

March come in with a little sun, little wind, little rain, little hail, little blowin snow, back to sun—all on the first! Nex day I'm pumpin the water Grammy Brook's courtyard, turn to lug it up our tenement steps and there Hen.

Wanna job?

❧

I'm workin the hotel with Hen! Greenwich Village where Auntie Eunice live, but not the Little Africa part. I never had a *real* job before: nine cent a day! We clean some, but mostly we be At Your Service to a guest. At the front desk they say, *I need a gal* or *I need a nigger*, then the concierge go *There*, point at me, and they say *Come on, girl* or *Move!* or *What a cute little pickaninny* or *What are you?* Sometime nice and sometime grumpy, sometime they gimme a penny tip! I pass along some a my earnins to my grammies and keep some. Wednesday the ninth my eighth day, I'm finished four o'clock, go home to Grammy Brook's. Auntie Eunice there! So busy workin, no time to visit her lately!

Auntie Eunice, I have a job! *Real* job. Near *you*, the Village!

So I hear, she say, lookin sad, *Daily Tribune* in her hand.

Wanna know what my job is?

Hush, say Grammy. Auntie Eunice is givin the news.

The article, I notice, take up a entire page.

The reporter, say my auntie, went down to the auction pretending to be an interested buyer. The sale took place one week ago over two days, Wednesday, March the second, and Tuesday, March the third, at a Savannah race-course. The condemned were kept several days prior in the horse sheds, identified by their catalogue numbers: Chattel 127, Chattel 231, ultimately to stand before a horde of boisterously laughing white beasts. The stipulation that families would be kept together—*family* was defined in the narrowest of terms. Yes, parents with small children were sold as a unit, but what of those parents' siblings? And the parents'

parents, no! A young mother of seventeen years of age would expect to be sold separately from her own mother of thirty-four, not to mention losing forever the embrace of her loving grandparents, these families had never been apart. The promise of unity was all they had! One young newlywed couple was not recognized as married in the eyes of the broker and thus were divided, the businessman's nuptial judgment suspicious given the young lovers' variant skills: she a rice slave, he cotton—economically expedient to sell them separately. When a young mother clutched her infant in protection, she was castigated by the louts: What was wrong with her? What was she trying to hide? But soon enough these minor hiccups passed, the gentleman planters back to their revelry, a military man among them claiming, quote: *We'll have all the niggers in Africa over here in three years—we won't leave enough for seed.*

Gran-Gran give a deep sigh, starin out the winda. Grammy just shake her head, shake her head.

The master must have suffered the remotest bruised conscience as he compensated each of the doomed with one silver dollar. This after he collects $303,850 for the two-day sale of four hundred twenty-nine men, women, children, and infants, the largest slave auction in U.S. history, *how?* This late in the day! I thought things were getting better! I'd convinced myself national emancipation *must* be around the corner! Then came the Fugitive Slave Act. Then came *Dred Scott.*

Auntie Eunice look like she gonna cry, then take a breath.

The writer of the article mentions that rain began as a drizzle while the slaves were exhibited for pre-sale viewing, then poured. Auntie Eunice read again: *As the last family stepped down from the block, for the first time in four days, the rain ceased, the clouds broke away, and the soft sunlight fell on the scene.* Folks have taken to calling those days the Weeping Time. I was at Maryam's all day until I came here, *I* wanted to weep! But *how* when *she* held strong, refusing to break? We must not despair, I say, we must not despair, but demand repair! Of our terribly failing social and political structure, the nation's abominations, there must be a reconstructing and compensation, and we must insist these reparations come swiftly! Then Auntie Eunice wipe away all the despair still streamin down her cheeks.

∽෧

Nex day's windy. At work, they say wait on a guest, Mrs. Reynolds from Florida who been in town a few days and leavin noon today. *Come on, girl*, she snarl. I follow her to her room, but when we get there already a little colored girl helper standin nex to the big bed. She sewin a button to a grown-up dress. When we walk in, she look up. Her left eye poked out!

Stop starin and collect my breakfast dishes, bring em down to the kitchen! And tell em at the desk one of their nigger porters put a scratch on my good chest!

Lucky Mrs. Reynolds's dirty breakfast dishes isn't many, I can bring em all down one trip, then come back up to be In Waiting. Mrs. Reynolds gone, but the girl still there. I'm glad herself has left because I do not want her to ask if I reported on the porter, which I didn't and won't.

What's your name?

The girl look scared! Look around, like somebody watchin us!

I'm Theo.

She look around again, then speak so low I can't hear.

Huh?

Sukie. Still the word soft.

Oh. How old are ya, Sukie?

Sukie look like I jus give her a test she didn't study!

Lemme see, I say, and walk to her. She back up gainst the bed but I come quick, nowhere she can turn.

I'm nine years of age and you a head smaller, so I put you at eight.

Eight? she say. I nod. Then she smile like she like that idea, say it again: Eight!

You like this job?

Sukie look at me like she don't know what to think!

I get nine cent a day plus tips! But I can tell Mrs. Reynolds ain't intent on offerin me no tip. You?

Her lower lip start tremblin. Then she look around everywhere everywhere everywhere, make sure nobody close. Then pull down the neck a her dress, show me top a her back, below her shoulder: *R* inside a circle, burned into her flesh. I jump back! She cover up again.

My eyes give her a head-to-toe. I never met a live slave before, didn't know I ever would! Gran-Gran and Grammy I only known emancipated. Auntie Maryam I only known escaped. But here a slave in action.

I come close, whisper: You oughta escape.

Her eyes go wild.

New York, I say. Free state.

Somethin red outside the winda. Klie! I run to the winda. Red, yella, green. I love kites! I say. These the first kites I seen this spring, look like seven out there!

Clink.

I swerve around. Sukie tryin to move. But now I see: Sukie's leg chained to the bed-post. I hearda slave chains but never seen one. I look at her. She look at me. She look like pain, and also like shame.

Maybe, I say, but can't figure what to say after Maybe. I see a flash and turn back to the winda. Blue kite!

Clink.

Sukie wanna come to the winda, but her chain don't reach longer n three feet, not close. Now tears in her eyes. She pull, *clink!* She pull, *clink!* Her tears comin, *clink! clink! clink!*

Did I hear that chain rattle?

And there stand Mrs. Reynolds. Where *she* come from? Sukie try to get back where she was when I come in, *clink! clink! clink!*

Don't you *move*, Sukie, don't you *dare* move! And what're *you* doin by that winda?

Sukie and me stare at her.

Escape?

No, ma'am! No, ma'am! cry Sukie.

Kites, my mouth say, but no sound come out. Mrs. Reynolds unlockin Sukie's chain.

Damn you! Mrs. Reynolds strike Sukie with her chain. *Damned niggers!* Crost Sukie's back, crost Sukie's legs. Sukie *hooooooooonk!* Like a goose!

Don't you *make* your sound, Sukie! Reckon you thought I wouldn't whoop you in the North?

NO, MA'AM! NO, MA'AM! NO, MA'AM!

I'll *kill* ya, ya black wench! And where you think *you* goin?

Mrs. Reynolds just taken notice a me inchin toward the door.

Little northern nigger, think you put ideas in Sukie's head? Come back here, yella bitch!

No! I tell her, and *bitch* sting: no one never call me that before! Sukie *hoooooonk*, Mrs. Reynolds whoop her legs, the chain start to drip red. Sukie fall, her leg bent funny. Stare at Sukie, I wanna go. I can't go.

Get up, Sukie! We're leavin for home in an hour.

Sukie try.

I can'ts, ma'am! I can'ts!

Get up! The chain strike crost Sukie's face. Mrs. Reynolds turn to me again.

Yankee blacky, get on back here so I can give you the same! And she raise the chain in the air, movin toward me.

I AIN'T NO SLAVE! And out the room I run, almost fly into a porter who tear into Mrs. Reynolds's room: *What's happening here?* but them's the last words I catch, race out the hotel, runnin to Auntie Eunice's. She at work but I know where the secret key is. I fall on Auntie Eunice's bed sobbin, the sobbin go on so long make my throat hurt. I remember Auntie Eunice once talkin about a story she read: *Twelve Years a Slave.* I remember the awful cold and hunger of the Depression, but I'd take penniless and homeless ten winters before I'd ever wanna re-live my five minutes a slave.

Auntie Eunice don't get back till late from her backstage duties at the Academy a Music, and when I wake in the mornin she's gone again, but I know she was here because I see the biscuit she left for my breakfast. She don't have to be at work till two on performance days, so I don't know where she is. I wanna tell her what went on at the hotel, and then again I like to erase what went on at the hotel from my brain like never happened. I wonder she might be at Auntie Maryam's.

She is, and still got that *Tribune* from two days ago, but now stead a sad, she mad.

There were no light mulattoes in the whole lot of the Butler stock, and but very few that were even a shade removed from the original Congo blackness, a point in their favor in the eyes of the buyer, for too liberal an infusion of the blood of the dominant race brings a larger intelligence, a more vigorous brain, which, anon, grows restless under the yoke, and is prone to inquire into the definition of the word liberty—how *dare* they! This, mind you, is the so-called abolitionist *Tribune*, implying that one as dark as you or I would not have the wit to even *consider* escape, let alone the ingenuity to make it a reality! How would this journalist explain *your* presence here, I wonder! Not from just below the border, but South Carolina no less!

Maybe he jus sayin that be what the buyers think, Auntie Maryam sigh.

No. If you continue, he expresses for the reader his own observations as if scientific fact: *The pure-blooded negroes are much more docile and manageable than mulattoes, though less quick of comprehension, which makes them preferred by drivers.*

If no mulattoes runnin round, say Auntie Maryam, maybe little bit a good news: nobody got the master for a father, no midnight visit to the womens. Or the little girls.

But Auntie Maryam don't look hopeful, jus tired. Enough bad feelin in the room I figure now not the time to bring up Sukie. Anyhow, what could they do? Her and Mrs. Reynolds long gone now, and Fugitive Slave Act and *Dred Scott* mean anywhere in America slave's a slave's a slave.

I start lookin through the old papers ready for the stove fire, hopin I might find somethin happy to share, but everything I see in the March 7 *New-York Times* look dull. Still, any story's better n slavery.

As the Rahway train, on the New-Jersey Railroad, was approaching the Jersey City Depot, the switchman let the switch turn on to a side track, on which there was a drill engine, attached to a train of cars. A severe collision was the result.

They don't say nothin.

The Metropolitan Police: Startling Disclosures of Corruption and Crime.

They don't say nothin.

Report from Augusta, Georgia, from March the fourth: *There have been heavy rains recently throughout the South, and the bad condition of the roads interferes with the forwarding of cotton and produce to market.*

And suddenly the wailin and the sobbin and the weep weep weepin from my aunties, like they was there in Georgia the whole rainy Weepin Time themself. Holdin each other, and wave me over to hold me which make me weep too, and weep harder rememberin Sukie can't. Through my tears seein Sukie longin to glimpse that kite, and hearin Sukie honkin the heartbreakinest noise I ever knowed.

Women's Rights

I'm a domestic!

Everybody turn to Maureen, jus walked through the door. Then cheerin: Grammy Cahill and Cousin Aileen and Cathleen and Auntie Siobhan and Great-Uncle Fergus. Ciaran look confused but smile, deductin this is some kind a good news.

Wait, say Cousin Aileen. You're just after comin from gettin the job?

I am.

It's Sunday! You're sayin ye won't be home Sundays, daughter?

Most Sunday evenins free, though I might be rotatin with another servant.

When do you start? ask Cathleen.

Tomorrow!

Rich, are they? say Grammy.

They are!

Have to be, say Cousin Aileen. All thanks to ye, Saint Joseph, she add, lookin at our Patron Saint of Workers statue.

But there's rich, and there's *rich* rich, say Maureen.

First of May: excitin doins altogether, say Great-Uncle Fergus. The movin-out and movin-in goin on in the street all day, and now this.

Did ye lose your Fiona and Sally with the rent increase, Siobhan?

Never, she answer Grammy. They always complain but know they won't find anything as nice for the price.

There's rich, and there's *rich* rich.

We *heard* ye, Maureen, say Cousin Aileen, and are presumin your new employers to be *rich* rich.

They are *not*, say Maureen. They're rich rich *rich!*

My family all happy for Maureen, but hard for me get *too* glad rememberin I didn't care for the maid work at the hotel, which I never gone back to since the day I met Sukie. Monday, as Auntie Eunice preparin to go to her own work, I report Maureen's news to her.

I understand their delight, she remark, standin in the corner a her bed-closet pullin up her knickers. A poor laborer can be used and abused, then tossed and replaced should they dare ask an extra penny. Once the fancy homeowners get used to a servant, however, they don't want disruption in their home, chaos. Come time for a raise, the maid has leverage.

What's leverage?

Power. Housemaids used to be good colored work. After emancipation, Mother was.

Grammy?

Auntie Eunice nod. I was small but I remember. Then the Irish came And the wealthy took a preference.

You like *your* maid job?

Always well to have gainful employ. And I am privy to beautiful music.

Can I go to your work with you?

May I. No.

How *come*?

Now her eyes to me, like she really considerin.

All right, you may have a peek before my start time. Go wash your face.

Hoho! Run to wash in the washtub water. Never thought she say yes!

I remember you brung me here when it first built! I say as we stroll east in the warm spring air.

You were only four.

I remember! But only got to see the outside.

When we get to Fourteenth and Irving, Auntie Eunice stop to gaze over it all, like she seein it anew, the grand tallness and bricks stacked neat, the high high giant bow windas. We walk all round it, then she take my hand and we enter through the back door, then into where's the stage and the audience seats. Big!

Eighty feet floor to ceiling, she say. Close your eyes.

She guide-walk me.

Sit.

I do.

Now look.

I'm sittin on a red chair, velvet soft! But I see no other chairs!

Where's the rest of em?

Stand, she say.

I do—and the chair seat fold up in on itself! And now I see *all* the chairs is folded up!

How you *do* that, Auntie Eunice!

New invention. They put springs in the seats to make them close when they are vacant so that people can walk through the rows. The Academy of Music has seats for four thousand audience members—largest opera house in the world!

Then I follow Auntie Eunice downstairs where people's makin a big scenery painting.

Good morning, Eunice.

Good morning, Hyacinth.

Now we're in Auntie Eunice's workroom: costume shop. Ladies sewin by hand and by machine, *clickety clickety clack.* On the floor here n there a scrap a satin, scrap a silk.

Look, Auntie Eunice say, standin by the big basins.

She turn a handle and the water flow right out, don't have to go outside to pump it! Now she grab a broom.

All right, sugarplum, I need to work. Run off now.

And you?

Auntie Eunice and me turn around. Pretty blond lady lookin older n Auntie Eunice but younger n Grammy, wearin a fur stole even though it's warm May. Smilin. Another white lady with brown hair nex to her.

Eunice, say Brownhair, this is Mrs. Heverworth, a great patroness of the Academy of Music. She requested to speak today with some of our back-stage labor and would like to know about the work you do here.

Then Brownhair glance at me, her face stop smilin.

My niece! say Auntie Eunice. I'm so sorry, Miss Jennings, she was curious about the Academy, so I—

Curious about the opera? say Mrs. Heverworth. I nod. How marvelous! What is it you like about it?

I think on that. The tuba.

Mrs. Heverworth laugh. Ah, my pet! *This* is why I have supported our new republican venture, the Academy providing good inexpensive seating *every-where*, not just in some segregated balcony as with the disastrous old Astor Opera House. Music should not be reserved for the elite! Music is for the masses! Eunice, are you as eager as I for Wednesday's *La Traviata* premiere?

Oh yes! say Auntie Eunice, I have heard the rehearsals and already Miss Piccolomini's astounding Violetta has brought tears to my eyes. But I must admit my partiality to last month's *La Favorita,* a most perfect role for Madame Gazzaniga. It's certainly a treat to be provided with consecutive programs in Donizetti's unmistakable bel canto mode, and truly a proper tribute given the great loss to the world of music with his passing eleven years back. And how perfect to follow with Verdi! given the obvious influence of the former's oeuvre on the latter's imagination.

Mrs. Heverworth look like she asked a two-bit question and got a three-dollar-gold coin answer. They keep talkin and I slip off, grabbin silk and satin snippets from the floor on my way out.

I got these from the Academy a Music! I tell Grammy Cahill that evenin.

Good girl! Grammy smile, lookin over the scraps.

I surely miss Maureen, sigh Cousin Aileen.

She's not been gone two days! say Great-Uncle Fergus.

Still! Didn't know how lucky I was, workin with my daughter, bein with her all day.

Sure she's five steps up from seamstressin, say Grammy. No rent: room and board free. And the power a housemaid assumes in those mansions: A raise I'll be havin or I quit!

❧

Nex day, I'm about to knock on Auntie Eunice's door, then hear voices.

Theo, come in! Do you remember my niece Theodora, Mrs. Heverworth?

Of course!

And there in the front-room (which Auntie Eunice still call a parlor like in Seneca Village) is a piano!

Your auntie and I had quite a chat yesterday! Her love of music was apparent, and she told me how she had long desired to organize a Sunday afternoon salon for negro ladies. Well! My husband and I had just purchased a grand piano, and we were looking for a proper beneficiary to whom we could bestow our old upright. And, *voilà,* I meet charming Eunice!

You are so kind!

My husband calls me impulsive. I say I'm decisive. Why vacillate when the obvious answer has come heaven-sent? And the instrument fits very nicely here.

Perfectly!

More than your appreciation of the great composers, I must say it was the mention of your women's cultural forum that affected me. When we bring our minds and spirits together, we women are a powerful force. Next Thursday the twelfth, I shall be attending the Woman's Rights Convention at Mozart Hall with my dear colleague Lucretia Mott presiding. As they have said in Paris as of late: *Solidarité!*

I don't know how I could ever repay you, Mrs. Heverworth!

She smile. Invite me to your first forum meeting. And then Mrs. Heverworth leave.

Can I come to the women's cultural forum?

May I, and it shall be called the *Ladies* Cultural Forum. So long as you wash your face first.

Okay! Why not *Women's* Cultural Forum?

Because colored women have always been labeled animals and whores! snap Auntie Eunice. Anything but *ladies*, a title reserved for white women. *We* are *ladies*.

Oh. I tap a couple piano keys.

Let us sit!

The two of us sit on the bench, her fingertips barely grazin the keys, like they magic she jus like to be near.

May the two of us ladies go sit in the foldin chairs and listen to music at the Academy of Music?

Auntie Eunice, eyes still on the keys, don't answer at first.

I haven't yet seen any negroes among the patrons. But perhaps. Perhaps. Then my auntie play a lively tune.

I didn't know you could play the piano, Auntie Eunice! With jus one finger! *Mary had a little lamb! Little lamb! Little lamb!*

Solidarité my arse, say Auntie Siobhan that evenin. Love to see the day those rich women rub elbows with the likes of us.

Have ye everything ye need, Cathleen? ask Cousin Aileen.

I'm after givin her all the ingredients she asked for, say Grammy. Jar, cotton scraps, cork

I supplied the cork! say Auntie Siobhan, holdin up the wine bottle. She brung it home full, but the grown-ups past it around and now nary a drop.

Scissors, whale oil, Grammy go on. Know how hard it is to find whale oil these days with the harpoon industry on its last legs?

Cathleen threadin the cord through the cork, payin the chatter no mind. Early dusk jus fell to deep dusk, everybody at Grammy's fadin to dark.

Can ye teach *me* to make an oil lamp, Cathleen? Ciaran ask.

We only got elements enough to make the one, but that'll do us fine, say Cousin Aileen. Miracle the seamstress piecemeal picked up, now needin light for the evenin home-work!

And with Fergus at the Central Park, ain't we rollin in it! say Grammy.

We can go to the Academy a Music with its inexpensive music for the masses!

Grammy and Auntie Siobhan and Cousin Aileen stare at me. Then roll their heads back, howlin.

First the Women's Rights gatherin, now the symphony, say Grammy, wiping a laugh-tear.

Did ye really think the *masses* was meant to include the dregs of Five Points? say Auntie Siobhan. With most lucky to have the one and only dress worn every day, worn to rags?

Remember the old Astor Opera House? ask Cousin Aileen. The poor had to climb that old narrow stairway to the benches in the cockloft, far and away from the aristocracy below.

Didn't stop the riot, did it, say Auntie Siobhan.

What riot? say me and Ciaran.

Foolishness! Happened around your birth year, Grammy say to me.

Year before, say Auntie Siobhan. 'Forty-nine. I remember, as I was but fifteen years of age.

The opera house also played plays, say Great-Uncle Fergus. 'Twas Shakespeare the night of the ruckus.

Macbeth, say Auntie Siobhan.

The elites were all for William Macready of England, who was playin the lead, say Great-Uncle Fergus, and the poor favored Edwin Forrest, our American-born star who'd performed for them previous in less stodgy venues.

'Twas a very cultural riot, say Auntie Siobhan with a crooked smile.

After a prior night of all sorts of cuisine hurled at the stage and *Down with the codfish aristocracy!* Great-Uncle Fergus go on, Macready was ready to pack his bags, but some fancy devotees urged him to stay.

Herman Melville, say Cathleen. Washington Irving.

Then, say Great-Uncle Fergus, some Tammany Hall personage gives out free tickets for Forrest aficionados to fill the rafters, plus thousands amassed in the streets outside, well, what more's there to say? The mob began hurlin pavin stones through the windows, set the buildin on fire!

The Seventh Regiment called in, say Grammy.

The Seventh well known to be made up of gentry toffs, say Auntie Siobhan. They opened fire.

Thirty-odd killed, say Grammy.

Then nobody speak a while.

Your eyes still seein in this dimness, Cathleen? ask Grammy. Cathleen nod.

Women's rights, women's rights, sure I don't understand the rich women wantin rights equal to the men, say Cousin Aileen. To work night n day? Like *us*? Grateful we are for the extra evenin work, but wouldn't I love to trade places, their life a leisure! Sure *I'll* go to your jabber meetins middle a the work week!

Auntie Eunice gonna start meetins with other colored ladies. Sundays.

Aul Eunice always busyin herself with some ennoblin scheme or nother, say Auntie Siobhan.

Hand me the oil, Cathleen say, and I pass the bottle.

Don't spill a drop, Cathleen! say Grammy. Expensive, very dear.

Can't say I can complain, say Auntie Siobhan, inheritin the Board and Publick from my dearly departed mate. How else could a woman run her own business?—the law always favorin the man. Makin my own rules, handlin my own money—the most satisfyin part of my marriage has been my widowhood!

Match, say Cathleen, and everybody go quiet while Grammy pick up our lone match from the mantle, pass it to Cousin Aileen who pass it to

Ciaran who pass it to me who pass it to the lamp-maker. Cathleen scrape it on the floor: *whoosh!* Her wick aglow.

'ᴌ ꠸ ꠹'

In the afternoon sun, Auntie Maryam pick her tomatas.

It will be an opportunity, Auntie Eunice tell her, for the ladies of our race to come together and discuss music and poetry and the great issues of our times.

What I gots to bring?

Yourself. And cucumbers for sandwiches?

Auntie Maryam keep pickin tomatas.

I know what you meant, what can you *contribute*. And I meant what *I* said: your pleasing self.

Take my cucumbers. Not me.

We gonna sing at the salon, Auntie Maryam!

Yes! You haven't yet come to see my piano! I know Bertha Williams can play.

You can play *too*, Auntie Eunice. *Mary had a little lamb—*

African ladies' societies have existed in New York for decades. It would not be a frivolous undertaking, a tea for senseless entertainment. Back in the 'thirties, petitions against slavery initiated by colored women's groups were so successful, the U.S. House of Representatives began to censor all debate on the matter, something that had never before happened in Congress on any issue. The restriction has been dubbed the *gag rule*, and it banned all petitions related to slavery for eight and a half years: 1836 to 1844!

How that good?

It demonstrated their fear of our might, the strength in our unity. We *threatened* those in power—the first step. We can be *change-makers!*

Auntie Maryam sigh and plant a potata seed.

One of those women's associations, the Ladies Literary Society, raised funds to aid escaping slaves. In 1838, one of those slaves was Frederick Douglass.

Now Auntie Maryam look up.

I know you worry. But secreting yourself away from the world is not the solution. If, God forbid, anything untoward were to happen, it would be *very* useful for you to have many allies.

Auntie Maryam swallow.

We have certainly had our disappointing setbacks, but we must remember the Republican party, only five years old, has recently made great strides into Congress. We are constantly told that immediate abolition is for unrealistic idealists, unicorn riders! *Yes*, we are told, it *will* come *gradually*, just be patient! But hasn't every great societal change been initiated by the righteous *im*patient? Theo, if you have to go, go!

Auntie Eunice noticin me hoppin one foot to the other, I *do* need the privy but don't wanna miss her talkin bout the salon! I run to the outhouse, empty my water! When I'm done, I hear Auntie Eunice lowered her voice, so I peek through the wood crack and prick up my ears good.

The African Society for Mutual Relief is the male equivalent of our gathering.

Now Auntie Maryam turn to her.

Publicly they assist the sick and orphaned and widowed and help with burials. And privately they have a trap-door that leads to a tunnel. You had just come through that tunnel and up through that trap-door an hour before you arrived at my mother's home.

Auntie Maryam eyes faraway.

I approached them, the Mutual Relief Society, inquiring as to how we as a newly established assemblage might work with them. I cannot vouch for the views of others there, but the gentlemen I happen to have met with were quite terse, and quite emphatic in their opinions that we ladies would be most useful performing *women's work*: as handmaids to our husbands, providing for them a comfortable, nurturing home so that *they* may go out into the world to do the important work toward freedom.

I ain't like them fancy ladies.

Auntie Eunice quiet a moment. I will *not* divulge your origins, though I can tell you if they knew, they would be honored to have a courageous refugee among us. All they will understand—yes, even as I introduce you as my sister recently come home, it *will* be apparent your educational background was less formal. Maryam: I would not *want* to be a part of a collective that eschews race prejudice while embracing class discrimination.

I gots to get back to the laundry.

Then Auntie Maryam walk up the steps to her house, Auntie Eunice heavin a silent sigh, and I come out the w.c. At her door, Auntie Maryam turn around to Auntie Eunice: I be there. Then she go inside.

Auntie Eunice smile, surprise and delight. Then turn to me.

If I'd been born a man, I would have made quite the persuasive lawyer.

❧

News from upstate: Sixty-year-old man bludgeons to death nineteen-year-old sickly daughter with a shoemaker's hammer! Religious fanaticism involved— read all about it!

Woman's Rights Convention upcoming at Mozart Hall!

I'm goin to the Woman's Rights Convention! I tell Hannah, whose eyes is on the newsboys when they oughta be seekin out customers.

Ya *are?*

If my Auntie Eunice'll let me! I ain't asked her yet. Ya gotta pick the right time or she'll say no.

Ya think the Woman's Rights Convention let me be a newsboy stead a a street-sweeper?

I'll ask!

❧

Sunday come: salon! And what Miss Bertha Williams is playin on the piano with two hands and all fingers got a lot more twists n turns than Auntie Eunice's *Mary!* Miss Bertha my grammies' age. The other two ladies is Miss Greene, around my aunties' age, and Auntie Maryam in her light-skin disguise. When Miss Bertha finished, we clap ladylike polite and hear a tappin at the door.

I must apologize for my tardiness, ladies! say Mrs. Heverworth, but there was a minor domestic incident. My maid was fetched by her brother to attend to her mother who was having a difficult delivery, and my home is chaos without my bridget.

My ma's Brigid!

Mother and infant? ask Miss Greene.

I am happy to report they are both well.

Mrs. Heverworth, say Auntie Eunice, I'd like to introduce you to my guests. Mrs. Heverworth is the kind patroness of the arts who presented me with the piano.

The ladies nod and polite half-smile.

This is Miss Hazel Greene. She and I once taught together at Colored School Number Three—

Ah! I should have *known* you were a teacher, Eu—*Mrs. Bennett*, say Mrs. Heverworth. How do you do, Miss Greene.

And this is my sister, Mrs. Wright, a laundress. Of course you've met my niece Theodora. And the pianist: Mrs. Williams.

Yes, I arrived a few minutes ago, but waited outside the door so as not to interrupt the music. Your playing is superb!

Thank you, Mrs. Heverworth.

And what a sublime piece! Who is the composer?

Francis Johnson, a Philadelphia negro.

A negro!

The first American negro to have a composition published as sheet music. He played many instruments but was most known for his virtuosity on the keyed bugle, which he likely learned from an Irish immigrant, Richard Williams. Maestro Johnson's band was for many years all black, but later he began to admit a few white musicians. He played for Queen Victoria at Buckingham Palace.

My!

May I offer you a cup of tea, Mrs. Heverworth? Piece of cake?

Yes, thank you, Mrs. Bennett. I must say, I am very impressed that you pulled your salon together so quickly! In five days?

Well, we are thus far only four ladies, plus my niece. I hope our gathering may grow, without exceeding a number that would jeopardize our splendid intimacy. One cube or two?

No sugar for me, but I would appreciate a bit of cream. As you are both teachers, were either of you fortunate enough to have made the acquaintance of Maria Stewart?

Yes! Of course! say Miss Greene and Auntie Eunice.

We should be very proud to say that she was a sister New Yorker for nearly twenty years, say Mrs. Heverworth. I had the opportunity to meet her once, and to tell her I was among the privileged few to have heard her exquisite oratory in Boston, before she resigned from public speaking.

Who's Maria Stewart? I whisper to Auntie Eunice.

Ah! Mrs. Heverworth smile at me. When William Lloyd Garrison established *The Liberator* back in the 'thirties, he immediately called for colored ladies to contribute, and fellow Bostonian Maria Stewart was the first to heed the call. An eloquent writer and lecturer for abolition *and* the rights of women, she was the first lady to orate between audiences of women *and* men, which tragically brought about her downfall. Harsh criticisms of the daring in her words, and the boldness of her actions to address mixed-sex audiences, finally wore her down. She relocated from Boston and resided for some time in New York City before removing again to retire in Washington City.

Did you know, say Miss Bertha, that Maria Stewart was married but three years when her young husband died? And the white executors of her husband's will maneuvered a legal theft that left Miss Maria penniless.

The white *male* executors, say Mrs. Heverworth.

Indeed, say Miss Bertha.

Ladies, we must struggle together! say Mrs. Heverworth, standin up. Our inaugural Seneca Falls women's rights gathering back in 'forty-eight was founded by five women, all abolitionists.

All abolitionists?

Mrs. Heverworth smile at me. Yes, my pet. And among the few men to attend that convention was your own Frederick Douglass, that great self-emancipated negro who is as well a staunch supporter of our women's cause. What was the motto of his newspaper? *Right is of no Sex. Truth is of no Color!*

Hurrah! I say.

Hear, hear! say Miss Bertha, raisin her teacup.

This Thursday we shall convene for our ninth Woman's Rights conference, and I shall proudly report to the delegates of your newly formed organization. Strength in numbers!

Can I go to the Woman's Rights Convention with you, Mrs. Heverworth?

It just popped out. I should've asked Auntie Eunice first! I glance at her, I know I'm gonna hear about *impertinence* later. But the expression on Mrs. Heverworth's face is somethin else altogether. Shock. Then, just a second, anger. Then sad.

One day, she say. One day, you will.

And somethin in the way she say it tell me she don't mean *One day when you grow up* because all the colored ladies here is grown-up, and suddenly I know ain't none of em invited to the Woman's Rights Convention.

Well, say Auntie Eunice. As you all know, we have come together to celebrate our culture, and to discuss the important issues of the day.

The ladies is slow to start, but then they begin on abolition and the Fugitive Slave Act and *Dred Scott*, and *tsk tsk* bout that old man upstate killin his sickly daughter with the hammer and everybody careful never ever to touch the important issue of the day goin on right in our room.

⁓

When Thursday the twelfth a May roll around, I head on up to Mozart Hall, Broadway betwixt Bond and Great Jones, which is north a Five Points but not far north as Union Square where the Academy a Music is. There go the ladies walkin in, wearin their big petticoat dresses like Mrs. Heverworth, none of em lookin colored or Irish or poor. A lotta ladies and also a lotta gentlemen, but almost all the gentlemen not with the ladies. Almost all the gentlemen very close to the ladies but just outside em, hootin n a-hollerin.

Women *should* have the vote! And birds as well since their brains are the same size!

Might I light your cigar, madam?

If your husband hasn't spanked you enough, I'll volunteer for the task.

Shave your mustache, madam?

I'm a shoemaker, say the spank-offer man lowerin his voice, and you might have heard we know what to do with a hammer.

Well, if it isn't Fido, my long lost hound. Here, boy!—and this man right up in a lady's face whistlin and barkin, and now I see the lady is Mrs. Heverworth. Some a the women huddlin, protectin each other from the tauntin gentlemen, but Mrs. Heverworth hold her head high. I can see the fear shinin in her eyes, her body tight but she keep walkin. The man follow her into the buildin, all the men followin the women into the buildin I know to keep up their rude-makin while the ladies try talkin about their rights. When everybody inside, the door close.

After the Ladies Cultural Forum meetin, I didn't wanna be Mrs. Heverworth's pet no more, but now I see some a the uptown ladies got their own kind a struggles if they're longin for somethin else in life besides Missus. If they want their strength in numbers, I think they got stuff to learn, and I'm hopin they will. Auntie Eunice said, *Hasn't every great societal change been initiated by the righteous impatient?* Then she brung the colored ladies together to be change-makers, while Auntie Siobhan makin her own change at her tavern, women's work, women's work knowin patience ain't never a virtue. *Solidarité.*

Steps

Sunday nights—and Thursdays, when business is light before the Friday and Saturday nighters. She closes the tavern, then goes.

Ciaran leanin gainst the buildin, his face-sweat turned to dirt lass hot Sunday a August.

Scrunch up your forehead all ye like, he go on. Never seen it yourself because *you* can't stay up that late.

I *can*!

Then meet me here tonight. Ten.

So here I be, Bottle Alley behind Baxter and Leonard hearin the church bell tollin ten, and after the sixth peal, I see my two grammies up there in the belfry dancin.

Wake up!

I jump! There Ciaran rollin his eyes. I fell asleep standin up!

Knew you couldn't stay awake. Here! Drink!

He hand me a tin cup. I don't wanna drink that coffee, thick and cold! But half the cup I down, and now my eyes wide: ready!

We hear the music a block away before me and Ciaran step inside the dance emporium. Packed! Hot! A colored man at the piano, Irish fiddler, colored with the banjo. Everybody dancin, everybody jaunty!

Only once did I ever attend a *ceilidh* back home, say Ciaran smilin.

What's a kay-lee?

Hoedown, Americans say. Partner dancin.

Well, what brings *you* two here?

Miss Fiona sittin with a drink. Now I notice Miss Sally on the dance floor, movin lively.

I never seen you outside a O'SHEA'S BOARD AND PUBLICK, Miss Fiona!

That's because I'm a work-at-home gal. But everyone needs a night free.

And there Mrs. Jewel and Mr. Jewel dancin! I never seen em merry since their baby girls died. Mrs. Jewel's belly startin to stick out a little. Then the music stop, and the piano-player say, Here we go!

The dance floor clearin, everyone backin away from the center, Ciaran and me cranin our necks to see. A Irish man and a colored man come out, shufflin and stompin, finger snappin, heel spinnin, *clickety clickety tap tap tap*, the fancy footwork! Everyone whoopin and cheerin, *More! More! More!* And they give us more! Then Ciaran touch my arm, point. As if I couldn't see myself who took the floor replacin the men.

Auntie Siobhan lift her dress so we spy her ankles, stompin and clompin, slip, slide, her feet so fast I hardly see em *rat a tat tat*tin like rain on the roof! Then a colored man dance right up to Auntie Siobhan, *click-stomp*in faster, then *she* go faster, then *he* go faster! They ain't partnerin, they competin! Everybody clappin and hootin *Tap it! Tap it! Tap it!* Auntie Siobhan win! Them both laughin. Then Auntie Siobhan go to the bar, leanin on it the sweat pourin, me happy the room so crowded she can't see me and Ciaran here seein her. Other people's dance-competin now, but hard for me take my eyes off my auntie. She swig her drink down, then turn to look right at Ciaran and me, give us a wink.

❧

Auntie Siobhan won the dancin last night!

Grammy Cahill's eyes narrow at me over her table, the top glintin in the hot sun. And how would *you* know that?

Oh, say nearby Maeve, Grammy's dearest friend and fiercest competitor, your aul granny's the *real* stepper in the family. Belle of Kerry, she was.

Grammy, who'd been gettin ready to snap at me for bein where I shouldn'ta been, now go a little pink. Then smile.

Oh, granddaughter, close your mouth before it fills of flies! What you saw last night when you were where you shouldn't've? They're the steps we brought over from the Isle. Yes, I had quite the click in my heels, stompin all over the county. Siobhan was the one I passed the magic feet on to.

Then I *click click* shuffle slip slide. Grammy take to laughin.

Look like your fancy feet moved down another generation, say Maeve.

Grammy's eyes look to the left, look to the right, no approachin customers. Then, sittin in her chair, her feet under the table start to move: *clickety tap click*.

Ah, there she doin the jig! say Maeve.

Right, now take this wool up to Cathleen. Need to keep it nice till we figure out what use it might be.

It's soft, Grammy!

Don't get it dirty!

I won't!

Reminds me of home. When your mother was your size, she *loved* the sheep. She *did?*

Found her nappin nestled into a ewe on more than one occasion.

I run out in a skip. The wool piece is big so don't think Grammy'll miss this little clump I slip into my gunny-sack. Deliver the rest to Cathleen, then head to O'SHEA'S BOARD & PUBLICK.

Auntie Siobhan! Where you learn them steps?

Her shelvin the new stock a liquor behind the bar.

What steps? she say, but little smile on her lips.

These ns! Then me shufflin and stompin and tappin. Auntie Siobhan throw her head back, the laughter.

Well. Was a time I spent most nights in the dance halls. You stay away from em! No place for a nine-year-old.

But where you learn em?

She shelve the last bottle, then look at me.

Tell ye a story.

Pull myself up on a barstool!

I've mentioned before when your mother was young, she loved to dance. Never said she was a *keen* dancer, but made up for it with her joy in the step. How she caught your father's eye, while I sat shy on the sides, flowerin the wall. But then somebody caught *my* eye, somebody steppin up a storm, turnin like a tornado!

Your dead husband Niall O'Shea!

No! This somebody's feet was enthrallin, liftin me to blue heaven.

I puzzle over that. Auntie Siobhan never mention no men in her life. I only know of her dead husband, and she don't like to talk about that one.

Eunice.

I wait for my auntie to go on, Eunice who? Then she smile.

My *Auntie* Eunice?

Open it wider and you'll be swallowin flies. *Yes,* your Auntie Eunice, queen of the dance hall!

Auntie Eunice don't go to dance halls! Auntie Eunice is temperance!

She no longer frequents our social emporiums, but *those* days. Auntie Siobhan sigh. I was enamored, week after week watchin her. Then finally work up my nerve. Stella up, my voice catchin. Ti ach me a step?

She *did*?

No! She laughed, sipped her drink. Yes, she'd tasted a drop or two in her time, but always respectable, never saw her except Saturday nights and never drank to drunk, just enough I'd wager to give her feet the courage. Turned out those were some of her last dance-hall days. Soon after she'd be teachin. And married.

If Auntie Eunice never give ya the steps, how'd you learn to dance so good?

Practicin, I got better. And the dance-hall men only *too* happy to help a young girl with the moves. One time, with Eunice on a rest, I was hoverin near her—well, who wasn't? She was the star! And seen her gazin at the dance floor, her eyes right on *my sister*, on *your mother* and her partner! And someone sneers: Four left feet between em, have they? expectin Eunice's approval of his ungenerous assessment. Now I might've been a shy dancer then, but never was I a shy fighter! I snatched up the critic by his collar, my fist reared back, then stunned to see another hand clutchin the same collar. Me protectin Brigid's step-honor, and her protectin Ezekiel's—and that's when I found out my sister's sweetheart, your father, was illustrious Eunice's brother!

Ah! But my parents didn't really have four left feet.

That's an expression, and in the realm of that expression, yes they did, but it was no one's business but theirs. Brigid was two years older than me and Zeke two more than Eunice, but your other auntie and me took it upon ourselves to chaperone the lovers home that evenin, makin certain they parted for two *separate* homes. This should've annoyed them, but the power of it. Their feelins for each other, Eunice and me could just sense ourselves disappearin before them. And not long after, weddin bells. Your ma and da may've never picked up the fancy steppin but nothin to worry on: You're here because they figured out all the moves they needed.

Let's tie the knot! Shit on the pot!

My singin get Auntie Siobhan to cacklin her head off, and me too! Then she say, No, that would be the theme music to *my* weddin. So walkin home behind your future parents, your Auntie Eunice and me chatted ourselves into friends. Close, for a while.

How come you and Auntie Eunice ain't friends still?

And Auntie Siobhan's voice go flat: Ask your Auntie Eunice.

Then Auntie Siobhan go back to her bottle inventory, I figure the conversation over. But after a minute: *clink clink clinkety clink*, I start hearin the glass. Auntie Siobhan holdin the bottles on her bar counter, makin em tap out the feet rhythm!

⁓

Nex day: *plink plink plink plink plink plink plink plink*.

I like your song, Auntie Eunice! Whatcha call it?

The major scales! Miss Bertha taught me. I'm taking piano lessons!

Plink plink plink plink, I take to shuffle stomp tap to it. Auntie Eunice stop plinkin.

Where'd you learn that!

I stare at her.

Did Siobhan take you to a dance hall?

No!

Liars go to hell!

She never took me, me and Ciaran snuck in!

Auntie Eunice's hands on her hips. You can't go to school but you can go to tippling houses! You're heading down a rotten path, Theodora!

Auntie Siobhan won her dance contest, but she say *you* was the dance *queen*!

Auntie Eunice's eyebrows raise, then I feel *my* eyebrows raise, not knowin what's comin next. Then she shrug.

Long time ago.

You know the steps? *True?* The Irish steps?

Irish? Those steps in the dance emporia are *African*, passed down the generations!

Grammy Cahill said Irish.

No! Then Auntie Eunice take a ponder. Well, I suppose they're both. Where the African and the Irish came together.

Like me!

She smile a little, play another scale. Then stop.

When Charles Dickens came to New York in the early 'forties, he was revolted by what he saw in Five Points and documented it in his *American Notes for General Circulation*. But there was one aspect of our neighborhood which enchanted that curmudgeon.

The dancin?

Master Juba.

Who?

William Henry Lane, lord of the step! I suppose I *was* admired for my foot moves in our regular dance hall, but wherever Juba made his appearance, *he* was emperor of the floor! Dickens was dazzled, this young negro's astonishing strides. I was fifteen when I began the night life, when I first saw him, he but nineteen and already crowned King. Sometimes he competed with John Diamond, the New York–born Irish step champion—on the dance floor, or on the theater stage to the tune of five hundred dollars *apiece*.

Feel my mouth stretch wide! Then close it before Auntie Eunice mention flies.

And I wasn't the only girl batting eyes Juba's direction. Women *and* men beguiled and bewitched by his maneuvers. He was nimble, he was spry, spin and roll his eyes sly!

You jus make up that pome, Auntie Eunice?

Yes! He could shuffle, he could fly, no one could take away their eyes! Or ears.

Where's he now?

Dead. Did a European tour and passed away there, not yet thirty. Auntie Eunice sigh, starin at the piano. I am a Christian, and I am for temperance, I no longer go to dance halls, a temptation for sin. But I do miss music. I was so grateful to Mrs. Heverworth for the piano: music right in my own home! And yet, until I have mastered the instrument on even a rudimentary level, and that may take a long, long, long, *long* time—Oh, I do miss the fiddle! And the banjo. And skilled fingers on the ivories. *Mary Had a Little Lamb* and the major scales *do* lose their charm after a time!

Then Auntie Eunice start tappin and brushin and clickin her fingers on the piano.

Auntie Eunice, you sure know the shoe rhythm!

She smile, her fingers still dancin.

Auntie Siobhan said the dance-hall days, you and her got to be friends.

Auntie Eunice stop finger-dancin and close the cover over the piano keys.

I've got to start supper, she mutter and disappear into her kitchen, the only music now the *clang bang* a pans.

⌁

Two days later's Thursday first a September, and I remember Ciaran sayin Thursday's the other night Auntie Siobhan go to the dance hall. There he be, got a horseshoe in his hand in the stalls behind the Spanish Company.

I can't go anymore, I got too used to the coffee. Fallin asleep at work Monday near got me sacked.

We only gone wunst!

You only gone wunst. 'Twas my third excursion. He hold the horse's right hind hoof in his left hand and hammer in the new shoe with his right.

My papa done that. Workin with the horses. How come you gotta change the horse's shoe?

Why didn't you ask your papa?

Because he died when I was two! Because I'm askin *you*!

Horses' feet change. Grow.

Oh.

Ciaran toss a old horseshoe in the corner with other old shoes, *clink*.

Can I hammer on a horseshoe? Bet my papa woulda taught me the trade if he lived. Bet I woulda been good at it. A girl could do it, like my cousin Hen, she's strong. Remember Hen, from your bowlin-alley days—

Shush! Your loud mouth carries, they come out wanna know why I'm s'idle I can be havin some chatty tea party!

What gonna happen to the old shoes?

Melted down to liquid, later to harden into shoes again.

Can I have one?

D'ye think my bosses would tolerate me just givin old metal away?

I watch Ciaran a while. I don't like what he just said so I guess I got nothin else to say. Then he go to the corner where the old horseshoes is, grab one, come to me and slip it into my gunny-sack.

Now scoot, he say soft, then back to start hangin on the horse's left hind hoof.

⌒〜〇

In the evenin, it's quiet at the tavern. Most every workin body only got Sunday off, if that, so Saturday's always the crowdest night, and Friday for the ones might wanna get a early start on weekend drinkin. While Auntie Siobhan's servin customers, I sip from her cup a coffee.

The dance hall rockin and a-rollickin, packed! Sittin on the floor betwixt chairs, betwixt two ones laughin and clappin, I wanna *be* on the dance space and do the step but fear hearin *Get that kid outa here*!

And there Auntie Siobhan. Four days since seein her fancy footwork on Sunday, I'm thinkin she *couldn'ta* danced *that* fast. But now I see my memory's right! Her feet quick, agile-tappin, my eyes can't keep up with em! Everybody clear the floor, everybody eyes glued to Auntie Siobhan's stylin steps!

And now two more feet next to hers, kickin up the skill even more! I look up at the face. I can't believe it! I look at Auntie Siobhan. *She* can't believe it! But there she be: Auntie Eunice grinnin and *clickety clack*in her legs like a blur like God himself blew bliss into her toes!

Then the music change and everybody out to the floor again. I can't see my aunties! I search for em, but don't want em to see *me* here, specially Auntie Eunice. There someone got a bun just like her—no, not Auntie Eunice. There someone with red strands flyin outa her rolled-up hair just like Auntie Siobhan—wait. Wait, what—? Somethin, I feel—I try movin but it don't move, fingers. Fingers reachin, fingers fiddlin under my dress, I scream!

Lightnin fass as their feet, both my aunties here, yellin and pokin at the man behind me, him glassy-eyed drunk, smilin like embarrassment shakin his head no, hands up surrender but my aunties keep up the harsh-talk, him backin to the door, backin out the door but them not lettin up, crowd partin to let em through and I right behind my aunties, us steppin outside the hot dance hall into the warm night, and now Auntie Eunice take her fancy feet and kick him in the shins, now his smile wiped off, *Bitch!* which trigger Auntie Siobhan to take the empty bottle she's holdin and crash it, slash his face, he screamin, and her: *Now ye're marked* and he pull back his fist but Auntie Siobhan quick with that jagged half-bottle at his throat and he stumble off fass, gone.

Disgrace to the race! holler Auntie Eunice after him.

Race? say Auntie Siobhan. Took him for mulatto, did ye? I was certain I heard a bit of Cork in that lovely moniker he dreamed up for ye.

Then they start arguin whether the man was colored or Irish.

Maybe both. Mutt, like me.

Well, what were *you* doing in there *anyway*, Little Miss Grown? Suppose your Auntie Siobhan finds it proper and fine.

And what were *you* doin in there, Miss Temperance? Today a holiday for teetotalers, is it?

I was not tippling! I just missed music, I didn't drink a drop! I'm thirsty!

Auntie Eunice storm down the street to the public pump, me and Auntie Siobhan followin. Auntie Eunice pump into her hands, drink, pump into her hands, drink, then turn to me.

You went looking for trouble, and found it!

Your Auntie Eunice is right. I told ye: dance emporiums not for little girls!

And if you wonder why, it's because they're full of *men*, as you just witnessed.

Can't trust them.

Beasts!

Dogs!

Swine!

Arses! *I'm* thirsty!

Auntie Siobhan stick her head under the pump, then wave for Auntie Eunice to pump. She do, and the flow come gushin into Auntie Siobhan's mouth, all over her face.

Swap! say Auntie Eunice and they do, Auntie Siobhan pumpin and Auntie Eunice's head under all unladylike, all unEunicelike, her tongue and face drenched in the rush. Then they both pump for me, and while I drink they look at each other's wet faces wet dresses and take to laughin and keep pumpin my fill and every time their gigglin almost wither, somethin in the seein each other have em roarin again.

My bladder, say Auntie Siobhan.

Makes two of us, say Auntie Eunice, and me and her follow Auntie Siobhan to O'SHEA'S BOARD & PUBLICK, round back to the outhouse. In the pitch black, me and Auntie Eunice stumblin, but drunk Auntie Siobhan who know her property like back a her hand walk sober straight. Polite, she let Auntie Eunice go first, and soon's she shut the door behind her, Auntie Siobhan slump against the privy outside-wall like asleep. Auntie Eunice come out, Auntie Siobhan go in, and by the time they're both through, church bells toll half-past.

Must be eleven thirty, say Auntie Eunice, yawnin. Time I'd be getting—

You shoulda stayed friends after my mammy and papa died!

They both stare at me.

You don't need em alive to be friends, you're friends now.

Our separation weren't about their passin. 'Twas about their burial.

I look at Auntie Siobhan. I look at Auntie Eunice.

Because your Cahill family decided to bury your mother in the Catholic cemetery where your father could never be.

How were *we* to know? Non-Catholic spouses was always welcome in the Catholic grave-yard!

Apparently not.

We didn't know that *particular* grave-yard had a colored ban! The downtown Irish cemetery was full. *Your Cahill family decided*—we decided nothin! The cemetery we used was the cemetery we could afford!

How about the colored cemetery?

Think we'd bury Brigid far from the Virgin's watch? We didn't know there was a colored ban! We didn't expect Zeke to follow so soon!

And on they go, the mystery a the family bicker now finally come clear. Anywhere but Five Points, race be reason enough for in-laws never to speak, I love Five Points! But yet and still, my families find cause for feud. What's the difference? I wanna say. Ain't my mother and father together in heaven? But I can see reasonableness from a kid be the lass thing they're havin. Voices gettin sharper, I don't know what they're sayin, I jus hear noise, noise, and feel a twinge between my legs that bad man put there, I don't like it I don't like it I don't like it.

Theo! Why're ye cryin, *mo stoirín*?

Sugarplum! What's the matter?

I don't know! I don't know!

Then the three of us sittin on the ground, me bawlin between em.

Can you find the Big Dipper?

Easy, I tell Auntie Eunice through my sobs, and point.

How about the Little Bear? ask Auntie Siobhan.

Then we're namin em: the Dippers and Bears, North Star, Cassiopeia, Leo the Lion, Scorpio and Sagittarius, the Triangle: everybody in the world know the night sky but callin em out never get old. Auntie Eunice say when she was a kid she thought the Milky Way was a silver path leadin to some magic world. Auntie Siobhan thought the Milky Way was where the sky was crackin open and one day we'd all get sucked through it. Then she say when she was little she thought Moon and the Mars was gonna get married one day, except when she say *Moon* she point to that bright gold star planet and when she say *the Mars* she point to the silver sliver, and Auntie Eunice say, Drunk! You can't even talk. *Mars. The* moon.

But I like *Moon and the Mars*, and I think maybe they *did* get married, Brigid and Ezekiel comin together and bindin two bright lights: the Brook and the Cahill, the Irish and the colored, the fiery and the calm—except that last is somethin both families brung. Took fire for my grammy and mammy and auntie and great-uncle and cousins to survive the Famine and the coffin ships, fire for my grammy and gran-gran and new auntie to survive slavery. And the calm keepin em all goin every day, whether food and comfort's bountiful or scarce. Moon and the Mars supplementin and complementin each other for it sure be a lonely sky without em both.

I got a idea, I say, and outa my gunny-sack I pull out the horseshoe and the wool. They look confused, then they look clear.

The park, say Auntie Siobhan.

Most of the new Central Park's still under construction, though the lower part opened for public ice skatin lass winter. But we know Auntie Siobhan means *the* park, the one my parents would remember—City Hall Park, which we figure is ground that'll always be undisturbed. We walk to it, kneel together. Auntie Eunice say The Lord Is My Shepherd, then Auntie Siobhan say Hail Mary Full of Grace, and then we take wool like the sheep my ma loved and a horseshoe like the work my papa loved and bury em together. Auntie Siobhan clutch my left hand and Auntie Eunice take my right, then it only make sense in the triangle they hold each other's. And now the sky light up. Green colors, yella, bright red-pinks. Lookin up, all our mouths open wide enough for a pack a flies!

We stroll up through Five Points, walkin north and west to Greenwich Village where Auntie Eunice delight Auntie Siobhan with her piano. Now my cyclids fallin, startin to win the battle gainst the coffee, but my aunties still chatterin. Middle a the night, I wake in Auntie Eunice's bed, snuggled between two aunties.

⌖

Aurora borealis! Largest solar storm on record!

Telegraph communications extinguished! Telegraph operators receiving electric shocks!

Northern lights visible as far south as Cuba!

Bright mornin I come out to the parlor, where my aunties whisper-gigglin over coffee, payin no attention to the newsboys outside. Then Auntie Eunice show a few dance moves to Auntie Siobhan, and Auntie Siobhan got a couple new toe tricks of her own to share, and maybe, I wonder, these might be their first steps back to friends. Jus like the powerful modern telegraph unhinged easy by the age-old northern lights, could be an old family grudge turn out to be no match against my aunties' rekindlin kinship with the *slide shuffle slide tap tap.*

Trap

Ch!

Mr. John O'Mahony stop. He jus come in the saloon through the back door, and Auntie Siobhan make a sound like *Sh!* but quicker so it don't disturb the goin-ons. The goin-ons is black cat with white streaks and half a right ear sittin up center a the floor whilst me and Ciaran and Auntie Siobhan on the sides stooped watchin.

Here it come: mouse run out from the right wall, cat's face snap to it. Mouse run crost the floor, cat's eyes follow. Mouse run off to the left wall, disappear. Cat stare. Cat start lickin its paw.

That's your mouser? say Auntie Siobhan to Ciaran. But Ciaran rollin on the floor, cacklin his head off.

Sorry! Sorry, I didn't know the cat'd be so, em . . .

Indifferent, I believe the word is, she say, and Ciaran find that funnier still.

Hadn't meant to interrupt, Siobhan. You'd said if the back door's open to come in—

That I did. I'll be gettin your tea, John.

Ya shoulda brung the cat what *won* the fight.

What's that? Auntie Siobhan say to me, Mr. O'Mahony's little wood box in her hand.

That cat—I point to what we're lookin at—and another was in a nasty tussle, Ciaran brung the loser.

He was mindin his own business, say Ciaran, when that white devil appears from nowhere and ambushes him! Scratchin, bitin, tore his ear off!

You watched the brawl and brought me the *defeated?* The victor, *that's* the mouser!

That white cat's crazy, mutter Ciaran. Pickin a fight just for the sake of pickin a fight.

Crazy cat's what I *need!* Attack anythin! Thank you, John.

I'll be seeing you in the morning, Siobhan. And Mr. O'Mahony leave with his swapped tea box.

I know a stray cat just have six babies under my Auntie Maryam's back outside steps! Maybe one of em's a mouser.

Newborn kittens are too small to leave their mother. And these fat mice would terrorize the poor thing. I need that champion cat, the one somewhere nibblin on this one's ear as we speak.

Well, ye won't be gettin it from me, Ciaran say. I seen that tabby pace the wooden fence behind the Spanish Company while I work, waitin to pounce, *I* shan't be the prey. Ciaran knead the black n white behind the ear and behind where the other ear useta be, make it purr.

There's bear traps and fox traps, why's no one yet invented a *mouse* trap? Auntie Siobhan sigh.

Você gosta disso? Ciaran say soft.

What?

Spanish, learnt it from some of my bosses at the Spanish Company, he tell her. Asked kitty if he liked my pettin.

What's today?

Tuesday, October the eleventh, I answer her.

And the rodents already settin up camp here, be an infestation come winter!

Nothin I can do, Ciaran say. I take a step close to that beady-eyed white cat and it hiss a cutthroat threat!

Make it worth your while? say Auntie Siobhan. Then she hold up a gold Indian-head dollar. Ciaran's mouth fly open.

One week. Bring that mad cat back by Tuesday the eighteenth: payment in full.

I can help! I like cats! Ciaran, me and you snag the white devil together: four bits apiece!

Another mouse run crost the floor. Black-n-white tabby comfy in Ciaran's arms raise a eyelid. Then back to its nap, never interruptin the purrin

Don't touch! Auntie Maryam say that afternoon.

I won't, jus lookin at em!

The stray cat had her litter under the steps leadin up to Auntie Maryam's door: a black one and a black-n-white, three tan, one white. Auntie Maryam warned when they got borned: touch and the mother abandon em.

I told Auntie Siobhan about em, she got mice, lookin for a mouser. But she say they too little.

Mm hm. Auntie Maryam sittin on her little porch-stoop knittin, both us outside enjoyin the chilly crisp sunny October-ness. She got long sleeves and gloves and her dress hang to her shoes, face covered in her garden net-hat so she don't gotta put on her light-skin disguise.

You comin to Gran-Gran's birthday Friday?

She nod. Only reach eighty wunst. Bring my turkey-kale.

I love your turkey-seasonin, Auntie Maryam! You the onliest person I know don't care for pork.

Then I see what she knittin: bootee.

Auntie Maryam! You fillin the Room of Hope!

She shake her head.

This for your Auntie Eunice.

I gasp! She look at me.

Guess they ain't tells ya. She not due till March, new mother wants to keep the word local, case somethin go wrong. You keeps the secret?

I nod.

You not happy bout Auntie Eunice?

I'm happy! she snap. Then soft: I'm happy. Just a bit blue, my own account. Eunice saze to me wunst, They only let me teach because I must be barren, all these years no issue. Her and me shared that. Now I gots no one share it with. Not even the cat.

What're you reading? Cathleen ask me nex day.

I look up at her on the couch, me on the floor, book in my lap. Ciaran on the floor crost from me, got that torn-eared cat wrapped round his neck.

Some new book my Auntie Eunice tole me to read, they gonna talk about it at the ladies' salon Sunday. Them dresses could fit *me*, Cathleen!

Simple children's smocks, she shrug. I need to finish by four, Ma'll pick them up for the Wednesday shipment tonight.

Where they ship em to?

Purrrrrrrr.

That cat has the loudest purr I've ever heard!

But it don't chase no mice! I tell her. Auntie Siobhan was mad! But Ciaran and me gonna get the mean cat for her.

What makes you think *you* can help me with that white feline?

You hold the cat, I hold the trap.

Ha! Ye mean ye watch it gash me till the blood leakin outa all my veins while *you* grip a burlap bag. And for that ye expect to split eight bits even.

Does your cat have a name? say Cathleen, her teeth snappin the thread.

Joaquim. Christened her this mornin.

Joaquim?

Spanish. One of my bosses has that name.

You need me! I say. Can't snag that mean cat all by yourself.

If ye want to be a part, the share is sixty-forty my favor, and *you* find the sack.

But—

More than fair! *You're* not riskin life n limb. And I'm the boss, you're the helper.

How do you spell *Joaquim?* Cathleen ask.

J-O-A-Q—

But you can't *do* it by yourself!

I get to work dawn, there she is: the white demon walkin the fence. Be there tomorrow crack of daylight with a burlap bag you want the forty coppers. Or don't.

Joaquim doesn't sound Spanish to me.

You know anybody Spanish? Ciaran ask Cathleen.

Spain's in the newspapers. America fighting Spain over Cuba, over Santo Domingo, I read the names of the people, of the places, they don't read like what you just said.

I know Spanish, I *work* for Spanish. Joaquim and Ramalho and Bartolomeu and João. Except I can't call em by first name, I gotta call em *Senhor.*

Cocks crowin nex morn, and there be the white cat, pacin top a the wood fence.

He look mean!

Because *she is* mean.

How you know *she*?

She's famous. Rumor is she had a litter, then went mad.

She lookin right at us!

Ciaran move so slight I ain't sure he did, till the kitty stop pacin and fire a hiss at him, hiss like Satan himself!

Maybe you was right the first time, Ciaran, maybe we can't catch that white cat.

For eight bits, we'll catch it.

But maybe we can get another cat. Them kittens at my Auntie Maryam's is growin, at least *one* gotta be a mouser! We'll bring all six to Auntie Siobhan, see which—

Sh!

Hiss!

I whisper, Look! It gonna fall, standin on that loose board.

Ciaran shake his head. She knows balance. Then he turn to me, me holdin the bag I brung tight, but the bag shakin! Ciaran stare at it.

I don't think that's gonna work.

I know! We need to leave that mad cat be!

I don't think the *sack's* gonna work.

He look around, spy a wood crate in the corner. He careful cautious move to it, pick it up, bring to where we're standin.

See that bottle?

I nod.

Put down the sack, then go pick up that bottle. *Slow.*

I look at him. He gimme a scowl. I do it.

Now, he say, go to the other side of the fence, throw the bottle at the cat.

No!

Shush!

Why you wamme hit the cat?

You *won't* hit it, you don't have the aim or the strength—

I *do*!

You don't, you'll just scare it. That's what I need.

No

Then gimme the bag and scoot. Dollar for me, zero for you.

I hit it, cat'll jump me!

No, I think the scare'll cause it to jump down *this* side, runnin *from* you.

Think or you *know*?

Even if it fall your side, it'll be runnin away, won't go after you.

Think or you *know*?

Never mind, do it m'self. Fraidy cat.

I'll do it!

I look at the cat. Cat glare at me. I creep round the fence, cat's eyes stuck to me all the while.

On the other side, I step light toward the white rotten pickets, kitty givin me the glower but now she gotta keep a watch both ways: me here and Ciaran to her left. I swallow, then rear back with that bottle when all a sudden a pigeon fly low on Ciaran's side, cat make a leap for it, fall! Pigeon screamin but fly off free. I scamper through the fence loose board just in time to see Ciaran slam that crate down top a the cat! Claws slashin through the slats, Ciaran: Ow!

Ciaran standin on the crate, below him paws, claws poppin out every-where.

Get up here with me.

My eyes big.

Jump!

I jump up, land on top a the crate with him.

I'm gonna get them rocks. You stay. Hear?

I nod. But I don't wanna!

Ciaran lift a big heavy rock, put it on the crate, then get another. The two stones in place, he tell me step off careful. I do.

She ain't clawin s'much no more, I say.

Wearin herself down.

We takin her to Auntie Siobhan's?

He shake his head. Not till I train her. Not till she answers to me.

Ciaran slow circle the crate, cat's eyes follow him.

Today's Thursday, he say, eyes on the caged critter, five days before the day she said bring the cat. In five days, that white devil'll be eatin out of my palm.

Cat make a low sound: growl from the throat.

First step to winnin an animal's trust: let it smell your hand, Ciaran say. Then stoop to the crate and hold out his fingers.

Cat slash Ciaran's fingers.

Ow! Fuck!

⌒♭

Eighty, say Gran-Gran Friday evenin, shakin her head. Can't believe it. Eighty!

Mijn gelukwenschen met uw verjaardag, Mama.

Bedankt, dochter. Gran-Gran thankin Grammy for the best wishes. That word I know's daughter, not doctor.

Grammy Brook and Auntie Eunice (who I only now notice got the barest hill of a belly) and Hen and light-skin Auntie Maryam and Mr. Samuel and Mr. Freeman gathered around Gran-Gran, and pigs' feet in vinegar and potatas and asparagus and turkey-kale: feast!

You have one day do again, which it be, Miss Lioda?

We ain't sure Gran-Gran heard Auntie Maryam, but we quiet a while in case. Then she turn to Grammy and speak: Emancipation Day. 'Twenty-eight.

I frown. But New York emancipation was eighteen twenty-*seven*.

What she mean, Grammy say, emancipation come to New York State July the fourth, eighteen and twenty-seven. By then, most New York black was free anyway, 'tweren't much sacrifice to the white economy. But emancipation only applied to those colored born before 1799. Whoever born 1799 to 1817, which was me: indentured servant till twenty-two if female, twenty-five if male. I was twenty-one so had to serve one more year. What Mama's sayin is emancipation for her truly happened a year later, when *I* was set free.

Jedediah, say Gran-Gran, smilin at Grammy. I love hearin Grammy's name!

But, Grammy go on, the worst: children born to mothers still slaves had to serve till age twenty-one! And my oldest, Henry Floy, just three.

My pa, say Hen.

Your pa, say Grammy.

My pa was free.

Yes! Grammy say. Lived free! till the epidemic took him too soon. Master Broek coulda let me go Emancipation Day and didn't. One more year, said he. But he also coulda held Floy till manhood and he let him go when I become free, for that I thank God.

Godsijdank, say Gran Gran.

So Emancipation Day 1827. And *our* family's emancipation: 1828.

Parade, say Gran-Gran.

Four thousand! say Grammy, takin Gran-Gran's hand. Four thousand of us marchin down Broadway, the master and mistress let me walk with the 1827ers. Happy Fifth of July!

Fif? say Auntie Maryam.

We was emancipated the fourth, but the fourth sacred to too many opposed to emancipation, ones liable to bring on the ugly hootin n hollerin.

Like Riot a 'Fifty-seven? I ask.

Like Riot a *'Thirty-four*, say Grammy.

I remember *that* one, say Auntie Eunice. Just turned four, but sealed in my consciousness.

What's Riot a 'Thirty-four?

Summer, Grammy answer me. White Lewis Tappan invites colored Reverend Samuel Cornish to sit with him for services at Laight Street Presbyterian. Cornish and Tappan both abolitionists.

Silk importer Tappan, Auntie Eunice say, renowned a few years later for his journalistic reporting on that *Amistad* case, the kidnapped Africans winning their freedom.

In 'thirty-four, Grammy say, those Presbyterians sposed to be enlightened people but ain't their feathers ruffled, black in a pew up near the front. Them days not too many abolitionists in New York, most a the antislavery white people was pro-colonization: free the blacks then ship em to Liberia quick! Tappan's affront smoldered till Fourth a July, some ruffians got rough at an abolition meetin in a church, others bullyin negroes outa the park. Over the followin days come more brawls, attacks on Tappan's home, and finally an out-n-out riot destroyin and lootin black property: the Mutual Relief Hall, churches and workplaces, homes wrecked to pieces, families with small children left penniless and homeless, this was *here!* Five Points! Dwindled the colored population. *That's* why negroes celebrate *Fifth* a July, not Fourth!

Amen! say Gran-Gran, then: Cake! Which I'm happy to hear as I been smellin it since Auntie Eunice brung it through the door.

～⌒

Saturday supper at Grammy Cahill's, everybody restin after the long work-week except Auntie Siobhan, already left for her busiest saloon night.

You heard a the Riot a 'Thirty-four, Grammy?

I have, granddaughter. Before we set foot on these shores, but the American Irish ahead of us remember it well. That Morse—one come up with the Morse code—hated Catholics. In 'thirty-four, he's writin articles for the *New York Observer*, come to be published in a popular sellin pamphlet. *Foreign*—? *Foreign . . .*

Foreign Conspiracy Against the Liberties of the United States, say Great-Uncle Fergus in his chair who I thought was sleep, eyes still closed.

Outlinin the plot by the Vatican to take over America. Foolishness! But the message spread like wildfire, and the ones hadn't read it *heard* of it and believed it. So, when in the summer of 'thirty-four a silly rumor catches on about a Protestant girl bein held against her will at a convent outside of Boston, a mob burns down the nunnery and goes after the nearby Catholic homes as well.

Beecher! say Great-Uncle Fergus.

Lyman Beecher, reverend father of the reverend Henry Ward, say Grammy.

Henry Ward preaches abolition in Brooklyn!

Cathleen chuckle. You mean, she say to me, he's an *abolitionist* preacher at a Brooklyn *church*.

His sister wrote *Uncle Tom's Cabin*!

Sure the Beechers are all abolitionists, say Grammy.

The offspring more radical than the father, Cathleen say.

And the father *also* riled up the populace with his anti-Catholic talk, say Grammy.

Abolitionists, Great-Uncle Fergus grumble. Some of these staunch foes of slavery is just as staunch against Catholic, I'll tell ye.

Which I'm afraid, sigh Grammy, has caused some Irish to put two and two together and come up with a mess of a sum.

❧

At the Sunday Ladies Cultural Forum, Auntie Eunice say, The preface and appendix make clear the novel is a highly autobiographical work of fiction. I understand the writer's desire for anonymity, but I am glad to know the author has been identified as a negro sister.

A published novel by a colored woman! say Miss Hazel.

Eight of us: me and Auntie Eunice and Auntie Maryam in her light-skin and Miss Bertha and Miss Hazel Greene who used to teach with Auntie Eunice, plus Miss Bertha's niece Mrs. Robbins, who got a baby belly a lot bigger n Auntie Eunice's, and Miss Sarah Daniels who teaches at the African Free School where Auntie Eunice went to school herself, and Mrs. Robbins's friend Mrs. Watkins.

I only wish our first literary creative work could have had a different title, say Miss Bertha.

But *Our Nig* is a perfect appellation! cry Mrs. Watkins. The way the poor girl was treated.

Yes, say Miss Sarah, I do agree. The double entendre as a term of endearment from the more humane members of the family and of derision from the cruel mother and daughter is ingenious.

Irony! say Miss Bertha.

I must say, I have had some spirited disputes with some of my white abolitionist compatriots over the content, say Miss Hazel.

Disputes? say Mrs. Watkins.

May I venture a guess as to the source of their discomfort? ask Mrs. Robbins. Might they have been troubled by the central theme—that a colored indentured servant of the *North* could be so horridly abused by her mistress?

Precisely! say Miss Hazel.

Oh, say Miss Bertha, the so-called enlightened blinding themselves to their own Yankee evil deeds!

For some, say Miss Sarah, I imagine it's a fear that the South could accuse hypocrisy.

The South would be correct, say Miss Hazel. Who buys the cotton from Dixie but the Yanks?

Still, the author did *not* intend this as a rebuke to *Uncle Tom's Cabin*, as some have alleged, say Mrs. Robbins, to Mrs. Stowe's criticism of the (Mrs. Robbins's eyes start rollin) Southern way of life.

The protagonist, Frado: a Topsy of the North! cry Mrs. Watkins. A tortured, tormented, battered, broken orphan! Six years old when she was left with that horrible white family!

I myself despised the ineffectual husband more than the tyrant mistress, say Miss Daniels.

For the man to have sympathized with the child, but too cowardly to stand up to his own brutal, conniving wife . . . say Miss Bertha, shakin her head.

I very much appreciated that Frado was willful, say Auntie Eunice.

Oh yes! say Mrs. Robbins. When Mrs. Bellmont would not even allow her a clean plate for her dinner—

Permitted to eat only after the white family finished! cry Mrs. Watkins.

Then the old beast mistress handing Frado her own filthy plate and ordering Frado to eat from it, say Miss Bertha.

To which Frado first had the dog lick clean! say Miss Hazel. She greatly preferred a canine's slobbers to her mistress's!

Everybody laugh at that one!

But of course, say Miss Sarah, as soon as poor Frado was alone with Mrs. Bellmont, the mistress beat her soundly.

The raw-hide, sigh Auntie Eunice.

The kicks! say Mrs. Watkins.

Slapping her precious little head, say Mrs. Robbins.

Denying her supper! say Mrs. Watkins. Whipping her! Propping her mouth open with that piece of wood and leaving her like that in the dark alone!

Everybody quiet.

Very frustrating, my discussion with my Caucasian colleagues, say Miss

Hazel. Oh, there were certainly some admirable radicals who praised the author's honesty and courage, but many others were loath to believe it could be anything but fiction, Oh no, *never* in the North! Some refused to read the book! And of course there are always those who assume a white person actually wrote it, how could *we*, with our small brains? So many whites who despise slavery, but admonish any suggestion of *equality*—

The child wrecked! Growing into adulthood sickly and penniless! and Mrs. Watkins break down sobbin.

Mrs. Watkins? say Auntie Eunice.

Of course she's distraught, say Miss Bertha, who among us was *not* affected by these truths? Frado's story was shocking but certainly not surprising—

It happened to me! Mrs. Watkins scream.

Everybody stare.

My father a cooper's apprentice, my mother a laundress. Then I woke one night: fire! I was so small, *I* escaped, but . . . And she bawlin again.

We're so sorry, Mrs. Watkins, say Miss Sarah.

This white family took me in, the *Quintons*. But in my case both wife *and* husband were cruel, *and* the children. The beatings! The loneliness!

Oh, poor dear! her friend Mrs. Robbins say.

Look at it! cry Mrs. Watkins, turnin to the appendix in the book. *She was indeed a slave, in every sense of the word*—

No, say Auntie Maryam, and because Auntie Maryam never speak, everybody turn to her.

Treated like slave, say Auntie Maryam. But Frado leave: eighteen. Not slave.

Mrs. Wright is correct, say Miss Bertha. Though Frado's youthful existence was a living hell, the effects of her maltreatment permanently impairing her, still, she was not locked into an entire life of subjugation. Her misfortune would be more accurately classified as indentured servitude.

Call it what you will! cry Mrs. Watkins. I was treated like *dirt. You* don't know! You've always had *everything*!

Vera! say Mrs. Robbins.

That's not so, say Miss Bertha. Mr. Williams and I have *struggled*. Yes, he is now a respected clerk, but he began as a porter at that hotel.

Papa worked hard! say Mrs. Robbins.

Respected in our *negro* community, say Miss Bertha, but at his place of employ? Hmph! He is a clerk *behind* the scenes, his workspace the broom-closet, why? So the hotel guests never have to see his black face. So the white clerks never have to come close to his black skin.

Mother, say Mrs. Robbins, puttin her hand gentle on Miss Bertha's shoulder. I never thought I see tears streamin down Miss Bertha's face.

He goes to work every day in suit and top hat, his dignity! But every day my husband is ridiculed. Twenty-nine years he has toiled for them—loyalty! And every evening, he returns home weighted down by the work, weighted down by the *humiliation. Oh! they treat me like a common Irishman!* he has lamented on more than one occasion.

Auntie Maryam's eyes snap to me, while Auntie Eunice and the other ladies try decidin which they gonna comfort, Miss Bertha or Mrs. Watkins.

＊

Tuesday mornin, Ciaran and me at the back alley behind Ciaran's workplace, dawn. White cat still in the crate but now a broke wood board been nailed coverin the top. Ciaran take the hammer claw and loosen the top nails, still holdin the board tight in place with his hands. White cat goin wild.

Guess we oughtn't take her to Auntie Siobhan's today? You said not till she answer to you, and don't look like she answerin to nobody.

He shrug. Said I'd give it five days, and it been five days. She's headed to Siobhan's. Then Ciaran lift the cat-in-crate like it weigh a ton and start walkin, ignorin the talons and the screeches. I run to catch up.

We walk into O'SHEA'S, and there stand Mr. O'Mahony, him and Auntie Siobhan swappin the mornin tea boxes.

What's *that?* say Auntie Siobhan, starin at that crate havin a fit.

Ciaran kick shut the tavern door behind him so cat can't escape.

We done it together so we gonna have to split that coin, Ciaran say and pour the cat out. White cat hiss like a python showin its fangs. Me and Auntie Siobhan scream, she snatch me and jump us both atop her bar counter, Mr. O'Mahony yelpin, trippin over his feet backwards! Evil white cat middle a the floor, flippin and screechin like still tryin to break free a that box, like she been struck by lightnin and jumpin electric, then all the sudden stop like a statue. Eyes sharp, ears pricked.

Boom! Cat fly crost the room, I catch my breath! Wait. Wait. And now here come white cat back, strollin: two mice hangin from her mouth.

Everybody gape froze. Then Auntie Siobhan scream again, but this time scream a joy, jig dancin the bar.

Mouser! she say. Oh, you done it, Ciaran, just what the doctor ordered! Worth your weight in gold.

Ciaran grin ear to ear. Least a dollar's worth, he say.

You earned it. Auntie Siobhan hop down from the bar goin to her till. Me and Ciaran laughin, even serious Mr. John near smile, but white cat, star a the show, pay us no mind, playin with the poor mice, let one run a few steps, then slap her paw down on the tail, drag it back, give the other mouse the same treatment, then claw em both a little, torture em to death. The mice screamin.

Poor mice, I say, sad.

Fifty, fifty, say Auntie Siobhan, holdin out two half-dollars.

Thanks! I say, reachin. Then I remember, stop smilin.

Forty, sixty, I say lookin at Ciaran.

Four bits, four bits, he say, and wink at me. Ciaran jus seem proud he done it, brung that mad mouser, now kindly sharin equal the rewards! I look at my shiny quarters. Ciaran grinnin, already pocketed his. Gainfully employed a year now, guess this all jus cherry-on-top to him.

Quite a show. Mr. John O'Mahony smile, headin for the back door.

Você é uma campeã, branca, Ciaran say gentle to the crazy cat.

Mr. O'Mahony stop, lookin impressed. All that, and you know Portuguese too?

Spanish, say Ciaran. Learnt from my Spanish bosses.

You're a champion, white, translate Mr. O'Mahony.

Ciaran smile, nod.

Portuguese.

Spanish.

Portuguese.

Spanish! I work for the Spanish Company!

Now Mr. O'Mahony go stock still. The Spanish Company?

Since last fall, say Auntie Siobhan. Since the comet.

They never failed in the Depression, say Ciaran. Secure.

Them jobs are keepers, say Auntie Siobhan.

Senhor Coelho Magalhaes said I have a great future with them.

Oh! say Auntie Siobhan, pickin up a whiskey tumbler. It'll be good to clean a glass and not worry bout mouse droppins. Though the lion's share of my customers never seemed to notice.

Do you know the business of the Spanish Company?

Ciaran stare at Mr. O'Mahony. Mr. O'Mahony's eyes look sharp and wild at the same time. Ciaran look away, say, They have *lots* of contracts, different . . . different clients—

The *Portuguese* are the ones who run the so-called *Spanish* Company.

Then, start Auntie Siobhan, why—?

Because the *Portuguese* know well that everyone knows well the business the *Portuguese* are well-known for.

And what business would that be, John?

Slaves.

We stare at Mr. O'Mahony. No sound but white cat lickin mouse blood.

Traffickers! Dealers! *Africa!*

Africa? ask Auntie Siobhan, her face a bafflement. But—that's not *possible!* The trans-Atlantic was outlawed ages ago!

Eighteen oh seven, I say.

Before we came to this country. Before we were born!

You've surely heard of the pirate ships, Siobhan. The damned Portuguese pirates, New York Harbor *infested* with them!

Auntie Siobhan look confused, look at Ciaran.

You *must* know, Mr. O'Mahony say to my auntie. *Everyone* knows!

How? Slave tradin in New York? With *all* slavery in New York illegal? Eighteen twenty-seven! I say.

The South has slaves a-plenty, she say, and birthin more every day, so why—?

Cuba, say Mr. O'Mahony. Brazil.

White cat suddenly jerk its head up to Ciaran, white cat keepin alert to Ciaran's moves, and Ciaran shiftin one foot to the other, his breath comin heavy.

Some *still* illegally shipped to Dixie, Mr. O'Mahony go on, but most further south: sugar plantations, gold mines. Brazil and Cuba have no interest in breeding, they work slaves to *death!* Mr. John weavin his worried fingers through his hair. So they need Africa to provide a constant supply. And New York getting fat rich in the transaction.

Ciaran wouldn't work for no slavers! I say, but it bother me he been so quiet. I look at him. He look at me. He look at cat eatin mice. He start walkin out.

Ciaran!

He keep walkin.

You think slavery's the South? Mr. O'Mahony say to my auntie. Slavery's survival is in the cotton manufactories: England. New England. New York.

Ciaran!

He turn around fass to me. It's *work!* *Steady* work, ye expect me to starve? Or not contribute to your grammy's household?

We stare.

I didn't know! When I started, I didn't . . . for a long time . . .

Ciaran swallow.

They sent me on an errand—a delivery. I'd been deliverin hundreds of messages for months, and the man I was deliverin it to'd stepped out so I was ordered to wait out in the cold till he returned. Freezin in the cold, tryin to keep my mind off the cold so I untied the string lock on the envelope, peeked at the form. A tear roll down Ciaran's cheek: *Male, twenties, strong build. Male, thirties, ricer. Female, mid-teens, breeder—*

Now not sure what my face doin, but Ciaran look at it, and his eyes narrow.

I've nothin to do with it! I never seen a slave, all I do's care for their horses, run their errands—

Auntie Siobhan step toward him: Ciaran—

You been eatin off my earnins!

Ciaran's eyes hard on me. My eyes hard back.

I don't eat your earnins! Not no more! Dirty money, I'll starve first!

Well, ye better not eat off Aileen's or Cathleen's neither because what in hell you think their manufactory make? Who'd ye think those little plain smocks Cathleen's makin was for? *Slaves!* Slave clothes, slave kids, *your eyes saw it, Theo!* You jus very easy shut down your brain.

I scratch at Ciaran's face, clawin wild like the white cat. He shove me back, then I'm flyin at him, knock him down on the floor, there's noise somewhere but I hear nothin outside a my own screamin, somewhere I see Auntie Siobhan flash by, Mr. O'Mahony tryin to pull me and Ciaran apart, then we do fly apart, me and him pantin, Auntie Siobhan wipin tears from her cheeks, now the only sane person in the room's the cat, starin like we all lunatics, then a ruckus from the street. Crowds, and *Sweet Jesus, did ye hear?* And *Lemme have a paper!* Then the door fly open, and there, just outside it, stand Grammy Cahill, the hordes all in the street beyond her.

Siobhan! Are ye after hearin the news?

Everybody in the street yellin, and I think *This another panic? Nother riot?* Everybody callin for a paper, everybody nose in the news or hollerin for a daily, the newsboys everywhere goin wild sellin em.

Negro insurrection in Virginia and Maryland!

Seizure of United States Arsenal!

Terrorism near the Capital!

Armed slaves and abolitionists!

Whites taken hostage! Civilian casualties reported!

Negro revolt at Harper's Ferry still in progress!

I walk out into the street. From behind me, I think I hear Auntie Siobhan and Grammy Cahill callin me back, fearin I might get trampled in all the crushin hysteria. I turn around and see them and Mr. O'Mahony, and I see Ciaran hard wipin the tears. Then I hear Grammy Brook—turn, there she be other side a the street, her and Hen and Mr. Freeman, them also fearin me gettin caught in some kinda stampede, wavin me over but I'm wedged, all the sudden I feel myself squeezed in the crowd, can't move, starin at my Irish kin on the south side a the street and my colored kin to the north and here I be: stuck, stuck, trapped in the middle.

1860

Words

January the 1st

My dearest Theodora Brigid,

Happy new year, mo leanbh! We miss you so so so much!

Sure I told you on the last letter and the one before and the one before that, but I need to make certain you heard: No slave work here anymore!! Not ever again! I'll tell you all about it if you come to the door, when I leave the letters your other grammy always saying you won't come to the door. I know you've been seeing your Auntie Siobhan but, see, she's kept her promise not to let me know when you stop by or I'd be there, wanting to hold you, kiss you. This letter will surely be wrinkled when it gets to you, my tears soaking it, Cathleen's tears for writing the words I'm saying.

Like a miracle a likeness of St. Anne the mother of Mary come to my table yesterday. St. Anne, the patron saint of family. I think she was wishing us all a new year, new start together. I pray for it.

All my love to you, a chuisle mo chroí.

Grammy Cahill

I come outa the bed-closet, show it to Grammy Brook.
What's that? she ask, pointin to the words before the sign-off.
Pulse of my heart.
She go back to stirrin the porridge pot.
We eat silent a while.

You know I ain't never kept you from your mother's people.

I look up.

I know. 'Twas *my* choice.

She stir her porridge bowl. Slavery's a machine, need all its parts to keep it runnin. The master and the overseer, the trader and the buyer, the manufacturer providin the chains, the whips. The clothes.

I nod, eyes in my bowl.

We eat silent.

Sewin no more slave clothes?

I look up. I nod. She stare at my eyes a long time. Then she sigh.

New Year's Day, she say. *Is* a good time. Fresh start.

Standin outside Grammy Cahill's door. Knock? I ain't never knocked on this door my whole life. I hear Grammy's murmur, Uncle Fergus's mutter, Cousin Aileen *May the saints watch over ye* and the wet come to my eyes. Push the door open.

Aaaaaaaaaaaah!

Grammy and Cousin Aileen run to me, Grammy cryin.

Theo!

Mo leanbh!

Theo! Cathleen sob from the couch. I'm so sorry! So sorry!

I gentle pull away from my grandmother and second cousin to go to her. On the floor, Ciaran sit, jus starin at me.

Never again, say Grammy, wipin tears but smilin through em. Our dear girl's come home to us, not another day our family ever be broken!

That one went on strike, say Great-Uncle Fergus, little smile, pointin to Cathleen. Wouldn't do the seamstressin, then stopped eatin. Everybody at everybody's throat.

Well, 'twas silly to starve yourself! say Cousin Aileen, glass eyes. Ah, such fuss! Well, ye *could* say we were providin a service: the slaves need clothes, don't they?

The room go dead.

I didn't *know*! Cousin Aileen cry to me in the silence. We didn't *know*, I'm only sayin—

We *should*'ve known! say Cathleen. How could I not see it? The little smocks, the poor little—Cathleen wipe her face. Very convenient. I'm a cripple, then act blind on top of it.

They *quit*, all that matters! Grammy say. A week after it all come out . . . And you not here . . . Piecin together other work was hard but they managed it, they managed it.

Making sure the other work was *not* slavery-contracted! say Cathleen.

And soon come time for the rich to commence their Christmas shoppin, the stores was hirin, say Cousin Aileen, turnin to our statue of the workers' patron. Thank ye, Saint Joe!

Oh, *mo leanbh*! Grammy come and hold me tight. Nothin the gentry was bestowin on one another a week ago could be grander than the new year's gift we got today. New *decade*! Eighteen sixty lookin very promisin!

Ciaran quit the Spanish Company? I ask, eyes on him.

Yes! say Grammy. Of *course*!

Now everybody lookin at Ciaran, his eyes on me. Then he get up, walk out the door.

January go by. My days at Cahill's at first few n far between, but by my birthday, Febooary the ninth—ten years of age!—I'm near back to splittin my time between my grammies. Ciaran always seem to make hisself scarce when I'm around.

❧

Near end a the month, Park street: everybody run for a gawk! Crowdin, followin him. Somebody famous in Five Points! Tall man! Lanky. Brown beard, wart above corner of his mouth!

Mr. Lincoln, how are you finding our city?

A fair sight different than Illinois, he say to the reporter. Man stand like a giraffe, squeak like a mouse!

Congressman Lincoln, did you attend church this morning?

I was indeed a member of the Sunday congregation at Reverend Beecher's Plymouth Church in your neighboring metropolis across the river.

Representative Lincoln, your senatorial debates of two years ago with Democrat Douglas continue to generate much excitement. Is it true you are considering a presidential bid?

Congressman Lincoln, you were not among the twenty-one prominent presidential candidates recently published by journalist D. W. Bartlett. Is your visit to our city a show of defiance to the naysayers?

Mr. Lincoln, sir, what will be the substance of your speech tomorrow evening at the Cooper Institute?

You will have to come and hear, Lincoln say, and now seem he really takin in Five Points, his eyes gettin a little worry, little sad.

Theo!

I turn. Friedrich wavin at me! Friedrich from racin in the bowlin alley, I ain't seen him in months. We follow everybody followin Mr. Lincoln, his tour guide chatterin to him, reporters shoutin at him, followin in Worth street east to the House a Industry where Mr. Lincoln disappear inside.

We mighta just near touched the next president a the United States! say Friedrich.

But it's only Febooary the twenty-sixth, my icy breath cloud provin my point. Election not till November!

Never too early to throw in the hat.

He from Illinois been to Brooklyn for church. I from New York *never* been to Brooklyn! Where *you* been, Friedrich?

Don't live in Five Points no more. My family removed to Little Germany.

Oh! You like Kleindeutschland?

Very good! He grins, me sayin it the way the Germans do. Sure, I like it. Though most a the time I'm down here workin. City Hall. I'm a baggage-smasher at the New York and Harlem station!

You like baggage-smashin?

Yes! Tips! Carryin baggage from the ferry terminals to the hotels, from the train depots to the hotels. I seen your cousin Ciaran there.

He ain't my cousin.

Anyway, that's why I don't race in the alleys no more. Busy.

New kids now, I tell him, most a the ones we raced with is gone. Remember Yacob? Now have to work with his father at the market. Remember Molly? Taken in by the House a Industry. Remember Christmas? I lower my voice: Lately I seen him at the docks with the grown-up thieves and robbers.

I know, Friedrich say regardin Christmas. We think on that a second, then Friedrich smile. Maybe Molly'll get a close-up gander at Mr. Lincoln.

We come in sight a City Hall depot. Okay, I gotta go back to work. But listen, you like to hear Lincoln at Cooper Institute tomorra night?

I stare at him.

Think about it. If ya decide yes, meet me here six and a half o'clock. That's exactly the time I leave, when the church bells ring it. Be here then or miss your chance.

I think they only let grown-ups in. Only grown *men*. How we gonna—?

Meet me here six thirty. Then Friedrich turn to the station: Help with your bags, ma'am? And jus beyond him Ciaran strugglin with a big trunk. Friedrich's twelve years of age while Ciaran won't be twelve till July, and Friedrich already a head taller. A flash of a second I catch Ciaran's glare at me.

⁓

At Grammy Cahill's, Cathleen seamstressin alone.

Ciaran ain't a very good baggage-smasher. I jus seen him, he could hardly lift the trunk!

Only work he could find after quitting the Spanish Company, and it's only for tips—nothing steady. He'd hoped to be a smithy. Taking care of the horses for that company, he'd gathered some know-how. Went looking for apprenticeships, but no smithy apprentice openings for Irish.

I don't care.

Cathleen glance up from snappin the thread, then back to her work.

I believe, say Cathleen, stickin the string through the eye, he felt very bad about it all. After it came out in the open that day at Siobhan's tavern, he started eating very little, eating seemed to make him sick. Then he quit.

Eventually!

Eventually. He thought about it a couple of weeks. No one forced him. I think he was struggling with it: the anger at himself.

He act angry at *me!* When *I'm* the one got a right to be angry at *him!*

I believe, say Cathleen, knottin the thread, he directs his anger your way because he hasn't yet figured out who he's *really* angry at, but seeing you always reminds him without you ever having to utter a word. Shame: a heavy load for a small boy.

Then Cathleen tip her head toward the wood stand. Open the drawer.

I don't know what Cathleen's talkin about, but I walk to the little table and do.

Ah! Cathleen, that's the prettiest baby dress I ever seen! I like that crochet rose you made!

For your Auntie Eunice.

Thank you!

From *all* your mother's family. She's due next month?

March the eighth, give or take!

I'll pray for her, say Cathleen, weavin in n out a the button holes. Beyond her, I notice a newspaper cut-out.

You put that on the wall?

No, she reply. Great-Uncle Fergus kept it, from December. *He's* the one delighted about Wood re-gaining the mayoralty.

I jus seen the nex *president* maybe!

Cathleen frown at me.

Mr. Lincoln! Out on Park!

Cathleen think.

I remember reading it now, the congressman's in town. *Former* congressman. He walked through *Five Points*?

I nod.

Well, that's impressive! Then murmur into her sewin, But a Republican president is doubtful.

Republicans spose to be against slavery. But you favor the Democrats like Great-Uncle Fergus?

I do *not*.

He always say Democrats the only ones lookin out for Irish.

That's not all they do, she mutter, snappin the thread.

The New-York Times

NEW-YORK, WEDNESDAY, DECEMBER 7, 1859.

Election of Fernando Wood for Mayor

Mr. Wood, after acknowledging the personal compliments which his presence excited, said: New-York has this day decided in favor of the Constitution and the Union.

{Cheers.} She has shown that however much a spirit of fanaticism and encroachment upon the constitutional rights of the South may arise over the North, she has, at least, stood firm by the rights of every section of the whole country; {loud cheers}

⁓

Auntie Eunice! Look what come from all my mother's family!

Well, isn't that pretty, she say, sittin in Auntie Maryam's rocker.

Be pretty with the bootees, say Auntie Maryam.

I'd wager a guess as to which one made it. You thank Cathleen and all the rest *Ow!*

Kick? say Auntie Maryam. Auntie Eunice nod, hand on her stomach. Since her belly got big, Auntie Eunice been stayin with Auntie Maryam and Mr. Samuel in the Room of Hope.

You give her the bootees you made? I ask.

Mm hm. Was time.

Eleven more days, smile Auntie Eunice. Give or take.

What you callin the baby?

Nathanial John, my auntie tells me. After Nat Turner—three a's in Nathanial, just like he spelled it—and after John Brown. Remember when the papers first called *Slave Insurrection! Negro Revolt!* never imagining the lead rebel was one of their Caucasian own.

What if it's a girl? I ask.

I want a son.

Why?

Sons can do things.

What things?

Vote.

Colored son?

If he owns property.

What if Mr. Lincoln become president? I saw Mr. Lincoln today! Maybe he be president and *everybody* vote!

Who?

He's famous!

My aunties wait for me to go on, but then I remember I don't know nothin else about Mr. Lincoln.

Oh, that Republican congressman, it come to Auntie Eunice.

Yes! Don't Republicans mean no slavery?

So they say. Well, I don't know that Lincoln stands a chance for the nomination. He was a representative for two years, and that's the entire of his federal political experience. And I don't know that the Republicans stand a chance to win. Such a young party, only the second time they'll be nominating a presidential candidate. But we'll send up a prayer.

Yes, say Auntie Maryam, touchin the pouch with the Arabic scroll round her neck.

He's speakin at the Cooper Institute tomorra night.

What an elegant venue! That magnificent Great Hall, I've watched them erect it, admired the progress every day on my strolls to and from the Academy of Music. And when they opened it last year . . . Oh, to be a fly on the wall!

My aunties start talkin more about the baby, and I notice on the table is *Echoes of Harper's Ferry*, the new book the ladies' salon gonna discuss, writings put together about John Brown. The page the book is opened to is Mr. Henry Thoreau's speech where he pleads for Captain John Brown's life: *These men, in teaching us how to die, have at the same time taught us how to live.*

Nex mornin, I'm peerin through the iron fence at the House a Industry, and there amungst the kids let out for fresh air stand Molly, who used to run with us. Mary Bree was adopted and shipped out West but, I come to know, most a the orphans the House a Industry keep and teach in their school.

Mornin, Molly!

Mornin, Theo!

You talk to Mr. Lincoln?

He talk to us! He come to our Sunday-school class yesterday.

What he say?

I fergit.

He talk about slavery?

No. Hm. He talk about bein poor. He said he was poor when he was a young'un too. But he look at us like we're poorer! He say, Do your best! Do your best! Then he stop talkin, like he wanna cry. I gotta go back in to school!

Later I'm reportin to Grammy Brook while she hang the whites. When I seen him Sunday, he look near to tears, lookin around Five Points. Then this mornin Molly say he almost cry in the House a Industry!

Gran-Gran in her corner chuckle. Grammy say, Back in the 'thirties, fearin a cholera outbreak, the city cleaned Five Points streets for the first time—mud and garbage and all kinds a manure, scrubbed it spotless. Underneath. paving stones! So many years and layers a muck, no one knew the streets were paved! And Grammy chuckle.

Whatchu knittin?

Blanket for the baby.

Everybody got a present for Nathanial John but me!

Grammy quiet a while, wrappin the yarn round her finger. Woman have a baby, it's a chance. Heads she pull through, tails she don't.

My ma was tails?

Grammy nod. So best present for the baby? Pray him and his mama survive and thrive: pray for the lucky cent.

⌒

At six thirty o'clock, I stand in front a the City Hall depot. Walkin up, I see Ciaran, then turn away before he see me. I find Friedrich, who look up and grin. As we start to head uptown, I snatch a last glance a Ciaran, who now stopped his work, gapin full-on at me and Friedrich walkin away together.

When the Cooper Institute come into view, I remember Auntie Eunice talkin about bein a fly on the wall. And all a sudden I know my gift: a report on Mr. Lincoln's speech! Somethin she can always tell the baby, especially if Mr. Lincoln become president! But now, standin with Friedrich starin from Third av where Eighth street become Astor place and watchin the gentlemen crowd into Cooper Institute, I suspect Friedrich don't got a real plan on how to get us inside. Then a couple a the gentry fellas start some kind a argument, and a few more join, and as it grow into some supreme fracas, Friedrich and me glide in. The auditorium is downstairs, underground. At first, we're flowin with the stream down the steps, no one notice us in the tight hubbub, look like it might be easy. Then we see a man at the audience door, givin a hat-tip greeting to each gentleman walkin through. Friedrich and me hide under the stairs, heart poundin in my throat. The ruckus in the hall get bigger, then quieter, then silent: speech musta started. No sound but occasional applause, and on one a these occasions, we slither out. Lucky us because the door guard gone. We slip in.

Mr. Lincoln on the stage. The Great Hall a the Cooper Institute like half a bowl, audience fannin out and up, speaker down in front. Hundreds! Us standin in the back. Once a man turn and gimme and Friedrich a dirty look, but then Mr. Lincoln say somethin causin people to cheer again, and the man turn back around.

But enough! This is all Republicans ask—all Republicans desire—in relation to slavery. As those fathers marked it, so let it be again marked, as an evil not to be extended, but to be tolerated and protected only because of and so far as its actual presence among us makes that toleration and protection a necessity. Let all the guarantees those fathers gave it, be, not grudgingly, but fully and fairly, maintained. For this Republicans contend, and with this, so far as I know or believe, they will be content.

And now, if they would listen—as I suppose they will not—I would address a few words to the Southern people.

You charge that we stir up insurrections among your slaves. We deny it; and what is your proof? Harper's Ferry! John Brown! John Brown was no Republican; and you have failed to implicate a single Republican in his Harper's Ferry enterprise.

Slave insurrections are no more common now than they were before the Republican party was organized. What induced the Southampton insurrection, twenty-eight years ago, in which, at least three times as many lives were lost as at Harper's Ferry? You can scarcely stretch your very elastic fancy to the conclusion that Southampton was "got up by Black Republicanism." In the present state of things in the United States, I do not think a general, or even a very extensive slave insurrection is possible. The slaves have no means of rapid communication;

nor can incendiary freemen, black or white, supply it. The explosive materials are everywhere in parcels; but there neither are, nor can be supplied, the indispensable connecting trains.

John Brown's effort was peculiar. It was not a slave insurrection. It was an attempt by white men to get up a revolt among slaves, in which the slaves refused to participate. In fact, it was so absurd that the slaves, with all their ignorance, saw plainly enough it could not succeed.

I don't hear the end a Mr. Lincoln's speech. I don't like his words, so I leave. And reportin his words no longer seem like such a good Havin-a-Baby present for Auntie Eunice.

☙

Middle a the night at Grammy Cahill's, feel my water. I go out to the front-room where Cathleen sleepin, Great-Uncle Fergus snorin, and Ciaran awake standin, starin out the winda. He don't turn around to me when I walk through for the chamber-pot, which I knew he wouldn't since we ain't spoke to each other since the mouser-cat in Auntie Siobhan's, since John Brown, since October. Empty myself outside the door and bring the chamber-pot back in and Ciaran full a tears.

I'm sorry! I'm sorry! I'm sorry! I'm sorry! I'm sorry!

Facin my direction with his eyes to the floor. He stop talkin but keep cryin, his sobs he gag silent so no one wake: jus me and him. I don't know what to say. He *oughta* be sorry so sure I'm not sayin It's okay. But I pre-ciate them words from him *sorry sorry sorry*, preciate he mean em.

Finally he calmer, calmer. Back to lookin out the winda.

Know why they call it *leap year?*

I shake my head. He didn't see me but guess he know because he go on.

Every year moves a day ahead. If January first is a Tuesday this year, it'll be a Wednesday next year. But add in a February twenty-ninth, and the next year leaps *two* days ahead.

Then Ciaran go quiet again. After a while I stand nex to him, both us starin out at the bright half-moon.

☙

Lincoln visits Beecher church and House of Industry!

Extra! Details of Lincoln's Cooper Institute address!

Lincoln address at Cooper Institute results in standing ovation! Read all about it!

In the afternoon, I walk up to Auntie Maryam's. The leap year tomorra gimme a extra day to figure out what to give Auntie Eunice before Nathanial John come on due date March the eighth.

Scream! What goin on at Auntie Maryam's! Another scream, I run in: Auntie Maryam! Auntie Eunice!

Auntie Maryam come runnin outa her and Mr. Samuel's bed-closet, I see Grammy Brook in there! I never seen her at Auntie Maryam's before! And there Auntie Eunice on the bed lookin sick! bad!

She havin the baby! You go in there, wait, and Auntie Maryam push me in the Room of Hope where I loud n clear hear Auntie Eunice hollerin holy hell other side a the wall! I see Grammy run out once, come back in with a pail a water she pumped. Seein me, she stop.

Pray!

She say it sharp, like I been assigned only one job and I ain't doin it. I fall to my knees in the cold room. Day turn to evenin to night, no supper.

I wake nex day, see someone put a blanket over me. Hear my colored women family in the nex room talkin soft. I slip in to Auntie Maryam and Mr. Samuel's bed-closet.

There Grammy and Auntie Maryam sittin on the bed, hoverin over Auntie Eunice, her baby suckin her. Mr. Samuel there too, standin, lookin all wonder.

That Nathanial John? I whisper.

Everyone turn to me.

No, say Auntie Eunice, then she look at the baby: Natalie John, meet your cousin Theo.

I come over, peer at the baby, her makin a fist. I never seen anything so tiny! And Auntie Eunice smilin like the whole world's grand even though she swore she wanted a boy.

Early girl, Auntie Eunice coo. Come early in the dark mornin, and early before due time.

Well, I ought to be gettin on home, Grammy say. Relieve Mr. Freeman, kind enough to stay with Mama.

Nattie John, Auntie Eunice say sof to her daughter. We'll call you that. You like it?

I'll mark her in the family Bible, say Grammy. Born February the twen-ty-ninth.

Born Leap Year! say I.

Born *free*, say Auntie Maryam, which cause tears to run down her face and Grammy's, and Auntie Eunice and Mr. Samuel's eyes fill up too, and all at once I know it's all right I didn't get a gift in time because that word Auntie Maryam just uttered mean Natalie John already been born with the greatest gift of all.

Smoke

Another terrible and mysterious tragedy became public yesterday, which, from present appearances, promises to unfold a chapter in crime of the most barbarous character.

This bout that abandoned sloop they found off Coney Island? say Grammy Brook, ironin whites.

Yes, say Hen, and keep readin aloud the *Daily Tribune*. *When boarded, the deck presented a most horrible spectacle, being almost literally covered with clotted blood and hair.*

Oh Father, sigh Grammy.

*On entering the cabin no person was visible, but large pools of blood lay on both sides of the stove, and in the companion-way. The star-board quarter was also stained with bloody finger-mark*s.

This is why I get fretful you girls don't come home. *You* I reckon at your other grammy's or Eunice or Maryam or your mother's sister's place, but *you* like sleepin out with the urchins now and then. I want you two to start tellin me exactly where you are! All times!

Them murders happen out on the water, pirate killin his own crew for the money.

Plenty murders *ashore* New York City, Hen!

On the floor lay a hammer weighing three pounds, to which, beside being bloody, was sticking a quantity of human hair.

Read no more!

I gotta go to work, and that quick Hen out the door, Grammy's face all worry.

Today's March the twenty-second, third day a spring, Grammy!

Mm hm.

Auntie Maryam tole me she's happy we all named her birthday first day a spring, in ancient Babylon spring started the new year! She think it still oughta be that way: rebirth.

From what Hen's readin, that'd mean the new year startin with the devil already scorin one against God.

Hen come home in the evenin, and nex night I stay at Grammy Cahill's. Night after is Saturday, and I'm back at Grammy Brook's, come to find out Hen ain't been home since Thursday.

I'm a whoop her! say Grammy, pacin, I tole her there's murderers about! And men doin bad things to little girls!

Gran-Gran stare at Grammy, worryin over Grammy's worry. Auntie Eunice here, arm around Grammy, whisper soft to her. Then Grammy go downstairs to fetch water.

The pirate got Grammy frettin! I tell my auntie. Hen always been in the street and never seem to bother Grammy much before.

You don't know. Adults *always* just have to send up a prayer for their children, and now . . . Your grammy says it's the pirate because the pirate isn't frightening as what she really fears. Not *that* pirate anyway. Blackbirds.

Blackbirds?

I don't mean *tweet-tweet.* Blackbirds: slave-catchers. Stealing colored folks to sell down South, they don't care if they're slave or free, grown or child. A little boy disappeared from Little Africa last week, his parents mad with grief. Georgie. You knew him?

I shake my head.

These things are very, very rare. You'll be fine as long as you *don't go wandering off alone, always stay where there's plenty of people!* Hear?

I nod. Then a commotion in the hall, Grammy fussin. In she come with Hen.

These streets are *treacherous*, think you're so smart no one can hurt you? *Take* you? They *can*, Hen! You got nothin to say?

I got a job!

That we know! What we wanna hear is why you didn't come home—

Not the hotel, quit it couple days ago. Cigar manufactory! Brooklyn!

We stare. Now I know what that smell is Hen brung with her.

Brooklyn?

Place hires lot a colored, Hen say to Grammy. Monday through Saturday, so I be back Saturday night to early early Monday morn.

And stay where in between?

I got a place.

Why you quit the hotel? I ask. I know my reasons, but wonder what's hers.

Tired a servin white folks. Shuffle for chicken feed, or crawl for chicken feed plus a tip. Look.

Hen stick her hand in her pocket, pull out dollar gold pieces, *clink clink!*

Pirate treasure! say Gran-Gran, who always pipe up from her corner at the sound a cash. Grammy holler at Hen: Why Brooklyn? Too far! Too dangerous! But everyone know it always end up Hen gonna do whatever Hen wanna do. She promise Grammy to always stay safe with the crowds, but I wonder if she bein truthful: Hen always favor her solitude.

Spring pass by. Then early May, Grammy tell Hen if she home for her thirteenth birthday on Thursday the seventeenth, she'll make a cake. So here sit Hen, playin a mouth-organ she bought with her earnins now she's rich. Take it out her lips.

Wanna job with the cigar manufactory?

I stare.

Seven cent a hour. Take home three or four a week, easy.

Dollars?

That's the kids' wages. 'F I was a black man, I'd be makin the most. Cigar-makers like ex–tobacco slaves with the experience: curin, fermentin, rollin. Black men make fourteen a week! White men only ten.

Black more n *white?*

The men. Some of em come out from Manhattan daily, worth the trip. White female usually make better n colored, but I'm fast: earn more. Six a week.

Dollar a *day?*

Long's I keep up.

Where you sleep?

You want the job?

I look to Grammy, makin the supper stew.

Ya know she'll jus figure you stayin with your Irish peoples.

❧

Nex mornin before dawn, before Grammy wake, Hen headin out, me slippin out to follow. Fulton Street Ferry: I never been on a boat before! I never been to Brooklyn before! More newsboys at the depots and terminals than in the street.

Republican National Convention in Chicago finishes today! Presidential nominee to be named!

Trial of Albert W. Hicks for sloop murders continues! Verdict expected by end of the month!

Radicals and moderates split at Republican convention!

Texas man burned at the stake for owning abolitionist tracts!

Seward the frontrunner for Republican presidential nom!

New York Harbor full a the big clipper ships and the freight barges and the rowboats and the steamboat ferries, traffic jam on the river!

East River's busy!

North River, Hen correct. Hudson.

And the dock: horse-n-buggies, men walkin horses, men haulin wagons, people quick-steppin everywhere, the hordes comin off the ferries while more masses scurryin aboard, Hen and me part a the hive. She give the man four coppers, raise two fingers: me and her. We on!

Squeeze into the banister space off the port side, gazin out onto the water. Still docked, I look up to the boat's tall chimney stack, down to the boat's big paddle wheels, around at the people chatterin, ladies in their long dresses and spring flower hats, men in their work cloaks and bowler hats, some people quiet-serious, thinkin on their day's work, givin a tired sigh. Then the paddle wheels take to turnin, boat slip out, slip into the frenzy a harbor traffic. Me and Hen wave down at some rowboat men, they wave back.

What's at island?

Governors, say Hen.

We start choppin up n down, I feel sick! Hen tip her forehead toward a big ship, mutter, We in its wake. Hen always mutterin, like hearin me but her eyes in the distance, mind always two things at once. I wonder if one a them big ships might be carryin Uncle Ambrose home. Or one of em's a pirate ship! All that's left a the crew's blood and hair and a cut-off hand like the pirate A. W. Hicks' ship except this would have to be a different pirate because Mr. Hicks been in trial all week and surely sentenced to hang soon. Then a little lurch and we're docked.

That was fast!

Twelve minutes, Hen mutter.

Twelve minutes! I think about when Grammy Cahill and Auntie

Siobhan and Cousin Aileen and Cathleen and Maureen and Great-Uncle Fergus and Meara and my mother crossed over from Ireland. Five weeks! Nothin but rags gainst the bitter cold, starvin! Then I think about when Auntie Maryam's mother crossed over from Africa, which was a whole lot worst.

Brooklyn! Pretty houses!

Fancy neighborhood, say Hen, knowin what I'm thinkin. This is Clover Hill, north part a the City a Brooklyn, facin New York. Brooklyn ain't all this.

We got on the Fulton Street Dock Manhattan, now we got *off* Fulton Street Dock *Brooklyn*!

Hen say nothin. I follow her walkin and walkin and walkin.

Where we goin?

Work.

Oh. When we gonna eat?

Dinner. Noon.

Lotta kids work at the cigar place?

If they can keep up. Factory likes kids, pay em a fraction of adult wages.

What's the difference between factory and manufactory?

One short for the other.

We turn into Sedgwick street. I see a giant cigar factory! Smell a giant cigar factory!

That it?

That's Lorillard's. We're next door.

Little white clapboard: WATSON'S TOBACCO COMPANY.

Lorillard's big: two hunnert n twenty work force, and Watson's only seventy-five, but each company got fifty colored workers, so at Watson's we're majority.

Hen go round back, knock on the cellar door flat gainst the ground, then step back. Cellar door swing up and open. A colored lady look at Hen familiar, then look at me: a question.

My cousin. She wanna work.

I follow Hen down and in. The cellar packed floor to ceilin with cigars in pretty boxes. Another underground room: big bales a tobacco, a colored lady and colored man tendin to the bales and leaves, sniffin and mix-matchin.

I follow Hen up the steps and now in a room with two long tables, benches on either side, and seated on the benches is cigar-rollers, mostly colored. Seated crost from each other but not lookin at each other, everybody eyes on their own work. The boss colored lady is Frankie. She squeeze me into a bench, tell me to do what everybody doin. She say I wanna keep my job, I gotta catch the skill fast. At first I can't fold the cigar right, the tobacco fallin out. Then my cigars too fat. Then my cigars too thin, or thin n fat messy. Frankie sigh, tell me stand, gimme a wood box and make me walk slow behind all the rollers. When I get near em, they throw their scrap into my box. Hen never look at me. Hen work fast, she one a the fastest rollers! When I done walked by all the people wunst, I look at Frankie. She sharp point for me do it again, and again, and again, and again, my legs gettin tired! Then a few rollers get up and leave. I look at Frankie. She point hard again, I keep movin. After a while, Frankie go to the door, fingers in the ends a her mouth givin a powerful whistle, and the ones that gone out the door come back and a few others leave. Eventually I feel a tap on my shoulder, look up. Hen tip her head for me to put down my box and follow her out. I put it down, race to her! Outside, race to the outhouse! Finished, I see Hen seated at a wood table in the spring warm with other colored ladies. I sit between Hen and a girl a little older. Crost us a lady ole as my grammies and another lady maybe Auntie Eunice's age. The younger lady take out a loaf a bread, tearin it apart.

I'm Mrs. Laurie, the older say. And you are?

Theo.

Theo?

Theodora, say Hen. My cousin.

Mrs. Laurie say, You will say *Theodora, ma'am.*

I don't wanna say that, but Hen gimme a side-eye, so I do.

Very nice to meet you, Theodora. This is Mrs. McCray, and you are sitting next to Carol Lee Williams.

Thank you! I say to Mrs. McCray, takin my offered bread. She parcelin it out to everybody.

What's your age? ask Mrs. McCray.

Ten. What's yours?

The grown-up ladies gasp so I figure I said somethin wrong.

I'm sixteen, Carol Lee Williams tell me.

What I miss? say a lady comin from the outhouse, older n Mrs. McCray, younger n Mrs. Laurie, big and lively, squeezin betwixt the ladies.

We were just getting to know Henrietta's cousin Theodora, say Mrs. Laurie, if we can get past her impudence.

Henrietta got a cousin? say the new lady. I always thought Henrietta dropped from outer space.

I look at Hen, thinkin she gonna get mad! She don't look up from her bread dinner, but first time I see a little smile cross her lips.

I'm Mrs. Niles, the new lady say. Nice to meet you, Theodora. You have very pretty hair.

Thank you!

That golden brown. And wavy.

Carol Lee has very pretty hair too, say Mrs. McCray.

What do you say, Carol Lee? say Mrs. Laurie.

Thank you, sigh Carol Lee, chewin, eyes in the distance.

Carol Lee's father is a full-blood Shinnecock Indian, say Mrs. McCray. That pretty straight black hair.

My mother wishes it mighta caught a *little* curl from her, say Carol Lee, whose mother I reckon is colored.

Well, the pirate gettin the verdict soon, say Mrs. Niles, tearin off a big chunk of her bread and stuffin her mouth.

Indeed, say Mrs. Laurie. And some exciting developments in Chicago. The Republican convention. They will be selecting the nominee today.

Less n they go the way a the Democrats, say Mrs. Niles.

Yes, say Mrs. Laurie tryin not to smile. The Democratic convention in Baltimore—a couple of weeks ago, has it been now? It did appear to have gone rather disastrously.

Fell apart, cackle Mrs. Niles. Fools couldn't agree on nothin since everything come down to slavery.

I saw the most marvelous illustration of the Republican assembly hall interior! say Mrs. McCray. They had to build it especially for the purpose you know, to fit in so many interested parties of the public. Seating ten thousand! The sketch revealed the view from the enormous balcony, where sat many lady spectators!

White women, Mrs. Niles say.

So it appeared, but how do we know there were *not* colored among the ten thousand? say Mrs. McCray.

Perfect acoustics, say Mrs. Laurie. The *Wigwam*. That's what they called the structure.

I don't like that, say Carol Lee.

Who's your man? say Mrs. Niles to the others.

Well, say Mrs. Laurie, Senator Seward is clearly the frontrunner.

Seward! cheer Mrs. Niles.

That would be good for New York, say Mrs. McCray. A former New York governor and present New York senator now elevated to president!

However, I believe the nomination of Seward, say Mrs. Laurie, would be a mistake for the Republican party.

What! say Mrs. Niles. Seward's the strongest abolitionist!

Quite.

Yes, say Mrs. McCray, Seward calls not only for prohibition of slavery in the territories but for the end of slavery everywhere. Seward the lawyer defended colored men *and* appealed in court for equality in education, in civil matters. Seward the senator spoke of a moral law higher than the Constitution!

I take this position, say Mrs. Laurie, because whatever happens in Illinois, whatever cheers and jeers are provoked by its outcome are all premature. The presidency will not be decided until November, and considering there is absolutely no Southern representation at the Chicago Republican convention, the party will have to choose a viable candidate to challenge the Dem challenger, once the Dems finally make up their minds as to whom that will be.

But did you see the Republican platform that was just put forth yesterday? ask Mrs. McCray. Carrying slavery to the territories is political heresy! Freedom is the *normal* position of the territories! *All men are created equal*, very promising!

Didja know the *all men created equal* part a the platform created an uproar? ask Mrs. Niles.

No. That cannot be! It's in the Declaration of Independence! say Mrs. McCray.

Mrs. Niles light up a cigar as she talk, one a the mistake ones woulda been thrown away. The conventioneers feared it would be a statement of negro equality. No no!—moderation: we oppose slavery, we do *not* advocate equality of the races. No no!—moderation: we oppose slavery on *new* soil and leave it be for the states already have it. The *promising* Republican platform is more *com*promising: state sovereignty.

And free homesteads, Carol Lee throws in. Protecting western settlers, I don't like that!

Abram Lincoln—start Mrs. Laurie.

Is it Abram or Abraham? ask Mrs. McCray. Or he goes by both?

No one seems to know, Mrs. Niles utter around puffs.

I saw Mr. Lincoln! He come to Five Points!

That's right, you *would* be from Five Points like our Henrietta, say Mrs. McCray, smilin. A Five Points mulatto. Your mother Irish?

I nod. But she died.

Aw. She shake her head.

Lincoln, continue Mrs. Laurie, blowin smoke from the cigar she jus lit, is the strongest candidate save Seward. He is a prominent Westerner from Illinois, he came into the convention with the support of Illinois and Indiana, and we'll need the western vote in November. Were my dear husband still alive, he surely would have agreed, and he was an eligible voter.

Remember the Liberty Party? ask Mrs. McCray, dainty lightin up her own cigar.

Still exists, say Mrs. Laurie.

Barely, say Mrs. Niles.

The Liberty Party was *always* confined to the margins, say Mrs. McCray, its abolitionist ideals considered extreme. And now abolition has moved to the main-stream, to the *presidential contest*—did you ever imagine it would happen in our lifetime? Then Mrs. McCray turn to me. The Republicans have reached out to your mother's people too. The right of citizenship to immigrants from foreign lands, that's on the Republican platform. When your Irish menfolk go to vote, you make sure they know that.

And railroad to the Pacific! Carol Lee cry, standin. I don't like that! Then Carol Lee charge back inside the manufactory.

Mrs. Niles sigh. Her Indian father. *Manifest destiny* they do not so heartily embrace. Then Frankie whistle for us to come back in for rest a the afternoon, all the ladies and Hen quick stampin out their cigars. I do the same task from the mornin except sometime I'm sent one floor up to deliver merchandise to the packin and shippin level at the top. End a day, Frankie scowl handin me my wages. Nine hours time seven cent is sixty-three, I know my sums and know how to check I ain't been shorted. *Clink clink!* in my pocket. Rich! Then walkin home with Hen, whatever home mean.

Mrs. McCray bring us bread dinner every day?

We each pitch in a nickel start a every week. She live near a bakery.

Oh. Them ladies your friends?

Got no friends. Jus people I work with.

Where we goin now?

Cheap eats.

Dark fallin, finally we reach the place: soup two cents, water free, so that's what we have.

And here two cent for the ferry this mornin, I say, holdin it out. Hen shake her head like she ain't takin it from me, lookin around at the people, mostly men, not like to greet em friendly but more jus keepin an eye. Before we leave she glance to see the lady runs the place ain't lookin and grind out a hill a pepper on the table.

Whatchu doin?

Hen slip a bottle outa her gunny-sack, scrape the pepper in it, cork it, shake it up. The water was already dark, so look like she been pepperin it a time.

Let's go.

I follow her out. Walk a while, then hear a sound, and some man appear outa the dark, grab both a us! I scream! Hen strugglin but don't scream, then sudden I feel a burn. The man scream. Hen threw her pepper water in his eyes! (a little got in mine) and while he hollerin, she take a knife to his thigh, he hollerin more! *Bitches!* But too blind to see us. Hen grab my hand, we run!

Barn in the night.

This where you sleep when you in Brooklyn? I whisper.

Barely see her nod in the dark.

That man find us?

His bad luck if he do, she mutter, and all a sudden I'm shakin all over. After a while, Hen start singin soft.

Say, brothers, will ya meet us
Say, brothers, will ya meet us
Say, brothers, will ya meet us
On Canaan's happy shore?

Glory, glory hallelujah
Glory, glory hallelujah
Glory, glory hallelujah
For ever, evermore!

What's that?

Walkin by some Brooklyn church one evenin, heard it pourin out. Some say it's a camp revival song. Some say slave song.

She sing it again. Then pull a little knife outa her gunny-sack, hand it to me. Case you need it sometime.

What if *you* need it?

Still got mine, this was an extry. In the dark, I see her chewin on hay.

One time I coulda used it. Dance hall. But Auntie Eunice and Auntie Siobhan beat that man away.

I know.

Auntie Eunice told you?

I know because it happen to every girl.

Some frog croakin.

What that man tried. That happen all the time to you in Brooklyn?

Not *all* the time.

Ever a man catch you?

Ribbit. Ribbit.

Hen. I don't think I wanna work at the cigar manufactory no more.

She chuckle. From the snarl on Frankie's face regardin your efforts today, I don't think that's somethin you need worry about.

You gonna get in trouble, bringin in a bad worker?

Hen shrug, shake her head.

I preciate you tryin for me though, I say.

Hen quiet. Then: Maybe thought it be nice workin with a cousin, see some family besides jus Sunday. Then she go back to hummin the Glory Hallelujah.

I don't know bout that song, Hen. I think it sayin every man's a brother, and some brothers I don't care for.

Hen think on this. Then fix her singin.

Say, sisters, will ya meet us
Say, sisters, will ya meet us
Say, sisters, will ya meet us
On Canaan's happy shore?

That one I join in to singin!

Nex mornin early before her work, Hen walk me to the Brooklyn Fulton Street dock, waitin for the ferry back to the New York Fulton Street dock. They come every ten minutes so I ain't got long to wait.

It's Saturday! You can come home too, Hen!

Be there after work tonight.

Republicans nominate Abram Lincoln for President!

Lincoln rises to the top on the third ballot!

Ohio delegation rumored to have been swayed to Lincoln by Chicago journalist's chicanery!

Friends of Mr. Seward shocked!

What! say Hen, and buy a two-penny paper. I look over her shoulder.

The New-York Times

NEW-YORK, SATURDAY, MAY 19, 1860.

The work of the Convention is ended. The youngster who, with ragged trousers, used barefoot to drive his father's oxen and spend his days in splitting rails, has risen to high eminence, and ABRAM LINCOLN, of Illinois, is declared its candidate for President by the National Republican Party.

This result was effected by the change of votes in the Pennsylvania, New-Jersey, Vermont, and Massachusetts Delegations.

Mr. SEWARD's friends assert indignantly, and with a great deal of feeling, that they were grossly deceived and betrayed. The recusants endeavored to mollify New-York by offering her the Vice-Presidency, and agreeing to support any man she might name, but they declined the position, though they remain firm in the ranks, having moved to make LINCOLN's nomination unanimous. Mr. SEWARD's friends feel greatly chagrined and disappointed.

Western pride is gratified by this nomination, which plainly indicates the departure of political supremacy from the Atlantic States.

Smoke n meers, mutter Hen.

You wanted Seward?

Hen nod. Then shrug. Well. Hopefully somethin nice'll still come out of it.

Nice like what?

Like war.

People start movin, and I get in the swarm loadin onto the ferry. The carriages and the carts and the horses and the people pack in, and I turn jus before I board and see Hen lookin at me, little smile on her face. I move through the horde, grabbin a spot near the banister to look out for the crossin. Take my lass look at the City a Brooklyn and surprised to see Hen still standin there, nobody near her, not seein me now and appearin a little sad. Grammy Brook useta say, If the whole marchin contingent turn west, you know Hen gonna go east, and till now I always figured Hen like it that way: alone.

Then the boat lurch and pull off. When I look again, Hen headed back up into Brooklyn, musta lit up a cigar because I see the smoke start to floatin over her head. Like some Indian smoke signal to say *All's well*. Or *All's well enough*.

Museum

I stand in the Franklin street hordes waitin for a lass look at him. His ferry to yonder island already docked, the other isle in the harbor that ain't Governor's. The handbills posted all over the walls a the Bowery.

FRIDAY, JULY 13TH

> Cruise to Bedloe's Island, enjoy beer and all you can eat oysters while watching the hanging of the notorious Pirate Hicks. One Dollar.

The crowd crushes. Albert W. Hicks, convicted a the bloody killin of his three shipmates, but at the last confessin to quite a few more murders. Somebody turn their head and I see him! Glimpse him through the swarm! Then gone.

What a circus! say Grammy Cahill, shakin her head that evenin after I tell her bout my peek at Mr. Hicks. Some show, takin a man's life.

He's a cold-blooded killer, so got his just deserts, say Cousin Aileen, crossin herself. And half the city treatin him like celebrity.

Whatever he is, a legal hangin party's shameful, say Grammy. *Civilization*, we call this?

Hm, say Great-Uncle Fergus, half-asleep in his chair. Ciaran already dead asleep on the floor, his usual state a bein since lass month gettin hired at the Central Park alongside Great-Uncle Fergus. Our apartment feel like a hundred degrees, I like the dog days outside but not the dog-day nights in.

Can I sleep on the front-room floor, Grammy? Cooler n the bed.

You can, she tell me.

Think of poor Maureen, sigh Cousin Aileen, tiny room off the kitchen of her employers. Maid to the gentry not always as deluxe a position as it might sound.

A little holler we hear from some of em fightin for sleep-space out on the tenement wood fire escape.

257

Can I sleep out on the fire escape, Grammy? Cooler n inside.

You can*not*. Those filthy men out there—never! I'll tie ye to the bed-post first!

〜

Sunday afternoon, I run into Ciaran on the street.

Ice cream? he offer.

Enjoyin my chocolate! Us sittin in the sun with our bowls.

How you get that Central Park job?

Mr. Fergus said they was needin more summer labor. Mr. Fergus told em I was fourteen years of age.

You jus turned twelve!

Eight days ago, and I look thirteen at least.

I wanna dispute it but can't. The family keep remarkin on his recent growth spurt.

What you do?

Sometime messenger, sometime pushin a wheelbarrow full a heavy rocks. Between the baggage-smashin and this, I'm gettin strong! and Ciaran flex his arm muscle.

Ice cream make ya stronger, the dairy. We oughta do this every Sunday.

Ye mean so long as I'm buyin for us both. He take a lick. They're about to move me, afternoon-to-evenin shift. After work Tuesday, I'll have that night to rest, then no work till Wednesday afternoon, so think I'll spend my Wednesday morn finally commemoratin my twelfth year.

If ya need somebody to have ice cream with—

Already have *other* plans.

Such as which?

Such as the museum.

I stare. You goin to *Barnum's American Museum*?

Ciaran smile.

I never been to Barnum's!

I know.

I'm mad! but don't let Ciaran know it. I *always* wanted to go to the museum, and sure I mentioned that to him! And I never heard *him* express any interest ever!

Why you look sore?

I'm *not*.

You could go if ye want. Fifteen cent for under ten years of age.

I'm not *under* ten, I'm *ten*, and it's a quarter for older! And if I *could get* in for fifteen, I still don't have it!

You don't gotta get loud.

My lass real job was the cigar factory, and it was for one day! And I bought a rattle from Grammy's table for my baby cousin, Nattie John, with my earnins so *I don't have the money for my admission to no museum!*

I have the money for your admission, say Ciaran, and take the lass bite a his vanilla.

Nex mornin, I wake late at Grammy Cahill's, everybody already gone to work. First thing I think: only two more days till the museum! But now I wonder, what if he was jokin? What if Ciaran get tired like he been from all the Central Park work and change his mind? Better I stop thinkin about it, gettin my hopes up.

Pay attention! say Cathleen, eyes on my sewin needle which she had to help me thread. You are ten and a half years of age now, well old enough to learn a livelihood. Look at your work. The spaces between the stitches should be even and—

I'm goin to the museum!

Cathleen stare.

Barnum's?

Ciaran tell me he take me with him Wednesday his mornin off!

Oh! Well, that should be an adventure. Siobhan went once, years back.

She *did*?

I hear the panoramas are quite nice. And the wax figures realistic.

Giant lady! Bearded lady!

Cathleen frown. Oh, I don't know about those.

The glassblowers! The big diamond jewel! Trenviloquists!

I'd like to see that!

Albinos! Siamese twins!

Oh, I don't know about those.

Seal play the horns! Bear dance the jig!

Tom Thumb, you must see him! Well, how could you not? Barnum's star attraction! Charles Sherwood Stratton: in his twenties now, but Charles alias Tom has been partnering with his older distant relative Barnum since he was four. A genius of character, Tom conjures Hercules! A Scottish highlander! Napoleon!

Tom Thumb performed for Queen Victoria!

I shan't hold that against him.

I thought maybe you didn't favor the human oddities.

Oh, I don't know about that word.

I'm bigger n Tom Thumb, and he's a grown-up!

People hired to *perform* are making a respectable, honest living. People hired to be *gawked at*? I am not comfortable with that.

I hear there's a elephant. I hear there's a whale!

Born for the stage! Barnum took notice of little Charlie Stratton because he was small. The showman had no inkling what a talent he'd discovered: gold mine!

Went with Fiona years ago, say Auntie Siobhan when I ask her in the tavern a hour later. The several floors of spectacle were worth the admission, though I was less enthusiastic about the dramatic entertainment. The Moral Lecture Room: big grand theater where Barnum brought in that European opera singer sometime before, where the likes of Shakespeare graced the stage, right up your aul Auntie Eunice's refined alley. All the pomp and circumstance, but I must say I'm partial to the Bowery Theatre just up the street.

Now Auntie Siobhan stoop and *tap tap* her fingers on the floor. The white mouser cat come flyin out at her, my auntie feedin her fish bits.

Here's a warnin: Barnum has little patience for people takin too long at the exhibits and has posted signs—*This way to the Egress*. Patrons wonderin what kind of fascinating show that might be, not knowing *egress* means *exit*, find themself outside on the street!

I was there once, say Auntie Eunice that afternoon. Nattie John sittin on her lap, playin with the rattle I bought for her.

You *were*? You never tole me!

Is it Colored Day?

Huh?

You know they only let colored in every so often.

I say nothin. I didn't know that!

I was twelve years of age when Phineas T. Barnum first came to town. Bought an old slave, blind from age, near paralyzed. Claimed she was nurse to the child George Washington, now a hundred sixty years old! The white folks believed it or they didn't, either way in proving their point Barnum's pocket got filled. Go under my bed and fetch my box.

In Auntie Eunice's bed-closet, I slip under the mattress and there the little wood chest. I bring it out. Auntie Eunice yawnin. She always seem tireder since Nattie John come.

Set it here on my lap.

What's that? I say, peekin into it.

Read it.

Marriage license! You and Uncle Ambrose!

Box is for things I need to keep. Or wanted to keep.

What's *that*?

Dried rose from my father's funeral.

What's that?

Open it.

I unfold the little cloth.

Why you keep a raisin?

Not a raisin. Nattie John's birth navel.

I gasp!

Read that.

Advertisement from a newspaper. On the bottom Auntie Eunice wrote *February 26, 1849.*

NOTICE TO PERSONS OF COLOR

In order to afford respectable colored persons an opportunity to witness the extraordinary attractions at present exhibited at the Museum, the Manager has determined to admit this class of people on Thursday morning next, March 1, from 8 A.M. till 1 P.M.

I was nineteen. All the excitement from the white people, I was wildly curious. To this day, I feel a certain thrill when, of an evening, I pass by that huge beckoning spotlight on Barnum's roof. I arrived seven and a half o'clock, early, as I'd anticipated a large crowd of negroes, and I was not wrong. Inside, I observed some very interesting displays, but my enjoyment was dampened by the implication that those few hours for which we paid just like the whites were considered some great gift bestowed upon us. Tom Thumb was a delight—and still a child then! I was very much looking forward to the Shakespearean drama. Had I been around a generation earlier, I could've seen negroes performing the bard, you should ask Mr. Freeman about that. But I was born into New York black freedom: too late for New York black art. So, after the magicians and the flea circus and the tree trunk under which it was claimed Jesus's disciples sat, the impresario offered culture. I suppose he wanted to show that plays need not only be for the most coarse of society. Who goes to the Bowery Theatre but rowdies and ruffians?

Auntie Siobhan goes to the Bowery Theatre.

So I eagerly took my seat for *Macbeth*, but quickly was dismayed to realize that parts had been excised! I came to find out that Barnum ordered the cutting of any text that might be construed as immoral.

Auntie Eunice sigh, then start ticklin Nattie John who answer with her baby giggle.

You seen colored Shakespeare? I ask Mr. Freeman at supper that evenin.

African Grove Theatre, catering to negro patrons back in the 'twenties, just before New York emancipation.

Why your Gran-Gran and me never got to go, say Grammy.

Couple of men from the West Indies established that venue, Greenwich Village. I saw Ira Aldridge perform there, colored Shakespearean actor who toured Europe to great acclaim: *Othello*, *Richard III*. But I was even more a devotee of the original work. One of the Caribbean founders wrote a play about an island slave uprising against the English masters. The colored theatergoers were enthralled by the performances, but the white audience members were too often trouble-makers, one time tearing the building apart. Naturally the police responded not by punishing the white thugs but by shutting down the colored theater.

∾

Tuesday night, I make a point to sleep at Grammy Cahill's. It bother me Ciaran come home from work in the evenin lookin tired, eat a little and fall asleep, sayin nothin bout the museum! I'll be mad if he forgot! But nex mornin, Wednesday July the eighteenth, he the one wake *me* up off the front-room floor, early.

Up up! he grin.

Just act like we belong, he say as we walk down Broadway, like all the sudden he unsure bout our chances for admission. I'll give em the money, don't look scared, look normal. Say you're nine years of age, that'll save me some cash in case the fifteen-cent rate is for under ten rather than ten and under.

And fast here we are, Ann and Broadway. On the first balcony, the band summonin folks in. Then a second balcony where folks already inside can look down at the street, but nobody there yet because the museum not quite open. Curvin around to take up half a block, four rows a big windas above the bottom floor, and the giant letters **BARNUM'S** above the fourth floor windows and **AMERICAN MUSEUM** just below them. On the wall between every winda, a big painting of an animal. A couple dozen flags from different countries posted from the edges of the roof, and an American flag with the thirteen stripes and thirty-three stars standin huge and tall. Just as big is the flag from the top tiltin over into the street: MUSEUM. Once I stood here on Broadway, watched a hot-air balloon fly off from the roof! Trinity Church bell start to tollin eight times.

Not so many folks wanna be at a museum eight a.m. so we walk right into the entrance hall, hardly any line. The floor marble, gasoline lamps, big animal paintings on the walls! Then the ticket man.

Ciaran put up the forty cent. She's nine, he say. Ticket man look at Ciaran, look at me, like he ain't sure. I look back all normal. Then ticket man eyes just on me.

No colored persons.

My heart leap to my throat! I wonder Ciaran gonna jus go in the museum without me!

People oftentimes mistake her for colored, he say. She's my cousin.

The man still look not certain, like he prefer to refuse Ciaran's money. But I'm middlin enough between Irish and black he can't be sure. He take the coins. We're in!

First come into a big room with many, many little lit-up windows. Look in one: pyramid, Egypt! Look in another: Colosseum, Rome! At the back: big, wide staircase, like a mansion! By the time we get through all the windas, it's gettin nigh onto nine o'clock, and the crowd startin to thicken already.

Second floor paintings high on the wall, pictures in glass cases, and in the back: elephant! Room so big, I didn't see it at first! But not movin.

Taxidermy, say Ciaran. Dead. Stuffed.

We touch its skin. I wish it was alive!

Hello!

We jump! There, set back in a alcove of the room stands the albino family! Mother, daddy, little girl. White hair, white skin, whitest white people I ever seen! They sell pamphlets about themself, fifteen cent to have a daguerreotype with them, some man and some lady do. Another alcove we surprised again: the giant Quaker couple! Man and wife, near touch the ceiling! The alcoves you don't notice till you come upon em. The Quaker man shake Ciaran's hand.

Oh, let's, John.

Liliana, we cannot pay for a photograph with *every* oddity!

But we're on holiday!

The man allows it. Mother, father, three children stand in front a the towerin couple. The little girl gimme a dirty look. Ciaran and me walk.

They sounded like the South.

New York's flooded with em in the summer, he shrug. The Central Park, always hearin the visitors with their Bamy talk.

I ain't heard it hardly ever.

Think vacationers comin to New York plan to tour Five Points?

Boo.

We jump!

Tom Thumb!

Hardly, little lady, say the little man. Commodore George Washington Morrison Nutt, at your service. Call me Thumb's under-study and I'll give you a kick under your knee. Then Commodore Nutt give a little kick in the air and kiss my hand. I giggle. Gunshot! But people runnin *toward* it stead a away!

There stand a man not much taller n Commodore Nutt. No arms. But loadin a pistol and firin it with his feet! Then he start cuttin up a valentine heart with his toes, all lacey dainty, and we see all the ones hangin he already cut up.

I'll have one of those, say a man, and they do a money exchange, regular-size man's hand and little armless man's foot, then the customer give his wife the heart. Now little armless man pick up some sticks, hit em on a little piano: music!

Can ya dance? ask a man.

He got feet, that's the one thing he *can* do, say another man, and most everybody laughin except one lady say *Don't say that!* while the no-arm man don't stop his chores, now pickin up a watch, puttin that gold disk between toes a left foot and windin it up with toes a right!

On one side a the big hall's a room a stuffed birds and live snakes. Anacondas! Glassblowers and a crystal-ball lady readin fortunes, a life-size Russian fort! Wax figures: one of em's Albert W. Hicks, the murderous pirate, and I remember Cathleen readin about Barnum visitin him in jail and payin him to make a plaster mold of his face. On the other side: water animals! Big glass boxes filled with big fancy fish. A *whale!* And nearby: the horn-playin seal! Then I see Ciaran headed to some secret exhibit.

NO! I yank him back nick a time before he go to THE EGRESS!

Third floor is the bottom entrance to the Moral Lecture Hall, the big theater which continue up into fourth and fifth floors. Also other saloons, which is what they call the halls: pictures a famous criminals loose in the world and more taxidermy—cougars and crocodiles and monkeys and bears—which make me say, I wanna see the *real* animals!

Ciaran lead us up to the fifth floor, top. A bubblin fountain in the center, windows on the ceilin open up to the sky—we can see the roof gardens and the giant spotlight! In the evenins, they switch it on, floodin its glow up n down Broadway!

Camels! Chimpanzees! Tigers! Den a serpents! And *huge* critters: rhino, two giraffes, ten elephants! The brown man guardin wear a turban and vest n trousers like India. There's a sign say HAPPY FAMILY with little birds and owls and squirrels and mice and monkeys, Prey and predator together, say another turban man. Down the hall: Grizzly Adams's dancin bears! Then a man call, A special performance by Chang and Eng, the Siamese twins: Saloon Five!

Me and Ciaran hurry with the other folks. We know the saloons now, and Five's on the third floor. Chang and Eng do a dance, perfect step! Then I see two boys, arms around each other's shoulders, do the Siamese twin dance like *they's* hooked together. Then a couple do it, then I grab Ciaran, us doin it, gigglin, Ciaran's arm huggin me *very* tight, till we hear somethin goin on in Saloon Six, fourth floor, and run up. Indian dance! Whoopin it up, then all us doin the Injun war whoop, laughin! Over there a dog runnin a sewin machine! Over there the club killed Captain Hook! My stomach growlin!

Come on, say Ciaran. He take me down to the third floor where the victuals for sale: oysters and ice cream and lemonade! Jus before we get in line, we hear a man claimin to take a measure a heads to tell the future.

Phrenology, folks! Modern science!

We move to that line. Ahead of us, we hear the man tellin some gentlemen they have a strong head for business. *I* do *run a successful shoemaking manufactory in Massachusetts. My tobacco plantation* has *been enormously profitable.* Their sons he predicts will go to fine universities, their daughters will be proficient caretakers in their rich homes. When Ciaran and me get to him, he ask our age, then tell Ciaran, Congratulations! Your brogue is nearly undetectable! before measurin our heads.

Yes. You will grow up to be very strong and very successful in outdoor work. And you, young lady, will make a fine domestic servant.

Ciaran get us one oyster order and one ice cream order to share. A lot more people in the museum now. I suck on a oyster, taste the ice cream. Salty sweet!

How come you ain't eatin your oysters and ice cream?

He shrug. Then he say, You know why that man said what he said?

What man?

Phrenology.

Oh. No. Why? while I let a slippery one slide down my throat.

Because we're Irish. And maybe he guessed you're Irish and somethin else.

Oh. Swishin my ice cream around the bowl.

Where I used to work, the Spanish Company. On the wall some of the bosses had pinned cartoons: Irish and colored, both lookin like apes. *Thomas Nast* the signature on most. Named right, *nasty* he is.

'F you don't want your ice cream, can I have it?

That's us: the manual laborer and the maid. That phrenologist sure saw no university *our* future.

I don't *wanna* go to no university.

Then you got no worries because he pegged you too stupid to.

He didn't say I was stupid!

He said we *both* are.

Well, I don't care what he think, I don't wanna go to no university but if I did, I would. He ain't no fortune seller.

Teller. And he never said he *was*, said he's a *scientist*.

I shrug, scrapin the ice cream bowl. I don't care what that man say, he don't know.

I start lookin around.

I never been to a place like this, Ciaran, sposed to be celebratin *your* birthday but feel like mine! This the best day a my life!

Ciaran manage a little smile. Then he reach over, touch my hair gentle. That I didn't expect, I jump back in my chair! He turn away, red. And all a sudden I feel somethin in my belly, somethin warm. Nice.

Ladies and gentlemen, Tom Thumb will be performing in ten minutes! Everybody run!

While we waitin outside the door a the Tom Thumb stage, we get a pre-show in the hall.

Oh, Jim Crow, I tink the ladies oughter vote.

No, Mr. Johnson, ladies am supposed to care berry little about polytick, and yet de majority ob em strongly tached to parties.

Everybody laughin. Two white men took charcoal and made their face black. In the story, one's a dandy, the other a dumb lazy nigger runaway slave. Next is a skit with a blackface dandy and blackface wench (but white men plays both), and the man say *I need to make a far* and pick up a poker, and the lady say, *Kin I help you, sweetums?* and nex to me I hear a man chucklin, whisperin, *Here it comes, he gonna poke her eyes out*, and now the dandy and wench wrestlin over the poker and sure nuff the dandy end up pokin the wench's eyes out make her blind, and the crowd roarin, holdin their hurtin belly-laughs because this was their favorite part they was waitin for. I look at Ciaran, his eyes on the show, grinnin. I didn't think it was funny but maybe it is, I start to laughin because everybody else is, and suddenly crost the circle I see that Southern girl who glared at me before, and now she laughin but her eyes on me, her eyes hard and cold like laughin at *me*, then somebody pull back the curtain entrance and we file into the Tom Thumb show. Seats fill fast: me and Ciaran left standin on the sides.

Out come Tom holdin the hand of a tall man, everybody cheer! Then the man sit in a chair nex to a little round table and set Tom standin on top a the table.

That's him, I hear whispered behind me. *That's P. T. Barnum.*

P. T. Barnum say things serious, and Tom get all the tomfoolery laughs. Then Tom become Napoleon and do the Scottish dance.

Now people start to pack into the Moral Lecture Room. Outside it's a sign on a easel.

UNCLE TOM'S CABIN
A MUSICAL IN SIX ACTS
The only just and sensible Dramatic version of Stowe's book represents southern Negro SLAVERY AS IT IS. In a word, this Drama deals with FACTS, INSTEAD OF FICTION. It appeals to reason instead of the passions, and so far as truth is more powerful than error, the impressions of this drama will be more salutatory than those of any piece based upon fanaticism without reason, and zeal without knowledge.

See the dramatization you've all heard tell of! say a man standin near the entrance.

All the characters you know and love! say another man. Little Eva, Topsy, and ole Tom himself!

You needn't wait till the evening, folks! Only at Barnum's American Museum can you see a show in the afternoon: the ma-ti-nee!

Wanna see the play? Ciaran ask.

I think: I ain't seen the Feejee mermaid yet! And I ain't seen the human skeleton yet! Or the mummies! But my legs is tired! I wanna sit! I look around at the people filin in, chatterin happy, chatterin eager. *Have you ever seen it? Oh, you're in for a treat! Little Eva will break your heart. Oh, but Topsy steals the show! I'se so wicked!*

I don't wanna.

Okay, Ciaran say. You wanna see the magician?

I think about October a lass year, Auntie Eunice's salon discussin *Uncle Tom's Cabin*. Auntie Eunice say, *The book sold three hundred thousand copies the first year, only surpassed by the Holy Bible!* and Miss Bertha say, *I appreciated the way Stowe challenged our anti-woman laws: if* Missus *Shelby could have had a say,* Tom *would never have been sold in the first place!* and Mrs. Watkins say, *Uncle Tom still such a young man with a young wife and small children, so heartbreaking!* and Miss Sarah Daniels say, *I appreciate that Mrs. Stowe readily admitted her inspiration by Josiah Henson's real-life slave narrative*, and Miss Hazel Greene say, *I loved the cleverness of Sam and Andy in playing the buffoon to confuse the slave catcher*, and Auntie Eunice say, *Shakespearean! The fool is actually the sage!*

You wanna see the ventriloquist? ask Ciaran.

And Miss Sarah Daniels say, *Topsy is an example of the literary "wild child" concept except* this *time the poor, unfortunate orphan is a slave!* and Mrs. Robbins say, *The saga of the benevolent master St. Clare challenges capitalism in his greedy reluctance to free his slaves*, and Miss Bertha say, *The book that invigorated the abolitionist movement!* and Mrs. Watkins say, *The ending is heartbreaking!* and Auntie Maryam say, *That Simon Legree— slavery as it* is, and Auntie Eunice say, *Unfortunately many more people have seen the stage adaptations than have read the book, and I hear those plays and musicals have taken shocking liberties.*

Last call for *Uncle Tom's Cabin*, say the man, and people pushin and rushin, and I look at Ciaran, grab his hand, and we race in. Usher lead us to sit in the second balcony—high up!

The curtain raise, and people start to clap, but the clappin get even louder as everybody see the scene: life-size steamship glidin on a painted river across the stage! Paddle wheels turnin and steam *puff! puff!* Now we on a plantation, and the slaves sing a happy song. When Topsy come out in the third act, whole audience cheer. A cute little white girl playin Little Eva, but some grown black-faced white man play Topsy doin some kind a clown dance like I never seen nobody ever do, then sing.

> *She used to knock me on de floor,*
> *Den bang my head agin de door,*

And tare my hair out by de core,
Oh! cause I was so wicked.

I'se dark Topsy, as you see,
None of your half and half for me,
Black or white it's best to be,
Ching a ring a hop, goes de breakdown.

'Tis Little Eva, kind and fair,
Says if I's good I will go dere,
But den I tells her, I don't care,
Oh! ain't I very wicked?

Whole audience laughin and clappin, Ciaran laughin and clappin. The end finally come, different from the book: Tom alive, Eva alive, all the slaves free! Everybody happy about it, *I'm* happy about it! Then all a sudden I'm certain that Southern family with that nasty little girl is here somewhere and also happy about it.

After the play, me and Ciaran ready to walk back uptown: me the ten blocks home to Five Points, him the seventy-plus to the Central Park.

I liked that play! You like it?

I read the book. It's different.

How so?

There weren't no Yankee reporter in the book.

Penetrate Partyside! Ciaran laugh.

He the only abolitionist in the play. How come he gotta be silly?

So was Sam and Andy, Ciaran smile.

In the book Sam and Andy was *smart* buffoons.

Who ever heard of a smart buffoon?

I kick a stone.

I didn't like the show before the show neither. With the blackface people.

Colored people likes minstrel shows too.

I turn to him. Says who?

Ask around.

I kick another stone. Ciaran shrug. Least *Uncle Tom* was a happy endin, everybody free. I gotta get to work. Hope Grammy have buttered greens for supper tonight.

In the book, it weren't a happy endin.

Then the play's better.

It's *not*.

You liked the endin!

So did all them Southern people.

Then maybe the play's a good thing: bring everybody together happy agreein.

I crost my arms.

I just spent a pretty penny on you so I hope your day weren't *all* a misery.

It was fun!

Grand.

But—

Let's stop talkin about the stupid play.

The book was sad! The book made you mad at slavery!

We *were* mad. Everybody in the audience wanted em freed—

I don't think nothin in that happy-slave play gonna urge nobody to stop slavery!

Ciaran stop walkin, stare at me. Quiet he say: It's just a show.

You ain't half-colored like me so guess *you* don't know!

No. All *I* know's near all my brothers and sisters died in the Famine before I was born, I know that catastrophe come from bad potatoes grown on bad land doled out by the damned British so if ye're askin about tyranny, I think that concept I got a pretty good grasp of.

So nex time let's watch a funny musical bout the Famine.

Now Ciaran's eyes narrow.

When I brought up the phrenologist, *science* peggin anything Irish or black destined for naught but the lowliest labor, *that* didn't seem to bother you long as you got the last bite of ice cream.

I *said* he didn't know nothin! But however mad he made *you*, you sure cheered up, enjoyin the black lady gettin her eyes poked out!

Ciaran's mouth fly open. Then he close it.

Guess we each found our own amusements. Like you laughin with all those white folks doin the Indian war whoop, maybe *you'd* prefer a show bout killin squaws and papooses.

What!

Or doin the Siamese twins dance, did ye also wanna dance with the armless man? Ye seemed so thoroughly delighted by shared organs and missin limbs.

You danced too!

I ain't the one pickin and choosin when it was jus fine to laugh at misfortune and when it 'tweren't.

Now *my* mouth fly open to answer, but nothin make any sense come to my head, and for a moment I wonder if the phrenologist mighta correctly pegged me stupid after all. Ciaran jus starin at me, I fly ahead leavin him in my dust, almost trippin over two little kids, a little dark boy and girl which make me think a Nancy and Elijah that died, lookin at the museum all wonder knowin they never be let in, and I hold in a cry. Head to Greenwich Village.

Auntie Eunice! Colored people enjoy minstrel shows?

I say it walkin through the door, before I see Nattie John suckin on my auntie. My little cousin quick turn her big baby eyes to me.

Did you see one at the museum?

I nod. Nattie John back to suckin.

How did you get in?

All a sudden I feel a shame, heat in my face.

Oh, Auntie Eunice say, lookin at me like she jus remembered my colorin. Well. She chuckle, sigh soft. It's all right to fool the white man every so often. So long as you don't try passing yourself off forever, because you can never fool yourself. Famous case: slave who looked white escaped with her husband, along the way them pretending they were mistress and servant.

Then she kiss Nattie John. Auntie Eunice know well and good what I done, pretendin white to get into Barnum's ain't nowheres close to the worthiness a that slave escape she mentionin. And I think she also know I won't never again be passin myself off as anything I'm not.

In answer to your question: Everyone likes minstrel shows, everyone wants to laugh. But negroes generally prefer the actors to be actual black people so we're laughing *with*, not *at*.

Nattie John cooin against her mother.

I never got that. From my ma.

You did. Brigid lasted three days after you were born, you got a few tastes of mother's milk. Then Auntie Eunice pat Nattie John's back, and she let out a big burp.

Nex day I need to see Cathleen. Go over Grammy Cahill's middle a the day, nobody but her home.

I'm ready to practice the stitches again.

Grand. Here's a little piece of fabric. And I want to see you tying it off to a knot when you're finished.

It take me ten minutes to get the dang thread through the eye—this time Cathleen won't help—and then I focus: push through pull through push through pull through, concentratin on my task, sayin nothin. I need to say somethin to Cathleen but not sure what.

How was the museum? she finally ask without lookin up from her work.

I start to mention the giant couple, then shut my mouth. Then start to talk about the play, then shut my mouth. Then the Indian dance, then the armless boy, then I almost bring up the live animals but for the first time realize those ten elephants looked awful cramped in that one pen. Then there's the stuffed dead animals, and suddenly the delighted gapin faces a the audience all day yesterday remind me a the delighted gapin faces I seen on Franklin street eager to watch A. W. Hicks get sent to the afterlife, and it come to me P. T. Barnum sure got a keen awareness of American amusement.

I liked Tom Thumb, I say at last.

Eyes still on her chore, Cathleen smile. That's all Ciaran had to say as well. Then my maimed cousin snap her thread and immediately push another strand through the needle-eye on the first try, like her eyes and fingers is the ablest on Earth.

Election

You may introduce yourselves, girls, say Miss Bertha at the Sunday, November fourth Ladies Cultural Forum.

Lavinia Clover.

Letitia Clover.

Twins! say Mrs. Watkins. How old?

We are now sixteen years of age, having celebrated our birthday in September, say Lavinia. She try to say it ladylike, but loud enough we can hear over Nattie John's howlin, Auntie Eunice back in the bed-closet tendin to her.

Their father owns a dry-goods store in the Thirties, say Miss Bertha.

Clover's! Of course, say Miss Hazel.

Unfortunately, say Letitia, business has waned in recent weeks.

It appears we are in another recession, Lavinia sigh.

Yes, say Mrs. Robbins whose toddler boy standin nex to her keep starin in the direction a Nattie John's hysterics. It seems to happen every third year now.

Just pray it doesn't plunge into depression, as the last time, say Miss Sarah Daniels.

Does anyone know how to calm an eight-month-old teething baby? ask Auntie Eunice, appearin at the bed-closet doorway with Nattie John screamin bloody murder.

Oh, the poor angel! say Lavinia and Letitia.

So was Lucifer, say Auntie Eunice.

Come here, precious, say Mrs. Robbins takin Nattie John, who start screechin louder, then reach for Auntie Maryam, who take her and she quiet down.

My sister Maryam has been kind enough to watch her niece while I'm working at the Academy of Music.

But hearin her mother's voice, Nattie John take to wailin again.

You need ice, say Miss Bertha.

You need rubber, say Mrs. Watkins.

You need whiskey, say Mrs. Robbins.

The iceman was here this morning, mutter Auntie Eunice, takin Nattie John outta the parlor again.

Well, say Miss Bertha, as we formed our cultural society eighteen months ago towards examining the issues of the day, I propose we devote today's session to the pressing news of this week.

Pressing and promising! say Miss Hazel.

But we need *every vote* to ensure Lincoln's victory! say Miss Sarah Daniels.

Indeed, say Miss Bertha. Given the intimidation and riots and fraud that are commonplace among *white* men at our city's polling sites, an eligible *black* voter may have legitimate reason for reluctance. But we must be strong.

And if our *men* cannot be strong as Mother suggests, say Mrs. Robbins, then we *women* must take matters into our own hands. Threaten a strike: if you are unmarried and your fathers and brothers are eligible voters, tell them to do so or you won't cook their meals! If you have a husband, there is plenty more to refuse.

If Lincoln is elected, do you think he can mend our ailing economy? ask Letitia.

I would *hope*, say Miss Hazel, that Mr. Lincoln's *first* priority would be emancipation, *everywhere.* After that: Lincoln is a man who worked himself out of poverty, so I imagine he has some idea of how to work the country out of recession.

Finally! Auntie Eunice say, enterin with a book and droppin herself in a chair. She'd been fighting sleep so forcibly, when I brought her back to the bed her eyes fell closed before I even gave her the ice!

I read a wonderful review regarding the costumes for *Rigoletto* at the Academy of Music, Mrs. Robbins smile.

Ought to be, since we were forced to work overtime all week. So! Let us commence the discussion. After seeing a fascinating profile in the press upon the book's American publication earlier this year, I was eager to ascertain my copy. I found the theories the author has put forth intriguing! Imagine: the prospect that species were not created in a state of permanence but rather are ever-evolving! What did you ladies think?

The ladies glance at each other, look down.

Quite frankly, say Mrs. Robbins, I was exhausted merely by reading the title.

I'm quite interested, say Miss Sarah Daniels, and intend to finish the work. But with so much happening at the moment, the election in two days, it was just impossible to find the time—

I recommended the book at the September meeting! You've all had two months!

I have to say, say Mrs. Watkins, I much preferred our discussions of *Our Nig* and Frederick Douglass's narrative and *Uncle Tom's Cabin*. What has the subject matter of this treatise to do with us?

It illustrates the development of our natural world! Are negroes not a part of that?

Yes, but—

And it has been embraced by the transcendentalists—Henry Thoreau, Louisa Alcott, Ralph Emerson—as evidence of the unity of humankind, thus bolstering their radical abolitionism!

I read it, say Miss Hazel.

Thank you, Miss Greene!

I understand the well-meaning enthusiasm of the writers you've cited, but I fear misinterpretation—whether unintentional or deliberate. How long before some disciple of this theory of natural selection decides that the negro race will naturally select itself into oblivion?

That's *not* what the book is saying!

It's in the title! say Mrs. Robbins. That is, if one has the energy to get through to the title's end. *Favoured* races?

But that's not what the author meant! The text must be *read* for content and context, *therein* lie the facts—

I couldn't agree more, say Miss Hazel, but *I* am saying facts never got in the way of bigotry, at which point Auntie Eunice take *On the Origin of Species by Means of Natural Selection, or the Preservation of Favoured Races in the Struggle for Life* over her head and slam it down on the floor. The ladies gasp! Auntie Eunice start to cry.

I'm so sorry! I've just been carrying such a burden. The additional hours at work and the baby teething, and of *course* I worry about the election, and oh, I miss Ambrose so dreadfully!

Oh, say the ladies, comin to Auntie Eunice. Please don't worry. You must care for yourself in order to care for the baby.

Thank you, say Auntie Eunice, wipin her tears. Thank you! Thank you!

Ambrose home soon, soothe Auntie Maryam. He alway come he back before ya know it, he saze—

Sezzzzz, Auntie Eunice hiss to Auntie Maryam.

After the ladies leave, Auntie Eunice hold a cool cloth over her forehead for her headache.

I'm so sorry, Maryam! You're so good to me, caring for Nattie John while I'm at work. I've never snapped at you before!

'S okay.

It's *not* okay! And how *dare* I complain about extra hours? This economy, I should be on my knees every night thanking God I *have* a job! Who am *I* to moan?

New mother, say Auntie Maryam. And free. Then, quiet, she go out the door.

Nattie John wake up hollerin but the ice calm her. Early evenin, her and Auntie Eunice nappin in the bed-closet. I weren't much interested in Mr. Darwin's book before, but after the ladies' lively debate, even though most of em didn't bother openin it, I sit in the front-room readin till the door creak.

Uncle Ambrose! I whisper. He carry flowers.

Well, Miss Theo! he whisper back, and gimme a hug and kiss. Baby asleep?

Her and Auntie Eunice. I like your purple daisies! They for Auntie Eunice?

He nod. Cornflower.

You come home for the election!

I prayed we'd dock in time. Lucky, I think the captain wanted to vote himself.

Auntie Eunice got a headache layin down but she sure gonna be happy to see you, Uncle Ambrose! She been missin you! She—

Natalie John has two parents, we hear from the bed-closet doorway behind us, but she'd never know it given only one's afflicted with the entire load, and when Auntie Eunice say that, ain't even a hint of a smile on her face.

Nex mornin, Grammy Brook gimme some pennies.

Bring me some bakin soda?

We makin a *cake*?

For the party.

Party?

She nod. This a very special election, so we gonna have a festivity. Hope it be a victory feast but, if not, we'll need the sweet consolin. You let Auntie Eunice know to come round tomorrow.

She mad at me.

What you do?

Nothin! She mad at *everybody*!

Hm. Must be the brain fever.

What's the brain fever?

Some women gets it after they have the baby. Or before their monthly. Some people gets it just because life's hard!

What make the brain fever go away?

Electin Lincoln be a start.

Daughter! cry Cousin Aileen a few hours later, always especially delighted to see Maureen if it ain't her regular Sunday night off which was jus yesterday.

Gettin me a rest! Maureen say, fallin on the couch nex to Cathleen. Those Carringtons are drivin me up a bloody wall!

Ye haven't quit, have ye? Ye can't! say her mother, who usually always lamentin the job took Maureen away. I'm desperate for work since they let me go last month, thank the saints they're still keepin Cathleen.

Sure it wouldn't have anything to do with them paying less for home piecework, say Cathleen pullin her needle through.

No, I didn't *quit!* snap Maureen. The missus is plannin some election-night party and sendin me errand-runnin all over Creation for it!

Suppose they're all rich, fancy Republicans, grumble Great-Uncle Fergus, him and Ciaran gettin their midday meal before headed to the Central Park, afternoon-evenin shift.

Mrs. Carrington goes for Lincoln, but *Mrs.* Carrington doesn't have a vote. Which don't keep her from naggin *Mr.* Carrington about *his* vote—the house turned upside-down with the bickerin! *You don't understand politics*, Mr. Carrington says to his wife. *I understand New York State has the most electoral votes, and New York will go Republican*, she retorts. *I understand New York will decide the election, do you want to be an outlier in your own state? Outlier?* says he. *Not in New York* City. *The mayor's a Democrat!* You *don't understand politics* or *economics, I run a bank dependent on the South, and if the South secede, smithereens!*

Smithereens! Me and Ciaran giggle.

If they only knew that word were Irish, reckon they wouldn't deign to utter it, Grammy remark.

What's *secede*? I ask.

Oh, it's just a rumor, say Cousin Aileen. Virginia says they'll *never* leave the Union.

If Lincoln wins, I wager Virginia's in for a surprise, say Great-Uncle Fergus.

Then Mr. Carrington goes out slammin the door, then Mrs. Carrington openin the door to scream after him, then slammin the door *again, crash! Maureen! A vase fell, get in here and clean up the mess!*

Breckinridge and the damned Southern Democrats, hard-line fire-eaters, ain't they never heard a moderation?

Thought you were Democrat dyed in the wool, say Grammy.

Am! *Northern* Democrat—Douglas. Well, the fusion ticket. Were the fusion ticket *everywhere*, maybe a hope: set differences aside for the sake of party unity, but no! Damned sectionalism!

What's *sectionalism*? Ciaran ask Cathleen.

What's *fusion*? I ask Cathleen.

Sectionalism, my cousin start, is inflexible loyalty to your section of the country, in this case the South sticking together, no compromise. Fusion—for New York, New Jersey, Rhode Island, and Pennsylvania, the three non-Republicans have been fused as one anti-Lincoln ticket. However, in the other twenty-nine states, there are four candidates: Douglas—Northern Democrat; Breckinridge—Southern Democrat; Bell—Constitutional Union; Lincoln—Republican. Except in the ten southern states where Lincoln—Republican was banned from the ballot altogether.

Dixie and its blasted Southern Way of Life, say Great-Uncle Fergus.

All Douglas is callin for's popular sovereignty: let the locals decide! But stubborn Virginia and Louisiana and the rest down there determined to dictate to us all!

Decide what? I ask.

The *Constitutional Union Party*, Great-Uncle Fergus say in a funny voice. Nothin but a Know-Nothin revival!

Let the locals decide what?

Slavery, Cathleen answer.

Leave it to the vote, that's all Douglas asks. Now my great-uncle turn to me. Sure it's not the hypocrisy of the Republicans, callin *No slavery* while kickin an Irishman under a stagecoach. *No slavery* and half them abolitionists pressin for blacks to be on a fast boat to Africa soon's their precious emancipation go through, *them's* the negroes' ally?

❧

There's an election night party at Grammy Brook's and none at Grammy Cahill's, so decidin where I'll be Tuesday weren't hard. I wake up that mornin, Grammy Brook nex to me, eyes wide, smilin.

Happy Election Day, sweet girl. And she kiss me, hug me tight.

Southern fire-eaters flooding the polls for Breckinridge!

Northern Democrats coming out for Douglas!

Lincoln predicted to reign triumphant! Read all about it!

Everybody come in carryin a paper: Auntie Maryam, Mr. Samuel, Mr. Freeman, Hen who come home from Brooklyn for the party. When Auntie Eunice walk in with Uncle Ambrose and Nattie John, the whole room take a breath, waitin to see if my auntie havin a good day or bad.

Well! Are we all prepared for President Lincoln? she say, smilin big, and everyone cheer. I remind em I saw Mr. Lincoln when he come to Five Points back in Febooary.

You're one of the few, say Mr. Freeman. After he won the nomination, he didn't do any stump-speech touring—just ran his campaign from his home.

Everybody chatterin and eatin.

Good you could be here for this, Ambrose, say Grammy.

Thanking God. When we lost Seneca Village, I lost my vote, but I wanted to be with my family when the party claiming to eradicate slavery took the White House.

Later on, Uncle Ambrose is holdin Nattie John, makin funny blow sounds into her belly and she cacklin her head off.

Is that your papa? Is that your papa? grin Auntie Eunice.

Hen start blowin the *Say, brothers, will ya meet us* on her mouth-organ, then *Say, sisters, will ya meet us*, everybody singin the *Glory hallelujah*. Sometime in the night I fall asleep, wake up hearin Grammy snifflin. Mr. Lincoln *lose*? I see Auntie Eunice's arm around Grammy, Gran-Gran in the corner lookin sad at Grammy.

I just wished they coulda lived to see this day! Grammy say.

I know, say Auntie Eunice soft.

Your papas, Grammy say to me and Hen, wipin tears. Henry Floy and Zeke. I can just see em sittin here, holdin their whole brood because they'd surely given you all a mess a little brothers and sisters! This is history, children! they'da said. Remember this!

You recall your papa? Auntie Eunice say to Hen.

A little.

What'd you remember?

Throwin me in the air, catchin me.

We was prayin, say Grammy, wipin her face. The cholera took your father and near took you, but you were *strong*.

Still is, say Auntie Eunice, sad smile at Hen. Then she turn to me. You can't remember your pa.

I shake my head.

Just like you. Never cared for school, even while Grammy begged him to go. But he could read. Read Thoreau's *Resistance to Civil Government* over and over! And never was there a more skilled smithy, shaming all the whites wanting dominion over the profession. He loved your mother, and when she died, he couldn't look at you for weeks, you were such a copy of her.

Eunice! say Grammy.

But then, one day he comes home after his long workday, and instead of his usual broth and bed, he picks you up out of your basket and leaves. I didn't know what to think! You couldn't have been more than eight weeks of age, I was afraid! Ignoring you all this time, and now taking you without a word? Zekie, I called. Zeke! No answer. Down the stairs and out the tenement, I followed my brother and baby niece through the streets. He brought you to the stable where he worked. I wasn't ten feet away, Zekie *had* to have known I was there but he never looked at me. Had a horseshoe in his hand that he showed you, and he only spoke to *you*, speaking soft to *you*. I could catch an occasional word: *mother, Brigid, luck*. And then he gently tossed the horseshoe to the nail: ringer! He brought you and the horseshoe home. It became yours. Your and your papa's routine, picking you up every evening after work and bringing you to ring the horseshoe. After a few days, I stopped following. This was private time: father and daughter. I gave you a soft dolly but nothing you loved better than that horseshoe, even when you couldn't lift the heavy thing, your tiny hand clutched it. By the time you were two years of age, when your papa would walk through the door, you would hold the horseshoe as best you could and say it: *Luck! Luck!* which meant you wanted your father to take you to ring the horseshoe.

Auntie Eunice go quiet a second.

You didn't understand. After the horse kicked him in the head . . . *Luck! Luck!* you cried to anyone and everyone, clutching that horseshoe, your eyes begging for your father who would never come again. One day I couldn't take it any longer. *There is no luck!* and I snatched the thing from you. I could hear you screaming as I ran out of the apartment and down the steps, over to the docks, to hurl it into the East River.

Auntie Eunice turn to Grammy. I'm sorry, Mother.

Always wondered where that horseshoe went, Grammy murmur.

Auntie Eunice look at me. You cried for days. Then you stopped. Forgot. The biggest regret of my life was taking that horseshoe from you and hurlin it into the river. To make my precious baby niece cry like that. And worse! When you forgot there was ever anything to cry about.

Now Auntie Eunice's tears comin fast, and she grab me and kiss me, and I nestle into her. Auntie Siobhan always givin me stories bout my mother but hardly ever I hear bout my father. I don't know how to tell Auntie Eunice how this story make my heart warm so I jus burrow my warm heart close to hers. In the night, I dream about swimmin undersea in the East River.

Abram Lincoln elected sixteenth president of the United States!

Lincoln wins popular vote and garners landslide in electoral college!

Lincoln takes New York State, trounced in New York City and Brooklyn! Tammany Hall morose!

Auntie Eunice run out and come back with a whole pile a newspapers, each one ringin in Lincoln as America's sixteenth. Cake for breakfast! Then Mr. Samuel head out to drum up the chimney-sweep work, and Auntie Eunice go to the Academy a Music, and Uncle Ambrose take Nattie John home with him, and Grammy get back to her whites for the whites, and Auntie Maryam go home to get to hers.

You didn't have to leave early to get back to the cigar manufactory?

Worked extra hours last week to take off today. Lotta colored did. Want another party? Brooklyn?

I don't know what Hen's talkin about, but she likes mystery and never disappoints so I let Grammy know where we're off to and follow her. On the way to wherever we're headed, she say the cigar ladies was plannin a celebration supper together this evenin at Mrs. Laurie's, who I met my single day of cigar-manufactory employment.

I been stayin with her, say Hen. Rent's cheap and beats a barn. I think she jus like havin the company.

The cigar ladies remember me, except the ones hired after my one day. More cake! Couple husbands here but this mostly feel like a ladies' feast. Mrs. Niles the funny one come late with a paper, readin aloud every state and the thus-far votin results. States for Lincoln get cheers, states for not-Lincoln get jeers. The afternoon party carry into the night. After everybody else gone, Mrs. Laurie give me and Hen dough-nuts she saved jus for us! And vanilla tea! And chattin friendly, Mrs. Laurie feel a lot nicer at home than at the manufactory. I start noddin sleepy because not much sleep night before. Me and Hen in her tiny bed, warm jus off the kitchen.

Nex mornin, I board the ferry back to New York. I'm thinkin bout goin to Grammy Cahill's but not eager to see everybody sad after the election. Well, Cathleen might be happy, but Great-Uncle Fergus surely won't. Get off Fulton Street Manhattan and walk up to the Points, stroll by O'SHEA'S BOARD & PUBLICK. Auntie Siobhan and Mr. O'Mahony out front, chattin and laughin. I never seen em together outside a their mornin tea exchange, and never seen him so merry, so I know who he voted for and who she woulda voted for if she coulda. They smile at me, and wink.

Walk into Grammy Brook's tenement and know somethin off. Cryin behind one a the neighbors' doors, but ain't everybody in Grammy Brook's buildin colored? Election-happy? Climbin the steps, the sound get louder, and all a sudden I know it's the Jewels. Lost both their baby girls, I know now their baby boy die too! But nothin I hear behind their door. The sound comin from Grammy's floor. The sound comin from behind Grammy's door, I run!

Grammy screamin and cryin, prayin to God. Mrs. Jewel sittin on the floor holdin her baby and prayin, Gran-Gran in her corner mutterin Dutch prayers, Auntie Maryam on the floor callin to Allah. Mr. Samuel on a chair, head down, Miss Lottie from crost the hall standin, head down. Middle a the room, Nattie John sittin up, whimperin, lookin scared.

Why we cryin? I sob to Grammy.

Nobody answer, jus keep on with their wails and prayers, but Grammy hold her arms out to me.

Oh, baby, she say, and I run to her, her clutchin me snug, me bawlin, Grammy's chin tight on my head, Grammy's hot tears fallin to my scalp. Now Uncle Ambrose rush in, eyes red and raw.

Everywhere! Asked everywhere, looked everywhere!

Academy of Music? ask Miss Jewel, barely hopeful.

Last night, I searched top to bottom! She didn't come home. She didn't come home! Now Uncle Ambrose bawlin. I should have gone to pick her up, brought her home!

Now why would you do that? cry Grammy. You didn't know! You didn't know! And now Nattie John screamin, and Mrs. Jewel's toddler boy start bawlin. Auntie Maryam pick up Nattie John *sh, sh* but Nattie John ain't likely to *sh* with the whole apartment lit up in the howlin again. Then in walk Mr. Freeman, hat in hand. Everybody go quiet, even the babies.

Asked everyone. The customers, the barbers—you know we get all the news. Nothing.

Grammy give a little cry, but everybody wait because Mr. Freeman seem to got more to say.

Mr. Thompson, white customer. He said he saw some strange white men walkin around. He had his suspicions. Mr. Freeman take a breath. Blackbirds.

Now everybody with the wild sobbin again, except for Mr. Freeman mumblin and and Auntie Maryam just seem to gone stone still. Blackbird, blackbird, Auntie Eunice taught me that word, I try to remember what it was.

Bounty hunter. Slave-catcher.

NO! I yell it to Mr. Freeman. Mr. Lincoln jus got elected president, Mr. Lincoln takin away the slavery!

He ain't president yet, Miss Lottie sigh. Fugitive Slave Act still effect.

I look around the room. Like my hollerin give em all a chance to take a breath between their own sobs. And now I see that what Mr. Freeman said weren't exactly news to everybody. Jus makin more likely what they already was dreadin.

But Fugitive Slave Act got nothin to do with Auntie Eunice!

Nobody say nothin.

Auntie Eunice ain't a slave!

Then I look to Auntie Maryam in her light-skin disguise.

I mean . . . ! I mean . . . !

Auntie Maryam hold out her arm, and I come runnin into the embrace she already got Nattie John in.

You mean, say Grammy, her throat catchin, after my mother slave forty-eight years, after *I* slave twenty-two years, *my daughter born free.*

Her word gainst theirs, say Uncle Ambrose, then he wailin again, and everybody joinin him. *Our* Weeping Time, and now, nex to the stove, I see the big pile a newspapers Auntie Eunice bought jus yesterday mornin. The *Tribune* and the *Times* and the *Sun* and the *Daily News* and the *Herald* heraldin the election to the presidency of the abolitionist candidate from the abolitionist party—all ready for the kindling.

1861

Education

What was Eli Whitney's significant contribution to America? ask Miss Sarah Daniels from Auntie Eunice's ladies' salon, standin in front a the class. Up go a hand.

Yes, Charles.

Charles, one a Miss Daniels's favorites, stand. Eli Whitney guaranteed the perpetuation of slavery.

Explain.

Cotton had been a luxury item because after the harvesting of the crop, the fibers had to be separated from their seeds, a slow and tedious chore. It was presumed that the economic impracticality of the cotton plantation would eventually render the slave system obsolete. Then, in 1794, Eli Whitney invented the cotton gin, a machine for seed separation that increased the speed of the task dramatically, thus reinvigorating excitement for the slave system as an exceedingly and terribly profitable enterprise.

Miss Daniels smile, which mean Charles gonna get another ticket. When you do good at the African Free School, you get a ticket, and you can save your tickets up to trade for a trinket. Last month, Charles traded his for a little wood horse. Charles is also a monitor which mean he get to run the class, and he sure cocky enough to like that.

All Auntie Eunice ever ask a me is go to school, so here I am. If I do this, be a good girl, surely she come back.

Grammy Brook wouldn't let me out the apartment for a week after Auntie Eunice gone missin. I like the outside! I tell Grammy Brook that Grammy Cahill gonna wonder where I am, and she say, I already stopped at her table and told her. On the eighth day, I say, Auntie Eunice'd want me to go to school, so for Auntie Eunice, and also after I showed her the knife Hen gimme, Grammy let me out. First I go to Grammy Cahill's table, who gimme a big hug and start fussin herself, like I better always let her and Grammy Brook know where I am every minute. Then I go to O'SHEA'S BOARD & PUBLICK, and as soon as Auntie Siobhan see me, she burst into tears. *After that time at the dance hall, me and Eunice promised to get together again soon. Never happened! Never happened!* Then she say anything Uncle Ambrose like from her tavern or medicine cabinet, he got it free.

Theodora, say Charles-as-Monitor, I would like you to spell *hypocrisy* and use it in a sentence.

The sentence seem easier so I do that first. *It's a hypocrisy when people say do this while they doin that.*

Mary Jane who's thirteen years of age and her crony Harriet who's twelve snicker soft so Monitor and Teacher can't hear em, then sneak me a sneer.

Say that again, Theodora, with proper grammar, say Miss Daniels, overhearin while tendin to the smaller kids.

When I first come to school lass November, Miss Daniels tell me how sad she feel bout Auntie Eunice. Since the pupils beginnin examinations now, maybe better I wait till January to start? I liked that suggestion! Then January come, and I figured her feelins for my family's troubles mean she be gentle on me, but I thought very wrong! She lemme know I *most assuredly* need to work on my *elocution* and my *penmanship*. Auntie Eunice always said improve my speech, so reckon this I do for her too, even if there ain't much reward in it: only *boys* let be monitors. Only *boys* get the cartography and navigation classes in case they wanna be seamen, *I* want the cartography and navigation classes! I don't want sewin instruction! I get enough Cahill seamstresses already tellin me how to do that! I like astronomy though, and that one for girls *and* boys. And I like geography because it keep changin. Miss Daniels recently added number seven to the list on the big slate, front a the class.

States seceded from the Union	States admitted to the Union!
1. 12/20/60 S. Carolina	1. 1/29/61 Kan. 34th state
2. 1/9/61 Miss.	
3. 1/10/61 Flo.	
4. 1/11/61 Ala.	
5. 1/19/61 Ga.	
6. 1/26/61 La.	
7. 2/1/61 Tx.	

I don't quite see how Kansas can be admitted as the thirty-fourth state if we already lost six of the prior thirty-three, then come Texas the seventh— don't that change the arithmetic? But I reckon whether the seceded states is really seceded is a matter a debate. New York City coulda been number two on the left list right after South Carolina if Mayor Wood got his way, crusadin for Democratic Manhattan to secede from Republican New York State. But he got outvoted.

Here's a couple biscuits and greens. You run em up to Uncle Ambrose, Grammy Brook tell me after school.

Grammy always givin me food to bring to Uncle Ambrose, like worry he starve otherwise. And everyone worry Nattie John starve with him, so she been livin with Auntie Maryam and Mr. Samuel. I don't mind my errands to Uncle Ambrose but then he always say come in talk to him. I useta like talkin to him when he come back from seafarin, but now he ask *How's school?* and I say *Grand*, then his eyes get glassy, and *Remember when your Auntie Eunice taught you to read?* And *Remember when Auntie Eunice used to make the sweet vanilla snow for you?* And *Remember the way our tenants in Seneca Village respected your aunt? loved her? Remember what a good teacher she was, old Colored School Number Three? Yes, Yes, Yes, Yes*, I answer polite, and that pretty much make up the entire of our conversations. Still, after a few visits I get use to it, and when the questions finished, Uncle Ambrose go melancholy quiet, and I get to look through Auntie Eunice's books or her clothes or her recipes, feelin like she here.

Once in late November when I'm sent to Uncle Ambrose with a cooked potata from Grammy Brook and egg-nog from Auntie Siobhan, I walk into the apartment and there talkin to Uncle Ambrose stand Mrs. Heverworth and some man must be Mr. Heverworth. First thing I think is she come to take back her piano since Auntie Eunice ain't here to play it. But Mrs. Heverworth jus smile sad at me and talk soff to Uncle Ambrose. Grammy said it be nice I make up Uncle Ambrose's bed for him if it messy and it always is, so I do that while they all chat quiet but Mrs. Heverworth the least quiet, her voice raisin to my earshot on words like *disgrace* and *crime* and *investigator* and *attorney*, and I glimpse Mr. Heverworth jus noddin and noddin. I recollect a few days ago when Miss Bertha and the ladies' forum ladies was here also for a talk with Uncle Ambrose but not so quiet: *We have our sources!* and *We're doing everything in our power!* while I sat away from em and turned the page in Mr. Darwin's book.

In December, I come to find Uncle Ambrose lookin through all those letters Auntie Eunice wrote him over the years while he was at sea which he read when he got home. Treasure! Can we keep readin through these when I come over, Uncle Ambrose? He nod, pullin the letter in his hand out the way quick before his tear soak it.

In the middle a January, Uncle Ambrose suddenly get it in his head to start strollin to the post office on Nassau street every day. We walk in. I look around, rememberin Gran-Gran once sayin the post office built as a Dutch church, then took over by the British durin the Revolution for a hospital and sometime a jail, then after the war back to a church, now the post office. *Anything for Ambrose Bennett?* my uncle ask the postmaster. As if Auntie Eunice's slave-master gonna let her write home occasionally. Or maybe Uncle Ambrose hope we's all wrong? Auntie Eunice never was kidnapped into slavery, she jus took herself on a rest somewhere, cure her brain fever? I tell Grammy Brook and Auntie Maryam and Auntie Siobhan and Grammy Cahill about our excursions to the post office. They all shake their heads and say nothin, jus like the postmaster shakin his head at Uncle Ambrose now.

But other people at the post office *do* get mail, and this gimme a idea. One day after midday dismission from school, I wait outside the House a Industry iron fence.

Afternoon, Molly!

Afternoon, Theo! she say, comin to me from the kids she was playin with.

Remember I toldja bout my friend Mary Bree useta street-sweep and people at House a Industry sent her away?

Molly nod.

I wanna write to her!

Molly stare at me, and I wonder did I say somethin foolish. Maybe she don't like the way I speak a the House a Industry. Maybe she reckon I know nothin bout letters. I don't! I never wrote a letter before! I never *got* a letter before! I don't even know if Mary Bree ever learnt to read or write!

I'll ask Miss Laird. She's the nice one.

Thanks, Molly!

I come back nex day, and there stand Molly with a lady lookin out the fence, look to be waitin for me.

You'd like to write to Mary Briana Cox?

I stare at her.

Her name used to be O'Doolin.

I nod!

You're the little girl who saved her life, brought her here the night she nearly froze to death.

I nod!

We cannot tell you of her whereabouts, but if you provide your name, we will certainly let her know you would like to hear from her.

Theodora Brook!

Very well, Theodora Brook. It will take some time for her to receive our letter—the travel distance from our post office and hers. Then we have no idea how often her family gets to the post office. Then, *if* she chooses to write to you, it will take some time for it to return to *our* post office. So I would allow at least a month or two before you expect to hear anything.

Thank you!

Don't get your hopes up! She may not remember you. She was a very little girl when she was adopted and her family brought her to her new home.

Seven! And now I'm eleven years of age, so she's ten.

Three years, Miss Laird nod. A lot would have happened.

A late Febooary mornin, I'm traipsin through the slush to the African Free School, and from the cloakroom I hear some a the girls in the class.

It's Febooary now. And ain't I warm, my raggedy cloak coverin up my raggedy dress!

Girls are gigglin. I never heard Mary Jane talk like that before.

Least the Febooary snow clean up my dirty face. We'uns calls it a Five Points bath!

That was Harriet, and the laughter bigger. I walk in. Five of em, and they all turn to me, the laughin all a sudden cut short. Them starin open-mouth, like shame, then look away quick, slink back to their seats. Mary Jane too, but she still carry a little smile she clearly want me to see.

All them years Auntie Eunice tryin to get me speak better. And these weeks Mrs. Daniels on me bout the elocution, but already I know nothin gonna give my education a boost as much as my warm cheeks and stingin eyes right now.

Feb. 23, 1861

My dearest, dearest Eunice,
         I have so much to tell you! Our daughter

That's as far as Uncle Ambrose got, wantin to write to Auntie Eunice while she away like what she done when he was at sea. He surely know I'm standin right behind him but he don't look up. Dip his pen in the inkwell, starin hard at the letter, dip his pen in the inkwell.

Nex day's Sunday, me rollin the wood ball to Nattie John, her laughin and laughin, tryin to roll it back. *Tee-oh!* she call me. Three and a half months since Auntie Eunice gone, and Nattie John finally stopped cryin for her, and I like Nattie John happy but also my lass night with my auntie come to me, when she told me I stopped cryin as a baby when I forgot my father.

Now my little cousin pull herself up from the table, take a wobbly step.

Auntie Maryam! Nattie John walkin! I mean, *Nattie John's walking.*

Auntie Maryam come in from her bed-closet smilin, say, She been doin that a few days.

Uncle Ambrose know?

Auntie Maryam shake her head.

He been tryin—*He's been trying* to write a letter to Auntie Eunice but don't—*but he doesn't* know what to say. I'll let him know bout—*about* Nattie John's walkin! I'll tell him—

Tell him come here, say Auntie Maryam, eyes narrow, *and see for hisself.*

❧

Monday at school, Miss Daniels make an announcement that the Colored Orphan Asylum need some after-school helpers. Any interested girls? *This* a female job I like! and raise my hand, but so does seven other girls! But some of em's too little, Miss Daniels only take the oldest volunteers: Mary Jane who's thirteen, Harriet who's twelve, Jenny who's twelve, and eleven-year-old me. The schedule'll start first week a March, but Thursday,

Feboo—February the twenty-eighth, we all go together for the introductory tour. Hour-long walk uptown: west side of Fifth avenue between Forty-second street and Forty-third. The main building is four floors with two three-floor buildings flankin each side.

One hundred forty feet wide, say Miss Jane McClellan, the white head matron welcomin us. She take us around first floor: kitchen and laundry, dining-room and bathing-room, infirmary. Second floor a the main building's a school-room for the babies. Second floor a each wing, we peek into the girls' school-room, the boys'.

Now to the basement, our guide say.

On the way down, we run into a noble-lookin colored man comin up.

Good afternoon, Doctor McCune Smith.

Good afternoon, Miss McClellan. The man smile at us. Good afternoon, girls. Then he disappear up onto the first floor. All the girls smile bright at Dr. McCune Smith! I know he run a pharmacy in Five Points, but not sure I ever laid eyes on him before.

In the basement's storage for food, storage for coal, and two playrooms—and there all the orphans! Miss McClellan take us aside from the kids and start lecturin on how we will care for the children at play and help them with their lessons. Any questions?

Jenny raise her hand. Miss McClellan, how often is Doctor McCune Smith at the asylum?

Miss McClellan smile. He is our resident physician, so as often as he can be, but he does have his private practice and his pharmacy. Are there questions about anything you've seen on the tour today. Harriet?

Miss McClellan, I have heard that Doctor McCune Smith went to medical school in Europe. Is that true?

Indeed. Despite his brilliance, no American college at that time would accept a black man, so he crossed the ocean: Scotland. From the University of Glasgow, he earned his bachelor's, master's, and medical doctorate. He has been in residence here these last eighteen years, serving our children as well as the black and white patients of his private practice, and I think that should answer all your inquiries about our illustrious doctor. Are there any questions regarding your upcoming duties? Jenny?

Miss McClellan, did you say Doctor McCune Smith serves black *and white* patients?

Walkin home after the tour, Mary Jane say, My parents know Doctor McCune Smith. They have been privy to his pharmacy back-room, where abolitionists meet and plan.

Snowflakes layin on Mary Jane's eyelashes.

Negroes were skeptical of the Colored Orphan Asylum at first, founded by white women to take in cold and hungry black orphans and then train them for menial labor. The community was won over after the hiring of the doctor as well as by some curricular changes.

Then Mary Jane go into a grocer for her after-school penny peppermint stick, which her parents provide her daily. A lone newsboy shoutin nearby.

President-elect Lincoln secreted to Washington City for inauguration! Arrives safely after Baltimore assassination conspiracy exposed! Read all about it!

Nex mornin, Friday March the first, I'm at school early.

Practicing your penmanship, Theodora?

Yes, Miss Daniels, I reply, even though my penmanship is no pen, jus chalk on slate.

Very good. Your poor auntie would've been so proud.

She's not dead!

Charles the Monitor, also early, look up at me like he ready to put me in the mental asylum.

I'm sorry, I say in a sincere voice, even though I'm not sincere at all.

I'm sorry, say my teacher, which coulda meant any number a things, but I just as soon not have her clarify which.

After school's Nattie John's first birthday! Auntie Maryam get in her light-skin disguise, and Mr. Samuel clean himself up from the chimney sweepin, and they put Nattie John in a new dress Auntie Maryam made for her and bring her to Grammy Brook's so her and Gran-Gran be part a the celebration, but everybody got a little clog in their joy with Auntie Eunice missin it. Hen here even though it's Friday not Sunday, Hen always seemin to get free from her work for cake. Just a week since I seen my little cousin, and now Nattie John walkin grand! She walk to Auntie Maryam laughin. She walk to Mr. Samuel laughin. She walk to me laughin. She don't walk to Uncle Ambrose and when he go to her she start screamin *Annie! Annie!*

which is *auntie*, Auntie Maryam. Uncle Ambrose jus sigh, look out the winda. We have cake, and later I'm walkin on all fours with Nattie John on my back. *Geeup!* she say. *Geeup, horse!*

How'd you decide Nattie John's February the twenty-ninth birthday was March the first instead of February the twenty-eighth? I ask Auntie Maryam.

Jus feel right.

Geeup, horse!

Your schooling has had an effect already, Theo, say Mr. Freeman. You're beginning to speak very well.

Thank you! I say, and it make me wanna work harder at it.

If I were any kind of man, say Uncle Ambrose, eyes still out the winda, I'd go down there looking for her.

The *South?* say Mr. Samuel. Stop talkin crazy, man!

That jus give the slavers *two* stead a one, say Auntie Maryam.

Hen starts playing the *Glory hallelujah* on her mouth-organ, and Nattie John get off me to go to her.

Well, the inauguration's finally here! say Mr. Freeman. Monday, at long last.

My Great-Uncle Fergus said Mr. Lincoln dressed up like a woman, fearin assassins.

No! say Mr. Freeman and Auntie Maryam and Mr. Samuel.

That was just a rumor, say Mr. Samuel.

He have a disguise, say Auntie Maryam.

Yes, say Mr. Freeman, disguised as a different *man*. The assassination plot was *real*.

Hen! Hen! say Nattie John, holdin out her hand for the harmonica, hopin Hen'll share.

What're you doin for work, Ambrose? ask Grammy.

I can't go back on a ship! I've got to be *here*, in case—in case—

I *know* you can't go back to the seafarin, but what *are* ya doin? To pay the rent? My daughter gonna wanna come back to her *home*.

I don't like to leave it! Except the post office. What if she comes? Ambrose—

Had a little tucked away, cash. But running low now.

Wish I could offer you some sweep work, say Mr. Samuel, but the recession, this damned recession.

Thinking of selling that piano.

No!

Everyone look at me.

You don't think she comin back to play it? I ask Uncle Ambrose, wipin the wet from my cheeks.

She's coming back! Then Uncle Ambrose look down. You're right. Have to save the piano for her. You're right.

⌒

During our introductory tour, Tuesday was the day I was assigned for my volunteerin, so Tuesday the fifth is my first time workin with the orphans at the Colored Orphan Asylum. I'm helping Miss Dahlia from the staff, colored girl, seventeen years of age. The littler ones keep us busy! But runnin after Nattie John gimme some experience.

You stop hitting him, Elijah! holler Miss Dahlia. I turn round to see what's the commotion.

Elijah?

The little boy look at me.

Elijah! Remember me? Theo?

Elijah shake his head.

You have a sister: Nancy.

Elijah nod his head.

I knew you all when we were little! Five Points! Nancy here?

She with the big kids. Then Elijah run off to hit that boy again. Half-hour later come bigger kids, and there she be, skinny n tall. I know her even before Elijah run put his arms round her.

Nancy!

She turn to me starin. I point to myself.

Theo! Remember? Five Points?

She stare.

You had Lucille the dog!

She stare. Then she say, One time you share your birthday apple?

Yes! You remember!

Kinda!

I thought you died! I heard you and Elijah caught a fever and died!

We caught a fever but we got better, and the Colored Orphan Asylum taken us in. I was five and now I'm eight. Elijah's six.

I'm eleven!

Then, there are other children to attend to, any Miss Dahlia behind me, so I start attendin to the other children, but Nancy start followin me around like the more she be with me, the more she'll remember, and Elijah mostly clingin to her. I'm happy to be with my old Lazarus'd street chums!

⤫

Anything for Ambrose Bennett?

No, the postmaster tells him the following Monday, but something for Theodora Brook. That be you?

Thank you! I tear it open, feeling Uncle Ambrose looking at me, like hoping Auntie Eunice might be writing to me if not him.

It's my friend, I say quiet. She used to sweep the streets, and Uncle Ambrose's face fall sad and a little mad, like if Mary Bree's letter hadn't've blocked up the postal service, Auntie Eunice's letter could've got through. I know I'm not ever coming with Uncle Ambrose to the post office no more for fear my mail be the wrong mail.

> Hello Theo I live Winsconsin house in the
> woods. I adopted by Cox. Mrs. Cox a teacher
> so I learn. I hafe my room. They don't hafe
> chilren just me. I like Winsconsin. I got boots.
> I miss kids 5 points. I'm 10!
>
> Mary Bree or Prudence.

There's all kinds of orphans. Nancy and Elijah at the Colored Orphan Asylum. Mary Bree, sent to House of Industry then adopted away to Wisconsin. Me, orphan lucky, lots of places to call home: Grammy's, Grammy's, Auntie Siobhan's, Auntie Maryam's. Then there's Nattie John, near an orphan since her mother taken away and her father too mournful to father. Been four months since Auntie Eunice been kidnapped to slavery, and seems like Uncle Ambrose become a slave to the sorrow of it.

Month later, parsnips in season at the market, Grammy make soup and send me to Uncle Ambrose with some.

You wrote to your friend? he asks. Take me a second to know what he's saying.

I nod. I'd written back to Mary Bree right away.

He gaze out the window a while, then turn back to me.

You help me write to your Aunt Eunice?

It's the same letter he started from February! Uncle Ambrose hasn't added a word, but I can imagine him pulling it out every day and staring at it, trying, trying.

April 11, ~~Feb. 23,~~ 1861

My dearest, dearest Eunice,

I have so much to tell you! Our daughter is walking now! Auntie Eunice, Im Theo helping Uncle Ambrose with your letter. Im going to the African Free School! My teacher is Miss Daniels. Im learning to speak proper. I like astronomy! I work with orphans at the Colored Orphan Assylm! Nancy and Elijah are there they didnt die! Write back when you can.

Love,
Uncle Ambrose and Theo.

April 11, 1861 (later)

I forgot to tell you Nattie John is one years of age! We had her February 29 birthday on March 1.

April 12, 1861

Also news Confederate shot at a Union fort in
S. Carolina which was the first seceding state
Tonight Hen came from the siggar manufactory even though its Friday not Sunday and said
that means war and danced a jig.

War

Printing House Square packed! The newspaper buildings—five stories! *six* stories! and high ceilings each floor! Park row facing the park, big letters: THE SUN, THE DAY BOOK, THE TRIBUNE, NEW-YORK TIMES, everyone wanting the first word on what Fort Sumter afire's to mean. Here come the papers!

THE NEW-YORK HERALD.

SUNDAY MORNING, APRIL 14, 1861.

THE WAR.

Are we at war?

What the paper says, answers Ciaran, eyes twinkling, looking over the **Topographical Sketch of Fort Sumter**.

While Ciaran's monopolizing the paper (*monopoly* was in our reading-vocabulary lesson), I look across the horde. There's a newsboy I know, except I didn't know he was a newsboy.

How do ye, Friedrich!

How do ye, Theo! How do ye, Ciaran!

How do ye.

I didn't know you were a newsboy!

They just hired a bunch of us yesterday, Friedrich answer me. Sumter! Newspapers workin overtime!

I work at the Central Park.

I heard, Friedrich tells Ciaran, then Friedrich's calling: *Fort Sumter surrendered and evacuated! Quarreling at Virginia State Convention over secession question, read all about it!*

Ciaran?

Voice behind us. Ciaran and I turn around. Staring at the man.

Ciaran Moore?

Ciaran nods. The man's brogue's thick.

Oh, it's grand to see ye! It's Aedan Moore, your cousin! First cousin to Riordan, your poor father. I remember your sister Moora, God rest her soul! Not long in the country, I'm only after arrivin four months ago.

Ciaran still stares.

Ye don't remember me! Sure you just a tiny one and I come a-singin.

> *A nation once again,*
> *A nation once again,*
> *And Ireland, long a province, be*
> *A nation once again!*

I remember! Ciaran's face glows bright. His cousin Aedan grins.

Come ere, boy. It's ketchin up we need to be doin!

This is Theo.

How do ye. Then he puts his arm around Ciaran, and they walk off together before I ever get a chance to tell Aedan how I do.

The New-York Times

NEW-YORK, MONDAY, APRIL 15, 1861.

PROCLAMATION BY THE PRESIDENT

SEVENTY-FIVE THOUSAND VOLUNTEERS AND AN EXTRA SESSION OF CONGRESS.

Thirty-four hours straight those blackguards bombarded the fort. A *United States garrison!* Outrage!

Thought you were all with the South, Fergus, say Grammy Cahill, looking over some of the wares she collected end-of-day yesterday.

I'm after supportin them to make their own choices, not to take cannons to infringe upon ours! To provocate against the nation!

Are we at war? I ask Cathleen next to me on the couch.

The president callin for seventy-five thousand volunteers, replies Great-Uncle Fergus, what's that tell ye?

Look, Theo, a new dress for ye! and she sets it on my lap.

Thank you, Grammy! I hold it up. It doesn't look pretty, but it's a little bigger than the one I'm wearing, and I need bigger.

Ye think he'll get the volunteers, uncle? asks Cousin Aileen.

Indeed he will! Look around at the fervor! After the affront of it! The dishonor!

Sure I hear it in the saloon, says Auntie Siobhan, who dropped in to share a morning cup of tea with Grammy.

I'll dart it for you, Cathleen says quietly, eyes on the dress. Then a little smile: You're starting to need it.

I look down at my chest. My teats beginning to protrude, right a little larger than left.

And, sighs my great-uncle, thirteen dollars a month. Pittance, but with everyone losin jobs . . . The Powers That Be call this *recession*, Mother of God! I swear there's more out of work now than durin the *de*pression three years ago!

They've mightily got the patriotic spirit altogether, says Auntie Siobhan. Also I've heard a whiff of future plans. Claimin the struggle on American soil'll be grand trainin for the comin war against Britain.

This is Cousin Aedan!

We're all startled, turning to Ciaran who just walked through the door with that man.

My father's cousin! From Kerry!

Everyone stares.

Aedan? says Cousin Aileen. The man stares at her. Aedan! We were kids together! Aedan, she repeats to Grammy and Great-Uncle Fergus. Part of Nora O'Grady's brood.

Nora O'Grady Moore, says Aedan.

Ah, Nora! says Grammy and Great-Uncle Fergus, now smiling.

Barely older than Ciaran is now when we left Ireland, weren't ye? Grammy goes on.

But Aedan hardly acknowledges, looking around our apartment with some kind of wonderment I can't unravel.

∾

Course we're at war, says Mr. Freeman Wednesday afternoon. Lincoln doesn't want to say because that would imply the Confederacy is a separate nation, but the president hasn't summoned seventy-five thousand volunteers for some peace time parade.

What about Washington City, where President Lincoln sits? I ask. Isn't that the South?

Washington City is where they're sending the Northern Volunteers first.

But Virginia seceded today! And at school they say Maryland's sure to secede when their lawmakers come back in session September, and Washington's sandwiched between!

The war'll be over in nine months, claim the purported political experts. Volunteers are asked to volunteer only three months, we are twenty-one million strong in the North! The South is a section of a mere six million whites with four million African descendants, and do you think they'd allow the latter to defend the so-called Confederate States of America even if they were willing to?

Nine months! says Grammy. Mary Todd probably already plannin the White House victory party for Christmas! Or maybe three, the three-month volunteers fix em?

But *everyone* must fight, says Mr. Freeman. The union would be greatly handicapped without the participation of negroes, especially as negroes have the strongest incentive toward action.

What incentive?

Emancipation! cry Grammy and Mr. Freeman and Gran-Gran a little slower from her window.

That's neither illusion nor delusion, says Mr. Freeman. See what's happening in Russia as we speak. The emancipation edict just enacted a few weeks ago, freeing the peasant serfs. It can happen!

Recruitin stations poppin up everywhere in New York! says Grammy. There's one out our window, look there.

Though I hope the Russian emperor's Emancipation Manifesto provides compensation. How can liberated people survive and thrive if there's no provision for reparation of the damage inflicted?

If the three-monthers have victory, Eunice be home by Fourth a July! cries Grammy, her eyes shining happy, hopeful. It can happen!

Mr. Freeman turns to her, his face looking like his mouth got ahead of his mind.

It can happen, he says quieter and less convincing, but Grammy smiles broad, settled into her reverie.

～

Rich! says Ciaran when I come upon him in the street, running some errand for his Central Park work. That's what Cousin Aedan said!

He's rich? I say, doubting it.

We're rich! Grammy! *Us!*

What! *We* are impecunious!

Ciaran frowns.

Poor! we're poor!

Well, here's what's what, Madam Scholar. There's poor and there's poor. Then all the sudden Ciaran starts tickling me, and I'm screeching the giggles before he runs off on his Central Park mission.

The next day a multitude of men are waiting in the line to sign up for the Volunteers. Some of the men are boys.

How do ye, Theo!

How do ye, Friedrich! What *are* ya doing?

He points to the line.

My brother Erich.

How old is he?

Sixteen.

But to volunteer you have to be between eighteen and thirty-five years of age.

Friedrich smiles.

Erich gonna *lie?* slips out before I remember my new grammar.

Nobody lies. They write *18* on a piece a paper and put it in their shoe, then when the recruiter asks How old? they say, I'm over eighteen! Friedrich cackles.

They won't believe him! He looks—But my sentence stops there, watching two boys not men walk out of the recruiters' office arms around each other, laughing and shouting: To Washington!

Wanna see poor?

We turn around to find Ciaran with a crooked smile, his eyes on me.

Huh?

Poor. Unless ye're a fraidy cat. Ciaran musses my hair. Fraidy cat, fraidy cat!

Hey!

Then Ciaran strides away. I see he's inviting me on some kind of secret adventure so I run to catch up, though I think it's rude he didn't even greet Friedrich standing right there. Down the block, I turn around to see Friedrich still looking at us, then shaking his head before turning to walk in the other direction.

Ciaran and I enter the Fourth ward, which is right next to the Sixth, the Fourth stretching out to the East River. Into a tenement with the door hanging by the hinges, down to the basement.

First I get the smell, put my hand over my nose. Then take in two women, three men, five kids. Ceilings low, rags hanging to dry. There's places like this in Five Points too, I've seen them. But lucky my grammies' places are aboveground.

Whatchu want? says a man.

No more room! says a woman, both of them irritated but not enraged. Like not able to summon up enough energy for enraged.

Ain't lookin to stay, says Ciaran. Her and me just here for my cousin Aedan.

He's the boarder, says one woman.

He ain't here, says the other.

High tide! High tide! says a little girl, and everybody jumps on the dirty bed. I feel it: wet seeping through the floor to my toes! Everybody goes quiet, like holding their breath. Then the water starts receding to mud.

Not too bad, says a woman.

Once flooded up to my knees! says a little boy.

Now a rumbling, moisture appearing in the walls, and everybody groaning. The smell getting worse, I run up and out of that tenement! Ciaran behind me.

It smelled like an outhouse!

Ciaran nods. The privy vault next door. Since they're in the cellar—

That was noisome!

Ciaran frowns. Wasn't that loud.

Noisome! Malodorous! Fetid!

Ciaran still stares.

It *stunk!*

Toldja. There's poor, and there's poor.

Bet your cousin not be too glad you brought me!

He hates that place, don't come home till late. Knew he wouldn't be here. Whatchu cryin for?

I'm not! Just my eyes burning, the smell!

Your hand over your nose, like some gentry woman doin the slums in Five Points.

What!

Wanna go on a carriage ride?

Ciaran's got my head spinning!

Carriage ride, the Central Park. The rich folks do them.

I know! So how you figure—?

Last week, I was spreadin the manure fertilizer. Jamey with his carriage came along, wantin to cross through our work area which wasn't allowed, but at that time I was the only worker there. Let me do it this once, said he, and I'll return the favor. And right then I named the favor.

Next morning five thirty o'clock, Ciaran and I stand next to Jamey and his horse and buggy, nobody but us and the spring birds chirping the dawn.

Aw, brought your girl? says Jamey.

I'm not his girl!

She's not my girl!

We'd said it at once. Jamey chuckles under his breath, taking out a blanket to cover the carriage seat, then lifts me up to sit on it. Ciaran climbs himself in.

And off! Into the park from its southwest corner at Fifty-ninth, up the west path, the horse *clip clop*, us bouncing. *This is the playground*, *This is the Promenade*, *This is the Parade*, Ciaran explaining everything I already know. And yet up in the carriage, the speed and the height give it all a newness.

Then Ciaran falls silent. Staring out at the trees.

Don't know why I took ye to Cousin Aedan's basement apartment yesterday, he says soft so Jamey can't hear. Shamed him.

I didn't tell—

Don't matter, I shouldn't've done it.

After a moment, he turns to me.

You have blood. You might be an orphan, but you've mother's and father's side both. Aedan's all I have.

That's pretty ungrateful after all Grammy's done for you.

I *do* appreciate! That's what I'm sayin! Her kindness out of love for my family, even though she knew me not at all, I love her for it! But Aedan. Remembers me a baby, remembers . . . I didn't just appear in the world an orphan of eight n a half! I have a history, same as you!

Ciaran leans his head back against our seat and sighs.

Don't matter. I'm losin him. 'Twas a shoemaker, but the recession. Boss closed the shop, fired them all. He asked me if the Central Park hirin. Ciaran shakes his head. He's volunteerin.

You kids goin to the march after? Jamey calls back to us.

Yes! I reply. Ciaran doesn't, his eyes on the trees and mind on who-knows-what.

Seventh Regiment, first unit en route to Washington City! Jamey goes on. And the *Baltic*, ship the Sumter soldiers retreated in's set to dock in New York Harbor today. And the monster meetin tomorrow—lots happenin!

What's a monster meeting?

Big rally in Union Square, Miss, thousands expected. Boost the enthusiasm, patriotism. How old are ye both?

I'm eleven, he's twelve.

Thirteen in July, Ciaran chimes in when I didn't think he was even listening, his eyes still on the passing scenery.

Well, ye're both a mite too young to volunteer then, Jamey chuckles.

She's a girl, Ciaran says.

I figured that out.

I like your horse, Jamey.

Aw, she's a moody one, Miss. But behavin today.

What's her name?

Aster.

Clip clop clip clop. The sun just peeking over the trees, squirrels scurrying, Jamey calling me *Miss*, I like that! I like riding high in the carriage, I like being high up high society. I turn to Ciaran.

It's grand that your cousin volunteered. The more volunteers, the faster we win the war!

Ciaran says nothing.

The faster we win the war, the faster we free the slaves!

Ciaran turns to me. That ain't what the war's about.

Yes it is.

No it's not. The war's to keep the United States united states. Pick up the pieces what splintered away and glue them back together.

And free the slaves.

Not *And free the slaves*.

Yes.

Ye're sayin after the slaves been slaves two hundred years, the country can just order the Southern planters to release them all in three months and said planters will politely oblige.

Three hundred and thirty-five years.

Did I hear ye say your cousin was lookin for work with the Central Park, Ciaran? calls Jamey.

Yes!

Shame. Lucky they provide *our* bread and butter, lad!

I wish the slaves be freed too, Ciaran mutters. But everyone says a lotta Southern slaves are sure to move to New York, and not enough work for a workin man as it is.

My face snaps to him.

A soldier's salary's barely nuttin, but better than the *pure* nuttin of hard times, calls Jamey. You know when the real customers have a carriage ride, *one* carriage ride, the fare could support a poor man and his family a year?

Ciaran and I gasp!

Don't think all that money goes to me! I got my bosses, I got the care of the horse. *I'm* not orderin steaks at Delmonico's with the damned filthy rich, which sure is where they come from before their leisurely ride through the park, *Girl, put that blanket under ye or I'll throw ye both out!*

Takes me a second to realize Jamey's yelling at *me*. Now I see I slipped off the blanket.

Pull it under ye! Ciaran snaps, and I do. I see we've gone east, approaching the impressive stone Willowdell Arch but suddenly I'm less in the mood for it. Yonder to the right, I glance a dog peeking out from a shrub, eyeing Aster. The blanket's scratchy. I move it just a little.

Keep it under! Ciaran hisses.

Why we gotta sit on it anyway?

Because Jamey don't want our filth infect on his respectable lady n gentleman customers.

I turn to Ciaran, who smirks: *Now* who's the noisome?

The dog comes barking at Aster, and she rears up whinnying. Jamey snatches the riding crop beside him, and when he's done with poor Aster, that whip's dripping red.

❧

Patriotic feeling all over the city!

One hundred guns fired in tribute at Ivy Green, Sixth Ward Democratic Headquarters!

Seventh Regiment to march down Broadway at four!

Taxes and meager land leave Russian serfs emancipated and emaciated!

New York businesses not donning the stars and stripes attacked!

Everybody in the city seems to be on Broadway, I'm crushed! Gotta push and shove to see the soldiers parade! Everyone cheering. Some crying.

Onward, brave Seventh! the people bellow. On!

Next day's Saturday: the Union Square monster meeting. I squeeze through the hordes.

The lower part of Bloomingdale, now Broadway, was to meet Bowery, now Fourth, said Mr. Freeman this morning, peeling his boiled-egg breakfast. *The surveyors saw the junction would have created an awkward angle, difficult for developing real estate, so instead they put a public square at the* union *of the two thoroughfares. How apt to rally at Union Square for the Union!*

Major Anderson who commanded Fort Sumter's the main speaker. The shot-through American flag hangs on the statue of Washington on his horse. Hard to move, hard to see through the crowd. I hear German.

How do ye, Friedrich!

How do ye, Theo!

Was your brother in the marching parade yesterday?

No, that was the Seventh. Blue-bloods, aristocracy. Erich's with the German Volunteer Corps, they don't leave till later in the week.

Oh.

He's right there. And my sister, see? And mother and father. That's my aunt Greta.

Sieg! Sieg! Freiheit für die Sklaven!

Friedrich's family looks happy, listening to the speakers, clapping. But his parents' arms around his brother, tearing through their smiles.

Can you understand German? I ask.

Course!

What's everybody saying?

Victory! Victory! Freedom for the slaves!

I stare at Friedrich. You don't think then the slaves'll come up to New York, and not enough work for a working man as it is?

Friedrich chuckles, eyes on the speaker. So say the Irish. My mother says, *You think our jobs are more secure competin against slavery?*

Liebling, I hear his mother murmur, her cheek against Erich's shoulder.

My father's a piano artisan, lowest of the low in the cabinet-makers. He and other Germans work at that new factory, Fourth avenue. Their bosses always tryin to divide the duties of the craftsmen, turn their expertise into somethin *un*skilled. And the founder and chief was born in the German Federation himself! Even if he Americanized his name to Steinway. The workers are maltreated and overburdened, but they keep fighting, together. Solidarity.

Solidarité, I mumble, remembering something from a while back.

Arbeiterbund. Founded by New York Germans but a coalition across American labor, openin its doors to every worker *without discrimination of occupation, language, color or gender*, that's the motto, my father repeats it every day! They denounce *all Slavery, whether white or black* and condemn *the heavy capitalists* whether Democrat or Republican.

Friedrich chuckles. Everyone's blood ragin to fight, what do they think the war's about? Negroes know. *Germans* know. And if President Lincoln doesn't yet know, he'll soon find out.

Tuesday I walk into o'shea's board & publick, which dons an American flag outside so is safe from patriotic attack, and then Auntie Siobhan and I join the spectators mobbing Broadway for the Sixty-ninth New-York Irish Volunteers Regiment march.

John! John!

I look where she's looking. There's Auntie Siobhan's tea-box friend Mr. John O'Mahony marching in the ranks! I've never seen him so happy! We wave wild to get his attention, and finally he sees us and waves back, smiling even brighter.

I whisper to my auntie: Has he volunteered for training for the coming war against Britain?

She whispers back: That might be a lovely added benefit, but John O'Mahony volunteered for the current war against slavery.

Surges in the crowd, and Auntie Siobhan and I get separated. I trudge through the throng. Here and there a soldier'll jump out of formation to give his mother a kiss. Or his girl a kiss. Wait. I *know* that girl.

Maureen!

She turns to me, smiles.

Emmet, this is my cousin Theo! Theo, this is Emmet!

How do ye, Theo!

They kiss quick again, then he pulls himself away to run and catch up with his unit. Maureen's eyes are on him vanishing up the street as she speaks to me: Ma already knows so you needn't worry about reportin the news, mouthy. Look. There's Ciaran.

We wave, but he doesn't see us. I try moving toward him. On the way, I get locked in a huddle.

A hundred thousand at the monster meeting in Union Square Saturday! says a woman near me. Didje hear?

We'll pray to Saint Sebastian, says the woman next to her. He watches over all the soldiers.

It's a brigade, I tell ye, says a man behind me.

It's not a brigade, says another. A hundred men forms a company, a thousand a regiment, three to five thousand a brigade. Michael! The man waves. That's Colonel Michael Corcoran, the commander. My cousin!

It's a *brigade*, and that's *Brigadier General* Corcoran.

Can you *read*? *Colonel* Michael Corcoran of the Sixty-ninth *Regiment*, it's all in the papers!

Aedan! I hear, and that's when I see Ciaran somehow got closer to me, though his focus is on a marcher, waving excited.

How do ye, Ciaran!

But then he drops his hand, disappointed. 'Tweren't him. Thought it was, but it wasn't.

There they are! says a woman next to the Sixty-ninth's-a-brigade man. Then she calls: Boys!

Our sons! says the man. Bradan and Padraig.

Both your sons volunteered? says the other man.

Plus two more, says the father.

Coinneach! calls the mother to another marcher.

Well. The father sighs. A soldier's pay's not much, but better n nothin.

Thank God the politicians and the military men say the war'll be over fast, says the mother. A lovely Fourth of July we'll all have! though her eyes shine like she's not certain.

Not *that* fast, another woman chimes in, though the three-monthers should be back soon after the Fourth. But *all* the boys home by Christmas.

My oldest sons'll have a little earnings to send to their families, says the father, and our baby boy to ours.

A little pay, says the other man, and the opportunity to serve his country.

Save his country, says the father. Sure, sure.

And free the niggers, says the first man with a grin.

Well, not goin for all that! the father laughs.

Friedrich said we will, I say so Ciaran can hear and nobody else. But Ciaran doesn't hear. *Friedrich said we will*, I say louder.

What? frowns Ciaran, eyes on the procession.

What that man just said. Friedrich said the war'll free the slaves.

Well, then maybe Friedrich oughta relay that message to the president by magnetic telegraph, since Mr. Lincoln appears to be unaware of the fact. Ciaran doesn't shift his attention from the parade.

All the Germans say that. Free the slaves.

Well, if the *Germans* say it.

Because it's true.

Now he half-turns to me while keeping an eye glancing over the marchers. I'm sorry about your auntie, Theo. I wish slavery *would* end, but listen: Lincoln offered general to a U.S. Army colonel who wanted to preserve the union and who called slavery evil. The officer considered it, but after his native Virginia seceded last week, he joined the Confederate ranks.

Who?

Name's Robert Lee, did ye hear what I just said? *A Confederate officer called slavery evil, the war's not about slavery.*

Yes it is.

He turns back to the parade. You have an annoyin pattern of makin bold assertions without botherin to provide any evidence to support them. If there were such a thing as a lady lawyer, you would not make a very good one.

Yes I would.

Aedan! Ciaran waves, then sees it's not.

If the war's not about slavery, what's the other differences of opinion we got with the South?

Ciaran keeps his eyes on the soldiers, says nothing. It occurs to me the ladies praying to Saint Sebastian and the men debating brigade-regiment seem to have stopped their own discussions to listen in on ours.

Huh?

I don't know!

Friedrich says his mother says workers who fear southern coloreds coming up to take their jobs seem to be overlooking the fact that they've been all along competing against *slave* labor, which is pretty harsh competition.

Well, then why don't you remove up to Little Germany with all your friends fightin for the slave?

A sudden whoop-cheer from everybody, but I missed why.

Friedrich *is* my friend. And his brother's savin the country, and he's only sixteen!

Then sure he'll make a fine bugle boy.

What!

No sixteen-year-old'll come to any combat.

He'll be part of it!

My *cousin*'ll be part of it! My cousin—

Who you don't even know.

Now Ciaran turns to me full on.

He's my *blood relation*. Livin in this country only a few months and now already off riskin his life for it.

You met him nine days ago, now gonna take out a lady's hanky, dab your eye to farewell him?

Ciaran's pupils are blazing, and I wonder if he might hit me like when we were little, but my lips sprung loose, too late to stop em now. Friedrich's brother'll come back a hero from freeing the slaves, *that's* what the war's about, *they* know. Coloreds know and Germans know, Friedrich knows. Friedrich says President Lincoln might not know yet but he's gonna find out, Friedrich says—

Friedrich! Ciaran growls and I jump back! just as everybody all at once starts cheering: end of the parade. Ciaran's face turns to panic.

That's not all! He looks at me wild. *That's not all!* and he pushes through the hordes toward the disappearing soldiers heading to the Cortlandt street ferry that's headed to Jersey City and the southbound train that's headed to Washington City.

A couple days later, I stroll up to Little Germany looking for Friedrich. There he is! sitting on the edge of the wooden sidewalk.

How do ye, Friedrich!

How do ye, Theo, he says quiet.

Your brother gone away to the war?

He nods. I sit with him, both of us silent a time.

What're you doin here?

I dunno, I answer, pickin at the dirt under my fingernails. Ciaran told me I ought to remove up to Kleindeutschland where all my friends are.

Friedrich chuckles.

He said the war's not about freeing the slaves. He said the Germans are wrong.

I'm sure he did.

He said the Confederate general Lee thinks slavery's evil.

And yet Lee owns slaves. Ciaran mention that?

I shake my head. We're quiet.

You've just been sitting here all day?

Since callin the mornin papers. Till I have to call the afternoon papers.

Down the street beyond Friedrich, some Kleindeutschland urchins start playing with a mangy dog.

Don't be a hero, Friedrich says soft. The last thing my mother said to him. Friedrich wipes away a tear. Then we saw him in the German parade. Then he's gone.

You don't want him to be a soldier and free the slaves anymore?

I liked when he was *going* to be a soldier, just. Felt different after he'd *gone* to be a soldier. Gone, gone.

The dog makes a low growl, and the kids scatter away, screaming and laughing.

He's only sixteen. They'll probably just let him be bugle boy.

They think he's *eighteen*. And only the little boys get to be bugle boy. And bugle boy's in the line of fire much as the rest.

But your mother said don't be a hero.

She meant no *extra* risks, don't *volunteer* for danger.

We're quiet a while, then Friedrich frowns. Then Friedrich says, Who said anything about bugle boy anyway?

I stare at him.

What *else* did Ciaran say?

The conversation suddenly jumped to some place I didn't steer it. And all at once the tears in Friedrich's eyes seem dried up by some internal fire.

Storming up Broadway, me panting to keep up with him. Dozens and dozens of blocks, Friedrich spittin mad, I don't know what'll happen next but I hope Friedrich sets Ciaran straight about the war without too much bloodshed!

Extra! Seventh Regiment arrives in Washington City, bedded down in the House of Representatives!

Seventy uprising Russian peasants killed by rich landowner!

We fly into the southwest entrance of the Central Park at Fifty-ninth, where Friedrich finally slows. Looking around. People strolling, chattering, ladies with parasols even though it's not yet summer, just a gentle late-April sun, and the kids in the playground in their fancy clothes screaming and hollering, nobody working, nobody a care in the world. Friedrich's mouth awe-wide, like Ciaran's cousin Aedan the day he walked through Grammy Cahill's door.

You've never seen the Central Park before, Friedrich?

But he's frozen from the shock of it all: everybody delighted, everybody easy.

This is called the Parade. The Parade's a meadow, and there's sheep. See,

Friedrich? and his face follows where I'm pointing. Not *dirty* sheep like the pigs sometimes in Five Points. *Clean!* Spotless white! Fluffy.

A hot tear falls from my eye, remembering Grammy telling me about my mother nestling with the sheep back in Ireland. And now a sheep comes right up to me!

Ah! Feel how soft, Friedrich!

He does, even if still dazed, both us caressing the sheep face. I think of Ciaran giving me this same Central Park tour from the carriage, and I start to see why it brought a smile to his face: feels grand to have the knowledge and to share it with somebody. I look up north to continue.

And there yonder? It's called the Promenade—

But that's as far as my sentence gets because suddenly I'm looking right at Ciaran staring back at us. What's he doing here? Doesn't he work up in the Nineties? He's pulling weeds. The boss must've told him to take care of the weeds in the lower part of the park where all the folks are enjoying themselves—wait. I *saw* him pulling weeds. I mean, I saw *somebody* pulling weeds when we came into the park but I paid no attention. All the visitors clean and serene and there's Ciaran, dirty worker here to serve them. Serve *us*, Friedrich's and my hands still stroking the sheep in our pleasantness. And Ciaran's face. Ciaran's face is *rage*—rancor and loathing and fury, in a second he's upon us, over to us so swift I don't have my head ready to warn Friedrich who turns to him just in time to get knocked down, Ciaran's fist meeting Friedrich's jaw, and now on the ground, swinging and knuckling, Ciaran's black hair and Friedrich's blond flying, rolling and punching and shrieking.

What did you say about my brother!

Here's what your damned war's about!

I'll wring your neck!

Get the hell outa my park!

The adults and children in their spiffy wear gawk. Some of the kids giggle. Some of the grown-ups grin, like these scuffling poor boys just provided them with the best Central Park amusement yet. In the brawl, I catch a glimpse of two bloody noses.

I gotta go back to work! screams Ciaran, yanking himself away. He hobbles north toward the woods, never looking back at us, most pointedly never looking at *me* as he wipes from his cheeks the blood and the mud and the tears. And everybody else shakes their heads and smiles, the impecunious back to work so the affluent can go back to play, like any regular old Thursday on the island of Manhattan.

Fighters

I am a man! says Mr. Freeman, standing in the barbershop. *That's* what I told them, *I am a man!*

From the street they tossed you out to? asks Josiah, sitting in his barber chair holding up the paper he's reading. The other barbers sit in their chairs holding their own dailies.

I was still *in* the street, mutters Mr. Freeman. They never let me set foot in the recruiting office.

What's that? asks Hen. Mr. Freeman appears startled to see us standing here, even though I'm sure he saw Hen and me walk in. He looks at where she's pointing. Boy's blue cap.

Some man brought his boy in for a trim, left without it, says Ben. Two weeks, reckon they're not comin back. Want it?

What you came for's in that sack, Theo, says Mr. Freeman. Don't tell me Hen's interested in making dolls too.

NO! says Hen, tucking her hair up under the blue cap.

She just came along because nothing else to do, I say.

You're the one at the Brooklyn cigar factory, says Josiah. Hen nods. They lettin people go?

I'm down to three days a week.

As you girls can see, says Ben, not much activity around here either.

What's in the bag is all that was collected this morning, says Mr. Freeman.

All *we* collected, says Josiah. *You* were out *not* volunteerin for the United States Army.

In the burlap sack is the cut hair which the barbers kindly saved for the two dolls I made: one for the Colored Orphan Asylum play-room and one for Nattie John. The hair is all white men's hair since all the barber-shop customers are white. Some of the beard hair's a little curlier.

The feds so cocksure the war'll be over in nine months, says Mr. Freeman, and look at the first major battle: disaster!

320

The retreat, reads the young barber Gus from his *New-York Times, was conducted in the reverse order of our march in the morning, and sharing comparatively little in the panic which characterized so painfully that retreat, and which seemed to be occasioned more by the fear of frightened teamsters, and of hurrying and excited civilians (who ought never to have been there), than even by the reckless disorder and want of discipline of straggling soldiers.*

The Washington City gentry came in carriages to the combat arena with picnics and opera glasses to watch the show! Mr. Freeman rails. They expected to toast a Union victory, only to turn tail with the rest of the Great Skedaddle! Disgrace! Do you know, after all the planning and anticipation, the Eighth New York State Militia walked off the battlefield the day before the big clash? Their three-months term expired, those ground soldiers just abandoned ship! Had it been *black* men—

Hot as hell *here,* says Ben, and *there? Virginia?* I'da walked off too.

And to hell with emancipation, retorts Mr. Freeman, fiery eyes.

I gotta go to the privy, says Hen, and disappears out back.

Don't you think three-quarters the negroes in this city wanna go fight them rebbies? Josiah asks Mr. Freeman. Woulda *loved* to've faced the elephant! But the recruiters refuse us, what's to do?

Fight! Fight to fight!

Or wait for the white North and the white South to kill each other off, says Ben. Then emancipation take care of itself.

Mr. BIRCH, reads the barber whose name I forget holding the *Sun, who took them to Bull's Run has returned, and reports that all the dead are not yet buried—*

No doubt, says Mr. Freeman. Five hundred dead, a thousand wounded—that's just the *Union* casualties!

The troops that have arrived here since the "Bull Run" fight, Ben reads from his *Herald, come with a distinct understanding that they are not about to participate in a fancy picnic excursion, as many of the three months' men seemed to suppose.*

You know about her aunt.

The men look at me, their bodies now solemn still, my heart beating quick.

Her aunt, Mr. Freeman continues, established a ladies' salon. When she went missing, think those women just sat back, hoped for the best?

They acted! Who do they know? Who might help? Lawyers and detectives, assessing their resources, you have to *stand up* for change!

The sitting-down men's eyes still grave on me.

We're at war, Josiah finally says quietly to Mr. Freeman. Beginning of the end. The South won't stay without slavery, but Lincoln won't let the South go, so whether they let us fight or not, look like the South gonna be made to give up slavery.

After that showing at Manassas? which is the last I hear of Mr. Freeman's reply because Hen just returned from the outhouse, hands in her pockets, and I follow her outside.

You got enough hair for your dollies?

Takes a few seconds to take my mind away from Auntie Eunice enough to hear and reply: shrug.

Now ya do. She takes her fists out and drops two huge clumps of negro curls into my bag, then takes off her cap.

Hen! Grammy'll whoop you, cuttin off all your hair! You look like a boy!

Thanks, she says and struts ahead.

Nobody's home when we get to Grammy's except Gran-Gran staring out the window. I look over the two rag dolls I made, trying to figure out the best way to attach the hair.

What's that?

New book, just came out. For the ladies' forum.

I thought you didn't go no more.

Miss Daniels at school said she didn't want to put pressure on, but the ladies missed me, and if I came she'd give me a school ticket, and if I get enough tickets I can trade them for a trinket.

Hen studies the cover—*Incidents in the Life of a Slave Girl*, by Harriet Jacobs—but says nothing.

I still didn't want to do it. Being there would make me feel bad without Auntie Eunice. But then Miss Bertha ran into Auntie Maryam and talked about how *Auntie Eunice would have wanted it*, and *Meant so much to her*, so we're both going again. In the book, Harriet Jacobs's name is Linda Brent. It's Auntie Maryam's book. She started it then put it down, said it was too hard to read, not difficult but sad, so she passed it to me, I read it fast! We don't talk about it till the Sunday August the fourth ladies' meeting but today's only Wednesday July the twenty-fourth, I wanna talk about it *now*! Even with the sad parts, what's grand about slave narratives is you know the slave must've made it to freedom to write about it!

But Hen isn't listening. Already sitting and reading.

I wake up early next morning to finish my dolls, then show them to Grammy.

Ah! You need to bring em to Ambrose, brighten his day. Then she glances at Hen. And I see where half their hair come from.

Hic, says Hen, reading the book.

When I saw your head, Grammy says, hands on hips and shaking her own head. Deserved more than the three smacks I gave your backside last evenin, but why bother? Too stubborn to cry no matter how stingin the switch.

Hic, says Hen.

Drink some water!

Hen looks up at Grammy. I did, *hic*. They won't go away, *hic*. Then Hen's back to the book. *Hic*.

❧

Hot! And school hotter still with the extra dog-days students packed in. With summer and winter come the kids from the uptown Manhattan farms. We never see them spring planting and fall harvest. City kids, we have school all year round. Dismission!

On the street, I glimpse Mr. Samuel with his straw and want to say *How do ye*, but then I see Mr. Freeman talking to him, Mr. Samuel listening and nodding, and I'm not in the mood for another big, loud speech from Mr. Freeman so I turn away to head up to the Village. Knock on Auntie Eunice's and Uncle Ambrose's door.

Yes? a lady answers. About Auntie Eunice's age. Big eyes, copper skin.

I step back!

Good afternoon. I'm looking for my Uncle Ambrose.

I'm sorry, dear. He doesn't live here anymore.

I race up to the Thirties!

Auntie Maryam! Auntie Maryam!

How do ye, Theo.

Tee-oh!

I made this doll for Nattie John, and Grammy said show it to Uncle Ambrose to brighten his day, and I went to Uncle Ambrose's and a lady answered the door!

What! says Auntie Maryam, her eyes like murder.

Baby! says Nattie John, eyes on the doll.

She said Uncle Ambrose doesn't live there anymore.

What? Now Auntie Maryam's eyes like fear.

Baby? says Nattie John.

Running back downtown.

Mr. Samuel!

Mr. Samuel puts up his hand for me to wait while he makes a straw sale to a customer.

Yes, Theo.

Auntie Maryam said to tell you but not to tell Grammy because it might worry her that a lady is at Auntie Eunice's apartment and she said Uncle Ambrose doesn't live there anymore!

Mr. Samuel frowns. I'll keep an eye out.

Friday July the twenty-sixth is Auntie Eunice's birthday, so Grammy makes a special dinner. She blesses the food and thanks God and thanks Auntie Maryam for showing her God's bounty from her garden so we're not quite as bad as others in this recession-depression and thanks Mr. Samuel for finding out Uncle Ambrose is staying at the Seamen's Home and prays the war'll be over quick which will bring Auntie Eunice back quick. That last prayer I've heard her pray morning noon and night but for the special dinner the prayer lasts a lot longer: *Two hundred and sixty-one days I lost my daughter* and *Thirty-one years of age she would be today* and *What a good daughter she is* and *What a good mother she is* and *What a good wife* and *What a good auntie* and *the Academy of Music* and *the Ladies Cultural Forum* and *What a good daughter* and *What a good granddaughter* and *What a good sister to her brothers* and *What a good sister to her foster sister* and *What a good daughter* and *What a good daughter* and *What a good daughter, Amen.* After dinner, people talk quietly.

Looking more like her mother every day, says Mr. Freeman gazing at Nattie John, who sits kissing the doll I made her between bouts of slamming its head against the floor.

Always treated me *jus* like a sister, murmurs Auntie Maryam. Like family.

Another person mighta fell into a brain fever and not come out, says Mr. Samuel. Losin Seneca Village, losin her teaching position. But she jus took up the opera house seamstressin, took it in stride.

My daughter's kidnapped into slavery, and her *husband's* the one fall into a brain fever. Why ain't he here?

He was bad when I saw him today, says Mr. Samuel. Wailin and weepin, I told him maybe he feel better be around family. But no answer, just cryin: *Eunice, Eunice*.

Nissy, says Gran-Gran to the window.

Ah! says Grammy teary, I forgot that! When Eunice was just a little thing, Mama use to call her Nissy. Thank you for that, Mama!

Must be a good book, Mr. Samuel smiles at Hen.

Hic, says Hen, turning the page.

Can we visit Uncle Ambrose at the Colored Sailors' Home? I ask.

He's not at the Colored Sailors' Home, says Mr. Freeman. The Colored Sailors' Home's in Dover street. Ambrose is at the Seamen's Home in Vandewater street.

What's the difference? *Hic*.

They are both boarding-houses for colored shipmen, Mr. Freeman answers Hen, but the Seamen's Home also provides services for negro mariners: clothes and equipment, finding them jobs, collecting their wages for them while they're at sea.

And other services, says Auntie Maryam.

I heard Albro and Mary Lyons at that Seamen's Home disguised a thousand refugees, says Mr. Samuel next to her. A thousand immigratin from the South to freedom! And he gives Auntie Maryam's hand a little squeeze, the couple smiling softly at each other.

Mrs. Lyons comes to the Colored Orphan Asylum sometimes. She gives presents to the orphans.

She's a very kind lady, says Mr. Freeman.

And a very fat lady, I add.

She earned it, says Grammy. Wearin her wealth. Ambrose is fortunate they took him into that home at a discount.

They sympathized with his situation, says Mr. Freeman.

I *told* him he'd lose Eunice's apartment if he didn't go back to the sea! says Grammy. How'd he think the rent get paid?

Well, Mr. Samuel sighs, he's hurting.

Who isn't?

Did Uncle Ambrose bring Auntie Eunice's piano to the Seamen's Home?

One a the ladies' salon ladies holdin on to it till Auntie Eunice come back, Mr. Samuel tells me.

Mrs. Robbins, says Auntie Maryam.

Can we visit Uncle Ambrose at the Seamen's Home?

No! Grammy tells me. Do you look like a seaman? Hen, drink some water! How you keep your job with all that hiccuppin?

I don't—*hic*—hiccup there—*hic*.

I think there's a parlor, Auntie Maryam says. At the home. People wanna visit.

Maryam, I heard you been keepin up with that Mrs. Heverworth, says Mr. Freeman.

Auntie Maryam nods.

No word?

Auntie Maryam shakes her head.

You think they're tryin? asks Grammy. That Pinkerton agency not often concern itself with negro abductions.

Can only pray, says Auntie Maryam.

You think I'm not? snaps Grammy.

How's the barberin business? ask Mr. Samuel.

Slow like every place else, sigh Mr. Freeman. Had it out with a customer today. Him claiming Lincoln panicked after Sumter, and it was *that* that did the most damage to the Union cause—the president's summons for militia and volunteers that incited the quick-succession secessions of Virginia and Arkansas and Tennessee and North Carolina. Then bringing up that resolution the Congress just passed, he and I got into it. *We'll see about that, sir!* I bellowed. *We'll see about that!* forgetting all about my razor scraping his throat.

You cut his—*hic*—throat?

What resolution? asks Grammy.

Not a drop of blood spilt, but he beat a hasty and hostile retreat without paying. I expected then my brother barbers in their worrisome idleness to have it out with me, but the resolution shook them all, shop quiet like a funeral.

What resolution?

Mr. Samuel turns to Grammy. Crittenden-Johnson. Congress affirmin the war bein fought to preserve the Union, *not* to end slavery.

Grammy looks around at everybody's faces, looking ready to burst into tears. Not true! Grammy cries.

Is true the resolution was passed, says Mr. Freeman, but what flim-flammery: the only way to preserve the union *is* to end slavery!

Tee-oh!

We all look at Nattie John, who is showing me that she pulled her doll's arm off, grinning as if her mutilation would make me proud.

Why you still readin that book, Hen? ask Grammy. This supposed to be a day about Auntie Eunice!

Tryin to—*hic*—finish.

I figured Auntie Maryam's book shouldn't leave our apartment so Hen's not reading it on the ferry where she might drop it in the Hudson or some such.

Thank you, Auntie Maryam says to me.

So she had to stop reading when she went back to work Wednesday and Thursday, today she's just picking up where she left off.

I don't wanna hear all that! I asked why she's readin it at all!

Hen sighs—*hic*—and closes it.

I swear that silly book's been givin you the hiccups, every time you read it!

Not silly, Mama, says Auntie Maryam, who rarely says *Mama* to Grammy. Slave narrative, what the slave have to go through. Then Auntie Maryam takes the book from Hen, reading from near the beginning: *But I do earnestly desire to arouse the women of the North to a realizing sense of the condition of two millions of women at the South—*

Why'd anyone wanna read that!

It *is* hard to read! Auntie Maryam couldn't even get through it!

I *will!* Auntie Maryam snap to me. I jus—jus needed a little rest. It remine me—it remine me—

It's a good book, Grammy! We're reading it for the Ladies Cultural Forum meeting in nine days at Miss Bertha's, Sunday after this one but, Hen, if you finish it later tonight, wanna discuss it with me?

Stop talking about that infernal book! And I'm surprised you still *have* that salon without Eunice. *She* started it.

Auntie Maryam looks shook by Grammy's hard eyes on her.

I *know* she started it—

Maryam, says Mr. Samuel.

We have it *for* her, we think she like we keep it. We take a collection for Mrs. Heverworth for the Pinkerton. We—

Nattie John falls, knot on her head, screaming.

Annieannieannie!

Grammy gasps. Auntie Maryam runs to Nattie John.

She call you *Mammy*? Grammy demands.

ANNIE! Nattie John bawling in Auntie Maryam's arms.

She call you *Mammy*? *You're not her mother!*

Auntie! cries Auntie Maryam. She sayin *Auntie!*

Nissy, says Gran-Gran, eyes out the window.

Aw, Mama. Grammy wiping the wet from her cheeks.

❧

Next day afternoon, Auntie Maryam and I sit in the parlor of the Seamen's Home. The table is fine wood, the chairs soft, intricate embroidery. Doilies, paintings, photographs in frames. I've never seen photographs of colored people before! Except Frederick Douglass.

This is Ambrose's little girl? says the nice man who's come to greet us.

Sure is, replies Auntie Maryam. Natalie John, seventeen months old. And this his niece, Theodora.

Well, I'm certain he'll be glad to see you all, and the man disappears into the other rooms. Nattie John sits on Auntie Maryam's lap holding her one-armed doll which I noticed she yanked bald in places. I look at the main framed photograph: obese Mrs. Lyons sitting next to a standing small, slim husband, which I realize is the man we just met.

Out comes Uncle Ambrose, smiling through tender eyes.

Maryam! Theo!

And Nattie John, says Auntie Maryam while Nattie John clutches her. She knows Auntie Maryam usually hands her to her father till she screams too much for anybody to take, but maybe Auntie Maryam doesn't want Nattie John to light up the Seamen's Home with her hysterics because today she doesn't remove her foster daughter from her lap.

Aren't they kind, taking me in? says Uncle Ambrose. They knew my . . . my situation—

Very kind, nods Auntie Maryam.

We were once neighbors. Seneca Village, the Lyonses two blocks down. Then they lost their property to the Central Park, like us. Albro filed a claim against the city and never compensated. Like us.

Now Uncle Ambrose gazes at Nattie John. Then looks to me.

That is a *good woman*, Theo, he says, pointing to Auntie Maryam. A good Christian—

Muslim, murmurs Auntie Maryam.

Her and Samuel took in my daughter. And I didn't know what to do with Eunice's clothes, books, *they're* storing them! And that Mrs. Robbins holding onto the piano, everyone looking out for my wife!

Uncle Ambrose, I say, I wish colored could volunteer for the Union Army. Make the war over quick, bring Auntie Eunice home quick. I bet volunteering would help you get over your brain fever.

Brain fever gives Auntie Maryam a little start. But Uncle Ambrose just smiles.

Sure wish I could, Theo. But I need to be here. When your Auntie Eunice comes home, I need to be here.

Somebody walks in from the outside.

How do ye, Jeremiah!

He breaks into a smile. How do ye, Theo! Miss Maryam.

Haven't seen you since running in the alley! Since you used to appren- tice chimney-sweep with Mr. Samuel and Hen.

I live here.

You're a *seaman*?

He laughs. Cabin boy. I'm twelve now, near grown. Then he ruffles my hair gentle and goes off into the other rooms. Nattie John pulls at Auntie Maryam to get down so she puts her on the floor. *Sit still. Don't touch anything!*

Maryam. Maryam! I've been thinking, I've been dreaming. I been having bad dreams, I need . . . What you think they have Eunice doing down there, huh? Picking that cotton in the hot sun? Hope they give her a hat, she. Or inside, the cleaning and the cooking? Maybe not, I love my wife but never was she the best cook! Uncle Ambrose chuckles, but the tears start streaming.

All the slave work, up with the last stars before dawn, not let sleep till the moon bright, long's she do her job, they leave her be, that the truth? Nothing else they ask of her? No whipping? No . . . ? She put in her toil then they don't bother her, she *left alone, left alone at night to sleep.* That the way?

Auntie Maryam's eyes on him, Uncle Ambrose's face a puddle of tears but no cry in his voice. Nattie John stares at him, left thumb in her mouth, her right arm clutching the doll amputee. Then she holds the doll out to her father: a gift.

꩜

I spend the night with Grammy Cahill and wake Sunday morning to a cool rain: relief from the heat. In the afternoon it clears, and I stroll to Grammy Brook's. Hen's frantically searching in the couch, through the bureau drawers, under the bed. Even Gran-Gran's turned from the window to stare at her.

What are you doing?

She stops, aware of me for the first time.

Where—*hic*—is it? Looking round the windowsill.

Where's what?

The book! Hic. The book! Hic. Peeking under a loose floor-board.

Incidents in the Life of a Slave Girl?

Yes! *Hic! Hic! Hic!*

I thought you finished it. Friday night late you said you finished it but too tired to talk about it, so I gave it back to Auntie Maryam when I saw her yesterday, when we went to visit Uncle Ambrose—

Hen's already out the door. I fly out after her.

I thought you were done with it! I say, trying to keep up with Hen's fast-walk in the late July simmer.

I was—*hic*. I was done readin but not done with the book, *hic*.—

Oh, I say but I don't know what Hen means. Do you wanna discuss it *now*? I ask, hopeful.

Hic.

It was sad. And true story, not fiction! Like the part when the new young mistress bride came and saw the old man who'd served the family his whole life hobble up for his little bit of food, and she said No! Slaves too old to work oughta be fed on grass.

Hen keeps walking.

And when Linda's auntie never got a decent night's rest her whole life because she had to sleep on the floor outside the mistress's bedroom at the mistress's beck and call. And since she got no sleep she had bad health and all her babies died before they were born or not long after, and then *she* died not very old, and the mistress was hoping to bury her in her white family's grave which was *unprecedented* so her slave would *always* be at her feet.

Hen keeps walking. I'm panting.

And when the lady goes to the white preacher and begs for comfort after they sold *all* her children, the last was her sixteen-year-old girl and she *knows* what'll happen to her, *knows* what'll happen, she's banging her chest like this—Hen, look, she's banging her chest like this, see? Look. Well, she's banging on her chest and crying for comfort, and Linda sees the preacher titter and turn red and cover his mouth with the handkerchief because he's trying so hard not to burst out laughing.

Hic! Hic! Hic! from Hen is all we hear now because I'm out of breath so stop speaking. Now we're at Auntie Maryam's front porch steps, her door ajar, and we hear talk from inside. Hen pushes on the door, and we step in soft.

Circle of men. Most must've brought their own chairs because Auntie Maryam and Mr. Samuel only have three. Mr. Samuel directly across from us, and the barbers, some chimney sweeps, I count fourteen in all. Mr. Freeman is standing. We hear *Bull Run* and *the Congress* and *the black man* and *Crittenden-Johnson* and *secession* and *the black man* and *the Union* and *OUR fight* and *the black man!* and Mr. Freeman who usually has plenty to say on all this is quiet, standing and presiding and listening, a vague smile on his face which I reckon is because he's the one called together this men's salon and all the men excited for it, at last all ready and eager and itching to take up arms—then everything stops.

Mr. Samuel had just noticed Hen and me, and now all the men have turned to us.

Lookin for your Auntie Maryam? Mr. Samuel asks.

We nod.

Took the baby out back in the garden for some sun.

Hen and I walk through the circle toward the back, the chatter picking up again as we go out. We stand at the top of the four steps leading down to the garden. Auntie Maryam, her face covered with the garden net-hat, sits in the grass, arms open for Nattie John.

Come to Auntie! Come to Auntie! Nattie John does her wobbling run to Auntie Maryam, them both laughing, falling in embrace. Then Auntie Maryam looks up.

How do ye, girls.

Tee-oh! Hen!

We stare back. Not just a friendly visit, we have a reason to be here but I don't know what that reason is. I reckon Hen knows but she hasn't shared that knowledge with me.

Girls?

I read that book, *hic*, that slavery book, *hic*, I kep thinkin it's all, *hic*, I kep thinkin it's, *hic*, I kep thinkin it's all because, *hic*, her master gonna make her, *hic*, I kep thinkin, *hic*, he gonna make her, *hic*, he gonna make her, *hic*—

That's right, says Auntie Maryam. Part a slavery, the woman's part. Master come in the night, he own you. *All* of you. This country. Auntie Maryam shakes her head.

Men do that, *hic!* Men *make* you, *hurts, hic!* Men make you hurts *hic* hurts *hic* hurts *hic!*

Auntie Maryam's eyes are soft on Hen, fourteen-year-old Hen. And suddenly I remember that night in Brooklyn a year ago: Hen with the pepper water and Hen with the knife and Hen always on the cautious lookout and Hen saying bad men doing bad things *happens to every girl* and suddenly I know whatever hurt happened to Hen was a lot more penetrating than any hurt ever happened to me.

It says, *hic*, and tears start streaming Hen's cheeks which is a much more astonishing sight than the tears from Uncle Ambrose. The *hic* book *hic* says *hic* slavery *hic* is *hic* terr—*hic*—ble *hic* for *hic* men *hic* men *hic* men *hic*—

Harriet Jacobs wrote *Slavery is terrible for men; but it is far more terrible for women.*

Ye *hic* Ye *hic* Yesssss *hic hic hic hic* Hen can't breathe from the hiccups, and Auntie Maryam puts her arms around her, and Hen's fists clutch her little bit of hair that's left, her fists by her temples, her body rocking back and forth, eyes shut tight tears but no sobs, just *hic hic hic hic hic* and little Nattie John sitting in the grass stares with her mouth open, and I stare and think of the men inside preparing to fight and the women outside who always had to.

Shoddy

The New-York Times

NEW-YORK, SUNDAY, SEPTEMBER 1, 1861.

IMPORTANT FROM MISSOURI.

PROCLAMATION OF GEN. FREMONT.
Head-Quarters of the Western Department

Circumstances, in my judgment, of sufficient urgency, render it necessary that the Commanding General of this Department should assume the administrative powers of the State. I do hereby extend and declare established martial law throughout the State of Missouri. All persons who shall be taken with arms in their hands shall be tried by Court Martial, and, if found guilty, will be shot. The property, real and personal, of all persons in the State of Missouri, who shall take up arms against the United States, or who shall be directly proven to have taken active part with their enemies in the field, is declared to be confiscated to the public use, and their slaves, if any they have, are hereby declared free men.

(Signed) J. C. FREMONT,

Major-General Commanding.

Hen grins as she reads it.

Know who Fremont is? she asks me. Western adventurer! Found a new pass through the Sierras to California! Planted an American flag top a the Rockies! The Pathfinder!

And first Republican presidential candidate, Mr. Freeman smiles. Lincoln was the second. But Frémont—his father French-Canadian—was the more radical abolitionist. Lawfully, he was to free only those slaves used in the service of the Confederate army. Frémont's proclamation freed the slaves of every Confederate *sympathizer*, effectively freeing every slave in

Missouri. Lincoln fears comprehensive emancipation will send the border states fleeing—ha! He'll have a *fit!*

Maybe Eunice is in Missouri, murmurs Grammy, sounding more sad than hopeful, causing all our smiles to fade.

In bed I wipe a tear, wishing Auntie Eunice were here, wishing I could share that news piece with her. The next evening, I walk up to the Academy of Music, stand outside and listen. But the strings and brass and timpani are interrupted by two fellows in their blue army uniforms, looking not much older than Friedrich's army brother Erich who's sixteen. They stumble out of a nearby pub.

> *John Brown's body lies a-moulderin in the grave,*
> *John Brown's body lies a-moulderin in the grave,*
> *John Brown's body lies a-moulderin in the grave,*
> *His soul's marching on!*
>
> *Glory Hally Hallelujah!*
> *Glory Hally Hallelujah!*
> *Glory Hally Hallelujah!*
> *His soul's marching on!*

Hen's song! New words! I laugh out loud: we're gonna win this war! The soldiers are too drunk to see me, arms around each other's shoulders and their free arm waving in the air. And now I notice those waving hands have no thumbs.

Couple of weeks later, I sit with Cathleen, her surrounded by a sea of deep blue material: Union uniforms! And coin for me to help her hem them!

The war's starting to turn a profit, she says with a crooked smile.

I concentrate: space my stitches evenly or she'll tear them out and make me start over.

Do you know who James McMaster is?

I shake my head.

Editor of *Freeman's Journal.*

That's the paper doesn't favor free men.

Correct, it is decidedly anti-abolition, and to that end McMaster has lately been writing quite rabidly on the administration in Washington City, calling those papers that are anti-slavery *slaves of the present despotism.* So yesterday Secretary of State Seward sent deputies to McMaster's office, just below Printing House Square, who handcuffed the editor in manacles confiscated from a slave ship, delivering him kicking and screaming to Fort Lafayette.

Where's that?

Island off Brooklyn. Army prison. Perhaps Mr. McMaster's cellmate will be the mayor of Baltimore, who just arrived.

A mayor in jail?

Yes, and it appears the inconvenience will rather undermine his plans to lead Maryland to secession.

We both giggle, which feels grand after the impasse between Lincoln and Frémont ended poorly a week ago. Lincoln had asked Frémont to comply with the congressional stipulations regarding emancipation, which is to say Lincoln urged Frémont to stop universally freeing slaves. Frémont's response to this respectful request was no. Then Lincoln ordered it.

Next afternoon, Wednesday the eighteenth of September, somebody comes up behind me mussing my hair all over creation.

Stop!

There stands Ciaran, grinning. But before I can let my anger fly: Buy you some oysters?

Fresh and tender! I slip them out the shell, sliding down my throat!

How come you're not at the Central Park?

Quit.

I almost choke on the meat.

He shrugs. They always start cuttin the employee roster nearin to winter.

I stop eating, staring at my feast. He laughs. Unemployed and fool-spendin! Not hardly. I got a new job.

Where! I say, back to slurping.

Delmonico's! Dishwasher boy, and this job secure: the rich love to eat in restaurants! If I fare well, promoted to waiter. Tips!

Delmonico's. I let the word roll over my tongue. What's it look like? Chandeliers? Red seats, like in the Academy of Music where my Auntie Eunice used to work?

He smiles. One day I'll give ye a tour.

~

Saturday dusk, Grammy Cahill comes home carrying her table, grinning.

War profit! More jobs for the war, more spendin! And Fergus and Aileen bringin home the weekly wages today! Then she sends me out for butter.

When I get back, nobody's speaking. Cathleen on the couch, and standing are Cousin Aileen and Great-Uncle Fergus, everybody staring blank at a rectangular piece of paper each holds in their hand. Grammy peers over my great-uncle's shoulder at his.

What's everybody reading?

They turn to me slow, just noticing I entered.

Money, says Cathleen.

Right then Maureen walks in.

Just a quick visit before I go to meet Emmet. They went out to some fancy mansion dinner so I'm free till tomorrow early-mornin Sunday breakfast!

Usually Cousin Aileen is fawning with every brief glimpse of Maureen, but now she's too dazed by the paper. Maureen looks from one to the other, then starts laughing.

Nothin to worry on, those greenbacks'll spend just as well as coin!

Greenbacks? I ask.

Maureen holds up her own. A paper with green highlights and the back nearly all green. The front has a 5 and the United States and PROMISE TO PAY TO THE BEARER **FIVE DOLLARS** ON DEMAND and a photograph of a statue of Columbia with her sword down at her side and a photograph of a man.

Who's the man? I ask Maureen.

Alexander Hamilton.

Who's that?

One of the aul ones. Each note *personally signed* by an official treasurer or comptroller! And see? Payable to trade for specie on demand.

We knew they were comin, says Grammy, all the announcements. We were eager for them!

But different seein them, says Cousin Aileen. How can it be five dollars when it's barely feather-weight? Maureen, what *have* ye got on!

What she's got on is some wide-legged affair, trousers puffed out and gathered at her ankles.

Bloomers! says Maureen. So comfortable. Mabel, the daughter, gave these to me, she no longer dons them, though they were her apparel of choice back in the fifties when it was scandalous. Now she wears her new whalebone corset under her new skirt which is slimmer to the fit, the latest Paris *haute couture*. She says hoop skirts are a thing of the past, even if most of America hasn't yet figured that out, especially the South. Anyway! Bloomers are so much less restrictive, more healthful!

When did *you* ever wear a hoop skirt? asks Cousin Aileen.

Never now!

You look like two balloons, says Great-Uncle Fergus.

I look like modernity, says Maureen. Like those greenbacks.

How can five dollars be paper? Cousin Aileen muses, back to her curious new compensation.

I seen a funny sketch in the paper, says Great-Uncle Fergus, woman in bloomers. *She's* the one goin to her beau's father to ask permission for his *son's* hand in marriage!

Grand! says Maureen.

I just don't trust it! says Cousin Aileen, eyes glued to that greenback.

Trust it, Ma, it's the new way. And helps with the war effort.

Her mother sighs.

If *this* is a worry, wait till ye hear about the comin income tax.

What! cry all but me.

Only for the rich, Maureen smiles, ye have to make eight hundred dollars or more annual, and ye know the rare times anyone round here clears even *three* hundred they're prayin thanks to the saints for a *very* good year.

Siobhan? asks Grammy.

Maureen shakes her head. I doubt she makes *that* much. But if she did, it's but three percent of income.

Grammy sighs. Maureen laughs again.

If Siobhan qualifies to be taxed, she's doin well. We're *all* doin well! Cheer up! The recession's over!

❧

Next morning early, I notice Ciaran's already gone, surprising since he returned late after the Delmonico's Saturday nighters. I walk out to the street humming *John Brown's body lies a-moulderin in the grave* which, since that night with the soldiers, I've heard on several occasions. And there's Ciaran, leaning against our tenement wall, reading a Sunday morning paper.

Morning.

He glances at me, then back to his paper, less rude than distracted.

You ever heard that song *John Brown's body lies a-moulderin in the grave, John Brown's body lies a-moulderin in the grave, John—*

Yes, he says, not looking up from his paper. I can tell he's in some kind of mood, but I'm not, so I continue.

Hen used to sing it *Say, brothers, will you meet us, Say—*

Your *point?* he asks, raising his eyes to me.

The Brothers Will You Meet Us was a Bible camp meeting song. Or a slave song. It's not about John Brown from the Harper's Ferry incident in Virginia. It's not Virginia anymore! Did you hear? The western part of Virginia doesn't want to secede from the Union, so they seceded from Virginia! Gonna make their own state! And that part of the state has Harper's Ferry, which is what that John Brown song's about—

No it's not.

Yes it is.

No it's *not*. John Brown was a Scotsman coincidentally bearin the same name as the abolitionist radical. Union army soldier, died months ago when the war first started, that's where the song came from.

It's about Harper's Ferry.

Not arguin with you, he mutters before turning back to his paper. And now I see he's been studying the war casualties list.

Searching for your cousin Aedan's name?

Ciaran snaps the paper closed and walks fast away.

ᕫ

An early October afternoon, I'm on a stool drinking tea in Auntie Siobhan's tavern. Miss Fiona and some man Great-Uncle Fergus's age sit separately with their drinks.

Did ye know Michael Corcoran of the Sixty-ninth's been taken prisoner by the rebs? asks the man.

At Bull Run, 'twas, nods Miss Fiona.

A Fenian founder! says the man, and thus I know the Fenians/Irish Republican Brotherhood aren't such a secret anymore, if they ever were—at least not in this pub. The man shakes his head. People are startin to feel a lot different than they did back in April, after Sumter.

Nine months they thought it'd be over, says Miss Fiona, now seven've passed with no end in sight. Still! We've a lot of determined boys, and it's grand combat trainin, do them well the next war.

Against the British? I ask. Miss Fiona winks at me.

And I hear there's quite a few Irish screamin the rebel yell with their *Dixie* comrades, fightin *that* side for the same reason, says the man. Every time I see a lad return minus a limb, I think *Why?* Why not call it off? Good riddance to the blamed South! We'll be grand without them!

But what about the slaves? I ask.

Sorry, Miss. They call it the War for the Union, not the War for the Slaves.

Then, says Auntie Siobhan, you must've been delighted last spring when aul Queen Vickie issued her proclamation of neutrality, recognizin the rights of your reb friends. Praps you can start wavin the Confederate stars and stripes in one hand and the Union Jack the other.

Who said I'm allyin with the South! roars the man. I said good riddance!

The same thing! *Call it off*, good riddance is our surrender! So we can leave Dixie alone to her lucrative dealins with merry aul England.

The devilish Union Jack! the man shouts. Woe to the one ever *dare* claim the blamed queen's *my* crony!

⟋⟋

A mid-month Monday, I'm at Grammy Cahill's having bread and honey for breakfast. Maureen walks in.

Mornin, all!

Don't you Mornin *me*, snaps Cousin Aileen, when I know where ye been your Sunday evenin off. Sure that Emmet'll bring ye to ruin!

You're the one I'm after, Maureen says to me. The missus is havin some big tea affair next month, needs extra staff. Good money. Interested?

Yes! I say, doubting the money's good but coveting the opportunity to take a peep at how the other half lives. Maureen stays for a quick bite, mostly ignoring her mother's grumbles. I head toward the door.

Pssst.

I thought Ciaran was still asleep, but now he's calling me from the floor.

Come to the back of the restaurant two and a half o'clock, not a minute before nor after.

I stand in the alley behind 2 South William street which is just south of Wall Street, Trinity Church bells ringing half past, presuming it's Ciaran's aforementioned promise of a Delmonico's tour he's about to make good on. The back door's locked, and just as I'm contemplating knocking, his head sticks out, his hand gesturing me in.

Huge! This kitchen's far bigger than an entire tenement floor! There's another dishwasher scrubbing a skillet and chewing tobacco. Ciaran shows me his big basin, says on busy nights there might be *eight* dishwashers. A baker rolls out sweet dough. Overhead hang all manner of pots and pans. Then Ciaran shows me to a door on the other side. Doesn't shut: it swings! Looking in at the dining area: chandeliers, red velvet chairs, lace table-cloths thrown over round tables—dozens of them!

Ciaran smiles at my gaping. Delmonico's, otherwise known as the Citadel, he declares.

A waiter standing near the door and looking over a book with a quill pen glances up at us, then back to his notes.

What's the baker making? I whisper.

Meet me in that alley—Ciaran points across the street—four and a quarter o'clock, and you'll find out.

Then a man appears at the restaurant entrance accompanied by others. He speaks to the waiter, who then shows the group to a table. Ciaran pulls me back into the kitchen while another waiter flies from the kitchen into the dining room.

Don't they already have a waiter? I whisper.

That was the host.

I didn't know the restaurant was open yet.

It's not. The man must've made a special reservation.

What's a special reservation?

Bribe. You go on, I got work to do.

There aren't any dirty dishes yet.

I got *other* work to do, *go*. See ye in the alley, and Ciaran starts sorting the salad forks and soup spoons and steak knives. The other dishwasher mutters in Irish to Ciaran, who makes some adjustment to his method.

I move to exit the way I came in, but then things start springing into action, and standing with my back against the door, nobody seems to notice me as the cook starts heating a pan and setting pots of vegetables on the burner and giving orders to another cook who says *Yes, Chef*, and the baker seems to start hustling his preparations a bit, and the waiter fills goblets with water and goes out with a tray of them and comes back for wine and brings it out and comes back for little foods and brings them out and comes back for wine and brings it out and comes back for bread and brings it out and comes back for salad and brings it out, and every time he goes from kitchen to dining room through the swinging door, I catch a glimpse of the party-of-eight table and hear their laughter, and after a while we hear arguing, and Ciaran and the other dishwasher glance at each other without pausing in their work, and the waiter goes out with plates of steaks, and in the flash of the swinging door, I see that the man who'd originally ordered the table has stood up and must've told a joke because the rest of the party, women and men, laughs merry. Then it gets quiet, and I turn to leave till I hear a song.

> *He's gone to be a soldier in the army of the Lord!*
> *His soul's marching on!*

I've heard it before—another verse of the John Brown's Body ditty.

> *Glory Hally Hallelujah!*

and then gasps and someone screams, and everybody in the kitchen including me rushes to the swinging door.

The man is still singing and now dancing *on top* of the round table, wineglass in his hand. His seven companions have pulled their chairs from the table and are standing, staring up at him in horror.

Wallace! implores one of the lady guests.

Then Wallace starts kicking: saucers and glasses and beef go flying, his people running and shrieking from the missiles.

I'll get Mister Simmel says the chef, racing up some back stairway in the kitchen.

Now Wallace sees us. He stops dancing and smiles.

My friends! My friends from the Isle, please join me!

A nation once again,
A nation once again,
And Ireland, long a province, be
A nation once again!

We can change it!

And America, long united, be
A nation once again!

Then some Metropolitans rush in, and Wallace says *No need to worry, the leprechauns will clean it up!* and Ciaran finally seems to notice me and glares so I scoot out the door as the coppers looking up at Wallace on the table start to respectfully reason with him, something new to me since in Five Points the police usually let their billy clubs do the reasoning for them.

I go collect some coal for my grammies, but when the church bells chime four, I race to the alley near Delmonico's and hop up to sit on a barrel. I don't want to miss Ciaran with that dough treat! Finally he appears.

Close your eyes.

I do. He chuckles.

I didn't say hold out your hand.

But I keep my palm open, and he lays something in it. I look. Strawberry pie!

Strawberry *tart.* Then he hops up on the barrel next to me.

The first bite I swallow fast! Then the second—wait. *Slow down, Theo!* my brain chides. *Make it last!* Then I notice Ciaran's just holding onto his treat, staring into the distance.

You don't want your tart?

Why, greedy, you want *both*?

If *you're* not gonna eat it—

Then Ciaran takes a bite, and I know he's not even enjoying it! Just so I can't have it! I nibble, the pastry a little bitter this time.

Coppers arrest that man? That Wallace.

I dunno. They all left agitated.

They didn't pay for their dinner?

Reckon he got a Delmonico's tab. Waiter got swindled out of his tip though. Ciaran shrugs. Usually I stay in the back, don't need to see any of the blamed customers.

Then Ciaran gives me the half of his tart that's left.

Thanks!

I take a bite of his. Then I look at the tart pieces in both my hands, feel a shame. Why'd I have to bite into his when I wasn't yet finished mine? What am I—dog marking its territory? Or cat, killing mice just for sport? Eat half then just splash in the blood of the rest? No, I'm no cat because I plan on not leaving a crumb! But still I'm a dog. I take another nibble, then look up to see Ciaran's eyes soft on me, then his face moving slowly toward mine.

He gonna kiss me! I don't wannim to kiss me! But maybe I do. Maybe I'll like the taste of his lips. But what if he takes the crumbs off *my* lips! I lick my lips quick before he can take those crumbs, and his face seems to be coming faster than his lips, and his eyes closed so I start to close mine but first I see something.

Cousin Aedan.

Ciaran's eyes snap open. He sees me looking beyond and behind him, and he swerves around fast, falling off the barrel backwards. But Cousin Aedan'd already walked by the alley and out of sight. Ciaran runs after him. I run after Ciaran.

Cousin Aedan! *Cousin Aedan!*

Cousin Aedan, right hand in his pocket, doesn't pause for Ciaran's beckoning calls but is moving slow so Ciaran and I easily overtake him, stand in front of him.

Cousin *Aedan.*

Now he stops. Stares at Ciaran, confused.

It's Ciaran! It's your cousin Ciaran, remember?

Cousin Aedan looks at him like he doesn't. Then he mutters.

I'm not hearin ye, cousin. Are ye sayin—?

Melted, says Cousin Aedan louder. *Knapsack. My uniform. Melted.*

Ciaran and I stare. Cousin Aedan stares at us, stares wild everywhere.

My rifle. Turn to a snake, bit me!

Cousin Aedan looks around.

Enemy. Enemy! Could've been my own cousins, Irish faces. Could've been my brothers!

He looks all over the ground.

Bodies. Bodies.

Then right at us.

Why would I be wantin to kill them? Why would they be wantin to kill *me?*

He's pointing to himself. The hand he's pointing with has no thumb.

Cousin Aedan's a lunatic! I say at Grammy Cahill's a half-hour later.

Grammy looks up from her boiling water on the stove, and Cathleen looks up from her sewing, and Auntie Siobhan looks up from her cup of tea.

He's back? asks Cathleen.

Ciaran and I saw him!

Bless him, says Grammy and crosses herself.

He got his thumb blown off! He said his rifle turned into a snake and bit him!

God help us, says Grammy.

Where is he? asks Auntie Siobhan.

We saw him near Delmonico's but he was walking uptown. Ciaran wanted to come after him but he had to go back to work, Ciaran couldn't decide between work and Aedan, then he turned around and Aedan was gone.

Mother Mary, murmurs Grammy.

He said his uniform melted. He said his knapsack melted!

Brooks Brothers, says Cathleen.

Everyone looks at her.

Sibling team, clothing merchants. Got a federal contract to make Union uniforms.

That the shaddy material I heard tell of? asks Auntie Siobhan.

Shoddy, says Cathleen. That's the name of the fabric. Now being exposed as just old rags they patched together. First rain, melts off their backs. Knapsacks cut from the same tawdry cloth. Then there are the boot sellers that glued wood chips together for soles, something that fell apart the very first march, whole series in the paper about it.

What about the gun that bit him? asks Auntie Siobhan.

J. Pierpont Morgan. Sold weapons to the Union. Purchased thousands of old guns for three dollars and fifty cents apiece, then peddled them to the army for twenty-two each. Some didn't work. Some backfired and shot off the thumbs of the men holding them. The war's making average merchants rich and rich merchants millionaires!

Grammy sighs. We need to go to mass. We need to pray. Those poor boys.

But *we* aren't Brooks Brothers! says Cathleen, eyes on the piles of blue she's sewing. And we aren't Opdyke's, manufacturing those slave children's clothes, never again! I shan't work for slave-mongering capitalists nor war-profiteering capitalists, *these* uniforms aren't shoddy! I tested them in water, good northern wool!

And southern cotton, says Auntie Siobhan.

We turn to her.

Wool!

Some parts, Auntie Siobhan concedes. And other parts cotton.

Cathleen stops sewing, gaping at the material.

July. Congress started allowin the North to buy cotton from the South for uniforms. You didn't read about it?

That can't be true!

'Tis.

Then we're supporting the rebels!

And aren't the Union generals enraged about it. But the president told them necessary evil.

Cathleen looks near to tears.

Aw, don't fret! Think of it this way: the Confederacy sellin its own defeat.

Cathleen still stares at the material like traitor, but picks up her task again, stabbing the needle through with fatal force.

Cousin Aedan *is* deranged. Way his eyes were darting around: mad!

Auntie Siobhan's eyes narrow at me. Whoever comes back from war calm and content, *they're* the mad ones.

❧

That Sunday, Grammy Cahill drags me to church: standing, kneeling, crossing myself. After all the Latin, Archbishop Hughes switches to English: The Irish will prove our patriotism in uniform, we'll support the Union cause in this war, a war that isn't about slavery. He dismisses abolitionists as a handful of aging fanatics who claim the Constitution is a pact with hell (even though now there's a whole slew of younger abolitionists too). Our priest likens the abolitionists to the other radicals he, as a decent Irish man, despises: the Young Irelanders. While Catholicism does not endorse slavery, he has no dispute with the slave-owners themselves so long as they take well care of their unfortunate servants. And anyway, he asserts, the abolitionists rant about the long-suffering Dark of the South while ignoring the long-suffering Fair of the North with starving Irish laborers clearly the worse off, no master to provide *them* free room and board.

> *If slavery could ever have become the cause of a civil war between the people, between the states, or between the inhabitants of the Colonies, the civil war would have begun eighty or a hundred and seventy years ago. Thus it follows that slavery cannot be the cause of this War.*

❧

The tea server is your guide, Miss Fitzgerald tells me in the enormous Carrington dining room, the day of my service with Maureen's gentry employers. She will initiate the move toward the table, but you should be so attuned to her intentions that for the guests it will appear you are moving as one. The server will fill the cup to three-quarters. At this point you will move to pour but be aware of the very rare subtle gesture from a guest indicating she would prefer to keep her tea black. *Never never never* step in between a conversation. The cream will raise the liquid one-sixteenth of an inch, we shall practice momentarily. The pitcher will rest on your turned-up left palm as you hold the handle with your right. Your grip should be firm without clutching. You will stand straight! Your weight will be evenly distributed on both legs, do not slouch, do not lean on one foot. Pay close attention to the introductions so that if you are called upon to serve any lady, you will know exactly who that lady is. Do not make eye contact. Do not speak! Unless spoken to, which is highly unlikely.

Maureen's the tea server, me cream-server next to her. Maureen always with the know-it-allness at home, I think she'll pass me a look of comfort, but her eyes dance all a-panic. When we got here, she whispered the kitchen's usually run by a different lady, nice lady, but that lady suddenly got married and left, and now Miss Fitzgerald who was second in command moved to boss, Miss Fitzgerald who Maureen said a week ago was just plain aul Sheila. Another lady, Darcy Healy, looking old as Gran-Gran, smiles warm at me and winks, and I sneak a grateful smile in return.

All us servers stand silent around the long table at the start of the affair while the hostess has the ladies introduce themselves. They each make a little speech about who they are and what they do which I usually would find boring but in this instance it mercifully helps me commit them to memory. Then the lady guests eat tiny sandwiches and tiny cakes and drink tea, and they all want cream except one who never gave a gesture but after I poured said *I did not want cream! Did I say I wanted cream?* bringing me near to tears and causing Maureen next to me to humbly *Sorry, ma'am! Sorry!* and fast replace her cup of *au lait* with black. After much *You are looking lovely today* and *That hat is magnificent* and *Your first grandchild—what a blessing!* Mrs. Carrington smiles and nods to Mrs. Dorchester, who stands: *If I may?* and gently touches her daughter Louisa Dorchester sitting next to her. Louisa, who had announced her age as twenty (the younger ladies offered their years during their introductions) stands, and her mother sits, and Louisa begins:

If we are mark'd to die, we are enow
To do our country loss; and if to live,
The fewer men, the greater share of honour.
God's will! I pray thee, wish not one man more.
By Jove, I am not covetous for gold,
Nor care I who doth feed upon my cost;
It yearns me not if men my garments wear;
Such outward things dwell not in my desires:
But if it be a sin to covet honour,
I am the most offending soul alive.

The Life of Henry the Fifth, Act Four, Scene Three. Then Louisa sits, and the guests applaud polite and smile.

Thank you, Louisa, says Mrs. Carrington. I hope all of you ladies saw Louisa's remarkable performance recently in *King Lear* at the Winter Garden. She played the part of Regan.

Because the actress who played Cordelia became rather friendly with the theater manager, says Louisa.

Louisa! says Mrs. Dorchester. We do not spread ugly rumors. Even if they are true.

Louisa kindly suggested this speech, says Mrs. Carrington, as an apropos introduction to our discussion. As you all know, we have gathered here to support the efforts of Doctor Elizabeth Blackwell, the founder and director of the New York Infirmary for Indigent Women and Children. Now, for the war effort, Doctor Blackwell is engaging in an honorable and ambitious plan to recruit thousands of ladies to serve on the Women's Central Association of Relief, tending to sick and wounded soldiers on the battlefield. Doctor Blackwell was born in England, immigrating to America as a child. Her family were very committed abolitionists.

As is everyone in this room, I presume, says Mrs. Henderson, looking around at all the guests. No Copperheads among us, are there?

Do we—are we expected to volunteer to tend to the sick and wounded? Louisa asks her mother, though everyone can hear.

Of course not, replies Mrs. Dorchester. Mrs. Carrington has beckoned us here as an invitation to perform our patriotic duty in *contributing funds* for the undertaking.

Elizabeth Blackwell's family was very close to William Lloyd Garrison! says Jenny, Mrs. Carrington's younger daughter, who is nineteen years of age.

Oh, Garrison is *much* too radical for me, says Mrs. James. Naturally I'm an abolitionist, but if slaves were *all* suddenly granted their freedom, the nation would be in complete chaos!

I don't like that term, *Copperhead*, says Mrs. Piper. Naturally I support the War for the Union, but what a cruel appellation for our Northerners who only wish for peace with the Confederate states.

Crueler than *slavery*? asks Jenny, stunned.

All right, says Mrs. Carrington, we shall keep our conversation regarding Doctor Blackwell free of any offense. As I'm certain everyone knows, she is our nation's first female physician.

I'm still not comfortable with that, says Mrs. Lindsay. There are *places* for a woman—

Which in this case is the hospital and battle infirmary, says Mabel, Mrs. Carrington's twenty-one-year-old daughter who gave Maureen the bloomers. She sits next to Louisa Dorchester.

Should we not say *Mrs.* Blackwell? asks Mrs. Newcombe.

She's *not* a Mrs., says Mabel. Mercifully for her.

If your fiancé could hear you speak like that! cries Mrs. Lindsay.

You think he hasn't? asks Mabel.

Miss Blackwell *was* rather squeamish, Mrs. Carrington begins again, but after a dying woman friend encouraged her, the doomed companion lamenting that she could not have been in the care of a female healer, Elizabeth was emboldened, and pursued medicine.

All the medical schools refused her, says Mabel, except Geneva Medical College upstate. She was so highly qualified for admission, the faculty couldn't bring themselves to dismiss her outright, so they cowardly passed the rejection responsibilities on to the student body, not anticipating that the boys would elect to admit a girl on a lark. She graduated top of her class!

You see! says Mrs. Myles. What talent that was nearly wasted! It reminds me of the plight of James McCune Smith of the Colored Orphan Asylum, our brilliant negro physician rejected by all U.S. colleges solely on the basis of his skin color, so where did he go? The University of Glasgow, an institution at *least* as prestigious as any in America!

A university in *Ireland*?

Scotland! snaps Mrs. Myles. Do you not own an atlas, Mrs. Cooper?

Ladies! says Mrs. Ostrow. Mrs. Carrington is trying to speak. And after this lovely tea, we certainly owe her that.

It *was* lovely! says Mrs. Frame. What an extraordinarily well trained staff. I must hire another bridget!

They *steal*, says Mrs. Lindsay.

Not *all*—starts Mrs. Frame.

My grandmother's brooch—invaluable! Vanished! I sent that Nora packing. *Oh no, mam! I swear on me sweet mammy's grave, I didn't! Please don't sack me, mam!* I did, and replaced her with a negress: *much* more trustworthy.

Ladies! says Mrs. Ostrow.

You're a very pretty little girl, Mabel whispers to me as I pour her cream. Maureen's cousin? I nod. Imagine: a genuine Five Points mulatto in our very home!

Doctor Blackwell is a treasure of our community, says Mrs. Carrington. Of the *nation*.

Doctor McCune Smith is *also* a treasure of the nation, says Mrs. Myles. He and his wife, Malvina, are very good friends of ours. They dined in our home just a month ago.

Ah! say the ladies.

Yes, such lovely people, says Mrs. Frame. James and Malvina have been guests in our home as well. And we are also *very* honored to have once hosted Frederick Douglass and his Anna.

Ah! say the ladies except Mrs. Myles.

I'm certain you have all read his slave narrative, says Mrs. Frame.

And a handsome man too, says Mrs. Henderson, and some of the ladies titter.

Have you read the *new* narrative? *Incidents in the Life of a Slave Girl* by Harriet Jacobs? asks Mabel.

Incredible story! says Mrs. Newcombe. I only wish the abolitionists had let her write it herself.

She *did* write it herself, says Mabel, eyebrows furrowed at Mrs. Newcombe.

Mrs. Newcombe smiles. It was in immaculate English. I don't think so, dear.

I think so.

Mabel, says Mrs. Carrington.

Mr. Garrison, says Jenny, looking shaky, *is* a radical.

I believe we have moved on from that topic, Jenny, says her mother.

How can we hold, Jenny goes on, that the abolition of slavery should come *gradually*?

All I'm saying—starts Mrs. James.

Frederick Douglass, says Mrs. Frame, became estranged from his former friend and ally Mr. Garrison given the latter's notion that the U.S. Constitution is pro-slavery, to the effect of Garrison promoting disunionism back in the 'thirties. He wanted *free* states to secede from the Union!

Garrison goes beyond emancipation, says Mrs. James, espousing *equality* of the races! Absurd!

I am aware that many object to the severity of my language, says Jenny, now standing, *but is there not cause for severity? I will be as harsh as truth, and as uncompromising as justice. I will not equivocate—I will not excuse—I will not retreat a single inch—AND I WILL BE HEARD*, *that* is Mr. Garrison! Is there any truer disciple of righteousness?

I told you that old man's married, says Mabel. Jenny's face snaps to her older sister's just before, near tears, she sits.

I would like to express how *vital* Doctor Blackwell's mission is, says Mrs. Carrington. In the war arena, there are combat wounds and there are *diseases*, and the latter are proving exponentially more deadly.

Mrs. Carrington, says Mrs. Lindsay. I came here today at your gracious behest, and I would like to think that my mind is open and receptive, but I have not at all been convinced that women *should* be on the battlefield. Two mornings ago, on the way to Haughwout's, I passed on the street a young man hobbling with crutches, no lower leg! Clearly a battle injury—

Yesterday *I* was in Haughwout's to purchase some glassware, says Mrs. Bradford, and I ran into that dreadful Mrs. Howell.

Ugh, says Mrs. Myles.

I tried to hide behind the lampshades but unfortunately she saw me first. *Good day, Mrs. Bradford!* she chirped. I squinted to protect my eyes from the glare of that garish necklace and gaudy diamond ring. And fur coat! True, yesterday was the second of November, but it happened to have been unseasonably warm!

Are we meant to be shocked? asks Mrs. Myles. Such behavior only mirrors that of all these who have sprung into wealth of late. They were among the schemers who sold our soldiers tins of rotten meat!

Indeed! After the mandatory etiquette of the greeting, I tried to discreetly move away, but she appeared determined to engage me in conversation, chattering about the Ball's Bluff defeat—with a *smile* on her face!

A *smile?* says Mrs. Henderson. Is she a *Copperhead?*

Mrs. Henderson! says Mrs. Piper.

No! At least I don't believe so.

Bull's Run last summer, then Ball's Bluff two weeks ago, sighs Mrs. Frame. Two major battles, two Confederate victories.

Her delight, continues Mrs. Bradford, appeared to manifest merely on the basis of her conversing with *me*.

As if you were social equals! says Mrs. Newcombe.

Mabel! says Mrs. Carrington. Stop that whispering!

And *giggling*, Louisa, scolds Mrs. Dorchester. We should have known not to seat you two together.

Between the defective victuals and the backfiring guns and that shoddy material, says Mrs. Myles, shaking her head.

The shoddy aristocracy! says Mabel.

What! say the ladies.

I hear it all the time at Pfaff's.

Pfaff's! says Mrs. Carrington, eyes rolling. My elder daughter has taken it upon herself to spend time with the poets and scalawags at that notorious saloon.

Walt Whitman is *not* a scalawag.

That, returns her mother, is a matter of opinion.

He's gotten such terrible reviews! says Mrs. Newcombe. They say he's quite vulgar.

Simultaneously, Jenny frowns and says *No!* and Mabel grins and says *Yes!*

Some of his verse *is* rather bawdy, but not all, says Mrs. Frame. I do enjoy the idea of singing America!

His words are exquisite! cries Jenny.

I hear America singing, recites Louisa very actorly, *the varied carols I hear—*

You've been to Pfaff's? demands Mrs. Dorchester of her daughter.

Only with Mabel!

You should read *Leaves of Grass*, Mabel suggests to Mrs. Dorchester.

But to hear Walt speak it aloud, says Louisa. Walt has such an elegant reciting voice! What striking blue eyes!

Which he constantly flashes at his coterie of young gentlemen admirers there, remarks Mabel, which disconcerts Louisa.

That unfortunate one-legged soldier! cries Mrs. Lindsay. I *do* hope this war ends quickly!

Well, the president has just appointed Mr. McClellan as the new Union general, says Mrs. Dorchester. Perhaps he will make that happen.

With the Union victorious! says Mrs. Myles.

And all slaves set free! cries Jenny.

I hear America singing! declares Mabel.

And on that affirmative note, says Mrs. Ostrow, I think it is time we made a collection for Doctor Blackwell's cause.

Thank you, Mrs. Ostrow, says Mrs. Carrington. Ladies, you will notice the envelope next to your teacup. If you could please specify on the enclosed card the details of your generosity.

And I believe I can speak for all in expressing our gratitude for *your* generosity, Mrs. Carrington, says Mrs. Dorchester, for hosting. As we inscribe our cards, perhaps Louisa will close our gathering with a little more recitation.

Oh! says Louisa, surprised and smiling, let me think. All right, I shall continue with *Henry Five*, but if you ladies will indulge me, I should like to embody a man. The army captain Macmorris.

Oh yes! says Mrs. Dorchester. Louisa is very adept with accents.

Well, I can't take credit for Shakespeare, says Louisa. He writes the Irish dialect right into the text. Such wonderful guides for actors!

Let us hear it! says Mrs. Cooper.

Louisa stands, and now does something odd with her body, making it bent with her eyes flitting around, speaking as if her teeth clench a pipe hanging from the side of her mouth.

> *By Chrish, la! tish ill done: the work ish give*
> *over, the trumpet sound the retreat. By my hand, I*
> *swear, and my father's soul, the work ish ill done;*

it ish give over: I would have blowed up the town, so
Chrish save me, la! in an hour: O, tish ill done,
tish ill done; by my hand, tish ill done!

All the ladies are tittering, some putting their hands to their mouths
to keep from cackling outright. I almost laugh because her accent is so
silly and so wrong, but feels like that's not exactly why everyone else is
laughing. Now Louisa starts hobbling around the room as if she had a
cane, more a very old man than an active army captain.

What ish my nation? Ish a villain,
and a bastard, and a knave, and a rascal. What ish
my nation? Who talks of my nation?

Now the ladies are bursting. Jenny doesn't join the mirth, looking near
tears again. Mabel glances at Maureen like she's considering plugging up her
giggles, then looks away and lets her glee roar. Maureen's face is hard stone, her
grip on the teapot handle clamped tight even though Miss Fitzgerald said firm
not clutching. Louisa picks up a butcher knife and makes big actorly toe-steps
around the table, suddenly rising up behind kind, elderly Darcy Healy who
stands with her little cake plate ready to serve. Louisa grabs Darcy in a tight
hold from behind, putting the knife to her throat. Darcy cries out and nearly
drops her plate, all of us gasping! and Louisa says, *I do not know you so good a*
man as myself: so Chrish save me, I will cut off your head.

And for a few seconds Louisa holds her grip, all of us dead silent and
gaping, not entirely certain whether Louisa just might go ahead and do it.
But then she lets go, giving old Darcy a little shove. As Darcy catches her
breath, trembling and hand clutching her chest, Louisa man-bows. The
ladies applaud so loud I half expect to see flowers tossed at Louisa's feet.

⁓

A couple of mornings later, I stroll over to Grammy Cahill's. Everybody's
gone except Cathleen sewing on the couch and Ciaran lying asleep on
the floor behind the couch. Cathleen's wearing the bloomers Mabel Carrington gave to Maureen.

If I want bloomers, I can make them my own blasted self! Cathleen says Maureen said. Then she almost ripped them in two! *Wait!* I yelled. *I'll take them!* Cathleen looks down at her outfit. They *are* comfortable, but I really don't understand what all the fuss is about.

I help Cathleen with the stitching for about an hour before I'm bored. As I get up to leave, I see Ciaran on the floor, his eyes wide open, and sad, and trained on me.

We walk downstairs together, and just outside the tenement entrance, he speaks.

I'm removin myself. Gonna live with Cousin Aedan.

I shiver in the early November cold.

He's in the Seventeenth ward now. Mackerelville. Fish shops, fish peddlers.

Mackerelville, I'm thinking, is the poorest next to Five Points and near all Irish. Fish, yes, but also, according to Harriet at the African Free School who just turned thirteen, *Mackerel means pimp, and that gives you a good idea about Mackerelville*, which I thought made it scarcely different from Five Points, but to Ciaran I say nothing.

That's all. I'm on my way to your grammy's table to tell her, but I wanted to tell you first.

We're your family *too*, Ciaran. You don't need to be blood-related for that.

This startles him. But I've *told* him that over the years one way or another, many times. Maybe he's just finally hearing me because his eyes water a second, then he hugs me quick and hurriedly disappears down the street.

Tuesday, November 7, I stare out Grammy Brook's window, listening to her cleaning the whites for the whites as she quietly weeps. First anniversary. President Lincoln elected a year ago, dancing! and the next day: my Brook family's catastrophe. In the street, a newsboy hollers, *Provisional leader Jefferson Davis now officially elected first president of the Confederacy!*

And a week after, this:

Navy captures two Confederate envoys on the British mail ship Trent!

United Kingdom threatening war on the Union!

Two wars we'll be fightin? worries a woman. I buy a paper to read it for myself, though I don't really understand the implications. Then, because

Ciaran's search for his cousin Aedan's name got me in the habit of looking over the war casualties, a list categorized by regiment and divided between WOUNDED and KILLED, I turn to that page.

EIGHTH NEW YORK VOLUNTEERS,

Killed.

Heinrich Schurz, private.
Erich Voigt, private.

Kleindeutschland's in the Eleventh ward, just east of the Seventeenth, and I make a point of going through the Seventeenth but see no sign of Ciaran. I walk through the Little Germany center, Tompkins Square, known locally as *der Weisse Garten*. I've rarely been in Friedrich's new neighborhood, and I don't know what street he lives in. Mr. Freeman told me New York's Little Germany has the most German speakers in the world next to Berlin and Vienna. People call Avenue B *the German Broadway*: shops everywhere, people everywhere, bustling. In the residential streets, I ask about Friedrich Voigt, brother of Erich Voigt, till somebody knows and shows me where. I try preparing my condolences. Nancy and Elijah who I thought died showed up healthy at the Colored Orphan Asylum, so I suppose the only dead people I've ever known are Charlotte and Clementine, the baby girl sisters downstairs from Grammy Brook. Is there something different to say for a grown-up? Erich was sixteen. Does that make him a grown-up?

I turn a corner ready to knock on the door but there he is, Friedrich sitting outside on the stoop of his tenement with his weeping mother, who I remember from the Union Square monster rally just before the very first troops were sent south. Friedrich's arm is around her, muttering German comfort, his face dazed, dark circles under red eyes, *Mutter, Mutter.* I stare, frozen. I've seen lots of sadness in Five Points, but this particular grief is new to me. After all the debates in school and at the barbershop and in my families' front-rooms, gazing at mother and son I finally grasp it: war.

From inside the building I hear a man's singing voice, German accent, hollow and sad and slow: *John Brown's body lies a-moulderin in the grave.*

Which reminds me of my argument with Ciaran, me saying the song refers to John Brown the insurrectionist and him claiming it's a soldier died in the war, but suddenly I got a flood of feeling that this man knows it's both.

1862

Battle Hymns

John Brown's body lies a-moulderin in the grave
Mine eyes have seen the glory of—
Mine eyes have seen the glory of—

Something's off. *John Brown's body lies a-mould'rin in the grave* is eleven syllables and *Mine eyes have seen the glory of the coming of the Lord* is fourteen, immediately followed by *He is trampling out the vintage where the grapes of wrath are stored*: fifteen. There's been so much talk about that poem just printed in the *Atlantic Monthly*, even the Ladies Cultural Forum had a big discussion on it three days ago at their February first-Sunday-of-the-month meeting, and Miss Bertha kindly gave Auntie Maryam and me her issue, saying she could buy herself another.

Maybe not meant to be sung, says Auntie Maryam next to me, Nattie John on her lap.

It is. Remember what Miss Daniels said at the salon? Some woman in a carriage with other people, all of them singing *John Brown's body*, and the soldiers all over Washington City heard and cheered. So somebody in the carriage with the woman said she ought to take the same song and write more dignified lyrics. See the last lines? *His truth is marching on, His day is marching on, Our God is marching on* just like in *Say brothers will you meet us*, just like in *John Brown's body*—stop!

I snatch away the journal just in time before Nattie John can reach it. Under it is the article Auntie Maryam tore from a paper about a ship captain accused of pirating slaves, so I quickly rescue this piece from Nattie John's yearning destructive fingers as well.

Trial soon, Auntie Maryam says softly.

Tee-oh! High up, high up!

Auntie Maryam sets down Nattie John who runs into my arms and, as requested, I lift my little cousin who will be two years of age in three weeks high up above my head, her giggling for all she's worth.

You think there'll be justice? You think he won't get off scot-free?

Inshallah, Auntie Maryam answers me. She always says that, but apparently God is *not* willing, has not *been* willing because whenever these cases have come up in the past, ships captured full of kidnapped Africans earmarked by way of New York for Dixieland or the Caribbean or South America, we are never surprised but always disappointed when *Not guilty* is the verdict invariably returned. I think of the sensational trial and hanging of Albert W. Hicks, pirate and murderer of perhaps dozens of white men, but *these* pirates who've ruined *thousands* of black lives are lightly chastised and sent on their way. I wonder if this particular captain might've worked for Ciaran's Spanish Company, if Ciaran might've met him. I know I'll never ask.

You usin the sulfur? Auntie Maryam stares at my brow.

Yes, I say, looking down, hating these bumps on my forehead!

Every day?

I shrug.

Have to use it every day, and Auntie Maryam's off to get the sulfur out of her cupboard to make the paste that surely won't dry up one blamed pimple. Then I head off to school, arriving just in time. I notice a new girl, mixture of some stripe but not obvious which. Negro her lips. Good hair, but I don't sense Irish. Always new kids appearing and old ones disappearing then appearing again, so I don't pay a lot of attention till mid-day break when Miss Daniels asks to speak to me, and there stands the greenhorn.

Abigail Coppin, our teacher introduces, Theodora Brook. Abigail has expressed interest in volunteering at the Colored Orphan Asylum. Theodora volunteers on Tuesdays after school dismission. Since you both live in Five Points, perhaps you could both volunteer Tuesdays, then have company on the walk home.

Yes, Miss Daniels, I say, surprised to hear Abigail's a Pointser since I don't remember seeing her before. Now Miss Daniels frowns, pushing aside my hair.

Theodora, I can't see your eyes! Why have you started dropping your hair over your forehead?

⟿

Monday evening, a drunk at o'shea's board & publick is railing about the *Trent* affair, when the U.S. Navy captured the two Confederate diplomats from the British mail ship. Ultimately, the rebs were released to avoid a larger conflict.

We shoulda gone to war against the Brits! the man intones. *Again!*

I sigh.

I'm closin up, Desmond, says my auntie. Kept my impatient little niece here waitin long enough.

The Bowery Theatre—I think that's where Auntie Siobhan's taking me! She said we'd go someplace special for my twelfth birthday, which was yesterday but theaters are closed on Sundays. Last week, she described a play she'd just seen at the Bowery: *Man and the girl foolin all the lords and dukes, the man's brogue thick as molasses! The audience yellin at the stage, actor finally turned to us—Is that what the lot of ye think? and we roared! Peanuts crunchin in our teeth, peanut shells crunchin in the aisles. Suckin on ham sandwiches and pork chops, and when we finished we dropped the bones on the actors' heads, now that's theater!*

On the way to wherever we're going, she buys me oysters from the street! But the Bowery Theatre is Bowery between Bayard and Canal, and we're going *west* on Canal.

What're ye frownin for?

I shake my head. Now *she* frowns, then breaks into a laugh. Ah, *mo stoirín!* You didn't think I'd be takin ye to that rowdy Bowery Theatre, did ye? No! But don't fret: 'tis a show we're gonna see!

On the east side of Broadway between Grand and Howard is the American Music Hall, a building I've passed a thousand times and never paid any attention to.

I look around the place, the other audience members. This arena is definitely nothing like the Bowery Theatre of my imagination. The venue we have found ourselves in doesn't seem to cater to the bawdy. The seats filled mostly by adults but also children, families, some of them respectable looking. Singers and jugglers, then a man comes out to introduce who—given the audience anticipation—I reckon is the main attraction. Fervent applause as a little girl takes the stage.

> *I'm a simple Irish girl, and I'm looking for a place,*
> *I've felt the grip of poverty, but sure that's no disgrace,*
> *'Twill be long before I get one, though indeed it's hard I try,*
> *For I read in each advertisement, "No Irish need apply."*

Alas! for my poor country, which I never will deny,
How they insult us when they write, "No Irish need apply."

Kitty O'Neil's ten years of age! Two years younger than I, and singing and dancing like somebody fully grown, entertaining a room full of cheering adults! The *No Irish need apply* clincher repeats over the subsequent two verses, but then the fourth changes it up a bit.

Now what have they against us, sure the world knows Paddy's
*   brave,*
For he's helped to fight their battles, both on land and on the wave,
At the storming of Sebastopol, and beneath an Indian sky,
Pat raised his head, for their General said, "All Irish might apply."
Do you mind Lieutenant Massy, when he raised the battle cry?
Then are they not ashamed to write, "No Irish need apply"?

I don't understand half of what Kitty O'Neil's singing, but I laugh and cheer with everyone else. The last verse all including Auntie Siobhan seem to know, and sing with the little star.

Ah! but now I'm in the land of the "Glorious and Free,"
And proud I am to own it, a country dear to me.
I can see by your kind faces, that you will not deny
A place in your hearts for Kathleen, where "All Irish may apply."
Then long may the Union flourish, and ever may it be,
A pattern to the world, and the "Home of Liberty!"

Everybody's on their feet clapping and stomping and whistling, Kitty curtseying ladylike. When the thunder of appreciation finally subsides, we sit and Auntie Siobhan says, Ye're having a nice time, love?

Yes! But as soon as I say it, I get a warm pain in my abdomen. We watch the last acts, the belly burns coming and going.

All those oysters, speculates Auntie Siobhan. You stuffed an awful lot into that twelve-year-old stomach tonight.

Finale: the man on stage whistling, then everyone joining in to sing *Dixie*. Why do Northerners sing that?

Everyone likes *Dixie*! my auntie replies. It's Lincoln's favorite song!

I don't join in. I *do* like the *Dixie* tune, but the words less: I sure don't wish I was in no land of cotton.

You been usin the honey on your face as I told ye?

I see Auntie Siobhan is peering close at my forehead.

Ye need to be usin it *every day*!

⁓

Next morning is Tuesday, February 11. At end-of-day dismission, I walk up to the new girl.

You still want to volunteer at the Colored Orphan Asylum, Abigail?

She nods. Abbie. Thank you for bringing me, Theodora.

Theo.

As we walk uptown, I tell Abbie I don't remember seeing her around Five Points before.

We just moved downtown. Used to live on West Thirty-second.

That's where my auntie is! Do you know her? Maryam Wright?

Abbie shakes her head, which shouldn't surprise me since Auntie Maryam doesn't really like to be out and about.

Abbie plays sweet with the kids and is properly firm when it's called for. They like touching her hair, which is a lot straighter than my wavy tresses. And mine's light brown. Hers is black. One of the matrons brings in little cakes some charity woman donated. The kids and I devour them. Abbie puts hers in her gunny-sack.

Olivia is ten years of age and having troubles with her sums. Abbie picks up a slate.

Here's a trick for your nines.

9
18
27
36
45
54
63
72
81
90

Look on the left side, top down: 1 2 3 4 5 6 7 8 9. Look on right side, bottom up: 0 1 2 3 4 5 6 7 8 9. And you could put a zero in front of the nine at the top, mirror image of 90, they're *all* mirror images! *And* each two digits adds up to nine! Abbie's face is bright, like this number magic delights her as much as she's hoping it will delight Olivia.

What *are* you? asks Elijah who just walked up to them.

Colored like you, says Abbie, not looking up from the slate.

Abbie and I leave the asylum, strolling down Fifth from the forties.

Why didn't you eat your cake?

I like to save sweets. Abbie smiles. I'll eat it in bed tonight.

We chat about how we like reading and astronomy, how I like composition and Abbie likes arithmetic, and about Mary Jane who's the new monitor for our level—how smart she is and how strict she is and how pretty she is and how stuck-up she is. Her appointment to the position is a departure, and perhaps a risk on Miss Daniels's part, from the boy-only monitor tradition. We short-cut through Union Square.

Red fox! Abbie cries.

So cute! But it's limping! Hobbling on three legs, holding up its front right paw. Abbie stoops, whistles, right thumb rubbing against her right index finger, beckoning. The fox staggers to her. I stoop beside Abbie. Something bit it, the injured leg bleeding. Abbie spits in the dirt, makes a mud pack, ever so gentle applies it to the wound. Then she's petting the fox, hugging it.

Foxy, she murmurs.

I hug Foxy, who appears to be a she. Abbie takes out her little cake and feeds it to Foxy. I wish I could bring Foxy home!

By the time we get to Park street in the Points, it's dark. I wave to Great-Uncle Fergus cleaning the streets, who gives me a quick wink and keeps working.

Who's that?

My uncle. My mother's uncle. He used to clean the streets, then he worked in the Central Park, then he near had a heart attack just before Thanksgiving so they sacked him, now he's back to street cleaning. He said *The blessing of the saints on us* that the city should take him back.

Your mother Irish?

I nod.

Where you and your mother live?

She's dead.

Where you and your father live?

He's dead.

Abbie stares. I point.

My Irish grandmother there. My colored grandmother there: Baxter.

I'm Baxter! Wanna see my apartment?

Yes!

Abbie's tenement is just around the corner, the colored section of Baxter between Park and Leonard. Grammy Cahill is with the Irish in the next block between Leonard and Franklin.

Whose fiddle? I ask after we climb to her fourth-floor apartment.

My father's. He plays saloons and fancy events.

Abbie shows me the doll she made. Pretty blue dress fanning out, flowy black hair down her back.

You made her hair from your hair?

My mother's.

Eyebrows and lashes too?

That was the hard part.

I comb Abbie's doll's hair, and Abbie begins combing my hair.

Your hair's pretty, she says.

I like yours.

Abbie starts braiding my hair, and I keep pulling out wispy strands to cover my bumpy forehead. When she's done, it's one thick plait that falls halfway down my back. She shows me a looking-glass. I smile and wonder what Ciaran would think of it, which causes a warm feeling in my stomach—not the painful burn, but a nice one. Since Ciaran removed to Mackerelville, I've only seen him twice, running to Delmonico's.

Abbie appears over my shoulder, smiling into the mirror. I smile. The other girls at school never took to me so Abbie's my first school friend.

Abbie's mother comes home carrying a gunny-sack. Her black hair is pulled up in a big bun, some strands falling out.

Ma! This is Theo. From school.

Good evening, Theo, Abbie's mother smiles. This should fit, Abbie, then her mother pulls from her bag a dress, like something she might have bought from Grammy Cahill's table. Abbie gasps and puts it on while her mother takes down her own hair to start from scratch pulling it up again neater. Abbie's mother's hair falls to her knees!

Your hair's pretty, Mrs. Coppin.

Thank you, she mutters, grabbing a needle and thread to hem Abbie's dress. I had a grandmother who was a full-blood Indian.

My stomach growls, and I think of supper at one of my grammys'. Abbie walks with me downstairs to the entrance of her tenement.

I was surprised what your mother said about having an Indian grandmother.

Yes, people can't always tell we have Indian blood, Abbie says not looking at me, staring into the street.

No, I mean from the looks of her, I thought your mother was surely full-blood Indian herself.

Abbie keeps her focus into the distance.

⁓

Saturday night must've been a wild time at Matt Brennan's saloon because here Sunday morning I'm looking at various shards of glass strewn across the back alley. Piece of a mirror: I pick it up. Doesn't seem like Auntie Maryam's sulfur and Auntie Siobhan's honey is helping my forehead at all!

How do ye.

I jump. Ciaran behind me, grinning!

How do ye! I smile. Then frown. You haven't stopped to talk since you removed. Just wave, running to Delmonico's.

Wanted to stop. But whatever free time I have, Cousin Aedan send me coal-searchin or scrap-collectin. So today I left a little early for work, hopin to see ye.

I smile again. As if I might've forgotten his face, I study it.

But now his smile fades. And I know why: he's looking at my pimples!

You like Mackerelville? I murmur, my fingers gingerly combing my hair over my forehead. Then I notice there's a few bumps on Ciaran's cheeks.

It's all right. Well, I have to get to work.

His eyes darting, and now I see that his smile had dimmed not from seeing *my* bumps but because of me seeing *his*. He gingerly covers them with his hand, trying and failing nonchalance like some grown man scratching his beard, as he turns on his way.

Tuesday in the Colored Orphan Asylum play-room, there's a show:

> *Will you come with me, my Phillis dear, to yon blue moun-*
> *tain free,*
> *Where the blossoms smell the sweetest, come rove along with me.*
> *It's ev'ry Sunday morning when I am by your side,*
> *We'll jump into the Wagon, and all take a ride.*

Nancy sings lovely! And the way she moves that marionette! Only nine years of age—she and Kitty O'Neil ought to make an act together! Everybody knows the chorus and joins in.

> *Wait for the Wagon*
> *Wait for the Wagon*
> *Wait for the Wagon, and*
> *We'll all take a ride.*

Nancy used to be a starving urchin on the streets of Five Points, I whisper to Abbie. Look at her now!

Listen to *me*! says her little brother Elijah, banging on a triangle and making a terrible racket. When the performance is over, Nancy shows Abbie and me the printed music.

WAIT FOR THE WAGON
Ethiopian Song
FOR THE
PIANO FORTE

BY

GEO. P. KNAUFF.

Knowing *Ethiopian* is another word for negro, it all reads to me like Geo. P. Knauff stole the song from colored. After the musical presentation, we help the children with their school-work, but just before we leave, Nancy graces us with an encore.

Come, all ye sons of freedom, and join our Union band,
We are going to fight the rebels, and give the slaves the land.
Justice is our motto, and providence our guide,
So jump into the Wagon, and we'll all take a ride!

I like that new verse! Abbie and I say at once, then laugh.

Nancy confides to us: I changed the words. It come from the South, it was *join our Southern band, We are going to fight the Yankees, and drive them from our land.* But my words fit better.

Walking home, Abbie and I sing Wait for the Wagon, trying to remember Nancy's lyrics. Then Abbie sings something not English.

That's pretty. What's it mean?

Chulëns means bird. It's a song about birds.

From your great-grandmother?

My mother. Her tribe.

Oh.

My mother's full-blood.

I'm looking at Abbie. She isn't looking at me.

My mother heard too many times *squaw* and when I was born *squaw and papoose* and spit in her direction and spit landing on her and after once it landed on baby me, she started teaching me *There's easier ways to get through life than letting people know all your business.*

We've entered Union Square Park. A goshawk guards her nest, swooping down to attack a squirrel on the trunk, the latter's hungry eyes on the eggs surely nestled in those woven twigs atop the branch.

My mother's family's on Staten Island, and when she turned seventeen years of age, she ventured off. She wanted to see the city. She came alone, no family, no friends. One night she was walking the Manhattan streets in the dark, and feeling fearful, she sang that bird song to herself to give her courage. Then she hears someone fiddling her very tune! She turns, and there stands a smiling man. That's how they met.

Your parents?

Abbie smiles. Then gapes delighted at something beyond me.

Foxy!

And there's our fox: running and playing with a dog! Her leg all healed, like she never had a limp. Abbie whistles, and Foxy turns to us. After rough-and-tumbling with that street mutt, now Foxy comes to Abbie and me—hobbling! Putting on a show! Abbie and I roll laughing!

What a cunning fox you are! says Abbie. I'm afraid we have no cake today.

But Foxy seems happy enough just getting our pets and hugs.

The next morning at school, some of the girls gather around Abbie to play with her long, straight hair, as they've been doing over the last week. At the start of class, Mary Jane walks to the front to become her typical despotic monitor self. When she turns her back, I roll my eyes at Abbie. Once Mary Jane catches me, then puts a division problem on the board and orders me to solve it, hectoring my every mistake. She doesn't call on Abbie because she knows Abbie's good at mathematics, but later she writes a sentence on the board and demands Abbie identify the part of speech of every word because she knows Abbie hates doing that. The sentence Mary Jane has chosen is from the Declaration of Independence, the last of the twenty-seven grievances brought against King George:

He has excited domestic insurrections amongst us, and has endeavoured to bring on the inhabitants of our frontiers, the merciless Indian Savages, whose known rule of warfare, is an undistinguished destruction of all ages, sexes and conditions.

Everybody goes quiet, waiting to see if Mary Jane gets the rise out of Abbie that she is obviously seeking. For several moments, Abbie stares at Mary Jane from her seat, not an eyelash twitching. Then Abbie walks to the front, marking the nouns and verbs and adjectives and prepositions, Mary Jane intermittently correcting, but as Abbie moves along the sentence, she limps to a degree perfectly on the border between credible and silly. I know the show's for me, Abbie's being Foxy to make me laugh, and I have to cover my mouth. Mary Jane looks from Abbie to me, not understanding the joke, nor can she quite prove my hand is covering my glee, so she can do nothing but glare at us both. At mid-day dismission, Abbie and I leave giggling our heads off.

I return for the afternoon session early, only Mary Jane there, eyes in a book.

You and Abbie are boon companions now?

I'm startled because she asks without looking up.

Yes, I say, wondering if Abbie would answer the same.

She's half-Indian.

I shrug, though Mary Jane isn't looking at me to see it.

You know the Indians signed a treaty. They're with the Confederates.

Now she looks up at me, staring into my face, but my face doesn't do anything.

They signed and shook hands—Indians and rebs: perpetual peace and friendship.

At that moment, we hear chatter, and the other pupils start filing back in. Mary Jane moves to the front of the class. I finally swallow, my mouth so dry, take my seat. In walks Abbie looking down, and I wonder what's wrong. Then she starts doing that limp, knowing I'm looking at her, and I have to put my fist into my mouth to gag the laughter. But a second later, it's no longer funny. A few times Abbie tries to catch my eye during the afternoon, but I keep my focus down in my work or up at the teacher or monitor. At dismission, I fly out the door, sensing Abbie's confused eyes following me.

❧

Customer at the barbershop, says Mr. Freeman chewing on Grammy Brook's potato stew that night, wanting to claim New York should've seceded, New York'll rise up and revolt against the war. I told him not likely since we finally voted that devilish Copperhead Fernando Wood out. Our *new* mayor's manufactory sells blankets to the Union army, it's in his *personal interest* to support the Union!

Didn't Mayor Opdyke's manufactory used to manufacture slave clothes before the war?

Mr. Freeman looks at me, looks away, shaking his head. And a member of the Free Soil Party all the while, he mutters. The hypocrisy of capitalists.

We hear a little mumble from Grammy in the bed-closet, her nightly prayer for Auntie Eunice's return.

Did Indians sign with the Confederates?

He looks at me, thinks. Then nods.

Last summer. Choctaws and the Chickasaws.

Why would they do that!

Choctaws and Chickasaws are Southern, embraced slavery before and *after* Indian removal.

And Cherokees, inserts Grammy entering the front-room, her prayer finished. Couple a hundred black slaves to the Cherokee died in the Indian removal, *our* tears shed on that trail too!

All the Indians Confederates?

No. New York Indians are Union. Mr. Samuel sighs. Shame. Indians and colored—think what we could be if we came together! But the Indian slavers played right into the master plan.

Divide and rule, I murmur, remembering an Irish history lesson someone gave me once.

Well, says Mr. Freeman, can hardly blame Indians for not wanting to pledge their loyalty to the United States government, given all that's gone on before. *Treaty* always meant feds got the treat, Indians got the cheat.

In the night, I wake up next to Grammy, my stomach waking me up, those pains again. Grammy's potato stew never gave me trouble before.

Next morning, I arrive at school just two minutes before it's called to order. I notice the little girls playing with Abbie's hair like normal, but Mary Jane and the bigger girls glance in Abbie's direction without coming near. From them I hear muttered *Indian rebs,* then one of them beating her fingers against her lips, effecting a war whoop and causing the others to snicker and howl. I'm sure Abbie saw me enter but she doesn't look up, her eyes in a book, paying no attention to the fawning tots. Mid-day dismission, *she's* the one running out quick. End of day, I head her off before she escapes.

Want to come to my apartment?

No.

And she turns to rapidly walk out the door with everyone else, Mary Jane and Harriet sneering in our direction. I wait for the others to disperse, then run to catch up with Abbie alone on the street.

I'm sorry!

She stops.

When you turn on me next?

I won't! I thought—

Chickasaws and Choctaws signed with the South, *I'm Lenape!* Don't you even know New York Indians?

I look down. Abbie walks fast ahead. I follow, but say nothing. At her tenement, she opens the entrance door, looks at me, considering. Then pushes it wide enough for us both to enter.

In her front-room, she takes out her doll and starts combing its hair, not looking at me.

Do you—do you want to comb my hair again?

No.

Tearing at the poor doll's hair.

I have Lenape family in Delaware. Delaware-Maryland border. We absorb blacks into the tribe, we're a station on the Underground Railroad, that sound Confederate to you?

A bald spot appears on the doll.

Huh?

I shake my head.

Where's Irish stand?

I stare at her.

New York Irish.

I still don't know what she means.

About half of em ready to make friendly with the rebs, *that's* where they stand.

Not *half*—

I wager your Irish family voted Democrat.

No! I mean, the women would've—if my Irish auntie could've voted, I know she—

What about your street-cleaning uncle?

I say nothing.

Voted against Lincoln, didn't he?

I say nothing.

Abbie shrugs. Good for him.

You a *Copperhead?*

Abbie laughs a not-friendly laugh.

What's so funny!

Lincoln promised to bring about the Homestead Act. Encourage white settlers to rush out and steal more Indian land, I *hate* Lincoln.

He might free the slaves!

Abbie snickers. I want to hit her. I remember Mr. Freeman's words.

Indians and colored, Abbie. Think what we could be if we came together!

Look at me! I *am* Indians and colored come together!

Not the way you *talk*. How about all those Indian slave-holders, colored never do that to *you*!

Lenape had no slaves! We'd never do that to you, you know what? If ever there come a day whites give blacks the gun, colored'll be right there shooting and stabbing and slashing the Indian women and babies right alongside the whites.

We *won't*!

And by the by, Indians have been enslaved too.

Not by negroes!

And blacks been slaves of blacks.

What!

My father performed for a ball in a hotel, he saw it. Visitor from Louisiana, New Orleans mulatto, brought his slave. The hotel owner thought the slave owner was white, hotel owner didn't recognize mulatto or he wouldn't have let him stay, but my father recognized it. The light-skins owning the dark.

Lie!

You should remove to New Orleans, you'd be happy there. Happy high-yellow mistress, bet you'd be very able wielding that whip.

I slap Abbie. Abbie slaps me back, and here we go: knock-down, drag-out rolling all over the floor. Pulling and pinching and punching, and suddenly I scream a scream even beyond the realm of our colossal rage. Abbie jumps back, staring at me. I hold my stomach tight, *the pain!*

What's the matter with you! Abbie cries. I didn't jab your belly!

Reach my hand under my dress.

You made me bleed!

I didn't!

Look!

That's not me. It's you.

I stare at her. I stare at the blood on my fingertips.

Wait.

Abbie goes into the bed-closet, comes back with an old rag. Rolls it up, shows me what to do. Then she heats water on the stove, makes tea from herbs. While I sip, she tutors me on womanhood and cycles and blood. My stomach pains start to subside. Then Abbie stirs up some other kind of paste and starts spreading it on my forehead.

It won't help, I say, feeling a hot tear roll down my cheek. My colored auntie and my Irish auntie gimme *their* remedies, nothing helps.

Couldn't hurt, she says. *I* use it.

You don't have pimples.

See?

After, Abbie talks quietly.

The southeastern Indians, so-called "civilized" tribes—Abbie rolls her eyes—*they* were the ones took after the slave-monger whites around them.

All the southern tribes?

Abbie shakes her head. Not all. Not the Seminoles. My papa made a song about them.

As if planned in a stage show, Abbie's father walks in the door right at that moment. His negro complexion's almost black as Auntie Maryam's African skin. He kisses Abbie and greets me, then grabs his fiddle.

Oh, I wish I was in the land of cotton

and I can't help but to smile and nod my head to the beat with Abbie. After the chorus, he stops.

That song's been played in the Mechanics' Hall two years, sung on the street. The composer supposedly wrote it right here, in his cold Bowery room pining for the warmth of the South. But come to light a couple of negro musicians who were that man's neighbors when he lived in Ohio claim he overheard *them* playing that tune which *they* wrote. So turns out the South stole the song from the North, and before that, the white North stole the song from the black North.

He picks at his violin a little, then chuckles. Know what the South like to sing now? And he starts the chords.

Abbie and I bellow in tune: *O Christmas tree! O Christmas tree! How lovely are your branches!*

They changed the words, says Mr. Coppin. The first shots of the war were fired by Baltimore civilians against the first Union soldier volunteers on their way south to Washington City.

The despot's heel is on thy shore,
Maryland, my Maryland!
His torch is at thy temple door,
Maryland, my Maryland!
Avenge the patriotic gore
That flecked the streets of Baltimore,
And be the battle queen of yore,
Maryland! My Maryland!

The despot, Abbie's father says, is Lincoln,
It fits the tune different from *O Christmas Tree*, I remark.
The scanning, he says, then shows me what he means.
Papa, can you sing your Seminole song?

From Caroline and Geor-a-gia,
Some people fled to Florida,
And other people took them in their fold.
The black escaping slavery,
The red defend their Right To Be:
The tale of red-black Semi- Seminoles.

Well, slaves they're still but now they're free
To keep their crops and families
For no one's ever ever ever sold.
Some other tribes mirror white men's ways
In how they beat and 'buse their slaves
But not the righteous Semi- Seminoles.

Escaped slaves called themselves Maroons,
And sometimes neath a bright full moon
Red crossed with black aside a cozy knoll
Which then begat a brand new breed
Of African and Indian seed,
And thus is born Black Semi- Seminoles.

Their harvest and their brood increased
As all would work and play in peace
Until here come the American patrol
To send them all far west of here
To starve and freeze, cry trails of tears.
Oh no no no, not Semi- Seminoles!

The red and black as one at war,
United giving whites what-for,
And while they're on their fit n fightin roll—
Plantations, they would give a yell,
And slaves would rise up and rebel
Together with Black Semi- Seminoles.

The red-black bond proved fierce and strong,
But whites have pow'r of might and wrong
And greed and fraud and scoundrel in their souls.
So to Indian Territory go
A tribe of grit and glory, oh
Our fearless red-black Semi- Seminoles!

Abbie and I come in on the Semi-Seminoles repeating line, and cheer when the song's over. Then Mr. Coppin pulls an apple out of his pocket and splits it between Abbie and me before retiring, catching a nap before his performance tonight. It's sour and I prefer sweet, but I'm hungry. I'm crunching, and I look at Abbie, who has her mouth wide open with the round half-apple stuck there, crossing her eyes and extending her arms out like a scarecrow, and I almost choke on the fruit and the laughter.

❧

Mine eyes have seen the glory of the coming of the Lord:
He is trampling out the vintage where the grapes of wrath
*   are stored;*

It fits! cries Auntie Maryam, delighted I figured out the scanning to make *Battle Hymn of the Republic* work with *John Brown's body*'s tune. A holler from inside the building, and we listen. Now silence again.

We are standing on Centre street in the late-morning chill outside the Tombs, which takes up an entire block of the Sixth ward. Centre, Leonard, Elm, Franklin. It *does* look like some Egyptian tomb, but officially it's the Halls of Justice, pretty words for jail. After everything that went on last evening, Abbie will wonder why I didn't come to school today, but when Auntie Maryam arrived at Grammy's early this morning, she'd said, *This is historic.* Grammy couldn't leave her whites so Nattie John stayed with her, and I came to stand with Auntie Maryam.

On the inside is Captain Nathaniel Gordon, about to put on a show for some marines and hundreds of invited guests: businessmen, politicians, reporters. The show will be Gordon's hanging by upright jerker, the latest experiment which means instead of the captain dropping through a trap door, he'll be snapped up into the air by weights and pulleys, theoretically breaking his neck to kill him quicker, less cruel but more unusual. Captain Gordon was convicted of *piratically confining and detaining negroes with intent of making them slaves*, and though that piracy act which carries the death penalty's been on the books since 1820, the captain is the first man ever to be found guilty and today, Friday, February 21, 1862, will be the first man to pay the price.

Miss Daniels at school and in the Ladies Cultural Forum was skeptical, thinking he never would be convicted. The law only came about, she said, because in 1820, given breeding, the United States decided it had enough slaves. It only came about because in 1820 the recent successful Haitian revolution had put the fear of God in white men's hearts—that too many blacks might suddenly spring back to bite the hand that whips them. Still, in spite of the cynical enactment, a few slave traders *had* been accused and tried under the legislation—all acquitted. But now the Republicans have won power: new day. When the verdict was returned, *Guilty* shocked us all.

The church bells start tolling noon. A few minutes pass, and now dozens of white men empty out of the Tombs, all in silk top hats, and we know it's over. According to the morning newsboys, the captain nearly cheated them out of the spectacle, swallowing strychnine powder at three this morning, but he was discovered, and doctors rushed in to save the patient so the state could kill him. There were much more powerful men in the illegal trans-Atlantic slave trade than Captain Gordon, but the executionee didn't have the influential family connections they did, the captain was just some nobody from Maine. And if the law meant anything, somebody, *somebody* had to be the first. I don't know how I feel about the state murdering Captain Gordon. I'd've been gratified if he and his bosses had all been sent to lifelong prison, perhaps some hard labor akin to which the Africans they'd abducted would have been subjected. But Auntie Maryam carries a smile that doesn't waver. When I look at her face, it seems to read satisfaction. No. It reads justice, at last. She softly hums the *Battle Hymn*, and when she gets to the third line, she opens her mouth to sing:

> *He hath loosed the fateful lightning of His terrible swift sword*

Her scanning is perfect.

Westward Ho!

Though Auntie Maryam doesn't like leaving her house and garden, she often visits Grammy Brook on Sundays, Mr. Samuel with her. But today something special feels afoot, excitement in her eyes. She reads like she's been doing it her whole life.

THE NEW-YORK HERALD.

NEW YORK, SUNDAY, MARCH 16, 1862.

President Lincoln on Thursday approved of the additional article of war, which goes into immediate operation, namely:—

All officers or persons in the military or naval service of the United States are prohibited from employing any of the forces under their respective commands for the purpose of returning fugitives from service or labor who may have escaped from any persons to whom such service or labor is claimed to be due; and any officer who shall be found guilty by a court martial of a violation of this article of war shall be dismissed from the service.

Grammy, Hen, and I stare at Auntie Maryam and Mr. Samuel. From their faces, seems like more than meets the eye.

Effectively, Mr. Samuel grins, annuls the Fugitive Slave Act.

Biscuits and gravy and tea!—best we have for a makeshift party at eight and a half o'clock in the morning. But happy as Auntie Maryam appears, I see she still wears her light-skin disguise, meaning she doesn't wholly trust it yet.

Month later, I'm at Grammy Cahill's, her taking me to Maundy Thursday mass. On the way back, I collect some violets to decorate our apartment for Easter.

Are they not lovely? smiles Grammy when we get home, putting them in water.

You should've picked some Virginia creepers in honor of our fearless military leader, says Cathleen, surrounded by papers.

Virginia creepers bloom in the fall, says Grammy as if Cathleen were being sincere while her tone brazenly drips of sarcasm.

Call him what you like! snaps Great-Uncle Fergus. I hear he is very popular among his Irish men.

Oh, I don't doubt that, Cathleen returns, every no-battle day being a good battle day. Tardy George, that's what Lincoln calls him.

Who's Tardy George? I ask.

Maybe *Lincoln* should be out there in the front line! retorts Great-Uncle Fergus.

What's Tardy George late for? I ask.

George McClellan, Cathleen answers me with her eyes still on our great-uncle, the major general, the *chief commanding officer* of the Union Army, how long have his men been in Virginia tiptoeing to Richmond? Snails'd get there faster!

So easy for civilians to think *they'd* make a better general than the general, says Great-Uncle Fergus. You criticize McClellan for not charging his boys into certain slaughter?

I criticize McClellan for dragging the war out! How many more will be slaughtered than if the war were already done?

Let me ask ye: D' ye think McClellan should be more like that Grant? Man in Tennessee?

Yes, Uncle! Shiloh was a Union victory!

And how many Union casualties for said victory? Killed and maimed?

Oh, says Cathleen, glancing at her papers. Well, the press hasn't yet provided those details—

Just wait till they do.

Have ye seen the cost of butter and eggs now? cries Cousin Aileen, entering from the outside. This war! Made jobs, but the profits the profiteers been reapin's inflated the price of *everything*!

Extra! Extra! we hear. *Slavery abolished in the District of Columbia!*

I race to the window, then turn back to my family.

Now *that* is good news! smiles Cathleen, returning my elation.

A blessin! declares Grammy.

Inflation, sure. Is it *three* dailies ye need to be spendin coin on every mornin, Cathleen? asks Great-Uncle Fergus as he walks out the door.

❧

A warm mid-May Sunday, Hen's free day from the cigar manufactory, she and I sit on the roof of Grammy Brook's tenement. The other tenants' laundry hangs, but because laundry is Grammy's livelihood, she never trusts hanging it outside our apartment as laundry hung on the roof sometimes disappears. A girl about my age on the next-door roof takes down dry shirts and socks while her baby sister sits near, sucking on a hunk of bread.

You hear? Emancipation: Georgia, Florida, South Carolina!

If it sticks, Hen answers my enthusiasm, puffing on her cigar. Don't forget when Fremont freed Missouri, Lincoln took it back. Hunter's the one created General Order Number Eleven abolitionizin the reb states you speak of, and *he* never consulted the president neither.

Who's Hunter?

David Hunter, major general of the Department of the South. He was *under* Fremont in the Department of the West when Fremont made his short-lived Missouri freedom decree, and after Fremont was relieved of his duties and Hunter assumed em, Hunter nagged Lincoln till he gave him the Dixie command. Now Hen smiles. Hunter always thought black men should be armed for the Union. After he declared Order Eleven, he formed a colored regiment: the First South Carolina, African Descent.

Colored regiment?

A flock of pigeons descends near the surprised toddler on the next roof, who must have dropped some crumbs.

Member I told you about that locomotive chase last month? Hen asks.

You said the Union lost.

But a sure fine effort. Civilian James J. Andrews led the raid, stealin the train, cuttin the telegraph lines to prevent rebs communicatin a warning, doin as much damage as possible on that Atlanta to Chattanooga track, come close to makin it all the way! Some good white men in this war. And now that we started bringin in some good black men, the tide's gonna turn, watch.

Shoo! Shoo! Shoo! says the older girl to the pigeons surrounding her baby sister, while the younger giggles her head off.

❧

Signed! says Miss Fiona, holding up a newspaper in O'SHEA'S BOARD & PUBLICK on Wednesday. Homestead Act! They need people to people the West so they have no meddlin stipulations, women can go!

Homestead Act, Homestead Act, mutters Miss Sally, sipping her drink. All she's talked about since she got the paper this mornin.

The West initially was still *east* of the Mississippi River, then Miss Fiona turns to me, right around the time you were born. Mississippi, Kentucky, Tennessee. Daniel Boone took us there, chopped his way through. The next West was land to the Missouri. Cross that river, and beyond is Kansas, Nebraska: Plains. Which includes Texas, Daniel Boone died at the Alamo, you know that? *Now* the West, the *Far* West is California, Oregon, Washington Territory, a continent of possibility!

To the Great American Desert, toasts Miss Sally. That's what they call those Plains. Sound invitin to you? she asks me.

Does indeed, answers Miss Fiona. Be nice to tackle the adventure with my boon companion.

She think she gonna take me out on some prairie, says Miss Sally, get kilt by some rattler. Or buffalo stampede, thinkin the thunder is signalin a merciful rain in the desert, no! Here come death hoofin toward us.

And don't forget the Indians, inserts Auntie Siobhan. They'll hardly be welcomin. And Kansas is still bleedin which, I tell ye, is the *true* begetter of this war.

Bleedin Kansas! echoes Miss Sally, then turns to Miss Fiona. You tryin to take me to a war zone!

How's Kansas the true begetter of this war? I ask my auntie.

Most of the Yanks sittin in Congress stomached slavery so long as they didn't have to see it, so long as it didn't threaten the Union. Then the Plains began streamin blood, Border Ruffian slavers versus the Free Soilers, tell ye it wasn't the question of slavery in the *South* that's brought us to death and destruction but the question of slavery in the *West*.

What about General Order Number Twenty-eight! cries Miss Fiona, turning to another page in her paper and snapping it open.

HDQRS. DEPARTMENT OF THE GULF

NEW ORLEANS, MAY 15, 1862.

As the officers and soldiers of the United States have been subject to repeated insults from the women (calling themselves ladies) of New Orleans in return for the most scrupulous non-interference and courtesy on our part, it is ordered that hereafter when any female shall by word, gesture, or movement insult or show contempt for any officer or soldier of the United States she shall be regarded and held liable to be treated as a woman of the town plying her avocation.

By command of Major General Butler.

As you well know, Miss Fiona continues, *her* avocation is *our* avocation, except *we* are paid, usually, and *we* reserve the right to *refuse* customers, usually. It seems Butler is rightfully becoming known as the Beast of New Orleans.

That would appear to defeat your argument favorin us movin West, says Miss Sally.

Sally—

And *maybe*, Miss Sally goes on, the white women just gettin a little taste a what the *slave* women—and here Miss Sally rubs her own dark skin for emphasis—been forced to put up with every day. Every *night*.

Things are getting freer, Miss Sally, I chime in. You hear? South Carolina and Georgia and Florida just proclaimed emancipated!

Lincoln rescinded that, Miss Sally answers me dry.

Benjamin Butler, says Miss Fiona, is a *Northern* man. Born in New Hampshire, raised Massachusetts, *that* masculine rough-house you well know is not restricted to the South. Wouldn't it be nice to make *our* way? *Our* freedom alone on the Plains, away from all that particular male sentiment?

Miss Sally sighs.

Have ye noticed the cost of salt lately? asks Miss Fiona. Of beeswax for your light-skin concoction? Inflation's dumped us in yet another depression, you prefer starvin *here*? How many of us live past thirty-five, our profession? The beatings, the disease, the drink. I'm offerin a chance for life!

Your forehead is startin to clear up, whispers Auntie Siobhan, and it's no lie—I saw it in a looking-glass—but I know she mentions it at this particular juncture seeing my long face since Miss Sally said freedom's been rescinded yet again. My auntie trying to cheer me a bit which, I'm ashamed to say, works.

❧

I just wanted you to know, Mrs. Brook, says Mr. Freeman to Grammy on an early-June Sunday, that it's a consideration on my mind.

Grammy stirs the stew.

And Josiah, another barber. We have discussed the possibility of heading out together. The economy, he sighs. Any dip and shave n a haircut's suddenly rendered a luxury.

What you *do* out there? demands Grammy.

Farm.

Westward ho! says Hen from the corner, lying on her stomach on the floor with a paper.

They even *let* colored homestead?

Oh yes, ma'am. The government wants to populate the West, I read the act. And plenty of colored settlements out there already: Ohio, Indiana. Michigan.

Yesterday in Atlanta, the Confederates hung James Andrews, the civilian who led the locomotive raid, Hen reports, sighing sad.

And negroes not new to the venture, many a slave followed his master cross-country in 'forty-nine to buy their freedom with the gold they excavated!

You'll be an explorer like Daniel Boone, Mr. Freeman! You know he died in the Alamo?

Daniel Boone, Mr. Freeman turns to me, got himself a plantation and a bunch of slaves, the adventurer making it on his own in the wilderness he was *not*.

Yesterday in New Orleans, Benjamin Butler the Beast hung a man for tearing down a United States flag after Butler warned in no uncertain terms no one was to touch it, Hen reports, not trying hard to keep the glee out of her voice.

Mexico, Mr. Freeman goes on, said no slavery in Texas, the province of Tejas. But the white *Texian* settlers came settling with their slaves and plantations nonetheless, with the United States Army backing them. Then one day Mexican General Antonio López de Santa Anna marched into the Alamo mission with the expressed aim of freeing the slaves, and the Mexican army *trounced* the gringos, I will *always* remember the Alamo! smiles Mr. Freeman as fondly as if he were there himself.

∽

The following Sunday evening at Grammy Cahill's, Ciaran walks through the door. I haven't seen him in a month!

Ciaran! we all say. He looks taller.

And he reeks! And sees us sneaking our fingers under our noses, his face flushing blood red.

The slaughter-house, he mutters.

Grand you got steady work with your cousin, Grammy says. Now go down to the pump and give yourself a good wash-off. Welcome home!

While Ciaran goes to clean himself, Great-Uncle Fergus mutters, Thought he worked at that restaurant.

Not in months, says Grammy.

He had to walk down to Delmonico's from the Seventeenth ward to the First, I insert, which is longer than his previous excursion of Sixth ward to the First, and with the lengthier travel, he came late a time or two.

And got sacked, says Ciaran entering, the stink greatly reduced. At least at the abattoir, I never have to see any blamed high society.

We all have soup. I'm so glad Ciaran came, and so mad it took him so long. I'm hoping he'll sit next to me on the floor to eat, and he does, telling everyone the latest goings-on in Mackerelville, both us trying hard not to smile and never never looking at each other.

Well, says Maureen after a time.

About to abandon your family again for that rascal, grumbles Cousin Aileen.

I spent half my free Sunday evening with you, says Maureen. Emmet only gets—

Bed-time! When's he marryin ye?

Before we move west.

Everyone gawks at Maureen.

The homesteadin doesn't go into effect till top of the year so there's time before we leave. Though they say it's good to already be there by January first: movin further west when you're already somewhat west beats the competition.

Maureen! cries Cousin Aileen. Ye can't go west! We'd never see ye again!

I'll write, Ma, and now Maureen's eyes start to shine. I'll write!

Fiona's been speakin of it too, says Auntie Siobhan.

Aw, they're goin nowhere, says Great-Uncle Fergus. Everybody sayin they're westward bound, goin west costs *money*. Got to pay a fee for the homestead, got to buy the farmin equipment, got to buy the wagon transportation. People talk of escapin Five Points, escape's expensive!

I expect Maureen to return with some clever response, but her eyes are wide, like all what Great-Uncle Fergus just said is new information.

I'm surprised Fiona would consider it, says Grammy. These young newcomers maybe, but amazes me *any* Irish who remembers the Famine would contemplate the harvest. Fiona may have been a Famine child but old enough to recall it. All of us were farmers back in Éire, but the soil turned on us. We lost the trust in the land, so Famine Irish in America: city folk.

Me and Cousin Aedan's thinkin of movin west.

My face snaps to Ciaran. I see him glance at me out the corner of his eye.

Not *far* west. Pittsburgh.

Pittsburgh? says Grammy.

Arsenal plant. Supplies to the Union, Cousin Aedan has another cousin there, no blood to me. Claims there's work for us both. The slaughter-house let a bunch go yesterday. Not the two of us yet but—and here Ciaran takes a big whiff of his shirt as if already sentimental for the stench—like Cousin Aedan says, Only time.

Friday night, Mr. Samuel gazes out his window, little smile. A newspaper open on the table.

Yesterday Lincoln signed the bill: slavery forbidden in the territories.

Like Oregon? says Auntie Maryam, sitting with Nattie John who chews on a biscuit. Pretty easy to forbid slavery in a territory got the exclusion laws: no blacks allowed.

Not interested in any blamed Oregon, mutters Mr. Samuel. California. That's what *I'd* like to see.

Cross the *continent?* cries Auntie Maryam.

Let me tell you about California. Under orders from their master, slaves Diddy Mason and Hannah and their small children walked from the state of Mississippi to San Bernardino, California by way of Utah, the master wanting to make him a Mormon settlement out on the coast. California's admitted as a supposed free state, but the law had contradictions. Eventually master decides he wants to remove to Texas, but Biddy and Hannah wanna stay put. With the help of local free negroes, including a black cattle rancher who employed free black and Mexican cowboys, Biddy and Hannah sued for freedom and, even with a former Dixie slave-ownin judge, *won.* California or bust!

I know about slaves goin west! says Auntie Maryam. Texas, Missouri, them states gettin settled by rich men wantin plantations, needin human chattel to work em. And slave-holders in the East only happy to sell misery. Bids on the block now sky high!

Homestead Act might finally be the chance for Africans in this country to be free.

I'm not goin west!

Even Nattie John's startled by Auntie Maryam's outburst, and I see now this is just the latest bout of an ongoing feud. I'm glad Auntie Maryam's fighting it! Why's everybody want to move away?

And when her mammy come home, don't we need to be here?

Mammy? asks Nattie John.

Yes, concedes Mr. Samuel, nodding, sighing. Yes. He turns the page of his paper, and I glimpse in bold: Six More Members of Andrews Raiders Hung in Atlanta.

Mammy! grins Nattie John, and this time it's clear she's addressing Auntie Maryam.

No! Auntie Maryam cries, horrified. You *has* a mammy, I'm your *aunt*ie, *aunt*ie!

On steamy Friday Independence Day, I see Abbie's head stuck under the intersection water pump. I wasn't in school yesterday, helping Grammy with some extra whites for the whites as her customers prepare for holiday visitors, so I never got to ask Abbie about her plans for today.

Wanna go to the fireworks tonight? Unless your family's doing something else for the Fourth.

I follow her back to her tenement. There sits her mother at the table, who looks up, smiles brightly at us.

Theo! Wanna help?

On the table are several flat pieces of ragged wood and pieces of charcoal, and part of a column torn from the *New-York Times*:

> The President has signed the following bills:
>   1. The Tax bill.
>   2. The Pacific Railroad bill.
>   3. The bill to Prohibit Polygamy and annul the polygamic laws of the Territory of Utah.

And on the walls—I can't remember what was there before, if anything, but I know it's not what's hanging there now, which are flat pieces of wood with sayings written on them. Abbie sits at the table with her mother, grabbing charcoal and wood to write.

Please! says Mrs. Coppin, pulling out the other chair for me. You schoolgirls have good penmanship!

On the table's an old rag laid flat with writing scrawled all over, and I see check-marks next to the scrawlings that match the text of the plaques on the walls. Abbie is making a new plaque for one of the passages still unchecked. My eyes rest on a hung plaque: sketch of an Indian.

Tecumseh! says Mrs. Coppin.

My ma's good at drawing, says Abbie.

These, says her mother, are all his quotations!

I walk around, reading to myself.

Show respect to all people, but grovel to none.

Sell a country? Why not sell the air, the great sea, as well as the earth?

Where today are the Pequot? Where are the Narragan-
sett, the Mohican, the Pauquunaukit, and other powerful
tribes of our people? They have vanished before the ava-
rice and oppression of the white man, as snow before the
summer sun.

Sleep not longer, O Choctaws and Chickasaws, in false
security and delusive hopes. Our broad domains are fast
escaping from our grasp.

When Jesus Christ came upon the Earth, you killed him.
The son of your own God. And only after he was dead did
you worship him and start killing those who would not.

The way, and the only way, to stop this evil is for all the
red men to unite.

He wanted us to come together—*all* of us, says Mrs. Coppin. *All* Indians! Only collectively can we defeat the white man: united we stand!

Mrs. Coppin smiles as she says this, but her bright eyes glaze, a tear peering from their edges. I turn back to Abbie sitting across from me. Upside down, it's hard for me to figure out which quotation she's writing but it's a long one.

Tecumseh was a Shawnee, says Mrs. Coppin, with his father's people, his mother a Creek. He fought in the Northeast and traveled as far south as Florida, gaining recruits. So eloquent, the whites compared his speechifying to their Henry Clay. Tecumseh rebuked the so-called peace chiefs who signed away land: When did it become theirs to give? The land is for all!

At the angle Abbie has turned the quote rag, I can now see which one she's transcribing.

Brothers, the white people are like poisonous serpents: when
chilled they are feeble and harmless, but invigorate them
with warmth and they sting their benefactors to death.

We had allies, her mother says. England, France, Spain. Tecumseh was a warrior-chief in that 1812 war, died there! But when it was all over, the white boundaries remained the same, what was the point? The only ones who lost that America-against-England war was Indians. Then Napoleon dies, and whatever remained of our alliance with France . . . Mrs. Coppin shakes her head. Spain surrenders independence to Mexico, then Mexico loses it all: New Mexico Territory, Utah Territory, California, Texas to the Rio Grande. Mrs. Coppin swallows, gazes at the words on the wall.

But the High Plains. All new landscape, all new climate, a foreign land to whites! Plains Indians been there centuries, let's see how the invaders manage *there*, *those* Indians!

Then Mrs. Coppin goes out to pump water for her supper cooking.

There, says Abbie, admiring her finished plaque. She turns to me. You don't have to do it if you don't want to.

Before your mother wouldn't admit to being a full-blood, now seems like she's ready to put on war paint.

Before was before the *Homestead Act*, snarls Abbie, *before* was before the *Pacific Railroad Act* staking claim across the continent. *Before* was before Lincoln opened the flood-gates.

I stare at her. Then I think about her father's black Seminole song. I sit, look at the quotes on the rag, and choose mine.

A single twig breaks, but the bundle of twigs is strong.

❧

Two weeks later, I walk into Auntie Siobhan's saloon at dusk. It's crowded, Roisin flustered tending bar.

Roisin, I call, wanting to know where Auntie Siobhan is.

Lincoln's a lunatic, grumbles a man on a bar stool to his neighbor. He already took half a million men after Bull Run, now *how* many more's he demandin?

As if to answer, at that very moment several drunk men take up a marching song.

We are coming, Father Abra'am, three hundred thousand more,

From Mississippi's winding stream and from New England's
  shore.
We leave our plows and workshops, our wives and children
  dear—

That's when the non-singers jump the singers, full-on brawl: fists and kicks and spit.

Stop it! Stop it! screams Roisin.

Well, chuckles the Lincoln critic's drinking companion, if the anthem was meant to inspire the fight in them, I wager it's done its duty!

I run upstairs looking for Auntie Siobhan to help moderate the political debate before her tavern's left in smithereens, though doubting she's at home or she'd already be here.

But up in the boarding-house, there's another fracas in process.

We'll fix you up, says Miss Sally to wailing Maureen. Fiona, where's your powder?

I stare at my cousin. Black eye. Bruises up and down her arms.

Leave the bastard, growls Auntie Siobhan.

I second that, says Miss Fiona.

Only when he's drunk, sobs Maureen. Other than that, a pure sweetheart, he is!

They all are, mutters Miss Sally.

We'll marry, move west, homestead west, says Maureen. It'll be better, dependent only on each other.

Are you ravin *mad?* asks Miss Fiona.

I second that, says Auntie Siobhan.

You're suggestin he take you out to the wilderness? asks Miss Sally. Just you and him, no neighbor to run to? Nobody around to notice if a wife suddenly disappears, no trace?

Before ye go, allow me to serve him up a hearty bowl of my mushroom stew, smirks Auntie Siobhan.

When did Theo walk in here? says Maureen. Don't you tell Ma, Theo! Your big mouth, it's none a your business!

Ye think Aileen didn't already see the bruises from *last* week? asks Auntie Siobhan.

The next morning, a brief but heavy shower provides some relief from sweltering late July. Walking Park street, for the second time in twelve hours I hear wailing.

A little sweeper girl, the latest Irish child to claim Mary Bree's old corner. There's generally less such work in the summer but today's rain has turned dirt to mud. The child looks so forlorn and so little. It occurs to me I must be growing up to be having these maternal protective thoughts, no longer thinking of a sweeper girl as my peer.

What's the matter?

She shows me. Barely a straw left in her broom.

I don't know what Mr. Samuel will think, but I look for him, her tagging along.

Strah-aw!

This is Kaelyn, Mr. Samuel. Not sure of her age, but she estimates eight.

I show him the problem. He considers, sighs. Gives us some straw.

Thank you, Mr. Samuel!

Thank you, mister!

Strah-aw! he starts calling again.

Thank you, Theo! she says after we've put it together.

You're welcome.

This is my friend Theo! she says to another urchin I don't know, who stares at me like I'm some prize Kaelyn beat him to. Now a woman approaches.

Sweep the corner for ya, ma'am?

I think how Nattie John will never have to raise herself like this because even without her parents around, we always have surplus family. And now I *really* feel like an aul one, suppressing a desire to go to my little two-and-a-half-year-old cousin right away and say, You don't know how lucky you are!

Monday, August the fourth, in the late afternoon, I wipe my sweaty brow strolling in the mugginess, when Grammy Cahill calls me over to her table.

Ye heard about the colored tobacco manufactory in Brooklyn? Fire were set to it! Ye've a cousin works there?

There's lots of colored tobacco manufactories in Brooklyn.

This one was Watson's.

I fly into Grammy Brook's.

Grammy! Grammy! But I see her pacing, her wild-eyed hand-wringing, and I know I know nothing she doesn't already. A few minutes later, Mr. Freeman arrives home early from the barbershop.

I just heard! Any news?

We shake our heads. He goes back out to see if there's any on the street. We wait.

Miss Lottie from across the hall bursts in. Did you hear? Anybody hurt?

We don't know. We wait.

Auntie Maryam and Mr. Samuel come just before nightfall. We only now heard! And Mr. and Mrs. Jewel from downstairs with their babies (two little boys after their two little girls died), and then Mr. Freeman returning, trying to piece together the news bits and fragments he'd collected, the apartment filling up, reminding me of the night we lost Auntie Eunice, full house makes me sick.

You all right, Miss Lioda? asks Auntie Maryam, noticing Gran-Gran at her window, her worried look and no one paying attention. My auntie walks over and puts her arms around her foster grandmother.

Nobody goes to bed. Finally, middle of the night, someone walks through the door.

Hen!

Everyone runs to embrace her, then steps back. Her arm's bandaged up. Cut on her cheek. Her eyes look sobbed-raw but now cold dry. She goes back to lie on the bed, no words, and sleeps most of the next day. Grammy and Auntie Maryam and I sleep with her like the old days, Mr. Freeman in his front-room rollout, Mr. Samuel on the front-room floor.

When Hen emerges from the bedroom Tuesday dusk, she looks at the *Brooklyn Daily Eagle* on the table.

The Irrepressible Conflict in Brooklyn.

SERIOUS RIOT BETWEEN WHITE MEN AND NEGROES.

The Former Attack a Tobacco Factory in which the Negroes are Employed.

ATTEMPT TO BURN THE FACTORY DOWN.

INTENSE EXCITEMENT.

The Arraingement of the Parties—They are Held to Bail.

Look, Hen! I say. The accused rioters were arraigned before a judge!
Biscuit and hog fat? Grammy offers her.

Hen looks around the front-room like she didn't hear. The men at work but Auntie Maryam's still here. Gran-Gran chews her biscuit slow, eyes out the window. Hen looks at the floor.

Good wages, she says soft, and colored got the skills, handed down and passed along from Dixie slaves. So course they come from other parts a Brooklyn, come ferryin from Manhattan, locals didn't preciate that. Local whites resent hirin from beyond the neighborhood, hirin black outsiders and payin em more. Saturday night. Sticky, soggy, two colored standin in the doorway a Grady's. Two white men say get out the way, they goin in to Grady's for a drop, black say *We got just as much right to the libations as you, just as much right to stand here*, white belts the black, fight! Broken up, but then the rumors, lies: black man insulted a white woman.

Always *that*, comments Gran-Gran, eyes out her window.

All a Sunday, threat in the air: if colored come to work, we live to regret it. *If* we live. We come to work. Not all: half went to the West Indian Independence Day merry-makin, what was left was five men, thirteen ladies, seven girls. Lorillard's next door, Lorillard's bigger, and when the black arrived seven a.m., boss sent em home in the avoidance a trouble, but at Watson's the twenty-five of us stayed. Whites gone home for lunch like regular, we stayed in with our brought lunch like regular, quarter to noon. Quarter to noon . . . *Hundreds*. The building surrounded, *Roast the niggers alive*, we hear, drunk boys and men, drunk Irish, bricks! We run to the top floor, make a fort, when they run in, run up to us, we hurl what we find: wood cigar molds, bottles, returnin the brick-bats they send flyin in, the scythe. And Mr. Charles. They break through and grab Mr. Charles Baker, beat him, near *kill* him. Tried to burn us down, but finally the police arrive. Arrested some whites, *arrested bleedin Mr. Charles.* Mob near *lynched* Mr. Charles and police arrest *him* . . . Hen sighs.

Mr. Freeman, Auntie Maryam says quietly. Last night, Mr. Freeman tole us he heard bout that. Police release Mr. Charles. Eventually.

You're not goin back, says Grammy, red eyes. I don't care how much they pay—

You don't got to worry, they let all colored go. Sacked *us*. *That*'ll teach the bullies a lesson.

I don't care! You'll work right here close to home from now on.

The bullies sure learned from *that*, all right, mutters Hen.

Wake up middle of the night: no Hen! I run down to the street. There she is, head stuck under the pump for a big gulp in the thick night, moon near full. She takes a start, then sees it's me.

How'm I gonna sleep, she shrugs. Slept most a the day.

She sits on the wooden sidewalk edge. I sit next to her. A distant rollicking from a pub.

Hen. When you said. Those white men. Those drunk white men attacked Watson's, drunk, bad . . . I thought you said . . . Did you say—?

Eye-rish, she hisses, eyes glowering in the moonlight, then turns away from me to go back inside. I stay out, staring at the pump, my mouth bone dry but this sudden sense I don't deserve to quench it.

Late morning, I'm awakened: Company! Company!

The person calling *Company!* is Gran-Gran in her chair, Grammy already gone laundressing. Near ten, and Hen still hasn't stirred. In the front-room, a gentle knocking.

Mornin, Theo.

Never before has Ciaran ever come to Grammy Brook's.

Mornin.

Heard about the cigar manufactory. Hen all right?

I nod. He waits for me to say more. I don't.

Well. I just come by to see how Hen's doin. And to say good-bye. We're headin out, me and Cousin Aedan. Pittsburgh, remember? I said?

I nod.

I just wanted to say good-bye. I'll be back when things get better. When the inflation comes down.

I know when people go west, even near west, they rarely come back, but I say nothing.

He sighs, looking around. Pittsburgh's not far. Comparatively. You hear they just discovered gold, Montana Territory?

I shake my head.

Cousin Aedan was ready to send us there! Let's go make a fortune, cousin! *No!* I thought. Too risky! That far, we *never* return! Ciaran shakes his head. He's my elder so I said it polite and true: *I'd rather starve here.* Then he backed away from that idea.

We gaze at each other. I glimpse a little muscle coming to Ciaran's arms, I never noticed that before. A few hairs above his upper lip. Ciaran just turned fourteen, me twelve and a half. I look down.

And up at him again. He nods and turns his sad eyes to leave, walking down the tenement stairs. I hear him on the lower steps, and suddenly I want to give him something. I need to give him something! but I've nothing to offer. I hear the outside door open and fall shut. I walk slow back into Grammy's, start to shut our door. Then I turn and race down the steps, out the door.

Ciaran! Ciaran!

He's walking away with his cousin Aedan, who must've been waiting just outside our tenement.

CIARAN!

Now he turns around. So does Cousin Aedan. I called before I figured out what I was going to say, I need to conjure it up quick.

Then I remember all the times Ciaran bought me treats.

If you get back while it's still warm, I'll buy *you* ice cream, Ciaran! If it's cold, oysters!

And slowly a surprised smile forms on his face, his eyes glassy as mine feel. I think he wants to say something in return but all he can get out's a nod.

Let's *go*, boy.

His cousin Aedan turns to walk away brisk and brusque, and Ciaran runs to catch up. Aedan appears to be saying things to Ciaran without looking at him directly, Ciaran nodding, nodding, once managing a glance back to me before they turn the corner and gone. My throat burns. Then a pounding next to me. A white man with a hammer posting a bill.

INDIAN TERRITORY

THAT

GARDEN OF THE WORLD,

OPEN FOR

HOMESTEAD AND PRE-EMPTION

In view of the early opening of the Territory, it is necessary for those who would secure Free Land and Homes in this magnificent country, to be prepared to start as soon as the lands are declared to be subject to Homestead Entry. The rush will be great, and early comers will have every advantage.

Every Person 21 Years of Age or Over will be ENTITLED TO 160 ACRES.

Whisper in my ear: Let em come.
I jump. It's Abbie, sneering at the poster.
Plains Indians waiting for you.
When I get back to the apartment, Hen's awake and has gathered her things into a little tramp pouch.
What are you doing?
Canada.
What!
Hen stares at the little bag holding her life's possessions.
Mrs. Laurie, my landlady—she's the one patched me up. Wrote to her

nephew up there, Ontario, asked if I could stay with him and his family. Time it takes for the note to get there and back is time wasted, may as well set to hoofin now. Because whether they take me in or not, I'm removin. Over the border.

Not even say good-bye to Grammy?

Talked to her bout it this mornin while you was sleep. She knew I weren't foolin. Said come up to the white folks' where she's workin for a so-long before I head out.

Hen ties her pouch. I feel my breath catching.

But *now*, Hen? Right when the war's come? Might soon be emancipation all over the country!

She stares out the window into the distance.

Maybe the war'll end slavery, and maybe it won't.

What!

Canada's the only guarantee. Freedom.

But her tone doesn't sound eager for Canada. It just sounds sad for America. And something new for Hen: disappointment. Discouragement.

Walk along the train tracks, I'll slip into a boxcar goin north.

Don't go!

She gazes at me, my desperation. Her face softens, and she walks back to the bed-closet. Returns with a cigar.

Lass one I wrapped. If you never smoke it, it's a keepsake. If you do, you always remember your first smoke so that's a keepsake too.

I stare at it, feel it. Memento, like what I couldn't find for Ciaran. Then she hugs me, which feels so out of character I forget to hug back. Now she walks over, hugs and kisses our great-grandmother.

So long, Gran-Gran.

Northward ho! Gran-Gran grins.

Which surprises Hen who isn't easily surprised. She laughs, and gives me a wink, and is out the door, gone. And not till late in the night, when I'm in bed with Grammy and hear some long distant train whistle do the sobs start to come, my fist tight over my mouth to mute them.

Epistles

Dear Mrs. Brook, Miss Lioda, and Theo,

We have just arrived in Independence, the Free State of Kansas! It has taken us merely sixteen days to travel to the center of the country—the _continent_. The marvels of modern transportation!

We rode the locomotive to Albany, and from there to our canal boat, skimming the Erie all the way to Buffalo to board the grand ship. Now I fully comprehend the appellation _Great_ Lake: Erie is an ocean! As I stood on the deck, as we drifted along that inland sea, I peered north, acutely aware of the proximity to Canada and what crossing over would mean.

We disembarked at Cleveland, where resides an uncle of Josiah's who offered a night's refuge. The uncle, Percival, was very accommodating but questioned our wisdom in venturing further west. Cleveland, he asserted, has been very good to his family (he has a wife and five children), and there are now numerous other colored settlements all over Ohio and Indiana and Illinois and Michigan and Wisconsin. A couple of savvy New York barbers could certainly find ready employment, he proclaimed. (His sectional state list, you may note, did not include nearby Iowa whose laws, while tolerating current black residents, prohibit any _new_ negroes from residing within its boundaries.) Lodging in many of these communities along our journey—friendly, self-sufficient black towns—served to pacify any doubts we might have had about undertaking this adventure. There _is_ a free United States for negroes! Josiah and I discussed Percival's recommendation, but no. Kansas we had dreamed of, and Kansas we shall behold.

So we carried on, mounting another stage to bring us to the next station, and the next, and the next. And at last we have reached our destination. The cornfields, the sunflowers! The endless sky! We are now prepared to commence the Santa Fe Trail, our design to settle further west in the state as Independence is much too near the border of raging, slave-mongering Missouri for our comfort.

Mrs. Brook, I must apologize again for my abrupt departure. The attack on the cigar manufactory felt symptomatic of an increasingly hostile environment for negroes in Brooklyn and our New York City, the building's near destruction only kindling my already burning wayfaring ambitions. By the time the Homestead Act goes into effect the first of the year, Josiah and I will have acclimated ourselves to the West, finding work and saving the capital to procure the necessities: tools, seed, livestock.

I already miss my dear Five Points "family." I shall write with details of our experiences here in the West from time to time and, once we are settled, very much long to hear from you. Most importantly, I shall not forget my promise to keep my eyes open for any sign of Eunice.

Lastly, I would feel remiss if I did not say that to this day I may still be sitting in Manhattan vacillating my decision had it not been for Hen's exodus—that a young lady of a mere fifteen years had the courage to take that step. Whatever our outcome here, Josiah and I shan't go to the grave with the shame of never having uttered "I dared."

Yours ever faithfully,
Homer Freeman

September 2, 1862

Dearest Theo,

It has been a long time since I have written
and now the words I etch are a blur through
tear-filled eyes: my dear mother is dead! Murdered two weeks ago today—by Sioux!

They are <u>animals</u>! Women and children
slaughtered! Yes, Dinah, a child of three years
of age, daughter of our good neighbors also
lay dead after the vicious raid. Why cannot
they fight with valor, as white men do? Dinah
was my heart, and my mother my everything.
She took me in when I was an abandoned
orphan, a poor street waif of Five Points.
God delivered me into the care of an angel on
earth too soon returned to Heaven. Why? We
did them no harm!

A year ago, my family and others journeyed
to Minnesota in search of a better life. Since
the announcement of the coming Homestead
Act, our numbers here have swelled. Until
recently, we have enjoyed a very cordial
relationship with the local Indians. Though
perhaps I should have been more alarmed
given the behavior of the agency men, which
has hardly been conducive to harmony and
mutual well-being. As I understand it, after the
sale of the land, some white agents, including
the <u>governor</u>, retained a healthy percentage
of the agreed-upon Indians' treaty sum for
unspecified "expenses," and what money they
have paid has been doled out not according to
the stipulated schedule but rather when and
if they have felt like it. Crops failed last year,

but there is a warehouse filled with foodstuffs that rescued the settlers. The starving Indians were refused these victuals, and when a few tried to steal into the stockpile, the punishment was swift, and in the aftermath one agent sneered, "Let them eat grass." So when a herd of Sioux returned with the war whoop, that agent was one of the first casualties, and I can hardly begrudge that slaying. But <u>we</u> are civilians!

I apologize for the excitable nature of this letter. I do not mean to assail you, my faithful old friend, but in truth I have just had another tussle with Daisy Iver. Daisy is also from Five Points though I did not know her then (and I don't think you did either, I've asked and she says she doesn't remember you). She is fifteen years of age, four years older than I and three older than you. Daisy was adopted through the House of Industry as I was, but she was less willing in her process. She did not wish to leave her mother, but her mother was given to drink and could not hold a proper paying position, so Reverend Pease did what was best for the girl. She traveled on the caravan train of children to be adopted in the West. As an older orphan, she was less appealing to potential parents, but the Ivers needed help with their large brood, and Daisy was eleven at the time so at a ripe age to assist with the babies and the chores. Daisy, however, has never been cooperative nor grateful. And from the start she has been opposed to our settlement here, claiming we are trespassing on Indian land when it was ceded by treaty! Well, I could not help, after

the massacre, to ask what she thought of her
beloved Indians now, to which she replied that
it never would have happened had we not
been here. And her adopted sister Baby Dinah
still warm in the grave! Incidentally Daisy, as
she debated me, donned two blackened eyes,
not for the first time, so apparently she had
already voiced these same opinions to her
grieving foster father.

I hope you do not find me cold, Theo. I
suppose you remember the sweet little girl
on the corner, trusting of all. It is true the
hardships of the West have in many ways
hardened my heart, but that only means
that I have grown wiser. It is also true that
many Easterners like to take some moral
high-ground, feeling safe now that they have
forced the Indians far inland.

Oh my friend! As Paul did for the Romans
and Ephesians, you have my promise
that I shall dispatch an epistle on a more
regular basis, as it feels selfish and cruel to
correspond only in days of despair. I hope
you will do the same and, if your news is
good, I shall receive it with pleasure and as a
treasure.

Even as I write, I hold in my hand a
wildflower that grew on the grave of
my blessed mother. I wish her death to
be avenged! I wish for peace! Are those
conflicting sentiments? Today I remember
President Jackson's avowal that Indians will
either yield to the white man or vanish.
Belatedly, I have been cheering for the latter.

In sorrow and in prayers,

Prudence Cox (your Mary Bree)

Sept. 15, 1862

Dearest Family,

Greetings from The Far West!

We just arrive this morning after 5 wks to Ft. Hall, Dakota Territory, ware we disembark our stage. I am writing from here because I dont know if we will have mail for the rest of our gurney. We about to take waggons for the remainder.

Other people on the same adventure have mosly been kind and generis. Majority white men, but some colored men too, and a few other women. Were sharing our waggon with a couple of these colored men, Hiram and Amos. Today they taught us to drive and shoot. And Fiona and me city dwellers – think of that! Between the 4 of us, we killed 2 bucks! One we gave to the local Soux, Amos said for peace and grattitude, and the people seemd glad. One of there young men Silver Cloud joined our party.

So tomorrow morning the 5 of us go to Grasshopper Creek, Montana Territory where we will try our hands at the gold-mining. Siobhan thank you for saying what if I set out with Fiona. She is a calm and capable companion, we will make very good partners in the home we shall stead together. She asked me to send her warm greetings to you. She misses Sally is writing to her right now.

Its hard to hold my eyes open! I must get some sleep before our early trek one last thing. If any of you see Emmet, please tell him I am alive and thrive in the west, and now I am not around to nag him about the drink, he is very welcome to drink himself <u>TO DEATH</u>.

Love to all,

Maureen

Sept. 24, 1862

My dearest Eunice,

Can you believe that in five days Nattie John will be two years and seven months of age? She is talking up a storm! Whole sentences! And walking, and running! Maryam takes very good care of her.

I am sitting in the parlor of the Seamen's Home. This letter is a copy because my first copy I had written over and over and scratched out so much, so now our dear niece Theo is writing for me, I wanted this letter pristine! It will be here for you when you return *soon, soon, soon!*

I don't know if you much hear of the news where you are, so you may not know that last month Pres. Lincoln met with five Washington City free negro leaders—a preacher, a teacher, a Freemason, et al.—right in the White House! Unfortunately, the conference seems just to have been for Lincoln to give a speech, a _lecture_ of how white and black will never live together in peace and equality, therefore you colored men of intellect stop being selfish and lead the negro race elsewhere! In case they were not in favor of the present American colonization settlement in Africa, Lincoln is now offering land in Central America. He made his speech and left the men, not deigning to wait for a response. But a reply quickly emerged from colored leaders near and far: No!

(Tho I must say sometimes I dream of your return, and our removal to Liberia, where no one would ever take you from me again.)

Tomorrow I ship out. I have not set sail since you were stolen from us, I have made my living by odd jobs, I have not wanted to miss your homecoming. But money has become scarce and, with the war, delivery of weaponry by ship has made sailing among the few dependable sources of income. It has occurred to me that perhaps God was waiting to see if I would show faith — that as soon as I leave, you will walk through Mother Brook's door, smiling at me when I return! Nattie John on your lap, her arms around your neck: "Mama!"

Theo drew the four-leaf clover for you. I am not at all opposed to enhancing my prayers to God with a charm.

Always,
Your loving Ambrose

Dear Theo,

    I was very happy to hear back from you after I wrote you last month as I had fear you might forget me out of sight out of mind. It was very hard to hear that your grammy & everyone have to go to the soup kitchen again thats how hard time's are.

    You wrote your confused where I am Lawrenceville or Pittsburgh, Lawrenceville is outside of Pittsburgh well there has been a lot of excitement here the Allegheny Arsenal. By now you have surely heard of the terrible Anteidam Battle on the 17th most casualties of the war so far & all in one day 17,000 wooded 3,600 dead. I am not sure who won the Union I believe but how can anyone tell with so many dead & wooded? Here is what most people do not know. We sufferred many losses here in Lawrenceville that same day. Here is what I did not write before. My cousin Aedan & I were duped because his cousin who wrote him to come is an old man near 50 and the work he said was for Irish its for Irish alright but almost all women & girls & a few children with fingers small & nimble to make the rifle cartriges. That's what regular people calls bullets but the bullet is the projectile in the front of the cartrige whereas the cartrige is the hole thing bullet & gunpowder & primer which ignites it all. So its mostly ladies & kids here in the labertory which means the pay is low 50 cents a day for me $1.10 for my cousin. However it has been honest & not unplesent untill the urgentcy of Antiedam caused everyone to work faster & then the accident. There are different theries such as reb sabotaj but it should be noted the DuPont gunpowder delivery which came in the wagon which somebody seen one of the wagon's horse's horse-shoes spark. The ladies here have been complaning to replace the hard stone road with something softer because hard wheels & horse-shoes on a hard road strikes sparks so our boss Mr. McBride had woodchips & sinders & sawdust laid down to soften the road but his boss Col. Symington had it all swept away to bring back the hard stone for reasons unknowen. Col. Symington is not well liked by the way since his son joined the rebs and daughter wore a Confederite rosette to church. Also Mr. McBride was prior a cooper by trade & he knew that in our situation it is dangerous to use a barrel twice because once you open a keg the 2nd time around it <u>never fits as tight</u> which he told the Col. but once again deaf ears.

    Cousin Aedan & I were working in the shell-filling room when we heard the first explosion, a boom like you can not imagine. We all rushed out. Screaming from the cartrige rooms, the ladies girls running on fire it was the most horrible sight & smell. & then another blast & then another and body parts, torso w/out a head. We were civillians working civillian defense for the Union & now everywhere the picture of front-line war except the corpses & limbs are female's. 78 died, mostly women and girls. This was 11 days ago. Yesterday there was some kind of tribunal & nobody went to jail but Mr. McBride who was mourning his daughter of 15 Kate who died in the blast got severly reprimanded for gross neglect & Col. Symington got scot-free.

We are back to work here & now someone had put it into Cousin Aedan's head to get work on the railway which would require another remove, Cousin Aedan always think he following the $. When they start building the trans-continental said this helpful person thier gonna need Irish hands well might be Aedan's hands but not mine. Plenty Irish already settled in Memphis after building the railways there, if the rebs win, that would mean settling in a different country. Memphis Irish working alongside colored & I'm sure the trans-continental also be built by Irish and colored who they ever find do it cheaper?

I wish I was home with you, I think of you always, always. Last night I had a happy dream you were in it & when I woke up hear I near cried.

Your friend always,
Ciaran

Fri O' 31

Dear Theo,

Do you know theres colored troops in Kansas? The 1st Kansas Colored Volunteers organized under Gen'l James H. Lane a jayhawker close to the border near Kansas City Missouri. Do you know what a JAYHAWKER is? A jayhawker is a guerrilla free-stater from Bleeding Kansas, do you know what a GUERILLA is? Its a warrior not with any kind of organized goverment or tribe. You will need to understand all this to understand this letter.

Gen'l Lane raised a regiment of colored men in August. He asked the president to let him do it but by the time the president finally got back to him with No the deed was done. So the unit is not mustered into federal service but it is mustered into Kansas service. The regiment is free men which are mostly escaped slaves from Missouri and Arkansas many of their prior escapes aided by jayhawker Gen'l Lane. Usally this would mean the slaves is contraband, do you know what CONTRABAND is? Contraband is escaped slaves run to the Union camps and enlisted in the aid of the soldiers but not allowed to be a soldier themself. So these escaped slaves should be contraband except under Gen'l Lane theres no contraband only colored soldiers. One of the soldiers is Lt. Patrick Minor, a colored commissioned officer!

Sunday came reports of bushwhacker activity along the Kan./Mo border so 1st Kansas colored men plus assorted officers and 5th Kansas Calvery scouts were ordered by Cap'n Henry Seaman into Bates County Missouri moving toward a guerrilla nest. BUSHWHACKER if you don't know is Confederate guerrillas. Next day the Kansas outfit occupied a civilian farm in order to ascertain intelligence and heres what it was: the Yanks is very outnumbered – 225 of us 1st Kansas vs. 400 secesh. SECESH is short for secessionist. The Union dug a fort and the farm was dubbed Fort Africa. Some long-range skirmishes happened the next day (Tues) each side getting a feel of the other, Wendsday the bushwhackers set prairie fires around Fort Africa. Cap'n Seaman sent out detatchments to investigate and ordered them to <u>stay within site of Fort Africa</u> but none of them did—bold or confuzed I reckon. The enemy attacked. The first detatchment was under command of only a private, Pvt. John Six-Killer a Cherokee and they got over-runned but we all jumped in for the next stage which was hand-to-hand combat. Which saved most of the rest of our men and the rebs end up withdrawing so then we're collecting the fallen for burial. The Union dead was Pvt. Six-Killer, Cap'n A. G. Crew a white man, and 6 colored men: Cpl. Joseph Talbot and Pvts. Allen Rhodes, Henry Gash, Samuel Davis, Marion Barber, Thomas Lane (no relation to the gen'l) plus 11 wounded. The rebs suffered enough casualties to send them retreating but that number is unnone. The Union casualties I believe would be the first colored casualties of this civil war. We buried our dead seeing organs cut out of stomachs, the grewsome terror frozen on their faces, the same face must have been on the face of that secesh I wounded (or kilt). Today is Hallowe'en but I never seen Hallowe'en like this before, as we dug the graves the terrible scars on the backs of our soldiers from slavery from the whip harder to look at then the battle butchery, some of the living told of slaves whipt till dead I think soldiers wounded or kilt at war never had to endure such torture. And the memory come back to me from late Sept. when Gen'l Lane who is a radical abolitionist read to us the Preliminary Emancipation Proclamation. Our cheers was out of formation but Gen'l Lane did not stop us.

The little note I have in here is for Grammy and Gran-Gran and is just love to them from Canada which is all they need to know, the military we keep between you and me.

In the field doing the burials I held in the tears and felt very proud when Cap'n Seaman and Gen'l Lane called us brave soldiers there proud of and very glad I heard tell of the 1st Kansas Colored Volunteers early on my journey to Canada so I could quick turn around and with all the rest of them go west young man.

Your cousin and ever-companion,
Pvt. Henry Brook (Hen)

Les Misérables

In walk the men.

Fergus Mcgillicudy?

Three of them. 'Twas just Cathleen and me home, but Great-Uncle Fergus came back for his mid-day meal.

Our records indicate you are eligible for draft enrollment. As you likely know, the ceiling's been raised: now all unmarried men up to *forty-five*.

We stare, frozen.

Then Great-Uncle Fergus cries, *I'm fifty-six if I'm a day! Ye can see that!*

They look at him like they can see that. Still, they interrogate. He passes their test. Still, they give him the suspicious eye as they turn to leave. *There's men voted who've claimed alien exemption, you can't have it both ways!*

Then they're gone.

Great-Uncle Fergus trembles like a leaf. *Knew* they'd be comin, heard they're goin door to door!

But there's no draft! I say. Only volunteers!

Draft *enrollment*, Cathleen answers me, eyes on our great-uncle. The law since July.

The election! cries Great-Uncle Fergus. Just three days ago, here they are already! I'm after hearin some's arrested and sent to the Tombs!

What's an alien?

Non-citizen, Cathleen answers me. Immigrant.

They're with them, our great-uncle now grumbles. That police superintendent, Kennedy, the whole force under Lincoln's thumb—*Republicans*. Goin after Irish, they know who we vote for! Already lost plenty of the Irish constituency, *why?* On the battlefield, *dyin* for this country! Man behind me in line whispered he spent three days in jail just for bein heard *complainin* about Republicans, *disloyalty* they call it: a crime!

And yet, I think but don't say, the Democrats won big anyway, in Congress and with our new governor Horatio Seymour. Tammany Hall rollicking all night.

The next morning, Saturday, November 8, Cathleen sits on the top step outside our apartment door. She pushes herself forward, lets herself down easy to the next step, pushes herself forward, down easy to the next step, pushes herself forward, down easy to the next step. Rests.

Grammy and I asked if she wanted help. She refused. We asked again, again, by the sixth *Are you sure?* she snapped sharp so now we say nothing. Cathleen pushes herself forward, lets herself down easy to the next step. When she finally touches ground level, her toes four feet from the entrance to our tenement, she smiles up at Grammy and me waiting with the old wheelbarrow, a late autumn chill whipping through the door crack.

This acquisition's a blessèd answer to our prayers, says Grammy for the tenth time, and its sale might bring our only food for the next month. Don't you two dare damage it!

The prayers Grammy referenced are related to the photography exhibit: *The Dead of Antietam.* I'd've gone early October when it first opened but, just as I was about to visit, I received that letter from Ciaran, and then Hen's arriving yesterday, their elaborations on headless torsos and detached limbs burning images into my brain, a flood of blood—no thank you, my mind's made enough gruesome pictures, I need no more. But Cathleen, always reading about life outside the apartment, has been especially in the doldrums about her confinement lately. All the press about Brady's battlefield portraits, the talk of the town, incited a yearning in my cousin that, for the first time, could not be quelled by merely perusing the papers on the event. Then lo and behold Grammy comes across this busted-up wheelbarrow: a way. We help Cathleen in, and I get behind holding the handles.

Fresh air! she cries, but it's the usual stink: garbage and manure. Still, crisp and sunny as we stumble along to Broadway and Tenth.

There are no longer the lines around the block like when the picture show first appeared, but a good thirty people are there before us, all standing on two legs, and just about every one of them stealing a glance at Cathleen, a few outright gawking. But my cousin doesn't notice or fakes oblivion well. The outside air seems to give her some magic engine, chatterbox spilling her knowledge a mile a minute:

Mathew Brady was born in the 'twenties upstate, so he says, but rumor has it he directly imported from the Isle. He came to the city in the 'forties just after the invention of the daguerreotype, he learned the daguerreotype process from Samuel Morse, yes the Morse code inventor and Catholic-hater, who in turn had learned it in Paris from Louis Daguerre himself. Brady photographed Abraham Lincoln when the candidate was in town two years ago, and Lincoln credits that portrait, along with his Cooper Institute speech, for his election, Brady's stately image having elevated Lincoln from his previous status as bumpkin. It was Brady's most famous work before the exhibit we are about to behold. But here's a secret.

Cathleen lowers her voice, and the nearby eavesdroppers in line subtly lean in.

These are not Brady's photographs. Oh, they are *legally*, all pictures taken by his employees are *officially* his. But the man on the ground was Brady's *assistant*, born-and-raised Scotsman Alexander Gardner. He arrived at the Maryland battlefield from Washington City two days past the strife, but there were still many, many, many images to capture as it does take time to bury hundreds and hundreds and hundreds of men. Imagine what this means, Theo! Alongside the articles in our dailies and the sketches in the illustrated gazettes, we may be embarking upon an entirely new form of journalism: the truth is in the photograph! We could—

No, says the guard. We have made it to the entrance.

But—

Who do you think you are? he cuts me off. Have you come to damage the floors of the gallery with that thing? Or to swing it around and knock the framed photographs off the wall?

My face is hot with shame and rage, and now Cathleen starts to cry! Which makes me want to slug the guard, and I'm on the verge of it when my cousin begins articulating through her sobs.

I only wanted to see if I recognized anyone, one of the soldiers I might have treated at Shiloh! Yes, I was there, a nurse, look at me! Pittsburg Landing, banks of the Tennessee, the rebs raided us, and I tended the wounded between volleys over those two days, *thousands* of wounded and dead! And as I bandaged a soldier's shoulder, in the cacophony of shooting I felt a sudden warmth in my back and collapsed. My spine! Both legs I still have but what good are they to me now? Then Cathleen raises her sobs up to an outright wail.

Let her through! demands one of the former gapers.

She's a wounded veteran sure as the fellas! says another till the guard enlists a man to haul the wheelbarrow while the gatekeeper himself carries Cathleen up to the second floor where the gallery is, gently placing her back into her vehicle. I don't know if Cathleen anticipated the trouble and had prepared the yarn, or if it came to her impromptu. Either way, my cousin's a wizard!

Were there lady nurses at Shiloh? I whisper.

She shrugs. Let them figure it out.

I'm doing everything not to grin, then hear a cry behind me. A husband and wife: he solemnly holding his hat in his hands, she with her hand over her mouth, looking as if she might be sick. They stare at a picture. And now Cathleen and I turn to the images hanging from the walls.

A corpse. His body twisted, left hand on his stomach. His right hand is crooked at the elbow and holds the back of his head. I wonder, Did the bullet enter from behind his skull? Except he lies on his back, as if shot from the front. Or lead hit him from both directions? His head is turned slightly away from his raised hand, his eyes . . . His eyes wide open, nothing but the whites. In another photograph, thirty or forty bodies have all been gathered in a long row for burial. The man in front—his frozen fingers are separated and curled, monster-like. Another image reveals President Lincoln talking to General McClellan and other officers outside battlefield tents. Another: killed horse, I know it's dead because horses don't lie on their stomachs. More than one picture is called *Burial Crew*, and what strikes me are the resigned looks on the faces of the men delegated the task: staring at the deceased, or looking away from them, a different type of deadness in the bodies of the breathing. There's a field hospital of little makeshift tents, and I notice Cathleen studying it, perhaps to embellish her story in case she's ever called upon to make use of her lie again. It occurs to me now that I haven't heard a peep from her, one who surely has plenty of relevant knowledge given her avid newspaper perusal. I see that she's just as stunned to muteness as I. As is everybody. Now I observe many bodies swatted down like flies next to a farm fence. The body closest to the camera, I can't see his face but I notice his left foot is shoeless and his right leg footless. Near him a body on its back, holes in the knee and chest. Another . . . I can't make it out. Where's his head? Which way is he facing? I count two arms—one raised in the air, floating inches above the ground, the other crooked and holding . . . a hat? War casualties we have sadly come accustomed to hearing about, reading about, but never has anybody not on the battleground *seen* them before. The awkward shapes of these men thrust every viewer into a brand-new awareness: death in war is not tidy and dignified but macabre and ugly.

Theo!

I turn around.

My dear, I haven't seen you in ages! Look how tall you've grown!

Good morning, Mrs. Heverworth, I try to say, but the words are caught in my throat. She nods sadly, looking around.

The photographs. Breathtaking, aren't they. This is my third visit.

I wipe my eyes and manage to introduce Cathleen. Mrs. Heverworth is a patronness of the Academy of Music where Auntie Eunice used to work. She gave Auntie Eunice a piano.

Your Auntie Eunice was my *friend*, says Mrs. Heverworth. She sighs. Such a strange coincidence to have run into you today. Of course your family is very much on my mind this week. The anniversary.

I say nothing, but it's probably not quite as awful as Mrs. Heverworth imagines. Yesterday marked two years since Auntie Eunice went missing. But September 22, President Lincoln came out with the Preliminary Emancipation Proclamation, setting the date for freedom one hundred days hence: the first of the year—still a long time if you're a slave, but it presented us with a dim light at the end of the tunnel. Grammy's been doing the count-down. Fifty-four days, she kept saying soft yesterday, wringing out her whites for the whites.

I have not forgotten you, my pet. Could you come to see me at my home later this afternoon?

I nod. I've never seen Mrs. Heverworth's home!

Then she turns to Cathleen and takes her hand, leaning down, her eyes tearing as she says: *You*, my dear, are a heroine, which lets me know the tall tale of Cathleen's military service has continued to circulate in the Brady studio.

⁓

Around two, I head up to Mrs. Heverworth's, which is one of the fancy north-of-Fourteenth-street mansions on Fifth avenue, Eighteenth and Fifth to be precise. A colored butler answers the door. Paintings in ornate gilded frames, fresh flowers in vases, a grand piano. A big bowl of apples and fist-sized pumpkins, the partaking of which I pray is in the offing. On a table is the expensive picture album of *Dead of Antietam* photographs that was on sale at the exhibit.

When Mrs. Heverworth appears holding a very thick book, I say, You have a very beautiful home.

Thank you, Theo. A slight smile on her face as she looks around, seeing what I'm seeing. We're comfortable, she remarks, which Maureen told me is what all rich people say. Ah, grown now! Our children in college.

She refers to a large painting of Mrs. Heverworth looking younger, standing next to a man, her husband presumably, and in front of them a boy and girl around my age.

For you, she now says, and hands me the tome. Very much worth reading. Usually I would add it to our library collection, but I don't imagine Mr. Heverworth would be interested, he is not inclined toward novels. And I remember the way Eunice used to like to stay current with all the new literature. The original was released in France last spring, premiering in New York over the summer.

Thank you, Mrs. Heverworth, I appreciate it. But I can't read French.

No no—this is English! The publisher just kept the French title. I suppose the English translation would be *The Wretched*.

Ma'am? says a colored maid appearing in the doorway.

Excuse me for a moment, Theo. Please help yourself to the fruit, says my hostess as she follows the maid out, so I know my eyes must have been glued to that bowl. When Mrs. Heverworth returns, she holds an entire apple pie!

For your family. A token of my sympathy.

Thank you!

She smiles sad, then grimaces, seeing me put the pie in my dirty gunny-sack, but how else will I get it home? Carrying it in my hands, someone's liable to take it. Then Mrs. Heverworth looks startled by the bowl—or the little that's left of its contents. She told me to help myself to the fruit, and fruit is also plural.

Grammy's very happy with the pie and the four baby pumpkins which she can add to her kale stew and the three apples, which means tonight and tomorrow we won't just have broth for supper and growling bellies for dessert. I read Mrs. Heverworth's book the rest of the evening, and in the morning, which is Sunday, I read it walking the street and almost get hit by a stage (*Look where ye're goin!* yells the coach driver), and in that moment when I look up, I notice a new girl at Kaelyn the street-sweeper's corner.

How do ye.

She stares at me.

Where's Kaelyn?

Jail.

Jail?

Stole bread.

Before I can ask the girl her name, she races off, like I'm in cahoots with the coppers and am about to make an arrest.

I run into Auntie Siobhan's tavern just in time to see that white cat fly across the floor, pouncing on some poor gray mouse. My auntie's at the counter, her head down in her figures note-book, adding up something.

Auntie Siobhan! Do you want to hear of a very strange coincidence?

They were heroic! says a male customer to his drinking buddy, two patrons here already so early in the morning. Meagher's brave Irish Brigade: valiant! All the papers said it, holdin the line! But the losses. The terrible, terrible losses.

Meagher was a Young Irelander, ye know, says his companion. The 'forty-eight rebellion.

I've been reading this book about a man imprisoned for nineteen years because he stole a loaf of bread, well, also because of his escape attempts, and then I go by the corner where a new street-sweeper girl's replaced Kaelyn because Kaelyn's in jail for stealing bread! Isn't that queer? The odd chance I'd be reading the fiction, then walk right into life mimicking it!

Two months ago Antietam was, and the news *still* tricklin in, says the first man. More than twenty thousand casualties! Two thousand Union *dead*! More than the rebs! And they call it a Union *victory*?

Auntie Siobhan!

She startles, like just now aware I'm here. *What?*

Kaelyn the street-sweeper's in jail because she stole bread, and I was just reading—

Little girl in jail for stealin *bread?*

I nod. She sighs.

Just like Shiloh! Just like Second Manassas! the man goes on. All of them more than twenty thousand losses! But Shiloh took two days last spring, that return to Bull Run end of summer took three. Autumn brings Antietam, which reached those numbers in *one day*, what a beastly year!

Poor little girl, says Auntie Siobhan. Don't suppose she has family to visit her?

I shake my head.

Poor lonely little girl.

No more, says the man. No more volunteerin, what I hear from *every* Irish, every one!

And don't think they'll draft us into those Indian wars out there neither, says the other.

That Sioux upstart was crushed weeks ago, dismisses the first.

Then Auntie Siobhan suddenly locates in her brain a vagueness of what I said before: What crazy kind of book ye're readin?

I show her and tell her. She frowns a moment, then throws her head back laughing.

Les Misérables, she corrects, very Frenchy. *Not* Les Miserables, ye're not reading about Lester from the Miserables family!

My face warm, eyes narrowing.

Listen, you might want to go upstairs, offer your farewells to Sally.

Miss Sally's going west *too?*

North. To Greenwich Village.

As I tear up the stairs, I hear the first man remark, One general said Meagher's brigade was so fearless, if ever he saw the Irish runnin to the rear he'd follow because the battle must surely be lost!

Miss Sally! Miss Sally!

Well, how do ye, Theo.

I don't want you to leave! Everyone's leaving!

Aw, come here.

I sit on the bed next to her, and she puts her arm around me, cuddling me close.

I whisper: Did Auntie Siobhan raise the rent?

No, no, she chuckles. Matter of fact, I was late last month, and I know a tenant two months in arrears. Your auntie might put on a show, hands on her hips sighing, but she's been very patient, very kind. With the inflation, she knows nowhere else we could afford, kicking us out is kicking us to the street.

Then why are you *removing*?

Miss Sally sighs. I guess it's just hard to be here without Fiona. She was my boon companion, you know.

I nod.

And. In the Village, there's a house of colored ladies, all in my trade, very welcoming. I kind of rather be very close to other colored now.

She holds me even tighter.

Things're changin. The tobaccery in Brooklyn. And all the papers claimin *Free the slaves and they come up take white jobs.* Not *my* job, my job's secure. But my *race*? Not so certain.

Sunday feels like a very nice day to visit somebody in jail, so after hugging Miss Sally and promising to come see her in the Village, I go to the Tombs. I realize I don't know Kaelyn's last name but I describe her to a guard. He's rude, and another guard is dismissive, but then a stern matron lets me in, muttering about somebody so little locked up in jail, glad she finally has a visitor. The lady leads me through a courtyard and into a wing of the prison, then into a room. I sit and wait. I try to think of something to cheer Kaelyn up but before I can think of anything, there she is with a different matron, who sits on a stool in the corner.

How do ye, Theo!

How do ye, Kaelyn.

I'm glad you come to see me! How're things outside?

I shrug.

I been in here two weeks! You're my first visitor! My brother woulda come, but he's in jail too. We stole the bread together!

You have a brother?

You never seen my brother?

I shake my head.

He's seven years of age and I'm eight! Or . . . I'm nine of years and he's eight, I forget but I'm oldest! When you were in the courtyard, did you see that bridge holdin the buildins together?

I nod.

That's the Bridge of Sighs, the condemned people gotta pass through it on the way to the gallows! This here's the Female Department. Next to us is the Boys' Department, and over there's the Men's, there ain't a Girls' because we're all together in the Female!

I'm sorry you have to be in jail, Kaelyn.

It's okay. You know what they have in jail? Food! Gruel! And sometimes a potato or apple, the Sisters of Charity takes care of the Females and the Boys! I'm not hungry no more! And the ladies in my cell is nice! I'm the only kid in my cell, the ladies call me Doll Baby and Sweetcakes, and sometimes they gimme some a *their* food! There was one other kid, Caroline, but she got released, now just me and the ladies gettin fat!

Kaelyn shows me her skinny arm, but I reckon it's less skinny than before jail.

Why don't you visit my brother? He don't got no one to see him.

Okay. What's his name?

Patrick! Patrick MacSweeney! He's in the Boys' Department.

Okay.

Before they put us in jail, we were playin a game, you have to think of an animal and a rhyme. I said, I am a bird, my tweet you heard. Then Patrick said, I am a cat, I'm big and fat. Then I said, I am a pig can do a jig. Remember that! Tell Patrick that and tell him it's his turn, then bring his turn back to me!

After I leave Kaelyn, I see another matron and ask about Patrick, but she says visiting time is over and walks me back to the entrance. School's tomorrow, so I make a plan to come see Patrick next week-end.

U.S. Military Commission sentences three hundred Sioux to death!

I stare at the newsboy. Then walk and search and walk and search till I spy a dirty penny on the ground. A *Times* costs two cents now (still less than a *Herald*, which is three), but a copper's enough to buy a damaged daily from a paper-collector in line for the scrapman.

The article couldn't've been any briefer.

The New-York Times

NEW-YORK, SUNDAY, NOVEMBER 9, 1862.

PUNISHMENT OF THE INDIANS.

Over Three Hundred of the Sioux Indians
Condemned to be Hung.

ST. PAUL, Minn.

Over three hundred Indians have been convicted by the Military Commission
at the Lower Sioux Agency as participators in the late horrible massacres, and
are condemned to be hung. Whether they live or die rests with the authorities at
Washington. The people of Minnesota, to a man, are in favor of their immediate
execution.

That's on page five of the total eight. But on page two, there's something more substantial: a letter.

What Shall be Done With the Sioux?

Under date of St. Paul, Oct. 10, Gov. RAMSEY, of Minnesota, in a letter to President LINCOLN, regarding the Sioux, says:

The conduct of these savages has shown that they are most dangerous when
least suspected, and that they are far less dreaded as open enemies than as pre-
tended friends.

Large numbers of our citizens regard with intense and inveterate hostility
these ruthless assassins of their friends, these ravishers of their wives and sisters
and daughters, and these destroyers of their homes and property.

By their infraction of treaty obligations, I suppose that the Sioux of Minnesota have forfeited all claim to the protection of the Government, and that the
disposition now to be made of them is purely a question of expediency which it
rests with the Executive to determine.

It is enough to say that the Winnebagoes are Indians, that, whether justly or
unjustly, they are strongly suspected of having been accessories to the bloody
plot of the Sioux, to justify the popular demand for their removal to some distant

MOON AND THE MARS 421

locality outside of this State—a measure as necessary to their own security in the present temper of our people as to the restoration of confidence among our citizens.

The Chippewas occupy a District in the Northern part of the State unfit for agricultural settlement, and inaccessable to military operations. It might be sufficient, in their case, to remove them farther north, at a distance from our settled border, and to place them under strict military and police restraint.

Trusting that these views may meet your sanction, and that they may be speedily accomplished by treaty or by force,

I have the honor to be very respectfully, your obedient servant.

ALEX. RAMSEY.

Stop it, Elijah! I told you not to pull Eleanora's hair!

Tuesday at the Orphan's Asylum, Abbie snatches Elijah by his shoulder, giving him a harsh shake, her furious eyes an inch from his frightened ones. It's the second time she'd given that directive, but she'd always been the patient one in the past so it's unnerving to see her snap. She wasn't in school yesterday, and didn't do much but grunt the entire trek to here. When it's time to leave, all she does walking back to Five Points is grumble: how spoiled and vain our classmate Mary Jane is (true), how the orphans at the asylum are rude and undisciplined (mostly false), how people just want a peek at *The Dead of Antietam* for the purpose of some grotesque thrill (unfair and debatable), and before I can pop out a syllable, she mutters something about needing to get home early, then races ahead leaving me behind which, given her mood, I find less an insult than a relief.

Next morning at school, I can see her disposition hasn't changed, so I just leave her be. We exit separately at dismission to face the remnants of a chilly downpour, and when I slip and fall in the muck, for the first time in my life I utter a curse, albeit under my breath.

Dammit is right, I hear, and there stands Abbie, reaching out her hand to help me up. I take it, but then slip again, pulling her down so now we both sit in the filthy mire, and are suddenly roaring from the farce of it all. When the mirth subsides, she says, There was this letter from the Minnesota governor in the *Times*.

I saw it.

She looks at me as if for comment. Feeling like I might step into a pit of snakes, I say nothing, so she continues: The Winnebagoes done *nothing* to the whites, the Chippewas forced from the East to Northwest are *far* from the whites but they want to push them farther! farther! As for the Sioux— this white man complaining they broke their treaty with the whites, and in the same breath proposes the whites break *their* treaties with the Winnebagoes and Chippewa!

I nod.

You got nothing to say?

Sorry, Abbie, I'm on my monthly, and I don't have any money for soothing herbs. (Which is true, but the larger issue is fear of saying the wrong thing.)

I'm on *my* monthly, that has nothing to do with the outrages!

You *also* on your monthly? Isn't that odd! Weren't we on our monthlies together last—?

Don't you dare say my melancholia is only my woman time!

I *didn't*—

Best thing about the monthlies is they force you to feel what you feel instead of tamping it all down tolerable like we do rest of the month.

Then she storms away, the mud tinting the ends of her pretty long black hair.

❧

Sunday I'm back at the Tombs, early enough to see Kaelyn and Patrick both. Kaelyn comes and says did I see Patrick and what was his turn in the game, and I realize I should have visited Patrick first.

That's okay, I'm in the middle of a different game with my cell-mates anyway, she says, ready to rush back to her lady friends, but first she tells me not to forget to see Patrick, and makes me recite the rhyme game till I'm perfect to the letter.

I ask the matron about Patrick and am told to wait, then she returns to escort me to the Boys' Department visiting room. There's a male guard near the door falling asleep, two older boys at work—one swabbing the floor and the other the walls—and a teeny little boy in the center.

Patrick?

Even though he's staring right at me, my utterance gives him a start.

I'm Kaelyn's friend. Your sister. She asked me to come see you. I'm Theo.

He doesn't move. I consider going to him, but his wild eyes and tense body make me think of a cornered animal, like one step in his direction and lightning fast he'd scurry away. I might've called Kaelyn rail thin but she seems downright plump compared to Patrick's state. Filthy, a barely healing black eye and assorted other bruises on his face and arms. He takes one step toward me wincing, and now I know the reluctance in his body is not only fear, but pain.

I speak softly: I just came by to say how-do-ye. I know Kaelyn, she asked me to pay you a visit.

He stares.

Kaelyn is doing fine.

Kaelyn come for me? His voice a whisper: hoarse, weak.

She can't. She's in the Female Department.

I go to the Female Department?

You can't, I say, laughing gently. You're a boy.

A whistle. Patrick's eyes snap terrified to the whistler, one of the older boys with dirty blond hair. Both boys sneer at each other, and at Patrick. Patrick begins to sob silently. The guard sleeps.

Aw, don't cry! Don't worry, Patrick, I bet they'll let you go soon.

And suddenly his sobs are screams, his fists twisting in his closed eyes.

Hey, says the guard, coming to life. HEY! What's goin on here?

Patrick! Patrick, listen. Kaelyn told me you and she were playing a game.

You want another taste a the strap, boy?

Patrick, *sh!* Sh, listen, wanna keep up the game? Listen: Kaelyn said, I am a bird, my tweet you heard. Then you said, I am a cat, I'm big and fat. Then Kaelyn said, I am a pig can do a jig. Your turn, Patrick! Your turn!

He keeps crying as he speaks, a sob between each syllable just before the guard yanks him away: I am a hen lock in a pen.

⤜⤏

A few mornings later, I hear *Sweep-oh!*

How do ye, Mr. Samuel!

How do *you* do, Theo. What's the news?

I know Mr. Samuel means my personal news, but I answer with a bulletin.

Three hundred Sioux to be hung!

I thought I was just relaying the report, but my voice surprises me with a little cry. He nods thoughtful.

Three hundred and four. But they can't hang anybody until the president signs off on it. As I understand the situation, he's reviewin the court transcripts now. He's a lawyer, you know.

Oh.

Mr. Samuel shakes his head. Don't know what there is to review. 'Twas a military court, they weren't obligated to provide any defense lawyer. As I understand the situation, the five-white-man military commission got impatient and started tryin em faster, forty in one day, some no more than five minutes, some a the accused not comprehendin a word of English. Why bother? Everyone knows the verdict, and the sentence: Death. Death. Death. Death. Death. Death. Death.

⁓

Middle of December, the review's over.

Abbie, President Lincoln commuted the sentences of two hundred and sixty-five Sioux! President Lincoln saved their lives!

I'm near yelling it. Abbie gives me a thin smile. School hasn't started yet, and we're supposed to be quiet and well behaved at all times, so the other students give me a surprised and judgmental look. I get closer to Abbie.

I mean, I know that means thirty-nine are still set to die. But that's only thirteen percent of the original, I say softly, hoping to impress mathematics genius Abbie with my sums.

She nods, her thoughts in the distance.

Who knows? Maybe more might get commuted—

Do you know what they mean by *commuted*?

I swallow. I don't know, but her tone doesn't sound promising.

It's an exchange. Most of the men will remain in prison until the day they die, their immediate executions were traded for a longer-term death sentence.

After that, I start keeping my conversations with Abbie minimal. She always manages to make me feel stupid, or like I'm not on her side, usually both. But with Hen and Ciaran gone, and Friedrich who I haven't seen in ages—I heard after his brother was killed, he got a job moving crates for some merchant on German Broadway—I'm pretty much left with no kid friends.

⌘

Next day, I stand in the soup line with Grammy Brook. It's one in the afternoon—our first and last meal for the day. Everybody in the line and everybody outside of the line reads papers.

THE NEW-YORK HERALD.

NEW YORK, SUNDAY, DECEMBER 17, 1862.

THE DISASTER.

Fredericksburg Abandoned by General Burnside.

The Army Safely Recrossed to the Northern Side of the Rappahannock.

ALL THE WOUNDED BROUGHT AWAY.

THE PONTOONS REMOVED.

The Terrific Struggle on Saturday.

ADDITIONAL   DETAILS.

Intensely Graphic Descriptions by Our Special Correspondents.

The Desperate Charges on the Right Wing.

Splendid Field Manœvering on the Left.

THE LAST MOMENTS OF GENERAL BAYARD

Scenes on the Battle Field After Sunset.

The Valor of Our Troops Praised by the Rebel Prisoners.

Our Loss Estimated at Eight to Ten Thousand.

Additional Names of the Killed and Wounded, &c.,   &c.,   &c.

Silence: you could hear a pin drop, except for the occasional gasp which I wager is when the reader gets down to the *Eight to Ten Thousand* part.

I go to Grammy Cahill's for the night, and in the middle of it my growling stomach wakes me. Here's Cousin Aileen asleep but where's Grammy? I walk out to the front-room. Cathleen sleeping, Great-Uncle Fergus snoring. Then I hear a little cry from outside our apartment door.

Grammy sitting on the step, wrapped in her old shawl. A sniffle.

Grammy?

Sh, she says softly, and I close the door and sit with her.

What's the matter? I ask, even as I think: What's not? Fredericksburg. The skimpy portion from the soup line. Tots in jail. The Sioux.

Ah, nothin, *mo leanbh*. This time of year just brings me a heartache sometimes. The three babies I buried back in Kerry, two of them just before Christmas. Then losin your mammy here, and Meara and her family. Only my Siobhan survivin.

Sorry, Grammy.

She shakes her head. I count my blessings. Siobhan and her publick house, she'd never let us starve. But I try not to bother her while the soup kitchen's offerin, she's feelin the hard times too, her tenants not makin the rent. Still, she won't toss them out. Never become the heartless landlords we had to live under back home!

A wind blows through the cracks in the walls, causing the old steps to creak.

First we smelled them. Like night soil, oh yes! our potatoes takin in the foul scent of the privy. We'd had the blight before, but nothin like this, nothin goin past one season into the next. And spreadin so fast, people desperate, squeakin through the rain-soaked peat, checkin this plant, that plant, that plant—*all* of them. The disease *in the soil itself!* What crops were salvaged were tiny and soft, a sodden mess. Your grandfather and me starin at it: the year's harvest, gone! We wailed and the children wailed, but whatever horrors were runnin through our heads, the comin reality we couldn't've imagined.

'Twas a gorgeous country. Our scalpeen jutted between the risin mountain and the drop to the sea, stunnin beauty right outside our door! The rich green of the land, and the rich green of the *sea*, teemin with fish! I remember tastin salmon once as a kid—a heavenly flavor! But grow up to have my own household, 'twas no longer available to us. The ocean's bounty, the hares that ran wild all over the countryside—they were the possession of the landlord, only the landlord and his guests could hunt and fish, any Irish caught partakin faced harsh penalties, eviction to the elements bein the most feared. And as the Famine took hold, d'ye think they'd gain a heart? No! The Hunger just made them more suspicious, more severe. More ready to throw entire families out into the cold!

We loved our tubers. Lumpers, we called them. Worst variety of potato, though I didn't know it till I ate my first American spud. Oh, there's *grand* Irish taters, just not on the rocky ground we were forced onto. But lumpers were fertile there! And we knew how to change them up: hot, cold, boiled, with onions, butter, mustard seed. We invented the mashed potato! And with a bit of milk, a few eggs—a hearty meal! And we were hearty souls!

Money none of us had. Cottage labor: we were compensated in potatoes, or with how many potatoes we were permitted to grow in our own gardens. We paid the rent in potatoes! And ten percent of it we were forced to tithe to the damned Anglican church! And when the Famine came, the blamed Protestants blamed *us*, said we Catholics were bein cursed for our popery! Christians, they purported to be, but when the Hunger took hold: no leniency! No Christian charity! Their mandate—no rent: eviction! And tear down the scalpeen while they're at it! Why on earth would they destroy the home? I wondered, humble as it was. Can't they rent it out to another poor family? But there wasn't another poor family could move in and pay the rent. The west and the south ravenous, they couldn't get blood from a stone.

Cattle. They wanted to clear us out, remove the house, and turn the land into cattle grazin, *there* the landlords could collect their capital.

Many of them didn't even live on the Isle. They were the British, or claimin to be descendants of British, wavin their Union Jacks proud on Irish land while residin in England or Scotland.

The States was generous. Well, there already were Irish here, broken-hearted by what was happenin back home. The American railroads carried packages to ships bound for Ireland free of charge. The American government removed the weapons from warships and filled them with supplies, *food*, rushed them to our shores! But the British even eyed a profit to be made there, demandin the ships first land in England so their cargoes could be transferred to *British* bottoms, and how much money did the English shipmen pocket on that arrangement! And how many starved in Ireland durin the delay! Finally world opinion embarrassed them enough they started lettin the ships go directly to the Isle.

The diseases. Typhus, *fiabhras dubh* we called it, black fever. Turnin the skin dark for a fortnight. Then: death.

One evenin, we heard our absentee landlord had come home for a visit.

We wanted to arrive early to beg him for mercy before the hordes appeared on the same mission, so we left in the early winter mornin, pitch dark still at seven. I'm after wakin the children, and could still see a flicker of hope in their starvin eyes, that morsel of shine left. Even with their collar bones protrudin, their hair fallin out in clumps, bald patches. We walked the road, the four miles to our landlord. Once on the lonely journey, a carriage appeared, and we rushed to it, but the passengers saw beggars approachin and hurried off, nearly collapsin over a bump in the road. The bump were a corpse, we knew it before we got there, and the carriage driver knew it too. I counted two more bodies along the way: the second layin with another not quite dead, but the four hungry rats couldn't wait, they nibbled on the dead and almost dead alike. I tried to shoo the animals away from the livin, but they paid little attention, one eyein my own skin n bones like I might be dessert.

Finally the landlord's big house appeared in the distance, but then, all at once, the children turned and ran in a different direction. How did they summon the energy? Where were they headed?

Grammy swallows.

The trough. My babies had seen the pigs and ran to eat the slop alongside the swine! Till the missus come out and shooed us all away, stealin from her livestock—we were nothin but vermin to her!

I put my arm around Grammy, who weeps in silence. Then she wipes her face, her eyes gone cold.

There was food in Ireland. Corn. That's what we called the grains—wheat, oats, barley, the potato blight didn't affect *those* crops, but they weren't meant for us: the landowners continued shippin them to England! Well, they sure couldn't line their pockets by handin it over to the starvin paupers they made to sow and harvest it! *Us*, the *original* inhabitants, the Indians of Ireland! And don't doubt they didn't have the sentries watchin close to make sure not a sprout of their merchandise was eaten by we the caretakers! The landlords did keep a bit in the country, enough for *themselves* to gorge on. While the priests were performin extreme unction to entire villages! Come, I need the Irish shantee.

I'm glad Grammy said that because I've had to go since I got out of bed. We walk out to relieve ourselves, then sit on a courtyard step, her putting her shawl around both of us, the tenement walls blocking the biting wind.

After you were shooed away from the landlord's house. That's when you came to America?

Grammy shakes her head.

Eventually England knuckled under international pressure and provided a daily soup—that is, for those of us they deemed qualified for it, and if ye weren't a dead ringer for dead, they wouldn't deem ye qualified. Soup as in broth, not a hearty stew, *that* would have cost too much. Some starved to death eatin that soup!

And the work. The pointless work required in exchange for the scanty suppers. Women and men breakin stones to build roads to nowhere, to erect bridges over no water. We could have looked for fertile land to cultivate, we could have built railroads, fished! But *productive* labor was forbidden.

Why?

Laissez-faire. They wanted us to earn our livin, literally—earn the right not to die! But the British were legally bound not to interfere in the economy. So the labor was *demanded* to be meaningless! Oh, now don't you start with the tears too. And Grammy wipes my face and holds me tight.

I often think of Ciaran, she says after a bit, always desperate for work, wishin to be of use. Sure his parents told him of those awful days, and I wonder how it all affected him. The need to work *for a purpose*!

Grammy sighs. I glimpse a rat peeking out from the w.c., and between Grammy's terrible stories and my sleepy head, for a second I mistake the large crumb in the rodent's mouth for human flesh.

And *then*. Lord William Henry Gregory.

Grammy spits sharply on the ground.

Damn him to hell! His Poor Law Amendment Act, *ach!* Two clauses. One: To provide the starvin with assistance in leavin the country and, believe me, said assistance was barely a cent over the ship fare, we left Ireland's shores destitute and arrived on America's worse! Hundreds of us huddled together below-decks, some boardin carryin the typhus, and more of those as we sailed. Lyin in their sick, all of us livin with the stench of the vomit, the diarrhea. Drinkin water was scarce, some of it stored in casks that previously held vinegar, contaminatin the supply! And the food. Bare minimum the ship provided per passenger, expectin we'd brought our own stock. *How?* We're fleein a famine! One out of three didn't survive our coffin-ship crossin, dropped overboard to the sharks, and I heard our death rate was better than some others.

That was Clause One. For those considerin stayin, Clause Two: All land more than a quarter of a statute acre had to be relinquished or we'd get no *outdoor relief.* D'ye know what they meant by *outdoor relief?* Food! How can anyone have a garden to sustain a family on land so small? So, at a time when the landlords could have shown compassion, could have provided for their deprived and starvin tenants and laborers, they chose instead to provide for themselves the thing they'd always wanted: removal. To cause the Irish to vanish from Ireland.

We buried your little uncles Colm and Ronan before losin your grampa Seamus. Brigid and Siobhan and I'm only after pattin down the earth coverin baby Grianne's grave when up to us walks the man offerin the papers, all officially worded under Clause One.

In the distance, a dog barks. I shiver in the chill, but right now Grammy seems to be engaging in enough bitter reminiscence to keep her warm till spring. We are silent a while, then at once comes a chorus of our growling stomachs here in the midst of what the papers tout as economic prosperity. It's Grammy's cue to take my hand and lead us both back up to bed.

‿◦

On Christmas Eve, Great-Uncle Fergus hobbles through the door after work. Ah, my achin back! he says. I'll be needin a soothin hot rag, or I'll never make my shift in the mornin.

Christmas ought to be a legal holiday! asserts Cousin Aileen.

When you all get home from work tomorrow, I have a little surprise for ye.

What! we all ask Grammy, eager.

Maybe a little stew. Maybe a little pork stew.

We sigh in anticipation. Then I remember I'll miss it. Since I'm spending Christmas Eve with this grammy, I need to spend Christmas Day with the other. Tonight supper's broth and a little cranberry bread that Grammy made with Auntie Siobhan's donated ingredients.

Did ye know they're kickin Jews out of the army? asks Cousin Aileen. Rachel at the manufactory told me about her eldest, Yosef, bein sent home.

Why would the president be kickin out the Jews? asks Grammy. Don't he need every soldier he can get?

The president didn't, says Cathleen. It's one Union general making some new rule for his department.

Which general? I ask.

Grant, Cathleen replies. Ulysses Grant. The Southeast commander. He expelled all the Jews in his jurisdiction: Kentucky, Mississippi, and Tennessee.

Civilians too? asks Grammy.

Civilians too.

Well, how can they—? Grammy starts to ask, then shakes her head, looking at our Mary statue and crossing herself.

I miss Maureen! cries Cousin Aileen suddenly, wiping a tear. Grammy puts her arm around her.

I'm sure she's having a grand Christmas in the West, Ma, smiles Cathleen, her own eyes full.

Strikin gold with Fiona, says Grammy.

At least out there she's far from the war, says Cousin Aileen. They probably forgot we're *in* war out there. Unless . . . Cousin Aileen's face turns to fret.

If you're worried about the Sioux War, says Cathleen, it's over. Or will be, day after tomorrow when they hang the thirty-eight.

Thirty-nine, I say, looking up from my book.

Thirty-eight. One of the condemned had his sentence respited. He's an old man, and it was decided those particular accusations of murder were clearly by the hands of a *young* man.

Did ye know, Grammy says, that the Choctaws sent money to Ireland? Durin the Famine? Remember, Fergus?

I remember.

We'd come over in 'forty-six, but course the Hunger was still ragin a year later when those Indians who'd suffered the Trail of Tears scarcely a decade before made a decision to send relief four thousand miles away. The Choctaw knew what starvation and cold was. Guess how they learned of *our* misery? From some Irish soldier forcin the Indians off *their* land!

Why must it always be like that? One afflicted under the heavy foot of power turnin around to stomp on the head of someone else.

Choctaws kept slaves.

Everyone looks at me.

Choctaws were southeast Indians, the slave-holding Southeast.

No one knows what to do with that, so everyone's quiet a while. I think about Tecumseh, Tecumseh said something important, how we need to bond together, fight together, but now I can't remember what it was exactly. *A twig breaks . . . A twig breaks . . .*

How did Lincoln decide? asks Grammy softly. The thirty-eight.

Cathleen says: General Pope, the local commander, said he was ready to *utterly exterminate* the Sioux if Lincoln empowered him to, the Minnesotans wanting to execute the execution order immediately, but it had to be signed by Lincoln. The president was pressured by General Pope that if he didn't quickly sign off on hanging all the accused, the settlers would settle it themselves with soldiers more than willing to assist: kill *all* the Sioux—women, children, elders. But Lincoln took his time anyway, reviewing each case. At first, he said only rapists would be put to death, but only two Sioux were thus accused, and Lincoln was fairly certain that would not quench the Minnosotans' thirst for blood. So Abe lowered the requirement to those found guilty of massacres rather than regular battles, which made thirty-nine now down to thirty-eight. Lincoln knew the settlers would not be happy but it was what he signed off on, *I could not afford to hang men for votes*, he said.

To Hell or to Connacht!

We turn to Grammy.

Isn't that what the bastard Oliver Cromwell said? Pushin us west on the Isle, and two centuries later the Famine pushin us off! Did ye know Andrew Jackson's parents were Irish? County Antrim, *Protestants*. Poor farmers, and still. That aul Indian-killer came from colonial stock, British-loyal. Was in his blood, no qualms about forcin a land's original people west. Or to hell.

The door flies open, and in walks Ciaran. He didn't write that he was coming home from Pittsburgh! I thought I'd never see him again! We all run to him but I'm mad Cousin Aileen and Grammy are closer and get to him first! He's taller and older, and can now embrace two women at once while looking over their heads, flashing his smile just for me, ear to ear.

⟳

Christmas Day at Grammy Brook's—the celebration less about the Messiah's birth than about a more current promise: one week till emancipation! In the evening after work, Auntie Maryam and Mr. Samuel and Nattie John come. And we have pork stew! And Auntie Maryam brings a little turkey stew for herself and anyone else wanting a taste. Gran-Gran grins over her soup. And that's our entire Christmas family. No Uncle Ambrose who's out to sea. No Mr. Freeman who's in Kansas. No Hen who everyone but me thinks is in Canada. No Auntie Eunice. So it's not the joyous holiday it could have been, but still an auspicious one. Except Grammy doesn't seem as hopeful as she did on November 7, Auntie Eunice's anniversary, and I think I know what she's feeling because it's what I'm feeling. Now that the date's drawn near, the questions: What if at the last minute they cancel emancipation? If it does go through, how will the slaves know they're emancipated? What does it mean if the whole country's emancipated and still Auntie Eunice doesn't come home? I bet Auntie Maryam and Uncle Samuel worry on this too, but they hold up their cups of tea and make bright smiles to toast it: Freedom!

After the meal, my adopted auntie and I wash the dishes.

Auntie Maryam, remember last winter when we stood outside the Tombs while they executed that slave-ship captain by upright-jerker?

Mm hm.

You think that's how they'll hang the Sioux tomorrow?

Everybody hears this and stops frozen to stare at me, like my Cahill family did yesterday when I mentioned that Choctaws owned slaves.

I don't know! Auntie Maryam finally blurts, looking fretful, looking angry and betrayed.

Theo! snaps Grammy, as if I bewildered Auntie Maryam on purpose which, only this second, I realize might be true.

Later, as we all sit around quiet, Auntie Maryam says, Captain Gordon, hung for that crime. I was glad. But been gladder the bigger ones in charge got it.

Snow! squeals Nattie John, looking out at the flakes softly falling.

Once the Preliminary Proclamation come out, Auntie Maryam goes on, seventeen negroes hung in Culpepper, Virginia. You heard it?

Grammy and I shake our heads. Mr. Samuel looks down.

They was charged with insurrection, but the only evidence was they was readin newspapers printed the proclamation. Most a them that was hung was free. I don't know if any was women.

Nattie John makes a circle with her finger on the window fog and giggles.

They rather us dead than free!

Nattie John is as startled as the rest of us, turning to her auntie and foster mother. Auntie Maryam swallows.

So I guess I don't believe in the death penalty no more. Long's it's around, seem like always the ones least deserve it gonna get it.

❧

The next day, I stroll by Abbie's tenement, stopping to stare up at her window. There used to be a white curtain with flowers, but now the curtain is black.

The new year will come, and Abbie and I will become friends again, but it won't ever be quite the same, which I'm starting to learn is what growing up is: scars that scab but never wholly heal.

And we'll hear of the three-day Battle of Stones River in Tennessee, fought over New Year's Eve and New Year's Day and resulting in—like Shiloh, like Second Manassas, like Antietam—more than twenty thousand casualties.

And on Sunday, January 11, page 3 of the *New-York Times* will fill the first two columns with a detailed report on the hangings that transpired at Mankato, Blue Earth County, Minnesota, on Friday, December 26, 1862. I will read that the thirty-eight condemned men, after being informed of the decision of the Great Father at Washington read in English and Dacotah, were permitted a farewell to friends and family, some of the partings impassioned, some of the doomed leaving a memento—a pipe, a lock of hair. Soon after, the men were chained in pairs, and the pairs chained to the floor preventing any movement. Periodically the keepers made some announcement regarding the captives' fast-approaching fate, which the Indians appeared to take with stoicism, even boredom. But as the hour drew near, and a Catholic priest began to speak, the elder Ptan doo ta let up a haunting wail, which one by one the men began to pick up, the sound resounding off the walls, and when I read this I shall think about Tecumseh saying *Sing your death song, and die like a hero going home.* The keening having comforted them, the men fell quiet, resuming their pipe-smoking until the Protestant minister began a speech which caused the wailing to erupt again, this second white religious man drowned out by the lamentation as was the first. Not long after, the condemned were escorted to the scaffold, a large square platform with beams that supported another square above: four perpendicular timbers from which hung thirty-eight nooses. In the middle stood the man who would drop the ax, slicing the rope to cause the platform beneath the thirty-eight to drop, leaving the men dangling, and when I read this, I'll think that if President Lincoln had not intervened, there might have been three hundred four executions, but if President Lincoln had never signed off on the Homestead Act in the first place, there might have been zero executions and zero killings of whites because there would not have been such an encroaching white threat. Outside the square were fifteen hundred soldiers on horseback in formation, and behind them several thousand Minnesota settler spectators jostling for view. The signal to hang was to be the third tap of the drum.

Caps were placed over the men's heads, the nooses fitted around their necks. At the first tap, each of the condemned warriors frantically reached out to hold his neighbors' hands, and each began shouting his own name:

1. Te he hdo ne cha—One Who Jealously Guards His Home
2. Ptan doo ta—Scarlet Otter
3. Wy a tah ta wah—His People
4. Hin han shoon ko yag—One Who Walks Clothed in Owl Feathers
5. Muz za boom a du   Iron Blower
6. Wah pay du ta—Red Leaf
7. Wa he hna—I Came (?)
8. Sna ma ni—Tinkling Walker
9. Ta te mi na—Round Wind (respited: not hanged)

10. Rda in yan kna—Rattling Runner
11. Do wan sa—One Who Sings a Lot or the Singer
12. Ha pan—Second-born Child and Male in a Dacotah Family
13. Shoon ka ska—White Dog
14. Toon kan e chah tay mane—One Who Walks by His Grandfather
15. E tay hoo tay—Scarlet Face
16. Am da cha—Broken to Pieces
17. Hay pee don—"Little" Third-born Child and Male in a Dacotah Family
18. Mahpe o ke na ji—One Who Stands on a Cloud
19. Henry Milord
20. Chaskay don—"Little" First-born Child and Male in a Dacotah Family
21. Baptiste Campbell
22. Tah ta kay gay—Wind Maker
23. Ha pink pa—The Top of the Horn
24. Hypolite Ange
25. Na pay shne—Fearless
26. Wa kan tan ka—Great Mystery
27. Toon kan ka yag e na jin—One Who Stands Clothed with His Grandfather or One Who Stands Cloaked in Stone
28. Ma kat e na jin—One Who Stands on the Earth
29. Pa zee koo tay ma ne—One Who Shoots While Walking
30. Ta tay hde don—Wind Comes Home
31. Wa she choon—Whiteman
32. A e cha ga—To Grow Upon
33. Ha tan in koo—Returning Clear Voice
34. Chay ton hoon ka—Elder Hawk
35. Chan ka hda—Near the Woods
36. Hda hin hday—Sudden Rattle
37. O ya tay a koo—He Brings the People
38. May hoo way wa—He Comes for Me
39. Wa kin yan na—Little Thunder

Watch Night

A jocular camaraderie replacing the competition among the chimney sweep-masters. The barbers laugh-talking outside their shop, even with it empty of customers. A skip in her step as Grammy irons her whites for the whites, chatting lively with Gran-Gran: something in the air! Saturday, December 27: Grammy's Christmas Day apprehensions about emancipation seem to have dissipated, replaced with gracious anticipation: *four more days.*

Pigs' feet at the market today! Grammy says in the afternoon, and pigs' feet I know is something we can afford. And potatoes for soup. Whyn't you run on up to Auntie Maryam's, invite em for Sunday dinner?

I stroll to West Thirty-second and knock. After an appropriate wait, I knock again, and the door is whipped open.

I was jus there Christmas! You know it cost me every time I leave the house, I gotta put on the light-skin concoction, and I done run outa ingredients! Can't afford to buy no more, you seen the price a beeswax lately? *Get in here, Theo!* Lettin all my heat seep out into the winter!

Auntie Maryam, who'd toasted our promised freedom two days ago, now appears to be the only colored person I know in a foul temper.

Tee-oh! Tee-oh! Nattie John grins, and I think it would be a good idea to keep the baby busy and us both out of Auntie Maryam's way. We play Pat-a-Cake, Nattie John squealing delight every time I put the cake in the oven for Nattie and me till Auntie Maryam growls we may as well stop playing that silly game because there'll be no cake *nor* bread—baking powder and yeast is too high.

Yease too high? Nattie John asks.

I need the privy, says Auntie Maryam, flying out the back door. When twenty minutes later she hasn't returned, I look out the window to see her standing in the cold, hands clutching opposite upper arms for warmth, glaring into the distance.

She'll be home soon, says Uncle Ambrose, beaming at Grammy the next day. Grammy nods, beaming back. My uncle came ashore yesterday, so here he is for Sunday dinner.

Two, says Gran-Gran from her corner, smiling at us and making a *V* with her fingers. Nattie John, sitting in the corner and playing with a clothespin, looks up to stare at our great-grandmother.

Three, Gran-Gran, I say. Still three days till emancipation. But close!

She means two emancipations, says Grammy. New York back in the 'twenties, and now: whole country!

Not the whole country, Auntie Maryam corrects, chewing on potato from her soup. Grammy kept the pork out of it for her.

Not the whole country, nods Mr. Samuel. Only the rebellious states.

Well, I'm sure one a those is who took Eunice! cries Grammy.

I know, says Auntie Maryam, squeezing Grammy's hand in apology. She be home soon.

Everybody colored debatin the proclamation, says Mr. Samuel. Grumblin: Some states not have to emancipate, nothin but Lincoln's military strategy! *I* say, slavery's a house a cards now, pull Dixie out n see what happens.

Which *are* the rebellious these days? asks Uncle Ambrose. It changes.

Ten states, I say, glad some African Free School knowledge is coming in handy. Alabama, Mississippi, Louisiana except for New Orleans and some of the parishes captured by the Union—

Wait, Uncle Ambrose interrupts. If the area's Union-controlled, that means they *keep* slavery?

No, says Mr. Samuel. But slave states never left the Union. *They* keep slavery.

House a cards! Grammy reminds everyone.

Texas, Arkansas. North Carolina, South Carolina, Georgia, Florida, and Virginia, but not West Virginia. West Virginia's the part that seceded from Confederate Virginia.

What about Tennessee? Kentucky? Uncle Ambrose asks me.

Kentucky wanted to stay neutral but the South occupied it, then lost it to the Union. Middle Tennessee we captured, western's still reb. Missouri was admitted to the Confederacy but never officially seceded from the Union.

Them border states, says Mr. Samuel. All kinds a in-fightin: debate and battle. Brother against brother—literally!

Everyone turns into themselves to ponder that particular tribulation.

I hear gonna be a special service Wednesday night, says Uncle Ambrose.

Yes indeedy! says Grammy. We be there early, get a good seat.

Reverend Henry Highland Garnet is a famous graduate of my school! I contribute.

Nattie John, stop makin all that noise! snaps Auntie Maryam, though no one else seemed to be bothered by my cousin's play-chatter.

I heard him preach time or two, says Mr. Samuel. Stirring. He got the gift.

He escaped slavery from Maryland at nine years of age with his family, I continue with the reverend's biography. They were pursued by slave-catchers.

I have a headache, I'm a lie down, says Auntie Maryam and goes into the bed-closet.

Years later the family went into dire straits, and he had to leave school to become a cabin boy on the sea. The slave-catchers came and his parents escaped but his sister was caught.

Auntie Maryam harshly pulls closed the curtain separating bed-closet from front-room.

They say Henry Garnet bought a knife, searching for his sister's kidnapper until his teary family convinced him to stop looking for more trouble and hide out on Long Island. He became a controversial minister, calling for slave rebellion back in the 'forties!

Ho ho! says Uncle Ambrose. Then I'm very glad to know the jubilee will be at *his* church, *his* preaching!

Maryland he escape from, observes Grammy, like Frederick Douglass. The luck to be born close to the Mason-Dixon.

And yet, Mr. Samuel says, my dear Maryam from South Carolina made it all the way north to us.

Yes! cries Grammy. Daughter Maryam. Miracle! Miracle!

From the bed-closet, I hear an irritated sigh.

Two, says Nattie John, now standing at Gran-Gran's chair, looking up at Gran-Gran's *V* fingers and *V*-ing back at her.

Two, Gran-Gran concurs. Two! Two! Two! Two! The very old and the very young together saluting our imminent freedom.

‿つ

Grammy catches a sale on yeast Monday morning and buys a little extra, then sends me to deliver it uptown to my aunt. I think Grammy just wants to make her feel better but I am not thrilled by the prospect of being around grumpy old Auntie Maryam third day in a row. At her door, I take a breath before clenching my fist to knock. Then I hear something and rush in.

Auntie Maryam!

She wails, Nattie John screaming sobs next to her.

Auntie Maryam! What *is* it?

Nothin! she utters between her cries. Nothin!

Then all three of us bawling. Auntie Maryam puts an arm around Nattie John and an arm around me, pulls us in close, our fast-flowing tears mingling. Gradually her weeping subsides, and Nattie John and I follow suit.

I guess I jus have a brain fever. I guess I jus keep thinkin bout all the slaves I knew never made it to freedom. My *mother* never made it to freedom! Born free in Africa, died on that damned plantation, not more n forty-five years of age, worked to death! And somewhere I got a older sister, sold before ever I got to meet her!

Then more sobs. Then quieter, Auntie Maryam swallowing.

Adam. Nearby plantation, his mother from Africa so him jus one generation removed. My mother brought there to breed, maybe Master wanna keep her Africa pure, I'm glad! No white blood in me!

Auntie Maryam wipes a loose tear.

Mama tole me was slaves in Africa. Maybe prisoner a war from another tribe. But where *she* come from, slave was a *person*, slave had *rights*! Could marry, have a family, crops. Africa never dreamed up what evil white can make. Then Auntie Maryam stands and goes to her cupboard. Now we got yeast, you help me with some dumplins? And like that, the crying spell's over.

She rolls up the dough, placing the balls into the popping grease.

The church service Wednesday be nice. But always the white songs.

Our songs nobody wanna hear, the free-born embarrassed for the slave songs, the escaped wanna forget, them songs brung us here! Now maybe they die out, no one remember.

What songs?

You ever hear a *Swing Low, Sweet Chariot?*

I shake my head.

Chariot's the Underground Railroad, the band a angels other side a the Jordan River is the conductors other side a the Ohio, what them words mean.

Auntie Maryam teaches me the tune. Nattie John tries to sing with us, then reaches for the dough, Auntie Maryam lightly smacking her hand.

You ever hear a *Follow the Drinkin Gourd?*

I shake my head.

The drinkin gourd we drunk outa, in the song it mean the Big Dipper, point to the North Star, escaped slaves follow it. You ever hear a *Wade in the Water?*

I shake my head.

A Bible meanin, but for truth if a slave escape, walkin through streams knock your scent off from the dogs.

I'm sorry about your mother and your friends who never got their freedom, Auntie Maryam.

Saw-wee, says Nattie John.

My girls, Auntie Maryam says, shiny eyes, moving the dough balls around in the popping grease.

And I'm sorry your mother died.

I ain't the only orphan, she says and kisses me on the cheek. I shrug.

I never knew my parents to miss then. But I feel sad for *other* orphans, the ones I see at the Colored Orphan Asylum. Or Kaelyn and Patrick in jail for stealin bread. Or Ciaran. He watched his mother die, came here to meet his sister only sibling left but her and her family burned to death before—

Your Irish family with them Irish tried to burnt down Hen's tobaccery? Auntie Maryam's tone is even, but her eyes have gone ice cold in perfect inverse proportion temperature to the sizzling dumplings.

⁓

Sweep-oh! Sweep-oh! Thee-o!

Tuesday morning, I turn to see Mr. Samuel grinning at me, and I laugh. Because he's a small man, standing next to him I realize that now I'm nearly tall as he!

Reckon you wonder how Auntie Maryam got to be so melancholy just before emancipation.

I stop smiling.

She told me, I say. Misses her mother. Sad for all the slaves she knows missed out on freedom.

He nods.

And somethin else, he says. I think. I think somewhere in her, that fury been sittin a long time. *Decades*, a whole life's rage. She been keepin it down, had it on a leash. But freedom comin, suddenly it all pourin out: storm. She got no room in her heart for the gladness till the madness and sadness move out, that what they doin now. Make sense?

I look at Mr. Samuel. I *want* it to make sense! Because I don't like feeling the bad feelings I've been feeling toward Auntie Maryam lately. Mr. Samuel winks, and his sooty sweep face all at once reminds me of Hen as a child sweep, and now I get my own bit of brain fever missing my cousin. Praying my soldier cousin who I haven't heard from since the one letter is still among the living, but the sadness'll pass, I'm grown-up now enough to know pain is passing. And eventually always comes passing through again.

Watch Night! says Grammy when I wake the next morning: Wednesday, December 31, 1862. Her dancing around the apartment. Dancing with me!

Free-dom! chants Gran-Gran, and Grammy and I step to her song. Free-dom!

Happy day—every negro happy in the street! Christians named New Year's Eve *Watch Night*, time for reflection and atonement, but this year black people own it, ours now and, I wager, forevermore. At five thirty o'clock, we start bundling up Gran-Gran in a shawl and blanket, getting her ready for the Watch Night service. Gran-Gran, who's never left the apartment for long as I remember, insisted she's coming in English and

Dutch: *Ik kom! Ik kom!* So gentle we help her down the tenement steps and out into the New Year's Eve chill and the ten blocks up to the corner of Prince street and Marion: Shiloh Presbyterian Church. Except we only get to eight and a half blocks, the line already reaching down between Spring street and Broome. The celebration doesn't start till ten, but here we stand at seven and a quarter o'clock, praying the church doesn't fill before we make it in. We look for Auntie Maryam and Uncle Samuel and Nattie John but we don't see them ahead of us, and soon we can't see the ones arrived behind us where Marion street angles away to become Centre. So many people, the collective body heat keeps the winter cold from dropping to downright freezing, but whatever the weather Grammy and Gran-Gran can't stop smiling. In a few hours, we will be a new country, liberated from the tyranny of chains. Not truly, not wholly, but close and no turning back. At the stroke of midnight, by the stroke of a pen, America will be a different nation—11:59 slave, 12:00 free.

At eight thirty o'clock, the line starts moving. We make it inside! and as we begin to take a seat, we hear, Mother! Miss Lioda! *Theo!*

In the first instant, I don't recognize her because I have never seen Auntie Maryam outside her house, out in public, without her lightening concoction. There she is, her shining dark skin making her beautiful white smile even brighter, even more illustrious, her gorgeous, soft African hair swept up onto her head: disguise no more. And wearing her splendid patchwork wedding dress. Beside her stand Mr. Samuel on one side and Uncle Ambrose on the other, joy bigger than the world in their faces, and in Mr. Samuel's arms there's Nattie John calling and squirming and reaching for me.

It's nine now, and the church is packed. Our order is Gran-Gran at the edge of the pew, the center aisle: the best viewing, next to Grammy next to me next to Auntie Maryam next to Mr. Samuel next to Uncle Ambrose, with Nattie John crawling between laps. Nearly a third of the congregation is white, which irritates me, as I know even with the church overflowing and many people standing, there are still plenty of colored people who never made it in. Unless these whites have all been radicals—a jayhawker from Bleeding Kansas or an Underground Railroad conductor or a John Brown soldier never apprehended—unless their abolitionist commitment has been to that revolutionary degree, I don't think they've earned the right to be taking seats from negroes, and most of these people look too *comfortable*, as Mrs. Heverworth would say, for that level of commitment. But like Auntie Maryam, I try to push out the madness and let in the gladness, that latter being pretty easy to absorb in this multitude of black faces, all beaming.

At ten o'clock, it begins. A prayer from a colored minister, then a hymn. More songs and prayers and speeches, not all the reverends black. One white man says *Emancipation is happening in England, Russia, Turkey, Washington City—all over the world! Shame on all the white clergy who were hirelings for slavery!* An escaped slave tells his story, not just of the brutality and godlessness—which brings tears to many an eye—but also of a massive uprising he purports was being plotted by many negroes in the South, only suspended by this civil war which, he has decided, was meant to be: God's punishment of America for the abomination of slavery as homes across the nation bury their dead, and with this I can now identify the likely handful of Caucasian radicals as the only whites who applaud this sentiment along with negroes.

In the second hour, Reverend Henry Highland Garnet comes to the pulpit. His words are eloquent, but in these last minutes, as the era of racially determined bondage—legally and socially accepted as natural, unassailable, and eternal—as one chapter of American savagery draws to a close, my mind wanders, my dream from last night abruptly coming back to me. Cataclysms: hurricanes and tornadoes and earthquakes reeling the country, as if white men controlled the heavens and depths of the earth, destroying the nation before they'd let emancipation transpire. I woke up hard. It was near dawn, and I fell asleep again. Now I was a slave on a plantation, and as I reached down to pick a cotton boll, someone grabbed my wrist. I looked up. *Auntie Eunice!* I was so happy to see her! I wanted to shout and dance but the cat had my tongue! I just stared, awe, and she smiled at me, and then I looked around. Hundreds of slaves—no. *Former* slaves, hundreds of free black people standing in the fertile fields but no one picking, everybody smiling, eyes on the rising sun.

It is five minutes before midnight, so now we all bow our heads in hushed personal prayer. The organist plays a dirge, then silence.

Near silence. Because I hear the tiniest peeps from Auntie Maryam to my right, her clutch of my left hand letting me know there are tears streaming her face, and the clutching of my right hand tells me Grammy is making the greatest effort to forestall a deluge of her own.

Now the choir begins *Blow Ye the Trumpet, Blow* thus we know it is midnight.

A dispatch from Washington is read, announcing that President Lincoln will sign the Emancipation Proclamation at noon today, and the cheer in response is thunderous and resounding. We are by no means dispirited by the twelve-hour delay because, as far as we are concerned, freedom has come. *Three cheers for Lincoln! Three cheers for Horace Greeley!* (Editor of the adamantly abolitionist *New-York Tribune*.) *Three cheers for freedom!* An avalanche of elation, more hurrahs and songs, and when all take up *John Brown's body lies a-moulderin in the grave*, Auntie Maryam is singing louder than anyone else. My beautiful auntie: newly adopted as a young woman into my family, someone born and raised in torture and grief, her body not even hers to rule till one night she did, nothing but life to cling to and she risked that in a treacherous, perilous journey of weeks following a star—now *there's* a story. Three cheers for Maryam Hathaway Brook Wright.

Gran-Gran, slave till age forty-eight, softly says, Free. Free. Free. Free. Free. Grammy, slave till age twenty-two, holds her and me tight, kissing Gran-Gran's cheek, kissing the top of my head, warm tears falling onto my scalp. It's well past one before Gran-Gran sleeps, with Grammy dozing, and Nattie John dreaming on Auntie Maryam's lap, the festivities showing no signs of stopping. Auntie Maryam's eyes are closed, gently rocking my little cousin and humming. At first I think it's a lullaby, but then hear it's that Sweet Chariot song, which the congregation does not sing because, just like Auntie Maryam predicted, the hymns were all composed by whites, those slave ballads may very well vanish from existence. And it occurs to me that the word *free* never came up in any of those songs she sang to me. Well, how could it? That surely would have meant a whipping from the master and, worse, divulged the song's secret message. I gaze at my auntie, and I remember a time when she made friends with squirrels who had the sense to destroy a slave bounty poster.

She gets to the verse, and I remember the words: *I looked over Jordan, and what did I see / Comin for to carry me home? / A band of angels comin after me* and here I change up the repeated line, whisper it in her ear: *Coming for to carry me free.*

Her eyes open, and she smiles so warm at me that suddenly in that moment all the world is love, freedom, love, freedom, love, freedom: amen.

1863

Fairies

Amusements.

BARNUM'S AMERICAN MUSEUM.

THIS EVENING at 7½ o'clock.
Thousands of ladies and children will embrace this opportunity to

SEE THE LITTLE FAIRY
SEE THE LITTLE FAIRY
MISS LAVINIA WARREN,
MISS LAVINIA WARREN,
MISS LAVINIA WARREN,
MISS LAVINIA WARREN,
THE QUEEN OF BEAUTY,
THE QUEEN OF BEAUTY,
THE QUEEN OF BEAUTY,

who, in addition to an exquisitely diminutive stature, though a fully-matured woman, has

A FORM THAT QUEENS MIGHT ENVY,
A FORM THAT QUEENS MIGHT ENVY,
A FORM THAT QUEENS MIGHT ENVY,
A FORM THAT QUEENS MIGHT ENVY,

and possesses every grace and accomplishment that

ADORNS A LOVELY WOMAN.

She is 21 years old.

ONLY 32 INCHES HIGH, AND WEIGHS BUT 30 LBS.

She is intelligent, every way interesting, and

ALWAYS CHARMS HER VISITORS,

Her matrimonial alliance with

GENERAL TOM THUMB

will prevent her exhibition after the close of her present
engagement at the Museum, and as

THE NUPTIAL CEREMONY TAKES PLACE,
On TUESDAY, Feb. 10,

but little time remains for the public to

SEE THE FASCINATING LITTLE LADY.

Her extensive wardrobe and numerous jewels enable
her to

APPEAR IN A DIFFERENT DRESS EVERY DAY,

which with her

"ENGAGEMENT RING,"

which she kindly exhibits to her visitors, adds new
charms to her own native loveliness. She is

ON EXHIBITION DAY AND EVENING,

From 10 o'clock, a.m., till 10 p.m.

ON THE PLATFORM IN THE MAIN HALL

Of the Museum at intervals, and

ON THE STAGE IN THE LECTURE ROOM

Admission, 25 cents.　　Children under ten 15 cents.

This Tuesday! cries Cathleen, eyes on the ad she ripped from the *Daily Tribune* while speedily weaving her needle in and out of the buttonholes. I want to know every detail!

Sure a blessin to have somethin in the news besides war, war, war, says Grammy as she prepares her wares for the day.

Lincoln rescinded that order castin out the Jews in those southern states, *that's* a blessin for the poor refugees, says Cousin Aileen. Though Rachel at work's sobbin. She was upset by the order, her young Yosef dismissed from the army, he wanted to fight! But now with him back on the battlefield, she says her people might've gained dignity and she lose a son.

Madame Demorest designed Lavinia's wedding gown!

We look at Cathleen, furrowed brows.

Madame Demorest. The famed *fashion* designer!

I'm helping Cathleen with hems. Her mind's usually on more serious news, so all her chatter about the celebrity wedding's a surprise. But then I remember when Ciaran and I went to the American Museum. She always did seem to feel some affinity with the so-called Living Curiosities.

I wager it will be a lovely ceremony altogether, says Grammy.

At fifty dollars a ticket, says Cousin Aileen, it *ought* to be!

That's the reception, says Cathleen. As for the service, fifteen thousand individuals *applied* for the privilege of witnessing it. Cathleen picks up a *Times*: *It was at first determined to make the affair strictly a private one, but the public desire was so great to see them that Mr. Barnum, who has kept modestly in the back ground, was compelled to yield to the pressure.* Cathleen laughs: Modest Barnum! *Next to Louis Napoleon, there is no one person better known by reputation to high and low, rich and poor, than he.* My cousin looks up from the paper. If Tom is the second most famous in the world, then Lavinia is third!

Did ye know Tom Thumb sent relief money to Ireland durin the Famine? asks Grammy. What a saintly soul!

The gifts! says Cathleen. Tiffany's will provide jewelry for Miss Warren. Silver coffee spoons plated with gold have been contributed from a lady of the gentry. Lavinia's slippers, a gift of Edwin Booth, the renowned actor. A pearl ring locket and chain, a bird watch, a silver watch, silver tea set, these are just a few of the offerings from the aristocracy. Not to mention the presents from many, many admirers of lesser means, the wedding of Lavinia Warren to Charles Stratton, Esquire, is the high society event of the year!

But isn't Tom Thumb rich already? asks Cousin Aileen as she wraps herself in her holey shawl, headed for the manufactory. Why would they need—?

The streets outside Grace Church will be thronged by well-wishers, Cathleen says to me, ignoring her mother. Get there early, get a good view. I want to hear everything!

In walks Ciaran.

Well, look who's here, smiles Grammy. Ciaran and his cousin Aedan are back in Mackerelville which, while only twenty-five blocks north and east, is a few wards away. That, coupled with Ciaran's perpetual state of working or looking for work, make his visits, as before Pittsburgh, few and far between.

Mornin, all!

Then his eyes settle on me. *Lá breithe shona duit.*

But my birthday's not till tomorrow!

Tomorrow's Monday, I might be called to work. Care for a birthday walk, Miss Thirteen?

Where're we going? I ask, following him down Centre street, watching my breath fog in the early February chill.

You'll see, he replies, a secret smile.

We are quiet a moment. Then I ask, Are you glad to be home, Ciaran? I'm deliberate in my word choice, wondering if he will reply indignant: *Ireland is my home!*

He stops walking. Are you glad to *have* me home? he utters quietly, worried eyes searching my face. I'd managed to suppress my smile just long enough to ask my question but, in reply to his, it's rushed back.

We halt in front of the depot: New York and Harlem Railroad. I frown.

We going someplace?

You told me once you always wanted to see Harlem. The Harlem draw-bridge.

It had been so long ago, I'd forgotten it had ever been a desire of mine, a little girl's dream junket faded with age. I don't say this to Ciaran. For the first time, I truly understand *It's the thought that counts* because my heart is very moved that he's kept this memory of me all these years.

We hear the horse *clip-clop*ping, pulling the trolley north from Ann street, and now I *am* excited. Ciaran pays and manages to squeeze us both on the crowded train. We stare out, watching our Sixth ward fly by!

Month ago, they broke ground in Sacramento, Ciaran murmurs, eyes on the swiftly changing scenery. The Pacific Railroad. They'll build it simultaneous from the west and from the east to eventually meet some-where in the middle. Soon we'll be able to take a train ocean to ocean, think a that! Traversin the continent!

Up Centre street, right on Broome to Bowery, then left going north, Bowery changing to Fourth avenue, past Union Square then up to Thir-ty-third street and drop into the tunnel: Murray Hill Tunnel, here we go underground, *clip clop* the horse, we don't see daylight again till For-ty-second! Now up the east side, continuing on Fourth av through the Sixties, Eighties, way up Manhattan Isle, and nearly an hour since we embarked, we reach the northern suburb of Harlem.

Streets here, but quiet, less houses. There are farms, and laborers tending them. Trees. Peaceful, idyllic. All the folks I see are white, some fancy, some not. Few passengers are left on the trolley as it nears its terminus.

Where'd you get the two bits for two of us riding? (Four bits, I hope, or we'll be walking the nine miles back.)

Ciaran's eyes on the countryside, a distant smile. Novelty Iron Works. Sporadic, but I arrive early every morn, cast foot a Twelfth av, and when a job comes, I'm there. Yesterday crack a dawn in the freezin, I wait. Bedplate. Bedplate's what supports a ship's engine, they'd just cast a *thirty-five-ton* bedplate, needed men to move it cross the yard, then hoist it up into the hull a the ship. *Lots* of men. *Strong* men.

Ciaran looks so pleased with himself, I have a devilish urge to remind him he's a *boy*, not a man. Still, he's a tall fourteen and a half.

And Cousin Aedan, Ciaran goes on as the car hits a bump and my stomach leaps. Longshoreman. He can't believe his luck, *every* man wants to be a longshoreman!

How'd he get it?

Right place, right time. Used to pay dollar fifty a day. Then, couple weeks ago, the bosses suddenly plunge it: dollar twelve. Uproar! Strike! Longshoremen looks out for each other, strength in unity! Greatly encouraged by the Longshoremen's United Benevolent Society what keeps the men in line. They tried to hold out, with the inflation even the one-fifty was hard, and the weekly work available four days at best, men got families. And the one thing always plentiful in hard times: scabs. Some could take it no more—better off to just pack up, head out: West. Or South. So it happens the day two or three quit, the company that lowered one fifty to one twelve raises it to one twenty-five, and that day in walks Cousin Aedan!

At 106th, we're approaching water: drawbridge! Ciaran and I exit the car and walk on the structure, gazing at the sparkling ripples below. A few yards upriver, a fisherwoman casts out her line.

He had to lie, Ciaran says, Harlem River reflecting in his eyes. He had to tell a tale, the longshoremen protects the jobs for family men, Cousin Aedan had to say he had a wife. He'd talked it over with Mary Clare at our tenement, shares the basement with us, her willin to pose as his missus. And didn't a few representatives a the Longshoremen's U.B. Society come out to our livin quarters to confirm it.

Fish in the water: *plop*.

Lads like me. Ciaran shakes his head. If we're young, no wife, no family, we don't get the job, the married Irish say we don't need it. As if we don't need food.

A man yells at us, and now we see a vessel approaching below. We move to the edge just off the structure and watch. A small craft gliding down the river. The bridge rises up and out, splitting itself. We both gape: the wonder of it.

❧

Next morning, I get to Grammy Brook's early before she leaves to deliver her whites. Our apartment smells divine.

Happy birthday, birthday girl!

Thank you, Grammy! What's baking?

Already baked.

Grammy hands me ginger cake. Sweet! Not much of it, but enough for Grammy, Gran-Gran, and me to have a breakfast bite.

Thirteen, says Grammy, shaking her head teary. He woulda been proud. By which I know she means my father.

Look what Cathleen gave me!

I'd spent last night with Grammy Cahill and already had my taste of birthday barmbrack this morning. And tied to my dress is the pretty crocheted heart brooch Cathleen made for me. *For the wedding*, she'd said. Then I tell Grammy how excited Cathleen is for Tom Thumb and Lavinia's nuptials, and that Auntie Siobhan told me to stop by tomorrow early for something from her, and then I recount yesterday's adventure, my journey to the Harlem drawbridge with Ciaran. When I get to the part about longshoremen protecting the jobs for family men, Grammy says, the Longshoremen's U.B. Society protect the jobs from *black*.

Mm *hm*, says Gran-Gran, eyes out her window.

You remember your cousin Marcus?

I shake my head.

Your papa's first cousin, your second. 'Thirty-two: five years after New York declared freedom, here come the New York cholera epidemic. Claimed my brother Cyrus. A longshoreman, and his son Marcus, about your age when his father passed, trained the same. Those days the jobs was *all* colored: buildin trades and crafts, seamen and shoremen, and free colored women had the good maid jobs, well, all them was the skills we brung from slavery.

I was a maid, I was a governess, I was a bookkeeper, Gran-Gran says to the window.

Now the rich folks only hire those girls from cross the ocean, Grammy continues, family name start O' or Mc, and you know what color the longshoremen come to be. Nobody but the boss likes scabs, but starve us enough, we'll take it. Refuse willin and able workers, and scabs you create. Marcus though—got tired a the struggle. When you were still little, he took his wife and his babies and his hope and headed north. Boston, last I heard.

I kept the household expenses, says Gran-Gran, I knew the worth of Master's land and manor and horses, which all together never added up to one percent of *my* worth.

❧

Tonight I stay with Grammy Brook and wake up to a sunny morn—the well-wishers gathering! That's what we are, thousands packing Broadway five blocks: Ninth street to Union Square, the only vehicles permitted being the numerous carriages of invited guests which make a steady parade. I arrived at ten and a half o'clock when it was starting, the sky clouding over. Ciaran stands next to me.

He showed up early at Grammy Cahill's but I wasn't there. She told him perhaps I was at Siobhan's since she'd promised me some belated birthday surprise so he raced to O'SHEA'S BOARD & PUBLICK where, at that moment, Auntie Siobhan was pinning on my dress—above Cathleen's crocheted heart—the white carnation she'd cultivated for me. With the wedding only a day after my birthday, she thought it might be nice to delay picking the flower so I could wear it fresh to the celebration. *Thirteen*, she'd said, wiping a tear. *Young woman now.* Then Ciaran walked in.

Stood out in the cold six to eight this mornin at the Novelty Iron Works, he tells me as we gaze at a carriage, freckled with sparkling diamonds! By eight, if day-workers ain't been hired, we likely won't be. Every mornin, I send up a little prayer for the day, but this was the first mornin the prayer was for there *not* to be work.

I look at him, and he blushes and turns away.

Didja hear they're goin to honeymoon in England? says a woman behind us.

Reckon they'll be visitin the queen again, her female companion returns. Tom's quite popular with the royals.

They got some big plans before Europe, a man chimes in. Headed to Washington City to be received by the president.

President *Lincoln*?

Spose he figures it's a nice diversion from war only war.

They come! someone cries, and we all scurry to look. But it's only another guest carriage.

Theo!

We turn around. There's Miss Bertha with her niece Mrs. Robbins from the ladies' salon.

What a big girl you're getting to be! says Mrs. Robbins. I keep telling Mother I can't believe how you've grown, how you look more like Eunice every time I see you.

I'm thirteen years of age today.

They gasp as if this news is just beyond belief. I introduce Ciaran.

How do ye, ma'am. How do ye, ma'am.

Very nice to meet you, Ciaran, says Miss Bertha, and I notice her eyebrows subtly raise toward Mrs. Robbins, as if having grasped fodder for later gossip.

Ah! breathes the crowd in unison, a carriage of red velvet passing by.

What a splendid event! cries Mrs. Robbins.

Indeed, says Miss Bertha, though I abhor crowds and am only here at the behest of my niece. May we please look for a spot where there is a *little* less of a mob?

After they've moved on, I say to Ciaran, It's grand you get work at the Novelty Iron Works, even if it isn't regular.

Ciaran, eyes on the march of carriages, frowns.

Not enough.

A great push and cry from the crowd, then we swerve back in place.

Did you know Tom weighed nine pounds and a half at birth? we hear.

Nine pounds and a half! her companion responds. Giant!

Lavinia weighed nine!

No!

Yes! Born to gentry, she was a schoolteacher in Massachusetts before she started performin with Barnum!

What I would love, Ciaran begins. What I long to be is a longshoreman. With Cousin Aedan. But it would be a miracle. Closed up, I *might* pass for eighteen, tall. But I'd need a wife.

Four hundred dollars! For a billiard table?

A billiard table custom-made for dwarfs! It's one of the most prized gifts, I'd love to see em play it!

But they always have those strikes.

For better wages, he answers me, decent treatment, sure. They let me in, I'd strike with em!

And then they bring in the scabs.

Vermin! he snaps.

The scabs is colored.

Ciaran turns to me.

They come!

The mass swerves forward. Another false alarm.

Correct. I wasn't gonna say it but since you brought it up: yes, for whatever reason, the scabs is mostly colored.

The reason is longshoremen used to be colored work, then taken over by the Irish.

Ciaran squints, as if that might help him better hear what I just said.

Theo!

There, in a carriage driving up Broadway, is Mrs. Heverworth waving at me. I wave and smile back, and see a little smile cross the face of her husband, gazing at her. He should be mortified by his society wife yelling like the rabble, from a coach in the procession no less. On the contrary, he seems charmed by a rare display of this side of her. I realize it's the first moment I truly like Mrs. Heverworth, touched that she could get past her proper refinedness and holler for me, so after they have passed and Ciaran makes a smart-alecky remark about my fancy friends, I don't have the heart to join in. But he interprets my silence as related to the previous discussion.

Long as anyone I know knows, longshoremen been Irish, maybe a German or two. And a scab's a scab's a scab, don't care what color.

Before the Famine refugees, before the 'forties, 'fifties, Irish work was black. And how's colored scabs if they're just taking back the jobs was taken from them?

To break a *strike*? Do you even know what a scab is?

Yes, I know what a scab is!

Stop him! Rascal! *Help!* Police!

A gentleman runs after a pauper who apparently snatched the former's pocketbook.

Keep your purse close to your heart, warns the woman behind us to her friend.

If my heart is between my breasts, then there my purse be.

Hey, looky there, says Ciaran, smiling, his eyes on the other side of the street.

Auntie Siobhan. Standing next to a man I've never seen before. They whisper and laugh hearty, throwing their bodies into the mirth. I make a little smile, but my heart's not quite in it, my heart's still in the debate.

Her sister, the bridesmaid. Even tinier than the bride!

You don't say!

Well, guess it don't matter since *I'll* never get a longshoreman's job anyway.

It *does* still matter, whether you get a longshoreman's job or not, I reply, to which Ciaran sighs heavily.

Since the engagement announcement, the museum's been selling twenty thousand admissions a day.

Twenty thousand!

Twenty thousand. I imagine when Lavinia accepted Tom's proposal, it thrilled Barnum more than when his own espoused Charity accepted *his*!

They come!

And this time they do come. The crowd rushes, crushes! I hear *ooh* and *aah* but see nothing! I have to report back to Cathleen. I want to see them for myself! I watch an urchin crawling between people's legs, I miss that I'm no longer little enough for that! Then Ciaran snatches my hand and makes some kind of in-and-out slinky maneuver through the throng, and here we are: front! Close enough to be shoved back with the horde by the police, but we see!

I gasp. Lavinia: I've never seen anyone so beautiful! That dress. The lace so delicate, the white gloves like a society lady. Like a princess! The crown of feathers placed meticulously on her hair, an angel's halo, just beholding her I feel like I need to wash my face! And arm-in-arm with Charles Stratton, Lilliput Tom Thumb! Followed by their little colleagues from the museum, groomsman Commodore Nutt (who I spoke with when Ciaran and I went to the museum!) and bridesmaid Minnie Warren, who *is* considerably smaller than her older sister. They'd stepped out of a big fancy coach with Barnum but I wish they'd come in their small chariot led by the pony, I wish I could ride with them in their wee chariot, I wish I was a little woman! The newspapers are wrong trumpeting it a fairy wedding, *the Lilliputian couple*, they *aren't* story-book, not magical. But when they call her the queen—*yes!* Regal. No, noble. American noble, like the finest lady and gentleman here, putting all these wealthy magnates in their carriages to shame. And there walking ahead is tall Barnum, face like a proud father. Barnum who would ordinarily garner plenty of attention but pity the poor souls behind us who, above all the heads, can see only the impresario but not the miniature magnificents!

We all watch them enter Grace Church, and the crowd does not scatter. The clock strikes half-past noon so the ceremony is on schedule. My prior irritation with Ciaran seems to have faded away. I'm beaming, and he beams at me, when we feel arms around us.

You two!

Auntie Siobhan! I give her a hug, and see the man next to her, grinning at us.

This is Kevin, she says.

Like the saint, he adds, winking. I haven't any idea which saint that might be, but I don't doubt some Kevin sometime must have gotten himself canonized.

A half-hour later, the doors open, Mendelssohn's triumphant *Wedding March* in C Major pouring out, and the radiant newlyweds appear, the crowd cheering. Glimpsing the couple exit onto the Grace Church steps is enough for me, I stand back to allow others a turn for a closer look as the Strattons and party walk to their Cinderella carriage, headed down Broadway to the Metropolitan Hotel on Prince street for the reception. Hordes follow, undoubtedly to form a multitude outside the party venue, but I'm quiet, Ciaran staying with me. The music has brought me back to a very different wedding: Auntie Maryam's union with Mr. Samuel in Grammy Brook's apartment. And here's Auntie Eunice explaining the new Mendelssohn tradition while hemming the beautiful wedding gown that my cousin Cathleen patched together from scraps Auntie Eunice found on Grammy Cahill's table. And here's Hen naughtily singing the bawdy *Let's tie the knot* song. And Auntie Eunice missing Uncle Ambrose on the sea, Uncle Ambrose—a whole man in body *and* mind, my entire family together and complete, we might've been in rags but that wedding *just* as regal, *just* as regal, and Ciaran softly asks, What *is* it?

The tears are streaming fast, I wipe my face fearing they'll freeze. The crowd has mostly dispersed, and suddenly I'm sobbing, we move away from the street to an alley, a back doorway shelter, and we sit, and I weep, and Ciaran gingerly puts his arm around me, opens his frayed coat and pulls me close under it, *Sh.* In the distance, we hear the newsboys already calling it.

Extra! General Tom Thumb and Lavinia Warren wed! The Lilliputians woo all high society!

And it begins to snow. Lightly, gentle enough I can see the design of every snowflake, *they* are the fairies! And the falling weather reminds me that it's cold, and I shiver, Ciaran holding me tight, warm and close.

The fairy couple receive guests at the Metropolitan standing atop a grand piano!

And now Ciaran's lips on mine. I shudder, I didn't expect it! And Ciaran pulls away, his fearful eyes tell me *he* didn't expect it! And now his blue irises form a question. I lean in to him. And we kiss, his lips and mine joining in a softness, and hold and touch and kiss and the snow falls. The newsboys' calls I still hear, but distant and fading.

London opens a train system in tunnels under the streets! You heard it! A railway underground!

Secretary of State Seward informs the French minister that America rejects France's offer to mediate our civil war!

Recent Tammany Hall mass shipyard and iron workers' meeting denounces hordes of southern blacks headed to New York to take jobs, read all about it!

The soft, fairy snowflakes alight on our eyelashes and lips and grinning teeth, and I know for certain no diamond-speckled carriage ever twinkled brighter.

Tourniquet

Penny for a veteran?

Our two windows are closed tight, gaps stuffed with rags, and still, muffled, we can hear him: the lad with the tin can and no legs. The veteran parked himself in front of Grammy Cahill's tenement a week ago. A biting late winter wind, the wedding of Tom Thumb and Lavinia just two weeks ago but feeling long past. It's the last Wednesday of February, and I'm missing school because after thirty minutes collecting coal, I didn't feel like going out into the frigidity again. I sit next to Cathleen under a quilt, she keeping her hands under the cover, sewing by touch. Even Grammy's found it too bitter to set up her table, but outside sits that wrecked soldier boy.

I feel so bad for him, says Cathleen. He doesn't look a day over fifteen.

And us frozen even *in*side, mutters Cousin Aileen. Paper-thin walls!

This headache's killin, says Auntie Siobhan, head on the table, arms crowned round her face.

Served our country and lost his limbs, now reduced to the panhandle, bemoans Cathleen. No one cares!

Ye're wrong, says Grammy. I invited him inside. *Come in out of the cold, lad! No one in our tenement would deny ye shelter from the gusts. Thank ye, missus,* came the reply, *but this is how I make my livin now,* and he went back to rattlin those nickels and coppers.

This headache's killin! cries Auntie Siobhan.

Don't come here complainin of the after-effects of drink, says Cousin Aileen.

It's not drink! Name the last time you seen me with any after-effects. I hold my liquor!

Aaaaaaaa! Cathleen and I scream.

And when did you two become the crowned princesses? Afraid of a damned rat.

You don't have to be here around them all day, Siobhan!

Ye talk like we have rats all the time, Grammy scolds Cathleen. We don't have rats all the time! And your shriek sent it right back in whatever hole it came from anyway.

Penny for a veteran? we hear again just before the bold rodent veritably leaps out of its hiding-place, Cathleen and I screeching, inciting Auntie Siobhan to pull out a pistol and *BANG!* the rat blown to smithereens, now everybody but my auntie screaming. I'd heard her once say she'd confiscated a six-shooter from an unruly patron and kept it around *just in case*, but why she happened to have it on her person now I'll never know. I would think the blast could only have exacerbated her headache but, on the contrary, a small smile crosses her face, as if this was the first bit of gratification she's felt all day.

∞

Sunday evening is March first, and we celebrate Nattie John's third birthday at Grammy Brook's, the third without Auntie Eunice. Uncle Ambrose is away at sea. Of course we all knew my auntie wouldn't just magically materialize after the president signed the Emancipation Proclamation two months ago—at least we knew it in our minds if not our hearts. The occasion seems to accentuate the reality that our sopping pre-1863 agony seems now to have been replaced with a dry resigned gloom. Nattie John cries a lot which Auntie Maryam attributes to teething, but I think my little cousin senses her birthday has just become a milestone for our grief.

The next evening, I'm having supper at Grammy Cahill's. It being Monday, a low-business time at the tavern, Grammy made Auntie Siobhan promise to be here and now worries that she isn't.

She's been fiery and dismal for a week, says Cousin Aileen. Leave her. She'll come around when she's ready, tornadoes always change direction.

That's why I'm after askin her to be here, seems she been needin the cheerin, says Grammy. Not like her to stay away without sendin word.

The blamed income tax, that's what's ailin her, claims Great-Uncle Fergus. With her business, I'd wager Uncle Sam came a-knockin for a pretty penny.

The income tax started a while back, says Grammy. Why would she be waitin till now to fret over it?

Maybe they didn't collect till now. Or! Maybe she thought she could get away with not payin, but they caught up to her. She tried hidin from the taxman, but he's a wily *axman*. Great-Uncle Fergus chuckles.

Ye don't think they'll be comin for *us*? worries Cousin Aileen. Ye need to make eight hundred a year, Isn't that what the paper said?

Six hundred! crows Great-Uncle Fergus. 'Twas eight hundred, but before the Act of 'sixty-one was ever put into effect, here come Act of 'sixty-*two*, droppin the minimum collectable income! Just watch. This time next year we'll *all* be excised by the damned feds!

The war effort, Uncle, reasons Cathleen. That's why President Lincoln—

Ye think I don't know why? *I* know why! Fund the war but not the warriors, why else that poor soul on our doorstep every day beggin for a copper?

Theo. You run over to Auntie Siobhan's? Lemme know all's well?

I go out and around the corner, the two-minute stroll to O'SHEA'S BOARD & PUBLICK. Roisin is minding the till alone, tending to just a few patrons, who sing.

> *We thought when we got in the Ring for Bales, for Bales*
> *We thought when we got in the Ring for Bales, says I*
> *We thought when we got in the Ring,*
> *Greenbacks would be a dead sure thing,*
> *And we'll all drink stone blind—Johnny, fill up the bowl!*

Roisin, where's Auntie Siobhan?

Sick. You might want to go up and see to her.

I ascend the stairs, knock. Auntie Siobhan?

She doesn't answer, but I'm certain I hear her. I push on the door.

She lies in her bed ghost-white and unaware of me, twisting and softly moaning. From under the edge of her blanket, a pool of blood has seeped.

Flying out of the tavern, screaming all the way to Grammy's. I know my words don't make sense but my hysteria is clear. Grammy and Cousin Aileen and Great-Uncle Fergus jump up, then Grammy turns to study her brother a moment before saying, No.

The women and I race to O'SHEA'S. Grammy and Cousin Aileen gasp at the sight of Auntie Siobhan, then quickly pull the sheet out from under her and start tearing it up. *Stanch the blood!* shouts Grammy before turning to me.

I need you to go get Philippa Hopkins. She lives at—

She colored?

She is! You know where she lives?

I nod. I hesitate.

Go!

I run to Greenwich Village. I'm out of breath fast but don't slow down, and when I get there, I knock hard. I was here only the once before, when newly wed Auntie Maryam bought herbs, hoping to fill the Room of Hope with a newly born.

What! snaps Miss Philippa as if I woke her in the middle of the night when it can't be much past eight. I apprise her of the situation, and she snatches some supplies and heads out. I didn't know she could move so fast, tiring me out!

Auntie Siobhan's tavern is now closed, and I imagine what kind of a time Roisin must've had tossing the drunkards out. Miss Philippa is soothing to Auntie Siobhan, soft touching her face, my auntie mumbling something scarcely coherent. You done good, you done good, Miss Philippa tells Grammy and Cousin Aileen and Roisin, the latter standing terror-frozen in the corner. Grammy's eyes are red and wild. Miss Philippa holds Auntie Siobhan's head up, helps her drink some herb mixture. A couple hours later, Miss Philippa says, All right, let her rest. And we all make a circle around sleeping Auntie Siobhan: Miss Philippa in the one chair, Grammy and Cousin Aileen sitting on either side of the bed, me sitting on the floor, Roisin standing. Eventually Grammy tells Roisin to go home, then finds a blanket in a bureau drawer and wraps me in it, telling me to lie on the little rug. Must be three in the mornin. Get some sleep.

At daybreak, Auntie Siobhan is awake but barely, talking soft to Grammy who still sits on the bed. Miss Philippa is gone, Cousin Aileen asleep in the chair. As Auntie Siobhan dozes, Grammy hums something soft from Éire. Then she quietly asks me, You know what throwin the baby is, *a chuisle mo chroí?*

I shake my head.

It's when a woman finds she has life growin inside her and needs to rid herself of it.

Oh.

Grammy hums.

That a sin?

Cordin to the law, it's legal till the quickenin. Till the woman feels it. After that, the person conductin the procedure is liable, never the woman.

That a sin?

Over the centuries, the church has gone back and forth on that point. The latest verdict agrees with the law: not a sin till it's quick.

Oh. Auntie Siobhan didn't feel it?

We could ask her after she wakes. Or we could mind our own business.

Grammy hums.

Then she says, I saw Ciaran couple days ago. He asked me to send his greetins to ye.

Couple *days ago*?

Theodora Brigid, I have a lot on my mind, I can't remember to pass along every odd message!

Sorry, Grammy.

She gazes out the window a few moments before speaking again. Close, you and he've been gettin. What happened to Siobhan—I don't want that happenin to you.

You can get a baby from kissing?

Grammy chuckles. No. That all you been doin?

I nod. And shrug.

I haven't seen Ciaran since Tom Thumb and Lavinia got married, he never comes around.

He said his cousin's been keepin him busy, odd jobs. That was the other part of the message.

It's quiet a while, and sitting up from my bedroll on the floor, I start to get sleepy again. Then Grammy begins to speak softly, and it takes me a few moments to become wide awake in the realization that she's explaining, in explicit detail, the precise course of action whereby I *could* get a baby, which is a cautionary tale as she promises to murder me should I be so foolish. The procedure itself: a shocking turn of events!

I sleep much of Monday. Walking uptown with Abbie to the Colored Orphan Asylum after school Tuesday, she asks, Did you hear the Cherokee are rescinding their secession from the Union and embracing abolition?

No! That's grand news!

I imagine it must feel especially glorious in the home of her red mother and black father. It's nice to see Abbie smile. I don't mention what I just read in the paper, the recent slaughter of the Shoshone and Bannock in Utah. According to the *Times*: *Our Indian war is over, short, sharp and decisive. Though Col. CONNOR cannot say, "I came, I saw, I conquered," he may report, "I went, I fought, I conquered, I exterminated," for such, indeed, was the fact. One man, who claimed to have visited the battle-field after the strife, said he counted 225 dead Indians, of whom ten were squaws.*

By Wednesday after school, my auntie is up and tending her tavern! (Though Grammy and I both come help this week in the evenings when it gets busier.)

Siobhan, says the sole afternoon customer, frowning at his *Daily Tribune*. You seen this?

The title of the article on the back page is National Militia Law. The legislation is written out in its thirty-eight-section entirety, no commentary. The man seems particularly perplexed by one paragraph.

> SEC. 13. *And be it further enacted,* That any person drafted and notified to appear as aforesaid, may on or before the day fixed for his appearance furnish an acceptable substitute to take his place in the draft, or he may pay to such persons as the Secretary of War may authorize to receive it, such sum not exceeding three hundred dollars for the procuration of such substitute, and thereupon such person so furnishing a substitute or paying the money shall be discharged from any further liability under that draft; and any person failing to report after due service of notice as herein described without furnishing a substitute or paying the required sum therefor shall be deemed a deserter, and shall be arrested by the Provost-Marshal and sent to the nearest military post for trial by a court-martial.

The customer whispers, Then a rich man pays three hundred dollars and gets himself out of the draft?

Wind creaking the counter, creaking the stairs to the boarders.

Anybody, I venture carefully. Seems *anybody* who comes up with three hundred dollars—

Poor man's lucky to make three hundred dollars *gross* in a *good* year! the customer cries. This is a rich man's clause! Rich man's ticket out!

❧

Saturday I help Auntie Maryam with her washerwoman work while telling her everything that happened with Auntie Siobhan, not including my bizarre conversation with Grammy.

When Grammy Cahill told me to go to Miss Philippa . . . I was afraid her medicine wouldn't work. Like with you. I mean, you wanted a baby and Auntie Siobhan didn't, but same healer. This time. This time, her herbs worked.

Auntie Maryam wrings out a sheet. Then she says without looking up from her task, It worked.

Nattie John laughs out loud, some mysterious entertainment she's making for herself.

Lost it. Miss Philippa's herb gay me the baby but it didn't stick. Miscarry. Bled like your Auntie Siobhan, Samuel had to run get Miss Philippa. Wonder that woman ever get a decent night's rest.

I stare at her. *Throwing* the baby nearly killed Auntie Siobhan, *losing* the baby nearly killed Auntie Maryam, *having* the baby *did* kill my mother, *why do women have babies?*

You hate her?

Auntie Maryam looks up.

My auntie Siobhan?

Why you say that?

I look down.

You think I hold it gainst her, I can't have a baby, she could and throw it away? Auntie Maryam waits for me to answer, but there's no need. She shakes her head, snapping out the pillow-case with vehemence. Women gots to figure out what they need to do for theirself. Lula, slave. Master always after her. When he give her twin girls, she drowned em. Whether that was a good decision or bad, I got no strong opinion, but what I don't believe is it was spite. I believe she looked at them newborn girls and already knew what life gonna be for em, to her was mercy, was mother's love. Master set to hang her, but up there with her noose necklace, she look so content and so peaceful and all relief, so master was cruel: yank her down, and right then taken her to the barn, aimin to plant more twins.

༄

Middle of the month, Cathleen shows me a patchwork quilt. Somehow she'd managed to find time to piece it together despite the recent large seamstress quotas.

Bring it to him, Cathleen tells me. Finbar.

I'm confused at first, then see her glance toward the window. So now Cathleen knows the veteran's name.

Sometimes I take the chair and crawl with it over to the window, and we chat while I work. Then, unnecessarily, Cathleen lowers her voice to a whisper: He's *not* fifteen, as I'd speculated. He's twenty.

Same age as Cathleen, I think, though she'll be twenty-one in a couple of weeks. She didn't tell him about the quilt, so when I hand it to him he's as much surprised as delighted, instantly looking up to the window where Cathleen has dragged herself.

Happy Saint Patrick's Day! she says though it's still two days away. Then she blushes, closes the cracked glass pane, and disappears.

You like to see it?

I'm startled.

You were starin at my stump, you like to see it? Finbar asks again, dry.

My face warms.

I don't mind showin. And he lifts one of his ragged pant-legs. I feel like I'm taking in *The Dead of Antietam* in real life, except the upper half of him's still alive.

Medic put on a tourniquet. Both legs.

What's a tourniquet?

Bandage round the wound, then twisted like a faucet, like a spigot on a barrel.

Finbar demonstrates, putting one fist on top of the other and twisting.

Stanches the blood flow.

I think how *stanch the blood* is a phrase that keeps entering the conversation lately.

Saved my life, if not my legs. Tourniquet halted the mad rush of blood—a temporary remedy.

Has your ma heard from your papa yet? That we hear from above, Colleen at the window again. Oh, Theo, I didn't know you were still here.

I leave, thinking how nice it would be to chat daily with Ciaran, the way Cathleen and Finbar do. Ciaran I haven't seen since the wedding kissing. I don't know where he lives to come visit him, and I reckon working all the time he can't find a few minutes to come see me. Or hasn't bothered.

⌒

On Saint Patrick's Day, I'm at the parade with Grammy and Auntie Siobhan and Cousin Aileen and, as the counties are marching by and everybody's cheering, here comes someone from behind, his two arms clutching me in a bear hug.

Ciaran! says Grammy, and he gives her a kiss on the cheek. Then he drily reports the latest bad news: a high fever left him on his back a few days, a theft and his and Aedan's meager belongings taken. These days Ciaran spends mornings hoping for work at Novelty Iron and, if not, searches for coal, then returns home to guard their sleeping spaces, desirable as they are in a dry area of the basement floor.

But it's Saint Patrick's Day! he smiles. I had to come out. And I know where you all always stand to watch!

Still, he doesn't stay long, seeming to worry about Cousin Aedan's likely reaction should they lose their enviable sleeping spots tonight. Ciaran turns just as the Longshoremen's U.B. Society marches by, disappearing into the crowd, me staring after him.

Just don't forget what happened to Siobhan, Grammy whispers in my ear.

Trudging through the crowds after the procession, people remark on their favorite floats and the majestic advance of the marshals on horseback and how nice to think of something not war. Then a newsboy calls, *Report from Richmond: Explosion in the Confederate Ordnance Laboratory kills more than sixty workers, mostly women and girls! Mishap set off by unfortunate Irish immigrant girl!* I can't believe it's happened again, a Southern replication of Pittsburgh which serves to silence any further commentary on the parade.

❧

Later in the week, I'm strolling up to Auntie Maryam's when someone calls out to me.

Miss Sally! I haven't seen you since you moved out of Auntie Siobhan's boarding-house!

What a lovely young lady you're becoming!

Thank you, I say, my eyes drifting to the crate she holds: salt and butter and flour and potatoes.

She smiles. Would you like some tea?

Miss Sally now lives with all colored ladies, and they are good cooks! A couple don't look much older than I. I'm licking my pork-grease fingers in the dining area when they retire to their bed-closets, preparing themselves for tonight's work, but Miss Sally stays with me.

Might feel like a recession to some, but not for *our* clientele. Business is good!

She sits back and kicks off her shoes.

How does Siobhan do?

She's doing well. She had a . . . She was a little sick for a while, but now good as new.

Yes, I heard somethin about that. She sighs. I miss her, and I miss Fiona. But! I love the ladies here. And sometimes—just nice to be around your own. Ya know?

A big fluffy yellow cat comes in whining, and Miss Sally quiets it with a little piece of fish, stooping and caressing its head as it gobbles.

Like another pork chop?

Thank you, Miss Sally, but I'm full. (True, but it still takes an almighty effort to be polite and refuse seconds.)

Well. I'd say *Don't be a stranger*, but you're at the age that too frequent visits might give inquisitive neighbors the wrong idea. So know you're welcome but, for your own sake, don't wear your welcome out.

She walks me to the door, yawning.

I shouldn't be so tired before work even begins! But the best thing about my job—after an exhaustin shift, I don't need to worry about the exhaustin walk home to bed. I'm already there!

Monday, March 23, spending my mid-day break from school wringing whites with Grammy Brook, we hear a pounding. I run to the door, and in staggers Uncle Ambrose holding his hemorrhaging head and sending us into conniptions. Grammy rips up a customer's sheet, and between this and Auntie Siobhan and the story Finbar told, I feel like this is some red-dripping nightmare I keep dreaming over and over. The blood is stanched, and Uncle Ambrose tries to catch his breath.

Shipping out. Word came there was a delay, don't come till ten o'clock. So nine and three-quarters, I'm heading to my sloop when I hear some foreman say, *I got enough niggers now, let's go*, then see a bunch of colored moving toward a docked schooner but somebody got there first. Irish. *Hundreds, everywhere*, took over the pier. Come to find out the long-shoremen been working for a dollar and a quarter, now struck for one fifty, these colored the scabs. Course they're scabs, how else they be offering black longshore work? The white clearly been standing there a while, but not till black faces appear do the whole wall of em come crushing down, and me not trying for longshoreman, my black *seaman* face they can't distinguish. Or don't. Stones. Sticks. Fists. Don't know if my ship sailed, but if it did, it did without me. Sorry, Mother Brook, to bring trouble to your doorstep, but here was closer than the Seamen's Home.

This is home.

He touches his bandage, sees fresh spots of red on his fingers.

Hunger or blood, he sighs. Seems that all the choice there is for a colored man.

Grammy tells me to stay with Uncle Ambrose while she makes a few whites deliveries. Then Mr. Samuel stops by covered in his chimney soot so I know Grammy told him as she made her local rounds. Then Auntie Maryam stops by with Nattie John so I know Grammy told her as she made her uptown rounds. Then Grammy's home.

Know the work I'd *like* to do? says Uncle Ambrose. Fight. But they don't want *that*.

Not in New York, concurs Mr. Samuel. Seymour. Governor Copper-head, him and our esteemed Mayor Wood both claimin emancipation means substitutin *niggerism for nationality*.

Massachusetts pullin together a colored regiment, says Auntie Maryam. Fifty-fourth Volunteers. Enlistin from all over!

Uncle Ambrose stares at her. I need to go!

One a my sweep competitors left for Boston yesterday, murmurs Mr. Samuel, eyes faraway. Negroes leavin the city, goin north to enlist because New York won't let em.

Plenty of white don't wanna enlist, says Uncle Ambrose, plenty of black do, how's Seymour being the white man's friend when black could help fill the New York quotas? And white getting angrier, angrier. Hunger or blood.

Uncle Ambrose stays the night with us, and a few days later, Grammy says, Let's us go see how Ambrose is doin, and she and I walk over to the Seamen's Home. Mrs. Mary Lyons, the very kind, very fat colored lady who runs the boarding-house with her petite husband Albro, says Uncle Ambrose isn't home now but we are welcome to wait in the parlor or leave a note.

He say where he goin? asks Grammy, little worry in her voice. I know she's greatly conflicted about Uncle Ambrose talking about joining the army.

Picking up some food items for me, says Mrs. Lyons, and Grammy seems relieved. Would you like a cup of tea and a cookie?

Yes, please! I say in my head, and Grammy utters the same minus the emphatic punctuation. We're sipping and munching when Uncle Ambrose returns, physically healing and mentally appearing much better, cheered that this morning he happened to run into two former pupils of Auntie Eunice's from Colored School Number Three in Seneca Village, the students relaying to him fond memories of what an exceptional teacher my aunt was. As he speaks, Jeremiah enters. He's fourteen now, slim and getting tall. His very dark eyes sparkle, his very dark skin shines, smooth and healthy clear. We haven't seen each other in some time.

How's Five Points? he asks me, as my grandmother and uncle continue engaging in their happy chat. And Mr. Samuel, my old boss?

I reply briefly, then ask, What's it like on the sea? Do you ever get sick from the waves? Scared?

It's the most peace I ever feel, he responds reflectively.

In the morning he has to ship out, sailing the Hudson to Albany, then Erie Canal to the West, but he'll be back in a couple of weeks. Maybe, Jeremiah goes on, if you're not busy with school or work, maybe if you don't have things to do with your family, maybe if it's a pretty afternoon, maybe you'd like to go for a walk.

Yes.

For a few days, Jeremiah takes occupation of my brain. Ciaran never comes to see me! And if he did, I don't want what happened to Auntie Siobhan to happen to me! But the longer Jeremiah stays away, the more I begin to doubt he'll even remember his invitation, and thoughts of Ciaran come flooding back.

An early April spring day, I walk up to Auntie Maryam's so I can play with Nattie John. They are outside in the garden, Auntie Maryam working at her washtub, Nattie John thrilled to see me. We roll in the grass a while, then she wants her ball so I take her inside to get it. The ball is newspaper that Auntie Maryam shaped into a sphere, then pasted and dried. I absently toss it up and down in my right hand, noticing on the table a newspaper clipping. Quotes from local Union soldiers in letters home regarding their thoughts on the Emancipation Proclamation. Given the confidential implications of some, the servicemen were apparently persuaded to share their inscribed opinions with the promise of anonymity.

> *I* for one (and I think it is so with a large portion of the Army) am disgusted with this war & its management. I did not come out to fight for the nigger or abolition of slavery. Much less to make the nigger *better* than white men, as they are every day becoming in the estimation and treatment of the powers at Washington. I would sooner see every nigger now free, *in* slavery, than see slavery abolished. And yet the *latter* seems to be the sole object of the Govt. Although I suppose it would not do to say so, openly, our officers & soldiers have no heart for carrying on a war on the principles those men & their followers advocate. It is not what they joined the service for, and they will not fight for them.
>
> —*New York officer*

There is much dissatisfaction existing in the army on account of the President's proclamation. Desertions are numerous and frequent. As the slaves become free only as our army advances, then who can deny we are fighting for the confounded nigger? The proclamation has done more to demoralize the army of the North than any good, practically or morally, that can possibly result from it.

—New Jersey soldier

The soldiers are down on the President's Proclamation, and our reg. is getting thinned out pretty fast by deserters. The soldiers swear they will never fight by the side of the damned Niggers.

—New York soldier

I shall try hard to get out. I am sick and tired of this Nigger War. A soldier has nothing to encourage him to fight for a lot of Nigger lovers at home.

—99th New York infantry officer

I have only nine months to serve and Uncle Sam may get all the nigger soldiers he can raise and scrape.

—New York cavalryman

The troops are loud in their denunciations against the President & the Abolition Cabinet generally & I have a faint idea that there will soon be a general uprising in the North to put an end to this war & decapitate some of the leading men in the Cabinet. Soldiers are constantly deserting & say that they will not fight to put niggers on a par with white men—that they had been duped & that they only enlisted for the preservation of the Union & nothing else.

—51st New York infantry soldier

Nattie John is suddenly wailing, and I realize I've mindlessly crushed her dried-newspaper ball to bits.

⁓

Friday the tenth of April, Jeremiah knocks on Grammy Brook's door. I'm not there but she passes along the message, and on Sunday the twelfth, he and I walk past the newsboys through the southwest entrance to the Central Park, West Fifty-ninth street.

Report from Richmond: Bread riots! Thousands of starved Southern women looting stores!

The sun is shining, wildflowers dotting the meadow, Jeremiah says he has to ship out again tomorrow. I ask him if he's afraid, given what's been happening at the piers. He says things have calmed down, no thug activity since Uncle Ambrose's incident three weeks ago. He feels very lucky to get so much work these days, though well aware much of it is due to the war. I tell him he *is* lucky—no, fortunate, lots of people want to be seamen but not everyone has the knack, and Jeremiah seems embarrassed and thanks me, and I'm having a very pleasant afternoon with him, just chatting, just smiling, except every quarter-hour I feel gripped by the fear that I might run into Ciaran. But the fright is always instantly followed by a fury: not a peep from him in weeks and he'd be here enjoying himself in the park? Then the anger replaced by the guilt that I would begrudge Ciaran an afternoon of peace, poor Ciaran who always seems to be working or looking for work, Sorry, Jeremiah, I missed that! What did you just say?

Before he repeats it, the racing gallop of a horse, everybody screaming and jumping out of its path. *Two* horses, racing carriages, the one packed with young white men, the other young men and a couple of young women, one of whom I swear is Mabel Carrington, the rich daughter of Maureen's former employer. They are all laughing, not appearing to have a care in the world, and are just as quickly gone.

Twenty-four hundred, says Jeremiah, as we stare after them.

What?

Eight rich white boys times three hundred dollars apiece, commutation fees. How much it'll cost to keep all of em outa the war. For them? Pocket change.

Next morning is Monday, and I should go to school but I take a walk instead. Up to the Academy of Music, where sometimes I go to think about Auntie Eunice. But I feel guilty because today I'm thinking more about Ciaran. About kissing after the wedding, Charles Tom Thumb

Stratton and Lavinia, and the brief embrace from him on Saint Patrick's Day, and then nothing else. Last night in bed with Grammy Cahill something occurred to me that hadn't before. I walk east.

What came to me in the wee hours was that maybe there's a very good reason I've seen so little of Ciaran. It could be that, akin to my nice stroll with Jeremiah yesterday, Ciaran has met some other girl. This would finally make sense of it all, and I'm angry with myself that it matters. I've come to the docks, and staring down into the water—sparkling, filthy as it is—my stinging, hot tears fall into the East River. If what I suspect is so, I should be relieved. How much time have I wasted missing him? Pittsburgh was one thing, but now just a few wards away and he doesn't come see me! If his attention's been captured elsewhere, he should have let me know, that would have been decent. Because even if we never put a label on it, what happened at Tom and Lavinia's wedding—that wasn't nothing.

I look up into the face of a man close to me, frowning at me, the whiskey on his breath strong. It isn't a leer. His expression is something else, something I can't quite put my finger on. I'm embarrassed by my tears and wipe my cheeks, then someone whistles and someone yelps and the man runs, suddenly *dozens* of men running, and I realize I just walked into some kind of throng, hundreds of what look to be all Irishmen wielding large sticks and descending upon a group of black men who just entered the sphere.

Drive off the damned niggers!

Kill em!

Lynch the sons of bitches!

The shouts are coming from everywhere, and I'm startled by a vague familiarity. The *lynch* voice. Christmas, the street arab boy who used to run the races in the alley. Now big, grown, and right next to him: Ciaran's cousin Aedan, who fires his own epithets against the company and against the scabs before hurling a large stone into a panicked black hub.

I'm paralyzed. The clanging of chains, thud of sticks on flesh: swinging and screaming and blood. With Aedan here, I cannot help but to wildly search, and pray not to find, Ciaran. A shot: all momentarily freeze, then see the pistol in the hand of a black man in self-defense, now set upon by the mob. Suddenly dozens of police out of nowhere, hopefully to restore order but for now only compounding the havoc. Another shot fired, and in the new confusion I see a narrow exit. Staying close to the shore, I walk quickly. Then run.

∾—ᴆ

Not just the longshoremen scabs, Mr. Samuel tells Auntie Maryam at their table that evening. Those drunk louts went after sweeps in the vicinity, I heard tell of it! Cartmen and porters, anybody colored!

Don't go back to work tomorrow! Auntie Maryam tells him, then turns to me. And stay away from those docks!

Other parts a the city. Didn't happen in Five Points, not where I work, where she lives, says Mr. Samuel, glancing at me. But your auntie's right. Stay away from the piers!

Don't go! sobs Nattie John, not certain whom she should address her directive to.

The clashes along the shore continue for three days while I travel between sleeping at Auntie Maryam's and at Grammy Brook's. On Thursday, I'm on my way to Grammy Cahill's and notice the newsboys have stopped yelling *mob* so maybe the longshoremen and the bosses came to some agreement. I walk through the door to see a sitting Ciaran who now abruptly stands, holey cap in his hands.

He's come every day since Monday searching for you, says Cathleen, not looking up from her sewing. When you're finished talking, I'd appreciate you coming back and helping me with some hemming.

Ciaran and I step out and, as he is closing the door behind us, Cathleen calls, still not looking up: Just don't forget what happened to Siobhan!

I run down the steps.

What happened to Siobhan? asks Ciaran, following me.

Nothing, I grunt, sick of being told to not forget about it.

Penny for a veteran? Oh, how do ye, Theo.

Who's that? asks Ciaran a block later, me walking rapidly down the street and him trying to keep up.

Finbar.

Theo, can you—? Do you—? *Stop!*

I turn around, arms folded.

What *is* it?

I say nothing. He swallows.

Cousin Aedan said you were there. I had to see you. Make sure you were all right.

I say nothing.

Why *were* you there?

Free streets. *I* didn't know some loonies would be planning their shenanigans.

He says nothing.

Were *you* there?

He frowns.

I'm not a longshoreman.

I stare.

Why would I be there? I'm not a longshoreman!

I turn to walk away.

No! I was *not there!*

I sigh. Lean against a building.

What else?

I look at him.

You're still sore at me.

What do you care.

I'm here!

I stare into the distance.

Because . . . Because I ain't been around to see you?

I grunt.

You ain't come to see me neither.

I don't know where you live!

Ciaran appears startled, as if this obvious factor never occurred to him. Why didn't you ask?

You wanted me to have the information, you'd've given it to me.

Why wouldn't I?

I look down, my foot tapping the ground in some rapid rhythm.

Five ten East Eleventh, at avenue A. The basement.

Then he's quiet a moment.

Cousin Aedan. Sometimes he makes it hard for me to leave. If I'm not doin one task or another, I'm not earnin my keep, that's why I didn't . . .

He swallows.

You can come see me every day, if you want. I'd like that.

And because such an invitation appears to negate the possibility of another girl, I almost smile. He leans against the wall next to me. The sky has grayed over, distant thunder.

He lost his job. They took most of them back today, but not the ones who yelled the loudest.

Two urchins race by: a little boy running, pushing a wheelbarrow carrying a littler boy, both screeching the joy.

He's talkin about leavin again. Somebody he knows who knows somebody else claims there's spring harvestin upstate, the chard and the rhubarb, fiddleheads and the fava beans. Course all I can do is remember our last travelin scheme. But he says—

Don't go!

My two words surprise me as much as him. Suddenly pouring rain, and we run for shelter in a dead-end alley, though we're already soaked, laughing, and then our hands on each other, our lips on each others'. I try not to forget what happened to Auntie Siobhan but that recent past feels blurred by the present of kiss kiss kiss.

⁓

Mid-May, Grammy Brook reads her paper. Look like ole Stonewall Jackson got hisself killed. Mistake: shot by his own men. Chancellorville.

Chancellorville or Chancellorsville? I ask.

Papers keep changing their mind bout the *s*, replies Uncle Ambrose who stopped by for a visit, eyes in his own paper.

We win at Chancellorsville?

North press doesn't want to say no, but see for yourself.

Uncle Ambrose shows me his *New-York Times*. **THE GREAT BATTLES IN VIRGINIA** followed by **THE CASUALTIES**, and under that three full-page columns of small-print Union names, a third of which are from Chancellorsville and most of those our state—and I wager most of those our city: 58th New-York, 82nd Ohio, 41st New-York, 54th New-York, 66th New-York, 104th Pennsylvania, 57th New-York, 52nd New-York.

A few weeks later, activity at the docks is again newsworthy.

The New-York Times.

NEW-YORK, TUESDAY, JUNE 9, 1863.

Strike Among the 'Longshoremen.

Yesterday morning at an early hour the 'Longshoremen commenced a great strike for higher wages, in accordance with their resolutions on Saturday last, when several of the parties who employed them received notice of the advance they would demand. At 9 o'clock groups of dock hands, assembled near the piers from East River to Pier No. 11 on West-street; and endeavored to dissuade men from taking their places, at the prices paid last week. They were generally successful. In about an hour, 500 'longshoremen assembled on the piers in the First Ward, and subsequently marched in a body to Pier No. 11, North River where they found a number of laborers engaged in removing a cargo. The laborers, having been notified by a leader of the crowd to desist, refused to comply, when the 'longshoremen at once attacked them, and quickly drove them off the Pier. Gangs of laborers are now working at several piers on the East and North Rivers, under the protection of a strong force of police. The strike already extends from Pier No. 8, East River, to Pier No. 11, North River. A riot is anticipated, and a strong police force is in readiness to quell it. The 'Longshoremen demand $2 per day, and 50 cents per hour after 7 P.M. Their employers have large posters out, offering employment to 1,000 dock hands at $1 50 per day; and also calling for an additional thousand men to load carts, &c.

I hear they're bringing in jailed army deserters and convalescin soldiers to break the strike, says Grammy Cahill.

Auntie Siobhan snickers. When they see what's waitin for em at the pier, I bet they'll all be wishin they were back on the battlefield.

I stare at her. It's not clear from the article whether these scabs are colored, but seems likely at least some are. I realize I'm not certain exactly where my auntie, who cheered abolitionist Lincoln's election, stands in all of this.

❧

Volunteers! says Auntie Maryam a week later, tending her garden, collecting cucumbers and kale. Walked by the enrollment office: over-flowin!

I help Auntie Maryam mainly by playing with Nattie John and keeping her out of the way. On the step, Mr. Samuel sits studying the newspaper, all concentration.

Men are volunteering again? I ask.

They got the spirit anew, she replies, since the rebs bein darin, pushin north.

The South coming *north?*

Don'tchu worry, they ain't gonna know what hit em in Pennsylvania!

(I think about the map at school. Pennsylvania's close!)

Surge of enthusiasm, feelin the threat, Mr. Samuel remarks, without looking up from his news. Doubt it'll last. State militia *has* to report for duty, the volunteers figure best to go on, sign up before they *get* signed up. Before their favorite regiments get *filled* up.

New York sendin more n any other state, says Auntie Maryam. Thousands!

Sixteen thousand militia, mutters her husband.

Rebs ain't gonna know what hit em! cries Auntie Maryam.

Mr. Samuel looks up for the first time, off into the distance.

Only five hundred fifty military left to protect the entire city, Mr. Samuel ruminates aloud, a worrisome frown. Then adds quietly, What if somethin go wrong at home?

Saturday, the Fourth of July, I stand in City Hall Park, Ciaran grinning next to me, both of us chins up: eyes on the fireworks. I vowed not to appear too eager and come knocking on his door frequently since I learned his address last April—and, besides, I fear running into Cousin Aedan, who never seemed so friendly to me. I only stopped by twice, Ciaran there for just one of those, and we took a brief Sunday stroll. But it's the holiday so maybe he won't be searching for work today, I thought. He nearly cried with delight when I came tapping on the basement entrance.

In the park before the pyrotechnics begin, we hear excited mumblings, rumors of positive war news from Pennsylvania though nothing yet confirmed. And debate regarding the possibility of the long staved-off draft. After two years of volunteer war, every day I fluctuate from believing there will never be a draft and expecting the first draft names to be called any minute. And when I lean toward the latter, I alternate between elation and dread.

A woman near us hollers at her unruly kids while her seeming oblivious husband turns the page of his newspaper. On the back I see an advertisement: *Gentlemen will be furnished promptly with substitutes by forwarding their orders to the office of the Merchants, Bankers and General Volunteer Association.*

⌒

Tuesday, July 7, details from the fronts have rolled in—Third of July: Union victory at Gettysburgh, Pennsylvania! Fourth of July: Reb surrender at Vicksburgh, Mississippi! (The spelling of both municipalities fluctuating in the papers regarding the end *h*.) Dancing in the streets! Stars and stripes hang everywhere, smaller flags people hold. Me stomping with Auntie Maryam in the Thirties, then move down to Five Points and step with Auntie Siobhan there. Look up, seeing Grammy Brook and Gran-Gran waving and grinning from the window. Over to Grammy Cahill's table, we do a jig. A woman offers us cake! People sing to that *Johnny, Fill Up the Bowl* drinking tune but now there are new words.

> *When Johnny comes marching home again, hurrah! Hurrah!*
> *We'll give him a hearty welcome then, hurrah! Hurrah!*
> *The men will cheer and the boys will shout,*
> *The ladies they will all turn out,*
> *And we'll all feel gay when Johnny comes marching home.*

I see Cathleen at the window talking down at Finbar.

Cathleen! Finbar! Want some cake?

I've eaten half my piece and tear the remainder in two, giving one chunk to Finbar and running up the stairs to give the other to my cousin.

Who stares at it. Dismal.

Cathleen! Why aren't you glad? We're winning the war!

She turns the *New-York Times* in her hand around so I can see the Gettysburg report she was reading: *The rebel losses are estimated at 20,000. Our troops are in the highest spirits.*

I know it's bleak, I say, but maybe this'll bring Robert Lee to his knees: surrender! I know it's sad, twenty thousand casualties, but they aren't all *killed,* some are just wounded—

Forty thousand casualties.

I frown.

If they estimate twenty thousand *rebel* casualties, and that very well may be an *under*estimate, does it not stand to reason the federal casualties would be in that vicinity as well?

We hear Finbar and turn to look down at him. He sings *When Johnny Comes Marching Home*, hollow and lonely, staring at the empty space where his marching legs once were.

In the dusk, I walk to Ciaran's tenement and knock on the basement door. Mary Clare, the one who posed as Aedan's wife for the Longshoremen's United Benevolent Society, answers, then calls Ciaran. He smiles wide, clearly surprised to see me again just three days after the Fourth. I'd managed to obtain another piece of cake, and give it all to him.

Happy birthday.

Saturday, Cathleen and Grammy and Auntie Siobhan and Cousin Aileen and Great-Uncle Fergus and I stare at the papers from yesterday and this morning.

The New-York Times.

NEW-YORK, FRIDAY, JULY 10, 1863.

THE DRAFT.

\-

THE ENROLLMENT COMPLETED.

Twenty-five Thousand Men to be Drawn in the City, and Seven Thousand in Brooklyn.

The Draft to Commence on Monday in the Eighteenth Ward, Eighth District.

The Draft has at length become a reality, and Monday next will be the memorable day on which it will be first enforced in this City.

THE NEW-YORK HERALD.

NEW YORK, SATURDAY, JULY 11, 1863.

The Draft in New York and Brooklyn.

It Commences To-day in the Ninth District.

FEELING IN THE CITY REGARDING IT.

WHO ARE LIABLE AND WHO ARE EXEMPT,

&c., &c., &c.

The long threatened draft in this city will commence to-day in the Ninth district, the drawing for which will take place at No. 677 Third avenue, corner of Forty-sixth street.

The enrollment has been completed in nearly every district in New York and Brooklyn, and nothing now remains but to carry out the requisite routine by this somewhat unpopular method.

The quota of New York is understood to be twelve thousand five hundred, while that of Brooklyn is set down at about five thousand. The preparations for this draft have been conducted in an exceedingly quiet and secret manner, and until yesterday no exactly positive information could be ascertained as to the precise time the draft would commence.

THE SUN

NEW YORK, FRIDAY, JULY 10, 1863.

THE DRAFT—*The Drawing to take place To-day*—It is understood that orders have been received by the Provost-Marshal, to proceed at once with the conscription in this city and Brooklyn. Our quota is 12,500, that of Brooklyn 4,000. The drawing will probably commence to-day in the districts whose rolls are completed. From the time an official notification is given, the drafted men will have but ten days allowed to find a substitute, or pay $300. The conscripts will be sent to Riker's Island previous to being organized. Although the number required from New York City is but 12,500, there will be 19,000 names drawn.

New-York Daily Tribune.

NEW-YORK, SATURDAY, JULY 11, 1863.

—The draft will commence in this city to-day in the Ninth Congressional District, and in the other districts on Monday, or as soon thereafter as possible. The total number of men required for the city (excepting one district the quota of which has not yet been made out) is 20,284. To this is to be added 50 per cent, making the total number to be drawn 30,426.

Well, says Cathleen. Well. Well, I guess now we know *something*.

Contradictions and utter confusion! barks Great-Uncle Fergus.

We *know*, Cathleen goes on, there *will* be a draft. We know it *will* be soon. Or already started.

We *know* it *will* cost three hundred dollars for the well-to-do to buy out of it, says Cousin Aileen.

Did ye know Lincoln's after settin unfairly high quotas for New York City? asks my great-uncle. In Democratic Manhattan?

That can't be, frowns Cathleen.

The governor said so! With all your readin, ye didn't see Seymour's statement on the matter? Not the millionaires of course. The millionaires'll pay their three hundred and walk free.

It's a terrible selfishness, sighs Cousin Aileen, but I just thank the saints nobody's eligible in our family.

Rich man's war and a poor man's fight, mutters Great-Uncle Fergus. I don't speak but think what he said is something I've overheard every day for weeks now from Irish on the street.

Imagine you'll be fillin the till tonight, Grammy says drily to Auntie Siobhan. Last drink before their names called.

Fillin the till started last night, says Auntie Siobhan. And I imagine *after* their names're called, the till'll be filled *double*. Though I suppose those'll be dragged off to Riker's Island before even a good-bye to their dear ones.

The fire laddies pretty outraged these days, says Great-Uncle Fergus. They always had the exemption from the state militia, but *now* eligible for the *federal* draft.

Things've been movin in the right direction, says Cousin Aileen. Gettysburg, Vicksburg. I'd be all for it, hit the rebs full force, get the war over with! if it weren't for the blasted commutation fee.

How can they do it! cries Grammy. Flaunt it at the poor!

They thought they were protecting the poor, sighs Cathleen. Lincoln, the Republicans. They feared if they left the cost of commutation to the open market, the price would go beyond reach.

Seem Lincoln and the Republicans already found the price-beyond-reach all by themself, grunts Great-Uncle Fergus. And why have it at all? Send the rich to the front-line too! *That* would be hittin them with full force!

Have ye noticed the sudden spate of old men walkin the streets? Auntie Siobhan smiles. This afternoon Brendan and Conan O'Sullivan walk into the tavern, their beautiful black hair turned grandfather gray. Conan's the older brother, but neither's more than thirty-five. Fellas! What happened? I cried. Ach! We was early grayers, but knowin the draft was comin, we figured time to stop dyein the hair. Now don't look a day under fifty, do we?

Maybe, offers Grammy. Maybe if this draft brings a surge of new men, new Yankee reinforcements. Maybe the secessionists will surrender quick?

Rebs are stubborn, no chance, returns Great-Uncle Fergus. Which suits plenty of Northern capitalists just dandy. Why should the war ever be over with the war profiteers windfallin!

That can't be true, Uncle! says Cousin Aileen. Prolongin the bloodshed for greed!

I believe it! he replies emphatically. I believe it, he repeats lamentably.

Do you know who Salmon Chase is?

Secretary of the treasury, Cathleen replies to Auntie Siobhan.

U.S. secretary of the treasury, his daughter livin in Manhattan, paradin around in the three-thousand-dollar shawl her father ordered from overseas. The talk at the tavern last night was her shoulder-throw was worth ten men's lives.

Aaaaah! Cousin Aileen cries.

Well, ye know who Attorney Lincoln worked for before he started politickin, don't ye, inserts Great-Uncle Fergus. Railroad companies! Land speculators! Corporations and nabobs, the rich! So he can talk about *Free the slaves!* and *Free-labor economy!* but you tell me: Where's that leave a poor Irishman?

One percent of New Yorkers now hold sixty-nine percent of the city's wealth, murmurs Cathleen.

Remember how we used to think about America, back home? muses Grammy. The land where every laborer is a possible gentleman.

It's important, swallows Cathleen. It's significant that Lee was stopped at Gettysburg. It was an ugly, bloody battle, but he *was* sent packing, he'll think twice before venturing north again, we have to remember the strides we've made.

That's grand, that's grand. And when ye holler down to *Penny for a veteran?* out there, do ye tell him, Aw stop givin out to me! Ye might've lost a couple of legs and buried a few pals, but Lee's back south so all's well.

Fergus!

The girl's right about one thing, he tells Grammy. Gettysburg. The way she's been mopin lately, watch, it'll come out: forty thousand casualties, I bet.

That's loony! Cousin Aileen snaps.

Watch, says he. And tell me, what's the point of it all except to make the rich richer?

Emancipation!

Everyone turns to me: the first word I've uttered. And all turn away. Then Grammy recruits Cousin Aileen into peeling potatoes with her, and the chatter in the room is anything *but* politics while my brain is flooded with conjecture of how the debate might have continued if I weren't here. If I didn't exist.

⁓

Soon after, I slip away from my Irish family and walk up to West Thirty-second. I love sharing Nattie John's bed in the Room of Hope, but tonight she touches my face, wiping away tears I didn't know were there. The next morning, Auntie Maryam says it would be very nice if I went to church with her and Mr. Samuel. Since Watch Night, Auntie Maryam walks everywhere, no longer chained to her home out of fear of slave-catchers. She'd prefer attending a mosque but as there are none around, she attends Shiloh Church, after hearing Reverend Garnet preach. She likes that Henry Highland Garnet is an escaped slave who gained an education, and particularly his outspoken pride regarding his African descendancy from Mandingo chiefs and warriors, his very dark skin invalidating white claims that all intelligent blacks have Caucasian blood in them. When I reply that I would rather not go, she doesn't put in her best Christian or Muslim effort to persuade me otherwise given that Nattie John always squirms in the pews, and this way I can stay home and tend to her. I'm teaching my three-and-a-half-year-old cousin a few words in the newspaper when her foster parents return.

News! smiles Auntie Maryam. Reverend Garnet talkin about a raid on the Combahee, South Carolina, month ago. They took a ship upriver, aimin to catch the slave-holders by surprise and emancipate the slaves.

Did they? Emancipate?

Yes! Seven hundred and fifty slaves free!

I whoop.

South Carolina! Maybe Hathaway. Maybe my plantation!

It gets better, grins Mr. Samuel.

The soldiers, says Auntie Maryam, was the Second South Carolina battalion. *Colored.*

I scream. Nattie John likes my screaming and screams louder.

And, says Mr. Samuel.

Their commander was colored, says my auntie. A colored *woman* commander in the Union army.

Mr. Samuel laughs. You can close your mouth now, Theo.

Reverend Garnet knows because was just published, abolitionist paper outa Boston, man writin her story. Seem she escaped from Maryland herself, and kep goin back. Led *dozens* to freedom!

Harriet, her name, says Mr. Samuel, then frowns, trying to recall. Harriet . . .?

Tubman, says Auntie Maryam. I think a my washtub, Harriet cleanin up America's mess! Now Auntie Maryam sweeps Nattie John and me into a warm embrace.

Good *some*body in the Union army got sense, she says. Here we got the best spy, best commander, best mission planner in the country. What kind a fools they be to pass her by because she black? A woman?

Marylander, I think. Like Frederick Douglass, like Reverend Garnet. If so many geniuses came from just the other side of the Mason-Dixon, just imagine the brilliant minds had the North been more accessible to the lower states!

But for now, I just soak up my brilliant South Carolinian escaped auntie's cuddle. And I think how very very nice to start the week smiling for a change, as I'd begun to dread Mondays, never knowing when there'd be trouble at the docks, or some other place where work is backbreaking and underpaid and dangerous and coveted.

I head back to Five Points in the afternoon, and on Eighth avenue in the Twenties, I'm surprised to see a procession. It doesn't appear to be a military event. And while there are many spectators enthusiastically, even zealously, cheering the pageant, there are at least as many with a glaring resentment, breathing heavy and threatening. And it hits me: the Orange Order parade. So long as we've kept to the Sixth ward, Five Points Irish

Catholics haven't had to witness this uptown annual grandiose flaunting of the 1690 battle in Ireland wherein Protestant William of Orange defeated Catholic James II. I turn around to move to peaceful Ninth avenue and continue south from there.

I begin to notice that many people are reading newspapers, peering scrupulously into them. I get to Grammy Cahill's table as a church bell strikes three, and though she is usually all business at work, she frowns, her eyes also in a daily. When she looks up to see me, she folds the paper.

Help me bring my table back up. Then you and I'll take a walk.

Grammy Cahill *never* takes time away from her wares! In the back of my mind, I find this concerning, but I'm too excited to think much about it. I carry the table up by myself. I'm plenty big enough: thirteen and a half!

We stroll along Park street under a burning sun, the sweltering humidity. Have I ever told you about the time I shook Frederick Douglass's hand? No! Where? *When?* He lives in Rochester! When was he in New York? Not New York. Cork.

She chuckles at the look on my face.

He was makin a tour of Ireland. 'Twas just after the publication of his narrative. A treasure map for any enterprisin slave-catcher hopin to kidnap him back to Maryland, he'd escaped but no free papers. So Mr. Douglass's abolitionist friends set up a speakin circuit to buy time, and the money it generated wound up buyin his freedom! Though, from what I hear, his lecture compensation was half that of the white abolitionist lecturers. He settled into our corner of Europe two years: Ireland, Scotland, England. Politically quite the savvy one—acceptin our graciousness but careful not to insult merry aul you-know-who, wantin to capitalize on their sense of moral superiority: *their* slaves, kept hidden away from Brits' delicate eyes and ears in the colonies, they'd freed decades before. What an embarrassment to America! Who just a while back dared throw up *All men are created equal* in England's face!

Grammy chuckles.

On the crossin over—not the dreaded coffin ships of our journey, no! Douglass traveled with well-to-do whites, a first-class ticket he had.

Negro with a *first-class ticket?*

Yes, but as a black man, he weren't given the cabin the fare implied but rather relegated to steerage. Grammy shakes her head. One day, his white cohorts are after invitin him to deliver a lecture on deck, which ye may not be surprised to know was *not* to the likin of the other American passengers. An uproar they caused, until the English captain threatened to put the rabble-rousers in irons. Did ye hear? He threatened to chain the *whites*! And sent one of his sailors to fetch the shackles lest the stunned ruffians doubt his sincerity on the point!

I grin. We're walking north on Bowery, which separates the Tenth and Fourteenth wards.

Landfall in Liverpool, and two days later, they crossed the Irish Sea to Dublin, startin their six-week tour of the Isle, and here Mr. Douglass got himself another shock. Poverty! The misery of our scalpeens! He witnessed the scrawny arms, heads low yieldin to the lords. He wrote about it, ye can read it! If the poor Irish had black skin and wooly hair, he scribed, he'd swear he'd seen us toilin on American plantations—and this *before* the Famine! A little like New York now. Look around!

I look around. The gaunt, hollow-eyed poor. And the drunkards lying here and there. Always a part of the landscape, but hard times the jolly or the fighting whiskey guzzlers seem to give way to this variety: the despairing.

No one would say the sufferin was equal to slavery. Irish weren't stolen and sold, whipped and raped. But our misery was vast. Even a former slave astonished.

But you said you *shook his hand*, Grammy. You didn't just read his words, you said you *met* him.

By divine providence. My younger sister Alannah, tryin to escape the scarcity, removed to Cork. Found work in the brewery. She'd been there almost a year when our mammy had a dream that Alannah was dyin and begged me go see her. Mammy could barely move anymore from the awful rheumatism or she'd gone herself, not wantin Alannah to die alone. I prayed Mammy's dream was wrong. It was September, and I hoped to return before the October harvest. I rode on the back of one sheep truck, then another, the old horse draggin along.

Alannah *was* ailin! Fever and vomitin, but I nursed her, she recovered. Mammy's dream didn't keep my sister from dyin alone: it saved her life! In a few days, Alannah was strong enough that we walked arm in arm through the Cork streets.

Like Grammy and I walking arm in arm through our New York streets now, I think, as we cross east into the Seventeenth ward. The despondency persists here, the faces frowning into their papers, but all that's coupled with something else. I'm startled to notice the hard looks directed at *me*, which Grammy doesn't seem to see. Grammy's mind in her story: another place, another time.

There he is! Himself—Mr. Douglass! First we catch sight of the crowd: the hordes surroundin him. Not a mob like on the ship. A swarm longin to hear his words! I didn't know who he was but found out quick, what with all the chatter. In Dublin, he'd heard *our* liberator speak, Daniel O'Connell, who condemned slavery in America unaware a former slave was sittin right in the audience! Douglass was shocked by the words, his heart warmed. Then someone introduced them, and O'Connell proclaimed Douglass the Black O'Connell! Grammy chortles. Our Dan was a man of many virtues, but humility was not among them!

So now Mr. Douglass had come to Cork. Sure Alannah and me couldn't afford the sixpence to get into the Imperial Hotel for his fund-raisin speech, so Mr. Douglass spoke to the destitute outside—a gift! And shook every hand! Includin mine! Oh, even there on the street, what an affectin speaker! And a pretty one too. I heard the galleries were *packed* with the ladies takin a grand glance. Grammy winks at me.

I'm not takin part in no fuckin draft, I hear a man ten feet from us say to nobody and everybody. A man near him with a flask toasts in agreement.

D' ye know what he said, *mo leanbh*? He said when he came to Ireland, he was shocked at the *absence of prejudice*. His phrase! The trouble on the ship was because of the Americans, but once he set foot on the Isle? Treated like the proper gentleman he was! He's after steppin onto stagecoaches and steamboats, walkin into the finest public houses and takin the finest seats, no one battin an eye! He grew quite famous as his time in the country went on, movin county to county, his reputation precedin him. But I'm of the opinion that those *first* days, when no one knew who he was but treated him respectfully all the same—I wager they were his most precious.

Grammy sighs, closing her eyes in the pleasure of the memory, then her eyelids raise.

Look at them.

Grammy gazes at a huddle of fellows, some appearing Ciaran's age. We're in Mackerelville, I realize—Ciaran's neighborhood. The young men glower. I'd never before glimpsed this flagrant brutal attitude when I'd visited Ciaran.

Hard for the fathers with families, says Grammy, and for these young ones too. Ah, they're good lads! Tryin their best! We came here searchin for a better life, and we *labor!* For the meagerest wages! But what happens when there's no work available, or work all the time but the inflation puts a loaf of bread out of reach? Boys, almost men: Idle. Hungry. Angry. And the lot of us crammed on this isle. Manhattan.

First day of the draft goes without a hitch!

The way the newsboy holds his *Herald*, I glimpse the back page. **THE DRAFT.** Followed by a few paragraphs, and that followed by tiny writing over several columns: hundreds of names. The conscripts. And I finally understand all the attention to the press.

Yesterday, clarifies Grammy. That newsboy's callin the calm a little early, but I pray it remains. She shakes her head. I feel it. A thickness in the air, powder keg waitin to blow. But let us pray not.

No keg, no keg, I repeat absently, softly. But I think about Grammy's words, and wonder: Even as she utters them, does she see what's right in front of us? Grammy, feeling the tension in our city, a tourniquet tightening, temporarily staving off the mad rush of blood. My Irish grandmother took me for a stroll to talk about Irish in Ireland treating a black man with respect. She knows who I am, my other family, this is why she's telling me the story, and telling it now. And still: a certain denial, blindness. She's never really seen me as anything but family, and family is Irish. Love is blind, and blind is dangerous.

A few years before Mr. Douglass docked in Ireland, she continues, there'd been a proclamation. Dan O'Connell signed it. So did Father Mathew, the famous temperance priest, thousands writin their names to the document, a message from Ireland to the Irish in America, encouragin our brothers to join in the American abolition cause! But the Irish here— Grammy sighs. Didn't take hold. Grammy clutches my hand tight. I don't know what we could have done from the other side of the ocean, but we had the spirit! Ah, *a chuisle mo chroí*, who knows what might've transpired!

Those days, Ireland was ready to fight for American negro freedom as well as our own!

Grammy smiles dreamily, shining eyes.

But bad timin. I returned from Cork, came home to our scalpeen—and smelled death in the soil even before I saw your grandfather's ghostly face: the potatoes startin to turn.

Grammy is in County Kerry, seeing soggy rotten tubers, smelling the stench, while I am in powder-keg New York, the Mackerelville neighborhood of the Seventeenth ward of lower Manhattan, staring at a cluster of men when there is a sudden parting and now I see standing among them Ciaran, his cousin Aedan right beside him. Aedan is yelling at him, something full of passion and fury, *work* I hear and *war* I hear and *nigger* I hear and Ciaran trying to make sense of it. Ciaran at fifteen years of age, and every time I think he can get no thinner he surprises me, but still a working-man's chiseled arms over his skin and bones. And turning his face just two inches, he finds me in his line of vision. His hungry, hollow eyes fixed on me hard, like daggers dipped in poison.

KEG

Next morning, I wake up at Grammy Cahill's in a sweat, daybreak already thick and muggy gray. I walk down Baxter toward Park, passing Abbie's tenement, and am surprised to see her just outside it, looking right at me.

Disturbance uptown! Wanna see?

Abbie grins. Her suggestion would mean playing hooky, or missing at least the morning subjects, mischief we've never done together before. But whatever this ferment is seems worthy of a peek.

A few blocks north of Five Points, we see men moving with intention, so we follow. Out to the west side piers, where there's clearly a strike going on but nothing violent occurring. *We'll not go!* men call out in unison, and this may explain the relative calm because whatever this dispute is, it doesn't appear to involve scabs. At any rate, the affair seems to be winding down, but now everyone seems to be headed further north, some banging on copper pans. Abbie and I look at each other—we would definitely be late to school if we continue uptown—and wordlessly agree to fall in with the flow on Ninth avenue. At corners, I glimpse an identical procession streaming up Eighth. Women and children are part of the parade, which ordinarily would imply something family-festive, except I notice in the hands of many marchers a stone or a shovel or a poker or a brick-bat.

We near the Central Park, where masses from every direction pour into the man-made meadows. Speeches are being spouted, but soon the multitude is on the move again. Many people have now separated from the crowd, strikers who have already struck and thus are done. Abbie and I try to move toward them but unfortunately we are caught in the current of those who are by no means finished, headed back south, then moving east on Forty-seventh. I'm aware that every inch of the street is packed with people—most Irish, but also some Germans, some native-born—many carrying placards and screaming the phrase written on them: No DRAFT! The air is perfumed with alcohol and purpose, and as I begin to wonder whether the march is the end in itself or if there might be a destination, we reach Forty-sixth street and Third avenue: the Ninth District Draft Office.

Ten a.m., they'll roll the lottery wheel, Mr. Samuel had said when I was at their house yesterday. Then a blindfolded man'll start drawin the names.

There are signs and shouting here just as at the docks, but now things feel considerably more chaotic. A shot is fired, which seems to set off harum-scarum: the building is suddenly being bombarded with street paving stones—windows breaking, façade crumbling. Abbie and I glance at each other, then hastily make an about-face, expecting everyone to do the same, but the discharge seems rather to have propelled the crowd more urgently forward, blocking our egress. A red fire engine is parked nearby, its horse terror-stricken. Many of the rock-hurlers are volunteer firemen, who bellow *Steal the draft records!* I turn to catch a glimpse of Ciaran joining in with another chant: *Down with the rich men!* He isn't twenty feet away but dozens are crushed between us. The horde lurches, and I lose my companion.

Abbie! Abbie! No sign of her, and I feel the panic rising as I keep calling, and one of those *Abbie!*s gets Ciaran's attention, his face snapping in my direction. The door of the draft office crashes, and the mob storms in.

Abbie!

What're you doin here?

How'd he get to me so fast?

Go home!

What are *you* doing here?

I got business. Go home, Theo!

Getting back to Five Points is of course precisely what Abbie and I have been trying to do, but Ciaran with that imperious tone will never know it.

No.

He tries to lower his voice to a confidential whisper, but with all the screaming, a whisper is just a shout in the receiver's ear.

Very well for you to be for the war since *you* won't lose family. *I* near lost my Cousin Aedan.

Why'd you shoot me that dirty look yesterday?

Ciaran stares at me like I'm a madwoman. *What?*

When Grammy and I were walking through Mackerelville, and you gave me the stinkeye. And don't lie and say you didn't!

Ciaran thinks on this, then says, We were talkin about work. We were talkin about the *lack* of work, what else is there to talk about? No jobs, bein paid pennies for movin *tons*, *that's* how much a bedplate to support a ship's engine weighs, *thirty-five tons*, so we try to stand up like men for proper wages only to watch some scab come and take our jobs for *half*-pennies and in the middle of that conversation if you happened to cross my line of vision maybe my mind was somewhere else, I hate to be the messenger of bad news but Extra! Extra! The world does not revolve around Theodora Brook.

Ciaran barely dodges a paving stone that whizzes past his temple.

Oh look who's shootin dirty looks now. Such an opinion about the war but no eligible men on your Irish side to be drafted, and colored *can't* be drafted so your colored uncles needn't worry neither. You got nothin to lose.

I hear him. And still see his glare from yesterday. And remember Grammy Cahill not seeing what was right before her eyes, the glowers in my direction, everybody in the neighborhood full Irish. But me.

And by the by, at the arsenal plant *I* was nearly *blown up* for the sake of this damned war, what do *you* care? Very well to take some *moral* stance, but *you*, you *personally*, Theo. What in the hell has the war to do with *you*?

I lean into his ear to hiss: I'm *black. Everything.*

The draft office erupts into flames. The crowd shifts madly—some scrambling away from the conflagration and others toward it—and in the rush I lose Ciaran.

Theo!

It's Abbie, looking petrified, and we start pushing ourselves out of the swarm. Some soap-boxer seizes the moment to stump for peace—and by *peace*, he means let the South and slavery be—and I swear I detect in his vowels the faintest sub-Mason-Dixon drawl.

Moving down Third av, we start to see very active rioting, though probably four-fifths of the throng are spectators dodging the flinging stones and flying glass. I remember how the near orderly demonstration on the piers differed from the makeshift rally in the Central Park which differed from the storming of the draft office, but there did seem to be some genuine unity of purpose in all those instances. These unruly mutineers before us now are something else altogether: utter drunken chaos. I hear a horse whinny and turn: astonishingly, the Third avenue streetcar is attempting to creep through the pandemonium. A shot is fired, and the unfortunate steed goes down, then *Get the nigger! We won't fight for niggers!* and several of the ruckus-makers yank a colored man off the vehicle and proceed to pummel him. Some of the onlookers cheer, most appear shocked and confused and appalled by this new development. I feel Abbie's trembling hand take mine, and I am at once profoundly aware that while my half-breed situation *might* allow me a pass, hers most certainly will not. We inch our way off Third moving west.

On Lexington, people have seized three-story homes, men digging up street cobblestones and hurling them through the windows. Women young and old, all Irish as far as I can tell, stand in the backyards cursing the bloody draft and cheering on their men and little boys who pitch out pots and books, chairs and mirrors *crash!* and very fine furniture, all raining down to be gathered by the ladies who haul the elegant goods downtown to adorn the lower-ward slums. I consider going in myself to see what commodities might make some nice items for Grammy Cahill's table when smoke begins seeping out of the windows. From one, wood shards start bursting and flying like popcorn, one charcoaled bit bouncing softly off my leg and landing at my feet. I pick it up, absently pocketing it, a souvenir, when Abbie grasps my arm, and I am jolted back to the reality that we have to get out of here, but how through all the congestion? My friend pulls me close to whisper: The Orphan Asylum. I nod—of course! The building is close, and the staff would surely shelter us an hour or two till all this blows over.

Cramming through the mob, I observe the taverns making a brisk business, a steady stream of customers flowing in and out the doors. In the street, like urban lumberjacks, men chop down telegraph poles, their axes glimmering with that newly store-looted glint, while women yank up the streetcar tracks with crowbars.

A huddle of men stumble out of a saloon behind us brogue-singing *We'll hang old Greeley to a sour apple tree! Our truth is marching on!* bringing to my mind a ghastly image of Horace Greeley, the wire-rim-bespectacled and balding editor of the pro-abolition, pro-war *Tribune*. And, as I remember now, a journalist who has long supported the worker standing up to his boss, so long as the worker didn't go so far as to strike. As the drunkards exit the tavern, some of them intentionally shove Abbie and me, especially Abbie. Some look at me through blurry eyes, trying to figure out what the hell I am. To the *Tribune*! one yells. Abbie and I keep moving west.

Caretakers at the Fifth and Forty-second Colored Orphan Asylum usher us in quickly. There is discord among the staff, some wishing to relocate everyone in the building, only to be answered with *Where? How?* Dr. McCune Smith is home ill today, and the physician in the building, Dr. James Barnett, keeps an eye on the street. I stand aside, baffled as to how it all happened. As if Abbie and I took one step out of Five Points into some alternate reality, some confounding bedlam from where all paths back to home have been closed off. We try to calm the frightened children, hoping the uninterrupted quiet in the neighborhood is a good sign.

It's close to four in the afternoon when we begin to hear the din nearing, and Dr. Barnett comes to warn the staff. Abbie and I join the adults, scurrying from room to room to gather the two hundred thirty-three orphans all in one place. I briefly glance out a window to behold a colossal mob filling Forty-second street, glowering at our building and wielding axes: *Burn the niggers' nest!*

When we are all gathered together, head matron Miss Jane McClellan softly asks the eerily silent children if they believe that God can deliver them from the horde. The children all nod, the staff nods, Abbie and I nod, but I'm not thinking Yes but rather a desperate Maybe! Maybe! Little Elijah, who must be eight now, has found me. I clutch his hand tight, his ten-year-old sister Nancy grasping his other. Miss McClellan now instructs us to pray and continue doing so until she gives us a signal to follow her, noiselessly, to the dining-room. And as we lower our heads, it crosses my mind that the simple, drab, but very neat uniform dresses worn by the orphans, with much gratitude to collections by colored women's charity societies, might seem quite handsome to the mob in rags on the street.

If there's a man among you with a heart within him, come and help these poor children! It is a distinctive Irish male voice that seeps in from the street, but the roaring in reply and the man's own screams clarify that his plea has been emphatically and savagely vetoed. Now I hear axes at the Forty-second street door, crazed voices, and my own heartbeat when Miss McClellan snaps her fingers once, and we open our eyes, all wiping away tears so we can see to file in behind her, silently. Elsewhere in the building, there is yelling and crashing and now a smell: burning. We exit through the back door onto Forty-third where we perceive a vast sea of rioters but, for reasons I can only speculate—more interesting targets on the other side of the street? A group ethos less inclined to attack hundreds of helpless weeping children?—we are not set upon. My last glimpse of the Colored Orphan Asylum is of flames bursting through the upper windows, and I turn away to see no more.

The staff hasn't any idea where to go for shelter but we are all led west. There have been rumors of colored refugees being harbored at the police station houses, so the school superintendent decides we should move toward the Twentieth Precinct building. I'm thinking it's a miracle that we have thus far stayed all together when Elijah, still holding my hand, asks, Where's Nancy?

And then I see that I and about twenty of the children have become separated from the rest! Thirteen-and-a-half-year-old me as the adult of the group! I try to remember where they said the station was. Thirty-fourth near Ninth? Or Thirty-ninth near Fourth? No! It *must* be Thirty-fourth near Ninth, we've been walking west! Stay with me, I order, the words quivering, tears streaming my face when I hear *Murder the damned monkeys!* just before I'm shoved forward.

We're surrounded, the mob taunting and swaying. *Those are some fine clothes you little niggers wear* and *Wring the necks of the damned Lincolnites* and *We burned the nest and we'll burn you*, and the children sob and I sob amid the yelling and the laughter and the loathing, and then a flock of young men charges into our circle, the children and I all shrieking, surely this is where we all die! when the leader speaks to the masses: *I'm Paddy McCaffrey, these men are stage-drivers from the Forty-second street line and these firemen are from Engine Company Number Eighteen, and we are here to deliver these children to safety. If you wish to object to our mission you might win, but we have enough firepower betwixt us to take quite a number of you down with us first!*

There is grumbling, but the Red Sea parts and, while our journey from there to Thirty-fourth and Ninth is hardly uneventful, the young Irishman and his team make good on their promise to bring us to shelter. Just before entering the police station, I look up and notice for the first time that the late afternoon air over Manhattan is darker than normal: smoke.

All the other children, including Nancy, managed to stay together with the exceptions of one little boy and one little girl who remain chillingly unaccounted for. We are first put into jail cells, but are moved when the cages are needed for the newly arrested and often bleeding rioters, the spaces rapidly filling beyond capacity. We now all stand in a passageway as there is no room for sitting. After some time, the police captain comes to see us and bursts into tears. He then begins shouting something at the officers. The children mistake this, believing he is howling at us and is about to turn us all out into the street, and momentarily there is mass hysteria.

Periodically, there are skirmishes at the door, rioters aware that the police are harboring negroes—there are other refugees besides the orphans—but the Metropolitans fend them off, firing their pistols into the mob and causing fast dispersions. Despite the weaponry, their favorable defense of us I find miraculous and heroic as the coppers are exponentially outnumbered. Their attitudes regarding our lot run the gamut, but even those police officers who are most resentful of the niggers taking up space do not regard us with the same unbridled abhorrence and revulsion they reserve for the mob.

By evening, we hear good news: the missing girl who had gotten lost in the multitudes was taken in by a kind white man, being sheltered in his own home. The missing boy had hidden in a dwelling near the asylum, alarming the white mistress who feared the rioters would target her house next. She asked for help from an Irishman who just happened to be passing by and just happened to have been employed as a mason by the Orphan Asylum for more than a decade. He wrapped the boy in cloth and secreted him to his own home, from where his daughter brought the child safely to the dwelling of a colored officer of the asylum. So *all* of the Colored Orphan Asylum children are now homeless but alive. I remember Miss McClellan's prayer.

Just before midnight, I hear rain and realize I need to relieve my bladder. I go out to use the privy in the back courtyard, which is protected by high walls. There is a long line, and I stand just inside the door, the police desk behind me, deciding whether I can hold it longer in the hopes that in the middle of the night there will be less of a wait, though that seems doubtful. And suddenly I feel a loosening in my stomach. Despite no food all day, I now need to do more than urinate and hope there will be newsprint still left in the water-closet to wipe myself. An officer enters through the front entrance, out of breath. I keep my back turned and my ears pricked.

We tried to cut him down. Clarkson street, but they. They wouldn't let us.

Silence.

We tried but they guarded him, their prize. They charged at us!

I'll confer with headquarters and let you know when it's time to go back.

Yes sir. But. With everything goin on, Captain, I don't know if sendin in some battalion of patrolmen to retrieve a body already dead's the best use of—

This is New York, officer, *not* the South, we don't just leave lynched black men hanging for show.

A couple of hours later, the rain begins to pour. I want to be home in my own shared bed with one of my grammies. I know my families are worried sick about me, I want to put their minds at ease, I want to go home. The rain doesn't stop and, because I no longer hear a distant rumble of deranged urbanites, I surmise the weather has proven to be a deterrent to the rabble. I feel uncertain about leaving the orphans, but then my absence would provide a little more sleep room for some of them. With children on laps, floor sitting-space has been somehow negotiated. I see Abbie sleeping down the hall, a little girl asleep on her lap and a toddler asleep on the girl's lap. I take out my charcoal wood shard from our earlier adventure in Lexington, and a piece of newsprint from the outhouse, and write GONE HOME. THEO, placing it in Abbie's hand, trusting she knows I'm wily enough to make it safely to Five Points and can convince the staff of the same. I move toward the door just as a rain-drenched officer enters in a frenzy.

We just shot into them! They were flyin up the steps after us, they *packed* the steps, men, women, children, we feared they'd torch the place with us *in* it! With *them* in it, it was madness!

Officer Murphy—

We shot, and the ones in front fell back causin a tumblin of the whole, some fallin over the banister five flights below, a boy who looked ten, he must've broke his neck! But they kept comin, and we shot! Women, children, it's all right? The jails are full, what could we do? We're after firin directly into them, *they kept comin!* And us *killin civilians,* sweet Mary Mother of Jesus they looked like my family! It's all right?

I have eased toward the entrance, but before I step out, I wait to hear the captain's reply. Softly he says, You did your duty, officer. These are *not* peaceful protesters. I was there when we were given the order, I do not believe Commissioner Acton came to his decision lightly, it was grim but it was clear: *Make no arrests.*

Outside, I am soaked to the bone within seconds. But the monsoon mercifully seems to have extinguished most of the active fires. I walk two blocks south, feeling relatively secure in the deserted city until I remember, according to that Metropolitan from earlier, that if I keep walking down the west side, I might pass Clarkson street and that hanged black man. I turn around to walk uptown, ten blocks, twenty, I keep moving north for reasons I can't say, thirty blocks, the rain pounding. Finally I turn east into the Central Park, stepping carefully into the blinding darkness, no sound but the occasional frog. A lightning flash and in the briefly illuminated world, I am terrified to have come across ghosts! I feel my breath intake but after this longest of days have learned well to make no further noise. Another flash, and I see that the ghosts are negroes, women and men, elders and children, silent and petrified and terrorized away from their homes, now saturated, now standing in the storm, hidden among a few trees and the newly planted saplings. Their eyes are at once alert and dead, and I realize my original assumption of ghosts was not far from the mark. And what did *they* see in the flare? A white girl? Irish girl? I move on so when the next flash comes, they might think they just dreamed me: a nightmare.

I come out of the park and proceed directly south on Sixth avenue, quietly but determined, the smell of smoke all over the city curtailed by the rain but still palpable. Anyone who sees me in the dark will likely mistake me for white, for Irish, and it *would* be a mistake. Tonight I don't feel half-Irish, don't want to feel *any* Irish. I think of how Auntie Siobhan sure knows her way with a brick-bat. Could she have been out there? With the brutes? *No.* She believes in abolition! But does she believe in the draft? And Great-Uncle Fergus—he was certainly putting up the fight with the Irish back in the 'fifty-seven riot (a minor altercation compared with today's calamity). My Irish family would never do anything to hurt me, but to them I'm not colored, I'm kin. In the beginning, Irish overwhelmingly signed up to defend the Union, but over time became disillusioned. In light of the draft, in light of the unjust commutation clause, in light of the terrible Irish losses at Antietam and Fredericksburg and Chancellorsville and Gettysburg, where exactly do my Irish relatives stand with regard to the *rest* of the negro race?

To imagine the viciousness I witnessed over the last fourteen hours from my Cahill dear ones seems preposterous. But what *does* make sense anymore? There was Paddy McCaffrey, I must remember that young Irishman who risked his life to whisk the lost orphans and me to safety. And the Irishman who'd called out, pleading with the mob not to attack the asylum, and the Irishman who had been a mason at the asylum and saved that stray boy. But the vast majority of Irish I've seen this day . . . What became of that poor colored man seized from the streetcar?

I'd pored over the *Dead of Antietam* photographs, I don't want that! I don't like war! But the South refuses to let go: the *peculiar institution*, as it is politely styled. War opponents speak of leaving the South alone, speak as if slavery is just doctrine, as if slavery is not *people*. As if the forced labor and lashing and raping and selling of human beings is in alignment with peace. Whites declared independence claiming *all men are created equal*, asserting *when a long train of abuses and usurpations evinces a design to reduce them under absolute Despotism, it is their right, it is their duty, to throw off such Government*, signing for liberation from tyranny with their right hand while whipping a slave with their left. They went to war to achieve *their* liberty. But *this* war. If the Union prevails, *this* might be the war to bring about *true* American freedom.

It suddenly dawns on me that the riot may have entered Five Points. I may come home only to find my neighborhood burned to the ground!— those tenements that house colored anyway. Fearing Grammy Brook and Gran-Gran, and further uptown Auntie Maryam and Mr. Samuel and Uncle Ambrose would be worried about *me* when *I* should be worried about *them*! The rain still pelting, and I remember the Weeping Time, the enormous slave auction and the sky opening up to mourn the horror of it, the utter depravity of humanity. And now I begin to notice that here and there I pass a person sitting in the street weeping, making them out by the light of a nearby pub or just hearing them in the darkness. Irish or some stripe of white. Colored people now can only weep in their hearts from their silent hiding places.

It's well past midnight when I enter Five Points. First I go to Abbie's tenement. Her parents are hysterical as I'd imagined, and embrace me with staggering gratitude when I tell them their daughter is safe at the Twentieth Precinct, adding warm tears to the cool rain on my shoulders. They have many questions but I tell them I haven't been home yet and need to go, which prompts Mr. Coppin to insist on walking me to Grammy Brook's tenement door, which incites Mrs. Coppin to argue that her husband as a black man is the most at risk so *she* should be the one to escort me. In the end, they both undertake the two-minute stroll with me to Grammy's building.

I ascend the stairs and as I push open the door, I hear the sharp intake of breath from inside, and I realize I've surely alarmed them as they couldn't be certain what demon might be entering. There sits Gran-Gran in her chair. And standing, all staring at me, all red-eyed and worn, are Grammy Brook and Auntie Maryam—and Grammy Cahill holding prayer beads and Auntie Siobhan.

They fly to me, and instantly we are all bawling, and the huddle then transports me to the couch, me sitting with a grammy on either side, Auntie Siobhan on the floor at my feet, Auntie Maryam gazing at me from her chair as if my presence here is a veritable miracle, and we all cry more. Their queries as to my whereabouts are rapid and multifarious, but I'm not yet ready to detail my long day except, between sobs, to say I was sheltered at the Twentieth Precinct station, and to gaze at them all, marveling at the sight of my black and Irish relations feeling like one whole family for the first time.

Theo, Theo, cries Gran-Gran. I cannot remember the last time I heard my great-grandmother utter my name, and I run over to embrace her tight, more whimpering. Which is when I notice the large hole in her window.

Happened in Five Points too, nods Grammy Brook, grave. Begun this afternoon. Put fire to our buildin! And next door, knowin they're colored. Then goin after the African Mutual Relief Hall, but the Metropolitans stopped all of it before the flames got goin good. Elizabeth Hennesy, woman my age over in Pell street, heard she got hit in the head when a whole bunch of em started throwin bricks at the colored houses there, but police come quick again. Seem she be all right.

That rabble got just what was comin to them, inserts Grammy Cahill. Dozens fallin in the street to be took to the hospital, on their way to the *jail*.

Then right before nightfall, we hear someone yell *The nigger cul-de-sac!* so we know they headed round the corner to Cow Bay, continues Grammy Brook, but all quelled fast again. We heard em just outside runnin their retreat, moved Mama away quick, just before the stone through her window. Grammy Brook sighs. Coulda been a lot worse.

Thank God it never took on like uptown, agrees Grammy Cahill, not that mighty mass evil. Nobody killed here.

Maybe the coppers came so fast because they *expected* the rowdiness would be here, says Auntie Siobhan. I swear most of the rascals were from outside Five Points. Sure *I* never seen them before.

Ya heard what happened to Philip White's pharmacy? asks Grammy Brook.

I shake my head, remembering the last time I'd been to that colored man's drug-store, picking up cold medicine for Grammy and seeing Mr. John O'Mahony of the Irish Republican Brotherhood/Fenians walking out with his own cure.

The mob came ready to loot and burn him down, but his Irish neighbors're after settin upon them and drove them away, says Grammy Cahill.

He'd always kindly extended credit to his customers, Auntie Siobhan remarks.

And Hart's Alley, says Grammy Cahill. The scoundrels enterin a passageway with a dead end.

Where, Grammy Brook picks up, the black *and* the Irish observin from their windows poured hot starch down on them, *that* was the dead end of their blamed invasions!

And if they decide to come back tomorrow, I sure know my way with a brick-bat, Auntie Siobhan winks, and I hug her, my tears streaming.

Grammy Cahill taps Auntie Siobhan. Go tell them—and my Irish aunt runs out to let Cathleen and Cousin Aileen and Great-Uncle Fergus know that I'm safe and home.

Hungry? asks Grammy Brook, and only because she's offered do I realize I'm famished, having not eaten all day. She boils a couple of eggs for me, serves them with a chunk of bread. My grammies chatter on, but Auntie Maryam in her wooden chair is quiet, half gazing at me, half lost in her own thoughts.

Went to see Sally up in Thompson street, Auntie Siobhan says after she returns, reclaiming her seat at my foot. The late mornin, when the rest of the city was berserk but the lunacy hadn't yet come to Five Points, askin if she and her lady friends would like to be sheltered up with my boarders for the duration. No, they wanted to stay and protect their house, fearin it'd be burnt to the ground. They were ready—the place a thick fog of steam from some concoction they'd whipt up, callin it the King of Pain: water, soap, ashes. Each and every one of em holdin a dipper: *We'll fling it on them and scald their very hearts out!* I worried they'd scald themselves, but they assured me they'd been practicin all day.

We are all laughing through our tears, then startled silent by Auntie Maryam's mirth abruptly transforming into a harsh sniffle. And suddenly I am aware of who's missing.

Where's Mr. Samuel? I ask, hearing the tremor in my voice. *Where's Nattie John?*

The baby's in the bed-closet, sleep, says Grammy Brook softly. Samuel . . . We don't know.

When things startin to turn, I come to Five Points, see if he here, cries Auntie Maryam, then answers the question by shaking her head.

When she come with Nattie John, says Grammy Brook, I went out lookin with her a while. Till things started whippin up local. She wanted to go home search her house again, I said *No*, you and my granddaughter will *not* go back. Not till it's over.

A large sniff slips from Auntie Maryam, then another, another. I want to go to her but, before I do, Grammy Cahill is there, gently caressing her back, humming something Irish and comforting. I stand up and walk to the bed-closet, peer in. Nattie John dreams, but her breath comes fast, anxious.

Haven't heard anything from Ambrose neither, Grammy Brook sighs, and then I remember that, unfortunately, he would not be in comparative safety at sea, that he had been ashore since late March when he'd come to Grammy's bloodied from the pier rampages.

We are still quietly chatting when the newsboys begin ushering in the dawn, abundantly more voices than usual.

Attack on the Ninth District draft office! Fires consume the surrounding tenements!

Armory at Second and Twenty-first besieged!
Colored Orphan Asylum burnt to the ground!
Negroes lynched!
Mayor's residence ambushed!
Police Superintendent John Kennedy beaten unconscious!
Ferries filled with negro refugees fleeing New York!

They won't be comin back, Grammy Brook mumbles regarding the last bulletin.

Auntie Maryam rushes out to buy some dailies, then sets them down and steps away, staring at them as if all at once gripped by terror. It takes me a few moments to decipher: a fanciful belief that there might be some word of Mr. Samuel within the columns until grasping that if Mr. Samuel's circumstances made their pages, the news could not be good.

Most of the papers seem more focused on damage to property than damage to persons, though a few are more enlightening.

The New-York Daily Tribune.

NEW-YORK, TUESDAY, JULY 14, 1863.

THE RIOT.

Relentless and cruel and cowardly as all mobs are, the actions of this at least are equal to any that have yet earned a record in history. "Pull down that d____d flag!" was their greeting to the Stars and Stripes. "Kill the d____d nigger!" was the infuriated howl raised at the sight of any unfortunate black man, woman, or child that was seen on the street, in the cars, or an omnibus. Resistance to the Draft was merely the occasion of the outbreak; absolute disloyalty and hatred to the negro were the moving cause. It was not simply a riot but the commencement of a revolution, organized by sympathizers in the North with the Southern Rebellion.

I thought they burned down the *Tribune*, I murmur. I heard something out there, about Horace Greeley. And the *Tribune*.

They're after tryin, says Grammy Cahill, then the police arrived. When the shootin commenced, it caused some kinda melee by City Hall, the park crammed with everyone fleein. Kept them from also tearin down the *Times* and *Post*, those neighborin buildings.

𝔗𝔥𝔢 𝔑𝔢𝔴-𝔜𝔬𝔯𝔨 𝔗𝔦𝔪𝔢𝔰.

NEW-YORK, TUESDAY, JULY 14, 1863.

There were probably not less than a dozen negroes beaten to death in different parts of the City during the day. Among the most diabolical of these outrages that have come to our knowledge is that of a negro cartman living in Carmine-street. About 8 o'clock in the evening as he was coming out of the stable, after having put up his horses, he was attacked by a crowd of about 400 men and boys, who beat him with clubs and paving-stones till he was lifeless, and then hung him to a tree opposite the burying-ground. Not being yet satisfied with their devilish work, they set fire to his clothes and danced and yelled and swore their horrid oaths around his burning corpse. The charred body of the poor victim was still hanging upon the tree at a late hour last evening.

At 1 1/2 o'clock this morning, Inspector CARPENTER, at the head of 300 Policemen, marched from the Police headquarters to take down the body. They had gone but a short distance before they were recalled to repel an apprehended attack on the headquarters.

Carmine street—so apparently a different victim than the one I heard the Twentieth Precinct police officers speak of, who was lynched in Clarkson street. I search for more information but the article doesn't refer to the murdered man again. Does this mean he hangs there *still*?

𝔗𝔥𝔢 𝔚𝔬𝔯𝔩𝔡.

NEW YORK, TUESDAY, JULY 14, 1863.

Although the community generally condemns the plundering and cruelty perpetrated by some hangers-on of the mob, yet there is an astonishing deal of public and private sympathy expressed in public places with the one idea of resistance to the draft. The laboring classes say that they are confident that it will never be enforced in the city, and that any new attempt will meet with still more serious opposition.

Fannin the flames, mutters Grammy Cahill shaking her head. Then she and Auntie Siobhan stumble home to their own beds, as Grammy Brook and I move into the bed-closet, barely able to hold our eyelids open. *Theo*! I hear as I walk into the room, Nattie John bright-eyed and ready to play.

❦

Grammy and I get a few hours' rest while Auntie Maryam, who can't sleep, watches over her foster daughter. My daybreak sleep is fitful, and in my waking moments I sometimes hear a distant cry from the street. Late morning, I emerge to find Grammy and Auntie Maryam at the windows. Five Points is quiet, people guarding their homes in defensive mode, but my grandmother and auntie listen to a few brave souls who ventured uptown and have returned to report that, the rains having passed over, the mob was already back in force by sunrise. A newsboy proclaims the latest from the battle front, something about General Meade and General Lee in Maryland, but we are all so caught up in New York City's own war that the other feels remote and irrelevant. I relieve Auntie Maryam of Nattie John, though my little cousin quickly grows impatient that my lethargy regarding our play is nearly as acute as Auntie Maryam's. We are on the floor behind her chair, and Nattie John's intermittent Where Uncle?—meaning Mr. Samuel—invariably evokes a shudder down Auntie Maryam's back.

In the afternoon, Uncle Ambrose walks through the door, and we rush to embrace him. Grammy had made pork-fat soup and serves him.

Some night, he softly says three-quarters of an hour later. He sits on the couch, Grammy and Auntie Maryam in the chairs, I on the floor staring up at him, Nattie John on my lap. Most of the Seamen's Home men left, but I stayed. They warned Albro and Mary, *Sooner or later the mob!* but they stayed. So I stayed.

Jeremiah? I worry.

Shipped out. Not back till next week.

I sigh relief. In truth, Jeremiah has not crossed my mind much since our afternoon in the Central Park, but I have a childhood attachment, having known him since we were little, he and Hen chimney-sweep apprentices for Mr. Samuel.

The stones started crashing through. And Mary and Albro Lyons and their grown children began using the stones to make a barricade against the rabble. Clever! Courageous! I joined in, and then, by some miracle, the fiends' attention was drawn elsewhere, and they moved on. Time passed. When it felt safe, just before dusk, the young people were delivered to some neighborly protective haven. But their parents refused to abandon their home and the business they'd built over decades—their rights as citizens! Colored men must be propertied to vote! As I once could, Seneca Village, when Eunice and I . . . Uncle Ambrose stops.

Their home saved? asks hopeful Auntie Maryam.

For now. The scoundrels envy their material wealth, prosperous negroes, and resent their abolitionist activities. So. We shall see. As I left last night, Mary and Albro sat together in their doorway, unwavering.

Just as Uncle Ambrose finishes his story, we hear an uproar and race to the windows. Rioters trying to force their way into the neighborhood have run into a wall of Five Pointers who must have been prepared to assemble at some signal. A shot rings out from an upper floor, and the invaders quickly scatter. A few minutes later, we warily return to our previous seats.

Where you been all night? asks Grammy. I was prayin you were on one a those ferries stuffed with colored people fleein the city.

After I left the Lyonses', I walked over to Dover street to check in on the Colored Sailors' Home. Uncle Ambrose sighs. It did not fare so well. The mob was already in the act of plundering William Powell's boarding-house when I arrived. As they were absorbed in their mischief, I was able to hide myself before any ruffians spotted me. Neighbors, predicting the horde would torch the house and likely bring down the adjoining homes, frantically removed their furniture to the backyards in the hopes of sparing their belongings. In this instance, the mob appeared satisfied with destroying the inside of the structure without setting it afire, leaving a shell of domesticity.

In the pitch black, an hour after the horde had moved on to other devilment, it occurred to me that perhaps the safest place to while away the night would be inside the ransacked abode, as it would be of little interest to the next passing huddle of looters. So that's what I did.

Early this morning, I found William Powell just outside, inspecting the ruin of his dwelling. As I walked out, he was naturally startled, not knowing who might emerge from the splinters. This is what he told me: From two o'clock until eight last evening, his terrorized family were trapped in their home, the demons beckoning outside. Eventually he managed to slip his wife, Mercy, and their children through their own roof to the roof of their next-door neighbor.

But, Grammy asks, isn't one a William Powell's daughters a cripple?

Yes! Sarah! William stayed to protect his home as long as he could until the throng finally broke in, and he was scarcely able to escape. By now it was pitch dark. Do you know who came to their aid? Their Israelite neighbor, lame himself! He took Sarah into his care. Despised by so many, and I have harbored my own enmity given the anti-war stance overwhelmingly embraced by Jewish merchants not wishing to impede their business with the South, but *this* man—this man has taught me not to prejudge, this precious Samaritan has earned my everlasting affection!

He sheltered them *all?* I ask.

No, that would have been too dangerous, but he provided rope for the rest of the family. They, including the women, clutched it like some trapeze act in Barnum's museum, managing to transport themselves from the roof of the five-story building to the next roof to the next, eventually lowering to the earth.

We all take a breath to picture and ponder that.

Things gettin any better, ya think? Auntie Maryam near whispers. Out there?

Afraid not, Uncle Ambrose says, though there have been changes since yesterday. The fire companies that incited some of the terror—now they all seem to have reformed and are on the side of vanquishing the mob.

Thank God, Grammy murmurs.

Is—? I begin. Is the mob different? Yesterday they were mostly Irish. Not today?

Uncle Ambrose looks at me and speaks softly. Yesterday the mob was mostly Irish. Today. As far as I can tell, *today* it is *all* Irish. Fueled by twenty-four more hours of whiskey.

You shoulda took the ferry away! cries Auntie Maryam. Samuel did! I know Samuel did!

Uncle? Nattie John asks Auntie Maryam. Now Uncle Ambrose looks around, suddenly aware of Mr. Samuel's absence and that it does not bode well.

꿍

The next morning, I wake just before dawn to hear some movement in the front-room. I walk out to find Auntie Maryam heading for the door.

Go back to sleep, she whispers.

Where're you going?

I got a errand. I be back!

It's not sunrise yet.

I be back!

I'll come with you.

No! Her eyes dart. Since the riots started, Grammy's insisted that Gran-Gran sleep with us in the bed-closet, and stubborn as Gran-Gran has always been about preferring to have the couch to herself, she has not argued. So now it's only Uncle Ambrose in the front-room snoring softly in a corner of the floor, and Nattie John sleeping on the couch next to where Auntie Maryam had slept, or not slept.

I had a dream, Auntie Maryam says. Samuel hurt, hidin in our house, if I don't get to him . . . !

I stare.

I have to go! and she quickly leaves. I watch her descending the steps at a swift clip, and after I hear her shut the downstairs door, I follow.

But she surmises this and is waiting right outside for me.

Theo. I'll never ever ask you another thing, just please please please stay.

You stay.

I *can't*!

Her tears stream. She turns, and I let her go, watching her disappear around the corner north onto Mulberry. Sweat beads on my brow, though I just stand still. The combination of nature and the numerous fires set all over the city promise that today is going to be the hottest all week. What *is* today? Wednesday? Wednesday.

I pursue Auntie Maryam at an undetectable distance. I'm not afraid, I tell myself, I'm not afraid. But I'm *very* afraid. Some in the mob might perceive me as Irish, others uncertain, and some will certainly detect my paternal heritage. Newsboys begin to appear, calling that the docks, the railroad stations, the roads north in Westchester County are all congested with multitudes of colored refugees.

The sky opens up, and the rain pours, always good news these days. I wonder if Auntie Maryam will reconsider her mission, but the deluge has not affected her stride: her rapid gait becomes no faster, no slower. We walk through the Teens to the Twenties to the Thirties, Auntie Maryam turning on her own West Thirty-second Street, and even half a block away and through the monsoon, I hear her scream, and I run.

The houses have been torched, her house—the front-room, her and Mr. Samuel's bed-closet, Nattie John's Room of Hope—ashes. And that isn't what has elicited the horrible sounds still emanating from her.

A black man hangs from a tree. His flesh appears to be universally bruised and slashed, his fingers and toes sliced off. We have come upon him from behind. I feel last night's pork-fat soup rising, burning in my throat. And now I notice the blood that covers this man is fresh, the culprits not yet far.

We have to go, Auntie Maryam.

I'm not certain how long she has known I've been with her, or if she realizes it only now, but she doesn't flinch, staring through the torrent.

I have to see.

Auntie Maryam—

I have to see.

She slowly walks around to the front of the corpse. Tears on her face but no cry in her voice when she states, That ain't him. Is it? That ain't Samuel. Is it?

I stare. The mutilated form seems larger than Mr. Samuel, but I really really really don't know.

No, I say.

She sighs relief, still gazing.

I didn't think so, she says.

And we turn and walk back to Grammy's.

❧

By late morning, the rain stops, and the torrid humidity returns. News-boys cry out yesterday's developments. The Brooks Brothers store at Catharine and Cherry streets, well known for the shoddy melting uniforms and knapsacks it sold to the military, was sacked. Army Colonel O'Brien, an Irishman who the day before ordered soldiers to shoot into hordes burning down buildings at Thirty-fourth and Second, was beaten to death. A calm speech was delivered by Governor Horatio Seymour to the mob in City Hall Park in which he addressed the rabble as *My friends!*

In the early afternoon, I lie on the floor where it's cooler, staring up at the ceiling. I glance at Grammy in her chair, sighing and far away. She has no intention of wandering into perilous territory to deliver whites for the damned whites, and surely the customers are gone anyway, rich enough to have fled the city. Blacks are not the only evacuees. The difference is that whites will likely return.

I hear a sobbing from just outside our tenement that nobody reacts to, not Grammy, not Uncle Ambrose, not Auntie Maryam, everyone staring at their own nothings. Not Gran-Gran, who's apparently looking right down on the weeper, spontaneous wails from the street lately having become a normal part of the Manhattan soundscape. Finally I sit up, walk over and look out. I leave our apartment, in no rush as I descend the stairs and out the door. Sit next to him.

Sorry! Sorry! Sorry! Ciaran says, wiping tears with the crooks of his elbows. He gulps big, and eventually the sobs subside. The ensuing silence is long, both of us staring out, not at each other. Somebody hammers, and I see a man on a lower roof covering his window in planks.

Monday mornin, Ciaran begins quietly. Cousin Aedan: *Let's go. Draft office.* I was confused but I don't argue. Don't know if you saw him, we got separated but he was there. So. We torched it.

Ciaran stops speaking long enough that I start to wonder if that's the end of the story.

We *torched* it, and it felt *good.* There's men says, Three hundred dol-lars, that's what an Irishman's life's worth to the government! I say they're wrong—*naught!* That's our value to the Powers That Be: see us, see *nothin!* But Monday, the draft office. *That* day they saw us.

Ciaran continues staring ahead. Then his eyes lower.

But the tenements caught. The nearby tenements, that weren't in the plan. No plan, but if there *were* . . .

A fly crawls up Ciaran's knee. His eyes on it, his mind elsewhere.

Peter Masterson's Black Joke Engine Company. Masterson's outfit right there, you saw em? Fire engine, well, I noticed no sign of them doin anything to put out the fires, then the Metropolitans arrived. The police arrived, chargin into the draft office to rid it of the damned invaders, I'm leavin! Shoved my way through the pack, found Aedan and let him know I was headed out *now*, at which point he let *me* know he'd no intention of quittin, things'd just gotten started. So I struck out for home alone, but. Ciaran sighs heavy. Caught in the crush.

He sits back against the tenement wall.

The army enters. About fifty convalescin soldiers, the Invalid Corps, well, all the able-bodied militias been sent to the front! So these recuperatin injured troops start tusslin with the horde, and at some point the terror sets in, and one of em makes a fool move, shootin into hundreds of fools, and that's when I manage to thrust my way through and out, runnin home to Mackerelville, shut myself in and stayed.

The fly on Ciaran's leg takes flight.

Aedan came home late, drunk and chatty. Kilt em. Soldiers who served, soldiers wounded in battle, these savages set upon two of em, bricks and clubs, walloped to a pulp. Then a third: chased to the river edge, flung to the rocks below, and in case that weren't dead enough, more stones hurled at the still body. Aedan imparts all this to me with neither glee nor remorse, himself a veteran sure as they but nothin to utter but *That's what happens*, shruggin, *That's what happens*. And after all that, from what I hear when the coppers got inside the office, they locked the draft records in a safe: protected and ready for the next lottery of names.

From the corner of my eye, I see Ciaran turn directly to me.

I'm sorry. The way I acted, the draft office, yellin at you. Two days ago. Feels like a month.

He takes a breath.

But I'm glad you went home. I saw you runnin off with that other girl, I breathed relief. Because things got pretty bad everywhere else after that, as I'm sure you've heard.

My eyelids heavy, I drop my face between my bent knees. I didn't go home. *Couldn't*, the *mob*. Abbie and I went to the Colored Orphan Asylum.

There is a silence that goes on too long, and I look up to find Ciaran gaping at me in horror.

But, I say, I'm glad to hear *you* went home. At least you weren't part of—

And his face a flood of tears again, no sobs this time but his breath heavy. I look ahead, sigh silent. Whatever next he has to say, I don't want to hear. Ciaran speaks softly.

All day, alcohol. Ye'd think Aedan'd be out cold all night. But restless, mutterin. Or singin: *We'll tie aul Greeley to a sour apple tree*. Or rantin, swingin his hands wild, the one with the thumb and the other without, sayin he fought that nigger war and any man's a fool to do the same, *that* sentiment he kept repeatin even in his sleep. Late next mornin, I go out to the privy, come back: he's gone. Mornin turned to afternoon, to evenin, to night. I'd no food all day and was hopin he'd be at O'Leary's saloon, where the men occasionally take pity on me, buy me a slice of bread.

Raucous. I didn't see him but if he *was* there, hard to know—people pushin their way in, pushin their way out, in, out, runnin to the tap then out to the streets. And these men decided as I'm fifteen, it's high time *I* take to the drink, and I reckoned it would fill my belly, and the men were buyin so I filled my belly and filled it and filled it more, then went outside to throw it up then back inside to fill it again. I was roarin when my bene-factors decreed it was time to venture out into the gallivantin night, and put their arms around me to drag me with them, this is the general sense of the situation as I recollect it through my blurred vision and whiskey brain. We fell in with a larger group that had a purpose and were led to Worth street.

Ciaran stands suddenly, taking a step forward, his back to me, hands on hips with thumbs in front, fingers clutching his lower back. His breath coming fast again. Then turns back around and, still standing, close to the tenement, leans his forehead against the building, eyes down, eyes closed.

The whore married a nigger, kill him. I hear it but don't understand. I don't quite understand but things startin to come clearer, I'm *startin* to understand, what I understand is I want to leave but can't, I can't get through the damned mass and here we are, how'd it come that we're inside? In an apartment, a basement apartment how many here? A hundred? *Two* hundred? In the middle the white woman holdin her mixed kids and they . . . They're beatin the boy with the butt of an ax and the spoke of a cart wheel, *a little boy* and I step forward: Stop it! Stop it, I say, Stop it—I say the words but can't hear em, scream the words but the mob's own noise is too great or. Or they don't hear because it's my heart screamin but my cowardice locks my tongue? *Her* screams are loud and clear: *For God's sake, kill me and save my boy!* She hurls herself on top of her son, which thrills the horde as it makes it easier to lay into her as well and it opens a path and I run. I could've jumped in with my body to shield the woman and her children, I could've started pummelin the demons, I could've run to the police! And hoped they didn't just peg me a drunk Irish rebel rouser and thrown me in jail or shot me on sight, but I ran. I ran home and cried and remembered my earlier thinkin about the government, the government and the gentry believin we're worth nothin and suddenly I felt if zero's what they think of *my* worth then they have many, many, many times overestimated it.

Ciaran's entire body trembles violently. I picture the terrorized family, wondering where the father is. Already murdered? And I am gradually aware that, because I don't know what they look like, in my mind I have replaced the father with the vision I've always carried of my own father, the woman being beaten: my mother. I am not the tortured boy but rather an onlooking sister, disconsolate yet oddly detached, as if I've always been aware of this scene's inevitability.

Aedan?

Ciaran answers my question with a vague shake of his head. Don't know, he whispers. He never came home.

Now, his hand quivering, he pulls out from his shirt a yellowed, crinkly old letter. Gingerly unfolds it and reads aloud.

> *My dear baby brother Ciaran,*
> *I have so longed to see you, and now at long last I shall! I cannot wait for you to meet my husband Colm, and your little niece. We will be so happy all together! And you will love America! Not every day is sunshine, but we always weather our storms. I have told my Regan*

that my little brother is coming to stay with us, her
uncle! She is still a toddler, but every morning she asks,
When will we see Uncle Ciaran? Soon! I tell her. Soon!
    All my love,
    Your sister,
    Meara.

There's a postscript with her address and your grammy's address, though I already knew it all by heart from her other letters.

Ciaran carefully re-creases the paper and puts it back into his shirt. 'Twas slipped into the other letter for my ma, he mutters. Fancy talk, from whoever she got to write it for her. Just like we always got someone to read and write for us.

He sits, but this time leaves several extra inches between himself and me, as if presuming I would no longer want him so close.

Went to Meara's grave this mornin. I was so hateful, I went to Meara's grave just to yell at her, *I wish I never came to America!*

Ciaran seems old, exhausted. Fifteen years of age, his face at first glance a baby's, at next ancient.

But when I got there. I couldn't tell her that. She just wanted what she thought was best, I couldn't tell her that.

A tear rolls down his cheek. In the still street, in the still, stifling air, a lone man walking his hog pumps water for the thirsty animal, then sticks his own head under. Elbows on my knees, I drop my face into my hands, tired, tired. Ciaran stands—boney-armed, frail, his eyes red and rubbed raw—and turns to me.

I lied to you.

I remember the deadness of Ciaran's irises when he first landed here as a small child. They gained vivacity over time but, at this moment, any light in them is gone. Not cold, but lifeless in their utter misery all the same.

I *did* give you the stinkeye that day with your grammy. I started to believe it. Slaves comin up from the South to take our jobs. And all I could think. Ciaran chuckles mirthlessly. All I could think is how you'd prefer that over a poor man like me. Well, you *should* prefer em, but not for their jobs. Because they're human, not *animals! Beasts*, we are! and the cry comes back to his voice. Irish died and died and died in this damned war, many times more than anyone else, *finally* we gain a little respect, and now . . . He shakes his head.

My trip to America was delayed. We'd replied to Meara but not heard anything back. Then Ma died, and the day before I boarded a ship to cross the Atlantic and be with my sister, I pocketed her written words. Took them with me walkin up from our scalpeen, up the mountainside, the landlord's sheep followin, to the peak to look across the sea, *beyond* the sea, hopin to catch a glimpse of America, a glimpse of New York! The soft rich green moss between my toes, aqua green of the Atlantic right there off the west Irish coast, how could I *miss* it? The beauty, the wonder right there in front of me!

Ciaran's eyes close. Then he slowly raises them and gazes at me for a long, long time. A sad smile, and he quietly walks away.

I turn into Grammy Brook's tenement, ascend the stairs. On the top step, just outside our door, Auntie Maryam sits wiping tears.

I weren't happy! I didn't mean okay they lynched that man long's it weren't Samuel! I didn't want it to be Samuel but that don't mean—that don't mean—

I know, I softly say, and sit with her a while.

In the evening, terror returns: mobs assemble outside the Park street colored tenements on and off, us all huddled in our windowless bed-closet. Miraculously, the police subdue the rabble every time before any further damage is wreaked.

The next morning, Thursday, the newspapers are full of hopeful tidings. Late last night help at last arrived: the 74th, then 65th Regiments of the New York State National Guard; in the wee hours, the 152nd New York Volunteers and 26th Michigan Volunteers; and just before dawn the New York 7th Regiment, increasing the five hundred fifty local troops to five thousand.

Mid-morning, Grammy Cahill and Auntie Siobhan drop by with non-alcoholic cider from Auntie Siobhan's tavern to hail the troops and their presumed extinguishing of the riots, a celebration I hope not premature. They have heard tell of residual scattered skirmishes uptown, but the latest misdeeds appear to be quickly suppressed. My Cahill family stand on either side of me, Grammy squeezing my hand, and at one point she whispers that Cathleen misses me, and I detect a faint worry in her tone. Then I think about their presence here with my Brook womenfolk three days ago, all praying for my safe return. I could just as easily have walked into Grammy Cahill's, but with everything exploding in the city, they intuited correctly which side of my family I would go to, and it occurs to me for the first time that my mother's family fears they'll lose me. When they leave, I stroll back with them.

I step through the door, and Cathleen and Cousin Aileen burst into tears, Cathleen waving me over so she can hold me, Cousin Aileen embracing us both. Great-Uncle Fergus stands, grinning through his own shining eyes: *There* she is! And then I notice sitting in the corner a new member of the household.

How do ye, Theo, he smiles.

How do ye, Finbar.

We didn't know, what with the mob showin up here and there, says Grammy Cahill. Invited him in.

And this time he accepted, says Cathleen, her warm eyes flashing in his direction.

Grammy searches her lean cupboard to feed me, treating me more like some guest than one of the family. After about an hour, I start glancing at the door. I feel a desperation from my Irish grandmother to hold me longer, I don't know how to tell her that I am not pulling away from my mother's family, I don't blame them, but right now, with negro New Yorkers facing sudden extinction, I need to be with my father's people. Cathleen seems to understand. Gazing at me with a sad smile, she gives me a quick, tight embrace: Don't be a stranger! Which is the catalyst for the rest of the family to start the process of hugging me in parting, then hugging me again.

On the way back I stop by Abbie's tenement in the hope that, with the recent military occupation of the city, it was safe for her to come home. Indeed, she'd arrived this morning. We fly into each other's arms crying, and I want to talk with her, or just be with her in silence, but I feel I need to get back to Grammy Brook's soon or they may start to worry, and Abbie's parents aren't yet ready to part with her so she can't visit me.

But my dear friend and I both know we can catch up in the coming days, weeks, years. Our whole lives ahead of us, which now promises to be a long time.

∾

In the late afternoon, Grammy Brook's door swings open.

Sam, Sam, Sam, Sam, Sam! Auntie Maryam flying into his arms.

But his embrace is confused. Mr. Samuel's eyes are wide and alert but seeming to see something we don't. We have him sit, we bring him water, soup. Three-quarters of an hour later with him unchanged, Auntie Maryam's joy turns into something else. *Sam?* As if she is no longer certain he's returned alive after all. He lowers his collar. An abrasion: friction from a rope. Auntie Maryam lets out a cry, then takes his hand and seems to count every digit: all there. And I realize she is thinking of the corpse we saw hanging on their street, fingers and toes removed.

They tried, he says, his first words since he walked through the door. He seems to be attempting to speak normally, but his speech is barely a whisper, so we lean in. They tried, he says again, then begins to weep silently, Auntie Maryam holding him and then his sobs come louder. This wakes Nattie John from her nap in the corner. She had been asking for her foster father all week but not like this, and when she runs crying into my arms, I'm not certain if it's because she doesn't recognize the broken being before her as her dear uncle, or because she does.

Half an hour passes, then Gran-Gran asks, *Het is voorbij?* Uncle Ambrose and I look to Grammy for the translation.

Yes, Mama, it's over, says Grammy, as if saying so will make it so. Then Grammy walks to Gran-Gran, hand on her mother's shoulder, both gazing out the window.

As it gets close to dusk, we all sit around in our own thoughts—me cross-legged on the floor, Nattie John quietly playing with my fingers as she falls asleep on my lap—when Mr. Samuel finds his voice.

Comin home. Monday. I saw the tide turnin, so walkin faster but they take me. Punchin, kickin, hundreds smashin me: a poker, shovel. Carry me west, I saw the tree prayed, God, God. Then the rope. Then you.

He turns to Auntie Maryam. You come to me, I saw you.

I know, says Auntie Maryam, the tears falling. I was there all the time, with you.

He clutches his chest.

Liftin me, I stretch my legs try keep my feet grounded. Then my toes. Then up, they got me, swing my legs, the rope rubbin, *snap*. Rotten. I come tumblin down. Fury, kickin me like *my* fault the rope broke, try again, *snap*, fall. Then somethin else come to em: horse n cart. They reckon the rope strong enough tie me to the cart, whip the horse, drag me to death. I'm tied to it, they smack the horse, I'm dragged! Not far. Horse stop, horse confused. Horse blind! Old and blind, afraid to move ahead. Somebody come along, I don't know who, someone come untie me. Hobble me to the police station, filled with colored people. There I been. Till now.

Nattie John, nearly asleep, murmurs *Horse blind*.

I heard some things in there, says Mr. Samuel. One police tell the story, that one echoin it to another, next shift. Names, though. Names I had to make special note of when they said em, mostly I just heard the colored this or the negro that or the nigger, when I heard a name I wrote it down, charcoal I had from all the burnins, I wrote it down.

Mr. Samuel takes out a newspaper page from inside his jacket. He has etched columns: *Mon*, *Tues*, *Wed*, with names inscribed under each.

Monday, he begins again, the East Eighties. Mob set upon Joseph Jackson, young man at work, gatherin dry food for cattle. Murdered him, threw his body into the East River.

Peter Heuston, dark-complexioned Mohawk maybe mistaken for black, maybe not, beaten severely and died at Bellevue today. His wife happened to've passed away three weeks ago, so their seven-year-old girl's an orphan.

Monday evenin, a few colored men jumped by a few Irish. Two a the negroes get away, the other only by shootin one a the whites. William Jones, a colored cartman, nothin to do with all this, just happen to leave his home to buy some bread. They grabbed him. Beat him, hung him, burned him to a crisp. And they wanted his body to stay swingin there: Clarkson street. Took a couple of attempts and hundreds a patrolmen before the police could take down his body.

Tuesday mornin, colored man steps into Leroy street from the Hudson, a seaman not aware the city's turned upside down. A white man named

Canfield come out of a groggery and asked the colored man's business. The colored man said he was lookin for a grocery store, whereupon Canfield and comrades-in-thuggery set upon the man, kickin and punchin, jumpin on his chest, droppin a small boulder on it. He was left in the street for some time, women and children starin at him, group of firemen walk by, look at him, move on. Two bypassers finally alert the nearest police precinct house. The victim was still breathin, put in a wagon to the hospital. Two hours later, he was dead. He identified himself at the end, but his voice was weak, so not clear if William was his first name or last. Or Williams.

Jeremiah Robinson dressed as a woman, fleein to the ferries with his wife and another woman. The horde recognized him as a man, murdered him, threw him into the river.

Tuesday night, a mob knocked on the door of the Derrickson family, who had a cellar apartment in Worth street, lettin the family know they had come to lynch Derrickson, who was black with a white wife. Derrickson managed to escape through the rear window, the family prayin that the mob would move on. Instead they beat a little Derrickson boy, and when his mother threw herself on him to shield him, they beat her worst.

I see Grammy glance at me, and realize I'd involuntarily shuddered.

They were able to wrest the boy away from his mother, took him to the street. Stripped his unconscious body naked, and while they were debatin the pros n cons a hangin him versus burnin, a grocer neighbor came out to chastise them. They prepared to hang the grocer, but the merchant had a pistol and quickly rounded up several German neighbors to back him up, and the mob left sulkin. Mother and boy in the hospital now, not lookin good.

Early Wednesday mornin, James Costello, a colored shoemaker, was chased by William Mealy, a white volunteer fireman and competitor shoemaker. Costello finally shot Mealy in the head, Costello then set upon by a few hundred rioters, beaten to death and hanged. His fingers and toes sliced off. This was West Thirty-second—and here Mr. Samuel looks to his wife. As I heard it, all the nearby tenements and houses was burned to the ground.

Auntie Maryam answers his unspoken question regarding their home:

a nod.

Plenty a room here, says Grammy, obviously a great exaggeration, and I remember being little and resenting newcomers Auntie Maryam and Ciaran taking up space in my homes, but now I nod agreement with Grammy's lie, and mean it.

Mr. Samuel has fallen silent so Uncle Ambrose speaks. Walked uptown a bit today, to hear the talk. People saying this is probably the end of New York City, they'll just close the whole metropolis down. I believe it.

We consider this, and in the quiet, I hope this is the end of Mr. Samuel's litany of atrocities. He always was sharp with facts, but right now I don't feel so happy that his mental agility came in handy. His soft voice breaks the silence again.

More yesterday. Augustus Stuart beaten by rioters, Seventh and Thirty-fifth. He ran away, then turned around to find whites in hot pursuit but this time they were soldiers he mistook for thugs. He fired at em, and in reply one took his sword, mortally woundin Augustus.

Samuel Johnson beaten near the Fulton Ferry, succumbin later to his injuries. Elsewhere in the city, his father had also been pummeled and miraculously survived, only to come home to his wife and dyin son.

Mid-afternoon: William Henry Nichols, in his young teens I gathered. Mostly women and children in his home, one a mother with a three-day-old infant when the rioters come, tearin her clothes off. Knowin colored males the most in danger, William Henry's mother rushes her son to the basement, where they and the others could see through a back window into the yard, watchin the newborn smash. Hurled by a member of the mob, the baby dyin on impact. The monsters axed the water-pipes, floodin the basement, forcin the refugees out. In the yard, William Henry and his mother were surrounded. The boy told the horde if they were goin to kill him, then please save his mother, which they did. A blow to the head with a crowbar, the boy expirin from his injuries today.

Abraham Franklin was a crippled coachman. Went to see if his mother was all right, Seventh and Twenty-eighth, when the mob stormed in. Beat him, set his mother's house afire, hanged Abraham from a lamppost in front of his mother. Soldiers arrived, the crowd dispersed, the soldiers cut him down, and as I heard it told more than once at the station house, he was alive. He raised his arm, he was alive, but the soldiers left him lyin in the street and left. So the mob returned. Hanged him again.

Now Mr. Samuel glances at Nattie John to make sure she's still asleep. She is, but he lowers his already soft voice anyway.

Then they started cuttin out his body parts. On a lark, some boy in his teen years started draggin him through the streets by his privates.

Mr. Samuel swallows. Seven-year-old Joseph Reed. Invalid boy, at home with his grandmother. Savagely beaten, the mob finally askin the youngster if he preferred to be hung or have his throat cut. At last rescued by a brave fireman, who carried the boy to a white landlady, who on her knees begged him to take the child away, fearin the mob. A German neighbor overheard the exchange and took the boy in. He isn't expected to survive the night.

Nattie John suddenly wakes and begins squirming, and I stand to move away with her, relieved to move away with her. I take her to the window, bouncing her and humming gently, feeling heartsick and destroyed and keenly aware of our good fortune. My family is scarred but we are intact. Close calls, but we lost no one. And my mother's family. Had any of them participated in the horrors, I don't think I could have set foot in Grammy Cahill's tenement again. But thank God they didn't have such ugliness in their hearts. These days have revealed in my city a distinct lurking viciousness I'm not sure I knew existed, but it seems for the most part my Five Points neighborhood has grown since its own racial rogueries of 'thirty-four that Grammy Brook remembers. And now my vision lowers to the ground.

It appears he has been there a long time, his eyes fixed on the spot where I stand. And now, because my eyesight is quite strong in the twilight, I can see the shine come to his eyes, the relief to catch sight of me, his smile melancholic and wistful but a smile all the same. He lifts his hand, a wave without movement, and while all the partings I've had with Ciaran over the years turned out to be so-longs, in this moment I know, and he knows, that this time it's good-bye for good: we won't be crossing paths again in this life. There's a number of poor New York Irish who've somehow found their way back across the Atlantic, and I hope that's where Ciaran's headed, where he might find some happiness, where he might make home. My own eyes water as I raise my hand to return the farewell, Nattie

John raising her hand because she's a little mimic, and Ciaran turns and in a few seconds is gone.

The next day is Friday, and in the morning we are speaking softly, reflecting on the week or doing our damnedest not to, when there is a sound outside our door, startling us to silence. We are all here now, my father's family, so who could it possibly be? The door creaks open. And, like with Mr. Samuel, I think we are staring at the walking dead.

Every negro I saw was in a panic, fleeing the city, I the only one moving in the other direction. I heard about the troubles but can't stop now. I'm coming home.

And Grammy Brook's apartment is flooded with tears again as we all fly into the arms of Auntie Eunice.

1878

Orphans

Hen pushes back from the table, from the empty plate where only minutes before had been a mountain of pancakes and sausages. *Full*, my cousin announces, patting a faintly rounded belly with a satisfied smile before grabbing the crutches, athletically quick on a leg and a half. At the doorway leading to the front-room, my veteran relation turns around.

Thirty minutes, I am reminded, or ordered, that vaguely commanding tone having been a part of Hen long before any military service.

I shan't be late.

And now I see Alma staring at the substantial remains on my plate with dismay.

I had plenty! Your cooking is delicious, Alma, but no one has the healthy appetites you and Hen have!

She finds this a grand compliment and smiles. Alma's very pleasing plumpness has finally returned after the years of scarcity. The Panic of 'Seventy-three brought about a dearth for several winters, but last year we finally began easing into recovery. Still, after all those punishing hard times in Five Points, this latest depression felt comparably manageable here in our quiet Albany corner.

I leave Hen and Alma's cottage to walk the twenty yards to *the house*, as we all call it—the two-story the rest of us share. The aunts are tending their garden as the heat of the July day starts taking hold. Auntie Eunice hands me pouches of freshly picked berries.

These are for Mrs. Heverworth, she says, as if I couldn't have guessed: fruits of the harvest in continuing gratitude for her providing our refuge.

The riots began on a Monday and spat their final sparks on Friday. There were those refugees who'd managed to escape New York in the early days, others who'd hid in the city under a pier or in a burnt-out building or in Central Park (to emerge starved after five days sans food) or shut up in their apartments praying for no unwanted visitors. The black exodus continued over the subsequent weeks and months. I believe the seeds of our own migration were planted that Saturday morning when Gran-Gran didn't wake. My family is in accord that her passing was not related to the week-long urban hysteria—she'd seen plenty of mob foolishness in her eighty-four years—but rather to Auntie Eunice's return the day before, permitting my great-grandmother Lioda Brook to sigh relief and decide now was a good time to make her exit while life was momentarily pretty good.

As Auntie Eunice explained piecemeal in the days following her home-coming, the day after Lincoln was elected she had been hit in the head and woke up chained and on a ship. Sold to a Virginia tobacco planter, someone ordinarily not as quick with the whip as Auntie Maryam's South Carolina master had been, but Auntie Eunice's voice had an uppitiness that unnerved him—he surely recognized the dialect of an educated North-erner, implying the illegality of her capture—and he was determined to beat that cadence out of her.

Rumors began to circulate of a Union contraband camp within thirty miles of the plantation. So, in February of 1863, after twenty-seven months of bondage, my auntie risked mutilation or death and escaped. *I just kept thinking about Nattie John,* she told us upon her return, though sitting in Grammy's tenement with her daughter a mere three feet away, my aunt seemed to have trouble just to look at her. By contrast, Nattie John had fixed her curious eyes on the interesting stranger in our midst.

Though there has been post-war testimony of abusive soldiers on some contraband camps, in Auntie Eunice's Virginia unit, so long as the escaped slaves did their assigned detail, they were left in peace. They were not exactly thrilled, as the chores often constituted working another planta-tion, but here there was one sharp departure from my auntie's existence of the last two and a quarter years: she began instructing the former slaves in reading. It was the first time she had resumed her role as teacher since the destruction of Seneca Village and Colored School Number Three, and the first time since November of 1860 that she felt something akin to hap-piness. She would have continued waiting things out on the camp till the end of the war, but then came the first case of smallpox, and quickly the second, and she knew she now had to find refuge from the refuge. Virginia to Maryland to free Pennsylvania, dozens of close-call episodes until at last she stepped off the ferry to home: the island of Manhattan, on a strange day when the boats were overflowing with negroes escaping it.

Word got around swiftly that Auntie Eunice had returned herself to us. We had quite a few visitors, a confusing time, our exuberance for my aunt's homecoming and simultaneous grief over Gran-Gran's passing in conjunction with the residual dispiritedness from the riots. Mrs. Heverworth came early on, dabbing her eyes with a cloth and speaking of those awful days when her husband, like other decent wealthy, rushed home to help protect the colored servants, inviting their families to be sheltered in the mansion.

A month later, Mrs. Heverworth paid us another call.

I am hesitant to bring this up. So many negroes have left—Manhattan is *conspicuously* whiter, have you noticed? I am loath to encourage more exodus, but I understand why our colored neighbors no longer trust the city. My husband and I. We have a few rental homes in Albany. Well, we'd be willing to sell. You could rent a few years till you've bought the house. I know your means are modest, and we are very willing to set the price within them.

It was not a terribly difficult decision. We expressed our sincere gratitude to our affluent benefactress but, in truth, we all believed this was a gift our dear departed Lioda had bequeathed: sanctuary in the city where she had found love so long ago.

The Heverworths were not alone in their generosity. There seemed to be an outpouring of altruism from some members of the have classes in the matter of basic relief and in arranging for the military to protect black employees at their jobs (lest the colored race become a burden on society). A week after the riots, the Merchants' Committee for the Relief of the Colored People Suffering from the Late Riots was established, setting up a depot on East Fourth street to offer clothing and money to survivors. Significantly, the organization relinquished its authority to distinguish between the deserving and underserving, handing all control to the good black radical Reverend Henry Highland Garnet.

In those fragile days, I was especially touched by the letter of one A. F. Warburton to the *Times*, an Irishman expressing his shame for the part his countrymen had played in the atrocities. (It is universally understood that he meant the terror inflicted against black New Yorkers—scores of incidents, including the outright lynchings—as opposed to the deaths of the terrorizers at the hands of police or by their own foolishness: getting trapped in a building they set fire to, etc. While there were exponentially more deaths of the perpetrators, they did not, as with the negro victims, involve unspeakable torture prior to the extinguishing of life.) Warburton laid out in specific terms, including his own financial contribution, how the Irish in America *alone* should rebuild the Colored Orphan Asylum, the widely accepted emblem of the week-long disgrace. *For the honor of that dear old Isle, let this work be undertaken at once, so that the smoking ruins of passion, prejudice and crime may be converted, by Ireland's sons, into a noble monument of liberal reparation and justice.* This sense of remorse sharply contrasted with many of the galvanized philanthropists who, while providing interim remedies, continued to condemn the impoverished rabble-rousers while never admitting to possible linkage between those days of tumult and their own three-hundred-dollar cut-rate exemption from the war. Ultimately it was revealed that the accusations of our then-Governor Seymour and on the street were true: the federal government *did* in fact set unfairly high conscription quotas for New York City, which is to say for the city's mostly Irish poor.

As it turned out, the asylum's founding and management by whites spurred many donors, Irish and otherwise, greatly invigorating its replacement: a temporary relocation just north of the city and government money available for rebuilding on the original site at Forty-second and Fifth. But wealth was moving into the area, and the same property owners who were outraged by the assaults on the orphans during the riots now insisted the replacement building be built someplace else. Eventually the institution settled at 143rd between Amsterdam and Broadway—our negro children's home now squarely in the farmlands of white Harlem!

The government was less forthcoming than the gentry regarding compensation to other black New Yorkers for loss of home, let alone loss of loved ones' lives. Those few victims who made claims were regarded with suspicion, reparations rarely awarded. Sleight of hand: The city ruled that if negroes fled their homes *before* the thugs had begun their destruction, then the plunder and pillage would be deemed an ordinary robbery—no restitution.

We moved into the Heverworth house September first, eight weeks after the riots, fifteen years ago. A peaceful area, the end of an old road at the edge of Albany. A palace! Two floors, four bed-closets! Grammy and I shared one, Auntie Maryam and Mr. Samuel another, Auntie Eunice and Uncle Ambrose the third, and the fourth and tiniest room was for Nattie John, close to both my aunties so she could be just as near to her dear foster mother as to the biological one she was getting to know.

Now I gaze at those ladies working in their garden hats. Our cultivated land here is many times larger than Auntie Maryam's little vegetable patch back in the city! Peas and squash are ripe, as well as potatoes, tomatoes, cucumbers, green onions, and my favorite: watermelon! Usually I'd be recruited into service, but they don't want me to get my travel clothes filthy. The women seem to have grown closer after our dear relation's return: my slave-born adopted auntie and my slave-made blood-relation auntie occasionally comparing lash marks on their backs and whispering of less visible, more private scars. To the rest of us, they speak little about their unspeakable ordeals. But once, not long after we moved here, I was walking by the tool shed and heard a tremendous wailing. I ran in to hold my sobbing Auntie Eunice, adding my own weeping but never questioning the precise memory that incited the present grief. As the bout subsided, my beautiful elder wiped her face and said, *Many slaves died before free, or searching forever and never finding family sold. Aren't we lucky.* Then she went out to collect the hens' eggs.

Manhattan's week of terror, which did not bring Uncle Ambrose quite so near to death as Mr. Samuel, appeared to provide an invigoration of the former. After his years as a broken man waiting for Auntie Eunice to return, her husband was able to nurse his wife's own broken spirit only until the end of the year before he was driven to sign up with the New York Twentieth Regiment of United States Colored Troops, the plans drawn up for the state's first negro corps with little objection after the riots. On March 5, 1864, there we were—Auntie Eunice, Auntie Maryam, four-year-old Nattie John, and I—waving our flags to cheer the 1,020 black soldiers marching down Fifth avenue, led by former police superintendent John Kennedy, who had recovered since his savage beating during the riots. We searched desperately for Uncle Ambrose (who'd mustered four weeks before on Riker's Island), then glimpsed him, and he saw us, grinning wide—a blessing, as it would be our last vision of him. The men were sent directly to the Department of the Gulf, and within weeks Uncle Ambrose would succumb to malaria in Louisiana. The estimate the authorities seem to have settled on for the Civil War dead is 625,000, 418,000 of which from disease. An astonishing 37 percent of all black soldiers would die in service.

Perhaps because the unimaginable of Auntie Eunice's enslavement and Mr. Samuel's near lynching were considerably more conceivable to my Deep South slave–born Auntie Maryam, she became the strength of the surviving household. She has thrived in the fresh country air far from the bustle of central Albany and a universe from Manhattan. Still, none of us is so naïve as to have proclaimed our new home some utopia. In our first years here, we were all disheartened, but not astounded, to learn that in 1793, after a fire destroyed buildings in Albany but killed no one, the Dutch hanged three accused slaves: Pompey, a boy not yet twenty years of age; Dinah, a girl of fourteen; and Bet, a girl of twelve. Still, our own decade and a half in the Hudson Valley has been mercifully placid. As I gaze at my auntie examining the corn stalks, her beautiful dark skin open to the sun and to the world, I realize I can no longer quite recall how she looked in her light-skin disguise, and I'm glad.

Inside the house, Mr. Samuel works on the whites for the whites. After a career of turning coal-black from the soot of whites' chimneys, now Mr. Samuel just wants to work at home and, if possible, to never ever see another white person again as long as he lives. They've reversed roles: Auntie Maryam out in the world collecting the laundry, and he confining himself to the safety of home to do it. Though he did make exceptions thrice: the April day in 'sixty-five when we all headed to the Capitol building in Albany, where Lincoln briefly lay in state before the funeral train continued on to Buffalo. (Later Auntie Eunice told us that assassin John Wilkes Booth, brother of the renowned actor Edwin—who was shocked, mortified, and disgraced by his brother's fiendishness—had managed to sneak into John Brown's military execution, nearly fainting at the sight of the hanging.) And in 1872 and 1876, Mr. Samuel went to vote. The Fifteenth Amendment guaranteeing all negro men the right was ratified in 1870, though these recent changes in the country—to wit, the dissolution of Reconstruction in the South —are of ominous portent.

In April of 1864, less than a year after Auntie Eunice had come back to us and our loss of Gran-Gran the next day, and as we had just begun the process of mourning Uncle Ambrose, Hen appeared. On top of all this emotional disorientation, the rest of the family had to get over the shock that Hen had not fled to Canada as they had been led to believe but had been on the front lines of battle, though my cousin's missing left lower leg certainly helped instill that reality. As for Alma, we all just thought what a kind, caring nurse to have accompanied her malmed patient home. By necessity, Nattie John was relocated to share Auntie Eunice's lonely bed—bringing mother and daughter together, a positive accident amidst the grief—so seventeen-year-old Hen and twenty-one-year-old caretaker Alma could occupy the small bed-closet. It didn't take long for us to realize Alma was here to stay and the implications thereof.

Grammy, finding happiness in now having all her grandchildren home, was noticeably more accepting of this Henry business than I. My foremost concern was my cousin's healing, so I held my tongue. *But*, I told my four-teen-and-a-half year old self, when Hen is well, we shall have a talk! This charade may have been expedient to maintain my cousin's male identity in the field, but it's time for it to end: Hen will have to be what Hen was born to be! Before my cousin had recuperated enough for me to enter into this discussion, however, I remembered Hen's dresses that never seemed to quite make sense, the chimney-sweep apprenticeship, the short hair, the pride and honor at the battlefront, and what Grammy had intuited finally dawned on me—that now, for the first time, Hen *was* what Hen was born to be. I've certainly never before seen my cousin so happy, frequently donning a big grin that's replaced the lower limb.

And now coming out of the house to work alongside my two kins-women is the third: Auntie Karimah. On Easter Sunday 1865, exactly one week after the Appomattox surrender, a woman knocked on Auntie Maryam's door: *I'm Peggy. I'm your sister.* Auntie Maryam was still an infant when her only sibling was given away, a five-year-old slave birthday present to a four-year-old white girl. After notes were compared and it became clear this was no mistake, Auntie Maryam had instant love for the sister she'd never before met. And there was a room, or would be soon. Nattie John's little bed-closet was tight for two grown women—we wouldn't have batted an eye about the crowding in Five Points, but in Albany: space! So, in a few weeks, Hen and Alma would finish the private cottage they'd been building on our property, and Peggy could move from the parlor couch to the small bed-closet. The common bond of my Southern relations became clear when the Fisk Jubilee Singers traveled through Albany years ago. My three aunties and I attended the performance, and Auntie Maryam and her blood sister knew most of the songs, slave spirituals that might have vanished from our history if it weren't for the Tennessee college choir saving the music in order to financially save their school. Peggy vaguely remembered their mother's religious practice, and Auntie Maryam schooled her in everything she herself knew about Islam. My new adopted auntie then changed her name to Karimah, and they created a mosque in the attic, which made me think of Auntie Maryam in our Five Points garret, performing her Muslim prayers there after she'd shooed all the squirrels away.

For a few years, Auntie Maryam had entertained a dream of taking President Lincoln up on his offer, bolstered by the majority-white American Colonization Society, to emigrate to Liberia. She longed to set foot on her mother's continent, the Mother Land, and wondered if living in a world of negroes might bring Mr. Samuel back to himself. But she reassessed her intentions after hearing too many tales of U.S. colored departing slave-culture America only to assume a master role on the other side of the Atlantic, instituting indentured servitude upon the native Africans. The whole repugnant irony left her sick and heartsore. She still often asks me about the Islamic west coast of the continent, or writes to our Nattie John with questions. At eighteen years of age, my young cousin has nearly completed the requirements for her baccalaureate degree at Oberlin College in Ohio. As for me, Auntie Maryam imagines I must have special access to the knowledge as an educator. Now twenty-eight, I've been a schoolteacher for a dozen years. I entered the profession here as a sixteen-year-old after a year at Albany Normal. I have chosen my occupation as have many negro women: the struggle of slavery finally over, we now heed the call to uplift the race. In answer to Auntie Maryam's questions about Africa, there doesn't seem to be enough information out there, but I report what I can find. The year chosen for her birth, the one I wrote in the family Bible so long ago, was 1831, which would make her fifty in three years, and she has vowed one way or another that she will see Africa by then, and her two sisters, by blood and by love, have sworn to accompany her. Will I be with them? I don't know what the future holds, but I find myself already imagining the wonder of breaking bread with my spiritual—and perhaps biological—sisters in a tribal village.

Across the way, I see Hen coming out of the cottage, Alma at her side. Though nimble on the ground, when pulling up into the wagon seat, my cousin invariably winces from the pain, which always pains me to see, and pains Hen to see me see. The first time I beheld Alma's eyes filling at the sight was the day I warmed up to her.

I'll just grab my hat and gloves, I call, a task I'd left till now so as not to witness Hen's struggle. I run into the house to retrieve them and, as I turn to leave, glance above the door at the items I'd nailed there when we first moved in: wool for my mother Brigid, who loved napping with sheep, inside a horseshoe for my smithy father Ezekiel.

I run out to kiss my three aunties so-long. I already visited Grammy Brook in the cemetery early this morning and apologized that I wouldn't see her tomorrow, but she knows we'll speak again as soon as I return in three days. Her heart took her last summer, and I have only very recently emerged out of that devastation. Seventy-two years of age. By a miracle, Jeremiah happened to be home from the sea at the time. He was a wonderful son-in-law, his addition to the family a decade ago inciting more living rearrangements: our one-room extension off the kitchen.

While I still lived in New York City, the only incident with my future husband that might have been labeled *romantic* was that single stroll through Central Park in the spring of 'sixty-three. But apparently he'd harbored great feelings, and when my family's imminent remove became known, he asked if he might write to me. Albany being the starting point of the Erie Canal, he was frequently here before shipping out, and began to call on me, though Grammy insisted these visits happen in our parlor or yard within her eyeview. I was eighteen and he nineteen when we wed.

Thanks to my powers of persuasion, but even more to the imperative of a teacher shortage, I was permitted to continue in my position at the colored school until which time I would become pregnant, Jeremiah and I repeating my dear Auntie Eunice's and Uncle Ambrose's teacher-wife/husband-seaman roles. I've never had to resign: it appears I am barren. Miss Irene, a local colored woman as skilled as (though less prickly than) Miss Philippa from Greenwich Village, has concluded some sort of twisting of my lady organs. My husband, who longs to be a father, has tried to be supportive of me in my distress over this, but it's difficult for him as it is hard to ferret out any distress. On the contrary, since the midwife's diagnosis, I can barely contain my glee. No pregnancies! Oh, I am very fond of children, something I discovered back in my own schoolgirl years volunteering at the Colored Orphan Asylum. But I've come to see that, while Auntie Maryam had a Room of Hope, mine is the Room of Ambivalence at Best. Perhaps my pupils, very precious to me, provide enough maternal gratification. Recently Jeremiah's times at sea have grown increasingly longer, and I have intermittently suspected infidelity, though that wouldn't quite make sense: I've never refused him intercourse. I think his absences are more logically explained by his sadness in knowing our nightly exercises are, in a literal sense, fruitless. I have broached the subject of adoption, which seems disappointing to him, but perhaps he'll adjust to the idea with time. Or maybe I should initiate a conference regarding an amicable separation. He could easily find a young, fertile wife, and it would make me happy to see him with his firstborn. And—in the hopes that the teacher shortage will rescue me again, this time from divorcée infamy—I could revel in my jubilant impotence. Well, we'll discuss our options when he is back ashore.

I walk over to the cottage and pull myself up into Hen and Alma's carriage—we call it that, though it's really just an old truck—tossing my carpet bag in the bed next to Hen's crutches. My cousin yanks the reigns, and old Buttermilk starts *clip-clop*ping toward the train station. I turn to wave at the three garden ladies, who are already waving back, and I wonder who else in the world is so orphan lucky as to have been born with two loving aunties and grown up to gain two more.

A vague, contented smile crosses Hen's face who, true to form, speaks only when spoken to for the twenty-five minute ride, and I speak little myself, my mind drifting back to the day of my cousin's homecoming fourteen years ago.

Started year before, Hen had muttered a few evenings after returning. Happen bout the same time as your draft riots. Honey Springs, Indian Territory. Enemy was the Twenty-ninth Texas, we whooped em. So now, April of 'sixty-four—Poison Spring, yes, that's what it was called, Poison Spring, Arkansas. Them white Texas rebs recognized us and wanted revenge on the niggers what took em. Also claimin we'd been lootin locally, true of the white Union, though not the Kansas Colored, but what we *were* guilty of they despised more: tellin every slave we see the Emancipation Proclamation happened. Tellin em to fight with us, and some a the First Kansas got a little rough if the slave wouldn't join, well, most a my brothers-in-arms had been slaves, seen the rebs and the bushwhackers slaughter their unarmed friends and family just for bein contraband, so reckon I couldn't hardly blame em.

We were down to half-rations, then quarter-. No rest. Then the officer discovered that five thousand bushels a corn, sent out a forage train to secure it. Starved and sleepless, and *still* when the rebs come, we held em two attacks. But the third. Decisive Confederate victory, and a hunnert eighty-two outa the three-oh-one Union casualties was First Kansas. No surprise, them puttin colored in front, but here's the thing: sixty-five wounded, a hunnert seventeen dead. How *that* happen? Dead always a fraction a the *wounded*, not other way round, once they're wounded they're outa fightin commission, let be for the infirmary or the cemetery. But in this case. In this case, the rebs went around *murderin* the black wounded. And murderin em vicious.

Miracle you with us today, Grammy had said softly.

Hunnert seventeen kilt, repeated Hen. Woulda been one eighteen I hadn't a played possum good. Choctaws was with the rebs, and just as brutal. Runnin over our dead n dyin with wagons, seein who could crush the most nigger heads. Somehow they missed me. Afterward, they desecrated the corpses.

Hen continued and I said nothing, but remembered again the generosity of the Choctaws, cold and starved on the Trail of Tears, who'd thereafter sent money to Ireland for Famine relief. Whatever I thought at the time Hen recounted this, I must have re-thought it in the ensuing years with the formation of the Buffalo Soldiers—black regiments so named by Indians as most were deployed in the wars against the Apache, Cheyenne, Arapaho, and Comanche, slaughtering by rifle or by starvation Indian men, women, and children. Just as my old friend Abbie once predicted would happen were negroes ever given the chance. And I think again of American Africans bringing forced servitude to Liberia—I shall never ever understand the contradictions of humanity. Those three ugly words Miss Fiona had uttered long ago: *Divide and rule.*

Hen and I arrive at the depot fifteen minutes early. Albany is the terminus, the train already in the station and boarding. I step down and grab my bag, then give a quick hug to my cousin, who responds with a subtle, manly tip of the hat.

My greetings to the O'Neills.

I'll relay them. I smile and hurry over to the ticket booth.

A half-hour later, I am gazing out the window onto the tranquil Hudson for the ride south. My eyes mist, recalling the last time I rode this train—five? no, *six* years ago, after receiving an urgent letter from Cathleen informing me that Grammy Cahill was on her death-bed.

My Irish grandmother was naturally heartbroken over my decision to leave the city. I was thirteen and a half, and she'd always assumed, barring her own passing, that she would see me grow into womanhood. The rest of the family were somber regarding my departure but not surprised: we had all just undergone a catastrophe wherein my father's people were the victims and my mother's people the victimizers. And yet it must be said, as conceded by even the most virulent anti-Irish press in the weeks following the madness, that while the vast majority of the New York City draft rioters were Irish, the vast majority of Irish did *not* participate and in fact condemned the atrocities, the racially motivated deeds in particular.

A man across the aisle in my locomotive car speaks sternly to the man seated next to him, grumbling about some item in his newspaper, and I bristle, detecting something Southern in his elongated vowels. And now the complainer's eyes rest on me, glaring, that old suspicion: What *are* you? And I am catapulted back to that ignominious day, the Dixie quality in that soap-boxer's voice after the draft office was set afire. There were those who'd theorized the riots were the making of Confederate conspirators and Copperheads, and there were some, but they appear to have been few and far between. That is not to say the South and its allies didn't cheer the horrors—riots having simultaneously sprung up in Brooklyn and other cities, though none so devastating as in Manhattan—but the reb-sympathizer dream that the rampages would ignite a great uprising against the war was quickly shattered. The ashes of the violence, in fact, brought about a great shame and the end of any Northern popular anti-war movement. New York City's Armageddon had postponed the enlistment process, but a few days later when the draft office resumed spinning the lottery wheel, there was no resistance (though still a goodly number of no-shows and defections to Canada). Moreover, a bit of a surge in volunteers occurred, and at this point there was no longer any ambiguity: the war was being fought to end slavery. Ciaran was part of that sentiment. Two weeks before our removal to Albany, I received a letter from him, not from across the sea in County Kerry as I'd presumed but from below the Mason Dixon in Maryland. Legally too young to be drafted, he'd walked into the recruitment office to volunteer, apparently adding three to his fifteen years of age, the enrollment agent never questioning the barely sprouted peach fuzz on his chin.

Several weeks before I'd received the missive from Cathleen, Grammy had begun suffering abdominal pain and, more alarming, blood in her stool. My Irish grandmother had been alone in her apartment those last two years since we'd lost Great-Uncle Fergus, run over in the street by a speeding stage, though Auntie Siobhan had visited her daily. The inflammation of the bowels had in no way affected Grammy's brain, so her memories were clear—of what a good granddaughter I was, accompanying her when she had to knock on the doors of the newly bereaved in the hopes of finding spoils of the dead to sell and thus prevent bereavement of our own. Grammy also shared a story I'd never before heard: being with my mother and me the first three days of my life and the last three days of hers. The way my ma held me, nursed me, ran her fingers tender across my lips. Grammy and I embraced often, and two days after my arrival came the evening my maternal grandmother dozed and didn't wake, Auntie Siobhan and Cousin Aileen and Cathleen and Maureen (who'd returned from the Far West years before) and I all around her. She was waitin for ye, Auntie Siobhan told me, and we all stayed up that entire night, embracing and laughing and crying and drinking Auntie Siobhan's whiskey to embrace and laugh and cry some more.

The train eases into the Harlem depot. I make my connection, taking the Harlem River Railroad south along Manhattan's lovely Hudson shore to disembark in the West Seventies. Houses have filled in considerably since my last visit. I turn into the single-floor dwelling on Seventy-third.

Come in! she calls.

The davenport and chairs are soft, a tasteful flowered print on ecru background. The room seems to have been freshly wall-papered, the air sweetly tinged by potpourri. I walk to the dining room, the table covered in lace and set elegantly: china tea set, crocheted doilies, and at the head and foot seated in their ultra-modern wood-and-wicker wheelchairs are Cathleen and our former war veteran beggar, Finbar O'Neill.

I know you're reserving your appetite for your luncheon, says my cousin, but a cup of tea and one crumpet you can manage.

I'll be staying tonight with Cathleen and her family and thus will return this evening for some special meal that she promises, but today I'll be making a couple of visits downtown. After I walk around the table to give Finbar a light kiss, followed by a warm embrace and many kisses to my cousin, we start catching up on news. I talk about my Brook family and my teaching, less about my marriage, the latter something Cathleen and I can confer on in private later.

Have you read about the developments of *Liberty Enlightening the World*?

I shake my head, wondering what scoop my ever-informed cousin has unearthed now.

The world's expo two years ago—the Centennial Exhibition in Philadelphia. Piece by piece, she's being created. They unveiled an enormous raised upper arm holding a torch. And now at the Paris Exhibition: her head! With a halo of seven rays, like the sun! The finished statue will be erected in New York, a gift from France.

Oh yes, I *have* heard of this! Where will they place her?

New York Harbor. Bedloe's Island.

Where that pirate was hanged? The one who murdered his shipmates?

The same! Her full body in robe, standing over a broken chain in honor of emancipation!

Truly?

Indeed! *Well.* It seems the French *intended* the chain to be quite prominent, but the Americans feared internal controversy. I imagine the compromise will be something comparably more subtle. And Cathleen rolls her eyes.

As we chat, I glance through the doorway into the workroom with the state of the art sewing *machine*. Cathleen had the talent, but how could it ever blossom when she had to seamstress morning to night? Then, 1864: Maureen strikes gold! The rewards did not exactly make her a millionairess, but they did provide supplemental cash (I'm *comfortable*, Maureen would chuckle, brandishing that gentry euphemism), and she returned from the West harboring an idea: bridging her sister's expertise with the fancy ladies she'd herself met during her work for the aristocracy. Betting on Mabel Carrington being the same glad-for-a-fad spoiled rich girl, Maureen offered her the double delight of both hearing adventures first hand from a female gold striker and commissioning a garment from a slum designer. Mabel was instantly intrigued but not prepared to part with money for a *completely* sight-unseen proposition. Then Maureen showed her some of Cathleen's crocheted brooches and napkins and, sans any conference with father or fiancé, the well-heeled young woman took the gamble. The fee included the material—and Cathleen's chosen fabrics were decidedly *not* shoddy—as well as labor, which Maureen as Cathleen's business representative set at a discount as a first-time investment toward future commissions, a number still exceedingly beyond any amount Cathleen would have dreamed of requesting. The blouse was a success, and Mabel proved herself useful by spreading the word among her upper-crust compatriots. Quickly Cathleen was making ladies' suits, cotillion dresses, even wedding gowns—Mabel's being the first. And of course her own: less extravagant but even more exquisite than Mrs. Tom Thumb's, in my opinion. All this income allowed my cousin, and husband Finbar as assistant, to work only a few hours a day while providing for themselves a very *comfortable* existence. Meanwhile, Maureen invested in I don't know what, but she seems to manage without working herself, living with her mother in Brooklyn. My gold-rich cousin could possibly run in the *nouveau riche* circles, but she doesn't seem to have the faintest desire to. Nor any inclination to marry. Miss Fiona, on the other hand, Maureen's partner in riches, discovered in Dakota Territory that she is a natural woodswoman, marrying some mountain man and living off the land.

I hear a ruckus in the parlor, and Cathleen and Finbar's boy and girl come running into the dining room, home from school for their mid-day meal.

Wash up first, Cathleen commands, then come greet Cousin Theo And don't wake the baby!

They rush off. I'd forgotten Cathleen had had a third! Must be toddling now.

How's Hen? asks Finbar.

The last time I'd visited, my Brook cousin had tagged along, muttering about seeing old haunts. We stopped in to Cathleen's, Hen not intending to stay long, but after being introduced to Finbar, the two crippled war veterans found they had much to talk about, comparing battle stories, and it got so late that my veteran kin wound up staying the night.

Hen is well, I reply, and sends warm regards.

Hi, Cousin Theo! says my grammy's namesake, little Eibhleen, making use of the new slang abbreviated greeting. She looks to be about nine years of age, and Conor about six, each of them holding the hand of a barely walking but widely grinning girl.

And who is this one? I ask.

Cathleen Junior! reply her siblings.

Such a Protestant thing, I know! says Cathleen. Junior, third. But I rather like that in America a *girl* can be junior.

They're *all* beautiful, I declare, and get out of my chair, stooping to gather my three little cousins in a fat embrace.

Back on the train, I head downtown to the Harlem River Railroad Thirty-first street terminus, where I emerge on Tenth avenue to walk south, then stop. First: three blocks north, just to acknowledge it—The police station at Thirty-fourth near Ninth that sheltered the orphans and myself. Thomas Acton, the president of the five-member Metropolitan Police Commission, was the man who came to the difficult decision to *make no arrests* of the rioters. I'd read later that he never slept the first seventy-two hours till the arrival of the military, ordering his officers to take in all refugees and asserting that the police will serve *until every man, white or black, can go anywhere on this island in perfect safety.* When time came for promotions in the succeeding months, officials who'd shown remarkably less courage and integrity were rewarded while Acton, the true hero, was overlooked. In other matters of injustice, of the few prison judgments meted out after the riots, the harshest penalty went to two Irishmen who stole a three-dollar hat (fifteen years' hard labor) while the mob leader who spearheaded the assault on the Derricksons—the bludgeoning of the white mother and her black son witnessed by Ciaran—was sentenced to only two years, an outrage that might be ascribed to racial bias as well as capitalism: our legal system's priority of property over people. Miss Derrickson's cry, *Kill me and save my boy*, proved prophetic: her son recovered from his injuries, while the mother died from hers a month after the incident. And seven-year-old Joseph Reed, as anticipated, did succumb to his own mob-induced fractures. Bitter irony: two days later, his Bermuda-born uncle, First Sergeant Robert John Simmons of the Fifty-fourth Massachusetts was captured by Confederates, also ultimately dying from his wounds. In the end, the official death toll for the five days of the New York City Draft Riots was just over a hundred, but those of us who survived the scourge maintain the true tally to be easily upwards of three hundred, and perhaps five.

Proceeding downtown, I gradually move east to Broadway—the buildings becoming taller, the infrastructure of urbanity: streetcars, stage and wagon traffic, lately a great confluence of criss-crossing wires overhead, and people people people. Passing Spring street, I look around at the new shops where once stood the second Barnum's. A fire consumed the American Museum in 1865, and the replacement here also burnt down just three years later. No human deaths in either, but terrified tigers and bears and zebras escaped the inferno to the street only to be shot dead by police, two beluga whales boiling to death in their tanks. I remember reading a few years ago about Barnum being strapped for cash from bad investments and wealthy Charles Stratton/Tom Thumb coming to the rescue. These days it seems sixty-something Barnum has undertaken a new enterprise: the traveling circus business.

I have reached Five Points. And despite the despicable events that drove me and my father's family away from the city, in my rare visits, when I enter *this* neighborhood, I cannot help but to feel I have come home. Still, the ward has changed dramatically. A few of the old businesses do remain, among them O'SHEA'S BOARD & PUBLICK.

Mo stoirín! my dear auntie cries as soon as I step into the pub.

Not so much of a *little* darling anymore, I'm afraid, I grin, and then we are hugging and laughing. The gray streaks highlight her red hair beautifully.

How's Eunice? she always needs to know first thing. As soon as I told her my father's sister had returned to us fifteen years ago, Auntie Siobhan had rushed over to see her.

Stronger every day, I respond invariably. Then Auntie Siobhan and I are chattering fast, catching each other up on six years of news.

Oh, I forgot my gloves! I got hot and took them off at Cathleen's.

Well, ye'll be returnin tonight to retrieve them, Miss Too Fancy for Naked Hands. And I hope ye're plannin to visit Eileen and Maureen in Brooklyn or they'll never forgive ye.

Tomorrow, I reply, as my auntie pours cider. We clink glasses.

You'd mentioned a Michael in a recent letter?

Auntie Siobhan shakes her head.

Haven't seen him in months—my choice, not his. After tryin marriage once when I was young, I reckon I'm happier without it. Lucky when that bastard died, he left me the public house. If women were allowed to make business on their own, I'd wager a lot fewer of us would walk down the aisle. Then Auntie Siobhan smiles. But there *are* exceptions. You have that handsome Jeremiah.

My husband had once stepped into the tavern to introduce himself during a Manhattan lay-over. *Well*, I begin, before telling her about my own marital struggles. She is quiet, listening.

Maybe we Cahill women just weren't meant for matrimony, my Theo, she says. The only one of us who settled well on that front is Cathleen. Speakin of which, you know I invited myself to your supper tonight. I'm snatchin every second I can get with my upstate niece!

Then she pours a shot of whiskey—*Tiny!* I plead, her serving larger— and we give a moist-eyed toast to Grammy.

After leaving my auntie's tavern, I walk to Baxter, looking up at Abbie's window. Two weeks after the riots, she and her family removed to Weeks-ville, one of several colored neighborhoods on Long Island just beyond Brooklyn (and perhaps a part of Brooklyn now, as the border keeps creeping further out) that was protected by armed negro sentries, wel-coming colored refugees during the strife and after. A year later, she, her black father, and her Indian mother packed up again, this time to settle in the Lenape community in Delaware that once served as a station of the Underground Railroad. My old boon companion and I corresponded a few years—I remember one special letter announcing her first child—but we haven't written in a while.

A block further, Grammy Cahill's tenement, where she lived till her death, is so dilapidated now I fear it might implode before my eyes. I walk back to Park, past where Grammy Cahill had once sat at her wares table, gazing at the new construction where our Brook home once stood. Five years after our removal to Albany, our tenement went the way of many of the old wooden buildings: burned to the ground. (Combustibility unrelated to race or riot.) I think of our old boarder Mr. Freeman, who seems to have fared well out west, according to his annual letters. He partnered with his travel companion, Josiah, to open their own barbershop, the clientele mostly colored men. He's married with several children he seems to dote on.

I stroll a block further to make a left on Mott, the street transformed by banners of red and gold, scripted with that curious Chinese writing. As instructed in the letter I'd received, I walk inside the building and up one flight, aware that I am not merely the only non-Chinese but also the only woman, though everyone seems to be too busy with their own concerns to notice or care. I step into the small second-floor restaurant, and at a table in the back, there he sits. At first sight of me, he stands, his lips part slightly. A good six foot tall now, slim as ever and a little worse for wear, donning a tan suit and a thick, dark mustache, but unmistakably him.

Theo, he says softly.

Good afternoon, Ciaran.

He pulls my chair out for me, and after I'm seated, goes back to his own, and now I notice that he moves with a limp, a cane resting against the wooden chair back. The smells are foreign but no less appetizing, and my near empty stomach roars. On my last trip to New York, I saw my first Chinaman—actually two Chinese men, chatting. But now to be in this humble dining room and hear the language everywhere, I feel like I just stepped off an ocean-liner docked on the other side of the world!

Ciaran has knowledge of the cuisine and, with my permission, orders for us both. The man with the long queue down his back brings the dishes, a deliciously spiced amalgamation of clams and sauce and vegetables and rice. As we dine, Ciaran asks about Albany, where he's never been, and I speak of its interest as a port city, although that distinction vastly pales in comparison to the port city we are now sitting in. I inquire about his family.

Two little girls, he says.

Yes, I recollect from your letter. Clare?

Clare's seven, he says, seeming pleased I'd remembered, and Meara's four.

Meara, I repeat softly. The sister in America he never met. We are mostly quiet during the meal. Shy, stealing glances. We haven't seen each other since he waved good-bye, looking from the street up to me standing in Grammy Brook's window fifteen years ago. What is there to say? Nothing and everything. When we are finished eating, I should be relieved that I can depart and end this awkwardness. But escape is not what I desire.

Would you like to walk?

As soon as the question is out of my mouth, my eyes drift to the cane, but before I have a chance to apologize for any faux pas, he says, *Yes.*

Outside, the consonant-based sound of the Chinese language permeates Five Points. There are still Irish but much less brogue, and a colored face is a rare sight. Ciaran and I stroll slowly in deference to his lameness, and begin playing *Remember when*: we used to race in the bowling alley? there used to be the black and Irish dance halls? we stood on the roof of O'SHEA'S BOARD & PUBLICK to watch the comet? Now a girl calls, Here's your nice hot corn, smoking hot, smoking hot, just from the pot!

I was pretty shocked to get your letter out of the blue.

It had been a month ago: the first I'd heard since that handful of missives from the front just after he'd volunteered. He pauses, as if considering his reply, eyes straight ahead.

Sweep for ya? a little girl in front of us asks. Her offer shames me somehow. We don't look fancy exactly, but we don't look Five Points anymore either.

Would you like an ear a corn? Ciaran asks her.

Yes! so he buys her one without having her waste her broom straws on us. We are in Bayard street. Ciaran looks around.

Things don't appear to have gotten any better.

They're worse, I mutter. When we were coming up, there were those who shunned us, but also charitable people who brought assistance if we could get past their condescension. Now with this new worship of commerce and industry, Rockefeller and Carnegie are the godly ones, and poverty the badge of sin. Henry Ward Beecher who was shouting *Abolition!* from his pulpit just a few years ago now enthusiastically espouses the new Ministry of Wealth!

I wait for Ciaran to comment, but he just nods, apparently agreeing but having nothing to add to my tirade. He seems to have grown into a quiet man. After a while, he speaks.

To answer your question, I knew I would be comin to New York today because *uuuuuuuuh!*

Ciaran stepped into a street crater!

Are you *all right*? I cry. I am reluctant to touch him, and at any rate he seems to have righted himself on his own.

I'm fine. It happens, he laughs softly.

From the war? I ask, eyes on his leg. Then think: what a stupid question. Where else would the injury have come from?

No—he starts. Then smiles and points.

The Italian man grinds a little organ, and a monkey does a dance! A new conglomeration of immigrants. I recognize the language from all the hours hearing opera outside Auntie Eunice's Academy of Music. I am delighted—till I remember our long-ago day in Barnum's Museum, and my second thoughts about all the so-called Living Curiosities, human and animal. We walk on.

My uncle volunteered. The colored troops. Died within a few weeks, malaria. Louisiana.

I'm sorry to hear that.

And my cousin Hen. Lost a leg, but survived.

Ciaran's brow furrows, trying to recall something. A scuffle ahead of us: white man and black man both trying to wiggle into the last space on a crowded streetcar. Somehow they both manage to squeeze in as the vehicle rolls off.

Hen! I remember her. The girl who could outrun all the boys!

Yes!

And now I see he's confused again, recollecting what I'd just said about Hen's military duty.

Cathleen is married—and three children! Did you know?

No!

She and her husband have a successful tailoring business.

What good news! he smiles. Then pauses. I was very sad to have missed Grammy's funeral. I didn't know she'd passed away until a year later.

We stroll quietly a while. Then I whisper: Listen.

Ciaran and I have arrived at the Academy of Music, which will always be *Auntie Eunice's Academy of Music* to me. We close our eyes: a sweet soprano in rehearsal. When the aria is over, we turn west.

My first battle, Ciaran begins. *Only* battle. Four months into my service, November 'sixty-three. Chattanooga. Almost six thousand casualties on our side, and we were named the victor. I was one of the casualties.

Children run screaming in front of us, and we pause to let them cross.

Prisoner of war. That was when I stopped writin to you. Ciaran glances at me briefly. My first letter, I told you that I needed someone to write to, and that it was fine if you didn't write back.

I feel the tiniest tremble in my hands. At the time, just after the riots, I didn't want to write back. And didn't think my decision through any further than that.

But I very much appreciated the one time you *did* write, to apprise me of your removal to Albany.

You're welcome.

I wait for him to speak again, then notice he's subtly trying to catch his breath. I slow down.

We prisoners were brought to Andersonville. Have you heard of it?

The Confederate prisoner-of-war camp?

He nods.

Yes. I can't remember the details but . . . It was bad. As I recall, it was very bad.

Georgia. Built to hold up to ten thousand P.O.W.s. I was one of more than *twenty* thousand. Captain Henry Wirz, the German-Swiss commander, would not allow prisoners to build shelters. Our daily food ration eventually dwindled to a half pint a cornmeal, three teaspoons a beans, and one teaspoon a salt. We drank water from the Sweetwater Creek, which was also where we relieved ourselves. Our ribs protruded, as did our eyes. I easily fell below a hundred pounds. My dreams were all of food, my nightmare was wakin. Dozens of prisoners died every day, thrown into a mass grave. I thought, *This* is the Famine. *Now* I understand it. This is the Famine.

He clutches hard on the cane.

But I wager few others were havin those thoughts. For the most part, they weren't from the Isle. The Irish Brigades had already been decimated by Antietam and Fredericksburg, Chancellorsville and Gettysburg.

I shudder, the word *Gettysburg* always inducing that reaction in me. The Irish brigades, comprised of the many thousands who volunteered for the Union before there ever was a draft, suffered the greatest losses by far in the war's deadliest battles. In Gettysburg, the final casualty count from both sides: *fifty thousand.*

One cold night, Ciaran goes on, some fracas in the camp. I've no idea what it was, but I saw the hole and took it. Fleein and hidin in the woods, livin off berries, a possum I killed by hand. Before the end of the war, Andersonville swelled to more than thirty thousand prisoners, *devils! Their* soldiers could have deserted rather than starve, but we were bound. And now so fashionable to lionize the Confederate officers, to turn gray privates into martyrs as if only *they* suffered, the Union *never* treated the reb prisoners so cruel! Barbarous!

Ciaran's eyes are wild, still incredulous.

After Appomattox, Wirz was tried and hanged.

Now a lengthy silence, and I realize Ciaran has finished his story. I begin carefully: Your leg injury. Happened in the battle?

He shakes his head.

Cousin Aedan once mentioned the railway in Memphis. So I walked— Georgia to Tennessee. No work left in the city, but wagonloads of Irish, veterans mostly, headin out to assemble the trans-continental. Ciaran chuckles. What kind of hogwash, buildin the Overland durin the Civil War! Sent us to Omaha, Union Pacific workin west to eventually hook up with the Central Pacific, them buildin eastward from California. The war long over by the time we finally come together May of 'sixty-nine, Promontory Summit, Utah. I guess I got a big head, the excitement of it all, because after all those years, it wasn't till the job was near done that I managed to sledgehammer my foot. Lost part of it, and if it weren't for a nearby digger from the Central Pacific patchin me up, I might've lost more, maybe my life. Ah Sing. We didn't speak the same language, but I knew to put my hands together like a prayer and bow my gratitude. Our work had been terribly backbreaking, and it was very clear to me that Ah Sing and his compatriots'd had it a lot worse. My oldest, Clare. Her middle name is Sing, after my friend. Julia found it pretty.

Julia?

My wife. Our Clare was named after Julia's dead mother.

I feel a twinge in my belly, then smile to myself. I knew Ciaran was married, and yet hearing him speak her name stirs up a flicker of ache. The marvel of puppy love—to imagine, after all these years, it would still have the slightest grip on me!

With the Overland complete, I poked about in the West a while. Then returned to Memphis, sharecroppin alongside colored. But I missed New York. Even after everything, I missed it! I was a tramp, hoppin trains north and wound up in Trenton. Reckoned I'd pick up a little local work, eventually make it to Manhattan from there. My veteran credentials helped me get some road building, even with the bum foot. And there I met Julia. So then I thought, All right. I assumed New York was callin me back, but now I realize New York was only there to guide me in the right direction.

Whoosh! We've wandered to Greenwich Village, and there it is above us: the Sixth Avenue Elevated! I had forgotten it was scheduled to open last month. I couldn't imagine what a train above our heads would look like, and glad the screech muffled my startled scream! Ciaran grins, looking up. We stroll under the line a bit, then walk east again.

Well, I believe it is now your turn to catch me up on *your* doins all these years.

I smile. Done some traveling myself.

Where?

I'm a teacher. I became qualified when I was sixteen, a few months after the end of the war. I went south.

South?

Since Southern law had forbidden slave literacy, the newly free were unlettered. Teachers were requested from every corner of the country. In the backwoods of North Carolina, my one-room school welcomed seventy-two students, the children I taught in the mornings, the adults in the afternoons. My youngest pupil was a three-year-old boy, my oldest a sixty-four-year-old woman.

Ciaran gapes, chuckles, shakes his head.

How long were you there?

Two years. But I missed my family. Naturally I didn't leave until I'd found a proper replacement. My pupils were sad to have me depart, the children especially took it hard. But the elders who'd lost children through slavery nearly kicked me out the door: Of course you must go to your people! Those two years—the most wonderful thing! To observe their grown children separated from them in bondage now, one by one, returning home! And so heartbreaking for the ones still waiting, hoping, having no clarity as to whether their sons and daughters, brothers and mothers were still alive, and the worse is the not knowing. I still feel a pinch of guilt for my selfish decision, but I'm glad I returned before I lost my grandmothers.

Selfish is *not* the word I'd choose, my companion remarks.

Ciaran, it was so exciting! Reconstruction! I count myself privileged to have been there, to bear witness. Negroes elected to the state legislature, and soon after my departure Southern negroes were on their way to sit in the House of Representatives in Washington! There was a chance, it was setting the country on the right path. Did you know of Thaddeus Stevens? White radical, House Republican from Pennsylvania strong-arming for emancipation, *he* wanted to confiscate four hundred million acres of Confederate land and give every adult freedman forty acres! Why *not*? The Confederates were *traitors*, and they *lost*—the spoils of war! And blacks the ones who'd tilled the land, Stevens knew the colored race *deserved* reparations, we needed a fair start! But Lincoln—God love him for ending slavery, but his desire to bring the country back together above all else, to kid-glove the defeated Dixie reprobates . . . Do you know the cause of our latest financial distress, the Panic of 'Seventy-three? It began with two brothers, two *white men*, one an investor in railways, the other the manager of the Freedman's Savings and Trust bank, the latter *embezzling money from unsuspecting freed negroes* to invest in his brother's venture only for it all to *fail* when the Dakota Sioux in no uncertain terms opposed the western train track, causing the Freedman's bank to fail and set off our latest national depression, and that *damned* contested election! That *compromise*, so now Republican Hayes is accepted as president so long as he appeases the Democrats by removing all U.S. troops from the South, no more protection of negro politicians, of negro voters, it's turning the clock back! This disgusting party system—anything to get a party member in office, even if that means doing nothing the party promised, doing nothing the party supposedly stands for! Why bother electing a president who will so bargain with the nonelected that the nonelected essentially won?

Here, says my companion, offering a clean handkerchief from his breast pocket, and I nod my gratitude, wipe my eyes and nose. I've never seen Ciaran in a suit before, and I feel sure it is his one and only. I'm touched he dressed so nicely for our meeting, but then, so did I.

You're right about all that. He is quiet in thought a moment. And you were very courageous. The violence against colored schools down there. You risked your life with the honor and bravery of a soldier.

I say nothing. I'm grateful for Ciaran's kind words but am still conflicted that my service was so brief. And now I remember how Jeremiah, not knowing when or if I'd be coming back, had waited for me. I hadn't asked him to, and felt guilty that he did. I very much appreciated his affection, or felt that I should. We married soon after I returned.

Quietly I begin again: I made one other long journey.

I feel the smile blossom across my face, warm my torso. I turn to him.

I went to Ireland.

He gapes. And now his entire body seems thrown into a cheer, even in his lameness.

Where! When! What did you see! How did you feel!

Three years ago, the summer after I'd turned twenty-five. I continued teaching back in Albany, and I saved money. My family's—*our* families' County Kerry, where I met dozens of relations—Cousin Aileen had sent me a list—and *those* cousins introduced me to others, though many more I found in the Famine cemetery. I had heard so much about the beauty, I was so eager to see the Ireland I'd dreamt of as a child. I braced myself for disappointment: How could it possibly measure up to my fantasies? It *far surpassed* them! *Nothing* could have prepared me for the richness, the green of the land and the green of the sea. The sheep! I slept nestled next to a ewe, like my ma!

Sleepin with the ewes, Ciaran whispers, and I can see I have brought back a fond and forgotten memory.

Then I traveled: The Burren. Cork. Dublin. Belfast. Ciaran: changes are happening! Well, after the nudging of some Irish Republican Brotherhood activity back in 'sixty-seven, who seem of late to have become rather agile with the bomb. There was the Land Act meant to protect tenants, though its complications rendered it more a gesture than a revolution. But it was followed by the Church Act, separating church and state: the people no longer pay tithes to the bloody Church of Ireland! *And*. There is now a truly robust movement for *home rule*: Ireland governing itself!

Hurrah! Ciaran cheers, and I do worry he'll hurt his leg but he appears to be in no pain.

I thought I would be drinking in the newness of it all, and there was some of that. But mostly, I just felt like I was coming home.

I knew it, he says, shaking his head and smiling. I always knew it.

We stroll a few minutes in silence. Then Ciaran carefully broaches: But aren't there laws against married women teaching?—and I see his eyes have settled on my wedding band.

Do you remember Jeremiah? One of the kids we raced in the alley?

I see Ciaran's mind working, trying to recall. He's the lucky one, then. Children?

I sigh. No.

Ciaran says nothing but I see the question in his eyes.

My body can't have any, and before you say anything else, let me tell you you will make me very angry if you say you're sorry. *I'm* not sorry! My mother died in childbirth, Auntie Siobhan *nearly* died . . . I sigh again, harsh and heavy.

He's quiet, looking straight ahead, his eyes moist, and I feel my heat rising. Does he pity me? Why is it that people can't believe a woman may not desire progeny?

Julia died, he says. Our second daughter was born. And I lost my wife a few days later.

I gasp.

Ciaran! I'm sorry! What I said—

It's all right. He swallows. She was really a sweet girl. A lovely, lovely girl.

I offer the handkerchief back to him, and he dabs his eyes. I gaze at Ciaran, wondering if he ever had a happy day in his entire life. Maybe back in Ireland, he should have gone back to Ireland. But he left the Isle at eight and a half years of age after his parents died, a precarious voyage to meet and be with his only remaining sibling and her family in America, who unbeknownst to him were already buried. I'll never forget the day he arrived at Grammy Cahill's, looking near dead himself. Was he ever mended, ever whole? As a child perennially in search of work—we all were, but there was something desperate in Ciaran's pursuit, as if in being of use he might find healing. Then he tried to make family with his older cousin Aedan who, last I'd heard, disappeared during the riots. And now to hear of the horrid P.O.W. abuse, and this Julia, the love he had at long last found and to have it taken from him, what misery! Ciaran and I were both orphans, but only I was orphan lucky.

But now I remember how his face lit up when he mentioned his daughters. *They* must provide him some happiness.

Where are the children?

With my wife's sister and her family, in Trenton. He smiles. They love their cousins, older than them. The construction work dried up, but I saw there was opportunity in the city. Have you heard of the telephone?

Yes, the newest apparatus. As I understand it, you can call someone without calling on them, I chuckle.

They were hiring a foreman, to supervise the layin of the lines. And Ciaran looks up to the crazy, convoluted wires in the sky.

I stay in the city Sunday night through Saturday, then take the evenin train to Trenton to spend the night and day with my daughters. I'm rentin the front-room couch from a widow and her daughter in Five Points.

You're able to ascend the poles?

Foreman. I work from the ground. I would never have been considered if it weren't that the man hirin happened to have been from my company. We saw Chattanooga together. And he seemed bowled over that I'd survived Andersonville.

I sift through all this a moment, then frown. But this afternoon we met for Sunday dinner. You curtailed your time with your daughters.

There's a weddin this weekend, my sister-in-law's cousin. They plotted the trip a while back, my daughters wanted to go. I didn't plan to attend, so I thought . . . A moment passes before he completes his sentence: I thought it might be a nice day to see my old friend.

We are suddenly pushed aside by an urchin running between us, a boy who looks as mutt-ish as myself, carrying two apparently stolen apples and running for his life, turning the corner to head downtown. Moments later, the pursuing copper appears, demanding, *Which way did he go?* and Ciaran and I both point north, sending the officer tearing off on a mission of futility.

Have you heard of Billy the Kid? I ask.

Sure. The West seems to have become quite wild, the bandits and the gunslingers. Like Five Points, with a lot more room.

He's *from* Five Points! There, or nearby, he was born poor New York Irish. Henry McCarty. Younger than us, just nineteen now. And an orphan. His mother had taken him out west. She took sick and he nursed her but watched her slowly die: consumption.

Ciaran nods.

He was a cowboy before a criminal. Worked a ranch for a Cork man, they both spoke Irish.

Truly?

So I've heard.

And now Billy a notorious outlaw, Ciaran murmurs. And after a pause: I hope he makes it.

So do I.

We cross Houston going south, the bell and horse *clip clop* of the streetcar approaching.

Ciaran. Whatever happened to your cousin Aedan?

He shakes his head. When I spoke to you, durin the riots. I saw him once more, the next night. Just long enough for me to tell him I was signin up for the army and for him to call me a fool and shake his fist at me, the fist minus a thumb. I never heard anythin else after that, all these years, so I imagine he died in the rampages of that week. I'd. I'd like to think . . .

Ciaran doesn't finish the sentence. We walk silently.

Then he breaks into a smile. Would you look at that.

I follow his eyes. We are at the corner of Broadway and Broome: Haughwout's Department Store. My old comrade turns to me.

Would you care to take a ride up in the elevator, madam?

We do! And it's just as terrifying (though exponentially less crowded) as it was that other time when we were kids, when it had just debuted as America's very first commercial passenger lift. We rise to the fifth and top floor, then step out, turning around to watch the metal box descend. Ciaran stares at it in awe, and then he speaks, and in his words I understand that it is not at the mechanism that he marvels, but this: We were children. *We were children.*

Twenty years ago, I say, though I'm certain he is speaking not just of the day the contraption premiered but about the whole of our extraordinary youth in poverty-stricken New York City.

I am now twenty-eight years of age—and a half! I laugh, which makes you . . . Ciaran! Today's your birthday!

'Tis.

Happy thirtieth!

Thank you.

As neither of us has the remotest desire to browse the extravagant merchandise, we go to stand by the large windows, gazing out. A breathtaking view of the city. *Our* city.

If we make it to our fifties, we'll see the twentieth century! I say. Can you imagine?

I can*not*.

A flock of pigeons flutters on the other side of the glass, just beyond our reach.

It bothers Jeremiah. He wants children.

I don't know why I utter this, our eyes still focused on the urban panorama. Perhaps because Ciaran was just so vulnerable in sharing his grief about Julia. Perhaps because we are old friends.

Sometimes. Sometimes I think the fair thing would be to leave him, set him free to find someone able to give him that.

A woman stands on the rooftop of a four-floor collecting her dry laundry. She happens to look up and see us, smiles and waves. We wave back.

It would be a sin, I suppose. Separating. You once told me I was a Catholic heathen.

And *you* replied you are only half-Catholic, half A.M.E. Zion, and while we still aren't facing each other, a giggle escapes my lips. From here we can look down on all the new telephone wires, such a mesh that I imagine if I were suicidal and threw myself out this window, I'd only be embarrassed by the multitudinous intersecting lines breaking my fall.

I'm hoping it won't affect my teaching position, I murmur. Married, though in my childlessness, they've thus far let me stay. But divorce? That might be a scandal too far.

How could they let you go? You're two heads smarter than everybody else. You always were.

The compliment catches me by surprise, my face growing warm.

An insane traffic jam is in progress just below us—a streetcar and a horse and buggy and a stage and a lot of yelling, and in the distance the remote whistle of the steam engine pulling the elevated train. Our city, where I was born and where Ciaran grew up. Where unbridled wealth begat unbridled poverty, a ticking bomb which fifteen years ago exploded into something vicious and depraved across our island, and yet. For the most part, our Five Points, the poorest of all, managed to rise above it all.

Ciaran stands to my left, our arms dangling at our sides, and now his fingers faintly graze mine, a touch so delicate as to be ambiguous, a place where he can easily back away should I demand it, and I demand it. A reflex, sharply pulling my hand back two inches from his, and he, respecting my response, moves his hands together, his right hand now loosely placed atop the left which holds the cane. How boorish to touch me like that in public! And knowing I am still a married woman! I'm now sorry I shared all that about Jeremiah and me, I'd no intention to provoke such a reaction.

And even if I weren't wedded, I've no time for foolishness. We no longer live in Five Points, and Five Points, at any rate, has changed. No more black and Irish intermingling freely. Recent laws ban Chinese men from bringing their women over, the world is closing up, or certainly this nation is. General Lee surrendered to General Grant, and what optimism there was in Reconstruction! But that grand dream was crushed, and if freed Southern blacks were never given their forty acres, and if a white man could be made responsible for freedmen's life savings and then callously gamble it all away, and if New York colored who lost everything in the riots never received reparations, and with the negro franchise currently under threat, how will future generations ever ever catch up with no economic foundation to start with? And now there is something in the South called Black Codes which, for minor infractions, sentence colored men to slave-labor prison, and there is something called sharecropping which sounds about a quarter-inch above slavery, and there is something called the Ku Klux Klan, and who won the war again?

And yet. The country is just a century old, and some would say it was newborn again in 1865, emancipation not even a generation behind us. That nation's a child, my Irish ancestors would say. A babe, my African ancestors would say. *We are just starting out.* And what possibility, our dear city holding it all: European refugees fleeing tyranny and starvation and black refugees fleeing southern terror, old settler progeny and new Chinese hopefuls, descendants of African abductees and descendants of the original people who've walked on this continent for thousands of years and all manner of immigrants imagining a new life: the great medley! *That* is the American experiment: our treasure, our promise. And grasping that richness, I reach over to grasp Ciaran's hand and feel him clutch mine fast and tight as, eyes brimming and hearts pounding, we look out on the magnificent potential of it all.

Anything can happen.

Postscript: Fact and Fiction

Moon and the Mars is a work of fiction inspired by real historical events. The central characters are created, but there are a few cameo appearances by real persons including Abraham Lincoln and others who may be less obvious: Jupiter Zeuss K. Hesser, German immigrant piano teacher and proprietor of Seneca Village's Jupiterville; John O'Mahony, the translator of *The History of Ireland, from the Earliest Period to the English Invasion* and co-founder of the Fenian movement; Dr. James McCune Smith, pharmacist and resident physician of the Colored Orphan Asylum; the homicidal pirate Albert W. Hicks; Mary and Albro Lyons, proprietors of the Seamen's Home; Dr. Elizabeth Blackwell (referenced at the wealthy women's tea), America's first woman doctor and founder and director of the New York Infirmary for Indigent Women and Children; Reverend Henry Highland Garnet, famed black radical and pastor of Shiloh Presbyterian Church; firefighter Peter Masterson and his Black Joke Engine Company; William Powell, proprietor of the Colored Sailors' Home; and Philip White, the African American pharmacist who extended credit to patrons and whose establishment was protected during the draft riots.

The human performers of Barnum's American Museum were all real, though they may not necessarily have been employed by Barnum's at the same time.

All of the named, and some unnamed, heroes of the draft riots were real. These include Colored Orphan Asylum head matron Jane McClellan who led the children out to safety, the Irishman who stood up to beg the crowd to spare the Asylum children, Paddy McCaffrey and the stagecoach drivers and firemen who rescued the strayed Asylum children, the Twentieth Precinct police captain who burst into tears at the sight of the orphans and did everything he could to protect them and the other black refugees sheltering in the station, those (including the Irish mason to the Asylum) who rescued the two stray orphans, Firefighter John F. McGovern of 39 Hose Company who rescued little Joseph Reed (who later succumbed to his injuries), the Jewish neighbor of William Powell who came to Powell's family's aid, and Metropolitan Police Commission president Thomas Acton. There existed a house of black sex workers who did indeed concoct the "King of Pain" for their self-protection.

All of the named victims of the draft riots, most of them detailed by Samuel, were real. Charles Baker, the black man beaten by the mob at the Watson tobacco factory and then arrested by police, and later released, was real, as was Elizabeth Hennesy, the black Five-Poinster injured during the riots. The murders of the convalescing soldiers at the draft office happened.

The names of the thirty-eight Dakota Sioux men (plus one whose sentence was commuted at the last minute) who were hanged in Mankato, Blue Earth County, Minnesota on December 26, 1862, were printed in the *New York Times* article that is referenced, but I used the names as identified, presumably more accurately, in the article "Names of the Condemned Dakota Men," *The American Indian Quarterly*, Volume 28, Numbers 1 and 2, Winter/Spring 2004.

All referenced news events and all stories called by the newsboys were real.

All newspaper quotations, when the paper is identified, are verbatim except that I have trimmed some and, in the interest of aesthetics, have not replaced the omissions with ellipses. Only once did I change a word: the *New York Herald* excerpt from July 11, 1863, erroneously makes reference to the Ninth District Draft Office on Third and Forty-ninth; I corrected this to Third and Forty-sixth. To the best of my abilities, I have assured that all edits have not changed the meaning of the original text.

I did not identify the newspaper that printed quotes from Union soldiers' correspondence regarding their opinions on emancipation because, to my knowledge, no such journalistic compilation existed at the time. The quotes themselves, however, minus proper ellipses, are real, as documented in Jonathan W. White's *Emancipation, the Union Army, and the Reelection of Abraham Lincoln* (Baton Rouge: Louisiana State University Press, 2014).

I made up the Black Seminoles song. "Battle Hymn of the Republic" was composed by Julia Ward Howe in 1861. All other songs are traditional or written/adapted by the composer that is named.

The text of the two runaway slave-bounty posters is accurate, except that I deleted the date of disappearance (which was a few months later in the year) from the one that is headlined "Mulatto Woman, Maria!"

I deleted some words of the Homestead Act poster, keeping, I believe, the gist of the message. The text of the advertisement for Lavinia Warren's exhibition at Barnum's American Museum constitutes the bulk of a lengthier announcement. The text of the advertisement for the Haughwout's store opening and its elevator is verbatim.

The extracted text from Archbishop John Hughes regarding slavery and abolition is quoted from an editorial written by Hughes that appeared in the *Illinois Staats-Zeitung*.

Last but not least, the moves in the dance hall that Siobhan and Eunice engage in reflect a mid-nineteenth-century amalgamation of African heritage stomping and Irish stepping that originated in Five Points. By the early twentieth century, this choreographic style became known as "tap dance."

Acknowledgments

I was very fortunate to have had a number of first readers, some who volunteered before I'd even asked. My undying gratitude to several who provided in-depth notes: Irishwoman Vona Groarke and Irish Americans Emily Daly and Kevin Hourigan as well as Rana Kazkaz (also for the Arabic translations), Cinda Lawrence, Catherine Mazur, Claudia Nys (also for the German translations), Moriel Rothman-Zecher, Naomi Wallace (also to her family for the Dutch translations), and my sister, writer Kara Lee Corthron. In addition, much appreciation to those who read and provided overall general thoughts: Nina Darnton, Iris Kinley, Michael Patrick Mac-Donald, A. J. Muhammad, Marina Shron, Cory Silverberg, Cori Thomas, and Michele Welsing. Thanks to Irishwomen Breda Stacey for some Irish words and Gina Breen for thoughts on Irish grammar and for consulting linguist colleagues, and to Gerusa Braz for the Portuguese translations. Ryan Opalanietet Pierce, founder and artistic director of New York's Eagle Project theater, served as the Lenape cultural consultant. (Thanks for the intro, Jen Marlowe!) Some of these names will be repeated below.

Harlem, New York City, has been my home for the last quarter-century, and while I love its ever-bustle, I am also exceedingly grateful for all the quiet spaces I was offered to focus on the book. I was granted residencies at MacDowell (twice), Blue Mountain Center (twice), Chateau de Lavigny in Switzerland, and Cill Rialaig in Ireland—and thank you, Cindy Cooper, for loaning me your phone while I stayed in that beautiful, lush, County Kerry middle of nowhere! Thank you, Rachel Jett, for allowing me a space in the National Theater Institute dorms. In addition, friends (many of them writers themselves) opened up their homes and a tranquil room: Joan Berzoff and Lewis Cohen, Kara Corthron and Tom Matthew Wolfe, Jennifer and Joseph Mazur, Tomas Medina, Cory Silverberg and Zoë Wool, and Naomi Wallace and Bruce MacLeod. I am wholly indebted to the hospitality in Ireland of Grace Wells in County Clare and of Michael Patrick MacDonald in Belfast during his Fulbright residency.

Michael provided me with incredible insights into Irish history, culture, and language, as well as an excellent reading list. He showed me around various parts of Belfast, and on another day Irish poet Scott McKendry (thanks for the intro, Tess Taylor!) gave us a tour of other neighborhoods, providing me with a more complete picture of the city, both Nationalist and Unionist.

Michael introduced me to his cousin, historian Brian Kelly, who kindly gave me a tour of Milltown Cemetery (graves of notable Irish personalities, including special plots for I.R.A. soldiers), and to his friend writer Michael Lee-Murphy, who also provided a rich window into Irishness.

Thanks to the Seven Stories gang for our second voyage together—for their belief in the book, dedication, and copious labor: Dan Simon, Veronica Liu, Ruth Weiner, Lauren Hooker, Silvia Stramenga, Stewart Cauley, Dror Cohen, Jon Gilbert, Nicki Kattoura. Much gratitude to fantastic freelance publicists Lauren Cerand and Yona Deshommes, and Copy Editor Extraordinaire Molly Pisani. And major appreciation to my dynamite agent Malaga Baldi.

I would like to acknowledge that this book was published in New York, which was originally a portion of the wide area on which the Lenape lived. That land, like most of this nation, was also cultivated in great part by Africans and African descendants in bondage.

I am a woman born to two African American parents. As far as I know, I am not Irish but, given my fair coloring, I'm a mutt like Theo, so who knows? Still, I am not culturally Irish, and my African American values spring from an era more than a century past the setting of *Moon and the Mars* and thus, in portraying characters so distant from my own experience, I surely have made plenty of mistakes, though a lot less than if I hadn't had the extraordinary consultation and suggestions of all the forenamed. That run-on sentence is a long way to say I hope readers can forgive most of my errors but, more importantly, please know that they are all mine.

—Kia Corthron

Bibliography

I consulted numerous sources in researching *Moon and the Mars*. In particular, I relied heavily upon five books:

Anbinder, Tyler. *Five Points: The 19th-Century New York City Neighborhood That Invented Tap Dance, Stole Elections, and Became the World's Most Notorious Slum.* New York: Free Press, 2001.

Bernstein, Iver. *The New York City Draft Riots: Their Significance for American Society and Politics in the Age of the Civil War.* New York: Oxford University Press, 1990.

Burrows, Edwin G. and Mike Wallace. *Gotham: A History of New York City to 1898.* Oxford, England: Oxford University Press, 1999.

Schecter, Barnet. *The Devil's Own Work: The Civil War Draft Riots and the Fight to Reconstruct America.* New York: Walker & Company, 2005.

Strausbaugh, John. *City of Sedition: The History of New York City During the Civil War.* New York: Twelve/Hachette Book Group, 2016.

The following is an abridged list of other sources I mined for content or used as inspiration. These do not include the many newspaper articles I already credited within the text of the novel. A few entries focusing on more recent events may be surprising for a novel set in the mid-nineteenth century but, in writing *Moon and the Mars*, I always strove to remain aware of the ramifications of the nineteenth century into the twentieth and twenty-first.

"1862 Dakota War: Minnesota's Other Civil War." ExploringOffTheBeatenPath.com

Aaron, Allen H. Patent: Seat for Public Building=s (folding chair patent). Patent No. 12,017, dated December 5, 1854; Reissued January 15, 1861, No. 1,126.

"Abraham Lincoln and the Election of 1860." AbrahamLincolnsClassroom.org

"Abraham Lincoln Visits Five Points." EphemeralNewYork.Wordpress.com, Oct. 15, 2010.

"Academy of Music 14th Street." EphemeralNewYork.Wordpress.com, Nov. 25, 2013.

"Academy of Music." NYCAgo.org/Organs

"Arrest of the Maryland Legislature, 1861." msa.maryland.gov

Amell, Robert. "The Big Picture of New York in the 1850s (Literally)" ManhattanUnlocked. Blogspot.com, May 19, 2011.

American Battlefield Trust. Battlefields.org

Andrews, Evan. "9 Things You May Not Know About Billy the Kid." History.com, Apr. 8, 2020.

"Aurora Australis: Magnificent Display on Friday." *The New-York Times*, Sept. 3, 1859.

Bailey, Anne C. *The Weeping Time: Memory and the Largest Slave Auction in American History.* New York, NY: Cambridge University Press, 2017.

Beard, Rick. "Lincoln's Panama Plan." *The New York Times* Opinionator Blogs, Aug. 16, 2012.

Beckenbaugh, Terry. "Battle of Island Mound." CivilWarOnTheWesternBorder.org

Bellis, Mary. "The History of Streetcars—Cable Cars." ThoughtCo.com Jan. 31, 2019.

Benjamin, Kathy. "The Sad Life of Billy the Kid." Grunge.com, Apr. 16, 2019.

Bentley, Rosalind. "How the 'Weeping Time' Became a Lost Piece of Georgia History: In Savannah, the Largest Single Sale of Human Beings in U.S. History." *Atlanta Journal-Constitution*, Mar. 2, 2017.

Bielenberg, Kim. "Is Shakespeare responsible for the 'stage Irishman'?" Independent.ie., Apr. 20, 2016.

"Black Civil War Soldiers." History.com, June 7, 2019.

Blackmar, A.E. "For Bales" song. Published New Orleans 1864. Library of Congress.

"Black Soldiers in the U.S. Military During the Civil War." Archives.gov, Sept. 1, 2017.

"Black Towns Kansas." SoulOfAmerica.com

Blight, David W. "Admiration and Ambivalence: Frederick Douglass and John Brown." The Gilder Lehrman Institute of American History. GilderLehrman.org

Boissoneault, Lorraine. "How the 19th-Century Know Nothing Party Reshaped American Politics." *Smithsonian* magazine, Jan. 26, 2017.

Boissoneault, Lorraine. "The Unheralded Pioneers of 19th-Century America Were Free African-American Families." Smithsonian.com, June 19, 2018

Bordewich, Fergus M. "Digging into a Historic Rivalry: As archaeologists unearth a secret slave passageway used by abolitionist Thaddeus Stevens, scholars reevaluate his reputation and that of James Buchanan." *Smithsonian Magazine*, Feb. 2004.

Bordewich, Fergus M. "John Brown's Day of Reckoning: The abolitionist's bloody raid on a federal arsenal at Harpers Ferry 150 years ago set the stage for the Civil War ." *Smithsonian* magazine, Oct. 2009.

The Bowery Boys/New York City History. "The Fabulous Former Fulton Ferry Terminal— And the Surprising Piece of It That Still Exists." Jan. 24, 2019.

The Bowery Boys/New York City History. "George Opdyke: The Mayor During the Civil War Draft Riots and His Unsavory Connection to New York's Fashion Industry." Aug. 16, 2013.

The Bowery Boys/New York City History. "Going Up: New York got its first commercial elevator 160 years ago." Mar. 23, 2017.

Brewer, W.M. "Henry Highland Garnet." *The Journal of Negro History* 13:1, Jan. 1928.

Briggeman, Kim. "1st Gold Strike in Territory That Became Montana Was 150 Years Ago." *Missoulian*, July 28, 2012.

Briggs, Amy. "Meet the 19th-century Political Party Founded on Ethnic Hate." *National Geographic*, Aug. 16, 2017.

Bristol, Douglas W., Jr. *Knights of the Razor: Black Barbers in Slavery and Freedom.* Baltimore: Johns Hopkins University Press, 2009.

Brophy, Alfred L. "Slaves as Plaintiffs." *Michigan Law Review* 115:6 (2017).

Brown, John. "Address of John Brown to the Virginia Court at Charles Town, Virginia on November 2, 1859." pbs.org

Brown, Lois. "African American Responses to *Uncle Tom's Cabin*." The Electronic Text Center, The Institute for Advanced Technology in the Humanities at the University of Virginia. utc.iath.virginia.edu, 2007.

Buchanan, James. Inaugural Address, Mar. 4, 1857. presidency.ucsb.edu

Burns, Ken, director. *The Civil War* (documentary). American Documentaries, Inc., Florentine Films and Time Life Video. Producers: Ken Burns, Ric Burns. Writers: Ken Burns, Ric Burns, Geoffrey C. Ward.

Calos, Katherine. "Brown's Island munitions explosion was worst wartime disaster in Richmond." *Richmond Times-Dispatch*, Mar. 4, 2013.

CandyGuy. "General Tom Thumb—The Most Famous Midget." TheHumanMarvels.com

"Casualties of Battle." National Park Service. nps.gov

"Cigar Shapes, Sizes and Colors." CigarAficionado.com, Nov/Dec 2000.

"Civil War Black Soldiers." CivilWarAcademy.com

Crawford, Amy. "The Slaves Who Sued for Freedom: New Research Uncovers a Littleknown Force for Abolition—Captives who Took Their Nasters to Court." *The Boston Globe*, Nov. 3, 2013.

Calomiris, Charles W. and Larry Schweikart. "The Panic of 1857: Origins, Transmission, and Containment." *The Journal of Economic History* 51:4 (Dec. 1991).

Catlin, Roger. "How One Mathew Brady Photograph May Have Helped Elect Abraham Lincoln." *Smithsonian* magazine, June 28, 2017.

Chaffin, Tom. "Frederick Douglass's Irish Liberty." *The New York Times* Opinionator Blogs, Feb. 25, 2011.

Champagne, Duane. "First Treaty Signed at Fort Pitt With Delaware for Trade and Alliance." Indian Country Today: Digital Indigenous News, Feb. 15, 2014.

"Chinese Immigration and the Transcontinental Railroad." Immigration Direct. uscitizenship. info

"Christmas Day in the United States." TimeAndDate.com

"The City: The Election Results Accidents Incidents. All About it. The Elections Yesterday." *The New-York Times*, Nov. 5, 1862.

Clausen, Carol, et al. "That Girl There Is Doctor In Medicine: Elizabeth's Blackwell, America's First Woman M.D." U.S. National Library of Medicine.

Clemens, Tom. "George B. McClellan (1826-1885)." Encyclopedia Virginia, Mar. 4, 2014.

Cohen, Michelle. "World's first streetcar began operation in lower Manhattan on November 14, 1832." 6sqft.com Nov. 14, 2016.

Cohen, Rich. *The Last Pirate of New York: A Ghost Ship, a Killer, and the Birth of a Gangster Nation*. New York, NY: Spiegel & Grau, 2019.

"Colonel John O'Mahony (1816-1877)." FenianGraves.net

Connell, Joseph E.A. "History—Irish Republican Brotherhood." Irishrepublicanbrotherhood. ie/history-irb

Connolly, Colleen. "The True Native New Yorkers Can Never Truly Reclaim Their Homeland." *Smithsonian* magazine, Oct. 5, 2018.

Conway, Henry J. Stage adaptation of *Uncle Tom's Cabin*, 1852.

Cook, James W. "Race and Race Relations in P.T. Barnum's New York City." LostMuseum. cuny.edu

Cruz, M. Dores. "Black Homesteading in the American Western Frontier." Oxford African American Studies Center. oxfordaasc.com

Cummings, Erica, instructor. "Role of Elizabeth Blackwell in the Civil War." study.com

Curriculum Concepts International. "Colored Orphan Asylum." Mapping the African American Past. maap.columbia.edu

Dabel, Jane E. *A Respectable Woman: The Public Roles of African American Women in 19th-century New York*. New York, NY: New York University Press, 2008.

"David Hunter." National Park Service, nps.gov. Sept. 21, 2016.

"Declaration of Sentiments" (from 1948 Seneca Falls Women's Rights Convention). National Park Service. nps.gov

DeCredico, Mary and Jaime Amanda Martinez. "Richmond during the Civil War." EncyclopediaVirginia.org

Deignan, Tom. "The St. Patrick's Day Parade." IrishAmerica.com, April/May 2006.

Dewulf, Jeroen. "Pinkster: An Atlantic Creole Festival in a Dutch-American Context." *Journal of American Folklore*, 126:501, Summer 2013.

Dewulf, Jeroen. *The Pinkster King and the King of Kongo*. Jackson, Miss.: University Press of Mississippi, 2017.

Dickens, Charles. *American Notes for General Circulation*. London: Chapman & Hall, 1842.

"Did Iowa Ever Pass a 'Black Exclusion' Law?" StateLibraryOfIowa.org

Diouf, Sylviane A. et al. "The Abolition of the Slave Trade: The Forgotten Story." Illegal Slave Trade essay. The Schomburg Center for Research in Black Culture, The New York Public Library, New York, NY, 2012.

Diouf, Sylviane A. *Servants of Allah: African Muslims Enslaved in the Americas*. New York, NY: New York University Press, 2013. (15th anniversary ed.)

Dolan, Patrick Terence, ed. *A Dictionary of Hiberno-English*. 3rd edition. Dublin, Ireland: Gill Books, 2020.

Dolkart, Andrew S. "The Biography of a Lower East Side Tenement: 97 Orchard Street, Tenement Design, and Tenement Reform in New York City." The Tenement Museum. Tenement.org, 2001.

Douglass, Frederick. Letter to W.R. (Women's Rights) Convention. ca. 1859. Library of Congress.

"Dred Scott v. Sandford" (1857). *The Supreme Court*, Thirteen/WNET New York, Educational Broadcasting Corporation, 2007.

"Dred Scott v. Sandford." *Oyez*, Sept. 19, 2018.

"The East Village, aka 'Mackerelville.'" EphemeralNewYork.Wordpress.

Duffy, Seán, general ed. *Atlas of Irish History*. 3rd ed. Dublin, Ireland: Gill Books, 2012.

Emmet, Robert. *Robert Emmet's Speech from the Dock*. 1803.

Etherington, Cait. "Life in New York City Before Indoor Toilets." 6sqft.com, Oct. 24, 2016.

Feinberg, Ashley. "19th Century New York Was Covered in an Insane Web of Telephone Wires." Gizmodo.com, Mar. 1, 2014.

Fenton, Laurence. *Frederick Douglass in Ireland: 'The Black O'Connell.'* Cork, Ireland: The Collins Press, 2014.

Fixico, Donald L. "When Native Americans Were Slaughtered in the Name of 'Civilization.'" History.com, Aug. 31, 2018.

The Five Points, painting, unknown artist, 1827(?). Metropolitan Museum of Art, New York, NY.

Flamming, Douglas. *African Americans in the West*. Santa Barbara, CA: ABC-CLIO, LLC, 2009.

Folsom, Ed and Kenneth M. Price. "Walt Whitman." WhitmanArchive.org

"Fortunes Made and Lost: The Panic of 1857." OhioHistoryHost.org

"Francis Johnson, 1792-1844." Archives.UPenn.edu

"Frederick Douglass." National Park Service. nps.gov

"Frederick Douglass." pbs.org

"Freedom at Antietam." National Park Service. nps.gov, Jan 27, 2018.

Freeling, Isa. "Black History Month: Black Theater in America Grows from Manhattan's 'African Grove.'" *New York Daily News*, Feb. 8, 2014.

Freeman, Rhoda Golden. *The Free Negro in New York City in the Era Before the Civil War*. New York & London: Garland Publishing, 1994.

Frick, John. "Uncle Tom's Cabin on the Antebellum Stage." The Electronic Text Center, The Institute for Advanced Technology in the Humanities at the University of Virginia. utc. iath.virginia.edu, June 2007.

Gallagher, Thomas. *Paddy's Lament: Ireland 1846-1847—Prelude to Hatred*. San Diego, New York: A Harvest Book/Harcourt Brace & Company, 1982.

Garfield, Leanna. "Incredible Photos of New York City When It Was Covered in Farmland." BusinessInsider.com Jan. 17, 2018.

Garnet, Henry Highland. *A Memorial Discourse*. Delivered in the Hall of the House of Representatives, Washington City, D.C. on Sabbath, February 12, 1865. With an introduction, by James McCune Smith, M.D.

Gasperini, Antonella, et al. "The worldwide impact of Donati's comet on art and society in the mid-19th century." The Role of Astronomy in Society and Culture. Proceedings IAU Symposium No. 260, 2009. D. Valls-Gabaud & A. Boksenberg, eds.

"George William Brown," former Baltimore mayor. msa.maryland.gov

Giesberg, Judith. "Explosion at the Allegheny Arsenal." History.net

Gilje, Paul A. and Howard B. Rock. "'Sweep O! Sweep O!': African-American Chimney Sweeps and Citizenship in the New Nation." *The William and Mary Quarterly*, Vol. 1, No. 3, Mid-Atlantic Perspectives (July 1994).

Gormly, Kellie B. "Sept. 17, 1862 — The Day Pittsburgh Exploded." *Pittsburgh Quarterly*, Fall 2017.

"Grand Emancipation Jubilee: A Night-watch of Freedom at Shiloh Church Great Excitement and Rejoicing Among the Colored People Prayers, Speeches, Songs, Dirges and Shouts." *The New-York Times*, Jan. 1, 1863.

Gray, Christopher. "Restoring a Richly Sculpted Venetian Palace (Streetscapes: The Haughwout Building)." *The New York Times*, Jan. 1, 1995.

Graetz, Rick. "Discovery Launches Montana Gold Rush." *Great Falls Tribune*, Sept. 10, 2014.

"Greenback." Museum of American Finance. moaf.org

Haberstroh, Dr. Richard. "Kleindeutschland: Little Germany in the Lower East Side." Lower East Side Preservation Initiative. lespi-nyc.org

"Harlem Village Farmland, 1820 – 1870." HarlemWorldMagazine.com, Jan. 9, 2014.

Harris, Leslie M. *In the Shadow of Slavery: African Americans in New York City, 1626-1863*. Chicago, IL: The University of Chicago Press, 2003.

Hawkins, Kathleen. "The Real Tom Thumb and the Birth of Celebrity." BBC.com/news/blogs-ouch, Nov. 25, 2014.

Hayden, Dolores. "Biddy Mason's Los Angeles: 1856-1991." *California History*, Vol. 68, No. 3 (Fall 1989).

Healy, Sarah. *A Compact History of Ireland*. Cork, Ireland: Mercier Press, 1999.

Heise, Kenan. "The 1860 Republican Convention." *Chicago Tribune*, Dec. 18, 2007.

Henken, Ted. "Black Neighborhoods Before Harlem." *Black New York: The Peopling of New York*. New York, NY: Baruch College, CUNY.

"Henry Highland Garnet." Biography.com

Hickman, Kennedy. "Great Locomotive Chase." ThoughtCo.com, Sept. 10, 2017.

Hider, Julia. "The Lost American Museum That Had It All." MessyNessyChic.com Jan. 12, 2017.

Hodges, Graham. "'Desirable Companions and Lovers': Irish and African Americans in the Sixth Ward, 1830-1870." In Bayor, Ronald H. And Timothy J. Meagher, eds. *The New York Irish*. Baltimore and London: The Johns Hopkins University Press, 1996.

"Homestead Act (1862.)" OurDocuments.gov

Howard, George, lyricist. "Oh, I'se So Wicked" sung by Topsy in a stage adaptation of *Uncle Tom's Cabin*, 1854.

Howard, Warren Starkie. *American Slavers and the Federal Law, 1837-1862*. University of California, 1963.

Hoyer, H. "New York, as viewed from Brooklyn-Fulton Street Ferry." Postcard photo. ca. 1860.

Hughes, John (Archbishop of New York). Editorial on abolition. *Illinois Staats-Zeitung*, Oct. 11, 1861.

Hugo, Victor. *Les Misérables*. France: A. Lacroix, Verboeckhoven & Cie, 1862.

Huston, James L. *The Panic of 1857 and the Coming of the Civil War*. Baton Rouge, LA: Louisiana State University Press, 1987.

Hyman, Tony. "Cigar Factories in 1885: Where They Were; What They Looked Like. A National Cigar History Museum Exclusive. CigarHistory.info, June 24, 2010.

Hyatt, E. Clarence, L.L.B. *History of the New York & Harlem Railroad*. Registered in Library in Congress, 1898.

Isaac, Ali. "6 Most Tragic Love Stories in Irish Mythology." AliIsaacStorytellr.co

"Irish Potato Famine: Coffin Ships." HistoryPlace.com

"Irish Republican Brotherhood—Fighting for Independence." ireland-calling.com

Jackson, Kenneth T., et al, eds. *The Encyclopedia of New York*, 2nd ed. New Haven, CT: Yale University Press, 2010.

Jacobs, Frank. "The Short Life of Little Germany, New York's First Ethnic Enclave." June 22, 2014. BigThink.com

Jacobs, Harriet. *Incidents in the Life of a Slave Girl*. Boston, MA: Published for the author by L. Maria Child, 1861.

"James McCune Smith." Consortium on the History of African Americans in the Medical Professions. chaamp.virginia.edu

"James McCune Smith." University of Glasgow Story. universitystory.gla.ac.uk

"Jennings v. Third Avenue Railroad Co. (1854)." NYCourts.gov/history

Jensen, Richard. "'No Irish Need Apply': A Myth of Victimization." *Journal of Social History* 36:2 (2002).

"John O'Mahony." LibraryIreland.com/biography

Jones, Jae. "African Grove Theater: The First Black Shakespearean Playhouse." BlackThen.com, June 2, 2018.

Joslin, Jeff. "Novelty Iron Works: New York, NY, U.S.A." May 28, 2019. Metropolitan Museum of Art, New York, NY.

Kappes, Alfred. *Tattered and Torn*, painting, 1886. Smith College Museum of Art permanent collection, Northampton, Massachusetts.

Kelly, Brian. "Gathering Antipathy: Irish Immigrants and Race in America's Age of Emancipation" in Johanne Devlin Trew, Michael Pierse (eds.), *Rethinking the Irish Diaspora: After the Gathering*. United Kingdom. Palgrave Macmillan, 2018.

Khomina, Anna. "The Homestead Act of 1862." USHistoryscene.com

Kidger, Mark R. "The Frequency of Appearance of Bright Naked Eye Comets Since 1750." *Instituto de Astrofísica de Canarias, E-38200 La Laguna, Tenerife, Spain*. Sept. 22, 1994.

Kim, Chloe. "Lincoln Ordered Execution of Dozens of Sioux Warriors, Commuted Sentences of Others." APNews.com. Dec. 31, 2018.

Kinealy, Christine. "The Black O'Connell." IrishAmerica.com, Oct./Nov. 2013.

Kinealy, Christine. "The Irish Abolitionist: Daniel O'Connell." IrishAmerica.com, Aug./Sept. 2011.

Kunhardt, Jr., Philip B., Kunhardt III, Philip B.; and Kunhardt, Peter W. *P.T. Barnum: America's Greatest Showman*. New York, NY: Alfred A. Knopf, 1995.

Lane, Fitz Hugh. New York Harbor 1860. Painting, 1860.

Laskow, Sarah. "The Forgotten Black Pioneers Who Settled the Midwest." AtlasObscura.com June 14, 2018.

Lepore, Jill. "Jill Lepore: Abraham Lincoln's 100 Days." *The New Yorker*, Apr. 29, 2009.

Lepore, Jill. *These Truths*. New York, NY: W.W. Norton, 2018.

Levine, David. "African American History: A Past Rooted in the Hudson Valley." *Hudson Valley Magazine*, Feb. 2017.

Lewis, Jone Johnson. "National Woman's Rights Conventions, 1850–1869." ThoughtCo.com, Mar. 17, 2018.

Library of Congress—Today in History, August 24. "The Panic of 1857."

Lincoln, Abraham. "Address on Colonization to a Deputation of Negroes." Collected Works of Abraham Lincoln, Vol. 5. Ann Arbor, MI: University of Michigan Digital Library Production Services, 2001.

Lincoln, Abraham. "Cooper Union Address." New York City, Feb. 27, 1860.

Lincoln, Abraham. "Message to the Senate Responding to the Resolution Regarding Indian Barbarities in the State of Minnesota." Dec. 11, 1862.

"Lincoln Arrives in Washington." History.com, Nov. 13, 2009.

"Lincoln's Funeral Train in Albany: 1865." FriendsOfAlbanyHistory.WordPress.com, Jan. 11, 2018.

Litton, Helen. *Irish Rebellions: 1798-1921*. Dublin, Ireland: The O'Brien Press, 2018.

Lynch, Suzanne. "Choctaw Generosity to Famine Ireland Saluted by Varadkar: 'The Choctaw family identified with the anguish, the spread of disease and starvation.'" *Irish Times*, Mar. 23, 2018.

MacDonald, Michael Patrick. *All Souls: A Family Story from Southie*. Boston, MA: Beacon, 2008

MacGuill, Dan. "Did Abraham Lincoln Order the Execution of 38 Dakota Fighters?" snopes.com, Mar. 14, 2018.

"Mackerelville." mingum.blogspot.com, Nov. 9, 2009.

Man, Albon P. "Labor Competition and the New York Draft Riots of 1863." *The Journal of Negro History*, Vol. 36, No. 4 (Oct., 1951).

"Man Wants Glory for Black Civil War Soldiers; First Troops Killed in Missouri Battle, Not in South Carolina." *Baltimore Sun*, Nov. 26, 1999.

Maranzani, Barbara. "The Most Violent Insurrection in American History." History.com

"March 23 1857—The First Otis Elevator is Installed in New York City." ThisDayInWorldHistory.com

Margino, Megan. "From Suburb to City and Back Again: A Brief History of the NYC Commuter." The New York Public Library blog, May 10, 2016.

Marrin, Richard B. "NY Harbor History: A Glance Back in Time." *Bay Crossings*, Apr. 2002.

Martin, Douglas. "A Village Dies, A Park Is Born." *The New York Times*, Jan. 31, 1997.

Marszal, Andrew and Tom Shiel. "What Was the SS Central America—or 'Ship of Gold'—and Why Did It Sink?" *The Telegraph*, Jan. 29, 2015.

Masur, Kate. "The African American Delegation to Abraham Lincoln: A Reappraisal." *Civil War History* 56:2 (June 2010).

McCarthy, Andy. "Class Act: Researching New York City Schools with Local History Collections. The New York Public Library, Oct. 20, 2014.

McCarthy, Joe. "The Gra-a-nd Parade." *American Heritage* 20:2 (1969).

McKinney, Roger. "Battle of Island Mound Marked First Time Blacks Fought in Civil War Combat." *The Joplin* (Missouri) *Globe*, July 30, 2011.

McKittrick, David and David McVea. *Making Sense of The Troubles: A History of the Northern Ireland Conflict*. London, UK: Viking, 2012.

McNamara, Robert. "The Colorful History of the St. Patrick's Day Parade." ThoughtCo.com, Feb 1, 2019.

Top of Form

Bottom of Form

McNamara, Robert. "Routes to the West for American Settlers." ThoughtCo.com, May 31, 2018.

Mikorenda, Jerry. "Beating Wings in Rebellion: The Ladies Literary Society Finds Equality." The Gotham Center for New York City History. gothamcenter.org

Miller, Benjamin. "Twisting the Dandy: The Transformation of the Blackface Dandy in Early American Theatre." *The Journal of American Drama and Theatre* 27:3 (Nov. 13, 2015).

Mirrer, Louise, et al. "Happy Fifth of July, New York!" *The New York Times*, July 3, 2005.

Monroe, Kristopher. "The Weeping Time: A Forgotten History of the Largest Slave Auction ever on American Soil." *The Atlantic*, July 10, 2014.

"More Songs About Ireland and the Irish: No Irish Need Apply, 1863." ParlorSongs.com

"More Women's Rights Conventions." National Park Service. nps.gov

Moser, Emily. "SmartCat Sundays: The New York & Harlem's Street Railway." The Harlem Line. iridetheharlemline.com, Aug. 28, 2016.

Moving Day (in Little Old New York), painting, unknown artist, 1827. Metropolitan Museum of Art, New York, NY.

Mulraney, Frances. "Honoring 10,000 Irish Immigrants Who Built the US Railroads." IrishCentral.com, May 10, 2019.

Mundie, James G. "Sideshow Ephemera Gallery: General Tom Thumb." MissionCreep.com/Mundie/gallery

Murphy, Matthew. "'They deliberately set fire to it ... simply because it was the home of unoffending colored orphan children': The New York Draft Riots and the Burning of the

Colored Orphan Asylum." New-York Historical Society Museum & Library: From the Stacks. July 16, 2013.

"Names of the Condemned Dakota Men," *The American Indian Quarterly*, Vol. 28, Nos. 1 and 2, Winter/Spring 2004.

The National Bureau of Economic Research, U.S. Business Cycle Expansions and Contractions. nber.org

National Humanities Center Resource Toolbox: The Making of African-American Identity: Vol. 1, 1500-1865. Report on the Improvement of Schools for African American Children in New York City from *The Anglo-African Magazine*, July 1859.

National Public Radio. "The Case for Tammany Hall Being on the Right Side of History." Interview with historian Terry Golway. *Fresh Air*, host Dave Davies. March 5, 2014.

National Republican Platform Adopted by the National Republican Convention, Held in Chicago, May 17, 1860. Contemporaneous poster.

"New York." The Maritime Heritage Project. maritimeheritage.org 2017.

New York Historical Society. "Examination Days: The New York African Free School Collection." nyhistory.org

New York Historical Society. "What was the New York Crystal Palace, and where was it located?" www.nyhistory.org/community/new-yorks-crystal-palace

"New York's "Fairy" Wedding of the Year, 1863." EphemeralNewYork.Wordpress.com.

Nielsen, Euell A. "Maria W. Miller Stewart (1803-1879)." Black Past, Feb. 11, 2007.

Nilsson, Jeff. "General Tom Thumb Gets Married." SaturdayEveningPost.com, Feb. 9, 2013.

"No Irish Need Apply: A Song of Discrimination." Georgetown University Center for New Designs in Learning and Scholarship.

Nokes, Greg. "Black Exclusion Laws in Oregon." OregonEncyclopedia.org

Norwood, John R. *We Are Still Here! The Tribal Saga of New Jersey's Nanticoke and Lenape Indians*. Moorestown, NJ: Native New Jersey Publications, 2007.

"An NYCHS Timeline on Executions by Hanging in New York State (Page 3: 1792 - 1794)" (Albany slave hangings). CorrectionHistory.org

O'Connell, Daniel. *Address from the People of Ireland to Their Countrymen and Countrywomen in America*. 1847.

O'Connell, Libby H. *The American Plate: A Culinary History in 100 Bites*. Naperville, IL: Sourcebooks, Inc., 2014.

O'Driscoll, Florry. "Religion, Racism, & Perfidious Albion: Irish Soldiers in the Union Army during the American Civil War." Paper, academia.edu

O'Loughlin, Jim. "Grow'd Again: Articulation and the History of Topsy." The Electronic Text Center, The Institute for Advanced Technology in the Humanities at the University of Virginia. utc.iath.virginia.edu 2000.

O'Neil, Kathleen, credited as lyricist. "No Irish Need Apply," 1862.

"On This Day in History: Comet Donati First Observed by Italian Astronomer—On June 2, 1858. ancientpages.com

Ortiz, Paul. "One of History's Foremost Anti-Slavery Organizers Is Often Left Out of the Black History Month Story." *Time* magazine, Jan. 31, 2018.

"Our Tribal History..." The Nanticoke Lenni-Lenape: An American Indian Tribe. nanticoke-lenape.info/history

"The Pacific Railway: A Brief History of Building the Transcontinental Railroad." Linda Hall Library: Science, Engineering, Technology. Railroad.LindaHall.org

Penniman, John. "Novelty Iron Works, Foot of 12th St. E.R. New York." Painting. 1841-44.

Peterson, Carla L. *Black Gotham: A Family History of African Americans in Nineteenth-Century New York City*. New Haven, CT: Yale University Press, 2012.

Piacentino, Edward J. "Doesticks' Assault on Slavery: Style and Technique in 'The Great Auction Sale, at Savannah, Georgia.'" *Phylon* 48:3 (Fall 1987).

Pildes, Richard. "Did Election Fraud Help Win the Civil War?" ElectionLawBlog.org, July 20, 2013

"Pinkster Celebration." *Historic Hudson Valley*, Apr. 11, 2018.

Pitz, Marylynne. "Allegheny Arsenal Explosion: Pittsburgh's Worst Day During the Civil War." *Pittsburgh Post-Gazette*, Sept. 16, 2012.

Poe, Edgar Allan. "The Murders in the Rue Morgue." Originally published in *Graham's Magazine*, Apr. 1841.

"Proclamation by the President." Lincoln rescinding David Hunter's Gen. Order No. 11. Freedmen & Southern Society Project. freedmen.umd.edu

Radeska, Tijana. "Tom Thumb's Fairy Tale Dwarf Wedding Attracted Over 10,000 People." TheVintageNews.com, Aug. 29, 2018.

Reilly, Lucas. "Why Do Students Get Summers Off?" mentalfloss.com Aug. 21, 2019.

Report of the Committee of Merchants for the Relief of Colored People, Suffering from the Late Riots in the City of New York. New York, NY: George A. Whitehorne, Steam Printer, 1863.

Ridge, John T., writer, and Lynn Mosher Bushnell, ed. *Celebrating 250 Years of the New York City St. Patrick's Day Parade*. Hamden, CT: Quinnipiac University Press, 2011.

Roche, Emma Langdon. *Historic Sketches of the South* (Ch. III: Illegal Traffic in Slaves). New York, NY: The Knickerbocker Press, 1912.

Rogers, W. C. & Co., lithographers. Lithograph: "Printing House Square 1868." *Jos. Shannon's Manual 1868*.

"Role in the Civil War." Harriet Tubman Historical Society. harriet-tubman.org

Rosenzweig, Roy and Elizabeth Blackmar. *The Park and the People: A History of Central Park*. Ithaca, NY and London: Cornell University Press, 1992.

Rury, John L. "The New York African Free School, 1827-1836: Conflict Over Community Control of Black Education." *Phylon*, 44:3 (Sept. 1983).

"Saint Patrick's Day Parade, 1872" sketch. Unique Identifier: SS2507043; Legacy Identifier: BU2717. Library of Congress/Science Source.

Sante, Luc. *Low Life: Lures and Snares Old New York*. New York, NY: Farrar Straus Giroux, 1991.

Schulz, Dana. "Kleindeutschland: The History of the East Village's Little Germany." 6sqft.com, Oct. 2, 2014.

Schulz, Dana. "Manure Heaps, Fat Melting, and Offensive Privies: Mapping NYC's 19th Century Nuisances." 6sqft.com, Dec. 11, 2015.

Schwantes, Carlos A. "The Steamboat and Stagecoach Era in Montana and the Northern West." Montana Historical Society. mhs.mt.gov

Semlak, John. "The Dead of Antietam: Alexander Gardner's Powerful Images from the Battle." explorenewyorkhitory.com, Oct 21, 2017.

"The Seneca Falls Convention." Library of Congress Digital Collections.

"Seneca Village Site." Central Park Conservancy. CentralParkNYC.org

Seward, William Henry. "Higher Law" speech delivered on the U.S. Senate floor Mar. 11, 1850.

Shaffer, Donald R. "A Violent Reaction to the Emancipation Proclamation." CWEmancipation.wordpress.com, Oct. 22, 2012.

Shaw, Madelyn. "Slave Cloth and Clothing Slaves: Craftsmanship, Commerce, and Industry." *Journal of Early Southern Decorative Arts*, 2012.

"A short biography of Elizabeth Blackwell." Printed a- nb

Simmons, Amelia. *American Cookery, Or The Art of Dressing Viands, Fish, Poultry, and Vegetables, and the Best Modes of Making Pastes, Puffs, Pies, Tarts, Puddings, Custards and Preserves, and all Kinds of Cakes, from the Imperial Plumb to Plain Cake. Adapted to This Country, and All Grades of Life*. Hartford, CT: Hudson & Goodwin, 1796.

Skrabec, Quentin R. *The 100 Most Important American Financial Crises: An Encyclopedia of the Lowest Points in American Economic History*. Santa Barbara, CA: Greenwood/ABC-CLIO LLC, 2015.

"Slave, Free Black, and White Population, 1780-1830." University of Maryland, Baltimore County. userpages.umbc.edu/~bouton/history407/SlaveStats

Smith, George H. "William Lloyd Garrison and Frederick Douglass on Disunionism." libertarianism.org

"Soldier's Pay in the American Civil War." CivilWarHome.com/Pay, Feb. 10, 2002.

"A Song That Is Now Rather Popular" [John Brown's Body]. *New-York Daily Tribune*, Feb. 28, 1862.

Soodalter, Ron. "Hanging Captain Gordon." HistoryNet.com

Soodalter, Ron. "Lincoln and the Sioux." *The New York Times* Opinionator Blogs, Aug. 20, 2012.

Spellen, Suzanne. "Walkabout: The Devil's Weed." Brownstoner.com/History

Stanley, Matthew E. "1st Kansas Colored Volunteers (Later the 79th U.S. Colored Infantry)." CivilWarOnTheWesternBorder.org

Steffe, William, lyricist. "Say Brothers, Will You Meet Us?" SecondHandSongs.com

Steward, Patrick and McGovern, Bryan. *The Fenians: Irish Rebellion in the North Atlantic World, 1858-1876*. Knoxville: The University of Tennessee Press, 2013.

Stowe, Harriet Beecher. *Uncle Tom's Cabin, or Life Among the Lowly*. Boston, MA: John P. Jewett and Company, 1852, following serialization in The National Era, 1851.

"Struggles Over Slavery: The 'Gag' Rule." archives.gov/exhibits/treasures_of_congress

"Sunken Treasure from Gold Rush-era Shipwreck To Go on Display." Feb. 20, 2018. CBS Interactive Inc.

"A Tale of the Tombs." CorrectionHistory.org

"Terror in Virginia: A Slave Insurrection Feared in Culpepper Seventeen Negroes Reported to be Hung, &c." *The New-York Times*, Oct. 21, 1862.

Thompson, Kathleen Logothetis. "Suing for Freedom: The Dred Scott Case." *Civil Discourse: A Blog of the Long Civil War Era*, Mar. 9, 2015.

Thoreau, Henry David. "A Plea for Captain John Brown." Speech delivered in Concord, MA, 1859; published in *Echoes of Harper's Ferry*, James Redpath, ed., 1860.

Tierney, Dominic. "'The Battle Hymn of the Republic': America's Song of Itself." *The Atlantic*: Nov 4, 2010.

Todd, Michael. "A Short History of Home Mail Delivery." *Pacific Standard*. psmag.com, June 14, 2017.

Tóibín, Colm and Diarmaid Ferriter. *The Irish Famine: A Documentary*. New York, NY: Thomas Dunne Books/St. Martin's Press, 2001.

Toomey, Daniel Carroll. "Where The Civil War Began: How the Pratt Street Riot determined the course of the war." *Baltimore*, Apr. 2011.

Trainor, Sean. "The Racially Fraught History of the American Beard." *The Atlantic*, Jan. 20, 2014.

Tremante III, Louis P. *Agriculture and Farm Life in the New York City Region, 1820-1870*. Doctoral dissertation, Iowa State University, 2000.

Tucker, Glenn. "Tecumseh: Shawnee Chief." Britannica.com/biography

Urwin, Gregory J. W. "'We Cannot Treat Negroes…as Prisoners of War': Racial Atrocities and Reprisals in Civil War Arkansas" (pp 213-229) in Bailey, Anne J. and Daniel E. Sutherland, eds. *Civil War Arkansas: Beyond Battles and Leaders*. Fayetteville, AK: The University of Arkansas Press, 2000.

"The Use of Black Powder and Nitroglycerine on the Transcontinental Railroad." Railroad. LindaHall.org

"U.S.A. Coins Sorted by Denomination." CoinDataBase.com

Van Deusen, Glyndon. "The Life and Career of William Henry Seward 1801-1872." *University of Rochester Library Bulletin* 31:1 (Autumn 1978).

Vinson, Robert Trent. "The Law as Lawbreaker: The Promotion and Encouragement of the Atlantic Slave Trade by the New York Judiciary System, 1857-1862. *Afro-Americans in New York Life and History* 20:2 (July 1996).

Vronsky, Peter. "*From Rebels to Revolutionaries: A Brief History of the Founding of the Fenians and the Irish Republican Brotherhood (IRB) in Ireland and the United States, March 17, 1858*." Fenians.org

Wade, Lisa. "Irish Apes: Tactics of De-Humanization." TheSocietyPages.org

Wadsworth, Kimberly. "Lavinia Warren: Half of the 19th Century's Tiniest, Richest Power Couple." AtlasObscura.com June 30, 2015.

"Walt Whitman." Poets.org

"Walt Whitman." PoetryFoundation.org

"The Weeping Time." pbs.org

Weidinger, Patrick. "10 Lesser-Known Historic Comets." Listserve.com, June 21, 2014.

Weiner, Jon. "Largest Mass Execution in US History: 150 Years Ago Today: Lincoln Ordered the Execution of Thirty-eight Dakota Indians for Rebellion—But Never Ordered the Execution of Confederate Officials or Generals." *The Nation*, Dec. 26, 2012.

Whitman, Karen. "Re-evaluating John Brown's Raid at Harpers Ferry." *West Virginia History* 34:1 (Oct. 1972).

White, Jonathan W. *Emancipation, the Union Army, and the Reelection of Abraham Lincoln*. Baton Rouge, LA: Louisiana State University Press, 2014.

Wilder, Craig Steven. "The Rise and Influence of the New York African Society for Mutual Relief, 1808-1865." *Afro-Americans in New York Life and History* 22:2 (Jul 31, 1998).

Williams, Phil. "Civil War: An Explosion Rocks Brown's Island." RVANews.com, Mar. 13, 2013.

Williamson, Harry A. *Folks in Old New York and Brooklyn*. Personal papers. Schomburg Center Manuscripts & Archives, New York, NY, 1953.

Wills, Eric. "The Forgotten: The Contraband of America and the Road to Freedom." *Preservation* magazine, May/June 2011.

Wilson, Harriet E. *Our Nig: Sketches from the Life of a Free Black, In A Two-Story White House, North. Showing That Slavery's Shadows Fall Even There*. Boston: George C. Rand & Avery, 1859.

Yee, Shirley. "The New York African Society for Mutual Relief (1808-1860)." BlackPast.org

"Ye May session of ye woman's rights convention—ye orator of ye day denouncing ye lords of creation" (political cartoon). *Harper's Weekly* 110 (June 11, 1859)

Zick, William J. "Black Composers and Musicians in Classical Music History." BlackPast.org

About the Author

KIA CORTHRON's first novel, *The Castle Cross the Magnet Carter*, won the coveted First Novel Prize from the Center for Fiction in 2016. It was championed by Pulitzer Prize winner Viet Thanh Nguyen, Robin D. G. Kelley, and Angela Y. Davis, among many others, and received rave reviews in the *New York Times Book Review* (Editor's Choice), the *Wall Street Journal*, and elsewhere. She was the 2017 Bread Loaf Shane Stevens Fellow in the Novel. She is also a nationally and internationally produced playwright. For her body of work for the stage, she has garnered the Windham Campbell Prize for Drama, the United States Artists Jane Addams Fellowship, and most recently the Horton Foote Award. She was born and raised in Cumberland, Maryland, and lives in Harlem, New York City.

MANHATTAN
1860

1 ✝ LITTLE AFRICA, GREENWICH VILLAGE
2 ✝ SENECA VILLAGE/CENTRAL PARK
3 ✝ 20TH PRECINCT POLICE STATION
4 ✝ AUNT MARYAM'S
5 ✝ NORTH DISTRICT DRAFT OFFICE
6 ✝ MACKERELVILLE
7 ✝ HARLEM DRAWBRIDGE
8 ✝ CITY HALL PARK
9 ✝ DELMONICO'S
10 ✝ MRS. HEVERWORTH'S
11 ✝ IRON WORKS
12 ✝ ACADEMY OF MUSIC
13 ✝ COLORED ORPHAN ASYLUM
14 ✝ LITTLE GERMANY
15 ✝ E. V. HAUGHWOUT & CO.
16 ✝ BARNUM'S MUSEUM
✦ ✝ FIVE POINTS NEIGHBORHOOD

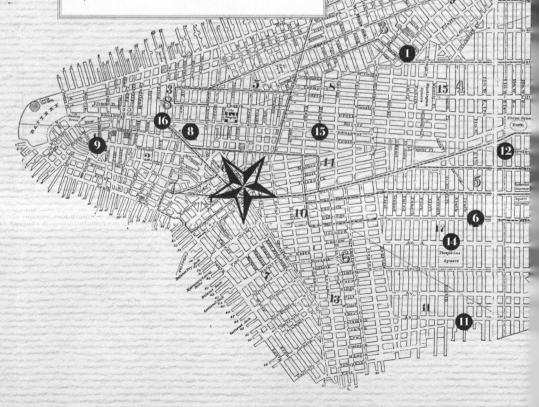